8-26-2010

Murder
When the Bell Tolls

Debbie Creamer

Copyright © 2010 Debbie Creamer
All rights reserved.

ISBN: 1451583230
ISBN-13: 9781451583236

On a chilly spring evening, Sara Michaels and her fiancé Paul Sanford were walking in the park. They stopped to feed the birds and watch some ducks land on the pond. They were talking and laughing. A man in raggedy clothes, holding a tin cup came up to them. Sara started looking in her purse for money to put in the cup. The church bells began to toll. Suddenly a shot rang out. Paul grabbed Sara's hand and slowly slumped to the ground. She screamed. The man in the raggedy clothes ran. She leaned over the body. "Paul, speak to me. Paul, are you alright." He lie motionless on the ground. Sara started crying. Another couple ran to Sara to see if they could help.

"Ma'am. I'm a doctor. Let me see if I can help." Sara got up and started shaking. Madison, put her arm around Sara's shoulder and tried to comfort her. The doctor came over to Sara. "I'm sorry ma'am. He's dead." Sara started crying. "Madison, call the police and tell them there's been a murder. Ma'am, you okay?"

"I think so. Where did that man in the raggedy clothes go?"
"I don't know ma'am."
"Please call me Sara."
"Okay Sara."

Several people came running when they saw two police cars and an ambulance pull up to the scene of the crime. Two officers approached the scene. "Hello Dr. Martin, Madison, ma'am. I'm Lt. Seth Parker, this is Lt. Mark Anderson. We received a call about a murder. Can you tell us what happened?"

Murder *When the Bell Tolls*

While the police were talking to Dr. Martin, Madison was trying to comfort Sara. "Was he your husband?"

"Almost. Paul and I were supposed to be married in two months."

"I'm so sorry."

"Thank you." Sara started crying hysterically when the ambulance drivers covered Paul's body with a sheet and put his body in the ambulance. Seth walked over to Sara and put his arm around her shoulder. "Ma'am, let's go over here and sit on the bench." Sara couldn't stop shaking. Seth asked the ambulance driver for an extra blanket. He gave it to Seth.

Seth put the blanket around Sara's shoulders. She couldn't stop sobbing. Once she stopped crying so hard Seth said "Ma'am, I know this is difficult but I need to ask you some questions about what happened."

"Okay."

"Can you tell me what happened?"

Sara told him what happened and about the raggedy dressed man.

"What about the man with the raggedy clothes?"

"He ran away. I remember I saw someone dressed in black clothing running away from the church. That person ran with a limp in their left leg."

"I know this is hard ma'am, but is there anything else you can remember?"

"It all happened so fast. I'm sorry Lt. Parker."

"It's Seth."

"Okay Seth. I'm sorry I can't remember anything else."

"That's okay ma'am. You've given us a lot of information."

"Seth, its Sara."

"Okay Sara. I need to get a little more information. I'll be right back."

"Okay."

Sara sat on the bench trembling. Madison Martin went over to her. "Sara, I think you should let Lt. Parker take you home. You need to get some rest. What was your fiancés name?"

"Paul Sanford."

"I'm so sorry about Paul."

"Thank you." Seth walked over to Sara. "Sara, how did you and Paul get here?"

"Paul picked me up. We went out for dinner then wanted to take a walk in the park."

"You've been through a very traumatic experience and are in no shape to drive. Let me drive you home." Sara didn't argue. She wanted to get home. As Seth walked Sara to his car Dr. Martin walked over to them.

"Lt. Parker, if she needs anything let me know. I asked her if she was okay and she said yes but I'm not so sure. Here's my card. Call me any time."

"Thanks Dr."

"Dr. Martin, Madison, thank you for your help."

"You're welcome Sara."

Seth opened the car door for Sara and helped her in. Lt. Anderson walked over to Seth. "Mark, I'm going to take Ms. Michaels home. I'll come back to the station after I'm sure she's alright."

"Okay, I'll see you back at the station."

Seth got in the car. Sara was still trembling. He turned the heat on in the car for her. She stopped trembling so hard. "Seth, I'm sorry about the tears."

"It's perfectly alright Sara. You've been through a very traumatic event."

"I don't understand why this happened. Paul and I were talking one minute and the next minute he's dead. Why?" She started crying harder. Seth patted her hand. They pulled up in front of Sara's house.

"Sara, let me help you inside." Sara wanted to object but she was too tired and terrified after what had happened. They walked up to the door, she unlocked it and walked inside. "Sara, let me take a look around and make sure everything's okay?"

"Why?"

"I need to make sure you're safe."

"Okay."

He walked around the inside of the house. When he came back into the living room he found Sara holding a picture of her and Paul. She was clutching it close to her body and crying. He walked over to her. His heart ached for her. He could tell how much she loved Paul. "Sara, are you going to be alright?"

"I don't know."

"Sara, is there anyone you'd like me to call?"

"Yes. Could you call Maggie and Kevin Sanford? They're Paul's parents. I don't have the strength to do it. I can't stop crying".

"Sure Sara. I'll call them for you".

"They're vacationing in Florida. Here's the number where they can be reached".

Seth put his arm around Sara's shoulder and tried to comfort her. "I'll call them as soon as I get back to the station".

"Thank you Seth".

"Now that I know you're okay; I need to get back to the station. I'll call you later and check on you".

"Okay Seth. I'll talk to you later."

"Do you need anything before I go?"

"No, I think I'm going to shower and change clothes."

"I'll talk to you later."

"Thanks again Seth."

Seth got back to the station. He had a bad feeling about leaving Sara alone. He knew there'd been three murders in the park in the past two months. The murders were getting closer together and this time Sara may have gotten a glimpse of the shooter. He was going through messages he had gotten about the shooting. He was going to start calling them back when he remembered Sara had asked him to call Paul's parents. He picked up the phone and called. The phone on the other end rang three times; then he heard "Hello, this is Maggie Sanford speaking."

"Hello Maggie, my name is Lt. Seth Parker. I'm from the NYSPD. Do you have a son named Paul Sanford?"

"Yes I do. Has something happened?"

"I'm afraid so. I'm sorry to inform you that Paul is dead."

Maggie gasped "Oh no! Are you sure it's Paul?"

"Was he engaged to Sara Michaels?"

"Yes he was. What happened?"

"Your son was shot and killed as he and Sara walked in the park earlier this evening."

"Oh my! Sara, is she alright?"

"She's in shock."

"I can imagine." Kevin walked into the house when he heard Maggie ask about Sara. Maggie was crying. "Do you know who did this?"

"No, but we're following every lead."

"Maggie, what's wrong? I heard you say something about Paul. Is that Sara on the phone? Let me talk to her."

Maggie turned to Kevin and said "It's not Sara on the line. It's Lt. Parker from the NYSPD. Paul was murdered."

"Murdered? Let me talk to the Lt."

"Hello Lt. this is Kevin Sanford. I understand from my wife that Paul was murdered?"

"Yes sir. I'm sorry to say that's true."

"When and how did that happen?"

"It happened earlier this evening. Sara and Paul were walking in the park when he was shot. The bullet hit him in the back of the head. He died in Sara's arms."

"Sara, is she alright?"

"She's in shock."

"Do you have any leads as to who could have done this?"

"We're tracking down all leads."

"I'd feel better if you'd put Sara under police protection. I'm really worried about her. I'm afraid she may be in extreme danger."

"I'll see what we can do about getting protection for her. Sara was so distraught I didn't get a chance to ask her what her occupation is."

"She's a seventh grade English teacher at a middle school near her home. Please take care of her. She's like family to us. We'll fly to New York tomorrow, and probably be there by noon. I'll call the precinct and give you a number where we can be reached. We'll probably spend most of our time with Sara. Please let her know we'll be there tomorrow".

"I will. Again I'm sorry about your son."

"Thank you sir."

After Seth hung up the phone he started going through the messages. He thought about what Kevin had said. "Mark, could you come in my office for a few minutes?"

"Sure."

"What's up Seth? You look worried."

"I am. Paul Sanford's father is convinced that Sara's in danger and I'm beginning to think so also. He wants us to put 24 hour police protection on Sara and I think we should. She may have caught a glimpse of the shooter herself." Mark gasped.

"How do you know that?"

Murder *When the Bell Tolls*

"She said she saw someone dressed in black running away from the church and that person had a limp in his left leg."

"Seth I agree. We need to make sure she's under constant protection."

"I'll take care of it. Have you found out anything from the calls you've made?"

"I've had some witnesses tell me they heard two shots instead of one and all of them said the church bells had started ringing when the shots were fired."

"What about the raggedy dressed man?"

"I've had several people say they saw him running south. No one except Sara and Paul saw his face."

"We have to find him. He may know something. I'll make some calls then I'm going back to Sara's house and make sure she's okay. I'll stay there until the end of my shift in the morning. I need for you to make arrangements for someone to take over for me in the morning."

"I'll do that."

"See what you can find out about the man in the raggedy clothes."

"I will."

Mark went out of Seth's office and started making phone calls. Seth couldn't stop thinking about what Kevin said. He wanted to make a few quick calls then get over to Sara's. He started making calls. After he talked to a few witnesses he was even more certain Sara needed protection. He walked out of his office. "Mark, I'm going to Sara's house. You have my cell phone number; call me if you hear anything."

"I will. I promise."

Seth left the station. He was halfway to Sara's house when his cell phone rang. He looked at the number; it was Sara. He felt panic building up. He answered it "Sara, its Seth. What's wrong?"

"Seth, I just got a call from someone claiming to be the killer."

"What did he say to you?"

Sara started crying. "He said he was watching me. Seth, I'm scared."

"Sara, I'm almost to your house. Lock all of your doors and windows. Don't let anyone in until I get there."

"Okay."

"I'll be there in five minutes." Seth turned on his siren so he could get there faster. Five minutes later he pulled in front of

Sara's house. He practically ran to the door. He knocked on the door. "Sara, its Seth. You can open the door now." She opened the door slowly. She had tears running down her cheeks.

"Seth, come in, I just made some fresh coffee, would you like a cup?"

"That sounds good." Sara went into the kitchen to get him a cup of coffee. She brought it to him and got herself a cup. She started shaking.

"Seth, I'm glad you're here. That call really unnerved me."

"I bet it did. Sara, can you tell me about that call? What did they say to you? How did they sound?"

"Seth, let's go into the living room. I need to sit down." They went into the living room. Sara sat on the couch and Seth sat in an overstuffed chair, facing Sara. "Seth, the voice on the phone was muffled. I couldn't tell if it was a man or a woman. They told me they're watching everything I do. They told me Paul got what he deserved. I can't imagine Paul doing anything to deserve that. He was a teacher. All of his students loved him and so did his co-workers." She started crying harder. His heart ached for her.

"Sara, I talked to Maggie and Kevin. They told me you're a teacher."

"Yes I am. I teach seventh grade English and writing at a middle school about ten minutes from here."

"How did you and Paul meet?"

"Paul's father's a retired dean from a college in New Jersey and his mom's a retired teacher from a high school in New Jersey. I met Paul about two years ago when I attended a teaching seminar in Queens. Paul's parents were some of the speakers at the seminar. Paul was there also. We met one evening after the seminars were over for the day, and hit it off immediately. He introduced me to his parents the last day of the seminar. We hit it off immediately also. I loved Paul so much. After my late husband Gary died of cancer eight years ago, I never thought I'd fall in love again; then I met Paul. He was such a wonderful, loving man. I don't know why anyone would do anything like this."

Seth wanted to throw his arms around her and hug her but he just patted her hand. "I know how you feel. I lost my wife about nine years ago because of a drunk driver."

Murder *When the Bell Tolls*

"Oh Seth, I'm sorry." Seth got up and started looking out the big bay window Sara had in her living room. Sara was still sobbing when she looked over at Seth.

"Sara, I almost forgot. Paul's parents said to tell you they're flying into New York tomorrow and they'll be here around noon. They're going to call the station and give us a number where they can be reached. They said they'd probably be spending most of their time with you though." Sara smiled.

"That sounds like Maggie and Kevin. Paul was all they had left. Maggie and Kevin made me feel like family from the first time we met. When Paul and I announced our engagement they had a huge party for us. They flew in from New Jersey just for that. They stayed several days and we had a wonderful time."

"They sound like wonderful people."

"They are."

"Sara, Paul's parents are very worried about you and so am I. Kevin asked if we would put 24 hour police protection on you and I assured him we would. I'm going to be staying with you until 8:00 tomorrow morning then another officer will take over."

"I know I'll feel better having you here." Sara went into the kitchen. "Seth, I'm going to make another pot of coffee; would you like another cup?"

"That sounds good."

Sara started making the coffee. Tears were running down her face. She was thinking about how she and Paul used to sit around and drink coffee at night before he left for his apartment. Seth walked over to Sara. He saw the tears. He rubbed his hand across her back in comfort. "Seth, I'm sorry about the tears. I was thinking about how Paul and I used to sit around drinking coffee at night before he went home."

"I did that to after my wife was killed. Marie and I used to stay up real late and watch movies, eat popcorn, and drink coffee. Our daughter Mary was grown up and in college by then". Seth knew that Sara was exhausted. "Sara, I'm going to get another cup of coffee. Would you like another cup?"

"Yes. I'll get it."

"You sit down in that chair and let me get it for you."

"Thanks Seth. I appreciate it."

Seth went into the kitchen and got two cups of coffee. He put them on a tray and brought them to the living room.

He set the tray down in front of Sara. She fixed it the way she liked it and Seth fixed his. "Sara, what do you like to do besides teaching?"

"One of my favorite things is the theater. I love the music, dancing and singing."

"I've always liked the theater; I'm partial to musicals."

"Me too. My favorite is Sound of Music and second is South Pacific."

"I like those two but my favorite is Jesus Christ Superstar."

"That's an excellent one too. Paul's favorite was Oklahoma. We'd go to the theater once a week during the summer."

"My wife and I used to go to the theater a lot." Sara started shaking. "Sara I can tell you're exhausted. Why don't you try and get some sleep?"

"I won't be able to sleep. I'm too upset."

"We can stay up and talk all night if that's what you want to do." Sara saw the compassion in Seth's eyes. She knew he meant it.

"Oh Seth, I can't believe Paul's gone." She started sobbing. Seth got up and started walking around the inside of the house. He looked out the bay window. Sara got up and went into the kitchen. She got out a pastry she had in the refrigerator and sliced it into several pieces. Seth walked into all of the rooms of the house checking for anything unusual. He came back into the living room. "Seth, I thought maybe we could have some of this pastry with coffee."

"Sounds good." Sara was rushing around in the kitchen getting things together. Seth came into the kitchen. "Sara, let me help you." She handed him a tray with the pastry, and coffee on it. She started crying and shaking. Seth put the tray down. He ran his hand over her back and tried to comfort her. He wanted to throw his arms around her and hug her but decided it was inappropriate. "Sara, let me help you to the couch then I'll bring the coffee and pastry in." Sara didn't argue, she just walked with him to the couch and sat down. She buried her head in her hands and sobbed. Seth brought the tray in the living room.

Sara sat on the couch and Seth sat in the overstuffed chair. Sara put a blanket over her feet. She started sobbing again. Seth rubbed his hand across her back. "Sara, what's it like to teach seventh grade?"

Murder *When the Bell Tolls*

"It's very rewarding but can be challenging at times."

"Would you mind if I changed into my gown and robe?"

"No not at all. Go ahead. I'll be fine out here."

"I'll bring out some extra blankets so we can put them over us if we get cold."

"Alright. That's fine." Sara went into the bedroom to change clothes. While Sara was changing clothes Seth looked out the bay window again. He thought he saw someone but looked away from the window when his cell phone rang. He answered it, "Seth Parker speaking."

"Seth, it's Mark Anderson."

"Hi Mark. What's up?"

"I wanted to let you know the man with the raggedy clothes was spotted at a local hospital. What would you like us to do?"

"Bring him in for questioning. See if he knows anything."

"Okay. How's Sara?"

"She's still really distraught and in shock. She says she won't be able to sleep because she can't get that image of Paul out of her mind. I told her we'd stay up and talk all night if necessary. Mark, I was wondering if you could send a car around the neighborhood. I thought I saw someone walking around Sara's house. I don't want to leave her alone or I'd check myself. I'm afraid Sara's in extreme danger."

"You may be right, I'll send some units out to patrol the neighborhood and let you know if we find out anything."

"Thanks Mark."

Sara returned to the living room carrying several blankets and a few pillows. Seth helped her put them on the couch. She sat down.

Sara started yawning. "Sara, why don't you try to at least get some rest? Tomorrow's going to be a very busy and trying day for you."

"Well maybe if I lean back and close my eyes, I can get a little rest. You're going to be right here aren't you?"

"Yes. I'll be right here."

"Good."

Sara leaned back and closed her eyes. She tried to relax by thinking about things that made her happy. She drifted off to sleep. Seth didn't want to let her out of his sight. He walked around the inside of the house checking outside to see if there was anything unusual happening then he checked on Sara. He pulled the blanket over her because she was shivering. His cell phone rang again. "Seth Parker speaking."

"Seth, it's Mark Anderson again."

"Mark, what's wrong?"

"The man in the raggedy clothes has disappeared."

"Disappeared? How? I thought you said he was spotted at a local hospital."

"He was but when the nurses and the security guard went to find him and check the last place he was seen, all they found were his clothes; nothing more. Sorry Seth."

"It's okay Mark. We'll just have to keep looking until we find him. Ask anyone who was in that area if they saw or heard anything. That will be a start."

"Right. Tom Monroe's going to relieve you in the morning. He'll be at Sara's at 8:00 A.M. Give me the directions on how to get to her house."

"Alright."

Seth was giving Lt. Anderson directions when he heard Sara stirring. "Mark, hold on a minute. I hear Sara stirring and I need to check on her."

Seth walked from the hallway into the living room. Sara was still asleep but very restless. He got back on the phone. "Seth, is Sara alright?"

"For now. She's asleep but very restless."

"I can imagine. I wish we had more to go on with a description of the man with the raggedy clothes."

"So do I but we don't. Sara may remember something about him at another given time but right now all she can think about is Paul."

"I can understand that. Seth, call in and let us know how Sara's doing in the morning. Let us know if you need anything."

"I will. Thanks for the information Mark." Seth closed his cell phone, walked into the kitchen and got himself another cup of coffee. He sat down in the chair and dozed off. A little while later Sara was awakened by a horrible memory. She sat up. "Seth, Seth are you here?" Seth awoke.

"Yes Sara, I'm here. What's wrong?"

"I just had a horrible memory. I feel like I know that man in the raggedy clothes from somewhere. I don't know where though. I suddenly feel really cold. I know it's 2:00 A.M. but I was wondering if you'd mind if I built a fire in the fireplace."

"Sara, let me build the fire for you." Seth built a fire. Sara pulled the blanket up to her neck.

"Thanks Seth."

"You're welcome, Sara, I need to walk around the inside of the house again and make sure everything's alright."

"Okay."

Seth walked around the inside of the house again. He went into the living room. He picked up a blanket. "Sara, are you getting warm now?"

"Yes, I feel a lot better now."

"Good."

"Seth, tell me about your family. You said you have a daughter?"

"Yes. She lives in North Carolina. We don't get to see each other as often as we'd like but we talk on the phone two or three times a week."

"That's great. At least you can talk to each other."

Sara suddenly turned pale. "Sara, what is it?"

"I remember something about the man with the raggedy clothes."

"What?"

"I remember his cup was empty, like he hadn't been there long." Seth's eyes got wide. He looked over at Sara; she was clutching her pillow and crying. He got up and sat next to her on the couch.

"Sara, you're exhausted. Why don't you lean back and try to get more rest? I promise I'll be right here." Sara leaned back and closed her eyes again. She kept hoping this was a nightmare and when she woke up Paul would be knocking on her door, but she knew that wasn't the case. She could hear Seth walking around making sure she was safe. She drifted off to sleep again.

At 6:30 A.M. Sara was awakened by the smell of fresh brewing coffee. She sat up on the couch. "Morning Sara."

"Seth, do I smell coffee?"

"You sure do. I drank the last cup a couple of hours ago, right after you went to sleep, so I thought I'd make a fresh pot this morning." She smiled.

"Thanks Seth. What time does your shift end this morning?"

"Sergeant Tom Monroe will be here at 8:00 A.M."

"Would you like to eat some breakfast before you leave?"

"Sara, you don't have to do that."

"I know I don't, but I want to. I have to eat anyway so why don't you join me?"

"Okay."

Sara went into the kitchen and made breakfast.

"Seth, would you help me take this food into the dining room?"

"Sure."

They sat at the table and started eating. "Wow Sara! This is great. I haven't had a meal like this for a long time. I can cook but nothing like this."

"I love to cook. Paul and I always liked to try new foods, so once a week we tried something different. It was fun to try something new and it was something we did together." Sara started sobbing again. Seth patted her on the hand. While they were eating breakfast the phone rang. Sara was hesitant to answer it.

"Sara, I'll answer it." He picked up the phone. "Seth Parker speaking."

"Seth, it's Maggie Sanford. We're at the airport getting our luggage. We were able to get an early flight out of Florida. We're going to be staying at the Ritz. We should be there in about three hours. How's Sara?"

"She's still in shock."

"Was she able to get any sleep last night?"

"Some. Would you like to talk to her?"

"Yes please." Sara got on the phone.

"Hi Maggie."

"Hi Sara. How are you sweetie?"

"I'm doing okay so far." She started to cry. "Maggie, I miss Paul."

"I know you do sweetie and so do we."

"Where are you now Maggie?"

"At the airport. We're getting our bags then going to the hotel. We're hoping to come by your house by noon, if that's okay?"

"That's fine. I'll be glad when you get here."

"Sara honey, it's okay to cry. Hang in there."

"Thanks Maggie. I'll see you when you get here."

"Okay. Will Lt. Parker be there when we get there about noon?"

"No, his shift ends at 8:00 A.M. Sergeant Tom Monroe will be here. Seth will be back tonight though."

"Good. We want to meet him. We'll see you later honey."

Sara hung up the phone and started crying harder. Seth put his hand on her back. "Seth, I miss Paul so much."

"I know you do Sara. I promise you, we're going to get the person or persons responsible for his death."

"Thanks Seth."

They finished eating. Seth took the food into the kitchen along with the dishes. "Let me help you clean up Sara."

"Seth, I couldn't ask you do to that. You're a guest in my house."

"Guest or no guest let me help you."

"Okay."

Sara filled the sink with soapy water and started washing the dishes. Seth dried them and set them on the counter. Just as they were finishing up there was a knock at the door. Sara looked at the clock. It was 7:45 A.M. Seth walked over to the door and answered it.

"Hello Tom. Come in and meet Sara Michaels."

Sara came out of the kitchen and walked over to Tom.

"Sergeant Monroe, this is Sara Michaels. Sara, this is Sergeant Tom Monroe."

"Hello ma'am."

"Please call me Sara."

"You can call me Tom."

"Okay Tom. I was just cleaning up from breakfast; would you like some breakfast and a cup of coffee?"

"Only coffee ma'am, I mean Sara."

"I'll get you a cup."

While Sara got him a cup of coffee, Seth told Tom, "Sara, had a rough night. We talked the biggest part of it. She's supposed to go to the funeral home and church today and make arrangements for Paul's funeral. She'll be with Paul's parents. Whatever you do, don't let her out of your sight. She may be in extreme danger. Tom I think I saw someone outside late last night. I couldn't make out anyone because it was too cloudy."

"Seth, I promise; I won't let her out of my sight."

"If something comes up, I want you to call me."

"I will."

Sara went to the dining room table and handed Tom his coffee. "Sara, my shift for the day is over. Call me if you need me."

"I will."

After Seth left, Sara looked at Tom and said, "Tom, I have some more things to put away, then if you don't mind I'm going to shower and get dressed before Paul's parents get here."

"Do you need some help putting things away?"

"That would be nice." He helped her put the dishes away.

"Tom, I'm going to shower now. I'll be out shortly."

"Okay."

Sara went into her bedroom, got out the clothes she wanted to wear and took them with her into the bathroom. As she was getting undressed she felt as though she was being watched. She got in the shower but still couldn't shake the feeling of being watched. When she got out of the shower she dried off and dressed quickly. After she finished getting ready, she walked into the living room. Tom was sitting at the dining room table reading the paper. He looked up and saw Sara trembling. "Sara, what's wrong?"

"Tom, while I was taking a shower I felt like I was being watched." He gasped.

"Did you see anyone?"

"No. I just had this feeling."

He walked around the inside of the house and looked out windows to see if he saw anyone. When he looked out Sara's bedroom window he saw footprints near the bushes. He knew someone had been there recently. He pulled out his cell phone and called into the station.

"Scott Marsh speaking."

"Scott, it's Tom Monroe."

"Hi Tom."

"Scott, I need a favor."

"Okay."

"Sara Michaels told me while she was taking a shower, she felt like she was being watched. She was. I found fresh footprints under her bedroom window. I was wondering if you could send an unmarked car over here to make impressions of the footprints. I don't want to leave Sara out of my sight."

"Sure, there will be a car over there shortly. How's Sara doing?"

Murder *When the Bell Tolls*

"She's hanging in there but she's still in a state of shock."
"I can imagine."
"Get that unit out here as soon as you can."
"Okay."

Tom closed his cell phone and walked into the living room where Sara was. He didn't want to scare Sara anymore than she already was. "Sara, I called the station and told him how you felt so they're sending someone out to investigate." Sara felt relieved.

"Thank you Tom."

"You're more than welcome. Seth told me Paul's parents are going to be here around noon; is that right?"

"Yes, Maggie called at 7:00 this morning and said they caught an early flight and were at the airport. They were going to go to their hotel and freshen up before they came here. She said she'd call and let me know when they'll be here."

"Can you tell me what they're like?"

"They're very nice, compassionate, and understanding. They have become some of my dearest and closest friends."

"That's great." There was a knock at the door. Tom answered it. "Hello."

"Hello, I'm Nancy Boyd. I'm the Principal at Sara's school. Is Sara here?"

He looked at her. "It's okay Tom."

"Come in ma'am".

"Thank you."

She walked in and walked over to Sara. "Hello Nancy."

"Hello Sara. I wanted to stop by and tell you how shocked I was to hear about Paul. You have my deepest sympathies as well as all of the staff at the school."

"Thank you Nancy."

"How you holding up?"

"I'm doing okay. Paul's parents are in town and they're going to be here around noon. They're staying at the Ritz. I'm really glad they're here."

"I know you are. I know how close all of you are. I want you to know you can take as much time off as you need."

"Thanks Nancy but I want to get back to work as soon as I can. I need to try to get my life back to normal."

"Is that man one of your relatives?"

"Oh no. It's Sergeant Tom Monroe with the NYSPD. I'm under police protection right now." Nancy gasped. "Nancy, let me introduce you."

"Nancy, this is Tom Monroe. He'll be here with me until 8:00 p.m. and then Lt. Seth Parker comes on duty until 8:00 tomorrow morning."

"It's nice to meet you Sergeant; I wish it was under better circumstances."

"It's nice to meet you too ma'am. I agree; I too wish it was under different circumstances."

"Sara, I need to get going. I just wanted to stop by and tell you how sorry I am to hear about Paul. If you need anything, let me know."

"I will. Thank you for stopping by."

As Nancy was leaving a florist van pulled up. Tom met the delivery man at the door. "Sir, may I help you?"

"Is this the home of Sara Michaels?"

"Yes it is."

"These flowers are for her."

"I'll take them." Tom handed the delivery person a tip and brought the flowers into the house. He sat them down on a table by the door. Sara walked over to the table and read the card. It was from some of her students and their parents.

"How lovely." She started sobbing again. Reality was starting to set in. Tom patted her on the hand. "Tom, I'm going to get myself another cup of coffee; would you like another cup?"

"Yes I would. Thank you." Sara went into the kitchen and poured two cups of coffee. She was thinking about how she and Paul used to spend their entire Saturday doing the things they loved to do together, like taking long walks, going to the theater, going to a dance or to a movie. Tears were running down her face when Tom walked over to her.

She handed him his cup of coffee. "Thanks Sara." She smiled. They talked for a little while.

The phone rang again.

"Sara honey, it's Maggie."

"Hi Maggie." Sara said choking back tears.

"Sweetie, how are you?"

"Not very well. I can't stop crying."

"Neither can I."

"Are you coming over soon?"

"Yes. We'll be over in about an hour. Will that be okay?"

"That will be fine."

Murder *When the Bell Tolls*

"We'll go to the funeral home first, then go to the church, make the arrangements there, then go out to lunch. Will that be alright?"

"That's fine."

"Is anyone there with you?"

"Yes. Sergeant Tom Monroe is here until 8:00 tonight."

"Good. I'm glad you're not alone. We'll be there in about an hour."

"I'll see you then."

"We love you Sara."

"I love you too."

Sara hung the phone up. "Tom that was Paul's mother. She and her husband will be here in about an hour. We have to make the funeral arrangements. I'm dreading that, but it has to be done."

"I know. I'll remain outside if you like."

"No. I want you to come in with us."

"Do you think Paul's parents will feel the same way?"

"I'm not sure; we'll see. I need to finish getting ready before they get here."

"Go ahead. I'll be out here waiting when you're ready."

Sara went into the bedroom. She started sobbing. She splashed water on her face then put on some make-up.

She walked into the living room about the same time someone knocked on her door. Tom answered it. "Hello."

"Hello. You must be Sergeant Monroe."

"Yes I am."

"I'm Maggie Sanford and this is my husband Kevin."

"Come in. Sara's expecting you."

"Hello Maggie, Kevin. Let me introduce you to Sergeant Tom Monroe of the NYSPD."

"Hello Sergeant."

"Please call me Tom."

Maggie threw her arms around Sara and they both started to cry. "Sir, please let me tell you how sorry I am about your son."

"Thank you Tom. Please call me Kevin."

"Kevin, Sara told me you're making funeral arrangements today. Is that correct?"

"Yes it is. We're going to the funeral home in a little while. Why do you ask?"

"I hope you won't mind having an extra person with you."

"Would that person be you?"

"Yes. Sara's under 24 hour police protection by order of Lt. Seth Parker."

Kevin sighed a sigh of relief. "Good. I was hoping you'd have her under protection. I'm afraid she may be in danger."

"So is Lt. Parker. She'll be under protection until the person or persons are caught, and sent to prison."

"What time does your shift end Tom?"

"8:00 tonight."

"Who will be here then?"

"Lt. Parker will be here. He'll be on duty until 8:00 A.M. Kevin, I'll wait in the car while you make the funeral arrangements if you want."

"Nonsense, you can come in with us."

"Thank you."

After Maggie and Sara had finally stopped crying so hard they walked over to Tom and Kevin. Maggie shook Tom's hand. "Tom. I understand from Sara you'll be joining us today."

"Yes ma'am."

"Please, call me Maggie. Sara told me she's been under police protection since last night."

"Yes she has. Lt Seth Parker insisted on it."

"Good. I'm glad. We've already lost Paul to a senseless death; we don't want to lose Sara too."

"No Maggie we don't."

"Sara's like a daughter to us. When we met her we really liked her and had hoped Paul would like her too. We all met at a teachers' seminar here in New York. We were elated when Paul told us they were engaged. We consider Sara a part of the family and she always will be." Sara looked at Maggie and Kevin; tears were running down her cheeks.

"Thank you both. I consider you family also."

"Is everyone ready to leave?"

"Yes."

They got out to the car. Kevin decided to drive. Even though they lived in New Jersey, Kevin knew his way around this area of New York. Kevin and Tom talked in the front seat and Maggie and Sara talked in the back seat. "Maggie, I'm so glad you got here when you did."

"As soon as we got off the phone with Lt. Parker, we started making arrangements to get here. We wanted to be with you. That's what families are for."

"Maggie, I can't believe he's gone. One minute we were talking about our wedding and the next minute he's on the ground dead." Sara started sobbing. Maggie put her arm around Sara and hugged her and held her close. Maggie started sobbing also. "Maggie, I want to do something special in Paul's memory but I wanted to ask you first."

"What is it sweetie?"

"I want to start a scholarship fund in Paul's name at the school where he teaches."

"Sara, that's a wonderful idea. However, I think we should also start a scholarship fund at your school also."

"Oh Maggie, that would be wonderful." They hugged each other. When they got to the funeral home, they all went inside together.

The funeral director greeted them. "Hello. May I help you?"

"Yes sir. We're here to make funeral arrangements for our son?"

"Okay. What's your son's name?"

"Paul Sanford."

The funeral director gasped. "Oh my! Please come this way." They followed him.

When they got into the room, Sergeant Monroe looked at Sara and said "I'm going to sit across the room so you can have privacy."

"Okay."

"If you need me, just call."

"Okay."

They made the arrangements. "Are you having the showing here or at the church?"

"Here."

"Okay. Is Monday alright?"

"That's fine.""What time?"

"4-8p.m."

"Are you having the funeral here or at the church?"

"We'd like to have it at the church."

"Is Tuesday alright?"

"That sounds fine."

Now that that's done there are two more things to be done. One is to pick out a casket." Sara started to tremble.

"I'll do that ladies. You stay here." Kevin went with the funeral director to the casket room. Maggie helped Sara sit down in a chair. Sara started to cry. Maggie put her arm around her and hugged her.

Kevin was trying to hold back tears when he came back. He wrote the funeral director a check for his services. "Please know I'm truly sorry for your loss."

"Thank you sir."

Tom got up and walked across the room. They all walked out to the car. Kevin and Tom talked on the way to the church. Sara and Maggie talked also. Maggie wrapped her arm around Sara's shoulder in comfort as they walked into the church. When they got into the church they were greeted by Pastor Jeff Akers. "Hello Sara."

"Hello Pastor Jeff."

"Sara, I was shocked to hear about Paul. How are you doing?"

"I'm not sure. This seems like a nightmare I can't wake up from."

He put his hand on her shoulder and tried to comfort her. Sara started to cry. Maggie walked up behind Sara and ran her hand across Sara's back.

"Pastor Jeff, let me introduce you to Maggie and Kevin Sanford, Paul's parents." He shook their hands.

"I'm sorry about Paul. He was a wonderful man."

"Yes he was." Kevin said.

"Pastor Jeff, I also want you to meet Sergeant Tom Monroe. He's with the NYSPD." Tom shook Pastor Jeff's hand.

"Hello Sergeant. I assume you're here because of Paul's untimely death."

"Well yes and no."

"Meaning what exactly?"

"Lt. Seth Parker feels that Sara may be in extreme danger because of Paul's' murder. Sara's the only witness to actually get a glimpse of the shooter. He's requested she be under 24 hour police protection until the person or persons responsible for Paul's death are in jail. Paul's the fourth person killed in or around the park in two months. We feel the murders are related." Pastor Jeff gasped.

"I'm glad you have her under police protection. Will there be police officers at the funeral?"

"Yes, several."

Murder *When the Bell Tolls*

"Good. That makes me feel better."

Pastor Jeff had all of them go into his office. "Did you get all the arrangements made at the funeral home?"

"Yes. The showing is Monday night from 4-8."

"Would you like to have the funeral on Tuesday or Wednesday?"

"Tuesday, if you don't mind."

"Is 10:00 A.M. alright with all of you?"

"That's fine."

Sara started feeling faint. "Sara, you alright? You look pale."

She looked up at everyone. "Yes, I'm okay. I'm just a little dizzy. I think it's because I'm a little tired."

"I need to know if there's anything special you want for Paul's funeral." They looked over the paper and decided everything should stay as they'd decided. As they got ready to leave Pastor Jeff said "Would it be alright if I spoke with Sara alone for a few minutes?"

"Sure."

Maggie and Kevin left the room. "Sara, I wanted to talk to you about how you're handling this."

"I'm not doing real well but my faith, my family and friends will get me through this."

"I'm glad to hear you say that. I understand you're under 24 hour police protection."

"Yes I am."

"I know this is difficult for you and I want you to know I'll be here for you, to help you spiritually and emotionally. If you need anything don't hesitate to ask. I feel like I'm not only your Pastor but also a friend."

"You are a friend."

"Sara, it'll take time but please don't try to do this alone."

"Thank you Pastor Jeff. I'll remember that." Sara felt the tears running down her face. Pastor Jeff handed her a tissue. "I'm sorry for the tears. I'm trying to be strong and brave."

"It's okay to cry. The tears are normal. No one will think any less of you or think you're weak if you cry because you're grieving over the loss of Paul. It's normal."

"Thank you for telling me that."

As Sara got up to leave she was overcome with dizziness. She grabbed Pastor Jeff's desk and tried to get her balance. "Sara, you alright?"

"Yes. I'm just having some problems with dizziness."

"Have you ever had problems with dizziness?"

"No. I've never had any problems with it. I really think it's stress related."

"I hope so."

"Please don't tell Maggie and Kevin about this episode. They're already worried about me."

"I can understand why. I won't tell them but you need to keep an eye on it."

"Thanks Pastor Jeff."

"I'll walk with you."

Pastor Akers helped Sara out the door and they joined the others. "Maggie, Kevin, Sara, if there's anything I can do, let me know. I want to help you through this difficult time."

"Thanks Pastor. We'll remember that."

They all walked out of the church. Maggie looked at her watch. "Wow! It's 12:30 P.M. is anyone besides me getting hungry?"

"I am starting to." said Kevin.

"Sara, what about you honey?" She didn't answer. "Sara?"

"I'm sorry, my mind was someplace else. What did you ask me?"

Maggie looked at her very compassionately and said "We're all getting hungry; what about you?"

Sara didn't feel much like eating but said "Yes, I'm a little hungry."

"Where should we go?"

Tom Monroe spoke up and said "I know a nice place. It's right down the road."

"Okay. Tell me how to get there."

Tom gave Kevin directions. They got to the restaurant. They went inside and the waiter seated them. They looked at their menus. "This place is famous for their chicken and desserts." Tom said.

"Chicken sounds good to me; me to." Kevin and Maggie both said. Sara felt sick to her stomach. She felt dizzy again.

"The chicken sounds good to me to." Sara said. Sara felt like her head was spinning and she felt nauseated. The waiter took their orders. Sara felt tears building up. Maggie looked at her and knew something was wrong. Sara was white as a sheet. "Would you excuse me? I think I'm going to be sick." She got up and practically ran to the bathroom. When she got into the bathroom she vomited once, then started crying. She walked over to the sink and vomited again. She started crying hysterically.

Everyone got worried when Sara wasn't back in a few minutes. "I'm going to check on Sara." Maggie said. When Maggie walked into the bathroom she found Sara sitting on the floor with her knees up to her chin, rocking back and forth, and crying hysterically. She walked over to Sara. "Sara honey, everyone's worried about you. Are you okay?"

I don't know Maggie. I vomited twice, I have the shakes and I can't seem to stop crying." Maggie hugged her and tried to comfort her. "Maggie, Paul's dead because of me." Sara said. Maggie gasped.

"Sara, why do you say that?"

"It was me who suggested we take a walk in the park. Paul agreed. If I wouldn't have suggested it, he would probably still be alive. I shouldn't have suggested it since we knew of the other shootings around the park. This is my fault." Maggie held Sara tightly.

Maggie was shocked and speechless. She didn't know what to say. Sara finally stopped rocking back and forth. "Sara, do you feel up to going back out with the others and eating something? It might help you feel a little better?"

"Yes; let me splash some water on my face then I'll be ready". Maggie helped Sara get up. Sara splashed water on her face then they went out to the table. Their food was just arriving when they got to the table. They sat down and started eating. Sara barely ate anything. She was still dizzy and nauseated. She started shaking. The waiter came back to their table and asked them if they needed anything or wanted any dessert. Everyone but Sara got dessert. She wasn't hungry. They finished eating. "Would you please excuse me? I need to use the bathroom and wash my hands."

"Go ahead Sara. I'll pay the bill. We'll wait here for you."
"Thanks Kevin."
"Sara, I'll go with you."

She didn't argue all she said was "Thanks Maggie." Sara and Maggie headed to the bathroom. After they finished they met the men and started walking to the car.

Since it was a twenty minute drive back to Sara's house, she leaned her head back, closed her eyes and tried to clear her head. Before she knew it they were at her house. Everyone went toward the front door. When Sara unlocked the door Tom said "Sara, I'm going to walk around the outside of the house and make sure everything's okay out here."

"Alright; we'll just go inside."

"I'll be in there in about ten minutes."

Tom walked around the outside of the house while the others went inside. He stopped when he got next to Sara's bedroom window. He looked down and saw more fresh footsteps. He went to his car and got his casting kit. He opened it up and made another plaster cast of the footprints. He let the mixture dry, then carefully removed it and placed it under the passenger side seat of his car. He got on his cell phone and called into the station. "Lt. Marsh speaking."

"Scott, it's Tom. I was wondering if you had someone come out here and make a plaster mold of those fresh footprints next to Sara's bedroom window."

"Yes I did. Why?

"It looks like there are more fresh footprints here. I made another set and put them in my car. I'll bring them in when I come in after my shift. Can you make sure you label the prints and put them in Sara's file?"

"I will."

"Thanks Scott."

"You're welcome. I'll see you when you get off."

"I'll see you then." Tom hung up his phone and knocked on the door. Kevin opened it and let him in.

※

While Tom was walking around outside; Maggie and Sara were in the kitchen cooking. Cooking was something that always made Sara feel better. Tom walked into the house. "Wow! It smells wonderful in here".

"Thanks Tom. Sara and I were just doing some cooking."

"We figured we'd cook up some food because if people stop by these next few days, I'll have something to offer them."

"That's a good idea. Do you need any help?"

"No. We can handle it, but thanks for asking."

"You're welcome."

"Kevin and I thought we could play some cards after we finish here. Would you like to join us in a game or two?"

"Sounds like fun. I'll go over and talk to Kevin until then."

"Okay."

Murder *When the Bell Tolls*

While Tom walked over to Kevin, Sara and Maggie finished up their cooking. They put the food in containers that could be reheated and stored in the refrigerator.

Tom started talking to Kevin. "Kevin, I didn't want to upset Sara anymore than she is so I think I should tell you about what I found outside." Kevin looked at Tom puzzled. "Sara told me she felt like she was being watched while she took a shower this morning and now I know why. There are fresh footprints beside her bedroom window." Kevin gasped. "I took plaster casts of the prints and put the casts into my car. I'm going to take them to the station after I get off. I'm also going to inform Seth Parker about this and he'll make sure she's safe tonight. I won't be here tomorrow, Lt. Scott Marsh will, but I'll make sure he knows what's going on also."

"Thank you Tom. I'll talk to Maggie about this tonight. I agree we shouldn't upset Sara any more than she already is. She's been through so much these past few hours."

"Yes she has."

Sara and Maggie joined Tom and Kevin in the living room. "Kevin, Tom you ready to play some cards?"

"Sure. Let me get the cards". Kevin walked over to a table next to the door and took out a deck of cards, a pad and pencil and walked back into the living room.

"Let's sit at the dining room table; there's more room." They got up and went into the living room.

"Maggie, I need to make a pot of coffee."

"Sara, just sit ; I'll make it."

"Okay. Thanks Maggie."

Maggie went into the kitchen and made a pot of coffee. She came into the dining room with a tray of cups and sat them down on the table. They started playing cards. They were in the middle of a game when the phone rang. Kevin answered it.

"May I speak with Sara please?"

"Who's calling please?"

"This is Peggy Miles".

Kevin turned to Sara. "Sara, there's a Peggy Miles on the line. Do you want to talk to her?"

"Oh yes. She's my good friend and a co-worker." He handed Sara the phone. "Peggy?"

"Sara honey, is that you?"

"Yes it is."

"Honey, I was so shocked to hear about Paul. How you holding up?"

"About as good as can be expected I guess."

"Is there anything you need"?

"Just your thoughts and prayers."

"You have that Sara. Who was that that answered the phone?"

"That was Kevin. Paul's father".

"Paul's parents are there with you now?"

"Yes, they got in about 6:30 this morning."

"Did you make the funeral arrangements yet or are you going to do that tomorrow?"

"We made the arrangements today. The showing is from 4-8 P.M. on Monday at the funeral home, the funeral is Tuesday morning at 10:00 at the church."

"Ralph and I will be there".

"Good. Peggy, there's something else I need to tell you."

"What is it Sara?"

"I'm under 24 hour police protection until the person who did this is caught, tried and convicted."

Peggy gasped. "Oh my. Are the officers who are there nice?"

"I've only had two officers here so far and they've been really nice. I feel safer with them here."

Good. I'm glad. Sara you sure there isn't anything we can do?"

"I'm sure."

"Are you going to church tomorrow"?

"Yes. I think Paul's parents are coming along. I know that a Lt. Scott Marsh, whom I haven't met yet, will be along too."

"I'd really like to meet Paul's parents."

"I'll introduce you."

"I'll see you tomorrow morning then."

"Okay. Thanks for calling Peggy."

Sara hung up the phone and walked back to the table. She sat down slowly. She was beginning to feel faint again but didn't say anything. They continued to play cards. There was a knock on the door. "Kevin answered it. "May I help you?"

"I have a delivery for Sara Michaels."

"I'll take it. Thank you."

He handed the delivery person a tip and took the flowers. "Look Sara, here's more flowers. Where would you like me to put them?"

"Put them on the fireplace mantel."

"Okay."

He walked over and placed them on the mantel. "Kevin, who are the flowers from?"

"Faculty members at Paul's school."

"How nice."

"That is nice".

They sat down and started playing cards again. Around 6:00 P.M. Maggie got up and went into the kitchen. "Is anyone hungry? I can heat up something."

"I'm getting hungry honey." Kevin said.

"Tom, what about you?"

"Sure I can eat something."

"Sara honey, what about you?"

"Nothing for me Maggie; thanks for asking. I can heat up the food Maggie."

"No just stay there, you need to rest."

"Thanks Maggie."

Maggie heated up some food and took it to the dining room. Everyone but Sara started eating.

After they finished eating Maggie cleaned off the table and took the dishes into the kitchen. "Maggie, since you wouldn't let me help you fix supper at least let me help you with the dishes."

"Are you sure you're up to it honey?"

"Yes. It'll help me feel better."

"Alright. I'll wash and you dry."

Sara smiled at her. "Okay."

They were just finishing up the dishes when there was a knock on the door. Sara looked at the clock. It was 7:45 P.M. "That's probably Seth. I'll answer it." Sara walked over to the door and opened it.

"Hello Sara."

"Hello Seth. Come in. I have some people here who want to meet you."

He went in. "Hello Tom."

"Hello Seth."

"Lt. Seth Parker, this is Maggie and Kevin Sanford; Paul's parents."

"Hello Lt."

"Hello, and please it's Seth". They smiled. "Sara, I need to talk to Tom for a few minutes then I'll be back."

"Okay."

Seth went out on the porch with Tom. "How did it go today Tom?"

"It went about as good as could be expected. I had to make some plaster casts." He gasped.

"Plaster casts? Of What?"

"Footprints. Sara told me she felt like she was being watched when she was taking a shower and getting dressed so I looked around and found footprints next to her bedroom window. I made a plaster cast of it. Sara's had a really trying day. She needs rest. Maggie and Kevin are terrific people. I know you'll like them."

"Thanks for the information Tom. Does Sara know?"

"No, we didn't want to upset her even more."

"I can understand that."

"Seth, I need to get back to the station."

"I understand."

"Sara, Maggie, Kevin, I need to get back to the station. I'll see you in a few days. Thanks for your hospitality and kindness today."

"You're more than welcome Tom. Thanks for your help."

"Goodbye Tom."

After Tom left Seth went into the living room. "Seth, you're the officer who called and told us about Paul aren't you?"

"Yes ma'am I am."

"Please call me Maggie."

"Seth, I'm Kevin Sanford, Paul's father."

"Hello sir."

"Please, it's Kevin. I understand you put Sara under 24 hour police protection."

"Yes I did. After talking with you, hearing what other witnesses heard and because of the other shootings in or around the park; I thought she might be in danger."

"I feel better knowing someone's here with her and will be with her at least until after we leave."

"I'm planning on having her under 24 hour protection until we get the person or persons responsible for the murders and they are incarcerated."

"That makes me feel better."

"We were playing cards before you got here. Would you like to join us in another game?"

"Sure, why not."

Murder *When the Bell Tolls*

They started playing cards again. "I'm going to get myself a cup of coffee, would anyone else like anything?" asked Sara.

"Coffee sounds good Sara."

"Why don't I bring the pot in and when it's empty we can make more?"

"That sounds like a good idea."

Sara got up to get the coffee. She walked into the kitchen, got out a tray, put the coffee cups, cream and sugar on the tray and when she went to pick up the tray she felt a horrible pain in her side. She set the tray down and grabbed the kitchen counter. She felt faint then felt her knees buckling beneath her. Maggie saw Sara struggling to stand up. She ran into the kitchen with Kevin and Seth close behind her. "Sara honey, what's wrong?"

"My side's hurting and I'm feeling faint again."

"Let's get you over to a chair."

Sara wrapped her arm around Maggie and they started walking toward the recliner in the living room. They got half way there and Sara collapsed. Seth kept her from hitting the floor. He picked her up and carried her over to the recliner. He laid her in the chair. "Maggie, Kevin I need a couple of pillows and some blankets." While Maggie and Kevin went to get the things they needed for Sara; Seth started checking Sara out to see if he could find any visible signs of an injury. He was moving her in the chair when he touched the left side of her shirt and found that it was soaking wet. He looked down and saw yellowish pus on her shirt. He gasped. Maggie and Kevin came back with pillows and blankets. Seth put a pillow under Sara's head and Kevin put a blanket over her. "Maggie, Kevin, I need to talk to you across the room for a minute".

"Okay."

They walked into the kitchen and Seth told them what he found. "Maggie, someone needs to raise that side of her shirt up and find out what's oozing onto her shirt."

"I'll do that right now."

Maggie, Kevin, and Seth walked over to Sara. Maggie gently raised Sara's shirt. She gasped when she saw a pink, hot to the touch open cut on Sara's side. Seth looked at it to and said" It looks like there's something in the wound, under the skin that's causing the infection. I better call..."

Debbie Creamer

Before he finished Sara opened her eyes. "Seth, Maggie, Kevin."

"We're right here Sara."

Sara tried to sit up but found she was too dizzy. "I'm so dizzy. What happened anyway?"

"Sara you collapsed on the way over to the chair. Seth carried you the rest of the way. Do you remember any of that?"

"No. Oww! My side really hurts."

"Sara, the reason it hurts is because you have an open wound that's infected. It's oozing and it looks like there's something in the wound, under the skin that's causing the infection. Do you have a family doctor?"

"Yes, but he's out of town for two weeks".

"This can't wait. Would it be alright if I called Dr. Martin?"

"Dr. Martin? I've heard that name before."

"He's the doctor who tried to help Paul in the park."

"Oh I remember him, he's really nice."

"I'm going to call him now, okay?"

"That's fine."

Seth looked thru his wallet for Dr. Martins' number. "Doctor Matins exchange, may I help you?"

"This is Lt. Seth Parker with the NYSPD. I need to have the doctor call me back because I have a very sick woman on my hands. She's vomited twice today, has had the shakes, and has felt faint and collapsed. There's yellowish pus coming out of a wound. Here's the number where I can be reached".

"I'll get in touch with him and he'll call you back within the next few minutes."

"Thank you."

He hung up his cell phone and went back over to Sara. She was shivering. "Did you reach him?" Maggie asked.

"I got his exchange. He'll return my call in a few minutes." Seth got another blanket and put it over Sara. A few minutes later Seth's cell phone rang. "Seth Parker speaking".

"Seth, this is Dr. Martin. I got a call from my service that you have an emergency".

"Yes, that's right Dr. I do."

"What's going on?"

"Do you remember Sara Michaels?"

"Should I?"

"She's the woman's whose fiancé was killed in the park last night".

"Oh yes. I remember her. What about her?"

"We have her under 24 hour police protection and tonight when I came on my shift Sara collapsed. She was unconscious for several minutes and couldn't remember what happened. Paul's parents are with her and they told me she vomited twice today, has been complaining about feeling faint and the worst part is she has a yellowish pus oozing out of a wound on her left side. It looks as if there's something in the wound, but it's under the skin. I really feel like you should see her. Her family doctor is out of town; I'm sorry to bother you but I didn't think this could wait."

"It can't wait. Give me directions to her house and I'll be there in a few minutes."

"Thanks Bob."

Seth gave him the directions. "Seth, keep her warm and give her plenty of fluids to drink."

"Okay."

He hung up his cell phone. "Dr. Martin will be here in a few minutes. He'll take good care of you Sara." Sara smiled. "He said to keep her warm and make sure she drinks plenty of fluids."

"Sara, you need to drink something. What would you like?"

"Some iced tea, if it's not too much trouble."

"It's no trouble at all".

"Thanks Maggie."

Maggie went into the kitchen and fixed some iced tea and took it to Sara.

Maggie handed the tea to Sara. "Thanks Maggie." She sipped the tea slowly.

About five minutes later there was a knock on the door. Seth answered it. "Dr. Martin, please come in."

He walked in. "Dr. this is Maggie Sanford; Paul's mother and Kevin Sanford Paul's father."

"Hello. I understand Sara's having some problems?"

"Yes she is."

"Where is she?"

"Over in that chair."

He walked over to Sara. "Hello Sara. Do you remember me?"

"Yes. You're Dr. Martin from the Park."

"That's right. I understand you haven't been feeling well and you have a wound that's infected."

"Yes sir, I do."

"Do you think if we helped you, that you could walk into the bedroom so you can lay flat while I examine you?"

"I can try". Seth and Kevin put their arms around Sara and helped her to the bedroom and laid her down on the bed.

"Maggie, I'm going to need your help also. I'm going to need you to be nurse and observer. Do you think you can do that?"

"Yes I can."

"Let's close the bedroom door slightly so we have more privacy and close the blinds also."

"What side of her body is the wound on?"

"The left side."

"Okay, let me examine her while she's lying flat then I'll need you to help me turn her on her right side".

"Alright".

"Sara, I'm going to check your throat, ears and eyes right now okay?"

"Okay."

"He checked her out and even listened to her heart. He pushed on her breast bone to make sure she didn't have any damage to her heart. "Maggie, can you help me roll her onto her right side?"

Once Sara was on her right side the doctor raised the left side of Sara's shirt up to her shoulder. He gasped when he saw the wound. "Oh my. It's no wonder she isn't feeling well. She has a bad infection. You were right; there is something under the skin that's causing the infection. Maggie I need to get some supplies out of my bag. Sara, please try not to move okay?"

"Okay."

Sara was scared and in pain. She had no idea how she got the wound on her side. The doctor came back with a scalpel, bandages, and something to numb the area with. "Maggie, I need you to hold Sara as still as possible. I'm going to have to lance that wound and take out whatever is causing the infection. Sara honey, I'm sorry this is going to hurt. I'll try and make it as painless as I can. It's okay to scream, cry, whatever you need to do but I need for you to lie as still as possible."

"Okay".

"Are you ready Maggie?"

"Yes I am."

Doctor Martin numbed the area. Sara started shivering. "Maggie does Sara have any extra blankets?"

"Yes, in the closet".

"I need you to put one over her." Maggie got a blanket and covered Sara up.

She patted Sara on the hand. "Honey, I'm here. Squeeze my hand if you need to."

"Thanks Maggie."

Dr. Martin lanced the wound and the infection poured out. He wiped it as clean as possible with gauze. Then he took an instrument and dug out what was causing the infection. He gasped when he realized they were bullet fragments. "Doctor, what is it?"

"Nothing. I'm just amazed that the infection didn't start sooner." He looked at Maggie with fear in his eyes. She knew something was wrong but didn't want to upset Sara anymore. Sara screamed when he started taking more pieces out. She was crying hysterically when he finally got the last piece out. He put some ointment on it and wrapped it in gauze. He patted Sara on the hand. "We're finished. I'm sorry that hurt like it did but you had some fragments buried deep inside the wound that I had to remove. I think I got all of them but I'll need to check the wound again in four days. I want you to rest, drink plenty of fluids and take this medication twice a day for the infection and this medication every four hours for pain. After I recheck your wounds in four days I will decide if you need more medication. If you run out of pain medication, call me. I'll get you more."

"Thanks Dr."

"You're welcome. I'm sorry about Paul."

"Thank you doctor."

"Sara, would you like to go back out in the living room?"

"Yes I would."

"Maggie will help you get dressed then we'll get you out in the living room".

While Maggie helped Sara get dressed Dr. Martin went into the living room where Seth and Kevin were. "What happened in there? Is Sara alright?"

"Sara's alright for now."

"What do you mean?"

"Her side was infected because there were bullet fragments lodged in her side." They both gasped. "Seth, I put them in a bag for you to take to the station".

"Thank you Doctor."

"What do you mean she's okay for now?"

"I gave her some medication for the pain and for the infection but she needs rest. When is the visitation and funeral planned for Paul?"

"Monday night and Tuesday".

"She should be feeling better by then. I want to see her again in four days. If the wound is healing that will be great; if it's not I may have to go back in and see if I got all of the fragments. We caught the infection in time. If she would've waited another day, she may have had to been hospitalized or could have died. I'm glad you called me. I want her to drink a lot of fluids also. She wants to come out here with you. I'm not sure Maggie and I can handle her; would one of you like to help me please?"

"Sure."

"Sara and Maggie don't know about the bullet fragments."

Seth and Kevin both headed for Sara's bedroom. Dr. Martin was in front of them. He knocked on the door. "Maggie, is Sara ready?"

"Yes; it's okay to come in."

They went in. Kevin went over to Sara and hugged her. Seth and Kevin bent down, put Sara's arms around their shoulders and helped her walk out to the living room. They sat her in the recliner. Dr. Martin looked at her and said "Sara, you need rest and I don't want you trying to get up by yourself; you'll rip the bandages. Maggie, Seth, Kevin, she'll need for someone to watch her constantly for the next few days. I want to see her on Wed. to decide on the next step of treatment."

"We'll make sure she has everything she needs. Thank you Doctor Martin."

"You're welcome. Sara, remember what I said and you'll be okay."

"Is it okay if I go to church tomorrow?"

"It depends on how you feel. If you feel up to it and you're not too tired that's fine but if you have a restless night then I'd suggest you don't go."

"Thank you so much for everything doctor."

"If you need anything, here's my card. Call anytime."

Seth walked Doctor Martin to the door. They went outside on the porch and talked. "Bob, I can't thank you enough for coming."

"I'm glad you called me."

"We only found one bullet at the scene of Paul's murder and some witnesses claim they heard two shots. Do you think this could be the second bullet?"

"As a doctor I would say it's only about one fourth of the bullet. The rest of it had to go somewhere else. Her wound looks like fragments of a bullet that went through something else first but there's no way it stopped there."

"Thanks doctor."

After Dr. Martin left Seth went back into the house. Sara was resting in the recliner. "Seth, thank you for calling the doctor when you did. We wouldn't know what to do if something happened to Sara. She's all the family we have left."

Sara smiled. "I appreciate that Maggie."

"Sara, even though you and Paul never got the chance to get married we still consider you family and always will no matter where life takes you. We've considered you family since you and Paul started seeing each other." Maggie hugged Sara. "We'll always love you Sara."

"I'll always love both of you." Sara started shivering.

"Sara, I have an idea. Why don't I make a fire in the fireplace to keep you warm, along with the two blankets you already have over you?"

"That sounds wonderful Seth."

"Let me help you do that Seth."

"Thanks Kevin."

While Kevin and Seth made the fire, Sara and Maggie talked. "Maggie, I feel so lost without Paul."

"I know you do sweetie. It'll take time."

"I know. I loved him so much."

"I know you did, but maybe you'll fall in love again someday and if you do don't let this horrible tragedy stop you from getting married or ever loving again. Sara you deserve love and happiness."

"Thanks Maggie." They hugged each other. The fire was roaring in the fireplace. "That feels good."

"That should keep you warm Sara. I'll keep it going all night."

"Thanks Seth. I'd appreciate that."

Maggie and Kevin looked at the clock. It was 11:00 P.M. They knew Sara had had a very traumatic day and she needed rest. "Sara honey, I think we're going to go back to our hotel if you think you'll be alright tonight."

"I'll be okay. Seth will be here with me."

"Okay but if you need anything you have our number, call."

"I will. What about church in the morning?"

"What time does your church start?"

"9:15 A.M."

"We'll be here at 8:15 A.M. If you aren't up to going to church we'll stay here, otherwise we'll leave here at 8:40 A.M., since it's 20 minutes from here to the church."

"That's fine."

"Do you know which officer will be going with us in the morning?"

"Lt. Scott Marsh will be here."

"Okay. We'll see you in the morning. Goodnight Sara, Seth."

"Good night Maggie, Kevin, thanks for everything."

Once Maggie and Kevin were in their car Kevin thought he should tell Maggie about what the doctor found. He reached over and clasped her hand. "Maggie, I need to tell you something the doctor told me about Sara. Before you get upset with me for not telling you earlier Seth, Dr. Martin and I agreed it was best not said in front of Sara right now. Seth will tell her later, after she's rested."

"What is it Kevin?" Maggie felt panic building up.

"The reason Sara's wound was infected was because there were bullet fragments in her wound." Maggie gasped.

"Bullet fragments?"

"That's what I said to. Seth told me several witnesses heard two shots fired the night Paul was killed, but they only found one bullet. Seth said they think the second bullet went thru something then grazed Sara in the side. They don't know what yet."

"Do they think the second bullet was for... I don't want to think it but do they think it was for Sara?"

"Yes, they do."

Murder *When the Bell Tolls*

Maggie gasped "Oh dear. I'm glad Seth and the other officers are there 24 hours. At least we know she's safe for now." They pulled into the hotel parking lot and parked their car. They walked into the hotel and to their suite. Their suite was beautifully decorated in blue with fancy curtains and big plush chairs. There was a bar and kitchenette in their suite. Maggie kicked off her shoes and so did Kevin. They looked at the clock. It was 11:30 P.M. They were both tired from the events of the day and knew they had an early morning tomorrow. They changed clothes, poured themselves some wine, and sat in the huge chairs and drank the wine.

Sara curled up in the chair and enjoyed the warmth from the fireplace. She was exhausted. Seth looked at her. "Sara, I need to ask you something."

"Sure Seth, what is it?"

"Do you have the purse you had with you the night Paul was killed?"

"Yes I do. It's laying on my dresser. I'll get it for you."

"You stay there; I'll get it." He walked into the bedroom and got the purse. He took it in the living room where Sara was. "Sara, is this the purse you were carrying?"

"Yes."

"Do you mind if I have a look inside?"

"No, but why?"

"I need to check for something."

"Go ahead."

Seth opened the purse and checked all of the seams. The last seam he checked he found what he was looking for, a bullet hole that went thru; that was when he knew Sara was the second target.

The look on Seth's face said it all. Sara knew something was wrong. "Seth, did you find what you were looking for?"

"Unfortunately yes I did."

"Seth, what's wrong?" He clasped Sara's hand. He didn't know how to tell her without upsetting her but knew he had to tell her.

"Sara, the reason your side got infected is because you had bullet fragments in your wound."

Sara gasped. She was shocked. "Bullet fragments? How did I get bullet fragments under my skin? That couldn't have happened unless I had been…" She couldn't finish.

"Unless you'd been shot. Sara, Witnesses have stated they heard two shots. We found one bullet at the scene but we didn't find the second bullet yet. I believe these bullet fragments will prove there were two shots and they were both fired from the same gun. Dr. Martin said he thought the bullet that grazed you went thru something first and after it grazed you it went into something else. Your purse is what may have saved your life. There's a bullet hole where the bullet went in and out but we still don't know where the rest of the bullet is. Can you remember anything else from that night?"

Sara thought about it. "That man in the raggedy clothes ran away from the scene, doubled over like he had a stomach ache or something. I'm sorry, that's all I can remember; I was leaning over Paul's body by then."

He squeezed Sara's hand. "That's okay. You need to try and get some rest. Are you warm enough?"

"Yes."

Sara suddenly felt fear building up. The reality of being shot was setting in. "Seth, you aren't going to go outside or in the other room are you?"

"No, I'll stay right here with you. It's alright. Just try to rest."

Sara leaned her head back and closed her eyes. Seth got a blanket, the paper and another cup of coffee then sat down in the overstuffed chair next to Sara. He could tell she was restless. After about an hour Sara finally began to relax and rest. Seth checked on her every fifteen minutes to make sure she was alright. When she was finally resting peacefully, Seth got up and walked around the inside of the house, shining his flashlight out the windows to check and see if anyone was outside that shouldn't be. He didn't see anyone. He sat down in the chair next to Sara and read the paper. He fell asleep. He was awakened when he heard Sara moving around in the recliner. "Seth, Seth, are you there?"

"Yes Sara, I'm here." He patted her hand.

"Thank you for staying in here with me."

"You're welcome."

"Seth, I need to use the bathroom, would you help me to the guest bathroom down the hall?"

"Sure."

Seth gently helped Sara get up. "Oww!"

"Sorry Sara."

Murder *When the Bell Tolls*

"It's not you. It's the bandages. It hurts to move but I think it might be because I've been in one place for so long."

"That's probably true. We'll take it nice and slow." Seth helped Sara to the bathroom. "Sara can you make it the rest of the way by yourself?"

"I think so."

"I'll be right outside the door if you need me."

"Thanks Seth."

When Sara came out of the bathroom she felt like she was going to collapse. Seth went over to her, put his arm around her waist, and helped her back into the living room. She looked at the clock. It was 4:00 A.M. She wanted to try and get more sleep if she could. Seth put another log on the fire.

"Thanks Seth. I appreciate it."

"You're welcome. Sara, would you mind if I had a glass of milk?"

"I don't mind. That sounds good. Would you bring me a glass of milk too?"

"Sure."

Seth went into the kitchen and poured two glasses of milk. He brought them into the living room and handed a glass to Sara." "Thanks Seth."

They drank the milk. Sara leaned her head back and closed her eyes. Seth took the glass from her hand and set it on the table. She fell asleep. Seth smiled as he watched her peacefully sleeping. He was so glad she was able to rest. He pulled the blanket up over her, then he put a blanket over him and fell asleep in the chair next to Sara. He woke up at 5:30 A.M. He went into the kitchen and made a fresh pot of coffee. He heard Sara begin stirring at 6:00 A.M. She opened her eyes slowly. "Seth, do I smell coffee?"

"You sure do Sara. I'm making a fresh pot."

"Thank you. I appreciate that." He smiled at her.

"What time is it Seth?"

"It 6:15 A.M."

"Seth, could you help me get up?"

"Sure."

He helped her stand up. "I want to shower and get ready for church; would you mind helping me walk back to my bedroom so I can get my clothes out for today?"

"Sara, I don't mind but are you sure you're up to going to church?"

"I'm not sure I'm up to it but I feel like I should go; besides I really want to go."

"Okay."

He put his arm around her waist and helped her walk back to her bedroom. "I'll wait out in the living room for you. If you need help let me know."

"I will."

Sara got undressed carefully, making sure to steady herself. When she took off the bandage she gasped. Seth asked "Sara, you alright in there?"

"Yes. I just took my bandage off, that's all."

"Okay; as long as you're alright."

"I am. I'm getting ready to step into the shower now."

"Be careful Sara."

"I will." Sara slowly stepped into the shower. She held onto the wall for support. She cringed when the water hit her wound. She started sobbing then crying. She missed Paul and the reality of what had happened had started to set in. She couldn't understand why anyone would want to hurt her or Paul. For the first time in a long time she felt vulnerable, and not because she was a woman. This was different. She dried off carefully making sure not to open up her wound. She got dressed, applied her make-up and some small jewelry. About thirty minutes later she called thru her bedroom door. "Seth, I need your help please." He came to her bedroom door and knocked.

"Sara."

"Seth, I need your help walking to the kitchen."

"Are you ready?"

"Yes."

He put his arm around her waist and helped her walk to the kitchen. He couldn't help notice how wonderful her perfume was and how lovely she looked, even though he could see the pain in her eyes. When they got into the kitchen Sara looked at the clock. It was 6:50 A.M. She started getting things out for breakfast. She had a lot of food fixed because she knew Maggie and Kevin would be there a lot and the police officers needed to eat also. "Sara, what are you doing?"

"Fixing breakfast. Are you hungry?"

"Yes, but you shouldn't be doing all of this. It's too hard on you."

Murder *When the Bell Tolls*

"I want to do this. What would you like? Waffles, pancakes, eggs or French toast? I personally feel like waffles."

"That sounds good to me. At least let me help you."

Seth and Sara cooked breakfast together. They went into the dining room at 7:15 A.M. to eat breakfast. "Seth. What's Lt. Marsh like?"

"Scott's a good police officer. He's bright, warm and friendly. He's only been on the force about eight years. He's younger than me but he's a good cop."

"That's good to know. Who's coming in this evening?"

"Officer Frank Hand."

"What's he like?"

"He's young. He's only been a police officer about two and a half years. He's a good officer. You can't help but like either of these officers. They're young, dedicated, polite, and friendly. I really like Paul's parents. They're wonderful people and they really treat you right."

"I love Paul's parents. They've always been there for me when I needed them; Maggie especially. When my mother died about ten months ago, Maggie came and stayed with me for a few days. Kevin had to teach at a seminar and couldn't get away. Paul, Maggie and I had a wonderful time together."

When they had finished eating Sara started clearing the table and taking the dishes into the kitchen. She was halfway there when the pain in her side caused her to drop the dishes in the middle of the floor. She grabbed her side and started sobbing. Seth put down the dishes he was carrying and went over to her. "Sara, what is it? Is it the pain?"

"Yes, I forgot to take my medication. Would you please get it for me?"

"Where is it?"

"On the table next to my bed."

"Let's get you over to a chair then I'll get your medicine." He helped her sit in the living room. "Stay here. I'll get your medicine." She sat sobbing in the chair. He came back with her medicine and a glass of water. "Here's you medicine Sara."

"Thank you Seth."

She took the medicine and immediately started to get up and clean up the mess from the dishes. "Sara, what are you doing?"

"Seth, I have to clean up that mess from the dishes."

"I'll do it you just stay there."

Sara started to object "But Seth, you're a guest."

"Don't argue, just sit."

"But Seth, Lt. Marsh will be here any time".

"That's alright. He can wait."

She smiled. "Okay. I'll stay here."

He smiled at her. "Good. Now let me get this mess cleaned up."

Seth had just finished cleaning up the mess on the floor when there was a knock on the door. "Sara, stay there. I'll get it." Seth answered the door. "Hi Scott. Come in."

When he walked in he saw Sara sitting in a chair. Sara got up slowly. "Sara, this is Lt. Scott Marsh."

"Hi Lt."

"Hello ma'am."

Sara smiled. "Please, call me Sara."

"Scott, I have few things I need to discuss with you that you need to know about Sara and this case. I haven't talked to the others yet but I will when I leave here. First of all, do not leave Sara out of your sight unless she is with Maggie or Kevin Sanford, or she asks you to go across the room so she can talk in private. Second, I had to call Dr. Martin last night because Sara collapsed. The doctor found out she'd been grazed by a bullet the night of the shooting. I have the fragments in a bag in my pocket. I'll take them to the lab and run a comparison on them. I think it's part of the second bullet other witnesses said they heard. Maggie and Kevin Sanford are Paul's parents. They're wonderful people; don't be afraid to ask them anything. If something comes up call me. I don't care what time it is, call me."

"I can do that."

"The Sanford's will be here around 8:20 this morning to pick Sara up for church."

"Okay."

"Lt?"

"Please, call me Scott."

"Scott, would you like something to eat or a cup of coffee or milk?"

"A glass of milk would be nice for now. I usually don't start drinking coffee until the afternoon."

Sara smiled. "I'll get you a glass of milk. Sara cringed when she got up.

Seth turned around and said "Sara, let me get it."

Seth got Scott a glass of milk, then looked at the clock. It was 8:05 A.M. "Sara, I have to go now but I'll call you later and see how you're doing. Ask Scott to help you if you need help."

"Okay."

"I'll talk to you later and see you tomorrow night Sara."

"I'll talk to you then."

"Goodbye Sara."

"Goodbye Seth."

When Seth walked out the door Sara felt sad. She didn't know why except for the fact she really liked Seth. Lt. Marsh was standing in the kitchen drinking his glass of milk. "Scott, it's okay to bring your glass of milk in here and sit down."

"Alright."

He walked into the living room and sat in the chair opposite of Sara. "Seth tells me you've been on the force about eight years."

"Yes ma'am. I mean Sara. I was in the military for eight years before that. The last three years I was an MP. It was challenging but very rewarding."

"I bet. My job is very rewarding but can be a bit of a challenge at times too."

"What type of job do you do Sara?"

"I'm a seventh grade English teacher."

"I can see where that would be challenging at times. Was Paul a teacher to?"

"Yes he also taught at a middle school."

While they were still talking there was a knock at the door. Seth told me that you weren't supposed to be moving around a lot so let me get the door." He opened the door. "Hello. May I help you?"

"I'm Maggie Sanford and this is my husband Kevin. We're here to pick up Sara". He looked at Sara.

"It's fine; let them in". Sara cringed when she stood up. "Good Morning Maggie, Kevin".

"Good Morning Sara."

"Maggie, Kevin, this is Lt. Scott Marsh. He'll be with us today." He shook Kevin's hand and nodded to Maggie.

Sara cringed again as she tried to walk toward Maggie. "Sara honey, stay there. I'll come over to you." Maggie walked over to Sara and hugged her gently. "Sara, you keep cringing; are you in a lot of pain?"

"Not as much as I was earlier. I took some pain medicine while Seth was here."

"Did you get any sleep last night?"

"Some. I had a hard time getting comfortable and I couldn't stop thinking about the night Paul was killed." Maggie hugged her again.

"I've been having trouble sleeping myself. Sara, honey, are you still blaming yourself for Paul's death?"

"I'm trying not to but I can't help thinking things would be different if I hadn't suggested we go to the park."

"Sara, Paul loved you. He would've gone with you wherever you wanted to go. Please don't blame yourself."

"Thanks Maggie."

"Are you feeling up to going to church?"

"Even though I had a rough night, I really want to go."

"Since it's 8:20 A.M. we need to leave in twenty minutes. Are you ready?"

"I need to get my shoes on and I'll need help with that. If I lean forward I get really dizzy."

"I'll be glad to help."

Kevin and Scott were talking when Maggie tapped Kevin on the shoulder. "Kevin, I'm going to help Sara get her shoes on. We'll be ready to go in about ten minutes."

"That's fine. Scott and I will talk more."

Sara and Maggie went into Sara's bedroom. "Which shoes do you want to wear Sara?"

"Since I'm wearing a black dress, I think I'll wear those black high heels that are in the front of my closet."

Maggie opened the closet and found Sara's shoes. "Are these the shoes you want?"

"Yes."

"I'll bring them to you."

"Thanks Maggie."

Maggie took Sara her shoes. Sara slipped them on and Maggie buckled them. She hugged her. "You ready to go sweetie?"

"Yes, I am." Sara and Maggie headed into the living room. "Well, ladies are you ready?"

"Yes we are."

After Sara locked up her house they went to the car ; Kevin drove to the church. "Maggie, I'm a little nervous about going to church today. It's the first Sunday in a long time I haven't had Paul with me. Having you and Kevin with me will help."

"Paul told me he really liked this church."

"He did. Everyone here liked him." Kevin pulled into the parking lot of the church and parked the car. The first service was just getting over. They headed to the church. As soon as Sara walked into the church; people started walking up to her and expressing their condolences. "Thank you," was her reply to them.

Pastor Akers walked up to them "Good Morning Sara, Kevin, Maggie, officer."

"Good Morning Pastor Jeff".

"Sara, you look pale. How you holding up?"

"Okay."

"Is there anything you need?"

"No, I'm okay so far."

"Don't hesitate to ask if you need anything."

"Thanks Pastor Jeff."

"We better take a seat before the service starts." When the service began Sara started sobbing. Maggie put her arm around Sara and hugged her. She felt better but still continued sobbing. She looked up and saw Maggie was sobbing also. The sermon was about keeping your faith after a tragedy. Sara started sobbing harder. The service got over ten minutes early. Pastor Jeff started heading to the door to shake hands with the people that were leaving. Sara stayed in the pews weeping. After Pastor Jeff was finished shaking hands with the people he came back in the church and walked over to the pew where Sara was. He stopped. "Sara, may I pray with you?"

"Certainly."

After he finished praying he said "Maggie, I have a strange feeling about Sara. Has something happened that I need to be aware of?"

Maggie looked at him and said "Pastor, Sara collapsed yesterday after we left here."

"Oh my, was it from exhaustion?"

"No; it was because she had an infection in a wound on her side. The wound was caused by a bullet."

He gasped. "What, when did that happen?"

"Apparently the night Paul was killed. According to the police there were two shots fired; they only found one bullet and the other grazed Sara in the side. She's in pain and trying very hard to deal with all of this."

"I can tell. It's a good thing she has 24 hour protection."

"Yes it is."

"If she needs anything or if you need anything, let me know."

"I will. Thank you."

As they were leaving the church they were met by Peggy and Ralph Miles. Peggy threw her arms around Sara and hugged her. They cried together. "Oh Sara, I'm so sorry about Paul." Sara cringed when Peggy hugged her. "Sara, what's wrong? Did I hurt you?"

"Just a little; I'll be alright though. Peggy, Ralph. I'd like you to meet Maggie and Kevin Sanford, Paul's parents.

"Hello Maggie, Kevin."

"Hello," they both said.

Lt. Marsh moved closer to Sara. "Is everything alright here Sara?"

"Yes Scott. This is my good friend and co-worker Peggy Miles and her husband Ralph."

"I'm Lt. Scott Marsh with the NYSPD. It's nice to meet you."

Peggy looked at her with compassion in her eyes. Sara cringed when she moved. "Sara, what's wrong honey? You cringe when you move?"

Maggie looked at Peggy and Ralph. "Sara has a wound that's infected on her side."

"How did that happen?"

"I'm not sure but the doctor told me I had bullet fragments inside the wound; that was why it was infected."

Peggy and Ralph both gasped. "Bullet fragments? Are you saying you were shot also?"

"Peggy, I don't remember. All I remember was talking to that man in the raggedy clothes, hearing a shot, watching Paul slump to the ground, and me leaning over Paul. Everything else is a blur right now."

"I bet. Ralph and I will be at the funeral home tomorrow night. I'm asking Nancy Boyd if she'll let me off for the funeral. If she doesn't, I'm taking off anyway. I want to be there for you."

"Thanks Peggy, Ralph."

"No problem Sara. We've been friends a long time. That's what friends do for each other." Ralph hugged Sara carefully. "Call us if you need anything."

"I will. Thanks Ralph."

"Maggie, Kevin, it's a pleasure to meet you. Wish it would've been under better circumstances."

"Nice to meet both of you. We've heard a lot about both of you."

"Well I guess we should be going. We'll see you tomorrow."

"Goodbye Sara."

Sara, Maggie, Kevin, and Scott left the church and headed to the car. "All of you wait here and I'll bring the car up to the front".

"Okay."

Scott stood outside and watched as Kevin walked to his car. Sara and Maggie stood inside the doorway. Kevin pulled up. Scott walked out with the ladies. Kevin and Scott started talking. Sara leaned back and Maggie put a pillow behind her head. "How you feeling sweetie?"

"I'm feeling a little better."

"Good."

"Kevin, I could use a cup of coffee," said Maggie.

"So could I Maggie. What about you Scott?"

"That sounds good."

"How about you Sara?" Sara was thinking about something else at the time and didn't really hear Maggie. "Sara honey, we'd all like to get a cup of coffee would you like some?"

"That sounds good. There's a little place down the road where the coffee is wonderful and the atmosphere is friendly. It's about five minutes from here."

"Sounds good. Give me directions."

Sara told Kevin how to get to the coffee shop. When they got there they had to look for a space to park. They got out of the car and headed inside. They sat down at a table and placed their order. "Oh may I have mine with a side order of strawberries?" Sara asked.

"Yes ma'am."
"Thank you."
Kevin and Scott talked.
"Sara, how did you know about this place? It's fabulous."
"Peggy, Carrie, and I used to come here a lot after school to grade papers and talk. We shared a lot of laughs, tears and secrets here."
"Peggy and Ralph seem like such wonderful people; have you known them long?"
"I've known them about 20 years. We met when we started teaching together, and we've been friends ever since."
"That's wonderful. I'm glad you have a friend like that."
"So am I."
The waitress brought their drinks and Sara's strawberries. They all started drinking their coffee. When Sara started eating her strawberries she suddenly remembered something about the man with the raggedy clothes. She gasped. "Sara honey, what is it?"
Sara looked at Maggie. "Maggie, I just remembered something about the man in the raggedy clothes," she whispered. "I really need to let Seth know but I don't want to wake him up."
"Sara, I don't think he'd mind if you called him. He'd want to know".
"I agree." Sara looked over at Kevin and Scott. "Would you all excuse me? I need to make a phone call."
"Is everything alright Sara?" Scott asked.
"Yes; everything's alright."
Sara walked outside, took out her cell phone and called Seth. "Seth Parker speaking."
"Seth, it's Sara."
Seth felt panic building up. "Sara, is everything alright? Are you alright?"
"I'm alright." Sara heard Seth sigh a sigh of relief. "Seth, I'm at Château Café with Maggie, Kevin and Scott."
"I love that place Sara."
"So do I. I hated to call and wake you but I remembered something about that man in the raggedy clothes."
"You did? What?"
"He has a strawberry birthmark above his ear, on his left cheek. The only thing that helped me remember is I'm eating strawberries and the shape was what I saw on his face."

"That will really help. Sara how you feeling?"

"I'm still sore but I'm feeling better."

"I'm glad. I wasn't sure you should have gone to church this morning but I'm glad you felt up to it."

"I wasn't sure either but I'm glad I went. Lt. Marsh is very nice Seth. I like him."

"I thought you would. How are Maggie and Kevin holding up?"

"About as good as can be expected. I was going to wait and call you later about what I remembered about that raggedy dressed man but I'm glad I didn't. It sounds so good and so comforting to hear your voice."

Seth smiled. "It's good to hear your voice too. I was a little concerned about you. I know how much pain you were in physically but I also detected the emotional pain you're feeling."

"Seth, I think reality is beginning to set in."

"I can only imagine what you're feeling. Sara, I'm glad you decided to talk to me about what happened. You can call me at anytime. I mean that."

"Thanks Seth. I have to go. We're going to go driving around for a little while then we're going back to my house."

"I'll call you later and check on you Sara."

"Thanks Seth."

"Goodbye Sara."

"Goodbye Seth."

Sara closed her cell phone and went back inside. Maggie looked at her smiling. "Were you able to reach him?"

"Yes. He was glad I called him."

"I figured he would be. Kevin is giving our waitress a tip. You ready to leave?"

"Yes I am."

Kevin returned to the table. "Were you able to make your call Sara?"

"Yes I was."

"You ready to go?"

"Yes."

They walked out to the car. They drove around looking at the flowers in bloom then went to Sara's. When they got to Sara's Scott said "Everyone, stay in the car while I walk around the outside of the house and make sure everything's alright."

"Okay. I'll park the car and wait for you to tell us it's okay."

Scott got out of the car and walked around the outside of the house. Everything seemed to be fine. He walked up to the porch and noticed a letter sticking inside Sara's door. He took the letter and put it on the inside of his jacket pocket. He walked out to the car. "It's okay to go in."

When they were all inside Sara looked at Maggie and said "Thank you for your help today Maggie, Kevin, It's appreciated."

"It's okay Sara. That's what families do for each other. Sara, you look exhausted."

"I am. This has been a very trying day for me. Would anyone mind if I laid down?"

"No, I think that would a good idea."

"Maggie would you come in the room with me and help me?"

"Sure".

Maggie and Sara went into Sara's bedroom. "Maggie, I'm going to use the restroom first then I need your help getting my shoes off."

"Alright, that's fine."

Maggie helped Sara into the bathroom. I'll be just outside if you need me Sara."

"Okay Maggie."

After Sara finished in the bathroom she came out and sat down on the bed. Maggie helped her take off her shoes. "Sara, lie down and try to get some rest. I'll stay in here with you if you'd like."

"I think I'll do that. You better tell Kevin and Scott so they don't worry about you."

"Okay, let's get you situated first."

"Alright."

Maggie helped Sara lay down on the bed. She got her a blanket and covered her up. "I'll be right back Sara."

"Alright."

When Maggie left the room Sara closed her eyes and tried to relax. Maggie found Kevin and Scott. "Sara would like for me to stay in her bedroom with her for a little while. She's lying down on the bed right now. I wanted to let both of you know that."

"I'm glad you did. I would've been worried about you if you wouldn't have."

Maggie smiled at Kevin. "Thanks dear. I'm going back in with Sara now."

"We'll check on both of you in a little while."

Maggie went back in Sara's bedroom. Sara tried to sit up but couldn't without cringing. "Sara honey, it's just me. Kevin and Scott know I'm in here with you. Lay back and try to get some rest."

Maggie held Sara's hand. Sara was restless, but finally drifted off to sleep. Maggie sat in the chair next to Sara's bed and checked on her every few minutes. Kevin came in to check on them. He smiled at Maggie then whispered "Is she asleep?"

"Yes, finally. She's restless but she really needs the sleep."

"I'm going to make a pot of coffee; would you like me to bring you a cup?"

"No, I'm fine."

Kevin walked over and kissed Maggie and hugged her. "I know you're exhausted too Maggie. If you go to sleep in here that's okay. Why don't you let me get you a blanket?"

"Okay."

Kevin got Maggie a blanket and covered her with it. He hugged her again. "You get some rest too. This has been hard on all of us."

After Kevin walked out of the room, Maggie leaned her head back in the chair and closed her eyes. Tears were running down her cheeks as she thought about Paul and Sara. She dearly loved Sara and hoped she could go on with her life after this was over. She thought about how much she was going to miss her conversations with Paul. Sara started moving around. Maggie opened her eyes to check on Sara. She could tell Sara was having a bad dream or something. She squeezed Sara's hand and whispered softly "It's okay Sara. I'm here honey." Sara relaxed and stopped moving around. Maggie closed her eyes again and leaned her head back. She fell asleep also.

Kevin and Scott talked in the other room. Maggie woke up about an hour later. She looked over at Sara, who was sleeping peacefully. Maggie needed to get up and stretch her legs. She walked around for a little while then went back and sat in the chair next to the bed. Maggie was in the bathroom when Sara awoke. "Maggie, are you here?"

"Yes Dear, I'm in the bathroom."

"Oh, Okay."

"I'll be right out."

"Don't rush. I'll wait for you."

Maggie came out of the bathroom. She went over and hugged Sara. "You look a lot more rested. Do you feel better?"

"Yes I do."

"Good. I'm glad. Kevin made a fresh pot of coffee. Why don't we go out and join the men?"

"That sounds like a good idea. Would you mind getting my slippers out of the closet?"

Maggie got Sara some slippers and helped her put them on. Her side still hurt when she bent over or moved a certain way. Maggie helped Sara walk out to the living room where Kevin and Scott were. When they got into the living room they found the men dozing. They both smiled. "Sara, let's get a cup of coffee and let them sleep." Sara and Maggie went into the kitchen and poured themselves some coffee. They went into the dining room and sat down at the table. Kevin and Scott woke up when they heard the ladies talking.

"Hello ladies."

"Hello."

"Sara, you look a lot better now. You don't look as tired. Do you feel better?"

"Yes I do Kevin. Thanks for asking."

They looked at the clock. "Wow! It's 2:00 P.M. I'm sure everyone's getting hungry. Sara why don't you let me heat up something to eat, then we can play cards or something?"

"That sounds good; but I can help heat up something."

"Okay, that's fine."

Sara and Maggie went into the kitchen to heat up something to eat. Maggie got the food out and Sara helped her heat it up. Once the food was hot everyone helped themselves. They ate at the dining room table. "Maggie, Sara, this is great. The food's excellent."

"Thank you Scott. Cooking is something I love to do."

They finished eating; Maggie and Kevin cleared off the table. "Is anyone up to a game of cards?"

"Sounds good to me," Kevin said."

That's fine with me," Scott said.

Murder *When the Bell Tolls*

"Sara, you up to a game of cards?"

"Yes."

"I'll get the cards."

Kevin came back with a deck of cards. He sat down and they started playing cards. Kevin dealt the first hand. While everyone was picking up their cards, Kevin was looking for a pen. "Oh, I think I have an extra pen in my pocket." Scott said.

When he reached into his pocket for a pen he felt the letter that was left on Sara's door. He took it out of his pocket. "Sara, I almost forgot, this was left on your door. I found it when I was walking around outside, after church." He handed her the letter and Kevin a pen. She gasped and started crying when she read the letter. She sat the letter on the table, got up slowly and walked over to the fireplace, sobbing the whole time. Maggie got up and walked over to her. She put her arm around Sara's shoulder and tried to comfort her. Sara trembled in fear.

Lt. Marsh had no way of knowing what was in that letter. He gasped in horror as he read it. The letter read: I'm watching you. I know who you are and where you live. I want you to know the killing isn't going to stop; until someone makes it stop. Someone else, just like your beloved Paul, will die on Tuesday, when the church bell tolls at 9:00p.m. I didn't kill you the first time but the next time I won't miss. Kevin looked at Scott, then he looked over at Maggie and Sara. Sara was crying and trembling. "What did Paul and I do to hurt that person so much?"

"Sara honey, you may not have done anything. This person is sick." Maggie said.

"Sara, I'm so sorry. I didn't know what was in that letter. If I would've known I wouldn't have given it to you."

"It's okay Scott."

Maggie was visibly shaken over the contents of the letter and so was Kevin.

"Sara, why don't I help you back to the dining room table?"

"Thanks Maggie."

Maggie helped Sara to the table, they all started playing cards again. Sara couldn't concentrate on the cards. She kept thinking about the contents of that letter.

Sara was still thinking about that letter when the phone rang. Sara jumped. "Sara honey, I'll answer it".

"Thanks Maggie."

"Hello Sara?"

"No this is Maggie Sanford."

"Maggie, it's Seth Parker. Is everything alright? You sound a little frightened?" Maggie was amazed at how well Seth picked up on the little things. She wanted to tell him about the letter but thought Sara should be the one to tell him. She knew now why Sara trusted Seth more than any other officer in the investigation.

"Something happened that was a little upsetting but I'll let Sara tell you about it."

"Is Sara alright?"

"For now."

"Can I talk to her?"

"Sure. Let me hand the phone to her."

"Sara, it's Seth. You alright?"

"Yes, I'm okay."

"Were you able to get any rest this afternoon?"

"Some. Maggie said I slept for about an hour and a half."

"That's good. That must have helped you feel better?"

"It did but then…" Sara started sobbing. She looked at Maggie.

"Sara, let me help you walk into the bedroom and you can talk in private."

"Thanks Maggie."

Maggie picked up the phone. "I'm going to walk Sara into the bedroom where the two of you can talk privately. We'll be just a minute."

"Okay."

Once they were in the bedroom Sara started to cry. Maggie hugged her. "I'm going out with the men. Come out when you're finished."

"Okay."

Sara was crying when she continued her conversation with Seth. "Sara, what's wrong? Are you in a lot of pain?"

"No, it's not that. It's just after I talked to you this morning, something else happened."

"What happened Sara?" Seth asked very compassionately.

"While Scott was walking around the outside of my house he found a letter stuck in my door. He forgot to give it to me until just now." Sara started crying hysterically.

"Sara honey, what did the letter say?" When she told him she heard a huge gasp on the other end of the line.

"Seth, Seth are you still there?"

"Yes Sara, I'm still here. Lt. Marsh handed you that letter when?"

"A little while ago. He said he forgot it was in his pocket."

"Sara, do you want me to come over there now?"

"Seth, I can't ask you to do that on your day off. Scott is doing okay and Maggie and Kevin are here. They'll probably stay until 11:00 P.M."

"Officer Frank Hand will be there until Lt. Marsh comes back in the morning. Sara, if you need anything at all please call me."

"I will Seth."

"I'll call you in the morning Sara."

"I'll talk to you then. Thanks for calling Seth."

"You're welcome. Goodbye Sara."

"Goodbye Seth."

After Sara hung up the phone with Seth, she sat on the edge of her bed thinking about the contents of that letter. She started to realize she may be in danger too, but from whom? She wondered. Seth sat in a chair at his house in complete shock about what was in that letter. He knew Sara was in extreme danger and he and the police department needed to do whatever was necessary to keep her safe. Then he remembered what was in that letter about another killing going to take place. Where and who? He wondered. What worried him the most was what the killer would do it to Sara if he caught her alone. He shuddered at that thought. Sara was still sitting on the edge of her bed when Kevin came in to talk to her.

"Sara, are you alright honey?"

"Yes."

"Was that Seth on the phone?"

"Yes it was."

"Did you tell him about the letter?"

"Yes I did and he got really worried."

"Maggie and I are worried about you too." Sara smiled at him.

"Thanks Kevin."

"Would you like to come out and join us?"

"Sure, but I need some help getting up."

"I'll help you". Kevin helped Sara stand up then helped her into the living room.

"Are you okay Sara?" Scott asked.

"Yes, I'm alright." Maggie hugged her. "I could really use a cup of coffee right now."

"Okay, I'll get it for you."

"I was hoping we could both go into the kitchen and talk."

"That would be fine wouldn't it gentlemen."

"Sure."

Maggie and Sara went into the kitchen and poured themselves a cup of coffee. Sara started pacing and shaking. "Maggie I'm scared."

"It's okay to be scared. I know I would be if I got a letter like that. I'd be terrified. You did tell Seth about the letter didn't you?"

"Yes and he was shocked."

"I bet. Sara, I'm really glad you're under police protection."

"Surprisingly, so am I."

Maggie hugged Sara and held her close to her as if she was trying to protect and shield her from further harm. They both walked into where the men were. They all started talking about things in general. Around 6:30 P.M. Sara asked "Is anyone besides me getting hungry?"

Maggie, Kevin and Scott said "Yes we are."

"Let me fix something then we'll eat."

"Sara, don't make anything really fancy and tire yourself out."

"I thought maybe we'd have spaghetti."

"That sounds fantastic. Would you like some help?"

"Sure Maggie".

Sara got out a pot and Maggie put the water in it and put it on the stove. While they waited for the water to boil Sara made a huge salad and got out some bread sticks from the freezer. She put them in the oven then checked the water for the pasta. Once the water was hot Maggie put the spaghetti in. Sara made a special salad dressing for the salad. When the food was ready Maggie and Sara started taking it into the dining room to eat. One of the plates was too heavy for Sara and she cringed and set the plate back down. "Sara honey, let me get that for you." Kevin said.

Scott grabbed the plates and silverware and brought them in. They sat down and started eating. "Sara, this salad's fantastic."

"Thank you. I think it's the dressing that makes it special. It's a recipe I found several years ago in one of my mother's old cookbooks."

They continued eating. When they finished Scott said "Wow Sara! That meal was wonderful."

"Thank you."

They looked at the clock. It was 7:15. Sara knew Officer Frank Hand would be there shortly. She started clearing the table and taking the dishes into the kitchen. Maggie and Kevin helped too. "Sara, I need to take one last look around the outside of your house before I end my shift."

"Okay."

Lt. Marsh went outside and walked around the house. Sara, Maggie and Kevin continued cleaning up from supper. "Sara, why don't you take a break? Maggie and I can handle the dishes."

"That's sweet but I want to help. If I keep busy, I won't think about missing Paul as much." Maggie and Kevin both understood and nodded. They all started doing the dishes.

Scott came back into the house. "Everything looks okay."

"Thank you Scott."

Five minutes later there was a knock on the door. Scott answered it. "Hello Scott."

"Hello Frank. Come in. Frank, this is Sara Michaels and Paul's parents Maggie and Kevin Sanford."

"Hello."

Sara was shocked to see how young Officer Hand was. He couldn't have been more than twenty five. "Come in and join us Officer Hand. I just made a fresh pot of coffee and I have milk, tea or whatever you'd like to drink."

"A glass of milk would be nice; and it's Frank ma'am."

"Okay Frank and it's Sara."

Sara went into the kitchen and got Frank a glass of milk. Scott told Frank about the events of the day. He gasped when he heard about the letter. "How's Sara taking all of this?"

"Pretty well. I think she's still in shock or denial right now. If there are any problems, call into the station."

"I will."

"Sara, Maggie, Kevin, I'll see all of you in the morning. You're in good hands with Frank."

"Goodbye Scott."

As Lt. Marsh was walking out the door; he turned to Sara and said "Sara, I'm going to take this letter to the station for evidence. I'll make sure all of the officers involved with this case see it."

"Thanks Scott."

He walked out the door and Sara took the glass of milk over to Frank. "Thank you Sara."

"Frank, Maggie, Kevin and I are cleaning up from dinner. Make yourself comfortable."

"Thank you."

They finished up then joined Frank in the living room. They decided to play a board game. They were almost finished with the first game when the phone rang. Kevin answered it.

"Hello. This is Marcus Cole."

"Marcus it's Kevin Sanford, Paul's father."

"Kevin, I heard you and Maggie were in town. I'm so terribly sorry about Paul."

"Thanks Marcus."

"How's Maggie doing?"

"Fairly well under the circumstances."

"I can imagine."

"She's trying to help Sara deal with all of this."

"That's why I called. I wanted to talk to Sara and see if there's anything she needs and to let her know how sorry I am about Paul. He'll be greatly missed. Is Sara doing alright?"

"She's doing better. Her physical wounds are healing and her emotional wounds will hopefully heal in time."

"Her physical wounds? What wounds?"

"You don't know?"

"No I don't."

"I better let her tell you. She's under 24 hour police protection because of all of this. Let me get her for you. Sara honey, Marcus Cole is on the phone for you."

"Marcus is so sweet. I'll be right there."

Kevin handed the phone to Sara. "Hello Marcus".

"Hello Sara. I wanted to call and tell you how sorry I am about Paul. He'll be greatly missed."

"Yes he will. Thank you sir."

"Sara I wanted you to know if you need anything, please ask."

"I will."

"How you feeling? I understand you have some type of physical wounds."

"Yes sir I do. I have a wound on my side that got infected because there were bullet fragments in it."

She heard a huge gasp on the other end of the line, followed by "Bullet fragments? So you were shot too?"

"According to the doctor I was grazed by a bullet. I don't remember getting hit, only Paul grabbing my arm and slumping to the ground."

"That's awful. I understand you're under police protection."

"Yes I am. The police and Kevin feel I might be in extreme danger until the person who did this is caught and in jail."

"I agree. I'm glad the police are there."

"So am I. Marcus, I'll be coming to your school later this week or next week. I want to start a scholarship fund in Paul's name at your school and at the school where I teach."

Marcus gasped in surprise. "Sara, that's a wonderful gesture. I need to go now but I'll see you tomorrow."

"Thanks for calling Marcus."

"No problem Sara. If you need anything let me know."

"I will. Thank you again."

Sara handed the phone back to Kevin. He sat it down on the table in the living room. They continued playing the board game. At 9:30 P.M. the phone rang again. Maggie answered it this time.

"Hello Maggie, it's Seth Parker. How are things going there?"

"They're going okay. We're playing a board game right now."

"That sounds fun. How's Sara doing?"

"She's doing okay. She's had a few times where she cries but that's normal given what she's been through."

"Yes it is. May I speak to Sara?"

"Sure, let me hand her the phone."

"Sara, it's Seth. I wanted to call and see how you were feeling now. I know you were really upset earlier when we talked and with good reason."

"I'm feeling better."

"That's good. How's Officer Hand working out? Is he doing okay?"

"Yes he is. He's really nice but he's so young."

"Yes he is. He's a good officer. If you need something, don't be afraid to call me."

"I won't. I promise."

"Okay. Sara, would you please let me talk to Frank?"

"Sure".

Sara handed the phone to Frank.

"Frank, it's Seth."

"Hey Seth."

"Frank how are things going?"

"They're going okay; why do you ask?"

"I'm just concerned about Sara and her guests. Did Scott tell you about the letter Sara received?"

"Yes he did. He said he was taking it into the station to add it to the evidence in this case."

"That's good to know. Did he tell you Sara's recovering from a bullet wound?"

Frank gasped. "No he didn't."

"Well she is. The doctor said she's to have constant supervision when she's walking anywhere or doing anything that might tear the bandages. After Maggie and Kevin go home this evening Sara will need you to help her do things. You can sleep in the chair in the living room while she sleeps either in a chair or in her bedroom. She'll ask you for help if she needs it. You need to make rounds of the house inside every two to three hours and once in the early morning around 6:00 A.M. Scott will relief you in the morning. Please take care of Sara tonight. I know you've never done anything like this before but it's part of our job as police officers to serve and protect and you are protecting someone, remember that."

"I will Seth."

"Frank, Sara knows if she needs anything she should ask. If something happens, I want to know about it, okay?"

"Sure Seth."

"Put Sara back on the phone for a minute will you?"

He handed the phone back to Sara. "Sara, I informed Frank of what he needs to do for you tonight. If you need me for anything, please call me."

"I will Seth."

"Okay. Try and get some rest tonight. I'll talk to you tomorrow morning and I'll see you tomorrow evening. Goodnight Sara."

"Goodnight Seth."

After Sara hung the phone up they went back to playing the board game they were playing. They finished one game then looked at the clock. It was 10:15 P.M. "Sara, you feel up to one more game?"

"Sure. Why not?"

They played another round. The game got over at 11:30 P.M. Maggie and Sara were both yawning. "Maggie, I think we should be going. Sara needs her rest and I know you're tired too."

"You don't have to leave."

"Sara honey, you need your rest. You know how to reach us if you need to."

Maggie and Kevin both walked over and hugged Sara. "Sara, we'll call you in the morning and make arrangements for picking you up to go to the funeral home and to see how you're doing. I think rest is the best thing for you now."

"I'm tired but I don't want to rush you."

"You aren't honey. We're tired also. I think all of us will feel better after we get some rest. I know I won't get much sleep but at least I can rest."

"Sara honey, we'll talk to you in the morning. Frank, take care of her. If she needs something don't be afraid to call. She has our number."

"Okay sir. Good night."

"Goodnight Sara."

"Goodnight Maggie, Kevin. I'll talk to you in the morning."

Frank watched as Maggie and Kevin walked out to their car. Sara was yawning when Frank got back over to her. "Frank, I'm going to get ready for bed if you don't mind."

"No, I don't mind. Go ahead. Sara cringed and walked very slowly as she tried to go into her room. Frank looked at her then remembered what Seth had told him about not letting her do things that could pull the bandages loose. "Sara, let me help you." He helped Sara walk to her bedroom. "I'll be right outside if you need me."

"Thanks Frank. I appreciate that." Sara walked over to her dresser and took out the gown she was going to wear. She undressed slowly, then took the bandage off of her wound. She gasped when she saw the huge mark. It wasn't as sore or pink but it still hurt. She put the ointment on it and put a fresh bandage on it then put her gown on. She started sobbing. She knew Frank would need blankets and a pillow in the living room. She got into the closet, got extra blankets and slowly walked out to the living room. Frank saw her coming and went to help her carry the things. "Frank, I brought you some blankets and pillows in case you want to sleep out here."

"Thank you Sara. I'll use them tonight. Would you like for me to keep the fire burning in the fireplace over night?"

"Yes, that would be nice. Frank, I'm really tired. Would you mind if I went to bed? Will you be alright out here?"

"I don't mind if you go to bed. I'll be fine. I need to make rounds every two to three hours anyway."

"Well alright then. Goodnight Frank. I'll see you in the morning. When I get up I'll fix you a nice breakfast before your shift's over."

"That sounds wonderful. Goodnight Sara. I'll see you in the morning."

Frank watched Sara walk very slowly into her bedroom. He grabbed the book he'd been reading, sat in a chair in the living room and began to read. He read for a little while then got up and walked around the house making his first set of rounds. He stopped and looked out the big bay window. The stars were shining brightly and the moonlight was shining directly into Sara's all seasons room. Everything looked alright for the time being.

Sara was restless. She tried to sleep but every time she closed her eyes she could see images of the shooting. She saw her and Paul talking, the man in the raggedy clothes, then Paul slumping to the ground. She started sobbing. She started thinking about Maggie and Kevin and how wonderful they were. She stopped sobbing, and started relaxing. She finally fell into a peaceful sleep.

After Frank had finished making rounds, he grabbed a cup of coffee, sat in the chair and started reading again. He

Murder *When the Bell Tolls*

finished his cup of coffee, took it into the kitchen, and was starting to head back to the chair when he thought he saw something outside. He grabbed his flashlight and went to the window. He shone the flashlight out the bay window but didn't see anything. He went back and sat in the chair in the living room. He dozed off and was awakened by Sara moaning in the bedroom. She was having a nightmare. He walked into her bedroom to check on her. "Maggie, it's my fault. Paul's dead because of me." He heard her say. Frank gasped and when he did it startled Sara. She opened her eyes. She was trembling. She saw Frank standing in the doorway of her bedroom. "Frank is that you?"

"Yes Sara it is. You alright? I heard you moaning and talking. I thought I'd check on you."

"I'm okay. I must have been having a bad dream or something. What time is it?"

"It's 3:30 A.M."

"Thank you Frank. Are you doing okay? Do you need anything?"

"I'm fine Sara. I already helped myself to a cup of coffee and now I'm going to put another log on the fire."

"Frank, help yourself to food or anything you need or want. Thank you for checking on me."

"No problem. You try and get some more sleep. I'll be right outside if you need me."

"Thanks Frank."

"Sara, do you need anything?"

"No. I'm going to try and get some rest. Thanks anyway Frank."

"Call me if you need me."

Sara sat up in bed trying to clear her head so she could sleep. She started shaking. She tried to think of something that made her happy. She thought about the theater. She smiled when she thought about the play the students in her school presented. They'd done a wonderful job and had enjoyed doing it. She laid down in bed and closed her eyes. She fell asleep quickly.

While Sara was sleeping, Frank was in the living room reading the paper. He got himself another cup of coffee. He looked at the clock. It was 4:15 A.M. He walked around the inside of the house again checking to make sure everything was alright. He went to Sara's bedroom door. He listened to make sure she was alright. He didn't hear her moving around so he assumed she was still asleep. He finished making rounds of the house and sat down to read. He fell asleep in the chair. At 5:30 A.M. he heard Sara moving around. He walked to her bedroom door to check on her again. He didn't want to frighten her if she was still half asleep. Sara heard him walking around. "Frank, is that you?"

"Yes it is Sara."

"I'm getting dressed right now but after I'm finished, would you mind helping me walk to the kitchen?"

"That would be fine. Let me know when you're ready."

As Sara got dressed she remembered it was Monday. Any other Monday she would've gotten up, showered, and gotten dressed for school but this wasn't any ordinary Monday. She started crying and shaking. This was the day she'd hoped she wouldn't have to deal with in a long time. She still couldn't believe Paul was dead. It still seemed like a nightmare. She finished getting dressed and went to the bedroom door. "Frank, could you come help me please?"

Frank appeared at the door. He helped Sara walk into the kitchen. Once they were in the kitchen Sara started fixing breakfast. "Frank, what would you like for breakfast? Eggs, French toast, waffles?"

"French toast sounds really good but so do eggs."

"How about I fix you both?"

"That sounds good. Do you need some help?"

"Yes. Could you hand me that pot and get the milk out of the refrigerator for me; then sit down and relax."

He handed her the things she asked for then reluctantly went and took a break. He admired Sara because of the fact she was still doing the things she loved but yet she was hurting. She'd been through a very horrific, traumatic experience yet she was opening up her home and heart to everyone. She's amazing Frank thought. He could smell the food cooking in the kitchen. He savored the aroma. "Sara, are you sure you don't need some help?"

"It's almost ready. What do you like on your French toast? Syrup, jelly, powered sugar?"

"Powered sugar and syrup."

"That's how I like mine too. I'll bring the syrup over to the table. Are you ready to eat Frank?"

Murder *When the Bell Tolls*

"Yes I am. It smells so good Sara."

Frank helped Sara take the food into the dining room. They sat down at the table and ate breakfast. It was 6:30 A.M. "Sara, do you always fix these big of breakfasts?"

"No. I usually only do that on the weekends. I don't get the time to do it through the week. I'm usually on my way to school by 8:15 A.M. I have to be in the classroom by 8:45 since classes start at 9:00 A.M."

"What's it like to teach seventh grade? I can remember my seventh grade year and it was one of the most difficult times of my life."

"It can be challenging but mostly, it's very rewarding. I have some very gifted and talented students."

"I don't think my seventh grade year would've been as difficult if I would've had a teacher like you."

Sara smiled. "Thank you Frank. That means a lot. It seems strange I'm not heading to school on a Monday during the school year."

"I bet it does. How long have you been teaching?"

"I've been teaching for twenty five years."

"Wow! That's amazing."

They continued talking and eating. About 7:25 they got up and started taking the dishes into the kitchen. Sara had made three trips into the kitchen with dishes when she stopped. She started feeling dizzy again and grabbed onto the table for support. Frank saw her struggling to stand. "Sara, you alright?"

"Yes. I just need a break."

"Let me help you to a chair."

"But, the dishes?"

"Don't worry about them. I'll take care of the dishes."

Sara didn't argue with him. He helped her to a chair in the living room. She sat down slowly. "Are you alright there, Sara?"

"Yes. I don't know what happened."

"I do. You're trying to do too much. Let me finish cleaning off the table then I'll take care of the dishes for you."

"Thanks Frank."

Frank got all the dishes together and washed them. He put them in the drainer to let them dry. He started to dry them but Sara said "Frank, I can put those away later. Thank you for washing them up."

"No problem Sara. What time do you need to be at the funeral home today?"

"Around three. We're having a private ceremony for the family members first."

"My girlfriend and I will try to be there. She gets off work at 4:00 P.M. She's a nurse at the county hospital." said Frank.

"Frank, I can't thank you enough for your help last night".

"You're welcome. It was my pleasure."

They looked at the clock. It was 7:45 A.M. There was a knock on the door. Frank answered it. "Hello Scott, come in."

"Hi Sara."

"Hello Scott."

"Scott, I need to tell you about last night. Sara, would you excuse us for a few minutes?"

"Sure."

Frank took Scott aside and told him "Sara had a fairly calm night, however she was having nightmares. She collapsed this morning. She's been trying to do too much. You need to watch her very closely today."

"I will. Maggie and Kevin Sanford will be with us also."

"Yes, I know. I'm not sure what time they're coming over today but Sara said they need to be at the funeral home by three."

"That's right; I remember her saying that yesterday. The next two days will be really rough for her."

"I know they will. She's a really nice lady."

"Yes she is. Who's coming in tonight after I get off?"

"Seth Parker. He told me last night he'll be at the funeral home by three. He thinks the more officers that are there the better it'll be for everyone."

"I agree."

"Sara, I have to get back to the station. I know you're in good hands with Lt. Marsh. I'll see you later."

"I'll see you. Thanks again Frank."

After Frank left, Scott walked over to Sara. "I understand you had a fairly restful night last night."

"Yes I did."

"That's good. I was hoping you'd be able to get some rest. Yesterday was difficult for you; I could tell."

"Yes it was. I didn't think it would be that difficult."

"I really like Paul's parents. They're such understanding people."

"They are good people. They've been so good to me. Scott, I'm going to get myself a cup of coffee; would you like a cup?"

"That sounds good."

"I have a lot of food. Would you like something to eat to?"

"No thank you. I ate breakfast before I came."

"Okay. If you want something to eat or drink, just ask. I have plenty."

"Thanks Sara. What time are Maggie and Kevin coming to pick you up?"

"I'm not sure. We didn't talk about that last night because I wasn't feeling well."

"You feeling better today?"

"Some. I'm dreading tonight and tomorrow though."

"I can imagine. I would be too."

The phone rang at 9:00 A.M. Sara answered it.

"Good Morning Sara. It's Maggie. How you feeling today?"

"Good Morning Maggie. I'm feeling a little better. I had a hard time sleeping last night, but I did get some rest."

"Good. I'm glad to hear that. Kevin and I were worried about you since Seth wasn't there with you. How did Frank do?"

"He did very well." Sara started feeling faint. "Maggie, can you hold on a minute? I need to sit down."

Sara heard Maggie gasp. "Sara honey, you alright?"

"Yes. I'm still having a little bit of a problem with dizziness."

"Are you sure that's all."

"I'm sure."

"Sara, Kevin and I thought maybe we'd come by and pick you up around 11:00 A.M. and take you out for a nice lunch. Since it's Monday the restaurants shouldn't be too busy. We'll have plenty of time before we need to get to the funeral home. Is 11:00 A.M. too early?"

"11:00 is fine. I'll be ready."

"Sara, which officer will be joining us for lunch?"

"Lt. Scott Marsh."

"Okay. Who's relieving him tonight?"

"Seth."

"Good. I'm glad."

Sara knew she needed to tell Maggie about the incident earlier with the dishes but she didn't know how. She knew Maggie was already concerned about her and knew it was going to be a long evening and an even longer day tomorrow; she needed Maggie and Kevin's support and help.

"Maggie, I need to tell you something that happened this morning and I don't want you to panic."

She could hear the anxiety in Maggie's voice when she said "Okay. What happened?" When Sara told her she'd collapsed after fixing breakfast and trying to do the dishes she heard Maggie gasp. "You sure you're alright honey?"

"Yes. I was just trying to do too much".

Maggie told Kevin what Sara had said and they agreed they should go to Sara's house earlier. "Sara honey, Kevin and I decided we'll come over in about an hour. We can talk for a little while before we leave; is that okay?"

"That's fine. I'll see you then."

Sara hung up the phone and walked into the living room and met Scott. "Sara everything alright?"

"Yes. That was Maggie. She and Kevin will be here in about an hour. They're going to take us to a nice restaurant for lunch before we head over to the funeral home. They'd planned on being here about 11:00 and leaving about 12:15 for the restaurant but after I told them about what happened this morning, they decided to come over early. Honestly, I'll be glad when they get here."

"I know you will Sara. They really look out for you."

"Yes they do. I'm glad they're around. I'm not sure I'd be able to handle this alone."

"I'm not sure I could handle something like this alone either. I know it's very difficult for you." Sara started shaking. Scott was afraid she'd collapse again. "Sara, let me help you sit down." He helped her to a chair, where she sat down slowly. She leaned back in the chair and tried to relax.

About thirty minutes later the phone rang again. Scott answered it. "Scott Marsh speaking."

"Scott, it's Seth. How's it going?"

"It's going okay so far. Maggie and Kevin Sanford will be here in about thirty minutes."

"How's Sara doing?"

"She's doing alright so far. She's had a rough start to the morning."

Scott heard Seth gasp. "What happened to cause her to have a rough morning? Did she get another letter, phone call, what?"

"No it's nothing like that. She collapsed earlier."

Seth gasped again. "She collapsed? From what? Her wounds?"

"She'd just finished cooking breakfast and was cleaning up when she collapsed."

"Were you there with her at the time?"

"No. Frank was. He handled it quite well under the circumstances."

"That's good to hear. Is Sara able to come to the phone?"

"Yes she is. Let me hand her the phone."

"Hello Seth."

"Hello Sara. I understand you've had a rough morning. How you feeling now?"

"Better. I think I was trying to do too much too fast. I have a hard time asking people for help."

"Sara now's a very stressful time. It's always okay to ask for help and especially now. I'm really glad you're feeling better. I understand Maggie and Kevin will be there shortly."

"Yes they'll be here in about fifteen minutes. Oh Seth, I wish I didn't have to do this. It still feels like a nightmare and I'm still waiting to wake up."

"I know the feeling. I really do. Are Maggie and Kevin going to take you somewhere for lunch or are you going to stay there and eat?"

"They want to take me to a nice restaurant. I probably won't eat much but Maggie says I need to eat to keep up my strength."

"It'll be good for you to eat a good meal. Maggie's right you know. You have to eat to keep up your strength. What time is the family service at the funeral home today?"

"We're supposed to be there at three."

"Okay, I'll be there by then. I think the more officers we have there the better things will go."

"I hope so. You know it's my fault that Paul was killed."

Seth gasped. "What do you mean by that?"

"Only that if I hadn't suggested we go for a walk he may still be alive today."

"Sara, you're not responsible for Paul's death. Please don't blame yourself. We'll catch the person responsible. I promise."

Sara started crying. "Thank you Seth. I guess I just needed to hear that. I kept having nightmares about the murder last night. It was awful." She couldn't tell him the nightmares wouldn't have been so bad if he was there. She felt much safer when he was there.

There was a knock on the door. Scott answered it. "Hello Maggie, Kevin, please come in. Sara's on the phone with Seth."

They walked into the living room and sat on the couch. Sara smiled when she saw them. "Seth, Maggie and Kevin are here now."

"I'm glad they're there with you. If you need me for anything, just call. I'll see you at 3:00 this afternoon."

"I'll see you then. Thanks for calling Seth."

"You're welcome. Call me if you need me".

Sara hung up the phone and turned her attention to Maggie and Kevin. Maggie walked over to Sara and hugged her. "Sara honey, we were so worried. Are you alright?"

"Yes. I'm alright. I had forgotten to take my pain medication and I was trying to do too much I guess."

"Sara, we're glad you're alright. We came earlier than usual because we thought maybe we could help you do something then we can decide where we're going to eat lunch. Scott said you were just talking to Seth."

"I was. He called to see how I was feeling and to find out what time the family service is today. He said he'd be there at three."

"Good. I'm glad he's going to be there. Now honey, what were you doing when you collapsed?"

"Taking the dishes to the kitchen and trying to get the extra food put away. Scott was helping me with the dishes."

"I got the dishes washed but not dried. I wasn't sure where they went and I didn't want to have Sara get up and collapse again."

"I'll dry the dishes and put them away. Is there any food that needs to be put away?"

"Just what's on the counter. I think I could manage to put it away now."

"Sara, there's no need for you to do that. We'll get your dishes and the extra food put away. I think you need to rest right now."

"I guess you're right Maggie. I hate having you do so much for me. You, Kevin, and Scott are my guests. I should wait on you not the other way around."

"Sara, we may be guests but we're still family. Family and friends help each other do things. We're glad to help."

"Thanks Maggie." Maggie dried the dishes, put them away then put the extra food away. When she was finished she walked over to Sara and hugged her.

"We're finished Sara. See it wasn't that big of a deal. We like helping you."

"Thanks Maggie, Kevin. It's hard for me to ask for help with anything. Seth said it isn't wrong to ask for help especially now, so I'm trying to remember to ask for help if I need it."

"Sara, how's your side doing?"

"It's better. It still hurts but not as bad. I still feel a little faint at times but I think it is getting better."

"I'm glad. I know that has to be painful."

"It is. I only imagined what it was like to be shot but now I know firsthand. I still don't remember feeling it at the time. Everything's a blur."

"I can imagine. Did you get any sleep last night?"

"Some. Maggie, I keep reliving that awful night. I keep seeing Paul slump to the ground and that person dressed in black, running away from the church, then seeing that raggedy dressed man. When will it stop? When?"

Sara started crying and Maggie held her next to her. Her heart ached for her but she too didn't understand why it had happened. She didn't have the answers to Sara's questions.

Kevin walked over to Sara and Maggie. He put his arms around both of the women and hugged them. He needed the same answers that Sara did.

At 11:30 A.M. everyone finally stopped crying. They decided to eat at a nice restaurant about thirty minutes from the funeral home. Before they left, Scott walked around the outside of Sara's house to see if everything was still alright. He finished and got into the car with Maggie, Sara, and Kevin. Kevin drove to a nice restaurant. They walked into the restaurant. The waiter seated them. Sara looked over at Maggie and smiled.

Once the food was ordered and the drinks were at the table Kevin looked at Sara. He could tell she hadn't had much rest or sleep but knew that was understandable under the circumstances. Scott and Kevin started talking and Maggie and Sara started talking. "Sara, I think you should take Nancy

Boyd's offer and take as much time off of work as you need; with that wound especially."

"I really wanted to get back to normal as much as I could but with this wound, I need a few more days."

"I think you need about three weeks off. Nancy said they'd pay you for any amount of time off you need."

"I'm going to take her up on that offer but just for the time you and Kevin are here. After you go home I'm going to need my work to keep myself busy."

"I agree, but you also need to ease yourself back in to things. I know. I had to do that when we lost both of our other children."

"Maggie, I know I'm hurting inside so I can only imagine how you and Kevin must feel. This shouldn't have happened."

"No it shouldn't have. However we'll always have our memories."

The food got to the table. They started eating. They talked about different things while they ate. Everyone was trying to avoid the subject of the funeral home. When they finished eating Sara and Maggie excused themselves and went into the bathroom to wash their hands. Sara started sobbing. Maggie put her arm around Sara's shoulder. "Maggie, I'm sorry about the tears. I'm really trying but I just can't seem to stop the tears."

"Sara, it's okay to cry. Kevin and I both have shed a lot of tears this week."

"Thanks Maggie. I needed to hear that."

"You ready to go back out and join the men?"

"Yes I am."

Sara and Maggie went back to the table. Kevin was paying the bill and Scott was leaving a tip. When the ladies got to the table, Kevin smiled at them. He knew how hard this was on both of them. It was hard on him too but he knew it was harder on them. Kevin checked his watch. "Maggie, Sara, it's 2:00 P.M. It'll take about thirty minutes to get to the funeral home. I guess we better get going."

"Yes. I guess we should." Maggie said.

Maggie looked over at Sara who was standing quietly with tears running down her cheeks. Maggie hugged her then they all headed out to the car. Kevin started driving to the funeral home and he and Scott talked. Maggie and Sara started talking. "Maggie, I'm so glad you and Kevin are here with me. You were with me when my mother died and that helped me deal with my grief easier but this time, I'm not even sure if that will help."

"Sara honey, we'll get through this together and we'll all grieve differently. That's okay. It's okay to be different. Don't hold your emotions back because we're here. It'll only make things harder for you. You're human, remember?" Sara smiled and then hugged Maggie.

They pulled up at the funeral home about 2:45 P.M. They got out of the car and walked into the funeral home. Sara started shaking. "Hello Sanford Family. I've prepared a special area where you can go as a family to grieve together. Most families use the time before the showing to console each other, pray together, or whatever they want to use the time for. I'll take you to that room now. It's adjoining so you may visit the casket also." He escorted them into the room. "There are chairs and couches so make yourself comfortable. I'll provide ice water and coffee also."

"Thank you sir. I was wondering if it would be possible to have a chair for Sara and Maggie out in the room where the showing will be. Maggie isn't able to stand for long periods of time and Sara's been terribly ill from an infection and the doctor doesn't want her on her feet for very long."

"That won't be a problem sir. I'll take care of that right now."

"Thank you sir."

While the funeral director was setting up the chairs in the other room; Sara, Kevin and Maggie consoled each other. He nodded at Kevin when he was finished. "Sara, Maggie are you ready to walk into the other room?"

Maggie and Sara both nodded their heads yes. Maggie clasped Sara's hand and Kevin put his arm around their backs as they walked to the casket. Maggie started sobbing. She leaned into the casket and hugged Paul and said her final goodbye. Sara started shaking. She still felt guilty about his death. Sara leaned into the casket and hugged Paul; tears were running down her cheeks. Then she whispered "I love you Paul. I'm so sorry."

Maggie cringed and Kevin gasped. He looked at Maggie. He pulled her aside. "What did Sara mean when she said she was sorry?"

"I'll tell you later."

A few minutes later Seth arrived. He was escorted into the room where the family was. He walked over to Kevin, shook his hand and offered his sympathy. He hugged Maggie and offered his sympathy then he walked over to Sara. He hugged Sara, then rubbed his hand across her back. "You doing okay Sara?"

"Yes. I'm doing okay. I don't think any of this has registered yet. I think after the funeral tomorrow reality may start to set in. I can't believe this is happening." She started crying and Seth hugged her again. Kevin and Maggie hugged her also. Seth hugged all three of them together.

Seth walked over to Scott. "Has Sara been okay after she collapsed this morning?"

"Not really. She almost collapsed two more times. Maggie and Kevin have been helping her and so have I. Seth, I'm glad you're going to be with her tonight. I know she'll be in good hands. It's not that Frank isn't a good officer, I just don't think he's capable of protecting her like he should. He's so young and inexperienced."

"I know he is but I believe in giving everyone a fair chance. Sara said he did okay."

"Sara's very sweet. I can't understand why anyone would want to hurt her."

"Neither can I and we have to make sure no one does. I want you to keep a close eye on Maggie and Kevin. I'll keep an eye on Sara."

"Okay. Didn't I hear you say Tom Monroe is planning on coming later?"

"Yes. He told me he'd be here at 6:00 P.M. He's off until tomorrow morning."

When Seth walked back over to everyone, Sara was starting to cry harder. Seth handed her a tissue, then rubbed his hand across her back. "Thank you Seth."

Everyone walked over to the casket and said their final goodbyes. Sara was crying hysterically. She kept saying "Paul, I'm so sorry. This shouldn't have happened. It's my fault. I'm sorry." They all gasped.

Kevin gasped and then looked over at Maggie. "Maggie, what does Sara mean by it's her fault? Is she referring to Paul's death?"

Murder *When the Bell Tolls*

Maggie looked at Kevin and Seth and said "Sara feels like Paul's death is her fault. She said because she suggested they take a walk in the park in the early evening, and Paul agreed it's her fault he was killed."

Seth and Kevin gasped. "That's absurd. She wasn't the one who killed him. Paul loved her and would have done anything for her. It was a simple walk in the park, enjoying each others company. It certainly isn't Sara's fault there was someone waiting to kill Paul and shoot her."

"Kevin, I know that. I've tried to tell her that but she insists it's her fault. I don't know what else I can do to convince her it's not her fault."

"Maybe I can do something to help. When my wife was killed nine years ago by a drunk driver, I blamed myself too. I thought if I would've been driving or been with her it might not have happened. The truth is; it would've happened regardless. Let me talk to Sara and see if I can convince her differently. I think once she gets through the grieving process she'll be able to think more clearly and rationally. I'll go talk to her now."

Sara was standing a few feet away from the casket. Seth walked over to her. "Sara, we need to talk for a few minutes before others start coming to pay their respects."

"Okay Seth. What would you like to talk about?" She asked as tears rolled down her cheeks.

His heart ached for her. She'd been thru a terrible ordeal and he didn't want to make it worse but he knew he had to try and get through to her about blaming herself. He thought carefully about what to say. "Sara, I overheard you at the casket telling Paul you were sorry. I asked Maggie about it and she told me you still feel like Paul's death is your fault."

"It is. We knew about the shootings around the church and park but when I suggested we go for a walk in the park Paul said yes. We wanted some time to talk, enjoy the fresh air and have a romantic walk. We had both been inside all day and the opportunity came up for us to enjoy the outdoors and we took it. A romantic walk would have been wonderful but why did I have to suggest the park?" She started crying hysterically. Seth rubbed his hand on her back.

"Sara, it's not your fault you suggested a romantic walk in the park. You and Paul were in love and needed some time together. It isn't your fault he was killed because of some crazed person. I know how you feel because I felt the same way when my wife was killed. I blamed myself too."

"Seth, does the pain ever go away? The guilt, the anger?"

"Yes it does but only if you have a lot of support from friends and family."

"Thank you so much Seth," she said and hugged him. Seth smiled.

The funeral director came into where they were all gathered and said "The visitation starts in five minutes."

"Thank you sir."

They went to the room where the people would come to pay their respects. Maggie and Sara both sat in the chairs provided for them. Sara started shaking. Seth and Scott stood off to the side so they weren't in the family line. Sara looked over at Seth. He nodded.

The funeral director greeted people at the door as they came in and showed them where to go. Sara was holding up fairly well until Peggy and Ralph got there. The three of them embraced and cried together. Some of Maggie and Kevin's friends came in next. Maggie started to cry as they came through the line. Maggie introduced them to Sara. "Sara honey, this is Elizabeth and Carl Harris. Two of our oldest and dearest friends. This is Sara Michaels, Paul's fiancé. We think of her as our daughter."

"It's a pleasure to meet both of you."

"It's a pleasure to meet you dear. I wish it could've been under different circumstances."

"So do I."

Since the line had dwindled down a little Elizabeth, Maggie, Carl, and Kevin talked for awhile. Sara heard Elizabeth tell Maggie "Maggie, Sara's so sweet and so attractive. I can see why Paul fell in love with her. How did they meet?"

"Sara's a teacher and a writer. They met at a teaching seminar that Kevin and I were speaking at. We fell in love with Sara when we met her. We'll always consider her family."

Sara smiled when she heard that. Seth walked over to Sara. "How you holding up Sara? Do you need anything?"

"I'm holding up okay. I could use a bottle of water if it's not too much trouble."

"It's no trouble. I'll be right back with your bottle of water."

Elizabeth looked at Maggie. "Maggie, who's that attractive man that was just talking to Sara?"

"That's Lt. Seth Parker with the NYSPD."

Elizabeth gasped. "NYSPD?"

"Yes. Sara's under 24 hour police protection."

"Why?"

"She caught a glimpse of the possible shooter and she was grazed by a bullet herself."

"Oh my goodness! Is she alright? How's she holding up?"

"She has her moments; like all of us but she seems to be doing alright."

"How's she handling the police protection?"

"She's doing okay with it. However, she'd rather have one or two officers with her instead of four or five. She likes Lt. Parker a lot and trusts him. There's another officer who'll be here later and his name's Tom Monroe. The other officer across the room is Lt. Scott Marsh. He's here until we leave this evening then Lt. Parker takes over."

"How do you and Kevin feel about Sara having to have 24 hour protection?"

"We're all for it. We want her safe. We've lost all of our children; we don't want to lose Sara too."

"That's understandable. Sara's very sweet. Maggie, other people are starting to come in. I think we should sit down and get out of the line." She hugged Maggie again then she and Carl sat in some of the chairs provided for the guests.

As soon as people started coming in again Sara got back in the family line. People from Paul's school were coming through the line then Sara saw Nancy with several students from her school. She tried not to cry but couldn't stop the tears. When Marcus Cole walked through the line he hugged Kevin and Maggie, then Sara. Students from Paul's school followed and Marcus introduced them.

Nancy came through the line and Sara started crying harder. Nancy hugged Sara, and the students from the school all hugged her at the same time. Maggie's friend's Elizabeth and Carl smiled.

A few minutes later Sara saw Tom Monroe walk in the door. He came through the line and expressed his condolences. He shook Kevin's hand and hugged Maggie and Sara. "I'm going to join Seth and Scott across the room. If anyone of you needs me for anything just ask."

He walked over to where Seth and Scott were. "Hello you two. Is everything going alright so far?"

"Everything's going okay. Sara's having a really hard time with all of this. You know she blames herself for Paul's death."

Tom gasped. "No. I had no idea. When and how did you find that out?"

"I found that out purely by accident. Sara was at the casket saying her final goodbyes and she actually apologized to Paul. She said she was sorry and that he shouldn't have died that way; that it was her fault. I talked to Maggie about it and she confirmed that. I talked to Sara about it. I think after she goes through the grieving process she'll think more rationally."

"I certainly hope so. Paul's death is certainly not her fault."

"Is there any news on the raggedy dressed man?"

"None. We can't locate him anywhere."

When the line diminished for a short period of time Sara excused herself for a few minutes. "Sara, you alright honey?"

"Yes. I just need to use the bathroom and splash some water on my face."

"Are you sure that's all?"

"Yes. I'm sure."

Maggie was worried about Sara. "Kevin, I'll be right back. I'd feel better if I went with Sara."

"That's fine. If anyone asks where you are, I'll tell them you stepped away for a few minutes and will be back shortly."

"Thanks Kevin. Sara honey, wait up. I'll go with you."

Sara stopped. She had tears rolling down her face. Maggie hugged her. They got into the bathroom and Sara started crying harder. Maggie held her next to her and tried to comfort her. She was crying to. Once they both stopped crying so hard they used the bathroom, and both of them splashed water on their faces. As they were getting ready to walk out the bathroom door Sara looked at Maggie and said "Maggie, when those children from the school hugged me all at once, that really tugged at my heart. They're great kids."

"It pulled at my heart strings too Sara. Those children really love you and I can tell how much you love them. Sara, the best thing you can do for them is to be you. They're starting the awkward years of their lives and if you show them it's okay to have and show emotions and it's okay to be themselves it'll be the best lesson you can teach them."

"Thanks Maggie."

"Let's go back out there and join Kevin. Sara, I know this is terribly hard on you but you shouldn't blame yourself. Paul's in a better place now. When he died, he died in the arms of the woman he loved, you. Sara always remember Paul loved you more than anything else. He really did."

Sara smiled. "Thank you for telling me that Maggie. I guess I never thought about it that way. I do know he's in a better place, it's just so hard to say goodbye."

Maggie hugged Sara. "I know it is honey. It's very hard to say goodbye."

They walked into the room where Kevin was. Elizabeth and Carl walked over to Maggie. "Is everything okay Maggie? We noticed you and Sara left together."

"Everything's alright. Sara's supposed to have total supervision because of an infection she has."

"What's the infection from?

"Bullet fragments in her wound, from when she was grazed by that bullet."

Elizabeth and Carl both gasped. "Are you and Kevin staying with her at night?"

"No. One of the police officers are there with her."

"What's going to happen when you go back home?"

"We understand from the police department that she'll be under police protection until the person who is responsible for Paul's death is behind bars."

"That's good to know."

"Yes it is. At least we won't have to worry about her as much as we would."

More people started coming in to pay their respects. Sara was doing alright until Art and his cousin Jack came into the room. Sara felt intimidated by Art; however she didn't know Jack very well. All she knew about either one of them was that Art worked as a teller in a local bank and he had hurt her severely and Jack was the manager at a local grocery store. Art had asked her out several times before she met Paul and she always turned him down. She wasn't ready for a relationship at that time.

When Art and Jack walked through the line they shook Maggie and Kevin's hand. When they got to Sara, Art squeezed Sara's hand until he almost broke her hand. She tried to break free of his grip without making a scene. Maggie noticed that Sara was uncomfortable around these men but didn't know why. Seth saw the look of fear in Sara's eyes and walked over to them and said "Sara, everything alright?"

"Yes Seth. These men were just paying their respects." She looked shaken up. He knew there was something she wasn't saying.

Seth whispered in her ear. "I know you are afraid of these men for some reason. I'll watch them constantly. Motion with your eyes if you need me. I'm going across the room."

After Seth walked across the room Art bent down and whispered. "Sara, you're still as beautiful as you always were. I'm sorry about Paul. The offer still stands. Anytime you want to go out on the town, I'll be glad to take you."

Sara, trying to be polite, smiled and said. "Thank you but not at this time."

Art smirked then he and Jack walked out the door of the funeral home. Sara was trembling and tried to pull herself together since other people were coming into the funeral home and getting in line to pay their respects.

Sara watched and waited until they were gone. She sighed. Maggie put her arm around her and hugged her. Other people came into the funeral home and got in line to pay their respects.

About an hour before the showing was over, Sara's best friend, who was recovering from cancer, walked into the funeral home. She got in the line. She shook hands with Maggie and Kevin but when she got to Sara, she hugged her. "Carrie, thank you so much for coming. I appreciate it."

"I know how it feels to lose someone you love. You're my best friend Sara and I want to be here for you like you've been there for me."

"Oh Carrie," was all that Sara could manage to say. The line dwindled down again and Carrie and Sara had a chance to talk. "Sara, I couldn't believe it when I heard about Paul. The news reports said you two were just walking in the park."

"We were. It had been a long week at school for both of us and we wanted some time to relax. Paul picked me up from work and we went out for dinner then went for a walk. I never dreamed it would be the last time he held my hand, hugged me, and the last time we'd ever take a walk together. I can't believe he's gone." Carrie hugged her.

"Carrie, thank you so much for understanding."

"You're welcome Sara. Are those two people standing up there with you Paul's parents?"

"Yes they are. Let me introduce them to you."

Sara took Carrie up to where Kevin and Maggie were standing. "Maggie, Kevin, I'd like you to meet Carrie White. My best friend whom I've known almost as long as I've known Peggy and Ralph."

"Hello Maggie, Kevin. I know I've already gone through the line but please let me offer my condolences again. I'm glad I've had a chance to meet you. I wish it would've been under different circumstances. I knew Paul some but not like Sara. She talks about you often."

Maggie and Kevin smiled. "It is nice to meet you Carrie. We too wish it would've been under different circumstances. Sara said you two have known each other a long time. How did you meet?"

"My late husband was a special education teacher at Sara's school and I was the secretary in the principal's office until I got my teaching degree twenty years ago. Then I became a seventh grade science teacher."

"Are you still teaching Carrie?"

"I'm on medical leave right now, but yes I am. I'm supposed to be back in the classroom in three weeks."

More people started coming in. "Carrie, Sara and I need to get back in line."

"No problem." She hugged Sara.

Carrie sat in one of the seats provided for the guests. The other people came through the line and expressed their condolences. At 8:10 everyone except for Maggie, Kevin, Sara, Seth, Scott, Tom, Carrie, and the Harris' were gone. The funeral director came into the room. "Would you like a few more minutes?"

They all looked at each other. Kevin could tell Maggie and Sara were exhausted. He knew no one had eaten anything since earlier. "Maggie, Sara, why don't we go somewhere and get something to eat and relax. This has been very trying for all of us and I think if we go somewhere and relax we'll all feel better. Carrie, Scott, Tom, would you like to join Maggie, Sara, Seth and I?"

"Thank you for the offer Kevin but I really need to get back to the station".

"Thank you for staying the whole time. We'll see you later".

"I need to get going too. It's been nice meeting you Carrie. I hope we can get together again sometime." Tom said.

"It was nice meeting you too. Sara, I'd love to join you."

"That's great. We'll enjoy having you."

They left the funeral home together. "Carrie, you're more than welcome to ride with us if you like."

"Thank you sir but I'd feel better driving myself in case I want to leave before you do, but thank you for the offer."

"I understand but Carrie, it's Kevin and Maggie." Carrie smiled.

They decided where they were going to go and got into their cars. It was a quiet ride to the café. Kevin looked in the rear view mirror and smiled, then turned to Seth and said "Finally, they're getting some much needed rest."

"That they are. I'm so glad. They both need it. I think Maggie's been Sara's strength through all of this and you've been like a rock to both of them. I know Maggie's a strong woman but this is more than anyone can take."

"I agree Seth. Maggie's trying to be a rock for me and for Sara, but that's Maggie. She's always been there when someone needs her. That's what makes her so special and Sara, I can't say enough good about sweet, loving, Sara. Sara's so gentle, yet strong, loving and compassionate. Paul dearly loved her. He once said that he'd never met anyone like her. She's funny, polite, and worldly, yet shy in her own way. I can see how Paul could fall in love with her. Maggie and I did when we first met her. We love her dearly too."

"I really like Sara too. We have a lot in common and she's so easy to talk to and so very understanding. However given what she's been through I'm extremely worried about her."

"So are we."

They pulled into the parking lot of the café. Kevin looked over the front seat. Maggie opened her eyes. Kevin smiled at her. He said softly "Maggie honey, we're at the café."

Maggie looked at Seth and Kevin then at Sara, who was dozing with her head on Maggie's shoulder. Maggie gently rubbed Sara's arm until Sara opened her eyes. "Sara honey, I hated to wake you but we're at the café."

"Oh, okay. Thanks Maggie."

Murder When the Bell Tolls

The men got out of the car and helped the ladies out. Carrie came up to them. "Hello Carrie. Are we ready to go inside?"

Everyone said yes and headed inside. Carrie and Sara started talking as they walked. "Sara, who's that handsome man walking with Kevin?"

"That's Lt. Seth Parker with the NYSPD. I'm under 24 hour police protection and he's the head of department in charge of protecting me. I really like him and I trust him. He's a good officer. Call him Seth."

Carrie gasped when she heard that Sara was under police protection. "Sara honey, why are you under police protection?"

"First of all because I may have gotten a glimpse of the shooter and secondly because I along with Paul was shot."

Carrie gasped. "Oh no! You were shot? I didn't know anything about that. Where were you shot?"

"I was grazed in my side by a bullet. I don't remember being shot only leaning over Paul's body. Apparently the bullet grazed me when it went through my purse. I didn't even know I'd been shot until I developed an infection in my side. A doctor came over and removed the bullet fragments and told me I needed to rest, drink plenty of fluids and take medication as prescribed; all of which I've been doing. I'm doing better but this day has been very trying."

"I can image."

They got inside and found a seat. All of the ladies sat together so they could talk and Seth and Kevin sat together. Seth wanted a chair facing Sara so he wouldn't have her out of his sight. The waitress brought them menus. All of them decided what they wanted.

Carrie, Maggie, and Sara started talking. "Carrie, you knew that Maggie was a teacher also didn't you?"

"I think I remember you mentioning that. You taught high school, right?"

"Yes I did. I loved it. You said you've been a teacher for twenty years. How do you like it?"

"I love it. I hated to have to take off these past few weeks but my treatments are causing a lot of side effects and weakness."

"Maggie, Carrie had cancer. She's taking chemotherapy. How many more weeks of treatments do you have?"

"I have one more treatment next week then I'm done. They were able to get it all."

"That's fantastic. I'm glad. Will you go back to teaching after that?"

"Yes I'm sure I will. I really love it and with Sara as my best friend, and co-worker I know I can do this."

Maggie smiled at both of them. "Carrie, did you know Paul?"

"Yes I did. Not as well as I know Sara but I remember the first time I met Paul. I thought Sara had to be the luckiest person in the world to have someone like Paul. Paul was truly a wonderful man and will be missed."

Sara started sobbing. "Thanks for being such a good friend Carrie."

Kevin and Seth were talking also. "Seth, Maggie and I are really worried about Sara. We're afraid of what will happen after we go home. She and Maggie are really close; they talk about everything. Maggie has never had someone like that that she can talk to. Is Sara going to be protected 24 hours after we go home?"

"She'll still be under 24 hour police protection until the person or persons are in jail."

"Seth, I know this is asking a lot but Sara trusts you. Maggie and I would feel better if you could arrange to protect her more often. We feel like she's safer with you and you can relate to what she's going through. Would it be possible for you to rearrange your schedule?"

"I have a better idea. How about I just stay with her 24 hours a day until the person or persons are caught, tried and convicted? I'd feel better if I didn't have to worry if the other officers were doing what they were supposed to be doing. I feel like Sara's in extreme danger. I don't mind going to church with her and we enjoy a lot of the same things. It would be my pleasure to stay with her then we wouldn't have to keep changing officers."

"I think that's a great idea. Let me talk to Sara and Maggie and see what they think. However, what will they say at the precinct?"

"It doesn't matter. I'm the head of the department and what I say goes. I really care about Sara. I'll do whatever it takes to protect her."

Murder *When the Bell Tolls*

Kevin smiled. "I'll discuss this with Maggie and Sara when we get back to Sara's house. I think both of them will agree with me that this is a wonderful idea. I know I'd feel better if you were the only officer there. I know Sara would be safe and you'd treat her right."

Seth smiled. "Yes Kevin I would."

The food arrived and everyone started eating. When they finished eating, Carrie, Maggie, and Sara, went to the bathroom. Once they were in the bathroom Sara, trying to keep from crying, started sobbing. Carrie walked over to her and hugged her. "Oh Sara, I know how hard this is for you. I wish there was something I could say that would make it better, I really do."

"Thanks Carrie. You're a true friend. Just being here helps."

Maggie hugged Sara too. "Carrie, I'm glad you're here."

"Maggie, Sara told me about her being shot and being under police protection. I'm glad she's under protection."

"So are Kevin and I. What do you think of Seth Parker?"

"I like him. He seems to care a great deal about Sara."

"He does. We have a lot in common and he's so easy to talk to. I trust him more than any officer that I've had protecting me," said Sara. Maggie smiled.

The women left the bathroom and went to meet the men. Seth and Kevin were waiting for them when they got there. "I paid the bill and Seth left the tip. Is everyone ready to go?"

"Yes we are."

As they started walking out to the parking lot Carrie looked at Kevin and said "Kevin, what do I owe you for the meal?"

"Nothing Carrie. It's on me."

"Thanks Kevin. It wasn't necessary but it is appreciated."

"I know it wasn't necessary but Maggie and I wanted to do it. You're Sara's friend and our guest. It was our pleasure." Carrie smiled at him.

As Carrie started walking across the parking lot Kevin said "Carrie, where are you parked?"

"Over by the street light."

"With everything that's happened I'd feel better if you allowed me to walk you to your car."

"Thanks Kevin. I'd feel a lot safer if you did."

"Seth, ladies I'll be right back."

Kevin walked with Carrie to her car and waited for her to get in. She still had her door open and said "Kevin, thank you again. I appreciate it."

"You're welcome Carrie. Be careful going home."

"I will. Thanks again." Kevin closed her car door and she drove away. He walked back to his car.

"Kevin, that was sweet of you to walk her to her car. She's been through so much these past three years. She lost her husband to cancer and now she's been dealing with cancer. She's lost all of her hair, wore a wig and…" Sara suddenly stopped.

"Sara, what is it?" Maggie asked.

"I just remembered something about the raggedy dressed man. Seth, you remember me telling you about what he looked like and how his hair was?"

"Yes I do. Why?"

"I think he was wearing a wig. I remember seeing streaks of brown hair mixed in with the blond hair on the back of his neck."

"That means we may be looking for someone who isn't homeless at all, but a second person involved in the murders. A set up person so to speak. Sara, let me call into the station now so the officers can widen their search."

While Kevin drove Seth called into the station. "Lt. Anderson speaking."

"Mark, it's Seth. I have a new lead on the raggedy dressed man. Do you have something to write this on?"

"Yes. Go ahead Seth."

"The person we're looking for may or may not have been wearing a wig and I believe he may not be homeless. It's possible he's the second person involved in the murders, the set-up person. Sara said she remembered seeing streaks of brown hair mixed with the hair on the back of his neck. We need to widen the search. Tell Tom to call me at Sara's tomorrow morning before he comes over."

"Okay, is there any particular reason?"

"I need to discuss something with him. It has to do with Sara being under police protection."

"Okay. I'll tell him."

"Thanks Mark."

Murder *When the Bell Tolls*

They pulled up to Sara's house. "Everyone remain in the car while I check around the outside and then we can all go in together."

"Okay Seth."

Kevin parked the car and waited while Seth checked around the outside of the house. He checked and made sure none of the locks on the house had been tampered with either, then he went out to the car and told everyone it was safe to enter the house.

Sara started sobbing when she got inside. Maggie hugged her. Maggie started sobbing too. It had been a hard day for both of them. Everyone could tell Sara was exhausted and in pain, she said "Would anyone mind if I changed into my nightgown and robe?"

"No, go ahead. Get comfortable."

"Sara, do you need some help?"

"That would be nice Maggie, thanks."

"We'll be back shortly."

"Okay. We'll be here."

When Maggie and Sara went into the bedroom Kevin and Seth started talking. "Seth, have you thought any more about taking on the task of protecting Sara yourself for 24 hours a day?"

"Yes I have. I've decided it would be a good idea. I need to have other officers canvassing the neighborhood at all times. I don't want to leave Sara in the house alone because I'm afraid someone may try to get in if I'm walking around outside."

"I'm glad you decided to stay on 24 hours a day. It'll be easier on Sara and I know she trusts you. I know you're the head of this investigation and you'll make sure Sara's safe at all times."

"Yes I will. Kevin I need to ask you something."

"Sure, what is it?"

"Since I'll be staying here, do you think it would be appropriate if I took Sara to the theater or to a movie myself? I mean I'll be with her wherever she goes anyway but if I want to do something fun and enjoyable for her."

Kevin smiled. "You mean like take her out on a date?"

"Yes, sort of. I wouldn't call it a date just something fun to take her mind off of what has happened, because I know when we catch this person or persons it'll be a relief but the trial could get ugly. I think that's when she's going to want to escape from things once in awhile."

Kevin smiled again. "I think that would be wonderful. I agree the trial could get ugly and really upset her. She's been through a lot these past two years and the less pain she has to deal with the better. If you think she'd enjoy something, I think it would be wonderful if you two did it together." He patted Seth on the back. "It's okay if you find her attractive and fall in love with her. Maggie and I understand. She's a wonderful person and we want her to go on with her life. We know how much she loved Paul and now he's gone. She deserves love and happiness in her life. She is and always will be part of our family. Just take care or her."

Seth smiled. "I'll take care of her. I'm glad you have confidence in me, and in my police department. I left word for Tom Monroe to call me in the morning before he comes in so I can discuss this with him and he can pass the word on to the other officers of the change in duties. However, we still have to ask Maggie and Sara if they approve of this. I'm supposed to get off at 8:00 tomorrow morning but I was planning on going to the funeral anyway. Tom's scheduled to be here at 8:00 A.M. I think I'll tell him to meet us here and we can all go to the funeral together, then after the funeral dinner I'll assume my duties as Sara's 24 hour police protection. Would that be alright?"

"I think that would be fine. We'll ask the ladies when they come back in here."

"That sounds fine with me. After the funeral tomorrow I need for you to take me to my place so I can get a few things like clothes and toiletries and my checkbook."

"That's not a problem. I can do that."

"Since I'll be staying here all the time for awhile, I'll dress in street clothes and blend in with everyone else, especially when I'm at Sara's school."

While Maggie was helping Sara change clothes they started talking. "Sara, I want to talk to you about something and I want you to think about what I am saying before you object okay?"

"Okay. What is it Maggie?"

"Sara honey, I think Seth Parker should be the only officer protecting you 24 hours a day. You trust him and I know you feel safer with him than any other of the officers. I'm not saying the other officers aren't good at their job but I know I'd feel better if Seth was the only officer protecting you."

Sara was shocked. She never thought she'd hear Maggie say that. She did trust Seth, more than she realized but she didn't know what to say. "Maggie, don't you think people might say something if Seth stayed here with me all the time?"

"No I don't Sara and even if they did, it doesn't matter. Your safety comes first. You mean so much to Kevin and I. I don't know what I'd do if something happened to you." She hugged Sara. "Sara honey, you and Seth have a lot in common." Maggie knew that Seth really cared about Sara.

"Maggie, if I agree to allow Seth to stay here all the time and sleep in one of the guest bedrooms; do you think it would be inappropriate if we went places that he'd want to go, like on a weekend fishing trip, or something like that?"

Maggie smiled. "No Sara I don't think it would be inappropriate. I think it would be wonderful for you to get away. I think the next few months are going to be really difficult and when they finally catch the person responsible for Paul's death and go to trial it could get really rough. You're going to need someone like Seth to help you through this. It's okay if you fall in love with him. I know how much you loved Paul and how much he loved you but he's gone now and Kevin and I hope you can go on with your life. You deserve love and happiness. You'll always be part of our family no matter what. We want you to be happy."

Sara was shocked. "Maggie, I was hoping you'd suggest Seth stay here all the time. I know I'll feel safer if he's here. I like the other officers but I really trust Seth. I feel like he really knows what he's doing and he cares about what happens to me and about catching the person or persons responsible for not only Paul's murder but possibly several others."

Maggie smiled. "We'll talk to the men when we get out of here. I know I'd feel better knowing if Seth will stay before Kevin and I go home this evening."

"Thanks Maggie. Do you think Kevin will object to having Seth stay here all the time?"

"No Sara, I don't think he'll object. I think he'll be relieved. He hated seeing you have to deal with so many different officers and not knowing if you can trust them. I think he'll agree to this. Let's go see."

Maggie and Sara walked into the living room where Seth and Kevin were sitting. "Hello Ladies." They both said.

"Kevin could I talk to you privately for a few minutes?"

"Sure Maggie."

"Maggie, Kevin you could go in my bedroom or the four seasons room. It's private there."

"Thanks Sara. I think we'll go in the four seasons room."

"Seth and I will go into the kitchen. I could use a cup of tea anyway."

"Okay. We'll be back shortly."

When Maggie and Kevin headed to the four seasons room Sara and Seth went into the kitchen. "Do you know what that's about Sara?"

"Maggie and Kevin talking privately? I assume it's about the fact that Maggie and I would like for you to stay here 24 hours a day. That you would be the officer protecting me. Maggie wanted to talk to Kevin first and see if he agrees to it. "Seth looked at Sara and smiled. "Seth, do you know something I don't"?

"Kevin and I had that conversation while you were changing clothes. He asked me if I'd consider staying here with you instead of constantly changing officers. I said I would if you agreed to it, and you did."

Sara smiled. She felt relieved that Seth was going to stay. She could try to get her life back to normal a little easier and quicker. She really liked Seth and found it comforting to know he'd be there. "Seth, I'm glad you agreed. I know I'll feel safer." Seth wanted to lean down and kiss her but he didn't; instead he clasped her hands and squeezed them.

Maggie and Kevin were talking. "Kevin, I've been thinking, it would be better if Seth moved into one of the guest rooms and stayed here all of the time. It would be easier on Sara and I know I'd feel better having someone I know we can trust and Sara can trust protecting her. I think she could get on with her life sooner. What do you think Kevin?"

Kevin smiled at Maggie. "I already had this conversation with Seth. He agreed to stay if we agreed it was alright and if Sara agreed to it. Besides they have a lot in common and Sara is entitled to happiness. Seth will make sure she's safe at all times. I know that."

"You know Kevin; Sara asked me if Seth was living in one of the guest rooms, if I thought it would be inappropriate if the two of them took a weekend trip together and just got away."

"What did you tell her?"

"I told her I thought that would be wonderful, that she could use the time away from here. It would help her move on more quickly."

Kevin smiled. "Seth asked me the same thing. He wanted to know if it would be inappropriate to take Sara to the theater, or a movie. He told me when the person or persons responsible for the murders are caught the trial could get ugly and he felt Sara might need to escape to something that makes her happy. I agreed. I also told him it was alright to fall in love with her, that we did the first time we met her."

Maggie smiled. "I told Sara the same thing. I told her we knew how much she loved Paul and how much he loved her but that he was gone and that she should move on with her life. She and Seth have a lot in common. I think he's the perfect officer to protect her. He'll treat her like a lady. Let's go tell them we think the arrangements should begin immediately."

"I know Seth asked me if I'd mind taking him to his house after the funeral tomorrow so he could pick up a few things. I told him I would. He said he was supposed to get off at 8:00 tomorrow morning but he was going to stay around and go to the funeral with us. I don't see why we can't go by his house afterward do you?"

"No, not at all. Let's go talk to them."

Maggie and Kevin walked out of the room and went into the kitchen where they found Seth and Sara talking and having tea. "Seth, Sara, you both know we were talking about Seth staying here 24 hours a day and we both agree that's what should be done. Having Seth here will make things a lot easier."

Sara and Seth looked at each other and nodded. "Seth, I think this should begin immediately. Is there anything you need to do at the station?"

"No. I'll talk to Tom tomorrow morning and he'll do the paperwork and we'll be done. It's set in stone that I'll be the officer protecting Sara. However there will be officers patrolling the neighborhood and if I become ill and cannot accompany Sara somewhere I'll see to it that Tom Monroe, or Lt. Anderson will replace me for the time Sara is away from here."

"That sounds great. Sara, which guest room would you like to have him stay in?"

"I'll show him." They all walked back to the farther guest room. Seth gasped when he saw the spacious bedroom, with a king size bed. The room was beautifully decorated in yellow. He had a six drawer dresser with a mirror, a computer desk with a computer, a large screen television, a walk in closet, a huge bathroom with a tub and shower, a large window, a ceiling fan and table lamps on all the tables. "Seth, this will be your room. I hope you like it. I'll get you some extra blankets and towels."

Seth was amazed. He'd only seen this room in the dark. It was beautiful. "Sara, this room's huge. I never expected anything like this."

"I'm glad you like it. It's one of my favorite rooms in the house and I always let my special guests stay in this room. Let me go get your things."

Sara walked down the hall. She opened the closet door and took out some towels and blankets. She took them back to Seth. "Here you are Seth. Some fresh towels and some blankets in case you get cold."

"Thank you Sara. Maggie, Kevin, I want to thank both of you for agreeing to this. I promise I'll protect her and take good care of her."

"We know you will Seth."

Sara was exhausted and knew Maggie had to be exhausted too. She looked at both of them. "I'm going to get a cup of tea, make a fire in the fireplace and relax by the fire before I go to bed. Would any of you like something?"

"I think I'd like to have a cup of tea also. It'll help take the edge off and help me sleep. I'll help you get the tea ready Sara."

They went into the living room. "Sara, why don't I get the fire going for you before we leave?"

"That would be nice Kevin. Thank you."

Kevin lit the fire, then went into the kitchen to help Seth and the ladies with the tea. When the tea was ready Maggie served everyone and they sat down in the living room.

Sara looked at the clock. It was 11:30 P.M. "Maggie, Kevin, what time will you be here in the morning?"

"The funeral's at 10:00 and it takes twenty minutes to get to the church. Pastor Jeff suggested we get there at least thirty minutes ahead of time so that means we should be there by 9:30 A.M. How about if we get here at 8:45 A.M.? Will that be enough time for you Sara?"

"Yes it will."

"Is that okay Seth or will you need more time to get enough officers at the church?"

"That will be fine. The officers have been informed that they need to be at the church at 9:00 A.M. I thought that would give everyone plenty of time to get things situated."

Maggie was so tired she was yawning. "Maggie you're so tired. Why don't you and Kevin go get some rest? I can tell both you and Sara are exhausted. I know this has been a very traumatic few days. Everything will be okay here."

"Sara honey, would that be alright? If you want us to stay longer we can."

"I'll be alright. I'm going to get ready for bed myself in a little while. Everything will be okay."

"How's your side feeling?"

"It's a little tender but it's feeling better. The medication is helping I think. Right now I'm so tired I'm ready to try and get some sleep."

Kevin and Maggie hugged Sara. "I think we'll be going so you can get some rest. If you need anything, you call. Otherwise we'll see you in the morning." They hugged Sara again. "Goodnight Sara, Seth."

"Goodnight Maggie, Kevin. We'll see you in the morning."

Seth watched Maggie and Kevin walk to their car and get in. He waved as they drove away. Then he came back into the house and joined Sara. He walked over to Sara. She had tears running down her cheeks. He rubbed his hand on her back in comfort. "You okay Sara?"

"Yes, I was just thinking about Paul."

"I figured as much. Would you like to talk about it?"

"Oh Seth, I miss him so much. I can't help think he'd still be alive if I hadn't suggested we go walking in the park."

"Sara, it's not your fault. There's a crazed killer out there who's picking and choosing his victims. You're forgetting you too are one of his victims, and you're the only one who survived."

Sara realized Seth was right but she felt so guilty and so helpless. "Seth, I know you're right but I feel so empty."

"I understand how you feel, I really do. I felt that way when Marie died. Sara, it's okay to cry and feel like you do. It might feel like you'll never stop crying but eventually you will."

"Oh Seth, thank you for understanding. It helps a lot."

Sara started to get up from the chair and go into the kitchen when she suddenly had a stabbing pain in the wound on her side. "Ow!"

Seth ran over to her. "What's wrong Sara?"

"It's my side. I suddenly have a stabbing pain in the wound. I wanted to get up and get another cup of tea before I went to bed but I can't move without having pain."

"You stay there; I'll get you another cup of tea. When you're ready to go to sleep, I'll help you walk into your bedroom."

"Thanks Seth. I appreciate it. I'm glad you agreed to stay."

"So am I; especially with you trying to recover from a bullet wound."

Seth went into the kitchen and got a cup of tea and brought it out for Sara. She fixed it the way she wanted it. "This tastes wonderful. Thank you Seth."

"You're welcome."

"Seth, would you mind sitting and talking for awhile? I'm not sure I'll be able to sleep even though I'm exhausted."

"I wouldn't mind, besides, there's something I've been wanting to ask you. I need to get myself a cup of tea also. I'll be right back."

Seth got himself a cup of tea, then went into the living room and sat in a chair facing Sara. The fire crackled in the fireplace. Seth looked at Sara and could see the tears welling up in her eyes. He could tell she was scared and grief stricken. He clasped her hands. "It's okay to cry Sara."

Sara started trembling. "Seth, this brings back so many memories. My late husband Gary and I used to sit around the fireplace and talk, late into the night. We'd eat popcorn and watch movies and snuggle on the couch, some nights even falling asleep on the couch, then after he died I met Paul. We spent a lot of nights sitting by the fire talking, watching movies, going into the four seasons room and looking at the stars. They were so bright from there. Now some crazy person has taken

Murder *When the Bell Tolls*

Paul away. I feel so empty and so vulnerable. I've never really felt that way before, but I do now."

"What you're feeling is normal. I think the reason you feel so vulnerable now is because you suffered a bullet wound. You're a victim of a crime. No one ever feels the same after they become a victim of crime. I've heard that many times from other victims. I also know how you feel when it comes to feeling empty. My wife and I did a lot of the same things you and Gary and even Paul did and when my wife was killed I felt something that you're not allowing yourself to feel, anger. Sara, it's okay to get angry. It really is."

"Seth, I don't allow myself to get angry because I am afraid of my anger. I don't want to be like my father when I get angry."

Seth looked at Sara. "What do you mean? Did he hurt you?"

"Yes he did and I've spent many years trying to process it. The pain is still there and when Art and Jack came to the funeral home tonight, I thought I was going to be sick. Art reminds me of my father and Jack reminds me of me, an obedient servant."

Seth gasped. "Sara that's what I wanted to talk to you about. Those two men that upset you so badly at the funeral home; how do you know them?"

"I know Jack because he's the store manager at the grocery store where I shop all the time and his unruly uncle is a bank teller at a local bank. Art's been trying to get me to date him since Gary died. He's so controlling of Jack I can understand why he'd do whatever Art told him to do. I remember one time when I was in the grocery store and Art was ordering Jack around. I walked down an aisle and Art came over to me and said something sexual to me and I slapped him. He grabbed my arm and told me I better never hit him again or I'd be sorry. After that I've tried to stay clear of him. As a matter of fact he's been trying to get a woman named Martha Mae Burns to go out with him and she keeps turning him down. She said she's afraid of him."

"I can understand why. He sounds really dangerous."

"Seth, I'm terrified of Art. He'll stop at nothing to get what he wants. Jack on the other hand is just the opposite. He'd do whatever Art wanted him to do just to please him. He's that way at the store. He goes out of his way to please people."

"Sara, I'm going to get another cup of tea for myself would you like another cup?"

Sara looked at the clock. It was 12:45 A.M. She was exhausted and ready to go to sleep. She thought about it and decided "No thanks Seth. I think I better try and get some rest. We have a big day ahead of us; one which I'm dreading."

"So am I Sara. It'll be a very difficult day and you do need your rest. Would you like for me to help you into your bedroom?"

"That would be nice Seth."

Seth helped Sara up from the chair then helped her walk to her bedroom. He waited in the bedroom while she went into the master bathroom. She came out then looked at Seth. "I'm sorry I don't have anything to give you to sleep in for tonight but Paul hadn't moved his things in yet and I got rid of all of Gary's clothes. Will you be alright for tonight? If not I think I can find something."

"Sara, I'll be fine. I'll have my things tomorrow. I'll manage for tonight. Go ahead and get in bed and get some rest. You know where I'll be if you need me."

Sara got into bed. She cringed when she moved. Seth helped her pull her covers up then helped her lie back. He patted her on the shoulder. "Goodnight Sara. If you need me just call."

"Goodnight Seth. Thank you for everything. I'll see you in the morning."

Seth left Sara's bedroom and went into the living room. He put another log on the fire, went into the kitchen, got a cup of tea, went into the living room and sat in a chair with the paper. It wasn't long before he was asleep in the chair. He woke up about two hours later. He got up and walked around the inside of the house looking out windows to see if everything was still alright. He walked over to Sara's bedroom and looked in. She was still sleeping peacefully. He smiled then went back into the living room and sat down in the chair. It was 3:00 A.M.

Seth read the paper for a little while then fell back asleep. Around 6:00 A.M. Seth heard Sara moving around in her bedroom. He got up and made a pot of coffee. Sara came into the living room. "Good Morning Sara."

"Good Morning Seth. Do I smell coffee?"

"Yes you do. I just started a fresh pot. How did you sleep last night?"

"Once I got to sleep, I slept pretty well. I didn't have any nightmares last night."

"Well, that's good. I checked on you at 3:00 A.M. and you were sleeping peacefully. I fell asleep in the chair in the living room and never made it back to the guest room."

"Seth, what would you like for breakfast? I have a lot of food already prepared in case someone from out of town stops by or decides to spend the night."

"I think I want something simple like scrambled eggs and bacon or maybe an omelet."

"Um. An omelet sounds good. Let me get the things together for the omelets."

As Sara was setting the things out to make omelets the pain in her side started hurting again. She grabbed the counter. Seth went over to her. "Sara, is it your side again?"

"Yes. It was fine until I bent down to get something from the lower shelf of the refrigerator."

"You need to sit down. Let me make the omelets."

"But Seth I..."

"Sara, I insist. Let me help you."

He helped her to a chair in the dining room; he went into the kitchen and started mixing up the omelets. They both decided they wanted western omelets so Seth cut up the ingredients and made the omelets. "Seth, do you need my help?"

"No. I got it. I used to be pretty good at making omelets; hopefully I still am. Well, they're ready. Let's see how they taste. You stay there and I'll bring yours to you and I'll bring mine in also."

Seth took Sara her food then went back into the kitchen and got his. He brought the pot of coffee and two cups out also. Sara smiled. They started eating. "Seth, this is wonderful. These omelets are great."

"Thanks Sara. I could still cook but I wasn't sure I still knew how to make omelets."

After they finished eating they looked at the clock. It was 7:05 A.M. Sara helped Seth clear off the table and get the dishes into the kitchen. Sara walked over to the sink and started washing the dishes. Seth was drying them and setting them on the counter to be put away. Suddenly Sara grabbed her side again. "Oww! My side's really hurting again. Seth I hate to leave the rest of the dishes but I need to sit down for a few minutes before I get dressed for the funeral."

"Sara, let me help you to a chair. You just sit there for a few minutes and I'll take care of the dishes, then I'll help you go back to your room so that you can get ready."

Sara wanted to object but she didn't. She let Seth help her to a chair. Seth did the dishes while Sara sat in a chair at the dining room table. Sara started sobbing. She dreaded the day. She watched as Seth washed the dishes then dried them and set them on the counter. At 7:50 he walked over to her. "Sara, Maggie and Kevin will be here in an hour. Do you think that will give you time to get ready?"

"Yes it'll be enough time. I really wish this day wasn't happening."

"I know you do. So do I but I'll be there for you and so will several other officers and Maggie and Kevin."

"That's true."

Seth helped Sara to her room to get dressed. As he was coming out of the room the phone rang. He answered it. "Seth Parker speaking."

"Seth, it's Tom Monroe. Mark told me you asked me to call you before I came over to Sara's. I would've called sooner but I got hung up in traffic on my way to work. What's up Seth?"

"Tom, there's been a change regarding police protection on Sara Michaels."

"What, do you want more officers for police protection?"

"No, only one. Me. Paul's parents asked me if I'd be willing to be the only officer protecting Sara. That means I'd be responsible for her at all times. I agreed and they set me up in a huge guest room that has almost everything a person would need to live in. The change is effective immediately. I do need a favor; two as a matter of fact. I was wondering if it would be possible to have police patrols every day and night about every three hours in the neighborhood and Kevin asked that if for some reason I cannot accompany Sara somewhere due to illness or whatever, if you'd be willing to accompany her for the day or evening?"

"That wouldn't be a problem. I'm scheduled to be at Sara's right now. What would you like me to do?"

"Come over and you can ride with us to the funeral home and eat with us. I'm going to have you stay with Maggie and Sara while Kevin and I get some things from my house to take to Sara's."

"That's fine. Seth can I ask a question?"

"Sure Tom. What is it?"

"Did Kevin ask you to do this because one of us messed up or something?"

"No it's nothing like that; it's just easier on everyone, including Sara if one officer is with her at all times and the others can concentrate on the case."

"I understand. I was just wondering. I'll be there in a few minutes."

"I'll see you then."

As soon as Seth hung up the phone he heard Sara calling him. "Seth, could you come help me please?"

He walked into her bedroom and found her clutching onto the dresser and trying get to her medicine."

"Sara, sit down."

He sat her down on a dressing table chair that she had in her bedroom. "Seth, I was trying to get my medicine. It's on my night stand next to the bed."

"I'll get it and get you a glass of water. You stay there." Seth got the medicine and a glass of water and gave it to Sara.

Sara took the medicine and set the glass down on the table, she started shaking. He rubbed his hand across her back to comfort her, then put his arm around her shoulder and hugged her. She just cried harder.

Once Sara stopped crying so hard she stood up and said "Seth, would you mind zipping my dress up in the back? I'm having a hard time doing that today."

"That's not a problem." Seth said as he watched Sara trembling.

He zipped up her dress. "Thank you Seth. I appreciate it."

"Sara, I'm going to get freshened up myself if you'll be alright."

"I should be alright. I only have to put on my make-up and jewelry. Maggie and Kevin should be here in fifteen minutes. Go ahead and freshen up. If I need you I'll call you."

Seth left the room and went into the guest room. He grabbed a wash cloth and washed off his face. He realized he needed to shave before he went to the funeral. He walked back to Sara's bedroom and knocked on the door. "Sara, it's Seth. May I come in?"

"Sure Seth."

"Sara, I hate to bother you with little details but I was wondering if you had an extra disposable razor I could use, also a toothbrush and toothpaste? I'd feel better if I could at least shave."

"Sure Seth. I'm sorry I didn't think about that last night. Let me get it for you. It's under the sink in my bathroom."

Sara got the things Seth needed and came back with them. "Here you go. Again, I'm sorry I didn't think about it sooner."

"Don't worry about that Sara. I would've managed if you wouldn't have had these things."

"I usually have those things around in case one of my out of town friends stops by and decides to spend the night and they don't have any of their own things. That happened last winter when a friend of mine from college came from New Jersey to visit and we had that massive snow storm that closed all the roads. She didn't have anything with her and no where to stay so she stayed with me."

"Sounds like you two had a good time."

"We did."

"I'm glad. I better get back to the guest bedroom and finish getting ready to go; Maggie and Kevin will be here shortly. I'll be out shortly too." Seth went back to his bedroom and started cleaning up.

Just as Sara finished getting her jewelry on there was a knock on the door. She walked to the door. "Hi Maggie, Kevin, please come in."

Maggie and Kevin hugged Sara. "You look nice Sara. Even though it's for a funeral you look nice. We brought you something."

Kevin handed the bag to Sara. She opened it up and tears started running down her face. She hugged both of them and said "Thank you both. I appreciate it. You're both so good to me. I wish we didn't have to go through this today."

"So do we Sara, but we thought this might help you feel better."

"It does. Thank you both again."

"Sara, where's Seth? We brought him a few things from the store like a clean shirt and some clean socks."

"He's back in the guest bedroom."

Murder *When the Bell Tolls*

"I'll take these things back to him."

"Thanks Kevin."

Kevin walked back to the bedroom where Seth was. He heard water running. He knocked on the door. "Seth, it's Kevin. May I come in?"

"Sure, come in."

"Seth, Maggie and I stopped at the store and brought you a few things we thought you might need this morning. We brought you a clean shirt, some socks, and an electric razor."

Seth gasped with surprise. "Wow, you two didn't have to do that. I was planning on getting my things today after the funeral."

"We know but we thought you might like a clean shirt and socks to wear."

"Yes I would. Thank you both. Now if I only had a pair of clean pants."

"I can do that. I think we're about the same size. What's your waist size Seth?"

"Thirty four."

"Perfect. So is mine. I brought a pair of my pants along in case you wanted a clean pair of pants."

"That's wonderful. I can't thank you enough."

"Here's the electric razor Seth. Would you like to use that too?"

"Yes. I think I'll shave first then put on some clean clothes. Kevin, would you like to stay here and talk while I clean up?"

"Sure. How did Sara do last night?"

"Fairly well. I checked on her a couple of times and she was sleeping peacefully. I was so glad. We talked for quite a while after you and Maggie left."

"Good. I'm glad you were here for her."

After Seth finished shaving he put deodorant on then put on the new shirt that Kevin and Maggie bought him. It fit him perfectly, then Kevin handed him the pants. He looked like an ordinary person now, not a police officer, which was what everyone wanted. He finished getting ready then he and Kevin walked out to where Sara and Maggie were sitting.

While Kevin was with Seth, Sara and Maggie were talking. "Sara, were you able to get any rest last night?"

"Some. I had a hard time getting to sleep. Seth and I talked until almost 1:30 this morning. I was exhausted but I was afraid I wouldn't be able to sleep and I was in pain too. That didn't help."

Maggie gasped. "In pain? From your side?"

"Yes. I've been having stabbing pains once in awhile since last night. I'll be alright today. I took my medicine and I'm going to take it with me in case I need it."

"I think that would be a good idea. Does Seth know about you having pain?"

"Yes and he's worried."

"I bet he is. When are you supposed to see Dr. Martin again?"

"I'm going to call him when we get back from the funeral and make an appointment for tomorrow or Thursday. He said four days and that would be tomorrow."

"I think as much pain as you've been in, you should call him before we go and get an appointment for tomorrow. I'd feel better if you did."

"If I get an appointment for tomorrow, I know Seth will go with me but I'd really love it if you'd be with me too. I'm not sure I'll remember everything he tells me."

"Let me know what time the appointment is and I'll be right there with you."

"Thanks Maggie."

"Here come the guys. Wow! Don't you look nice Seth?"

"You do look nice Seth. Where did you get the clean clothes?"

"Maggie and Kevin brought them."

"Maggie, Kevin that was sweet of you. I felt bad because I didn't have anything Seth could wear so I'm grateful you brought him something."

"It's no big deal. Sara, why don't you try and call Dr. Martin's office now? We have about ten or fifteen minutes before we have to leave."

Kevin looked at Sara very concerned then looked at Maggie. "Is there any particular reason why that can't wait until we get back from the funeral?"

Maggie looked at Kevin and said "Yes, there is. Sara's been having stabbing pains in her side since last night. She's supposed to see Dr. Martin tomorrow or Thursday anyway. I told her I'd go with her. I think she needs to make the appointment as quickly as possible."

"I agree. She was in terrible pain last night and this morning."

Kevin gasped. "I had no idea she was having that rough of a time."

Sara dialed Dr. Martin's office. "Dr. Martin's office, may I help you?"

"Yes. This is Sara Michaels. Dr. Martin came to my home the other night and cleaned out a wound I have on my side. He instructed me to come in and see him in four days so that he could check the wound. Four days would be tomorrow. Is there any way I could make an appointment for tomorrow?"

"I have an appointment opening at 11:00 A.M., 1:00 P.M. or 3:00 P.M. which would you prefer?"

"Let me check. Maggie, which is easiest for you?"

"I think 11:00 would be best."

"I'd like the 11:00 appointment please."

"Okay. I have you down for 11:00 tomorrow morning Ms. Michaels. We'll see you then."

"Thank you."

Sara hung up the phone. "Sara, I guess it's time to head to the church."

"Yes, I guess it is." Sara said with tears running down her cheeks. Maggie hugged her.

The sun was shining and it was such a beautiful day that Sara couldn't believe she was going to a funeral on such a beautiful day. She was thinking: If Paul were still alive we both would have taken our students outside for class, just to enjoy the sunshine. I can't believe he's gone.

They got in the car and Kevin started driving. It was a quiet ride because everyone was very somber. Sara wept quietly and so did Maggie. They parked in the church parking lot. Kevin held Maggie's hand as they walked inside. Seth took Sara's arm and walked with her.

Pastor Jeff was waiting for them when they arrived inside the church. "Maggie, Sara, Kevin, you may go over to the casket then take a seat in the front row. We've reserved the front rows for family and close personal family friends, like Peggy and Ralph Miles."

"We have very close personal friends and their names are Elizabeth and Carl Harris. We talked to them earlier this morning and they'll be here shortly."

"Maggie, Kevin would it be alright if Carrie sat up here with us also?"

"That's fine."

"Carrie? Do I know her Sara?"

"I don't think so Pastor Jeff. She isn't a member here but she's a member of St. Peter's Methodist Church. She's a co-worker and my best friend who's battling cancer right now."

"I'll be sure to have the ushers bring her to the front when she gets here."

"Pastor Jeff, this is Lt. Seth Parker; he's my personal police protection."

"It's a pleasure to meet you officer."

"Please, it's Seth, and it's a pleasure to meet you sir."

"Seth, what's involved with being Sara's personal police protection?"

"I'm with Sara at all times regardless of where she is. At school, here at church, at home, the grocery store, etc. Maggie and Kevin asked me if I'd be the only officer to protect Sara because it's easier on her and she trusts me. Sara fixed up a huge guest bedroom for me and that's where I sleep at night when I'm not up making rounds. I walk around the inside of the house every two or three hours to make sure there isn't anyone or anything outside that shouldn't be or anyone inside that shouldn't be. I've also requested there be officers patrolling every two or three hours. I want to make sure Sara's safe."

"That sounds like a wonderful plan, but what happens if you're sick?"

"I've made arrangements for that too. I told Sara I'm looking forward to coming to church with her. I've been going to a lot of different churches and never found one I can call home. Sara says she thinks I'll be able to call this church home. I hope so. I like what I've seen already."

Pastor Jeff smiled. "You're welcome anytime. I wish you could've been here before this tragedy."

"So do I. I'm going to join Sara at the casket then I'll take my seat."

Seth joined Sara, Maggie, and Kevin at the casket. They all held hands and said a prayer together. Sara started crying and so did Maggie. The men helped them to the front pews and helped them sit. A few minutes later Sara heard. "Sara, honey I'm sorry we're late. We got hung up in traffic."

Sara looked up to see Peggy and Ralph standing there. They hugged her and Maggie and shook Kevin's hand. They went up to the casket and said a prayer. "Peggy, Pastor Jeff said you're to join the family in the front pew."

"Oh what an honor."

Peggy and Ralph took their seat. "Peggy, you didn't see Carrie out there did you?"

"No, I didn't. I did see Nancy and several of the administration heading inside."

A few minutes later Elizabeth and Carl Harris arrived. They went up to the casket then over to Maggie and Kevin. They hugged both of them then hugged Sara. "Elizabeth, Carl, we'd like for you to sit in the front pew with the family."

They both gasped. "Are you sure? Isn't there anymore family coming?"

"I don't think so. We're waiting on Carrie White to get here yet."

"Is that Sara's friend that has cancer?"

"Yes it is."

"We saw her getting out of her car when we were heading inside."

Carrie came inside and went up to the casket. She bowed her head and said a prayer then found Sara and hugged her. She looked pale but Sara was glad she was there.

The other people came into the church and the funeral service began. Sara and Maggie wept the whole time. Kevin, Maggie, and Sara all held hands through the whole service. Seth reached over and clasped Sara's hand to let her know he was there for her.

After the service was over Maggie, Kevin, Sara, and Seth were escorted to the waiting limousine and seated inside. The others filed out of the church and into their cars. They drove out to the cemetery where the conclusion of the service took place. Everyone started heading back to their cars to drive back to the church for the dinner following. Sara didn't want to leave the graveside. She started crying hysterically. Reality had set in. She couldn't stop crying. Kevin and Seth helped her back to the car.

"Sara honey, you okay?"

"I will be. I can't believe this is happening. It doesn't seem real but it is. Why did this happen?" She started crying harder. Maggie hugged her.

"This seems so unreal for all of us Sara."

They arrived back at the church and the men helped the women out of the car. Sara saw an array of several police cars as she headed inside. She knew she was safe but it didn't ease her grief.

Everyone got in line to get their food. Maggie was walking behind Sara as she went to the table to sit down. Carrie, Peggy, Ralph, Elizabeth, and Carl all came over to their table. Tom, Scott and Frank also joined them. They all sat down to eat. The food was excellent and everyone had a chance to talk and catch up on things. Elizabeth, Carl, Maggie, and Kevin all talked while Sara, Carrie, and Peggy talked. Seth, Tom, Scott, Ralph, and Frank all talked. "Carrie, Peggy if you'll excuse me I need to go to the ladies room. I'll be back in a little while."

Peggy could tell something was wrong with Sara other than just grief. "Sara, would you like for us to come with you?"

"Yes I would, thank you."

As soon as Sara stood up she cringed in pain and grabbed the table for support. "Sara, you alright?" Carrie asked her.

"Yes, it's just the pain in my side. I've been having problems with it since last night. I'll be okay."

Peggy and Carrie looked at Sara very concerned. Maggie hadn't seen what was going on because she was talking to Elizabeth. The three of them started walking toward the restroom. Once they got there Peggy said "Sara, let me see the wound on your side."

"It's nothing really. It's just a flesh wound."

"Let me see it. You might need more ointment on it."

"You'll have to unzip my dress to see it."

Peggy unzipped the zipper just far enough to get to the wound. She gasped when she saw the deep wound. It was pink but not hot to the touch. It was very sore though. "Sara, it looks like it's healing but it's still pink. I think you should stay off of your feet as much as you can for the next few days that might help."

They washed their hands and started heading out to the table. They were halfway there when Sara stopped in front of them. Her knees buckled and Seth saw her start to fall to the floor. He ran to help her to the floor gently. He laid her down on the floor. "Peggy, Carrie, get some wet paper towels. We need to get her fever down. Where's Maggie?"

"Right here, what's wrong Seth?" Before he could answer Maggie saw Sara lying on the floor. "Oh no! Sara! Seth, is she going to be alright?"

"I think so. I need to get her fever down and she needs to rest. The stress from all of this has been too much for her. Peggy and Carrie went to get her some wet paper towels."

"Seth, there's a lounge where she can lay down and relax for awhile away from all of this." Ralph said.

"Good, can you show me where it is?"

"Sure, but it's upstairs. I don't think she can make the steps."

"That's not a problem. I'll carry her up the steps. Please show me where the room is."

Seth picked up Sara and carried her up the steps into a private room with a couch and several chairs. He laid her down on the couch. "Are there any blankets around that I can cover her up with?"

"I don't know but I can find out. I'll let Pastor Jeff know you're up here and let Maggie, Peggy, and Carrie know. There are restrooms across the hall."

"Thanks Ralph."

Seth took off his suit jacket and put it across Sara. Peggy, Carrie and Maggie came up shortly afterward. Peggy put the damp towels on Sara's forehead. "Seth, what can we do to help?"

"Ralph went to see if there were any extra blankets. Peggy, you and Carrie could check to see if there are any regular towels I can use so that we can keep wet towels on her forehead. Maggie, I need for you to stay with her while I go get some more paper towels."

Peggy and Carrie went to the kitchen area and asked for three towels to use. They were handed four. "We'll wash them and I'll bring them back Sunday."

"That's not a problem Peggy; just take care of Sara."

Ralph came back with several blankets and a couple of pillows. "Ralph, could you help me put these pillows under her head?"

Ralph raised Sara's head just enough that Maggie could fit two pillows underneath. Seth came back with more paper towels. "Good. I see you brought several blankets. We may need them. Let me put these wet towels on her head then we can put more blankets over her."

Peggy and Carrie came back with the towels. "Seth, they gave us four towels. Will that be enough?"

"That will be fine. Peggy, would you go across the hall and get two towels wet with cold water and bring them back here please?"

Carrie and Peggy went across the hall and got the towels wet. "Peggy, do you think Sara will be alright? Her side looked really bad."

"I know her side looked bad. I think she'll be alright if she does what the doctor says. Besides from what Maggie has told me Seth will make sure Sara's well taken care of. He really cares about her. Let's get these cloths across the hall."

As Peggy and Carrie were walking across the hall Pastor Jeff was coming up the stairs. "Peggy, how's Sara?"

"I don't know. We're heading to the room where she is with these wet cloths. I know she was unconscious when we were in there earlier."

"I know this has been hard on her. I just hope she'll be alright." He looked at Carrie and said "I don't believe we've met. I'm Pastor Jeff Akers."

"I'm Carrie White. A co-worker and Sara's best friend. We've known each other for a long time. She's been so wonderful to me by helping me get through the tragic death of my husband and now going through cancer. She's such a wonderful lady. I hate seeing her go through all of this."

"So do I. Let's go see how she's doing."

They all walked into the room. Peggy handed Seth the wet cloths. Pastor Jeff walked over to Sara and took her hand. He said a prayer for her. "Seth, has she been like this the whole time she's been here?"

"No. She was still awake when I brought her here. She asked me where we were going and I told her someplace where she can rest and I promised her I'd stay with her."

"Seth, is there anything I can do?"

"Pastor Jeff, Sara needs a doctor. Dr. Robert Martin has been treating her for this infection. Is there any way you can reach him at his office?"

"I can try. Should I tell him to come here?"

"Yes. Sara has an appointment with him tomorrow morning but she needs to see him now. If he can't come here ask him what we should do." Jeff picked up the phone in the room where they were and called Dr. Martin's office.

Murder *When the Bell Tolls*

"Dr. Martin's office. How may I help you?"

"Hello. My name is Pastor Jeff Akers. I'm calling because one of my parishioners is very ill. During the funeral dinner we had to take her somewhere quiet because she collapsed. She's unconscious right now. She has a high fever, and the infection site is pink but not hot to the touch."

"Okay sir. What's the patient's name?"

"Sara Michaels." He heard a gasp.

"Sara Michaels? Didn't she attend a funeral today for her late fiancé?"

"Yes she did and I think all of the stress caused a lot of this?"

"That may be; where is Ms. Michaels now?"

"She's in a room resting. She has cold compresses on her head and three blankets over her. I think the doctor needs to see her. I understand she has an appointment tomorrow anyway."

"She does but the doctor needs to see her right away. Give me the address of the church and I'll pass it along to the doctor."

"Thank you. Do you have any idea how long it will be before he gets here?"

"He's finishing up with a patient right now, it shouldn't be more than thirty minutes."

"Thank you. I'll watch for him." He looked at Seth. "Dr. Martin's nurse said he should be here in about thirty minutes. How's she doing?"

Sara was stirring. "Seth, Maggie, help me please. Maggie, Seth, are you there?"

Maggie clasped Sara's hand. "I'm here Sara. Seth's here too. So is Peggy, Carrie, Ralph, and Pastor Jeff. How you feeling honey?"

"Like I've been run over by a truck."

"I would imagine. Honey, Dr. Martin will be here in about thirty minutes. He wants to check you out."

Sara started to panic. "Dr. Martin, why?"

Seth walked over to Sara. "Sara, you don't remember do you? You collapsed in the dining hall. I brought you up here so you could rest."

"I don't remember anything except having this horrible pain in my side while I was talking to Peggy and Carrie then waking up here."

Maggie stroked Sara's face gently. "Sara, everything will be alright. Dr. Martin will check you out and we'll get you back home where you can rest. I think you need rest and maybe a stronger dose of medicine. This has been very trying for all of us."

"Pastor Jeff?"

"Yes Sara."

"Thank you for everything you've done for me and Paul's family. It is appreciated. Thank the ladies in the kitchen for helping with the dinner. It is much…" Sara passed out again before she could finish her sentence.

Maggie tried not to panic but was overcome with fear. "Sara, Sara, can you hear me? Sara?" Seth leaned over and could tell that Sara was breathing. "Seth, is she alright? What's happening?"

"Maggie, she passed out again. She's breathing on her own which is a good sign. I think her fever's coming down but we need to keep her warm. Could someone hand me another blanket?"

They all watched helplessly as Sara lay on the couch still unconscious. A few minutes later Kevin came up with Dr. Martin. "Seth, where is she?"

"She's in here. She has been in and out of consciousness."

"Let me have a look." Dr. Martin went over to Sara. He leaned over her. "Sara, it's Dr. Martin. Can you hear me?" He clasped her hand. "Sara, squeeze my hand if you can hear me." There was no response." How long has she been like this?"

"About an hour? She was having trouble with pain in her side last night and this morning. We didn't want to call you because of the funeral today. Is she going to be alright?"

"Yes but she needs another dose of medicine and a lot of rest. I need to check the wound on her side to be sure that it doesn't need to be lanced again."

Sara started stirring. She opened her eyes. "Sara, thank goodness you're awake. Dr. Martin is here and wants to check you out is that alright?"

"Yes, I guess so. What happened anyway?"

"Sara, you collapsed again. Seth brought you up here so you could rest."

"Where's Seth?"

"Right here Sara." He walked over to her and clasped her hand. "Sara, Dr. Martin needs to check the wound on your side okay?"

"That's fine."

"Sara, I'm going to have Maggie help me roll you onto your right side okay?"

"Okay."

Maggie helped Sara onto her right side and held her still. "Maggie, would you unzip Sara's dress down to the wound please?" She did. The doctor checked the wound. When he touched it she cringed. "Sara, is it still that tender?"

"Yes it is."

"The infection is clearing up but I think you need a different medication for the pain and swelling. I'm going to give you a dose of that medication right now. It should start working in about fifteen minutes. The only side effects you may have are dry mouth and tiredness. You need a lot of rest. Do you have an appointment to come back and see me about that wound?"

"Yes I do. The appointment is for tomorrow morning."

"Good. You can let me know how the medication is working. I'm also going to give you a sedative. If you have any problems sleeping, I want you to take one of these."

"Okay. Dr. Martin, thank you. I appreciate you coming here on such short notice."

"Sara, I'm glad I could help. I'll see you in my office tomorrow. If you need me for anything else today or tonight, just call my office."

"Thank you again doctor."

As Dr. Martin was leaving Maggie walked out the door with him. "Dr. is she going to be alright?"

"With rest and the medication she should be alright. It might take awhile. She must be under supervision at all times while she's on this medication."

"Seth's staying in the guest room at her house now. He's there 24 hours a day. He'll make sure she's alright when we aren't there."

"Good. I've given her enough medication for another five days. Hopefully by next week she'll be feeling better. The stress from all of this has made it worse. When you're with her make sure she drinks plenty of fluids and try to keep her stress level down. Do fun things with her. How long are you going to be here?"

"We are staying two weeks."

"Good. That will help her a lot."

"Thank you again doctor."

⚜

After the doctor left Maggie went over to Sara. She rubbed Sara's shoulder. Sara smiled. "Thank you for your help, all of you. Maggie, can I speak with you privately please?"

"Certainly."

Sara looked over at Seth. He nodded that he understood. Everyone left the room. "What is it Sara?"

"Maggie, I hate putting the burden of all of this on you and Kevin. You have enough to deal with."

"Sara, you can't help the fact you were wounded by a bullet yourself. It's not a burden. That's what families do. They help each other out when they need to."

"But Maggie, I never legally became part of your family."

"Legally or not you're family and always will be."

"Thanks Maggie." Sara said as she hugged her.

"Maggie, I'd really like to sit up now. Do you think that would be a problem?"

"I don't see why. Let me get Seth in here to help me."

"Okay."

Maggie opened the door and looked around. Everyone was sitting in chairs down the hall talking to each other. Kevin had gone downstairs. "Seth, I need you please."

He came out of a room with a Styrofoam cup of coffee. "Yes Maggie, what do you need?"

"Sara says she feels like sitting up and I was wondering if you could assist me with that."

"I'd be happy to."

They walked into the room and helped Sara sit up. "I feel a little dizzy. Maybe that's from getting up to quickly or from lying like I was."

"It's probably from lying like you were. Maybe if you just sit there for a few minutes you won't be as dizzy."

"Maggie, what about the people who came to the funeral? Aren't they going to be upset because you and I aren't down there?"

"Nonsense, they're eating and talking with each other. I'm sure there are some concerned people down there but I'm sure they understand the stress this has caused both of us; besides Kevin is down there with them now."

"I guess you're right but I'd still feel better if I was down there with them."

"You sit there for a few minutes then we'll see about going back downstairs."

Maggie walked over to Seth. "Seth, Sara wants to go back downstairs. What should I tell her?"

"If she feels up to it that's fine but she doesn't need to tire herself out. People are going to be leaving right away. Have her stay there for a few more minutes, then we'll see."

Carrie walked over to Sara. "Sara, I'm so glad to see you sitting up and awake. You gave us quite a scare. Are you feeling better?"

"Yes I am. I don't know what happened except I had a terrible pain in my side."

Carrie hugged Sara. "I'm so glad you're going to be alright. I don't know what I'd do if something happened to you."

"Thank you Carrie. You are a dear friend."

"Sara, I have a doctor's appointment at 2:00 this afternoon. I need to go home, get cleaned up then leave for my appointment. If there's anything you need, don't hesitate to ask."

"Go on Carrie. I'm getting ready to go downstairs anyway. I need to see some of the people before they leave. Thank you for coming Carrie. It means a lot."

"You're welcome Sara and again I'm terribly sorry about Paul." She hugged her, then went down the stairs to head out to her car.

Seth looked at Maggie and Sara. "I don't want her walking out to the car alone. She needs protection also. I'll have Ralph get Tom Monroe for me and he can walk her to her car. "Carrie, hold on a minute please. I don't want you walking out alone. Ralph, do you remember Tom Monroe?"

"I think so."

"Would you mind having him come up here please? Tell him I need to talk to him."

"Alright; I'll go get him."

As Ralph was going down the stairs, Elizabeth and Carl Harris were coming up. "Excuse me, but is Maggie up there?"

"Yes ma'am she is; so are Seth, Carrie White, Sara, and my wife Peggy."

"Is everyone all right? They've been gone awhile?"

"Yes. Everyone's alright now. Sara collapsed from exhaustion and they brought her up here so she could rest. They're in the second room on the right side of the hall."

"Thank you sir."

Maggie sat on the couch next to Sara and hugged her. They were talking when they heard "Where are Sara and Maggie?"

"We're in here Elizabeth."

Elizabeth and Carl walked into the room. They gasped when they saw how pale Sara looked and how concerned Maggie looked. "You two alright? Maggie, we got worried when you left abruptly and didn't come back; now we understand why. What happened?"

"Sara collapsed from exhaustion and from the infection she is dealing with. I was really worried about her. We called the doctor and he came and gave her some medicine and he wants her to rest. I think that's the best thing for her to do. Witnessing Paul's murder devastated her. She's blaming herself."

They both gasped. "It's not her fault Paul was murdered."

"I know that and you know that and I think deep down Sara knows that but right now she's blaming herself. I think once she goes through the grieving process she'll see that none of this is her fault."

"Hopefully she will. I'm not sure how I'd react if I witnessed a murder either. The poor thing. Maggie, if she needs anything or you and Kevin need anything don't be afraid to ask."

"Thanks Carl, Elizabeth; we appreciate it."

"Maggie, is everything alright?"

"Yes honey it is. Carl and Elizabeth just came up to see if we were okay since we hadn't been downstairs in awhile. I told her we were alright."

"Carl, Elizabeth, I'm sorry I haven't been down there. I'm not sure what happened except I remember eating then walking to the bathroom with a few friends; the next thing I remember is waking up here."

"Maggie told us you're exhausted physically and emotionally. We both understand that. Carl and I would like to invite you, Maggie, Kevin, and Seth to our house for dinner one night while Maggie and Kevin are still in town. I'll prepare the food honey; you don't need to fix anything. We only live a few miles from here. We'd really like to get to know you better."

"That sounds good. We'll discuss it and let you know when it would be best."

"That's fine. Maggie, we need to get going. If there is anything we can do, let us know. Sara, the same goes for you."

"Thank you both for coming. We appreciate it."

"You're welcome Sara. Hopefully we'll see you later in the week. Goodbye Maggie, Sara."

"Goodbye Carl, Elizabeth, we'll see you later in the week."

About five minutes later Tom came upstairs. "Seth, I was told you wanted to talk to me."

"Yes. I was wondering if you'd mind walking Carrie out to her car? I'd feel better knowing someone was with her."

"That's not a problem. I'd be honored to do that. You ready to go Carrie?"

"Yes I am."

Carrie hugged Sara one more time. "Sara, I'll see you later. If you need something ask."

"I will. Thanks for coming Carrie, Tom. I appreciate it."

Tom and Carrie headed outside. "So Carrie, how long have you known Sara?"

"About twenty years. We've worked together all those years. She's the sweetest person I know. Tom, I enjoyed our conversation earlier."

"So did I Carrie."

"Well, this is my car. Thank you Tom."

"You're welcome Carrie. If you need anything here's my card. Just call me."

Carrie smiled at him. "I will. Thank you again."

After Carrie left, Tom went back inside. He went up to where everyone else was. "I got Carrie to her car alright. She thanked me. She's really nice Sara."

"Yes she is. We've known each other for a long time. I should try and go downstairs. I feel like I've let everyone down or made them feel like I was snubbing them. I really need to go downstairs." Sara said.

"If you think you're up to it now we'll all go together."

"Maggie, I need to try."

"Let Seth and I help you up."

"I'm still a little unsteady on my feet but I think if all of you are with me, I can do this."

"Peggy, Ralph, Sara is ready to go downstairs but she can't do it by herself. Seth and I will hold her up on each side if you'll walk behind us that would be great. If she starts to collapse again we'll stop."

Maggie and Seth each got on one side of Sara and held her hand as they descended the steps. Sara felt wobbly but kept her balance. When they got to the bottom of the steps, Kevin was waiting for them. He hugged Sara. "Sara, I'm glad you're alright. You gave us quiet a scare."

Other people came up to Sara, hugged her and told her how sorry they were about Paul. Sara started sobbing again but thanked all of the people. When the last of the people were gone and Sara, Seth, Kevin, Maggie, Tom, Ralph and Peggy were the only ones left; Pastor Jeff came over to them. "Sara, I'm so glad you have all of these people around you for support. Maggie, Kevin, I'm sorry about your son. He was a wonderful man and he'll be missed. I'm glad I had the honor of meeting you and anytime you're in town you're welcome at this church. Again I'm sorry for your loss. Sara, if I can do anything let me know. Let me know how your doctor's appointment goes tomorrow. I'm concerned about you."

"Thank you Pastor Jeff. I appreciate it."

"We're going to take her home so she can rest. Thanks again Pastor Jeff."

Everyone left the church together. "Sara honey, I wish there was more we could do."

"Just supporting me and being here with Paul's parents and me today is wonderful. I couldn't ask for more. Thank you both for coming."

"You're welcome. Sara when do you think you'll be coming back to school?"

"I'm not sure yet but soon. I want to try and get things back to semi-normal as soon as I can. I don't think things will ever be normal again or at least not for awhile."

Murder *When the Bell Tolls*

"Peggy, I can guarantee she probably won't be back for another ten days at least. The doctor told her she won't be able to go back until her side is completely healed and that will probably take two weeks. We're leaving in about two weeks so that will work out great."

"Sara, take it easy and if you need anything, don't hesitate to ask."

"Thanks Peggy, Ralph. I appreciate that."

Ralph and Peggy got in their car and drove off. "Tom, could I talk to you for a minute?" Seth asked.

"Sure; what's up?"

"Tom, I need to have Kevin take me to my house to pick up some things since I'm going to be staying at Sara's all the time; Sara needs to get home and rest. I don't want to leave Sara and Maggie alone in that house with a craze killer on the loose. Would you mind staying with them while I get my things? That way Kevin and I won't have to hurry and if we get stuck in traffic I know Sara and Maggie will be safe."

"Not a problem. I enjoy Sara and Maggie's company. They're such nice people."

"That they are. Thanks Tom."

They walked back over to the car where Kevin, Maggie, and Sara were waiting. Sara was already in the car with her head leaned back trying to relax. The men got in. Tom got in his patrol car. "Sara, since you need to get home and rest I'm going to have Kevin take all of us to your house, then Tom will stay with both of you while Kevin and I get my things together. Will that be okay?"

"That will be fine."

"Tom's going to follow us to your house so stay in the car until he walks around the outside of your house to make sure everything is alright."

"Okay."

Sara fell asleep on the way to her house. The medication the doctor had given her had helped her relax enough to sleep. Maggie leaned her head back and fell asleep too. Kevin and Seth were talking. "Kevin, I hope you don't mind taking me to my place so I can get a few things."

"I don't mind at all. I'm glad Sara and Maggie are finally able to get some much needed rest."

"So am I; that's why I suggested Tom stay with them while we go to my place."

"I'm glad you did. I know they'll be safe with Tom there. I feel better knowing you're staying with Sara 24 hours a day. Sara's very special you know."

"Yes I know that."

They pulled up to Sara's house. Seth and Tom both got out of their cars. All of you stay here until we make sure everything is alright."

"Okay Seth, Tom. I'll just park the car and we'll wait."

Sara was still asleep in the back seat when they arrived at her house. Maggie awoke and looked over at Sara. She gently touched Sara's cheek. When Sara awoke Maggie and Kevin were smiling at her. "Sara honey, we're at your house. We're waiting for Seth and Tom to tell us it's alright to go in."

"Okay. That's fine. Maggie, Kevin, thank you for helping me today. I really appreciate it. I wouldn't have been able to handle any of this if you hadn't been here. I still can't believe this is happening. I feel so numb."

"Honey, that's what families do. They support each other and love each other. We love you dearly and always will." Maggie hugged her.

Seth and Tom were almost ready to go inside when Tom said "Seth, come look at this."

Seth walked over to where Tom was. There were all sorts of flowers and rose bushes. On one of the bushes was a piece of cloth and some blood. "It looks like whoever has been watching Sara may have cut their arm or leg on one of these thorns. The cut is deep enough to cause the person to have more than a small band-aid on it."

"It sure is. Tom take this piece of cloth back to the station and have it analyzed."

"Okay. Seth, do you think since you are staying with Sara all the time the killer will continue to stalk Sara or even contact her?"

"Yes I do. The only people who know I'll be here at all times are the people at the station, Maggie, Kevin, Peggy, Ralph, Carrie, and of course Pastor Jeff. I know none of them are going to say anything. I think it's best that way. This person will make a mistake and that's when we'll get him. I think we should go join the others and let them know it's okay to go inside. We don't need to let Sara know about this. She's very fragile at the time and I don't want to terrify her."

"I agree. Sara's such a wonderful person. Seth I really like her friend Carrie White."

Seth smiled. "I do too. Peggy and Ralph are nice too. Let's get going."

Seth and Tom walked to where Sara, Kevin, and Maggie were. "It's safe to go inside now."

They walked up to the porch. Sara unlocked the door and they went in. Seth helped Sara to a chair. She sat down at the dining room table and Maggie sat down with her. "Maggie, Sara, Kevin and I are going to leave and go get my things. Tom will be here with you if you need anything. Tom, you know what you need to do. We should be back in about an hour."

"Goodbye Kevin, Seth. Please be careful."

Seth and Kevin left. "Sara, Tom, I could use a cup of coffee. What about you?"

"That sounds good." Tom said.

"Yes it does. Maggie, do you need my help?"

"I got it Sara. You stay in that chair and rest."

Maggie went into the kitchen and made a pot of coffee. Tom and Sara talked. "Sara, I know this has been a very trying few days for you. How are you feeling now?"

"A little better."

"I'm glad. I was really worried about you at the church."

"Thanks Tom. I appreciate the concern."

"Sara, I realize this might not be the right time to discuss this but I wanted to ask you about your friend Carrie."

"What do you want to know about her?"

"I know you two have been friends for over twenty years. I was wondering if you could tell me what she's like as a person."

"Carrie's a very sweet, warm, caring, compassionate person with a love for children. Her passion is children with special needs. As a matter of fact, some of her students are special needs children. She's wonderful with them and they love her. When she developed cancer eight months ago, it was devastating to all of us. She's a real trooper. She's been a wonderful support for me with everything I've been through. Before and even after I met Paul and we started dating Carrie, Paul and I would go out to eat together once a month, go to the theater, to a show on Broadway, a ballet and once a month we had a ladies night out. We always had a lot of fun. Carrie loves to dance and sing. Before she became ill she was a flutist with the New York Municipal Band. She had to sit out this year though and it's been really hard on her. They were getting ready to start their season in a few weeks and she was hoping to join them again this year but she didn't think she had the strength."

"Wow! She sounds like quite a lady. I talked to her a little bit earlier."

"She is."

Maggie came into the dining room carrying a tray with a pot of coffee, cups, sugar and creamer. She sat it down on the dining room table. "Thanks Maggie. Maybe I can enjoy a cup of coffee now that I feel more rested."

"Sara, you have been through a terrible ordeal; you and your body are exhausted. It may take a while before you feel totally rested."

"I know once I get a good night sleep, I'll feel a lot better."

"I think it would help me too but I can't sleep. Every time I close my eyes I feel like I'm reliving that awful night in the park. I feel like there's something I should be remembering but I don't know what it is." Maggie hugged Sara.

Kevin and Seth started talking. "Kevin I appreciate this. You know you didn't have to do this."

"I know, I wanted to. It means a lot to Maggie and I that you agreed to do this."

"Kevin, there's something I need to tell you. I didn't tell you this before because I didn't want to upset Sara anymore than she already is." Seth told Kevin what he and Tom had found.

Kevin gasped. "You mean you actually found a piece of cloth outside her window?"

"Yes we did. Tom's going to take it back to the station where it'll be analyzed. I don't know if we'll get anything off of it but we have to try. There was enough blood to suggest a fairly deep cut."

"I'm glad you didn't tell Sara. She's been through enough already. Have you or Tom told Maggie?"

"No. We thought we'd let you tell her when the two of you are together."

"That's a good idea. I'll tell her tonight on the way to our motel."

Murder *When the Bell Tolls*

They arrived at Seth's house. Kevin was surprised at the neatness of the house. Seth had been a widower for nine years yet his house was extremely neat and clean. "Seth, do you need some help getting your things together?"

"I could use some help picking out clothes to take with me. I don't want everyone knowing I'm a police officer, because people will open up to me more; but I don't know what type of things are allowed at Sara's school. I know I need two suits and ties but I don't know about the rest."

Kevin helped Seth pack the things he needed. They finished packing and started heading out the door to go to Sara's when Seth noticed the light flashing on his answering machine. He listened to the messages and wrote down the numbers. They walked out the door and headed to the car.

Once they got in the car Seth said "Kevin thanks for your help. I appreciate it. I know it doesn't seem important but I really want to fit in at Sara's school; when I'm there."

"I can understand how important that is. Teenagers dress so differently these days, but they also notice how the adults are dressed and they respect them. Sara's school has some of the nicest students and staff you'd ever want to be around. Paul always said he loved going to Sara's school because everyone was so nice."

Seth smiled. He looked down at the messages in his hand. "I guess I should have my phone shut off for now. I'll have them call me on my cell phone."

They pulled up to Sara's house. "I really hope Sara's feeling better. I'm worried about her."

"So am I Seth. The stress she's been under along with the bullet wound has been too much for her. Maggie and I are doing our best to help but we aren't sure what else to do."

"Didn't I hear your friends the Harris' say they'd like for both of you and Sara and I to go over there for dinner this week?"

"Yes but Sara said she wasn't sure she'd be very good company."

"Well, I think she should go. It would do her good to be with other people."

"I agree. Seth, maybe you can talk to her and convince her to come. I'm sure Maggie will talk to her too. Maybe that will help."

"I'll do what I can. I think she's so overwhelmed right now and that doesn't help. Maybe in a couple of days she'll feel like going somewhere. I'll have Maggie talk to her too."

They arrived at Sara's house. Kevin carried Seth's things up to the door. Seth knocked on the door. "Tom, it's Seth and Kevin. Would you please open the door for us?"

Tom opened the door for them and they took Seth's things inside. Maggie and Sara were sitting at the table; Sara was weeping quietly. "Maggie, Sara we're back. Is everything alright?"

"Everything's alright."

"Seth, would you like some help with your things?"

"Kevin's going to help but you're welcome to help too Tom."

"Sara, Maggie, will you be alright?"

"Yes, we'll be fine. We'll call for you if we need you."

"Okay."

The men went into the guest room where Seth was staying. "Wow Seth! This is really nice."

"I think so too. This room has everything I need except a kitchen."

They talked while they put Seth's things away. Sara and Maggie were talking in the dining room. "Maggie, thank you for taking charge when we got home. I felt so scatterbrained and confused that I'm not even sure I would've remembered how to make coffee."

"Sara, it's normal to feel like you do after you've lost a loved one. I haven't told Kevin but I feel that way too at times."

"Maggie, I feel so lost, so empty without Paul." Maggie hugged Sara as they both wept. Suddenly Sara started feeling faint again. "Maggie, I think I need to lie down. I'm starting to feel dizzy and queasy again. I don't know what's happening to me."

"Let me help you to your bedroom where you can get comfortable."

"Alright."

Maggie helped Sara stand up; they started heading into Sara's bedroom. Suddenly Sara just stopped. "Sara, you okay honey? Sara?" She collapsed in Maggie's arms. Maggie could hardly handle her. She started yelling "Seth, Kevin, Tom, come quick. I need your help."

All three men came running to find Maggie struggling to hold Sara up. Tom took one of Sara's arms and tried to stand her up. It was no use. They laid her on the floor. "I'll take her into her room. Maggie would you come help me please?"

Seth picked Sara up and carried her into her bedroom. He laid her down on the bed. Maggie covered her with a blanket. She gently stroked Sara's hair. She started moaning and stirring. "Sara, can you hear me?"

Sara opened her eyes. "Maggie, how did I get back here?"

"Seth carried you back here. You collapsed in my arms."

"Thank you Seth. I don't know what happened. The last thing I remember is Maggie and I were walking back here then I started feeling dizzy. Everything after that's fuzzy."

"Why don't you rest for awhile? If you fall asleep that's alright. We'll all be here when you wake up."

Tom leaned over. "Sara, get some rest. Seth and I need to fill out some paperwork anyway for him to be here twenty four hours a day. If I'm not here when you wake up, I'll stop by tomorrow sometime during my shift and see how you're doing. What time's your doctor's appointment?"

"11:00 A.M."

"Get some rest. I'll see you later."

Sara laid her head back. Maggie sat in the chair next to the bed. "Sara, would you like for me to stay or would you prefer to be alone?"

"Would you please stay? I don't want to be alone right now."

"I'll stay. Just close your eyes and try to rest."

"Thanks Maggie."

Sara closed her eyes and tried to rest. She felt tears running down her face. She kept thinking about Paul and about all the fun times they had together and how much she missed him. She started shaking. Maggie clasped her hand in comfort. Sara finally went to sleep.

Maggie didn't want to leave Sara's side. She was afraid she might lose consciousness again. Maggie was so tired herself she fell asleep in the chair. When she hadn't come out of the room for awhile Kevin and Seth went back to check on

her and found her asleep in the chair. "Let's not wake her. She's exhausted too. They both need the rest."

"Let me make sure Sara's alright though." Seth said as he walked over to the bed. He watched Sara breathing and knew she was alright. They walked out of the room and went back into the living room where Tom was.

"Seth, are they both alright?"

"They're both alright and both of them are asleep. That's the best thing for them right now. This has been hard on both of them."

"Tom, you're welcome to stay for awhile, have coffee, and eat something, whatever. Your shift doesn't end until 8:00 P.M. anyway and it's only 1:30 P.M. Kevin and I are probably going to sit around and talk."

"That's fine. I'd love to stay. I think I'm going to go get myself another cup of coffee."

Tom got himself a cup of coffee and joined Kevin and Seth in the living room. "Kevin, I really liked your friends Elizabeth and Carl Harris. How did all of you meet?"

"They were both teachers at the school where I was a dean. Elizabeth was a psychology teacher and Carl was an English teacher. We got to be friends during the school year and over the summer became even closer friends. We started having cook-outs and going to dances and movies together; before we knew it we became inseparable and that was forty-five years ago."

"Wow! That's a long time to be friends."

"Yes it is and we couldn't ask for better friends; they're like family."

They continued talking and drinking coffee. About an hour and a half later Maggie came into the living room. "Hey Sleeping Beauty. Do you feel better?"

"Yes I do. I feel a lot more rested. I don't want to stay out here too long. Sara was starting to stir and I want to be in the room with her when she wakes up."

"We all understand."

"I'm going to head back into Sara's bedroom now. After Sara wakes up I'll come out here and make some more coffee and something to eat. I better get going."

As Maggie started heading back to Sara's bedroom, Kevin got up and followed her. "Maggie I'll walk back there with you." They walked back to Sara's room together. Kevin looked at Maggie compassionately, hugged and kissed her then said "Maggie, you doing okay? I know how hard this has been on all of us."

She smiled at him. "Yes Kevin I'm okay. I'm just really worried about Sara. She seems to be doing as well as can be expected under the circumstances but we're here with her most of the time. What's going to happen after we go back home to New Jersey?"

"Maggie, Seth will be with her. The two of them have a lot in common; besides, we only live two hours from here. We can come back anytime." He hugged her again.

Maggie went into the bedroom. Sara was starting to wake up. She opened her eyes and saw Maggie smiling at her. "Hello Sara."

"Hello Maggie. What time is it?"

"It's about 4:00 P.M."

"Have I been asleep all that time?"

"Yes you have. How do you feel now?"

"A lot more rested."

"I'm glad. I promised the guys I would make a fresh pot of coffee for them after you were awake."

"That sounds wonderful. Could you help me up and hand me my shoes and I'll go out with you?"

Maggie helped Sara sit up and put her shoes on, then she helped her stand up. They walked into the living room together. The smell of fresh coffee filled the air. "Do I smell coffee?" Sara asked.

"Yes, I started a fresh pot." Seth said.

"That was sweet of you. I'll fix us something to eat for dinner." Maggie said.

"Maggie, would you like me to help?"

Maggie knew how much Sara liked to cook and how much it helped her deal with a lot of things so she said "Sure, but I don't want you doing too much."

Sara knew Maggie was protecting her and taking care of her. She smiled at Maggie. "Thanks Maggie. Why don't I get out the food and you can heat it up?"

"That sounds good."

While Maggie was heating up the food Seth, Tom, and Sara started talking. "Sara, do you feel any better?" Tom asked.

"Yes I do. I feel more rested."

"That's good."

"How's your side feeling now?"

"It's feeling a little better. I think a lot of it was because I've been extremely tired. I usually stay up fairly late during the school year, grading papers, planning lessons, whatever is necessary."

"You may stay up late then but you're usually not under the stress that you've been in and I know you've been having flashbacks of the night Paul was killed; that hasn't helped. I'm glad you're feeling better though."

Maggie started putting the food on platters to take out to the dining room. "Maggie, that sure smells good. What can I do to help?" Tom asked.

"Would you mind helping by taking the food out to the dining room?"

He grabbed a couple of plates and so did Seth and Sara. They set the food down on the table. Maggie was getting a tray with the coffee pot, creamer, sugar, and cups ready to bring in also. Kevin walked into the kitchen and hugged Maggie. Seth, Sara, and Tom smiled. Kevin whispered something to Maggie and she smiled. Kevin picked up the tray and brought it into the dining room.

They sat down at the dining room table and ate. After they were finished eating they drank coffee. Maggie started clearing off the table. Sara helped her and so did Seth. "Tom, I understand from Seth that you're second in command at the station."

"Yes I am."

"So how will that work with this investigation now that Seth's staying here twenty four hours a day?"

"It'll continue the same as it always has except we won't change officers. The officers involved in the investigation will spend more hours in the field, or patrolling the area. We want to make sure Sara and the rest of the people are safe. Seth has my cell phone number if something comes up that he feels I should be aware of. However, he's still the lead officer on this case and what he says goes."

"How do you feel about Seth staying here all the time?"

"I'm all for it. He has been asking for an assignment like this for a long time. He's one of the best undercover officers we have. He used to do it all the time but when his wife died he wanted to do something different. He's been a police officer all his life. Sara's in good hands."

"I agree. I really like Seth. He cares about people in general. Now that Paul's gone, Sara's alone again and I hope this isn't going to destroy her. Sara's a strong woman but seeing someone she loved being murdered right in front of her; I know it'll have some effect on her."

Maggie, Sara, and Seth came back into the room. "Does anyone want any more coffee, tea, or anything?"

"Nothing for me." Tom said.

"Me either." Kevin said.

They looked at the clock. It was 6:00 P.M. Sara usually went to the theater. Sara had already told them she wouldn't be there that week because she and Paul were supposed to go to dinner with Carrie. "It seems strange not to be going to the theater tonight. I usually help with something behind the scenes at the little theater for the up and coming stars. I usually go on Tuesday nights when I can but they knew I wasn't going tonight because Paul and I had made plans to go out to dinner with Carrie, and those plans have changed too. My whole life has changed now." Sara said, tears welling up in her eyes.

Maggie walked over to her. "Sara honey, it'll be alright. Maybe next Tuesday evening you, Seth, Kevin, and I can all go to the theater together and work on something together. I used to be involved in the theater when I was teaching."

"That's right you were. I know you really enjoyed that."

"It'll be okay. I know you want to try and get on with your life as normally as you can and this is the best way. Don't wait until we go home to start doing what you like to do. We'd love to come along and see some of the things that you do, besides teaching."

"I'd like that too."

Maggie and Sara hugged each other. Seth looked over at Tom. "Tom, you can stay here until the end of your shift in a couple of hours or you can take off early and I'll vouch for you that you were here the full twelve hours. You've been such a huge help today; you deserve a much needed break. I think we're going to play cards for a little while so it's up to you."

"I think I'll stay. We can all play cards. Besides Kevin beat me last time in Gin Rummy, it's my turn to win for a change."

They all laughed. Kevin got the cards and they sat at the dining room table. They were having so much fun they lost track of the time. It was 9:30 P.M. before anyone realized it. They were all talking and enjoying themselves when the phone rang.

Tom answered the phone and his face became ghostly white. Seth walked over to him. Tom hung up the phone and looked at Seth. "Tom, what is it?"

"Seth, there's been another murder. Just down the street from the church, across from the park."

"Oh no! Do they know the name of the victim?"

"Yes. It's Peter Edwards."

Sara gasped. "Peter Edwards, the stock broker?"

"I don't know about that; they never told me that. They did tell me they think the MO is the same because there was someone dressed up as an old man holding out a tin cup. Apparently Peter was going to give the man some money when he was shot."

"Oh my! Just like Paul." Sara said.

Seth looked at Sara. "Sara, did you know Peter Edwards?"

"Yes I did. I did business with him because I have some money tied up in the stock market and he helped me with that."

"Tom what did the station say?"

"They want one of us to get over there as quickly as possible. Would you like me to take it this time?"

"If you wouldn't mind. Call me as soon as you find out something."

"I will Seth. Maggie, Kevin, Sara, I hate to have to leave like this but it's important I go."

"We understand. Thank you for your help Tom and be careful out there."

"Thanks, all of you. Seth, I'll call you on your cell phone as soon as I can."

"Thanks Tom and be careful."

After Tom left Sara, Kevin, and Maggie sat quietly at the dining room table trying to process what they had just heard. Sara was stunned. "I can't believe what has happened."

"Sara, how well did you know Peter; other than he was your stock broker?"

"I knew him quite well. He was a very bright, intelligent, young man with a very promising career. He was very personable, and charming. He also worked in the Art industry. His girlfriend was an art dealer."

"His girlfriend? Do you know her name?"

"Sure. I told you about her last night. Her name's Martha Mae Burns. She owns an art shop about two blocks from the park. Paul and I used to see her and Peter walking there a lot."

The look on Seth's face told Kevin there was something seriously wrong. Kevin wanted to talk to Seth about it but he didn't want to upset Maggie or Sara. Seth looked at Kevin. "Kevin, I need some help with something in the guest bedroom, would you please come and help me?"

"Sure Seth. Ladies, we'll be back shortly."

Kevin and Seth walked back to the guest room. "Seth, what's going on? The look on your face says there's something terribly wrong?"

"That's because there is. I believe Sara's in even more danger than we first thought."

"Why?"

"Because of the girlfriend of this last victim. She and Sara know each other and they also know a mutual acquaintance that could possibly be our shooter or raggedy dressed man, or just someone who knows something. I don't think we should tell Sara at this time but after we've checked everything out I'll talk to her and let her know what's happening. I can't risk putting her in even more danger."

"I agree. Maggie will be upset enough about the piece of cloth you and Tom found. I can't imagine how she'll feel when she finds out about all of this."

"The only difference in this case is that someone dressed up like an old man, not a man in raggedy clothes. We got a description but no one saw or heard the shooter. It was on a street corner."

"Seth, do what you need to do to protect Sara. She's all we have left. If you need anything let us know. We'll do whatever it takes to protect her."

"I'll keep that in mind Kevin. We better go back out there before they start to worry."

While Kevin and Seth were talking, Maggie and Sara were cleaning up the dishes and the table. "Maggie, I can't thank you and Kevin enough for everything you have done for me these past few days. I don't know how I would have gotten through them without both of you."

Maggie hugged Sara. "You're so sweet Sara."

Seth and Kevin came back into the living room. Kevin looked at Maggie. She could tell something was wrong but didn't say anything. They looked at the clock. "Oh my, It's 10:00 P.M. Sara you need your rest. I think maybe Kevin and I should go so that you and Seth can both relax for the evening."

"Maggie you don't have to go."

"I know but I'm tired and I know Kevin's tired, and I really think you need rest."

"What time will you be here in the morning?"

"Is 9:30 A.M. too early?"

"No, that's fine."

"Goodnight Sara. We love you honey."

"Goodnight Maggie, Kevin. I love both of you too."

Seth watched to make sure Maggie and Kevin got to their car. Once they were in their car Kevin decided to tell Maggie everything he knew so far. Maggie could see the concern on Kevin's face. "Kevin, I know something's wrong; that's why I suggested we leave now. Can you tell me what it is?"

"Maggie, there are two things actually. First, while Tom and Seth were walking around the outside of the house they found a piece of cloth with blood on it, stuck to one of the bushes beside Sara's bedroom window." Maggie gasped. Secondly, what I have to tell you is really going to upset you."

"Kevin, if it concerns you or Sara please tell me."

"Alright; it has to do with the phone call that Tom took."

"The call about another murder near the park?"

"Yes. Seth feels Sara may be in even more danger than anyone thought because she knows the victim and his girlfriend, and the part that's going to upset you is this: Sara and the victim's girlfriend may know the shooter and or the man of different disguises." Maggie gasped.

"How's that possible?"

"According to Seth, it was something Sara told him in confidence but apparently they both know this person. I don't know how though. Seth does and he said he'd follow all the evidence and leads and see where it takes them. He promised to do whatever it takes to protect Sara. I told him to let us know if there's anything we can do to help."

Murder *When the Bell Tolls*

"I'm glad you did. I can't believe the person who shot Paul and Sara is someone who knew both of them. My question is why?"

"That's my question too. Sara's safe for now though."

Kevin drove to their motel. Meanwhile back at Sara's, she and Seth started talking. "Sara, you alright? You suddenly got very quiet after I asked you about Peter."

"I'm okay. I'm just trying to process the whole event. Martha is a wonderful person. I can truly understand what she's going through. The horror of the incident and the questions. My biggest question in all of this is why." She started sobbing again and Seth rubbed his hand across her back in comfort.

"Seth, I'm tired but I know I'm not ready to go to sleep. I'm too uptight right now to sleep."

"Sara, I have a suggestion. Why don't we watch a couple of movies, and try and relax?"

"That sounds good. Pick out the movies you'd like to see."

Seth picked out a comedy that lasted about two and a half hours. He put it in the DVD player and they settled down on the couch to watch the movie. They grabbed a blanket and threw it over their legs for warmth. They were enjoying the movie and for the first time since Seth had met Sara she was laughing. He smiled.

The movie was just getting over around midnight when Seth's cell phone rang. "Seth Parker."

"Seth, it's Tom."

"Hello Tom. What did you find out?"

"The victim was shot in the back of the head with the same caliber gun as Paul and the other victims. The victim was seen talking to an elderly gentleman with a tin cup just before he was shot. The elderly gentleman got away before the police got there, even though two men chased him into an alley. The men said they lost him when he went around the corner."

"This man is a master of disguise. It's no telling where he is now. Have the officers check the location the man was last seen and see if they can come up with something. Let me know what you find out but wait until morning unless it's an emergency."

"How's Sara doing Seth?"

"She's doing alright. We watched a movie and I'm getting ready to get both of us a cup of coffee. Sara says she's too uptight to sleep so we will probably talk for awhile. Thanks for the update Tom. Do you work in the morning?"

"Yes I do. Right now I just want to go home, shower, get into bed and try to get some sleep."

"I want you to do that. I'll talk to you in the morning. I'll call you at the station. Get some sleep."

Seth hung up the phone and walked back over to Sara. She had a concerned look on her face. "Was that Tom?"

"Yes it was."

"Seth, do they have any leads?"

"No, but it looks like Peter was shot with the same caliber gun and the same way Paul was shot. I believe there's a connection. I don't want you to worry about that right now. Why don't you tell me about some of the things you and your students do at school?"

"Well, it's an English class but I also teach them about writing. The students seem to enjoy the different styles of writing. That also teaches them how to write letters, poems, whatever with proper grammar. We take several field trips too. We go to the art museum, visit a television studio, go to the zoo, and a lot of other places. I have the students write a paper about their experience in these places. On nice days like it was today I would've taken my students outside for class. They always enjoy that."

Seth smiled. "It sounds like fun. I could see where writing a paper on their experiences could be difficult and challenging but also very important."

"I think it's helped several of my former students succeed in their classes. I've had several of the teachers from the high school say that several students from my classes have excellent grammar and writing skills. I feel pretty good about that. I try to make learning fun."

"I think you're doing that. Now I know why your students sent that lovely bouquet and why they all hugged you together at the funeral home. You are very special to them, Maggie, Kevin and a lot of us."

Sara had tears in her eyes. "Thank you Seth. That means a lot."

Seth clasped Sara's hands. "You're welcome Sara. I'm going to get myself a cup of coffee; would you like one?"

"No, I don't think so. I'm so tired, I think I'm going to try and get some sleep."

"I think that's a good idea. Let me walk with you to your bedroom."

Seth helped Sara back to her bedroom. He helped her into her bed. "Sara, do you need anything?"

"No, I'm fine Seth. Thank you for your help."

"You're welcome. If you need me I'll be back in the guest bedroom, just call me."

"I will. Thanks again. Goodnight Seth."

"Goodnight Sara."

Seth left Sara's room and went into the kitchen to get another cup of coffee. Since he was used to staying up at night because of the shift he usually worked he wasn't tired. He took the coffee and went into the guest room. He turned on the television and when he did he saw the story about the murder in the park. He heard them say the murder probably took place about 9:00 P.M. because witnesses said they heard shots fired as the church bells began to ring. Seth was thinking: Oh dear; it's the same MO and probably the same person who murdered Paul. We have to find the man of many disguises. He always seems to be there when the murders occur. How is he connected? I have to make sure Sara is not out of my sight. It's just too dangerous.

Seth started walking around. He decided to get on the computer in his guest room. He got onto the internet to research the other murders in and around the park and the church across from the park. He gasped when he saw all the similarities. He knew he had a serial killer on his hands. He just didn't know who and how they were all connected.

When he looked at the clock it was 3:00 A.M. He decided to check on Sara, make a walkthrough of the house, then try and get some sleep. He walked back to Sara's bedroom. He walked through the door and saw her sleeping peacefully. He smiled. He was glad she was able to sleep. He knew she was really going to have traumatic days ahead of her but he knew she was a strong person. He hoped she would lean on him for support after Maggie and Kevin left. He knew what it was like to lose someone due to someone else's carelessness but he had no idea what it was like to lose someone to murder. Looking at Sara and knowing how bad she was hurting inside made Seth want to get this serial killer even more.

After he left Sara's room he did a walkthrough of the house and everything looked alright. He walked back to the guest room and got ready for bed. He got into bed and tried to sleep; he kept thinking about Sara's reaction when two men showed up at the funeral home. She was actually afraid of one of them. He'd have Tom check both of them out in the morning. He wanted to find out as much as he could about these men. He wanted to talk to Sara more about the man she called Art.

Seth set his alarm to go off at 7:30 A.M. He wanted to check on Sara again. The alarm didn't go off. He woke up at 7:45 A.M. He dressed in blue jeans and a short sleeve shirt. He walked back to Sara's bedroom. He looked in but didn't see Sara. "Sara, Sara, are you alright?"

"Yes I'm alright. I'm just brushing my teeth."

"It just scared me when I didn't see you."

"Sara came out of her bathroom. She smiled. "I'm okay. Wow, you look so different. I'm not used to seeing you out of uniform. You look great. I like it and you'll fit right in with other people. I'm going to lay out the clothes I want to wear today but before I get dressed, I want to shower. Would you mind staying close while I shower in case I need you?"

"That's not a problem. I'll wait out in the living room. I can hear you from there."

"That's fine but first would you mind getting something out of the closet for me? I'm unable to reach up and pull that blouse off the hanger."

Seth got the blouse for Sara and handed it to her. She put it on the bed along with her slacks that she had intended to wear. "Thank you Seth," she said and hugged him. "I appreciate it."

Seth was stunned. He never thought she'd hug him. He smiled. He knew Sara was trying to move on with her life and he was starting to see more of the person she was every day. "I'll wait for you out in the living room."

When Seth got to the living room he sat in one of the wing backed chairs in front of the fireplace. He wanted to be close enough to hear Sara if she called for him. He heard the water in the shower. He walked into the kitchen and put a pot of coffee on, then returned to the living room. He heard Sara turn the shower off. He headed into the kitchen to get a cup of coffee. He heard Sara walking around in her room. She was dressed and walking to her closet when she felt that stabbing pain in her side. Her knees buckled and she fell to the floor. "Seth, please come help me." Sara cried.

Seth ran into Sara's room and found her on her knees, crying and holding her side. "Sara, what's wrong; is it your side?"

"Yes it is. Seth please help me stand up."

He helped her. "What were you doing?"

"Trying to get my shoes on. I got this stabbing pain in my side and I just fell to my knees."

"Sara, I'm so glad you're going to the doctor today. Hopefully he can do something to help with the pain."

"I hope so." Seth helped Sara over to her bed. She sat down on the bed and he put her shoes on her. He looked up at her. She looked so helpless and vulnerable. "Seth, could you help me into the living room?"

"You sure you're ready?"

"Yes I am."

Seth helped Sara into the living room. "Seth, do I smell coffee?"

"Yes you do. I made a fresh pot and I was hoping to surprise you with breakfast too but I got up too late."

"Seth, that's sweet but I can make us breakfast. What would you like? I think I still have some of that egg casserole left over. It just needs to be heated."

"How about I fix you some blueberry pancakes along with some bacon?"

"That sounds wonderful. I usually don't have time to eat very much for breakfast unless I get up extremely early or have everything prepared the night before. I usually have cereal and toast for breakfast. I'd love to have pancakes and bacon for breakfast. Do you need some help?"

Seth knew Sara wanted to help but he didn't want her doing anything to cause her side to hurt either so he said "Well, why don't you get the silverware and napkins out and I'll do the cooking?"

While Sara got out the silverware, Seth mixed up the pancakes and started cooking them. "Those pancakes smell good. I haven't had pancakes in a while either. That's something I usually fix if I'm making brunch on Saturday. I used to have brunch here twice a month. Carrie, Paul, Peggy and Ralph would come. We took turns having brunch at our houses. When Carrie got sick Peggy and I both volunteered to do her Saturday; it was just too much for her."

"That was nice of both of you."

"We both enjoyed it and it was something we all could do together. I think that's why I made so much food Saturday when Maggie was here. It was supposed to be my turn to fix brunch."

Seth finished up the pancakes and started cooking the bacon. Sara got out napkins and coffee cups. She got out juice glasses and dessert bowls. She got into the refrigerator and got out some fresh fruit "Seth, I'm going to make a fresh fruit salad. Do you want some?"

"That sounds good. Are you going to be able to handle doing that or do you need some help?"

Sara knew Seth was only trying to spare her any more pain than she was already feeling. "I think I can handle it. If I need help, I'll ask."

Seth smiled. "Well, the pancakes and the bacon are ready. I'll put the platters on the dining room table and come back and get the coffee, creamer, sweetener, coffee and juice cups."

"I'm almost finished cutting up the fruit for the fruit salad. Would you mind taking these bowls with you?"

She cringed when she handed him the bowls. "Sara, do you need help?"

"I'm not really sure. This is a different type of pain. The wound is burning now. I'm not sure I can carry this big bowl over to the table."

"Why don't I help you to the table first so you can sit down. I'll get the bowl and bring it in here."

Once Sara was situated at the table Seth brought the big bowl of fruit salad in. "Sara, this looks good."

They started eating. "Seth, these pancakes are absolutely wonderful. I detect a hint of something, I'm not sure if it's nutmeg or cinnamon."

"It's cinnamon. It's one of my special ingredients in pancakes. I think it brings out of the flavor of the blueberries."

"It does. I never thought of that." They ate and talked. When they were finished eating they started clearing the table and taking the dishes into the kitchen.

Murder *When the Bell Tolls*

Seth saw Sara cringe as she picked up the plates. "Sara, leave those plates there. I'll get them."

"Thanks Seth."

He finished clearing the table and started doing the dishes and cleaning up the kitchen. Sara put the leftovers away and grabbed a towel to start drying the dishes. They finished cleaning up at 9:00. "What time did Maggie and Kevin say they'd be here?"

"Maggie told me she'd be here around 9:30 A.M."

"That's in about thirty minutes. We have the kitchen cleaned up and everything's put away; is there anything else that needs to be done before we leave today?"

"I was going to start a load of laundry but I just don't have the energy. I'm sure Maggie will help me with that. Seth whatever things you have that need to be washed or freshened up please get them together and I'll wash them also. It seems so strange for me not to be teaching today."

"I bet it does. Do you feel the same way in the summer?"

"I do for about the first couple of weeks until I get used to being home and able to get caught up on some of the things I didn't get around to doing before. I shop during the week and in the day time not after I leave the school. I can actually go into the bank and do my banking, you know, all those little things that I can't do when I'm working."

"I know how that is. Since I work the night shift I sleep a lot in the day and don't always get to get things done when I'd like to either."

At 9:20 A.M. there was a knock on the door. Seth answered it. Maggie and Kevin were surprised to see Seth out of uniform too. They both smiled. "Kevin, Maggie come in please."

Sara walked over to Maggie and Kevin and they both hugged her. "How you feeling Sara?"

"A little weak but I'm not as tired."

"Sara, you look a little pale."

"She's had a rough morning."

"Why? What happened?"

"She's had a few incidents with pain in her side. I made her sit down and rest but now she told me her side feels different. It's burning."

"I'm glad you have a doctor's appointment today. If you didn't I'd take you to see the doctor myself."

"I appreciate that Kevin, I really do."

"Did you two have breakfast?"

"Yes. Seth made the most wonderful blueberry pancakes and bacon. I really enjoyed them especially since I usually only get to have them once in awhile and very seldom through the week unless school's out. I wanted to start a load of laundry before we left but Seth doesn't want me doing anything while I have this burning pain in my side."

"He's right. You shouldn't. Where's the laundry; I'll get a load started for you and I'll toss it in the dryer when we get back."

"Maggie, you don't have to do that?"

"I know, but I want to."

"The clothes are in a basket in my bathroom. I'm not sure where Seth's things are."

"I'll get my things together."

"I'll get a laundry basket for your room while you're getting your things together."

"Sara, where are the laundry baskets; I'll get it for him. You should rest."

"The baskets are in the hall closet on the left side."

Kevin walked to the closet and got a basket. Maggie walked back to Sara's room and got her clothes basket and brought it up. She sorted the clothes and put a load in the washer.

It was 10:05 A.M. when Maggie got the laundry started. "I got the load of laundry started. You both had a few white things but not enough to make a regular load so when we get back; I'll put the whites in on a small load. I don't want to leave with the dryer running so I'll wait until we get back to put the clothes in the dryer."

"Maggie, thank you so much. I really appreciate it." Sara said.

They talked for a little while. It was a little chilly outside so at 10:30 A.M. they all got their jackets on. Sara cringed while she was trying to put her's on. "Sara honey, let me help you." Maggie helped her with her jacket and they left for the doctor's office.

Once they arrived at the doctor's office, Seth helped Sara out of the car and Kevin helped Maggie out. Seth was helping Sara walk inside. They had only taken a few steps when Sara squeezed Seth's hand. He knew something was wrong. He whispered "Sara, what's wrong? Is it your side?"

"Yes. It's really hurting now."

"Put your arm around my back and I'll help you inside."

Maggie turned around right as Sara was putting her arms around Seth's neck. "Sara, what's wrong honey?"

"It's just my side. It really hurts and I'm not sure I can make it inside without some help."

"Seth, do you need more help?"

"No, I've got it. However, could you see if there's a wheelchair available for Sara to use until I can get her inside?"

Kevin went inside and checked to see if there was a wheelchair available. He came back out with one. Maggie helped Seth set Sara in the wheelchair. Seth pushed Sara into the doctor's office. The nurse was shocked when she saw them. "Hello, I'm Maggie Sanford. We brought Sara Michaels here for her 11:00 appointment. She's in a lot of pain so we put her in the wheelchair just to get her inside."

"Sara Michaels? The same Sara Michaels the doctor had to attend to yesterday?"

"Yes ma'am."

"Please bring her in here and we'll get her set up in a room." Maggie took Sara into the room the nurse had directed her into. "I need to get her vital signs." The nurse took the vitals, wrote the information down, then turned to Sara. "I would imagine you're in pain honey. I need for you to remove your slacks, and lay down on the table. The doctor will be with you shortly. Here's a blanket to cover up with. Ma'am, you may stay with her."

"Thank you nurse."

"Maggie, would you please help me remove my slacks? I have to take these shoes off first."

Maggie helped her remove her shoes and her slacks. Maggie gasped when she saw the wound on Sara's side. It was extremely pink and oozing. She knew why Sara was in so much pain. Maggie helped Sara lie down. "Maggie, I'm cold. Could you please cover me up with that blanket?"

Maggie had just covered Sara up when the doctor knocked on the door. "Yes."

"Is it alright to come in?"

"Yes it is."

Doctor Martin walked into the room. He gasped when he saw how pale Sara was. "Hello Sara."

"Hello Dr. Martin. Do you know Maggie Sanford, Paul's Mother?"

"I met her yesterday at the funeral. Are you still in pain Sara?"

Before she could answer she grabbed her side and cringed. Dr. Martin grabbed a few things out of the cupboards and sat them down on a table next to the examining table. He looked at Maggie and Sara. "Sara, I need to check your wound. I'm going to roll you over on your right side, okay?"

"Okay."

Once she was on her right side he could check the wound better. He gasped when he saw it oozing. He touched the area and she whimpered. She was trying to be brave while Maggie was in the room with her. He shone a light on the wound. He thought he could still see something in it. "Sara, I need to get my nurse in here because I'm going to have to lance that wound again and I need the nurse to hand me different things."

Sara was scared. "Can Maggie stay in here with me? Please?"

"Well, it's usually not allowed but in your case, I'll allow it."

"Thank you Doctor."

He got on his intercom system and called his nurse into the room. Before she got inside Doctor Martin said "Sara, would you please excuse me just a minute?"

He met his nurse outside the door. He told her what was going to happen. I need for you to have my wife answer the phone, take messages, and run the office until we are finished. I need you in here."

"Yes doctor."

The nurse found Madison and told her what the doctor had said. "No problem. I was almost finished with the books anyway. Did you say he was going to have to lance someone's wound open?"

"Yes I did. This woman is in terrible pain and the wound is infected; he's had to see this woman three times in four days."

Madison gasped. "This patient wouldn't be Sara Michaels, would it?"

"Why yes it would, why?"

Madison gasped. "That poor woman has been through so much since seeing her fiancé murdered right in front of her. Sara's such a sweet person, I hate that this is happening to her. What room is she in?"

"Room 3."

Madison walked down to room 3. "Madison, did Dixie tell you what I need for you to do?"

"Yes she did and I'll gladly do it but I was wondering if it would be alright to say hello to Sara?"

"Sure, go ahead."

Madison walked over to where the doctor had pulled the curtain so that they could prepare to lance Sara's wound. She poked her head around the corner. "Hi Sara. Do you remember me? I'm Madison Martin, Doctor Martin's wife."

Sara smiled. "Yes I remember you. You were the lady that was so nice to me after Paul was shot. Are you a nurse?"

"No, I do the billing for my husband and occasionally run the office while the nurse is busy. I understand you've had a really rough time since your fiancé was killed. My husband told me that apparently you were grazed by a bullet also. My husband will do what he can to make you better. I wish you all the best Sara."

"Thank you Madison."

The nurse came into the room and she and Dr. Martin came behind the curtain. Sara started shaking. She was scared. Dr. Martin tried to comfort Sara. "It'll be alright Sara. We just have to lance the wound; I think there may still be some fragments inside that are causing the infection. If that's all it is I can remove them and antibiotics will do the rest. If that's not the problem I may be able to see what is. I want you to hold Maggie's hand and squeeze it when the pain gets to be too much or to help comfort you. I'm going to numb the area with Novocain now. Maggie, would you come over here on this side and hold Sara's hand?" She did. "Nurse, I need you over here."

Sara started shaking as Doctor Martin put the liquid Novocain on her side. Maggie squeezed her hand and whispered "I'm right here honey."

Sara winched and started sobbing as the doctor cut the wound open. Dixie gasped when she saw shiny slivers inside the wound tract. The infection was oozing and she was trying to wipe the skin as the doctor grabbed a different instrument. "Sara honey, there are several tiny fragments inside the wound that I wasn't able to see the other day. I'm not sure they were in the wound at the time. It looks like they may have been buried underneath some skin and worked their way into the wound. I must remove them. I know it'll be very painful and I'll do what I can to keep the pain level down. Sara, I want you to squeeze Maggie's hand when the pain gets unbearable. Maggie, I need for you to talk to her about something she enjoys; something to try and help her focus on anything but the pain."

"Okay doctor. I was wondering if someone would mind telling my husband and Seth what's happening."

"Not a problem. I'll have my wife do that." He got on the intercom and asked Madison if she'd inform Seth and Kevin what was happening. "Take them into my office. You can answer the phone in there if you need to."

Madison went into the waiting room and asked for Seth and Kevin. They stood up. "I need to talk to you for a few minutes. Would you come back here please?" There was one other person waiting in the waiting room and it was a pharmacy rep. "Sir, I'll be with you in a little while. He nodded as Kevin and Seth went with Madison.

"Is something wrong ma'am?"

"Well yes and no. Sara's undergoing a very difficult procedure to remove more bullet fragments that were lodged under the skin and went into the wound tract. It's a painful procedure but the doctor has done this several times. Maggie's with Sara. Sara asked that Maggie be allowed to stay with her. That's usually highly unacceptable but the doctor made an exception in this case."

"Does the doctor think that the fragments were the problem?"

"I'm not sure. You'll have to ask him. The whole thing should be over in about thirty minutes. You can stay in here if you like. Help yourself to coffee. Restrooms are down the hall on the right."

"Thank you ma'am."

After Madison left the room Seth and Kevin looked at each other. "I can't imagine the pain Sara's going through. She's been through so much and has never complained. She's always been there to help when she's needed. She's a wonderful person. I can't imagine why anyone would want to hurt her. Seth, have you talked to anyone from the station today?"

"No. I was supposed to call Tom Monroe but I thought I'd wait until we got back from here. He worked late on that new murder case last night and I told him he didn't have to go into the office until ten; I told him to get some rest. It will also give him some time to follow up on some leads. When I talk to him I need to pass on a couple of names that keep coming up in this case. Kevin, I really want to get this guy."

Meanwhile Maggie was talking to Sara about the theater and a movie that she and Kevin had seen while they were vacationing. Sara relaxed but cringed as Doctor Martin removed the fragments. Suddenly he gasped. "What is it doctor?" Maggie asked.

"There's a tear in the muscle I didn't see before. The bullet must've pierced the muscles and allowed some of the fragments to go into the muscles. That's why I didn't see all of the fragments before. Dixie, shine that light on that area so I can see if I've gotten all of the fragments."

He looked at the wound twice. He made sure all of the fragments were out; he rinsed the wound with an antiseptic, stitched up the tear in the muscle, then cleaned the wound on the outside. He put ointment on the open wound and a clean bandage too. "Maggie, this dressing needs to be changed at least once a day and if there's a lot of drainage, twice with this ointment applied whenever the bandage is changed."

"Okay. I'll make sure that gets done."

"Sara, all of the fragments are out now. You'll have some pain so I don't want you lifting anything for three days and light activities as tolerated. Don't overdo it and get plenty of rest. I want to see you back in a week."

Dixie and Dr. Martin helped roll Sara back onto her back. She cringed. "Sara, I'll prescribe something for the pain. I want you to take it every four hours as needed. Do you have any questions?"

"No I don't think so except when do you think I'll be able to go back to work?"

"Not for at least ten more days. I want to make sure your side starts to heal and your infection clears up. It'll take that long for the medication to run its' full course."

Sara was disappointed but understood. "Thank you for everything doctor. I appreciate it."

"You're welcome. Let me help you sit up."

After he helped Sara sit up he looked at her and said "If you need anything just call. You may get dressed now. After you're dressed you can pick up your order for your prescription at the desk. Dixie will assist you."

"Thank you again doctor." He walked out the door. Maggie helped Sara get her slacks on. They went out of the examination room and headed to the desk to pick up the paperwork. As they were coming out of the room Kevin and Seth were coming out of the doctor's office. They were both visibly shaken from what they'd been told. They walked over to Sara. "You ready to go?"

"I have to get my paperwork and give them my insurance information."

"Sara, I'll get the paperwork for you." Seth said.

"But what about the insurance information?"

"Don't worry about that. I'll take care of it." Seth said.

"But how? You don't know the information."

"I'll take care of it. Maggie, you can take her out to the car."

Dixie helped Maggie get Sara to the car. Thank you Dixie."

"You're welcome. Sara, do as the doctor told you with that wound and it should heal. If it's not any better in three days, please call me and I'll let the doctor know."

"I will and thank you for everything."

The nurse had orders to stay with Maggie and Sara until Seth and Kevin returned. They talked for a little while then Kevin and Seth got to the car. "Thank you Dixie. Your help's appreciated."

"You're welcome. Just take care of Sara and call and make an appointment."

"We will. Thank you again for your help."

As Dixie went inside Kevin and Seth got in the car. Sara was leaning back trying to get comfortable and rest. "Sara, I can imagine the pain you're in right now. Is there anything we can do to help?"

"I could use a blanket and a hot cup of soup or coffee."

"Kevin, there's a sandwich shop down the road from here. They serve everything from sandwiches to soup and coffee.

Would that be alright Sara? We can get it to go so we can eat it at your house."

"That's fine."

Seth gave Kevin directions to the sandwich shop. When they got there, Seth decided he should stay with the ladies while Kevin ordered and paid for the food. Maggie said she'd go with him because it was such a huge order. Sara was resting in the back when Maggie rubbed her on the arm. "Sara honey, I hated to wake you but we're at the sandwich shop and need to know what you'd like?"

Sara sat up to see which sandwich shop they were at. She recognized it because she'd been there several times when she took her students on an outing and they ate there at lunch. "I want a roast beef on rye with mayo and pickles on the side. I'd like to have French onion soup in a bread bowl."

"That sounds good. I think I'll have the same thing except I want mustard instead of mayo." Maggie said.

"Kevin, I want a large cup of coffee with that." Sara said.

"Okay. I think I have everyone's order. Maggie are you coming with me?"

"Seth, I know you can handle things; you don't mind if I go with him do you?"

"Go ahead. He needs help carrying the order anyway. Sara and I'll talk until you get back."

Maggie and Kevin left to place the orders. "Sara, I'm so sorry you had to go through that painful procedure today. I wish there was something I could do to help ease the pain."

"Seth, you're so sweet but time will heal the pain. I'll have to take medication for the pain. I really wanted to go back to work after Maggie and Kevin went home next weekend but the doctor told me I couldn't go back for ten days. It's only a minor setback. I could use the rest anyway.

"Here come Maggie and Kevin. They have their hands full. I need to help them." Seth got out of the car and helped them get into the car."

"On the way back to Sara's Kevin said "Wow! That food smells good. I hope it tastes as good as it smells. I didn't think I was hungry but after smelling that food I am."

They got to Sara's. Seth got out and walked around the outside of the house while Kevin parked the car. Seth gave them the all clear sign. He walked out to the car and helped

Kevin get Sara into the house. They went into the house and Kevin and Seth helped Sara sit in a dining room chair. Maggie got plates and eating utensils and brought them into the dining room. They opened up the sacks and set out everyone's food.

Everyone started eating. Sara was having trouble eating. The anesthesia had worn off and Sara was beginning to feel the pain from the procedure she just had. "Sara do you need some help?"

"No, I think I can handle it."

"Just ask if you need any help. I know it's just soup and a sandwich but the bread bowl is hard to pull apart."

"It is but I really think I can do it; but thank you for the offer."

Seth and Kevin started talking about baseball and who they thought could go to the World Series. They were talking about one of Sara's favorite sports, football. She had to smile when Seth and Kevin disagreed on who was better in football the Jets or the Giants. She was an Eagles fan herself but rooted for the Giants too.

They were almost finished eating when the telephone rang. Seth picked it up. "Seth Parker."

"Hello, is Sara there? This is Suzann, her sister in-law."

"I didn't know she had a sister in-law. She just had some surgery done earlier today so she's still a little groggy. Let me get her." He looked at Sara. "Sara, there's someone on the phone named Suzann; claims to be your sister in-law."

"She is. She's Gary's sister. Her husband's captain of a cruise ship and were out of the country the last time I knew. Just hand me the phone please."

Seth handed her the phone. "Hello."

"Sara, It's Suzann. Steve and I just heard about Paul. We were in the Virgin Islands until yesterday. We didn't hear about any of this until late last night and it was too late to call you then. When is or was the funeral?"

"The funeral was yesterday."

"What was that I just heard about you having some sort of surgery?"

"Suzann, Paul died from a gunshot wound to the back of the head. Apparently two shots were fired and one of them grazed me in the side. I had to have a procedure done because the wound got infected. Oh Suzann, it was awful. One minute Paul and I were talking and laughing and the next minute he's dead." Sara started to cry. Seth walked over and ran his hand over her back.

"Sara, who was that handsome sounding gentleman who answered the phone? He said his name was Seth Parker."

"Yes. He's Lt. Seth Parker with the NYSPD. He's here along with Paul's parents Maggie and Kevin Sanford."

"How are Maggie and Kevin taking all of this?"

"Fairly well. Maggie's been my rock through this. She and Kevin have been wonderful."

"That's wonderful. However, why is a Lt. with the NYSPD there? Is he a friend of the families?"

Sara wasn't sure how to answer that. "Well, yes he is. You see, ever since Paul was murdered, I've been under twenty four hour police protection."

Suzann gasped. "Why?"

"I'll let you talk to Seth about that."

She put Seth on the phone. "Hello Suzann. I understand you have some questions about why Sara's under police protection. Well, first of all Sara's the only person who may have caught a glimpse of the shooter, second of all she herself received a bullet wound, thirdly we think she may have also been the target and we now think she may know who the shooter is. She's in extreme danger and we need to make sure she's safe at all times."

"Oh I definitely agree. Sara's very important to us. Thank you for looking out for her. May I speak with her again please?"

He put Sara back on the phone. "Sara honey, Seth sounds so nice yet so authoritative. What's he like and what are the arrangements that have been made to keep you safe?"

"Seth's very nice, very gentle and caring yet very much in charge of this investigation. Paul's parents really like him and so do I. Paul's parents like him and trust him so much they made arrangements with the police department for him to stay with me twenty four hours a day. He'll sleep in one of my guest rooms. He'll go where I go. He'll be a plain clothed officer at the school where I teach. I like that arrangement better than before when there were officers changing shifts every twelve hours. I trust Seth more than any of the officers that have been here."

"I'm so glad Sara. He does sound really nice. Sara, you're beautiful, talented, sweet, loving and in the prime of your life. I know Gary and Paul both would want you to move on with your life."

"I know you're right. Maggie and Kevin have told me the same thing. I can't seem to focus on anything except what happened to Paul."

"I know that has to be hard for you. I can't imagine how I would feel if I saw Steve murdered right in front of me."

"Suzann, the worst part is there have been four other murders with the same MO committed within the past three months. I got a call and letter from someone claiming to be the killer. Seth sent that letter to the lab to be analyzed."

Suzann gasped. "You got a call and letter? Sara, you need to be extremely careful. We don't want anything to happen to you."

"Where are you and Steve now?"

"We're at our home in Miami. Steve and I are scheduled to leave again in four days. This is the start of the busiest time of the year for cruises. Do you need anything?"

"No. I think I'm fine for now."

"Sara, Steve thinks it is a good idea for you to have a number where you can call if you need to reach us, while we are on the ship. Do you have a pencil and paper?"

"Yes I do. What's the number?" Sara wrote the number down and repeated it to make sure she had it right.

"Sara, if you need anything don't be afraid to ask."

"I won't; thanks Suzann. Where are you going on the next cruise?"

"Our cruise ship is scheduled to go to Australia. It's a fourteen day cruise. We have a lot of land time. We'll call you from there. Are you going back to work next week?"

"No. The doctor told me I wouldn't be able to go back to work for at least another ten days. That's alright though because Paul's parents aren't leaving until then anyway. That will give me more time to spend with them."

"Sara, I need to go. Call us if you need us. We'll fly up to see you soon. We love you Sara. Please be careful."

"I love both of you too. Thank you for calling. It means a lot."

When Sara hung up the phone, she had tears running down her face. Maggie walked over to her and hugged her.

Murder When the Bell Tolls

Sara just started crying. Maggie held Sara close to her and comforted her. After Sara stopped crying so hard Maggie asked Sara "Honey, who are Suzann and Steve?"

"Steve's Gary's brother and Suzann's his wife. Steve's a captain for a cruise liner and Suzann's the cruise director. They always travel together. They were out of the States when Paul was killed or they would've been here. Paul never met them but they knew him from my letters and calls. They were so happy we were going to get married. They're wonderful people; they have always been so supportive. Maggie I know you'd like them."

"Maybe, Kevin and I will get to meet them someday."

"I hope so. I know Paul would have liked them. He loved it when I told him about some of the places they'd gone on their cruises. It was amazing." Sara was starting to feel really weak.

"Sara, I can tell you're exhausted. Let me clean up from lunch. You just stay there and rest. I can handle it."

"Let me help you." Kevin said.

Seth helped get things together also. Seth could tell Sara needed to rest in a different chair or in her bedroom. He turned to Kevin, "Kevin, I think Sara really needs to rest. I think she needs to be somewhere other than the dining room table. Would you help me get her over to the living room chair?"

"Maggie, would you mind?"

"I was going to suggest that too. Go ahead and help Seth; I can handle this."

Seth and Kevin helped Sara stand then helped her to a chair in the living room. "Would you like a blanket Sara?"

"No, I'm comfortable, but thanks for asking."

"Seth, I need to help Maggie."

"That's fine. I need to call the station anyway."

Seth took out his cell phone and called the station. "Tom Monroe speaking."

"Tom; it's Seth. I was calling to see how things are going on this case."

"There isn't much more to tell you than I told you yesterday. No one saw the shooter. We think from the location of the head shot the weapon was fired from off the roof of the church or from somewhere close by. I have officers over there looking for any evidence. How's Sara doing? I know she was in terrible pain yesterday."

"She's doing a little better. There was a good reason she was in pain. Some of the bullet fragments tore a muscle in her side and embedded themselves inside the muscle. As Sara started moving around, the fragments moved and lodged themselves into the wound tract and made the wound infected again. She had to undergo some type of procedure to remove the fragments, repair the muscle then clean the wound. They've given her pain medication and so far she's doing okay, but the doctor has said she's not to do any lifting, or anything stressful for at least ten days. She can't even go back to work for ten days. The doctor wants to see her back in a week. He'll tell her then if she'll need to undergo another procedure or if the wound is healing."

"That's horrible. I wish there was something I could do to help her feel better."

"I know you do. I have something I need for you to do for me. I need you to find out as much as you can about a man named Art, who works as a teller at the US Bank and a man named Jack, who's a store manager at the Shop N Save. Let me know what you find out."

"Sure Seth, but what are we looking for?"

"I'm not sure. A connection to these murders. I believe Sara and Martha Burns may know the man of many disguises and or the shooter. That could be our connection but I don't know for sure. I want to know where they live, if they're married, anything you can find. It's really important Tom."

"I'll get right on it Seth. I'll let you know what we find out."

"Thanks Tom."

Seth hung up his cell phone. He walked over to Sara. She was asleep in the chair. He smiled then walked over to Maggie and Kevin. He whispered "Sara's asleep. I'm going to put a blanket over her so she doesn't get cold. She doesn't need to get sicker."

"I agree. After you do that let's play some Gin Rummy. We won't disturb her that way."

"That sounds good." Seth walked over and put a blanket over Sara then went over to the dining room table where Kevin and Maggie were sitting.

Kevin started dealing the cards. "Seth, were you able to reach the station?"

"Yes, I talked to Tom and told him about the two men Sara told me about. He's going to check them out."

Maggie gasped. "What men?"

"Remember I told you last night they thought Sara and this latest victim's girlfriend knew the shooter, raggedy dressed man, or both?"

"Sara kept saying she felt like she knew the man in the raggedy clothes, but she didn't know from where."

"She may be right. If she does she may be in even more danger than we thought."

"Seth, it's a good thing you're staying here with her. I feel a lot better knowing you're here."

Sara starting talking in her sleep. "Art, please, I'm sorry. I didn't mean to say that. Please, please…" She fell back to sleep.

Maggie and Kevin looked at Seth horrified. "Seth, would Art be one of the two men who may be involved in Paul's murder?"

"He could be. He's a person of interest."

"Do you have any idea what she was talking about just now?"

"No, I have no idea. Hopefully it was just a nightmare." Seth didn't want to tell Kevin what Sara told him about Art. He thought she should tell him herself if she wanted him to know.

They continued playing cards. Maggie got up and made a fresh pot of coffee and took it into the dining room. About thirty minutes later Sara awoke. "That coffee smells good."

"Hello Sara, I'm glad you were able to sleep. Do you feel better?"

"Yes I do."

"I'm glad. Would you like some coffee?"

"Yes please."

"Sara, would you like for Kevin and I to help you over to the dining room table?"

"That would be nice Seth."

Kevin and Seth helped Sara stand then they walked her over to the dining room table. "What card game are you playing?"

"Gin Rummy and Seth's beating me big time." Sara smiled.

Maggie came back with a cup of coffee for Sara. They started playing cards again. At 5:30 P.M. there was a knock on the door. Seth answered it. "Hello Seth. Do you remember me? I'm Peggy Miles; Sara's friend."

"Oh sure. Come in."

When she hugged Sara, Sara cringed. "What's wrong, did I hurt you?"

"No. I just had to have a procedure done today to remove more bullet fragments from my side and apparently some of the fragments tore a hole in some of the muscles in my side. They had to be repaired and the fragments had to be removed so I'm still pretty sore."

"I would imagine. Do you have any idea when you'll be able to come back to work?"

"In about ten days. The doctor says it takes that long for the medication to run its course."

"Hopefully this will take care of it. The reason I stopped by was I wanted to see how you were doing after yesterday and I wanted to invite all of you to my house tomorrow night for supper, if you're up to it."

"I'm not sure Peggy."

"Peggy, we'd love to come. What time would you like us to be there?"

"Is 6:30 P.M. too late for you?"

"No, that's perfect. Is there anything you'd like for us to bring?"

"Just yourselves. It's casual so you don't have to wear anything fancy. Sara, Carrie's going to be there too."

"I'm looking forward to spending time with all of you. I hope I don't ruin the whole evening because of how I feel."

"We'll have fun. We'll eat, talk, and play some board games."

"That sounds like fun. We'll be there."

"Sara, I need to get going. I just stopped by on my way home from work to check on you and ask you to dinner. I still need to stop at the grocery store on my way home to pick up some things for tomorrow night. I'll see all of you tomorrow."

"We'll see you. Thanks for stopping by Peggy."

"Let me make sure you get to your car alright."

"Thank you Seth."

Seth walked Peggy to her car. "Seth, is Sara alright? She looked pale."

"She's going to be alright but that procedure was hard on her today. Peggy I need to ask you a question."

"Sure Seth, what is it?"

"Do you know someone named Art that works at the US Bank?"

"The name sounds familiar but I'm not sure I know who he is; why?"

"I'm not sure exactly but I think he may have something to do with this case. We'll see you tomorrow night. Be careful going home."

Seth watched as Peggy got in her car. "Did she get off alright?"

"Yes. I made sure she got in her car."

"That's good. Peggy's a wonderful friend, teacher, and confidant."

"She's worried about you Sara." Sara smiled. "Is anyone getting hungry?"

"I am." Kevin said.

"So am I." Seth said.

"Sara honey, what about you?"

"I could eat something but I don't really feel like anything big."

"Okay, we'll have something light."

"Maggie, why don't you let me help you fix something. I feel so useless not helping with anything."

"The doctor said you weren't suppose to do any lifting or anything strenuous for at least three days, but I think I can find something you can help me with." Sara smiled. "I thought maybe we'd have tacos. Would you be able to cut up the things that go into them?"

"Sure. Let's see we need onions, tomatoes, lettuce, there's sour cream, cheese, and black olives in the refrigerator and the taco shells are in the cabinet next to the stove." Sara got everything they needed and cut up what was necessary. She put everything into small bowls so that everyone could fix the tacos the way they wanted, then she took the bowls into the dining room and set them on the table.

Maggie cooked up the hamburger and heated up the chicken strips for the tacos. Once she did that she and Sara took the meat and the taco shells into the dining room and set them on the table. They all wanted iced tea to drink so Maggie made a pitcher of iced tea and brought it into the dining room. Seth brought the glasses in. They were on a higher shelf that Sara wasn't able to reach without tearing the bandages on her side.

They sat down at the table and began eating. "Sara, how far away do Peggy and Ralph live?"

"They live about five miles from here. It only takes about ten minutes to get to their house."

"I'm glad Peggy invited all of us for dinner tomorrow. I'd like to get to know them a lot better than I do. I only know Peggy from the conferences I've met her at during my teaching career and I've only talked to Ralph a couple of times. They both seem like such nice people." Maggie said.

"Sara, when Ralph was helping me at the church he was eager to help and seemed like he knew how to take charge of a situation. Didn't you tell me he was a stock broker?"

"Yes, he's a manager of a brokerage firm. As a matter of fact Peter Edwards worked in that firm. He was one of their stock brokers; that was why I went there."

Seth gasped. "Peter Edwards worked for Ralph Miles?"

"Yes. That's how I met him and Martha."

Kevin looked at Sara very concerned, then looked at Seth who had a shocked look on his face. He was convinced there was a connection between Paul's murder and Peter Edwards' murder but he wasn't sure yet. Peggy had said she wasn't sure if she knew Art, but there had to be a connection somehow.

"Sara, how well did Paul know Peter?"

"He didn't know him very well. He only knew Peter was a stock broker in Ralph's office and he was my stock advisor. Why?"

"I'm not sure." Seth didn't want to upset Sara by telling her he was convinced Paul and Peter's murders were related. He would have to go back and look at the other murders before he could be sure.

They finished eating; Seth and Kevin helped Maggie clean up. They insisted Sara stay at the table. Seth didn't even have to say what he was thinking. Kevin already knew. He knew Sara was in extreme danger. Seth took out his cell phone. "I need to cell into the station. I need to ask Tom a couple of things."

Seth called the station. "Tom Monroe."

"Tom, it's Seth."

"Oh Hello Seth. What can I do for you?"

"A couple of things."

"Sure. What are they?"

"First of all, are you on duty tomorrow?"

"Yes, but I'm going in at 7:00 A.M. instead of 8:00 because Frank has to leave early; his girlfriend has a doctor's appointment early and he needs to take her because her car is broken down. Why do you ask?"

"Well, I was wondering if you had any plans for tomorrow night?"

"No, just go home and crash on the couch after I do a load of laundry why?"

"How would you like to go with Sara, Maggie, Kevin and I to Ralph and Peggy Miles home for dinner?"

"That would be great but why?"

"Carrie White's going to be there and she'd like to see you again. I told Peggy I would ask you."

Seth could almost see Tom smiling over the phone. "Sure, but what time's dinner?"

"6:30. I can arrange for you to get off at 6:00 P.M."

"That would be wonderful. I'd love to see Carrie again."

"I know, that's why I asked you."

"I'm glad you did. Seth, you said there were a couple of things you wanted. Was that all?"

"No. I need all the files we have on the five murders in and around the church and park in the past two months."

"I'll get them for you. Would you like for me to drop them off at Sara's when I get off at 8:00 tonight?"

"That would be great."

"Seth, what are you looking for?"

"A connection. I have a feeling these murders are all connected but I don't know how yet. I think those two men I asked you about have something or everything to do with the murders. I just don't know what. Maybe there's something we missed or overlooked in the files. I'll go over them carefully and see if I can figure out what it is. Tom thanks for your help."

"You're welcome Seth. I'll see you later."

Seth hung up the phone and went into the kitchen to help Maggie and Kevin with the clean-up. Sara was sitting alone at the dining room table and turned to Seth and said "Seth, would you mind getting the phone for me? I'd like to call Martha and give her my condolences on the death of Peter. Martha's a friend and I know how she feels."

Seth got the phone and handed it to Sara. She called Martha. The phone rang twice. "Hello." Said a tear filled voice.

"Martha?"

"Yes, who is this?"

"Martha, it's Sara Michaels. I heard about Peter and I wanted to call you and tell you how sorry I am. Peter was such a wonderful person and he was a friend, just like you."

Martha started to cry. "Oh Sara, I feel so lost without him."

"I know. I feel the same way about Paul. Is there anything I can do?"

"You already have. Calling and talking to me is the best thing you can do. I heard you've had a hard time since Paul was murdered. How are you doing?"

"A little better. Having Paul's family with me has helped. They're wonderful people."

"Peter's father is flying in from London tomorrow and his mother will be here in the morning. Sara, this just seems so unfair."

"Yes it does. Martha if there's anything I can do let me know."

"I will. Thank you so much Sara. It means a lot to know that your friends care."

"Yes it does. Goodbye Martha."

"Goodbye Sara."

Sara had tears running down her face when she hung up the phone. She could identify with the fear, pain, and anguish that Martha was going through.

"Sara, you alright honey?" Maggie asked.

"Yes. I know how Martha feels. I could sense the anguish and pain. She thanked me for calling her. I want to make sure I keep in touch with her. She's a nice person and she's a friend. Luckily she wasn't with Peter when he was killed. She was closing up her shop for the night. He was on his way over to see her when he was killed."

"That's awful. The person responsible needs to be caught."

"Maggie, Kevin, I promise you we'll find this person and they will pay for their crimes. Sara, I wanted to tell you I talked to Tom and asked him to come to Peggy and Ralph's tomorrow night for supper. Carrie's going to be there and Peggy stated Carrie would love to see Tom again and wanted to know if he'd come for supper. He said he would but I have to make the necessary arrangements so he can get off early enough to join us."

"That sounds great. I know Carrie will enjoy the company. She's a wonderful person. She's had to deal with so much the past five years. She lost her daughter to bone cancer, then lost her husband and now she's dealing with cancer herself. I think she and Tom will get along great. He's a good person. He's honest, fair and a good police officer."

Seth smiled. "That he is. He asked about you. He's going to be stopping by on his way home from work tonight. I asked him to bring me some files from the station."

"Oh, okay. What time do you think he'll stop by?"

"Probably around 8:30 P.M. He has to give a report and finish up his paperwork before he gets here. I know he wants to see you Sara."

They looked at the clock. It was 7:45 P.M. "I'll make a pot of coffee, if Tom wants to stay for awhile we'll have coffee."

"That sounds good Sara. Would you like my help?"

"Yes Maggie, I would."

Maggie and Sara went into the kitchen to make the coffee. Sara got everything ready but she couldn't lift the pot that was full of the water. Maggie took the full pot of water and poured it into the coffee maker. Sara put the coffee in and turned the machine on. "Sara, you're quieter than usual since you talked to the woman whose boyfriend was killed near that church; what was her name?"

"Martha. Maggie I want to help her because I know how she feels but I can't stop thinking about how Paul was killed and how I feel either. I don't know if I could help when all I can feel is guilt and sorrow."

"I understand the sorrow and grief but why guilt? Do you still feel like you did something to cause Paul's death?"

"I don't know how I feel about that. I keep having nightmares about what happened and I can't make any sense of them. I miss Paul so much Maggie."

Maggie threw her arms around Sara and hugged and held her. "I know you do and so do I. As the days go by it'll get easier but there will be things that remind us of him every day. I know when the Daffodils are in full bloom, I think about my daughter. She loved Daffodils. She would always say Mom, the world has finally awaken from its' winter nap. They're fond memories I'll always cherish."

"One of my favorite memories of Paul is his love of the outdoors. I remember last spring when he came over and helped me plant my garden and plant those rose bushes out my bedroom window. He planted the Joseph's Coat next to the window because he knew it was my favorite. When they bloom, I will always think of him." She started crying again.

Kevin and Seth were talking in the dining room out of earshot of Maggie and Sara. "Seth, I heard you say earlier you think the murder that happened last night and Paul's murder are related. Do you know how; other than you think Sara and this other woman know who the shooter or the man of many disguises is?"

"I know there's a connection to both of these murders. I'm having Tom bring over the files from the five murders we've had in or around the church and park in the past two months. I want to see if there's any connection and if there is what. Kevin, I'm not sure if you remember but there were two men who came to the funeral home to pay their respects. Sara was terrified of one of the men. I asked her about them and all she told me was their names and where they worked. I'm having Tom check them out. I think they may have something to do with the murders or know who does. I'm afraid Sara's in even more danger than anyone thought."

"Seth, I'm glad you're here with her all the time. Please, please protect her. She's so very special to us."

"I know. I promise you, I'll protect her."

The coffee had just finished brewing when there was a knock at the door. Seth answered it. "Hello Tom, come on in."

Tom walked in carrying a huge stack of folders in his arms. Seth took them from him and set them down on the dining room table. "Hello Tom." Everyone said.

"Hello everyone. Sara, I understand you had to undergo a painful procedure today. How you feeling?"

"I'm weak but feeling a little better. We made a fresh pot of coffee; would you like some?"

"That sounds good Sara."

"Have a seat Tom. We were going to start playing some cards. Would you like to join us in a game of Gin Rummy?"

He looked over at Seth and smiled. "You bet I would. I have to beat Seth in this game. He always beats me so it's my turn to beat him."

Sara was getting herself a cup of coffee when the pain from the procedure took over. She grabbed the counter in the kitchen and cringed. Kevin got up and ran to her. "Sara, you alright?"

"Yes, I just need my pain medicine."

"I'll get it for you Sara."

"Thanks Maggie."

"Let me help you to the dining room table."

"Thanks Kevin."

Maggie came back with Sara's medicine. Sara took the medicine and sat at the table shaking from the pain.

Tom looked at Sara with compassion and empathy in his eyes. "You going to be alright Sara? Is there anything I can do?"

"I'll be alright Tom. The doctor told me I'd have pain for awhile. It's better than it was though. Thank you for asking. The one thing you can do to help is join us in a game of cards and enjoy some coffee."

"I can do that."

They sat down and started playing cards. It was 10:30 before they realized it. "Oh my, look at the time. It's 10:30 P.M. already. Kevin, we should go. Sara needs her rest."

"That's true. She does. She's had a very difficult day. Sara honey, will it be alright if we went back to our motel?"

"Yes. I'll be alright; besides both of you need your sleep too. You both have been such a big help to me and so supportive. I appreciate all you did for me today. It means a lot." Sara hugged both of them. "Thank you again."

"You're welcome Sara. You mean a lot to us. We'll come by in the morning and see how things are going. Goodnight Sara, Seth, Tom."

"Goodnight Maggie, Kevin be careful going to your motel."

"I'll make sure you get to your car safely. Sara, you stay with Tom; I'll be right back."

Seth walked with Maggie and Kevin out to their car. "Seth, please, please protect Sara." Kevin pleaded.

"I will Kevin. I promise both of you, I'll find the person responsible for Paul's murder and for the attempted murder of Sara."

"Thank you Seth. Goodnight, we'll see you and Sara in the morning."

"Goodnight. Be careful."

After Maggie and Kevin drove off Seth stood on the porch for a few minutes, then he walked around the outside of the house to make sure everything was alright. He didn't see anything so he went back inside. However, Art was lurking around down the street. He hadn't seen Seth and Seth hadn't seen him. Since Seth had his own car in front of the house Art had no way of knowing Seth was there. He saw the patrol car there and decided to stay where he was until he saw the car leave. He thought now that Paul was buried Sara wouldn't have police protection anymore.

While Seth was walking around outside Sara and Tom were talking. "Tom, I'm glad you're coming tomorrow night to Peggy and Ralph's. Do you know them at all?"

"I only know them from yesterday at the funeral. They seem like wonderful people."

"They are. Peggy helped me my first year as a teacher at the school where I'm teaching. I knew Carrie because her husband was a teacher there and Carrie was a secretary in the office. When Carrie became a teacher I helped her the same way Peggy helped me. We've all been friends since then. Carrie's a wonderful person; the cancer has slowed her down though. She only has one more treatment and they think she'll be done. She's a little self conscious about losing all of her hair. I told her I thought she looked cute with the hats' she's been wearing."

"I thought the hat she wore to the funeral looked wonderful on her."

Seth walked in the door. "Kevin and Maggie got off safely and I walked around the outside of the house and everything seemed to be alright."

"That's good. Seth, Sara I think I'm going to take off also. I have to be at work a little earlier than usual and it is getting late. I'll see both of you tomorrow."

"Tom, why don't you meet us here and you can go with us or follow us in case you want to stay later or leave earlier?"

"That sounds good. Seth could you arrange it so that I could get off work at 5:00 so I can go home, shower and change clothes?"

"Yes, I'll arrange it. Tom, now that I'm officially staying here twenty four hours a day, you're in charge at the office. I'll write up something stating you're to receive a pay raise and overtime as needed. Does that sound fair?"

"Wow! I never expected that but yes, it sounds fair. Thanks Seth."

"You deserve it. I'll walk with you to the door. I don't want to leave Sara alone."

"Goodnight Sara. Thank you for the coffee and card game. I'm glad you are feeling better. I'll see you tomorrow night."

Goodnight. I'll see you then."

Tom squeezed Sara's hand then headed toward the door. Seth started walking with him. "Seth, I'll see you tomorrow to." Tom walked out the door and got into his car. Art was lurking behind some bushes two houses down. He watched Tom get in his car and leave. He thought the police protection was officially over. He smiled, got out of his black outfit and walked over to his car, parked two blocks away and drove off. He decided it was time to pay Martha a visit.

Sara and Seth decided to stay up and talk for awhile. "Sara, I'm glad we're going to Peggy and Ralph's for dinner tomorrow night. It may help you feel better."

"I'm sure it will. I always loved going to Peggy and Ralph's. They have a beautiful home. What Gary, Ralph, Paul and all of the guys enjoyed was Ralph's game room. The guys would go in there while we women talked."

Seth smiled. "I can understand that. When we would go to Marie's sister's house, she had a pond behind the house and in the summer all of the men went fishing and all of us went swimming or boating in the evening. In the winter we played hockey on the pond."

"That sounds fun. Seth, I'd like to have a cup of coffee. Would you like a cup?"

"That sounds good. You stay there; I'll get it."

Seth went into the kitchen and got the coffee. He came back and he and Sara sat in the living room. "Seth, I'm glad I called Martha."

"So am I."

"She was understandably tearful and grieving but there was something else in her voice that I detected. I can't tell you what but it was different, almost as if she was begging me to stay on the phone with her."

"Sara, did she say anything about what happened other than what she has been told?"

"No. The only thing she said was when Peter didn't call or make it to her house she knew something was wrong. He'd talked to her earlier in the day and they'd made plans for the evening. She told me he'd always call if he was going to be late. Seth, I know how she sounded now. It was fearful, unsure, worried."

Seth gasped. "Sara, excuse me a minute. I need to call into the station."

He took out his cell phone and called the station. "Mark Anderson."

"Mark, it's Seth."

"Hey Seth, how's it going?"

"It's going okay. Mark I have a favor to ask."

"Sure Seth, what is it?"

Before Seth could say anything, Frank yelled "We have a report of a possible burglar at the home of Martha Burns."

Seth heard Frank over his cell phone. "Mark, that was what I was going to ask. I was going to ask you to send a patrol car over to Ms. Burns house. The suspect is possibly our shooter."

"What? Are you kidding?"

"I wish I was but I'm almost sure of it. I think all of our victims knew the shooter or the man of many disguises or both. Get over there now and let me know what happens."

Seth was pale when he hung up his phone. "Seth, what is it? Is everything alright?"

"Sara, how well do you know Martha?"

"I've only know her for about two years but I'd consider her as a friend why?"

"While I was on the phone with Lt. Anderson, a call came in of a possible burglar at her home. Units are on their way over there now."

"Oh no. Not her too."

"What do you mean Sara."

Sara thought about what Art had done to her and had hoped since Martha kept turning him down for a date, Art hadn't hurt her. She trembled at the thought. Seth looked at Sara. "Sara, you're trembling. What's wrong?"

"It's nothing Seth. I was remembering something from after Paul and I were engaged. It's nothing really."

Seth looked at her concerned. No matter how much Sara trusted Seth she wasn't ready to tell him what Art and her father had done to her. If Art was found to be involved with the crime she'd tell Seth then but not until then.

Sara finished drinking her coffee. "Seth, I'm really tired. I think I'm going to get into my gown and go to bed."

"I think I'm going to get ready for bed too Sara. Let me help you up and help you back to your bedroom."

Seth walked with Sara back to her room. She was trembling. "Sara, you're trembling. You sure there isn't something you want to talk about?"

"I'm sure Seth. I'm just really tired and in pain."

"I can understand that. Would you like me to hand you your medicine?"

"Thanks Seth."

Seth waited for Sara to finish getting ready for bed before he left her room. She came out of the bathroom in her robe. She almost collapsed on the floor. Seth put his arm around her and helped her to her bed. "Thank you so much Seth. I don't know why I feel so weak and so tired."

"I do. You had that procedure done today and the doctor says you need rest."

Sara smiled. "Thanks for your help Seth."

Seth smiled. "It was my pleasure. I'm going to change clothes myself and stay in the guest room. I need to go over the files Tom brought for me. Would you like for me to turn off the light in here when I leave?"

"Just a minute. Let me turn on the light by the bed. Would you please hand me that paperback book over there. I want to do some reading before I go to sleep. Sometimes reading helps me relax."

Seth got the book and handed it to her. He noticed it was a mystery novel by a local writer. "Here's your book Sara. Do you need anything else before I go back to my room?"

"Only to tell you goodnight."

"Goodnight Sara. I'll turn the overhead light off for you. I'll check on you before I go to sleep. Try and get some rest."

"Goodnight Seth."

Seth left the room. He picked up the files he had laid on the hall table and took them into the guest bedroom with him. He set them down on the desk. He opened the files, wrote down things he thought were important then turned on the computer to make a list of the things he had written. After looking at the files he knew all of the murders were connected; it was why he hadn't figured out. At 1:30 A.M. he decided to call it a night. He got the files together and set them on the desk. He used the bathroom, then went to check on Sara.

He walked back to Sara's room and looked in. She was sleeping peacefully with her book left open across her chest. He picked up her book, marked the page where she was, then closed the book and set it on the table next to the bed.

He walked out of Sara's room and walked back to the guest room. He set his alarm for 7:00 A.M. He wanted to make sure he was awake in case Tom called when he came on duty; he also wanted to be up to fix breakfast for Sara. He got into bed and had no trouble falling asleep.

Seth woke up when his alarm went off. He shaved and got dressed, then went into the kitchen to fix breakfast. He was a little bit nervous because Sara wasn't up yet. He started a pot of coffee, then went to check on her; he knew it was unusual for her to sleep past 6:30 A.M.

Seth walked to Sara's bedroom and looked in the door. He saw her stirring. He smiled, then walked into the kitchen and started cooking breakfast. Sara got up, went into the bathroom and washed up. She came out, got dressed then headed into the kitchen. "Good Morning Sara. How did you sleep?"

"Good morning Seth. I slept fairly well. Do I smell crepes?"

"Yes. I wanted to surprise you and fix my specialty for breakfast."

"Crepes? I haven't had those in years. I think the last time I had a crepe was when Gary took me to this tiny little French café in Queens the year before he died. I don't even know if it's still there but the food was fantastic."

"I remember that place. I don't think that place is there anymore; I think they turned it into a restaurant. I haven't been there in awhile either but Tom has. He said the food's good. He told me they moved that tiny café to somewhere by the park and renamed it."

"Seth, didn't you tell me Tom brought some files over for you?"

"Yes I did. I went over some of them last night. I'm convinced more than ever that all of these murders are connected; I just don't know why yet. Sara did you know any of the victims beside Paul and Peter?"

Murder *When the Bell Tolls*

"I knew Fred Sweeney, the second victim. He went to church with me, but I didn't know the other two. You really think these are all related? I don't think Paul knew the other two either."

"I do think they're related and I'll figure out why."

"I know you will. Let me help you with breakfast."

"Sara, you need to take it easy."

"Please Seth, I feel so useless."

He gasped. "You're not useless. You're recovering from a bullet wound. It'll take time. However, if you want to help, let me hand you some silverware and napkins and you can set them on the table."

Sara set the silverware and napkins on the table. She cringed on her way back. "Sara, the crepes are ready for the filling. What would you like?"

"Blueberries. I love blueberries."

"So do I. Do you want cream cheese also?"

"Oh yes. That sounds great."

"Why don't you sit down and I'll fix it for you and bring them over to you?"

Sara walked to the table slowly and sat down. Seth brought the crepes in. "Seth, these look so good."

Seth sat down at the table and they ate and talked. After they finished eating Seth got up and started clearing off the table. "Let me help you." Sara said.

Sara started helping clear off the table. She stacked the dishes together then got the silverware together. She grabbed the silverware and started heading slowly into the kitchen. She got about halfway and had to stop. She grabbed her side and stayed where she was. Seth walked over to her. He had his hand full of dishes but he set them down on the glass coffee table in the living room. "Sara, you alright? Do you need some help?"

"Seth, could you help me to the chair please?"

Seth helped her to the overstuffed chair and helped her sit down. He took the silverware from her. "I'll take the dishes into the kitchen and clean-up. I want you to rest."

"But Seth, this is my house; I should be doing that not you."

"Sara, you're supposed to rest. You're recovering from a bullet wound, besides, I'm living here too so I plan on helping you out as much as possible."

"Yes but your job description is supposed to be to protect me and go where I go. I hate the fact it includes doing all of this for me."

"Sara, my job description is to do whatever is necessary to help and protect you. After all the police motto is to Serve and Protect."

Sara smiled. "I guess you're right; that helps me feel a little better."

Seth washed up the dishes and cleaned up the kitchen, then put on a fresh pot of coffee. He joined Sara in the living room. "Seth, I'm a little nervous about going to Ralph and Peggy's tonight."

"Why, they're some of your best friends."

"I know, but I feel so lost and so sad."

"Sara, you're grieving; that's natural. Peggy and Ralph know that, I think that's why they invited you to dinner. They want to try and help you get through the grieving process a little faster."

"I grieved when Gary died but nothing like this. When Gary died it was almost a blessing. He'd been suffering for so long, but Paul was a vibrant, happy, loving, man with his whole life ahead of him until someone took that away from him. It's not fair."

"No Sara, it not fair but the person who took Paul's life will pay for it; I promise."

"I guess Maggie and Kevin will be here in about an hour. Would you mind if I took a shower now?"

"Go right ahead. I'll take one after Maggie and Kevin get here that way I know someone will be here to make sure you're alright."

Sara smiled as she headed into her bedroom to shower. When she got in her room she laid out the clothes she wanted to wear to Peggy's and put her perfume, and make-up on the table. She knew it would probably take her an hour to get ready, especially since she had to be extra careful with the open wound. She took a shower, put her robe on that was on the back of the bathroom door, wrapped a towel around her hair and walked into the bedroom to get dressed.

Sara was dressed and putting on her make-up when there was a knock at the front door. Seth answered it and Sara heard Maggie's voice, then she heard Seth say "Sara's in her room. She said she was going to shower and change into the clothes she's going to wear tonight."

"Thanks Seth. I'll see if she needs any help."

Maggie went to Sara's bedroom door and knocked. "Sara, it's Maggie. May I come in?"

"Sure."

Maggie looked at Sara and smiled. "My you look nice Sara. How you feeling today?"

"Better. I slept much better last night."

"That's good. Do you need some help with anything?"

"Actually I do. My side's been bothering me a lot and I was wondering if you'd mind helping me brush my hair."

"I'd be glad to."

Maggie brushed Sara's hair then discussed the make-up she should wear and the jewelry. After Sara was ready she walked into the living room. Kevin and Seth both smiled when they saw how lovely Sara looked. It was nice to see her looking better. "Sara, you look very nice. It's good to see you with a little more color in your face. How are you feeling?"

"Better. I think I'm sleeping a little better."

"That's good. I was hoping you'd start sleeping better."

"Would anyone mind if I took a shower and changed clothes? I didn't want to take a shower until I knew there was someone here to help Sara in case she needs something."

"That's understandable. Go ahead. We'll take care of Sara."

Seth headed back to the guest room to shower and change clothes. "Sara, I'm so glad you're feeling better. Are you still having nightmares?"

"Some but not as bad. Now that the funeral is over they don't come as often. I can't stop thinking about that raggedy dressed man. I know I know him from somewhere."

"Sara, has Seth told you he thinks that Paul's murder and this last murder are connected?"

"Yes. He told me he feels all five of the murders are connected. He's trying to figure out why."

"Sara, the man in the raggedy clothes may be the key, but let's not worry about that tonight. Let's just have a good time at Peggy and Ralph's and leave all of this behind."

"I wish I could but I feel so guilty for Paul's death."

"Sara honey, it's not your fault."

Seth came back from taking a shower. Sara couldn't believe how nice he looked in dress casuals. "Seth, you look like you're ready to go."

"I am. Do you think I'm dressed alright?"

Sara looked at him and said "Seth, you look fine. As I matter of fact, I think you look wonderful."

Kevin and Maggie smiled at each other. They knew Sara was trying to move on with her life. They knew how hard it would be for her after what she'd been through. "Sara, I was wondering if you felt up to doing some shopping. I want to get myself some new shoes before tonight. Would you feel like going to Macy's?"

Sara's face lit up. She didn't get to go to Macy's very often so it would be a lot of fun. She thought about how she felt. "How did you know Macy's is a store I love to go to but because of my work schedule I can't always go when I want to?"

"Being a former teacher myself I know sometimes there are conflicting schedules."

Sara walked over to Maggie and threw her arms around her. "I'd love to go Macy's."

"Are you up to it?"

"I think so."

"Great. Seth, you don't mind do you?"

"Goodness no. My late wife used to shop there too. Our schedules conflicted a lot so we had to go on the days I was off. We always had a lot of fun. When our daughter was little we used to go to FAO Schwartz too. I think it'll do Sara a lot of good to get out of the house and start going places again."

"I agree." Kevin said.

"I almost forgot; I need to call into the station and make sure Tom got there and that he's still going to be able to join us for dinner."

Seth called into the station. "Tom Monroe speaking."

"Tom, it's Seth. I was checking to make sure you got into work alright and to make sure you're still coming tonight."

"I wouldn't miss tonight for anything."

"Maggie, Kevin, Sara and I are going to Macy's for the day. Sara says she's up to it and I think she needs to go and get out again. She's been inside since Paul was killed. The only time she got out of the house was to make funeral arrangements and the funeral itself. She needs to have some fun. I used to love going to Macy's; there's something for everyone."

"There sure is. Am I still supposed to follow you to Peggy and Ralph's tonight?"

"Yes. Be here by 6:00 P.M."

"I will. Have fun today Seth."

"I will and we'll see you tonight."

Seth hung up his cell phone. "Tom's going to meet us here at 6:00. I hope that's alright."

"That's fine. I was going to suggest you tell him to be here by 6:00. I know we'll be back by then. I want to get Sara home by 4:30 or 5:00. I want her to have a chance to rest before we leave."

"That's a good idea. While we're out would you mind stopping by the post office so I can tell them to forward all of my mail here?"

"Not a problem."

"Kevin, could I talk to you privately for a few minutes before we leave?"

"Sure Seth. Let's go into the guest bedroom."

Sara and Maggie started talking. "Maggie, Seth made the most wonderful breakfast this morning. I tried to help but the pain from my wound stopped me. He fixed crepes with cream cheese filling, covered with powdered sugar, drizzled with chocolate sauce and topped with whipped cream. They were so good."

"It sounds like it. I'm so glad you're feeling better. I know this has been hard on you. It's been hard on all of us, that's why we thought a day of enjoyment might help. If you get too tired we'll sit down and rest. We don't have to hurry."

"Maggie, I think I'll wear flatter heels to shop then change into my pumps when we get back."

"That sounds like a good idea. Do you need some help getting your shoes on?"

"I could use the help, thanks."

While Maggie was helping Sara with her shoes Kevin and Seth were talking. "Seth, what's wrong?"

"I think I found the key to Paul's murder along with the other four. The key is the man of many disguises. Sara keeps saying she feel like she knows him from somewhere. I'm convinced all of the murders are connected, and that's one of the pieces. I need to figure out why they're related. I think Sara's another piece of that puzzle."

"Sara, why?"

"I'm not sure. I really think she knows the identity of the man of many disguises and maybe the identity of the shooter. Right now the only connection I have between Paul's death and Peter Edwards death is they knew each other from the stock market. I don't think that's the reason they were killed. I think it's something else. I promise you, I'll do what it takes to protect Sara."

"I know you will Seth. I'm glad you're coming along with us to Macy's. I'll have someone to talk to. Maggie starts shopping and becomes oblivious to me or anything except what she's looking for. Sara, that's different. Sara pays attention to others and sometimes misses out on things that are important to her."

"I hope you won't mind if I look for a dress shirt and pants. I only brought three pair with me and I need some nicer clothes to go to church with Sara and maybe take her a few places that require dress attire. Sara told me yesterday I'll fit right in with the staff and students at her school."

"You will. Sara teaches at a wonderful school. The students are very educated and well-mannered. However, they dress, act, and talk like teenagers, which isn't all bad. Sara says a lot of her students former and present ask her for advice on many things and she tells them the best she can."

"We better get back before they think we left without them. Kevin, I haven't told Sara I think I know what the connection is in these murders. I'm afraid it'll really upset her and she's been through enough right now."

"I agree. I won't say anything to her or Maggie."

"I think that might be best. I appreciate that Kevin. Thanks for trusting me."

Seth and Kevin went into the living room where Sara and Maggie were. "I had to change my shoes. It's too hard to walk around Macy's in pumps."

Kevin and Seth smiled. "Is everyone ready to go?"

"I know I am." Maggie said.

"So am I." Seth said.

"Sara, you ready honey?"

"I'm nervous but yes I'm ready to go."

They got their things together and walked out the door. They drove to Macy's. They got inside and the ladies decided to go to one department and the men were going to another. "Sara, here's my cell phone. Let's meet back here at 2:00."

"Seth do you think it's okay to leave Maggie and Sara out of our sight?"

"I don't want to let either one of you out my eyesight but we can still go to different departments; just let us know where you're going next."

"Okay Seth."

Seth wanted to look at men's shirts; he and Kevin went into that department while Maggie and Sara went to the shoes. Maggie and Sara both found a pair of shoes they wanted to try on. "Maggie, what do you think? I really like these shoes and they're so comfortable but I'm afraid when I wear them it might make me look too sexy."

Maggie smiled and even laughed a little. "Those shoes make you look very attractive. It's okay to look sexy and beautiful. I like those shoes too. I think you should get them if they're comfortable."

Sara smiled. She decided she'd get the shoes. They tried on several more pairs and both ended up buying three pairs of shoes each. After they paid for the shoes they went into the jewelry department. They both found something they liked. Sara wasn't sure she should spend the money so she decided not to get it. Maggie knew how much Sara wanted the necklace she had just seen and kept it in mind.

They'd been shopping about an hour and a half when Sara looked at Maggie and said "Maggie, I really need to sit down for a few minutes. I feel really dizzy and tired."

They found a couple of seats and sat down. Sara looked pale. "Sara honey, you alright?"

"Yes. I just need to rest for about ten minutes then I'll be alright."

They sat in the seats for about twenty minutes then got up and went to the make-up counter. They both got something they wanted. Kevin and Seth stayed sitting down. Maggie checked her watch. It was 12:30. "Seth, Kevin are you getting hungry?"

"Yes we are. Let's find a restaurant and get something to eat."

They left Macy's and found a sandwich shop around the corner. Since it was a beautiful day outside they decided to sit outside and eat. They got their food, sat down and ate. They talked and laughed while they ate. They finished eating and walked back to Macy's. "Seth, Kevin, Sara would you mind if I went back into Macy's. I saw something I wanted but didn't buy it because we needed to take a break. I promise I'll be right back."

"We don't mind Maggie but you're not going in there alone. I'll go with you." Kevin said.

While Kevin and Maggie went into Macy's Sara and Seth walked down the sidewalk. "Seth, did you find what you wanted at Macy's?"

"Yes I did. I found three nice shirts and a couple pair of pants. I really needed the pants too. What did you find?"

"Well, I found three pairs of shoes, and some make-up. I wasn't sure about one pair of shoes but Maggie talked me into them and I'm not sorry I bought them. They're comfortable."

Maggie and Kevin were inside Macy's. "Maggie what did you forget?"

"Jewelry. Sara's had a really hard time dealing with all that's happened and today she saw a necklace she really liked; she even had the clerk let her try it on. She wanted to buy it but decided she wouldn't. You should have seen the look on her face when she tried it on. She told me it was a necklace Paul was going to buy for her. I think we should buy it for her and surprise her."

"I think so too. Let's wait until we get ready to go back home before we give it to her. That way it'll really be a surprise, besides I think anything that reminds her of Paul right now will really upset her even more."

They got to the jewelry department, bought the necklace, and had it gift wrapped. Maggie slipped it into her huge purse so that Sara wouldn't see it. They went back outside to find Sara and Seth. When they got outside they saw Sara and Seth talking and laughing. "Hello you two."

"Did you two find what you were looking for?"

"Yes, but because it is so bulky the store said they'd hold it for us until we can pick it up tomorrow morning."

"That was nice of them."

Kevin looked at his watch. "Well it's 1:30. Sara are you ready to go back to your house or do you still have shopping to do?"

"I'm ready to go back home. I really need to rest."

They got in the car and went home. Seth checked the outside of the house, waved to the officer driving past the house then they went inside. Sara kicked off her shoes and went over to the overstuffed chair. Maggie helped her sit down. She leaned her head back, closed her eyes and fell asleep.

Maggie hated to wake Sara up but it was 5:30. "Sara honey, it's almost time to go. Are you going to wear your pumps?"

"Yes, I'll get my shoes on and brush my hair, then I'll be ready to go."

Sara put her shoes on and while she was brushing her hair she felt like she was being watched. She continued brushing her hair. She got up and walked into the living room with a puzzled look on her face. Seth looked at her. "Sara, what's wrong?"

"Maggie, Kevin there's something I need to talk to Seth about privately for a few minutes. Would it be okay if we went into the four seasons room?"

"Is something wrong Sara?"

"I'm not sure. I need to talk to Seth."

"Okay."

Seth and Sara went into the four seasons room, they left the door open slightly. "Sara, what's wrong?"

"Seth, it may be nothing but while I was brushing my hair I had a feeling like I was being watched. After I got up and walked across the room I didn't feel that way anymore. Maybe I'm just being paranoid."

Seth looked at Sara with a concerned look on his face. She looked vulnerable and so scared. He put his hands on her arms and looked her in the eyes. "Sara, I don't believe you're being paranoid. You may have more of a real reason to feel like you do. Is this the way you felt when you told Tom you felt like you were being watched?"

"Yes. Seth, I'm scared." Sara started crying and Seth rubbed her arms trying to help ease her fear. Seth wiped Sara's tears."

"I know. I'll try and ease that fear as much as I can. I think it's an even better reason to be going to Peggy's tonight; so you can try and get your mind off of all of this for a few hours."

"Thank you Seth."

"You're welcome. We better get back or Maggie and Kevin will know something's wrong."

"Seth, please don't tell Maggie and Kevin about me feeling like I was being watched."

"Sara, what you tell me is only repeated to other officers if it pertains to this case. Right now, we don't know if anyone was out there or not, so I see no reason to upset Maggie or Kevin. Let's go to Peggy and Ralph's and enjoy the meal and the socializing."

Sara and Seth went into the room where Maggie and Kevin were. At 5:45 there was a knock on the front door. Seth answered the door. "Hello Tom. Come in. We were just getting our things together to go."

"Hi everyone."

"Hi Tom."

"Seth, you look a lot more dressed up than me."

"It won't matter. We're going to enjoy ourselves."

"Is everyone ready to go?"

"I think so."

They walked out the door and got into the car. Tom got into his car and they drove to Peggy and Ralph's. When they got there they rang the bell. Peggy answered the door. "Well Seth, Maggie, Kevin, Sara come in." She hadn't seen Tom standing behind Seth. Seth was 6 ft 3 inches tall and Tom was 5 ft 8 inches tall. When they started walking in the door Peggy saw Tom coming along. She grabbed his hand and whispered "Tom, Carrie will be thrilled that you're here. Let's surprise her." He nodded.

Seth, Maggie, Kevin, and Sara knew Peggy wanted to surprise Carrie with Tom's presence so they walked in ahead of him. "Hi Sara, Maggie, Kevin, Seth, it's nice to see you again."

"Hello Carrie. We're glad to be here."

Peggy was standing in front of Tom. Carrie reached down to get something out of her purse when Tom stepped out from behind Peggy. Carrie looked up and gasped with surprise. "Tom, I didn't expect to see you here tonight. It's great to see you."

Murder *When the Bell Tolls*

He smiled. "Hello Carrie. I'm glad to be here. When Peggy invited everyone she asked Seth to get in touch with me and ask me if I wanted to come. I couldn't say no when I found out you were going to be here."

Tom couldn't stop staring at Carrie. She looked so beautiful in her red dress and pumps. She was wearing a big hat with a red ribbon and some of her beautiful brown hair, that was starting to grow back, was sticking out from under the brim. Carrie smiled.

Everyone smiled. "It'll be about twenty minutes before supper's ready. I got a late start. I got home from teaching later than I thought I would."

"I know that feeling." Sara said. "It's happened to me more than once."

"Me too." Carrie said.

"Make yourselves comfortable. I'll finish up."

"Do you need any help Peg?"

Peggy knew Sara was recovering from a bullet wound and Carrie was still weak from her treatment. "I could use some help but Sara I don't want you lifting anything. Remember what your doctor told you."

Carrie, Maggie, and Sara went into the kitchen to help Peggy finish up. All of the men sat and talked. The women came into the huge dining room with food and drinks. Sara carried the silverware in. They sat at the table and began eating. "Peggy this is wonderful."

"Thank you. It's something easy and quick to fix. Something I've found myself having to do a lot lately, especially since this is the last quarter of school."

They talked, ate and laughed. After dinner the ladies started clearing the table and taking the dishes into the kitchen. Sara stopped halfway into the kitchen. She had a severe pain in her side and her arms were full of dishes. Seth got up and went over to her. "Let me take those."

He took the dishes from her. She was still holding onto her side when Seth took the dishes into the kitchen. "Thank you Seth." Sara said trying not to cry.

"Sara honey, you alright?"

"I am now. I need to take my medicine."

Sara took her medicine and the ladies did the dishes and cleaned up the kitchen. "Well ladies we're done with the clean-up would you like to play a board game?"

"Sure. What about everyone's favorite game, Monopoly?"

"Guys, how about a game of Monopoly? We'll get into teams. There's eight of us so we can play four teams?"

"That sounds good."

"I'll get the game."

Peggy came back with the game and everyone got into teams. Tom and Carrie were together as were Maggie and Kevin, Sara and Seth, and Peggy and Ralph. Ralph was the banker of course. They had a wonderful time playing the game. Sara and Seth were the ones winning. At 11:00 P.M. Maggie and Kevin said "Wow! It's 11:00. Sara, Seth, I think we'll be going back to our motel now if that's alright. Are you ready to go home or would you like to stay a little while longer?"

"I think I'm ready to go home. I'm tired."

"Peggy, Ralph, thank you so much for the enjoyable evening and for the wonderful meal, and thank you for allowing us to come along with Sara. She means a lot to us."

"Maggie, Kevin, you're welcome any time in our home. Sara's like a sister to both Carrie and I. Thank you all for coming. It was wonderful."

"Peggy, Ralph, thank you for inviting me. I really enjoyed myself. I wasn't sure I would but it really helped me a lot. Thank you for allowing Seth to come along, for always being there for me. It means a lot. Carrie, Tom I enjoyed your company too. Thank you both for everything you've done. I'll see all of you later."

"Goodbye everyone. We'll see you later."

"Seth, I'll talk to you sometime tomorrow. I'm off tomorrow unless there's a break in this case. Thanks for showing me how to get here. I really enjoyed the evening."

"You're welcome. We'll see all of you later. Thanks again."

Tom and Carrie stayed a little while longer. At midnight Carrie said "I think it's time I get ready to leave. It's midnight and Peggy you have an early day tomorrow. Hopefully, I'll be back teaching in three weeks. Thank you for inviting me and for the wonderful surprise. I really enjoyed myself. I'll talk to you later."

"Peggy, Ralph, I should be going too. Thank you for inviting me. I enjoyed myself."

"Thank you both for coming. Be careful going home."

"We will. Thanks again."

Murder *When the Bell Tolls*

Tom and Carrie walked out of the house together. He walked Carrie to her car. "Carrie, how far away do you live?"

"About ten minutes."

"Carrie, I was going to stop and get a cup of coffee at the all night diner, would you care to join me?"

"I have a better idea. Why don't you just follow me to my place and I'll make us a pot of coffee and we can talk. I wanted to ask you a couple of questions about Paul's murder anyway that I didn't want to ask with Sara there. She's been through enough and I didn't want to upset her even more."

"That sounds great. You lead and I'll follow."

Carrie and Tom both got in their cars and left.

Sara had fallen asleep in the car on the way home. Seth told Kevin he could let them out then they could go to their motel but things changed when they got to Sara's. Seth could tell someone had been there. He tried to talk to Kevin without waking Sara. He whispered "Kevin, I think something's wrong. Someone's been here. Stay in the car and keep Sara and Maggie in the car. I'm going to have a look around and see what I can find."

Maggie, who was almost asleep perked up when they stopped. She looked over at Sara who was sleeping peacefully. She looked at Kevin. "What's wrong? Why aren't we walking Sara into the house?"

"SHHH! We don't want to wake Sara. Seth said to stay here while he checks things out. He seems to think someone's been here."

They waited while Seth walked around. Seth gasped when he looked on the back door. He found a picture of Paul and Sara at the park the night Paul was murdered. There was an x thru Paul's face. There was a note attached that said. I'm watching you. Check all of your doors. Seth walked around to the front door and found a picture of Sara, with a towel wrapped around her head and drying off with a towel. Seth gasped. "Oh Dear! I can't let Sara see this picture; they need to know at the station that someone's stalking Sara."

After he'd walked around the outside of the house again and didn't see anyone he walked out to the car. He had a horrified look on his face. He looked in the car and saw that Sara was still asleep. He was relieved about that. He had to try and hide the pictures from her, at least for tonight. "Seth, you're back." Kevin whispered.

"Kevin, would you get out of the car for a few minutes. I need to talk to you privately."

Kevin got out of the car and Seth told him what he had found. "That's not all. I need to show you something."

Seth showed Kevin the picture of Paul and Sara in the park then the picture of Sara getting out of the shower. "Oh my Word! How did they get those pictures?"

"My guess is the killer took them. I believe he's stalking Sara. She's been the only one who caught a glimpse of the shooter. I'm convinced Sara knows the shooter and not by choice."

"Seth, can you keep her safe?"

"Yes. I know Tom's off tomorrow but I'm going to call him and tell him about all of this. He'll send additional patrols around. I could do that but I put Tom in charge. It's still my case, but I'm letting Tom take the reins because right now I want to make sure Sara's safe."

"I agree. Is there anything Maggie and I can do to help?"

"I'm not sure yet. Are you two coming by here tomorrow?"

"We were planning on it. We thought maybe we would take you to the Art Gallery. That's always been one of Sara's favorite things to do."

"I'd love to go to the Art Gallery. What time are you coming?"

"Is 3:00 P.M. too late? We thought we'd take both of you to supper after that."

"I think that would be fine. It'll give Sara a chance to rest."

"Seth, you know I have to tell Maggie about the pictures and that someone's stalking Sara."

"I know, but tell her to try not to worry."

"I will."

Maggie opened her eyes. "Hi Seth. Sara's really sleeping."

"I know. I hate to wake her but I need to get her inside."

Maggie rubbed Sara's arm. "Sara honey, you're home. You need to wake up so you can go inside."

Sara opened her eyes halfway, looked at Seth and smiled. "Sara, you're home. Let me help you inside."

"Goodnight Sara, Seth. We'll see you tomorrow."

"Goodnight Maggie, Kevin, thank you for taking us tonight. I really had a good time. We'll see you tomorrow."

Kevin started to help Seth get Sara inside. "Kevin, it's alright. I can get her inside. You go ahead and take Maggie to the motel. We'll see you tomorrow."

"Are you sure you don't need my help?"

"I'm sure. Thanks for the offer. Goodnight."

Seth had checked the locks on the door and noticed that none of them had been tampered with, which was a relief. He helped Sara to the house. She unlocked the front door with her key and they went in. "Seth, I could use a cup of coffee before I go to bed, how about you?"

"That sounds good. I'll make a pot."

"Seth, would you mind if I changed clothes while you're doing that?"

"Not at all. Go ahead. I think I'm going to change my clothes too."

Sara headed to her bedroom and Seth headed to the guest bedroom.

At Carrie's place, Tom helped Carrie out of her car. They walked into her house. The house was beautifully decorated in yellow, blue, and mauve, with the kitchen decorated in a warm and inviting rust color. "Tom, why don't you have a seat in the living room and I'll get a pot of coffee started?"

He went into the living room and sat in a soft wing backed chair. He looked around and saw the room decorated in mauve and earth tones with a huge Grandfather Clock in one corner. She loved owls and had pictures and knick-knacks of owls throughout the room. He heard her moving around in the kitchen. He thought about how lovely she looked but also about how weak her body was from the cancer. "Carrie, do you need some help?"

"No, I can handle it"

"Okay."

While Tom was sitting in the chair and looking around the living room, he saw a picture of Carrie and her family. His heart ached to know that both her husband and daughter were dead. They looked like such a happy family. He wished he had known them before they died.

Carrie was in the kitchen getting everything together. She was a little nervous about having Tom in the living room. She thought about how nice kind and considerate he was. She thought about how he took care of Sara, her best friend. She was worried about Sara and she knew that Tom might be able to ease some of that fear, however, she was quite smitten by Tom.

She walked into the living room, carrying a tray with a silver coffee pot, two cups, and some cream and sugar. She set the tray on the wooden coffee table in the living room. "Coffee's ready. I brought this tray in."

"Carrie this is a beautiful home. Did you decorate it yourself?"

"Most of it. Sara and Peggy helped too. Before my husband died we had all new carpet and draperies put in. He didn't get to enjoy them very long, but he enjoyed them for awhile. It was his idea to put in a fireplace since we have such terrible winters here. I'm glad he did. It's kept me warm for awhile but I'm going to have to get more wood before next winter."

Carrie poured the coffee for both of them. The clock chimed at 12:30. They both started drinking their coffee. "Tom, I have a couple of questions about Sara that you may or may not know the answer to."

"What are they Carrie?"

"First of all did I hear you right when you and Kevin were talking that Seth thinks all of these murders might be connected somehow?"

"Yes, I'm afraid that's true. Seth believes Sara may know the killer or the man of many disguises or both."

Carrie gasped. "Oh my, does that mean Sara may be in even more danger than anyone thought?"

"Yes it does but don't worry Carrie. Seth will do whatever it takes to protect her; she couldn't be in better hands. Carrie, do you know anyone who works at the US Bank named Art or the Manager at Shop N Save named Jack?"

"Yes, I know both of them. Jack is as nice as can be. He's always courteous and thoughtful and goes out of his way to please the customers. Art on the other hand is a deceitful, angry, and very unhappy man who can make many people miserable. Why do you ask? Does one or both of them have anything to do with the murders?"

"We're not sure."

Tom poured himself another cup of coffee. "Carrie, would you like another cup?"

"Yes please." Tom poured her another cup. "Thank you Tom."

"Carrie, I'm really having a good time this evening. I haven't enjoyed myself this much for several years since my wife died in 9/11."

Carrie gasped. "Your wife was killed at the World Trade Center?"

"Yes, she worked in one of the financial offices there. She was a secretary."

"Oh Tom, I'm so sorry. I didn't know."

"It's okay. I don't talk about it very much. I've tried to move forward but sometimes it's just so painful."

"I know how that is. It's only been eighteen months since my husband died but for three years I took care of him all the time. I didn't have a life. I'd do it again though. I miss him but like you I have to try and move on. When I was diagnosed with cancer four months ago I was devastated."

"I bet. How are the treatments going?"

"I have one more treatment then I am done for six months."

"That's great. When's your last treatment?"

"Tuesday. I have to be there at 10:00 A.M."

"I'm glad you're doing better. I wanted to tell you all evening how lovely you look. That red looks great on you. I was afraid I was under dressed for the evening."

"Thank you Tom. I think you look very handsome in the outfit you're wearing. I don't think I've seen many police officers in street clothes unless they're undercover officers and I don't know many of them."

The clock chimed at 1:45 A.M. "Wow! I didn't know it was that late already. I better go and let you get some sleep."

"I didn't realize it was that late either. I've really enjoyed being with you Tom. I really had a good time at Peggy and Ralph's too."

"I really enjoyed being with you. What are your plans for tomorrow?"

"I don't have any plans. I thought maybe I'd take a walk and enjoy the sunshine. I always like to walk everyday that I can; it helps me think more clearly."

"What would you think about a picnic in the park?"

"That sounds fun. What time?"

"I'll pick you up at 10:00 A.M. Wear something comfortable and bring a jacket. I'll fix the picnic basket so that you don't have to. Do you have a spare blanket?"

"Yes, do you want me to bring it?"

"Yes. I better go, so you can get some sleep."

Carrie walked with Tom to the door. She was smiling, almost grinning. She was really looking forward to the picnic. "I'll see you in the morning Tom."

"I'll see you Carrie. Goodnight."

Seth and Sara were talking about the events of the evening. At 1:00 A.M. Sara went to bed. Seth walked around the inside of the house checking to make sure everything was alright. He was almost to the guest room when we looked into the four seasons room. He looked outside twice to make sure everything was alright. He went into the guest bedroom and got into bed but had a hard time going to sleep. He couldn't stop thinking about the pictures he'd found. He finally fell asleep.

Seth was restless. He kept tossing and turning. He woke up at 6:00 A.M. He got up and got dressed. He went to check on Sara. He walked back to her bedroom and looked in. She was still sleeping peacefully. He was relieved. He knew she needed the rest; he wasn't sure how he was going to tell her about the pictures or even when. He walked to the guest room and got out the files Tom had brought. He kept going over them trying to find the missing link.

At 8:00 A.M. Seth heard Sara walking around. He walked into the kitchen and made a pot of coffee. Sara walked into the living room wearing her gown, robe and slippers. "Good morning Sara."

"Good morning Seth. Have you been up long?"

"I've been up about two hours. I had a hard time sleeping."

"So did I Seth. I kept having nightmares."

"Nightmares about what? Paul's murder?"

"Yes."

"Sara, you remember Maggie and Kevin are coming over at 3:00 this afternoon to take us to the Art Gallery then take us out to dinner."

"Yes I remember. I want to make sure I wear something comfortable. I was so happy to see Carrie happy last night.

Murder *When the Bell Tolls*

She and Tom really hit it off. Carrie hasn't been that happy in a long time. She's been through so much. When her husband died, a part of her died also. I saw that spark of happiness again in her last night."

"I noticed that too. Tom's had a rough time too. He lost his wife in the attack on the World Trade Center. He was never the same after that."

"That's awful. I really like Tom. I think he and Carrie are meant to be together. I think this will help both of them."

"I agree. Was there anything in particular that you needed to do this morning, before we go?"

"I was hoping to go to the grocery store and I need to go to the post office and get some stamps so I can mail out the thank you cards from the funeral. I don't feel like driving and I'm not sure I feel like shopping but I really do need a few things."

"I'll drive and remember, I'll be with you so don't try to do everything by yourself.

"Would you mind if I took a shower before we go?"

"No, go ahead. I have some things I want to go over. I need to call Tom anyway. I know it's his day off but I told him I'd check with him."

Seth helped Sara walk back to her room so she could shower. When he was sure she was alright he went into the living room, took out his cell phone, and called Tom. "Tom Monroe speaking."

"Tom, it's Seth."

"Hello Seth."

"Tom, I know it's your day off but there's something I thought you needed to know."

"What's that?"

"Last night when we got back to Sara's; there were signs of someone being there, so I walked around the outside of the house and you wouldn't believe what I found. Taped to Sara's back door was a picture of her and Paul the night Paul was murdered. His face had an x thru it and on the front door was a picture of Sara getting out of the shower. There was a note attached that said, You're being watched. I haven't told Sara yet. I'm trying to spare her the pain."

Tom gasped. "Do you have any idea who took those pictures?"

"Not a clue. Tom, Sara and I are going to the grocery store and post office this morning; I was wondering if you'd want us to run the photos over to you while we're out."

"I would say fine but I won't be here. I have other plans."

"Okay, that's fine. You work this weekend don't you?"

"Yes. Why don't I swing by Sara's tomorrow afternoon and pick them up."

"Call here first. I may take Sara to my place then out to dinner; it depends on what Maggie and Kevin have planned."

"Sure Seth. I'll talk to you tomorrow."

As soon as Seth hung up the phone Sara walked into the living room. "Seth, what would you like for breakfast? I feel like a bowl of cereal, some fruit, and a cup of coffee."

"That sounds good to me."

They both went into the kitchen. They each got a bowl of cereal, some fruit, and some coffee. Sara had a breakfast bar in her kitchen with a couple of bar stools so she and Seth decided to sit there and eat. When they were finished they cleaned up and got ready to go.

Right when Sara and Seth were getting ready to go out the door, the phone rang. Seth answered it. "Sara, it's Maggie."

"Good Morning Maggie."

"Good Morning Sara. How you feeling today?"

"Better. Seth and I are going to go to the grocery store and post office. We'll be back in time to go to the Art Gallery with you."

"Good. We'll be there at 3:00. I wanted to tell you we made reservations this evening to go to the dinner theater. We thought you might like that."

"Maggie, that sounds fun. We'll be looking forward to it."

"Do you think you're up to going to the store?"

"Seth said he would help me. I think I can handle it if someone's with me. I don't hurt as much today."

"That's good. I'll let you go and we'll see you later."

"Thanks Maggie."

Seth and Sara walked out the door and got into Seth's car to go to the grocery store. While they were shopping they saw Martha. "Hello Sara."

"Hello Martha. How are you doing?"

"I'm doing alright. I don't think any of this will seem real until after Monday when we bury Peter. He'd asked me to marry him and I said yes. He was going to come by and we were going to celebrate the night he was killed." Martha started crying.

Sara tried to hug her gently. "Martha, I understand." When Martha hugged Sara back; Sara cringed.

"Sara, did I hurt you? You cringed when I hugged you."

"No, you didn't hurt me I'm just recovering from a infected wound and I'm still a little sore."

"Did you cut yourself or what? That seems like a strange place to have a wound."

"It happened the night Paul was killed. It'll be alright in a few days. Is there anything I can do for you?"

"Just pray that they find the person who did this."

"I do. Do you have the funeral arrangements made yet?"

"Yes, Peter's body is being shown on Sunday evening and the funeral is Monday at the Catholic Church, down the street from my shop."

Seth came up behind them. "Sara, everything alright?"

"Yes Seth it's fine."

Martha looked at Sara. "Martha, this is Lt. Seth Parker with the NYSPD."

"Hello Lt. Parker. I'm Martha Burns."

"I'm so sorry for your loss ma'am."

"Thank you sir."

"Martha, Seth's the head of the investigation into Paul's murder and he's working on Peter's murder also."

"Oh. Why is he with you Sara?"

"Sara's under police protection because she's the only one who caught a glimpse of the person who murdered Paul. She's been receiving calls from someone claiming to be the killer."

"I can understand why she's under police protection then. I need to finish my shopping. Peter's family will be here tonight and they're coming to my house for dinner and my folks are coming in tonight also; they're going to be staying with me."

Sara grabbed her side. Seth grabbed Sara's arm to help keep her on her feet. "Sara, you alright?" Martha asked.

"I will be. I just get pains in the wound every once in awhile."

"Please be careful Sara."

"I will. I'll see you Martha."

Just as Sara and Seth were finishing up shopping they saw Jack talking to a customer. Sara wanted an excuse for Jack and Seth to meet so she pretended to not know where something was. "Hello Jack."

"Hello Sara. How are you today?"

"I'm doing better."

"That's good."

"I was wondering if you could remind me again where the boxed Jello is. I always forget."

"Sure Sara. It's down aisle five."

"Thank you Jack."

Seth walked up behind Sara and knowing Sara's plan went along with it. "Sara, did you find what you're looking for?"

"Yes. Jack told me it was in aisle five."

Jack looked at Seth and trembled. "Sara, do you know this man?"

"Sure. This is Seth Parker, he's a friend of mine."

"Hello Seth, I'm Jack. I'm the manager here; if you need anything just ask me; I'll be glad to find it for you."

"Thank you Jack."

Sara and Seth went down aisle five and grabbed four boxes of jello. They wanted to make the inquiry look real. They took their things to the check out, paid for their groceries and started to leave. "Goodbye Sara, Seth. Come back anytime."

Seth smiled. He knew Jack was hiding something so he casually said "Thank you, we will."

They headed to the car. Seth put the groceries in the car, then helped Sara into the car. They drove about a mile to the post office. Seth helped Sara out of the car and into the post office; they bought stamps then went back to the car.

They got back to Sara's and Seth took the groceries inside and Sara started unloading them. Seth helped her. The light on her answering machine was blinking. Sara went to check her messages.

At 10:00 A.M. Tom knocked on Carries' door. When she answered it he stood stunned in the doorway. She had a canary yellow shirt and blue jeans on with a big brimmed hat, and just a hint of make-up. She looked so beautiful. "Come in Tom. I was just getting the blankets ready and I fixed us a thermos of Lemonade so that we have something to drink."

"Good. I didn't think about that. You look fabulous. I like that hat."

Carrie smiled. "Thank you Tom. Would you like a tour of the house?"

"Yes, I would."

Carrie walked him around the house and in one room he saw flutes, guitars, and an upright piano. He saw a lot of owl paintings and in another room he saw nothing but books, and an antique oak desk that was still shiny. "That is my room where I go when I grade papers or want some quiet time. I do most of my reading in here. The bedrooms are down the hall as is the laundry room. When this house was built we wanted it to be on all one level, because my late husband had trouble with his knees from an old sports injury in college and steps caused him a lot of problems."

"This is a beautiful home Carrie; I love the flower gardens out front."

"I've always enjoyed flowers. "Tom smiled because he had a beautiful bouquet of flowers for her in his car.

"Carrie, you ready to go?"

"Yes, let me grab the thermos and the blankets."

"I have the picnic basket in my car. Let me assist you to the car."

Tom took Carrie's elbow and they walked out to the car. He walked around to the passenger side of the car and to Carrie's surprise there was a bouquet of flowers sitting on the front seat. Tom reached in and grabbed them. "These are for you Carrie."

She smiled, then hugged him. "Thank you Tom, they're lovely."

He helped her in the car and they drove to the far end of the park. He got out of the car and helped her out. It was a beautiful sunny day. Carrie had to put on her sun glasses because the sun was so bright. "I have a surprise for you; something I hope you will like."

"I like surprises."

A horse drawn carriage with a driver pulled up next to them and stopped. Carrie gasped. "Tom, how did you know I love to take carriage rides?"

"Peggy told me." Carrie smiled. "Your carriage awaits you Carrie."

He helped her into the carriage. They talked and laughed through the entire ride. "I haven't done this in a long time."

"So you're enjoying yourself?"

"Yes I am." She leaned over and kissed him on the cheek. He smiled.

The carriage ride took about an hour. They got back to where they were going to have a picnic. Tom helped Carrie down from the carriage then they got the blankets and food out of the car and set them underneath a shade tree. Carrie got the plates and silverware out from the picnic basket. She poured both of them a glass of lemonade.

"Carrie, I hope you like cold fried chicken and potato salad. I made it this morning."

"That's fine Tom."

"Carrie for dessert I'm going to take you to the best place in town for chocolate."

"Um, sounds great."

After they finished the main course, they walked across the park to a chocolate shop. Carrie got chocolate truffle ice cream and Tom got German Chocolate ice cream. They sat at one of the outdoor tables and ate, then started walking back to the car. They got to the car. "Tom, I'm really enjoying myself and I hate to stop but I need to rest."

"I understand. Why don't you just lie down on the blanket and rest?"

"Okay."

Carrie laid on the blanket and closed her eyes. Tom couldn't stop watching her. She was so beautiful. He sat down next to her and closed his eyes to.

Carrie opened her eyes and looked around. She saw Tom lying on his back on the blanket looking up at the sky. She turned onto her side so she was facing him. She touched his shoulder. He looked over at her and smiled. "Hello Carrie."

"Tom, I'm sorry. I didn't mean to fall asleep"

"It's alright Carrie. I understand."

"What time is it Tom?"

"It's 3:00 P.M."

"My goodness. I didn't realize it was that late. I usually go for a walk around this time of the day when I'm not teaching. I know we walked earlier but I need to walk at least two times a day; it really helps and the doctor said it's helping my body heal faster."

"Well, it's pretty quiet here now; where do you usually walk?"

"I like the peace and quiet of the hiking trails in the woods. There's not a lot of noise and it's a flat area to walk, not bumpy like a lot of areas. I usually wear headphones to have something to listen to besides silence."

"Would you like to have some company on your walk today?"

"That would be great but do you think you can walk three miles?" She grinned.

"Watch me." He laughed.

They left for the trails. When they got to the edge of the woods Tom went down first and helped Carrie. They started walking side by side. "Carrie, how long have you been walking like this; I mean three miles at a time?"

"I've been doing this for several years. I had to take a break when my husband got sick and came back to it but I've had a hard time since I've been sick. I just got back in to walking two months ago."

"I walk a lot with my job too. Seth does too. He and I both used to be pretty good athletes."

"It shows." She smiled.

Carrie was surprised when she had to stop after only going half way. She'd only gone a mile and a half. She started breathing hard. Tom stopped and looked at her. "Carrie, what's wrong?"

"I'm not sure. I just need a few minutes to rest."

"Okay. Let's take a break."

They sat on a bench that was on the trails for people to stop and rest or just watch the wildlife. Tom rubbed Carrie's back trying to help her breath better. She sat up and looked at Tom and smiled. "Are you ready to continue walking?"

"Yes."

They'd gone about a mile when they saw some turtles come out from the bushes and a beaver walk in front of them. They stopped to enjoy the animals. Tom put his hand on Carrie's back as they watched the animals. "Isn't that beaver cute? I wonder where his home is?"

"It's no telling. There are a number of places around here that he could have built a home."

Two ducks flew overhead and they watched as they flew past them. When they both looked down they were looking into each others' eye. Tom leaned over and kissed Carrie very

passionately on the lips and she responded likewise. She felt something inside she hadn't felt for a long time and so did Tom.

They held hands as they finished walking the rest of the way. They got off the trails and went over to the blanket and sat down to rest. They got up about five minutes later and started getting their things together to go into the car. They loaded the things into the car and stood there not knowing what to say to each other.

"Carrie, it's 4:00 P.M. Would you like to go somewhere for coffee?"

"Yes but I was wondering if we could do something first. I was wondering if you'd mind taking me to the place where Sara and Paul were before Paul was murdered?"

Tom gasped "Are you sure you want to go there?"

"Yes. I need to see for myself that awful scene. I want to try and help Sara with this but I need to see the scene for myself."

"Okay, let's drive there. It's on the other end of the park."

When they got to the spot where Paul was murdered Carrie stood quietly and said a prayer, then she looked over at the church. "Tom, is that the church where the shooter hides and waits?"

"Yes. It looks like you can see the entire city from the roof of the church."

"Then the shooter knew exactly who he was shooting at and waited until that person got in his line of fire and Sara happened to be in that line of fire too."

"Seth thinks that Sara may have been a target but because of the way she was standing the shooter missed her and the bullet went through her purse, grazed her in the side and went full force into something or someone."

Carrie was getting a strange feeling and said "Tom, I think we better move on. I'm getting bad vibes from standing here."

They started walking to the car. "I know we said we were going to go get coffee but I'm starting to get hungry so instead of the coffee shop I know a nice little place that serves food and has great coffee that we can go to."

"That sounds good."

They got in the car and went to a little restaurant that Carrie had only heard about. They walked inside, sat down and waited for the waiter.

Murder *When the Bell Tolls*

Sara was checking her messages. She had one from Carrie telling her she was going to be gone all day and she would be with Tom. Sara smiled when she heard that message. Then there was a message that caused Sara to feel panic. It was the person who claimed to be the killer. He told Sara his next victim was going to be a woman. Sara started sobbing and trembling. She was terrified.

Since Seth was in the other room he didn't hear the messages. He walked into the living room and found Sara, sitting in a chair with her knees up to her chin, crying and rocking back and forth. He walked over to her. "Sara honey, you're trembling. What's wrong?"

"Seth listen to the messages on the answering machine."

Seth walked over to the phone and listened to the messages. He smiled when he heard about Carrie then gasped in horror when he heard the message from the shooter. "Oh my! Who is this poor woman and when will this happen? When Sara heard the message the second time she trembled harder. Seth looked at Sara and realized she could be the target. He knew she was terrified. He walked over to her, put his arms around her, and hugged and comforted her.

About fifteen minutes later there was a knock at the door. Sara was so terrified she ran and hid in her bedroom. Seth answered the door. "Hi Maggie, Kevin come in."

"Hello Seth." They looked around for Sara. "Where's Sara? Is she asleep?"

Seth wasn't sure what to say. "No, she's not asleep. She's back in her bedroom. I'll go check on her."

Seth walked back to Sara's bedroom. "Sara. It's Seth, you can come out; it's safe."

She came out from her walk in closet still shaking. "Sara, Maggie and Kevin are here. Do you want me to tell them you'll be out in a few minutes?

"Would you please. I need to pull myself together before I go out there or they'll know something's wrong?"

"Sara, something is wrong. It's alright to be scared even terrified. I know Maggie and Kevin would understand."

"I'm sure they would but Seth I'm so scared I can't stop shaking."

He put his hands on her arms. "It's alright. I'll protect you."

"Thanks Seth. I need a few minutes to freshen up."

"Okay, I'll tell them."

Seth left the room so that Sara could freshen up. She stood in the middle of the room still sobbing but she'd stopped trembling. She thought about how Seth's strong but gentle hands and arms on her arms made her feel so much safer. She was glad he was there. She went into the bathroom, splashed water on her face then reapplied some of her make-up, she straightened her blouse and slacks then went into the living room to greet everyone.

When she went over to Maggie, Maggie could tell she'd been crying. "Hello Maggie, Kevin. Sorry I kept you waiting, I wasn't happy with my make-up."

"It's alright dear. Are you ready to go?"

"Yes."

They left the house, got in the car and went to the Art Gallery. They admired several of the paintings but Sara was admiring the pottery and hand blown glass.

After they finished up at the gallery, they went back to their car and went to the restaurant where Maggie and Kevin had made reservations.

When they walked into the restaurant they waited to be seated. As they were being seated they walked past Carrie and Tom's table. Tom was holding Carrie's hand across the table. Sara was still shaken up from the phone call earlier but when she looked up and saw Carrie and Tom she had to smile. "Carrie, Tom what a surprise to see you here. I got your message. I didn't think I'd see you again today."

"Hello Seth, Maggie Kevin."

"Hello Tom, Carrie."

They were all talking when the waiter said "Would you follow me please?"

"Tom, Carrie we'll talk to you later."

"Okay."

As Seth walked past Tom he whispered. "I need to talk to you about something that happened at Sara's but it can wait until morning. Enjoy your evening with your beautiful lady."

Seth joined the rest of the group; they sat down at their table. He and Sara looked at each other and smiled. Seth could still sense Sara's uneasiness. They ordered their food, then Sara excused herself to go to the ladies room. "I'll go with you."

Seth got up too. "Sara, you alright?"

"Yes. I just need to wash my hands."

"Okay." Maggie looked at both of them puzzled.

While Sara was washing her hands tears were running down her cheeks. Maggie knew something besides Paul's death was bothering Sara. She knew because of the way Seth talked to her and what was said between them. Maggie hugged Sara, then very compassionately asked her "Sara honey, what's wrong? I know you're having a hard time dealing with Paul's death and so am I but I know something else is bothering you. Can you tell me about it?"

Sara looked at Maggie and started crying harder. "Maggie, it has to do with Paul's murder."

Maggie gasped "What happened? Did you remember something else?"

"No. Seth and I went to the grocery store and post office this morning and everything was going okay. I saw Martha, you know the latest victim's fiancé"?

"I remember Seth saying that."

"Well we talked for awhile and I introduced her to Seth. Jack, the store manager was standing there hanging onto my every word too, so I was careful about what I said. We brought the groceries home and Seth unloaded them. After I put them away and rested for awhile I noticed that the light on my answering machine was blinking. I had two messages. One was from Carrie and the other one was from…" Sara started crying harder.

"Sara, was it that message that upset you?"

Sara nodded her head yes. After she stopped crying so hard she looked at Maggie and said "The message was from the person claiming to be the killer. He said the next victim will be a woman. Maggie I'm so scared. What if he means me and if he doesn't who will it be? Carrie, Peggy, who?"

Maggie gasped. She was horrified at what Sara had just said. She threw her arms around Sara and held her tightly. Maggie trembled at the thought. Once Sara stopped crying so hard she looked at Maggie. "I'm sorry about that outburst Maggie."

"It's perfectly alright honey. I think I would've done worse than that."

"Maggie, I'm so scared, but having Seth with me really helps. I feel so much safer."

"I know you do. What do you think about Carrie and Tom, Sara?" Maggie said trying to help ease Sara's uneasiness.

"I think it's wonderful. They both need someone to talk to, go places with, enjoy the little things that make a relationship special."

"I agree. Seth really cares about you. I can tell that."

"He's good to me and I really feel safe with him."

"Are you ready to go back and join the men?"

"Yes, maybe our food is here. I'm starved."

Maggie rubbed her hand on Sara's back as they walked back to the table. Seth let out a sigh when Maggie and Sara came back to the table; so did Kevin. "We're glad you're back. We were getting worried."

"Everything's alright. We were just talking."

Shortly after they sat down, their food was delivered. They started eating. They were halfway through their meal when Tom and Carrie came back to their table. "Are you enjoying your meal?"

"Yes, the food's wonderful." Sara said. "Did you enjoy your meal?"

Yes we did. I'm going to take Carrie home now. Seth, I'll talk to you in the morning."

"I'll talk to you tomorrow. Be careful."

"Goodbye all."

"Goodbye Carrie, Tom. It was nice to see you."

Tom and Carrie left and they finished eating. Everything was going fine until out of the blue Art walked into the restaurant. When Sara saw him she felt panic building up. She gasped then dropped her fork. She started trembling. Maggie saw fear on Sara's face. She looked up and saw a man standing across the room but didn't recognize him. Seth saw the fear on Sara's face. "Sara honey, what's wrong?" Maggie asked.

Sara didn't want to tell her about Art. She tried not to panic when she said "It's nothing. I'll be fine."

Seth turned around and saw Art standing across the room. He knew Sara was terrified of Art but didn't know why. "Maggie, Kevin could you excuse Sara and I for a few minutes?"

"No problem but Seth, what's wrong?" Is there anything we can do to help?"

"I need to talk to Sara for a few minutes."

"Okay. I'll get the check."

Seth and Sara went into a small hallway near the back of the restaurant. Sara started trembling harder. "It's alright Sara. I'm here and I'm going to protect you."

"Seth, if he sees me, he'll walk over here and I don't want to speak to him. I changed my bank because of him. I'm so afraid of him. Maggie wants to know what's going on and I can't tell her. I told her about the call and she didn't know what to say or do. She was very understanding though. Seth I'm sorry I can't stop the tears."

"It's okay to cry Sara. You know that."

He put his arm around her shoulder and hugged her. "Thanks Seth. We better get back. I wish I knew what to tell Maggie."

"Sara, I promise you'll be safe when I'm around."

They went back to the table. Seth found out how much the bill was and offered to pay half, but Kevin said it was their treat. Kevin paid the bill and they started heading out the door. Sara glanced to her right and saw Art sitting in a booth alone, with a martini in his hand. He didn't see her and she was glad. They walked out the door. Seth, Maggie, Sara, stay here and I'll go get the car."

Kevin walked across the parking lot and came back with the car. Sara was still shaking. Maggie hugged Sara. "Sara honey, you okay?"

"Yes. I just want to get home."

"It won't be long."

Kevin started driving and it wasn't long before they were at Sara's. "All of you stay here, I'll walk around the house and make sure everything's all right."

They stayed there while Seth walked around. Kevin couldn't stop thinking about what Seth had found last night. He hoped everything would be alright. Kevin hadn't even told Maggie about what Seth had found. He was glad he hadn't.

Seth came back and they went inside. It was still early. "I'm going to make a pot of coffee if no one minds."

"That sounds good Maggie. Would anyone mind if I got more comfortable?"

"Go ahead Sara."

She walked back to her bedroom and closed the door so she could change clothes. She couldn't stop thinking about

Art being at the restaurant. She wondered if it was him who was watching her and if it was, why."

She changed into her night clothes and went into the living room. The coffee was done so Maggie got cups and poured coffee into them. They sat down at the dining room table. "Sara, I'm really worried about you. You look tired and worried? Is something happening we don't know about?"

Sara wasn't sure what to say. All she could think about was Art and how terrified she was of him. "Nothing happened. I'm just really tired. It's been a very busy couple of days."

"That it has. Do you feel up to playing some Monopoly Sara?"

"Sure. I always have fun when I play that game but this time there are no partners. We play for ourselves."

"That's fine."

While Kevin got out the game, Seth checked his cell phone to see if he had any messages. There were no messages so he sat down and they played Monopoly for hours. At midnight Seth looked at Maggie and Kevin and asked "Would either of you mind if I took Sara to my house tomorrow for awhile. I need to get a few more things and check my answering machine, even though I told them to forward my calls to my cell phone. I want to bring over some food and some other things."

Kevin smiled "That sounds fine. Maggie and I wanted to do some sightseeing while we were here anyway. Sara, would it be okay if we didn't come by tomorrow?"

"It'll be fine. I want you to enjoy yourselves while you're here."

"Sara, you sure it'll be okay?" Maggie asked.

"I'm sure. I'll miss not having you here with us but I'll be fine."

"Are you planning on going to church Sunday?"

"Yes. Seth and I are going to go to the 9:15 A.M. service. We'll go to the coffee hour before that then go out for brunch after church. Coffee hour starts at 8:30 A.M. if you'd care to join us."

"That sounds good. I know we can find our way back to the church. How about on Sunday, we meet you in fellowship lobby at 8:20 A.M.? We'll all go to church together then go out to brunch."

"That sounds good except for one thing."

"What's that Seth."

"I pay for brunch this time."

"Well, okay."

They looked at the clock. "Kevin, it's after midnight. I think we should go so Sara can get her rest."

"Kevin, you won the game this time, but next time I'll win." Seth said.

Kevin smiled. "Sara, Seth, we'll see both of you on Sunday. Enjoy your day tomorrow."

"You two enjoy sightseeing and we'll see you Sunday."

Carrie and Tom decided to make some popcorn and watch a movie together. They decided on a comedy. It was a chilly night so Tom made a fire in the fireplace for them. They watched a couple movies. Tom looked at the clock. It was midnight. He looked over at Carrie who'd fallen asleep on his arm. He smiled, then bent down and kissed her. She opened her eyes. "Carrie honey, it's midnight. I have to be at work in the morning so I better go home so I can get some sleep and you're exhausted."

"Tom, I enjoyed myself today. It's the most fun I've had in a long time. Thank you."

He kissed Carrie again. "I had a wonderful time too. Would it be okay if I called you tomorrow from work?"

Carrie smiled. "Yes it would."

As he walked out the door he said "Goodnight Carrie. I had a wonderful evening."

"Goodnight Tom. So did I."

After Tom left, Carrie went into her bedroom and changed clothes. She got into bed and for the first time in a long time was able to rest peacefully. She felt something inside she hadn't felt for a long time; passion.

Sara and Seth talked for a little while, then Seth took the dishes into the kitchen to be washed. He washed them and Sara dried them. Seth could tell something was troubling Sara. "Sara, would you like to tell me what's troubling you?"

"I keep thinking about the man in the raggedy clothes and the shooter. I know I've seen the man in the raggedy clothes before. I feel like I've seen him several times since the shooting; then there's Art. I have this strange feeling about him. I really do, maybe it's because of what he did to..." Sara couldn't finish.

Seth walked over to Sara and put his hands on her arms. She felt the strength and power, yet gentleness and compassion in his touch. "Because of what he did to who or what?"

Sara started to cry. "It's because of what he did to me Seth. It's me. What happened at the restaurant was because I thought Art was following me for some reason."

Sara could hear the compassion in Seth's voice when he asked "Sara, can you tell me what Art did to you?"

"Seth, I'm just not ready to talk about it. All I can say is it was awful, humiliating and undeserved."

"Sara, whenever you're ready to talk about it; I'll listen."

"Thanks Seth. That means a lot. Maybe after Paul's killer is caught, I can deal with all of this. It's just so overwhelming."

"I know it is Sara. We'll catch this person. Soon I hope. I can tell your exhausted. Why don't you go try and get some sleep. We don't have to get up early and we don't have to hurry to get to my place. It shouldn't take but maybe an hour at my place, it's just the drive that takes time. Since tomorrow is Saturday it won't be as bad."

"Well, I am tired. Seth I'll see you in the morning. Thanks for being understanding. Goodnight Seth."

"Goodnight Sara."

Sara walked slowly back to her bedroom. Seth put the dishes away then headed back to the guest room to change his clothes. He knew Sara had a very trying day so he decided to sleep in a chair in the living room so if she needed him, he wouldn't be far. He had a bad feeling about how the night was going to go.

He changed clothes, then went into the living room and sat in the overstuffed chair. He pulled a blanket over him and went to sleep. About four hours had past when he heard Sara talking in her sleep. He got up and went to her bedroom door and listened. "Art, I'm sorry. It won't happen again. Please, please stop. It hurts, it hurts. I'm sorry." Was what he heard her say. He got really worried especially when he heard Sara start crying harder, then scream. He ran into her room. "Sara, what's wrong?"

Sara had tears running down her face, she was trembling, and breathing extremely hard. She looked at Seth. "Oh Seth, I had the most horrible nightmare."

Murder *When the Bell Tolls*

He rubbed his hand across her back. He knew she was having flashbacks but didn't want to tell her then and upset her even more. He knew that Art had done something really awful to her; but had no idea what. "Sara, it's alright now. I'm here. You're safe."

Once she realized what Seth had just told her she felt more at ease. "Seth, I'm sorry if I woke you."

"Sara, everyone has nightmares sometimes. It's good to have someone to talk to about them when they happen."

"I can't remember what this one was about, except it had to do with Art."

Sara stopped crying so hard. "Sara, do you think you can go back to sleep?"

"Yes. I feel better knowing you're here. Thanks Seth."

"You're welcome. Goodnight again."

"Goodnight."

Seth wasn't sure whether to leave the room or not. He was afraid Sara would start having flashbacks again. He knew she would eventually remember where she knew the man of many disguise from and it could be disastrous. He walked out of the room and went back into the living room. He sat in the chair but couldn't rest enough to sleep. He was worried.

When morning came, Sara awoke and walked out to the kitchen. She saw Seth asleep in the chair and smiled. Her side was feeling better so she decided to try and fix breakfast. She decided on French toast and bacon. She made the coffee then started cooking. Seth woke up when he smelled the bacon cooking. He looked into the kitchen and saw Sara. He smiled. "Good Morning Sara."

"Good Morning Seth. I hope you like French toast."

"I do. Were you able to go back to sleep after your nightmare?"

"Yes I was. I didn't have any more problems sleeping."

"That's good. You're cooking breakfast for me, I'm going to cook lunch for you at my place. We can sit down and eat, then go for a walk, do some shopping, then go to a nice restaurant for dinner, then I thought I'd take you to the symphony tonight. Lt. Anderson wanted to go but he has to work and can't so he gave me the tickets. Would you like to do that?"

Sara smiled as big as she could. "I'd love to do that. I haven't been to the symphony for a long time."

"After breakfast, I'll help you clean up the dishes then you can change clothes then I'll change my clothes and we'll go to my house for a couple of hours."

"That sounds great."

They sat down and ate breakfast. "Sara this is really good. It tastes different than any French toast I've eaten."

"It's probably because I put almond extract in it."

"That's what that wonderful taste is. It's really good."

They finished eating and cleaned up the dishes and the kitchen. "Seth, I'm going to shower now, then get into some comfortable clothes. Do you think I should take my clothes that I want to wear tonight along with me or are we coming back here first?"

"We can come back here first before we go to dinner. I'll shower at my house and change into the clothes I want to wear tonight while I'm there. You go ahead and shower; I'll put the dishes away and wait for you to finish."

Sara smiled as she headed back to her room. Once she got there she walked into the bathroom and got ready to shower. She took a shower, got out and put on a pair of jeans and a button down blue shirt. She brushed her hair then put on a hint of make-up. She walked into the living room where Seth was sitting. He looked up at her and smiled. "My, you look nice."

"Thank you Seth."

"I'll go back and change clothes now then we can go."

"That sounds great. I think I'll give Maggie and Kevin a call just to let them know we're getting ready to leave for your house."

"Okay."

Sara found the phone number for the motel where Maggie and Kevin were staying. She called the number and the phone only rang once when Maggie answered.

"Hi Maggie; it's Sara."

"Good morning honey. How are you?"

"I'm doing okay. I called to let you know Seth and I are going to be leaving to go to his house in a little while and you'll never guess where we're going tonight."

"Where honey?"

"Seth got free tickets to the symphony. I'm so excited. I haven't been there for awhile."

"Sara, how fabulous. I'm sure you'll enjoy yourself. We're going to the Empire State Building and maybe do some shopping."

"That's a busy day. Enjoy yourselves. We'll see you tomorrow morning around 8:25 A.M."

"Yes you will. I'm so glad you called Sara. I was worried about you."

"I know. That's one reason I called."

"We appreciate it. Have fun and we love you. Goodbye Sara."

"I love you too. Good bye."

After Sara hung up the phone Seth came into the living room. "Were you able to reach them?"

"Yes I talked to Maggie. They were getting ready to leave also."

"Are you ready to leave Sara?"

"Yes I am."

Seth and Sara left for his place. "Seth, have you heard from Tom yet today?"

"No. I'm going to call him from my place around 10:00 A.M."

"I hope he and Carrie had a nice time together last night. I know Carrie hasn't had a night out for a long time, especially since she was diagnosed with cancer four months ago."

"Tom hasn't gone out in awhile either. He's been on dates but only to the movies or a concert in the park. I've never seen him happier."

They got to Seth's house. Once he parked the car, he walked around and opened the door for Sara and helped her out of the car. When they got inside Sara was amazed at how neat everything was. Seth picked his mail up off the floor. He went through it, found the bills to be paid, checked the rest of the mail and put the bills where he would remember to take them with him when they left. He checked his answering machine; there was a message from his daughter. She wanted him to call her. He smiled when he heard her voice.

"Seth this is a really nice home."

"Thank you. It seems a little emptier than usual. There was a message on my answering machine from my daughter Mary. She wants me to call her sometime this weekend. Would you mind terribly if I called her right now?"

"No, go right ahead."
Seth called his daughter.
"Mary, it's your dad."
"Hi dad. It's good to hear your voice."
"It's good to hear your voice also."
"Dad, I wanted to tell you something. I've met a young man from New Jersey. He's a resident doctor at a local hospital in New Jersey. He comes here on his vacation because his sister lives down here. We started going out and then writing letters back and forth. Dad he's asked me to marry him and I said yes."
"Mary honey, that's great."
"But dad, there's one thing I need to tell you. I'm moving to New Jersey where Clayton has his practice. That means I'll only be about a two hour drive from you. Dad, I'm so excited."
"I'm so happy for you. It'll be nice to have you closer to home."
"Dad, was there a reason you haven't returned my call earlier?"
"Well yes there is. I'm working on a serial killer case. One of the victim's fiancés' caught a glimpse of the shooter and she's the only witness. I've moved into her home because she's under twenty-four hour police protection. She's being threatened by the killer and we think she may know that killer."
"Dad, please be careful."
"I will."
"Dad, what's this woman like? Is she good to you?"
Seth laughed. "Mary, Sara's a seventh grade school teacher and a writer. She couldn't be any nicer if she tried. She cooks for me, does my laundry with hers, and we talk about a lot of things. She's having flashbacks about the night of her fiancé's murder. She witnessed it and he died in her arms."
"Dad, that's horrible. How's she holding up?"
"Other than a gunshot wound in her side and the horror of what happened on her mind she's holding up alright. She'll be going back to work not this week but the next. I'll be at the school with her."
"Dad, you're going to be a plain clothed officer again?"

"Yes and I'm looking forward to it. I've met a lot of her friends and co-workers and they're really nice." Seth went out of ear shot of Sara but could keep her in his sight. "Mary, I don't want Sara to hear what I'm about to tell you."

"Okay Dad what is it?"

"I've fallen in love with Sara but I'm trying to be professional. I think she feels the same way about me but her fiancé was buried last Monday. Mary, she's a very beautiful woman on the inside and out. I haven't felt this way about a woman since your mother died. Sara's so wonderful, but I'm not sure if I should pursue this any further."

"Dad, I'm happy you found someone that makes you feel happy. I think if the two of you love each other I say go for it! I'd love to meet her. She sounds like a terrific lady; don't let her go. Dad it's okay to fall in love again."

"Thanks Mary."

"Dad, I'm coming to New Jersey this summer, would it be alright if I stayed at your house while Clayton's at work?"

"I may not be there but sure."

"I'll call you with the dates. Take care of yourself and Sara. I'll see you in a couple of months. Good bye Dad. I love you."

"Goodbye Mary. I love you too."

Seth walked over to Sara. "Sorry about that Sara. I hadn't talked to Mary in awhile and she wanted to tell me she met a young man who's a resident doctor on staff at a hospital in New Jersey. They've been dating and he asked her to marry him. She said yes and she's moving to New Jersey. Oh Sara, I'm so happy. Mary and her husband will be living about two hours away."

"That's great Seth. I'm happy for you."

"Sara, could you help me decide what clothes to take along and what I should wear tonight?"

"Sure, no problem."

They walked to Seth's bedroom and picked out clothes, shoes, and a jacket for him to take back to Sara's; then they went into the kitchen. Seth opened the refrigerator. "Sara, there's a lot of food in there. I'm not sure what to take and what to freeze."

"I'll go through it for you."

"Thanks Sara."

"Sara, I'll help you do that but I want to call Tom. I can do both at the same time."

Seth started helping Sara go through the food. He looked at the clock. It was 10:20 A.M. "Sara, please excuse me while I talk to Tom."

"Okay."

Seth called Tom. "Tom. It's Seth."

"Hi Seth." Tom said rather groggy.

"You sound tired."

"I'm just a little tired. I left Carrie's house last night at midnight and got home about 12:15 A.M. and went directly to bed."

"You didn't leave until midnight?"

"No, we were watching a couple of movies."

Seth smiled. He knew Carrie and Tom would be seeing a lot of each other. "So you enjoyed yourself."

"Yes I did. Carrie's a very sweet, loving, intelligent woman and I really enjoy her company."

"I can tell. I need to talk you about something I found at Sara's the other night when we came home from Peggy's."

"What was it?"

"Two pictures." He told Tom about the pictures. Tom gasped.

"Does Sara know?"

"No, I haven't told her. She's been so upset I didn't want to upset her anymore."

"I understand. Do you still have the pictures?"

"They're at Sara's house. Could you stop by after work and pick them up?"

"Sure. Any luck with making a connection as to why the murders are related?"

"Not yet, but I'm getting closer. Did you find out any information about Jack and Art?"

"The only thing I found out about Jack is that as a young teenager he was accused of stealing from the store where he worked and he's Art's cousin. Art on the other hand is a different story. He's been accused of assault on four different occasions and all of the times the charges were dismissed because the person he assaulted wouldn't testify against him. By the way all of the victims were women."

"Oh my goodness. Did he just physically assault them or was there more?"

"It doesn't say. Why?"

Murder *When the Bell Tolls*

Seth thought about how terrified Sara was of Art and that he did something awful to her but she couldn't talk about it. "I was just wondering. Are you going to see Carrie again?"

"I hope so. I'm going to call her right away and ask her if she'd like to have lunch with me. I'm planning on going with her Tuesday for her last cancer treatment. She said after this treatment she doesn't have to go back for six months, and that's just a check-up."

"I'm glad you two are together and very happy. I'll call you later on if something changes but Sara and I are going to the symphony tonight. Mark gave me his tickets because he has to work and couldn't get off."

"Enjoy yourselves and tell Sara I said hello."

Seth hung up the phone and walked over to help Sara. They finished going through the refrigerator. Seth looked at the clock. It was noon. "Sara, I have a couple of things I need to do then I'll fix us some lunch. Are open faced sandwiches and mashed potatoes alright?"

"That sounds good."

Seth went into this bedroom and grabbed a couple of things that he hadn't thought about until he talked to Tom. After talking to Tom, Seth was convinced Sara was one of Art's victims. He didn't know whether she even filed a complaint. He wondered if Martha was one of Art's victims also.

He walked into the kitchen where Sara was doing up some of the dishes she'd emptied. Seth smiled. "Sara, you didn't have to do that."

"I know, but I wanted to."

"I got done what I needed to get done, so let me fix you some lunch."

Seth fixed lunch and they sat down at the small kitchen table he had and ate. "Seth, this is really good. I appreciate you fixing lunch for me."

"I told you I would. Besides, it makes up for all the wonderful meals you've made for me and for the other officers. It's a lot more enjoyable to cook if you have someone else to cook for."

They finished their lunch and cleaned up. "Sara, would you like to take a walk around the neighborhood?"

"Sure. I always enjoy walking."

"After we get back, I'll take a shower and get ready for this evening. We'll go back to your house and your can change clothes there."

"That sounds good."

They started walking. "Sara, when I talked to Tom this morning I told him he sounded tired. He said it was because he was tired. He left Carrie's last night at midnight."

Sara smiled. "At midnight? What were they doing, just talking?"

"No; Tom said they were watching movies and talking. He left at 12:00 A.M. He was going to call Carrie and ask her to meet him for lunch today. He even wants to go with her for her last cancer treatment next week. I think he really likes her."

"I think he does too and I'm so glad. Tom's a very nice man and Carrie's so sweet. I can see how they'd get along great together."

Tom called Carrie after he hung up the phone with Seth. "Carrie, it's Tom Monroe."

Carrie beamed. She wasn't sure he'd call her back but she'd hoped he would. "Hi Tom."

"Carrie, I was wondering if you'd be free around 12:30 P.M."

"Yes Tom I am, why?"

"I was wondering if you'd like to meet me at the station and we could go to lunch together."

"I'll be there."

"Great, I'll see you then."

Carrie beamed with excitement. She put on a nice skirt and blouse and another large brimmed hat. Then she put on a hint of make-up and some perfume then got in her car and drove to the police station to meet Tom for lunch.

Rebecca Segrest, a very attractive, intelligent, and polite young woman, who worked at the bank where Art did was closing up the bank for the day. Art had asked Rebecca many times if she'd go out with him and she always turned him down. After she locked the doors, she and Art were supposed to count the receipts for the day and lock them in the safe before they went home.

Murder *When the Bell Tolls*

After Art counted the receipts and Rebecca locked them in the safe they were headed out the door." Becky, let me walk you to your car."

"Thanks Art but it's daylight. I'll be alright."

Art was furious. He was going to have Rebecca one way or the other. He walked up behind her and when she went to unlock the door of her car, he hit her over the back of the head with a binder he had taken from the bank. Since the parking lot for the bank was behind the bank, Art knew he had time to get her into his car. He picked her body up and carried her over to his car. He put her body in his car and drove to his house in the country.

Once they were at his house he carried her into the house and took her up to his bedroom where he tied her to the bed. He walked out of the room and went into his study. His head was spinning. He finally had one of the women he wanted. She wasn't Sara but she'd do. Art wanted Sara to be his wife more than anything. He'd been rejected so many times but Sara was different. She was always sweet, and polite until that day in the store when he was ordering Jack to do something and Sara told him to stop; he had to teach Sara a lesson she wouldn't forget, just like the other women who rejected him. Martha for one.

He was writing a letter in his study when he heard Rebecca moaning in the bedroom. He smiled as he walked into where she was. She was shocked when she saw him. "Art? Where am I? How did I get here?"

"You're a guest in my home my dear. I hope you like your accommodations."

She realized her hands were tied to the bed. She tried to pull free. "You can pull all you want. I can guarantee you won't get free."

"Art, what are doing? Why do you have me restrained?" The look on his face sent terror through her body. He laughed an eerie laugh. "What are you going to do to me?"

He sat down on the bed next to her, leaned over and kissed her. She cringed. She wanted to get away from him but couldn't. She started to cry. He wiped her tears. "You and I are just going to get to know each other better this weekend."

"Art, please untie me."

"And have you run; I don't think so."

"What are you going to do to me?"

"I'm going to let you see what happens when you continue to reject me, and mock me. Then I'll make you love me the way I deserve to be loved." He leaned down to kiss her and she turned her head away from him. He jerked her head back toward him and slapped her as hard as he could across her face. She screamed and started crying harder. "Shut up! You know you deserved that and so much more."

"Art, I'm sorry."

He was so furious he slapped her again. She just cried harder. She laid on the bed and trembled. He looked over at her swollen face. She had tears running down her face and he smiled. He looked over at her, then bent down and touched her arm then her chest. She wasn't as beautiful as Sara or as sexy but he had her and he was going to take advantage of the situation. He knew she didn't have a boyfriend, no family around and all of her friends were out of town for the weekend. No one would miss her until Monday when she didn't show up for work. That gave him plenty of time to set his plan in motion.

He unbuttoned Rebecca's shirt, removed it then removed her slacks. She was lying on the bed crying and in her underwear. He smiled. "Rebecca, you're more beautiful than I thought. I need to finish what I was doing so you can lay there and think about us and how things could've been. I'll be back shortly."

He walked into his den and finished writing a letter, then he called Jack at home. "Jack, it's Art."

Jack wasn't thrilled but said "Hello Art."

"Jack, you have another assignment to do for me on Tuesday night. I have a very beautiful woman in my house as a guest or should I say as my prisoner for the weekend. No one will even know she's missing until Monday when I call her off of work. Tuesday night I'll take her to the alley by the church. I want you to be dressed up as a police officer when I bring her to the alley. You'll talk to her and I'll finish the job. Do you understand?"

"Art, I don't want to do this anymore. I saw Sara yesterday and it almost destroyed me to see how devastated she looked. Art, I really like Sara and I feel bad because of what happened to her."

"Sara, Martha, Allison, Susan, they're all responsible for what's happening. Sara in particular. Now do as you're told."

"Alright Art. Do I know this woman?"

"Yes you do and believe me she's getting what she deserves. I'll call you Monday night with the details."

"Alright, but I don't like this."

"You don't have to like it, just do it."

Sara and Seth went back into Seth's house; he took a shower and got dressed in the clothes he wanted to wear to the symphony. Sara, looked around and saw a book she wanted to read. She knew Seth wouldn't mind. She picked it up and started reading. She got so involved in the book she didn't hear him walk back into the room. He cleared his throat and Sara looked up from the book. She was stunned. Seth looked so handsome in his three piece navy blue suit. "Wow Seth. You look really nice."

"Thank you. I was hoping you'd like it. Are you ready to go back to your house?"

"Do you mind if I take this book along and read it?"

"No, go right ahead. I've already read it. I finished it the night before I became your twenty four hour house guest." She smiled.

Seth locked up his house and they walked to his car. He started driving. "I wonder if Carrie and Tom were able to get together for lunch."

"Me too. I'm sure Carrie made every effort to get there."

"I wonder where they went for lunch."

"I bet it was some place very special."

"I hope so."

Carrie met Tom at the station. When she walked in everyone smiled. Most of them knew Carrie and really liked her. When Tom saw her he smiled and she smiled back. "Hello Carrie. I'm not quite ready to leave. Have a seat and I'll be ready in a few minutes."

"Take your time. I can wait."

Everyone could tell Tom was smitten by Carrie and vice versa. Three officers raced to find her a seat. Lt. Marsh offered her his chair. She sat down in the chair. Tom finished what he needed to do then he and Carrie walked out the front door of the station. "Carrie, you look very lovely today."

She smiled. "Thank you Tom. I'm glad you invited me to lunch. I couldn't stop thinking about last night. It was absolutely wonderful."

"It was for me too. I thought we could go to that nice little restaurant a block from here."

"That's fine."

"Do you mind walking there?"

"No, I like to walk."

Tom reached for Carrie's hand. They held hands as they walked down the block to the restaurant. When they got to the restaurant they found a table right away. It was a booth in the back, away from everyone. The waiter took their order and they talked while they waited. "Tom, I'm sorry I fell asleep before you left last night."

"It's not a big deal. I fell asleep too."

They smiled at each other. "Are you able to do this very often? I mean come to a restaurant like this for lunch."

"I can do it more now than I could before."

"Why?"

"When Seth volunteered to be the one staying with Sara twenty four hours a day, he put me in charge. He's still the head officer on this murder case but I run the operation as needed and keep him up to date on what's happening. He tells me what needs to be done and we work together that way."

"That's good."

The food arrived and they started eating. After they had finished their lunch, Tom paid the bill and they left. Tom and Carrie held hands as they walked back to the station. Halfway back they stopped at a candy shop. "Oh look, they have my favorite candy. Chocolate truffles." Carrie said.

Tom took Carrie into the candy shop and bought six truffles for her. He handed them to her. "Thanks Tom, but you didn't have to do that."

"I know but I wanted to."

They came out of the candy shop and walked a few more steps. There was an alley between two buildings. "Carrie, let's go into this alley for a few minutes."

She looked at him puzzled but did as he asked. Once they were in the alley he pulled her close to him, threw his arms around her and kissed her passionately. She melted like butter in his arms. "Carrie, you're so beautiful and such a warm, caring, loving, intelligent woman. When I'm with you I feel something inside of me I haven't felt for a long time and never thought I'd feel again. I love being with you."

Carrie didn't know what to say. She felt the same way. "I feel the same way about you. I couldn't stop thinking about last night."

He held her closely and kissed her again. "Carrie, I'm off on Tuesday. I was wondering if you'd like some company when you go to your last treatment."

She smiled. "I'd love it, except the treatment makes me really tired. They told me this one shouldn't make me sick though."

"That's good. How long does the treatment usually last?"

"It varies. Sometimes, it's two hours sometimes it's more."

"That's alright. I want to be there for you. We'll make arrangements Monday evening after I get off work."

"Sounds good."

"Carrie, I need one more kiss before we go back to the office."

They kissed each other and they both knew at that moment they were more than friends, they knew they were meant to be together. They came out of the alley holding hands and walking the rest of the way to the station. Tom walked Carrie to her car. He kissed her one more time and opened her car door for her, checked the car to make sure it was safe, then helped her into the car. "I'll call you tonight. Goodbye Carrie. Be careful."

"Goodbye Tom. I will."

Back at Sara's, Seth sat in the living room while Sara changed into the clothes she wanted to wear to the symphony. She put on some make-up and some jewelry and went into the living room. Seth was reading the paper and dropped it when he saw Sara standing there. She looked absolutely radiant and stunning in her blue off the shoulder dress, pearl necklace and earrings, and blue pumps. Seth just stared at her. He was speechless. "Sara, you look stunning," was all he could manage.

She smiled at him and said "Thank you Seth."

"Sara, you ready to go?"

"Yes."

Seth and Sara left for the restaurant.

Back at Art's Rebecca kept pulling on the restraints trying to get her hands free. Art came in. "Becky, I think you've had long enough to think about how it'll be between us." He leaned down and touched her shoulder, he lowered her bra strap and she started to cry.

He looked her in the eye and said "Now you're going to do exactly as you are told aren't you Becky? If you don't I can guarantee you don't want to find out what happens then."

"Get away from me you jerk?" Rebecca shouted.

He grabbed her by the hair and yanked her head up. "That's what I'm talking about. Young lady you have disrespected me for the last time."

He untied one hand at a time from the bed and turned her on her stomach. "You're going to pay for that remark Becky and I mean pay for it."

"Art, please I'm sorry. Don't hurt me."

"It's too late for sorry Becky. All you would've had to do was go out with me one time."

"Art please, if you don't hurt me, I promise we can go out as much as you want. Please, please don't hurt me."

"Shut up!" He yelled at her as he removed his belt.

"Please don't do this Art."

"Since you don't seem to know what shut up means, I'm going to show you what it means." He took the pillow case off of the pillow and gagged Rebecca's mouth with it.

Over the next ninety minutes Rebecca would suffer the worst pain she'd ever felt in her entire life. She screamed, cried, and begged but nothing helped. Art was like a mad man on a mission. He finally left the room. Rebecca laid on the bed crying and terrified.

Art went back into his den. He tore up the letter he'd previously written and wrote a different letter. He reread it then laughed his eerie laugh. He sat at his desk and listened to Rebecca crying in the other room, plotting his next move.

Seth and Sara arrived at the restaurant. The waiter escorted them to their table and handed them menus. Several other couples kept staring at Sara. Some of them knew her as their child's teacher, others knew her through Paul. While they were deciding what they wanted one of Sara's students' mother walked over to her. Sara was afraid the mother would be critical of the way she was dressed.

"Ms. Michaels, it's good to see you getting out. How are you doing?"

"I'm doing okay."

"I heard you were under twenty four hour police protection; at least until after the funeral? Is this one of the officers."

"Yes. This is Lt. Seth Parker. He'll be the officer that will be at school with me when we're there and he'll accompany me everywhere."

"Hello. I'm Ann Peterson. My daughter Karen is a student in Ms. Michaels class."

"Nice to meet you Mrs. Peterson."

"Ms. Michaels, surely you didn't get this dressed up to come to this restaurant?"

"Oh no. Seth got tickets to the symphony tonight. I wasn't sure I should go but my friends tell me I have to move on with my life, so that is what I'm trying to do."

"I can understand that. I'd recommend the spaghetti; it's excellent."

"Thank you Mrs. Peterson. I'll keep that in mind."

"I'll let you eat in peace. I had to come tell you how glad I am to see you getting out. When do you think you'll be back at school?"

I'll be back in two weeks. I'm looking forward to coming back. Thank you for stopping by."

"No problem. Glad to see you're feeling better. By the way, you look fabulous."

"Thank you Mrs. Peterson." Sara smiled.

After she left the waiter took their order. "Sara, she's right you know. You do look fabulous. It's nice to see you smile too."

"Seth, I'm so excited about the symphony. I wanted to go last year but Paul wasn't feeling well that night so we didn't go, then everyone got busy and there didn't seem to be enough time."

"That happens a lot but I remember I always told Marie we should always make time for what's important in life, especially family."

"That's very true. I realize how important that is now."

Their food arrived and they ate and talked. After they finished Seth paid the bill and left a tip. "Seth, I need to wash my hands."

"I'll walk back to the restrooms with you."

They got back to the restrooms. Sara went in while Seth waited outside the door. Sara came out shortly and they headed to their car. Seth opened the door for her and helped her in. He checked his watch. "It's 6:00 P.M. The symphony starts at 7:00 and it'll take us fifteen minutes to get there from here. Do you want to get there forty-five minutes early or would you rather sit in the car and talk?"

"Let's get there early. We can look around and take in everything."

"I agree. To the symphony it is."

When they got to the symphony, Seth parked the car, then helped Sara out. They went inside. Sara couldn't stop smiling. She was so happy.

Back at Art's he realized it was 6:00. He was getting hungry and he thought maybe Rebecca was too. He walked into the room where she lay on her stomach crying and in pain from what he called learning a lesson. He put his hand on her welted back and ran his hands over her welted body. He leaned down and kissed her. "Becky, I'm going to untie your hands from the bed. After I untie your hands from the bed I'm going to tie them in front of you, then we're going downstairs and you're going to fix supper for both of us. You better not try to run or you will receive more of what you got earlier only worse; do you understand?"

"Yes Art." Rebecca said through tears.

He untied her hands from the bed and pulled her up. She screamed from the pain when she stood. He grabbed her wrists and tied them together in front of her and pulled her into the hallway. He pulled a gun out of his back pants pocket and put it to her head. "I've never had a woman cook a meal for me in their underwear. I'm looking forward to it. Now move."

Rebecca trembled and cringed as she went down the steps. When they got into the kitchen Art got all of the food, pots and pans, and cooking utensils out that she needed to cook with. He untied her hands. "Now, I'll be right behind you watching everything you are doing; don't think about doing anything stupid. Get moving."

Rebecca cried harder as she prepared the meal for Art. She was furious at him for kidnapping her and then for hurting her like he did. She cringed every time she moved. Art walked up behind her and slapped her on her very sore behind. "It smells good. I hope it tastes good."

Rebecca cried harder. "You know Becky, you're lucky. You probably never knew what real pain was until you decided to disrespect me. All of you woman who think I'm not good enough for you have never known true pain. You're experiencing mild pain compared to what I felt when I was growing up. My uncle; Jack's father used to beat me until the back of my legs and my butt were raw. I always had to spend the summers with them and that happened on more than one occasion. So you're very lucky my dear. Now finish our supper!"

Rebecca felt sorry for Art after he had told her that, however she found herself being forced at gunpoint to fix supper for him in her underwear. She trembled. "Art, the food's ready. I need some plates to put it on."

He got the plates. She put the food on the plates and tried to make it look nice. He grabbed the plates and set them on the table, then he grabbed Becky and pulled her over to the table. He pulled the chair out for her. "Sit down and eat dinner."

Rebecca screamed and jumped up as soon as she sat down. Art was furious. "Sit down in that chair right now or you'll find yourself leaning over that chair, having a wooden spoon used on your back side. Is that what you want?"

"No sir."

"Then sit down."

She cringed when she sat and had a hard time staying seated. "Art can you at least tell me why I'm here?"

"You're here because I want you to be my guest this weekend. I want to show you all of the things we can do together. I want you to see I'm just as good as you are."

They ate quietly and after they'd finished Art pulled Rebecca up out of her chair. "Get over there and wash those dishes!' he ordered. She did as she was told. After that was done he tied her hands in front of her again and forced her to go back upstairs.

At 8:00 P.M. Tom called Carrie. "Hello Carrie, it's Tom." She smiled. "Hello Tom."

"Carrie, you doing anything tonight?"

"No why?"

"After lunch today I couldn't stop thinking about you. I was wondering if you'd like to get a cup of coffee. I'm leaving work now and can be there in about fifteen minutes."

"That sounds good. I'll be waiting for you."

Tom smiled as he got in his car and drove to Carrie's. When he got to Carrie's she answered the door with a big smile on her face. "Hello Tom. Come in for a few minutes. I have to get some different shoes on."

Carrie got different shoes on and went out to where Tom was waiting for her. He was smiling. She walked over to him and they embraced and kissed each other. "How did work go for you today? I know you're trying to put together more pieces of this murder case."

"It went okay but we still can't find the connecting pieces. It's a real mystery. Carrie I wanted to ask you if you had a cell phone."

"I did at one time but I don't anymore why?"

"I think you should have a phone to carry with you in case you run into problems. I can get you one."

"Thanks Tom but do you really think it's necessary?"

He kissed her again then said, "Yes. As close as you live to the park I'd feel better knowing you had a way to call for help if something happened. Please, let me get you one. I'm supposed to stop by Sara's tomorrow during my shift anyway; Seth has something he wants to give me pertaining to Paul's murder. I'll swing by and drop the phone off then. I'll call you first though."

"Okay. That would be fine."

"Are you ready to go?"

"Yes I am."

They got into the car and drove to a nearby coffee shop. They both ordered a Chai Latte and a biscotti. While they waited for their order they continued their conversation. "Carrie, when are you suppose to go back to work?"

"Not soon enough. After I have my last treatment Tuesday they said if everything goes well, I can go back to work that following Monday. I'll be so glad to get back. I miss the students."

"I bet, and I'd bet they miss you." He smiled and reached for her hand across the table. The server came with their order. They drank their lattes and talked about different things.

Murder *When the Bell Tolls*

As they were leaving the coffee shop they saw Martha leaving her Art shop. "Hello Martha. How are you doing?"

"Hello Carrie. I'm doing okay. How are the treatments going?"

"Good. I take my last treatment on Tuesday then don't have to go back for six months."

"That's great. I'm so happy for you. Are you going to be able to go back to work?"

"Yes. I should be going back in about a week. Martha, do you know Lt. Tom Monroe?"

"Yes I do. Hello Lt."

"Ms. Burns. I never really got a chance to tell you how sorry I am about Peter."

"Thank you Lt. Carrie, I didn't know you knew Lt. Monroe."

"I didn't until I met him at the showing for Paul Sanford."

"Paul Sanford? Wasn't that Sara's Michaels' fiancé?"

"Yes it was."

"How's Sara doing? I saw her the other day and she looked tired and worn. She said she was trying to recover from some type of wound on her side."

"Yes she is. I saw her last night and she seemed like she was feeling better."

"That's good, but how did she get the wound on her side?"

"The night Paul was murdered, she was shot also."

Martha gasped. "I had no idea. That's horrible."

"Would you like to join us for coffee Martha?"

"Thank you but I can't. I have a house full of people that have come here for Peter's funeral." She started to cry. Carrie got up and hugged her. "I need to get going. Thank you for everything."

After Martha left Tom and Carrie decided to leave too. They walked out to Tom's car. It was a beautiful evening and the stars shone brightly in the sky. Tom helped Carrie into the car and they drove the few blocks to the park. "Carrie, it's so beautiful tonight. I thought maybe we could take a walk around the park."

"I'd love that."

Tom helped Carrie out of his car. They held hands as they walked around the park. They were walking by the pond. Tom looked at Carrie and could see the beautiful brown curls of her hair sticking out from under the big brim of her hat. Her hair shone in the moonlight. He put his arm around her and hugged her, then he leaned over and kissed her. She felt so special. They continued walking around the park. Carrie got a cold chill when she saw the yellow police tape around a statue where the latest murder had taken place. "Is this where the latest killing took place?"

"Yes it is. The other officers and myself combed this area with a fine tooth comb and came up with nothing. Hopefully, we'll find the person responsible for these murders before they strike again."

"Hopefully for Sara and Martha's sake."

Tom and Carrie walked to the car. He got in and took her home. He walked her to her front door. They embraced each other and kissed passionately. "Tom, thank you for taking me for coffee. I had a nice time."

"I enjoyed it too. You look really tired. Will you be alright?"

"Yes. I think I just need a little extra sleep tonight. I'm planning on going to church in the morning but I can still get a little extra sleep."

Tom smiled at Carrie. "What time is your church over?"

"It gets over at 11:30 A.M."

"How about I call you about 2:00 P.M. and I'll make arrangements to bring the phone by then?"

"That sounds good."

He hugged and kissed her again. "I'll talk to you tomorrow."

"I'll talk to you then. Thank you for tonight. Goodnight Tom."

"Goodnight Carrie."

Carrie looked at the clock. It was 10:00 P.M. She changed her clothes, grabbed a book and curled up in a chair to read. She fell asleep reading.

Sara and Seth were enjoying the symphony. Sara felt more relaxed than she had in days. During the intermission Seth waited for Sara to use the restroom, then he used the restroom and they both got something to drink and talked for the fifteen minute break. They headed back to their seats for the rest of the performance.

Murder *When the Bell Tolls*

Rebecca sobbed the whole time Art was forcing her to go upstairs. Once they were upstairs Art threw her on the bed on her back. She screamed from the pain. She was terrified. "Now we're going to get to know each other a little better."

Rebecca endured another three hours of humiliation and pain. After it was over Art looked at her and said "See, now that wasn't so bad was it?" She spit in his face and he slapped her as hard as he could across the face four times then tied her hands to the bed. "It's 11:00 P.M. I'm going to bed so I can get up and go to church in the morning." He laughed his eerie laugh as he walked out of the bedroom where he left her tied to the bed. He got half way down the hall when he turned around and went back into the room. "Becky, I'll be back in two hours to let you use the bathroom. I'll come in every two hours during the night and check on you. Sleep tight."

Rebecca trembled and sobbed quietly as she heard him close the door behind him. She tried frantically to get loose but couldn't. She wore herself out trying to get free. She finally fell asleep.

Two hours later Art came into the room. "Becky, I told you I'd be back in a couple of hours to check on you." He untied her hands, then helped her walk to the bathroom. She used the bathroom then he took her back into the bedroom and tied her back to the bed. He handed her a glass of water. "Drink this."

She did. A few minutes later her head was spinning and she felt extremely tired; her body started to shake. Art watched as the water, mixed with a sleeping aid took effect on Rebecca. As she closed her eyes he smiled. "I'll see you in the morning Rebecca. Sweet dreams."

Seth and Sara were leaving the symphony at 10:30 P.M. "Seth, that was wonderful. I had a wonderful time. I didn't realize how much I needed to get away from everything and relax. I can't thank you enough."

"Sara, when Mark asked me if I wanted those tickets I didn't have to think twice. I knew it was the best thing for you. You've been through so much this past week and you needed to get away. I'm glad you enjoyed yourself."

While they were walking out to their car they looked up at the sky. "The stars are magnificent tonight and that moon is so bright."

"Yes they are."

Seth helped Sara into the car. When they got to Sara's, he helped her out of the car. She opened the door and they walked in. Sara noticed she had some messages on her answering machine. She was almost afraid to listen to them.

Seth looked at her and said "Sara, I know that message on your machine the other night upset you so why don't you let me listen to them with you?"

"Okay. That would be great."

They listened to the messages together. There was a call from Tom confirming he'd be there around 2:00 tomorrow to pick up something from Seth, there was a message from Maggie, Peggy, and Carrie also. Sara took off her shoes and tried to get comfortable. "Seth, would you mind if I got into my gown and robe?"

"Go right ahead."

She went into her bedroom and changed clothes. She took her medicine for her wound, then went out to where Seth was. "Sara, would you like a cup of coffee before you go to bed?"

"I don't think so tonight Seth. I'm exhausted. I think I'll go to bed right away if that's okay?"

"That's fine. Do you mind if I make myself a pot of coffee? I need to do some paperwork before bedtime."

"That's fine but don't forget we need to be at the church by 8:20 in the morning. We need to leave here by 8:00 A.M."

"I'll set my alarm for 6:30 A.M."

"Seth, thank you for an enjoyable evening. I really needed that."

"You're welcome."

"Goodnight Seth. I'll see you in the morning."

"Goodnight Sara."

Sara and Seth got up at the same time. Sara got her church clothes on then walked into the kitchen. She made a fresh pot of coffee. Seth came into the kitchen dressed in his church clothes. "Good morning Sara."

"Good morning Seth. I set out some Danish for breakfast and the coffee's almost ready. I hope that's alright?"

"That's fine, since we're going to go to brunch anyway."

Once the coffee was done, they sat down at the breakfast bar and ate. "Sara, I'm looking forward to going to church

Murder *When the Bell Tolls*

with you this morning. I've been looking for a church to call home for a long time and I think yours is it."

"I'm glad you like my church. Pastor Jeff is wonderful and so understanding. I've belonged to that church for a long time. Everyone's so nice; they'll treat you like family."

They finished eating, then cleaned up the dishes. "Seth, I need to put some jewelry on and my shoes, then I'll be ready to go."

"I need to get a couple of things also."

They both went into their rooms and did what they needed to do. Sara decided she wanted to wear a different blouse so she took off the one she had on and walked over to her closet to get a different one. As she was putting on her blouse, she felt like she was being watched. When she turned around she saw someone peeking under the shade of her bedroom window. She screamed and pulled her blouse closed and ran into her bathroom. Seth ran into her bedroom. "Sara, what is it?"

She was terrified. "Someone was looking into my window. They peeked under the shade and took a picture while I was changing my blouse. They ran when I screamed. I'm sorry Seth."

Seth got on his cell phone and called into the station. "Tom Monroe speaking."

"Tom, it's Seth. Sara just saw someone looking into her bedroom window while she was changing clothes. They ran when she screamed. I caught a glimpse of the person. They were wearing Navy Blue Pants and a jacket. He was a white male, 40-45 years old, about 5 foot 8 inches tall, about 175 lbs, with brown curly hair. He ran west after he left here. I don't want to leave Sara alone. Could you please send a car to see if you can find him? We're leaving in about twenty minutes for church. You know where Sara goes to church if you need us."

"Seth, I just dispatched two cars to the surrounding area. They'll report back to me with what they find. If I need to talk to you, I'll call you on your cell otherwise, I'll talk to you this afternoon. Is Sara alright?"

"She's shaken up but I think she'll be alright for the time being. I need to go check on her. Thanks Tom."

Seth went back to where Sara stood shaking. She felt violated and humiliated. She had no idea who the person was. Seth stood in front of Sara. She cried harder "Seth, I'm sorry I screamed and scared the person off but it startled me. I feel so embarrassed."

Seth put his hands on Sara's arms and looked her in the eye. "Sara, it's okay. If you wouldn't have screamed I wouldn't have known he was there."

"Were you able to contact the station?"

"Yes. I talked to Tom. He dispatched two cars to patrol the area and if they find this person they'll take him in for questioning."

Sara started shaking harder. She moved closer to Seth and leaned against him. He put his arms around her and hugged her until she stopped shaking so hard.

Sara looked at the clock. It was 8:05 A.M. "Oh Seth, we need to get going or we'll be late."

"Sara, are you sure you're alright to go?"

"I'll be fine as long as I know you're there with me."

"Let's go then."

They got in the car. Seth kept looking over at Sara. She seemed so quiet. "Seth, you don't have to tell Maggie and Kevin about this do you?"

"I won't tell them if you don't want me to. They want to help."

"I'd rather you didn't tell them. I don't want them thinking I'm not capable of handling things."

"Sara, what you tell me is in the strictest of confidence. I don't reveal anything unless I feel it pertains to the murders, and even then I use discretion."

"Thank you Seth. I appreciate it. All of this just seems unreal and so overwhelming." He patted her hand.

When they got to the church at 8:25 A.M., they saw Maggie and Kevin getting out of their car. Seth parked the car and got out; he helped Sara get out. Maggie and Kevin stopped in the parking lot and waited when they saw Seth and Sara just pulling up.

"Good morning Seth, Sara."

"Good morning."

Sara was still shaken up from what had happened earlier. Maggie could tell something was wrong. "Sara, everything alright dear? You seem distracted this morning."

Sara looked over at Seth. "Everything's alright Maggie."

Murder When the Bell Tolls

Maggie looked over at Seth and saw a look of concern on his face. She knew something was wrong but didn't push the issue. They walked into church together and went into Fellowship Hall. Maggie and Kevin enjoyed doughnuts and coffee, while Sara and Seth just had coffee. Several people came up to Sara to express their sympathy over the death of Paul and several talked to her for a few minutes. She introduced them to Seth, and they welcomed him with open arms.

When it was time to go up to church, they headed upstairs. On the way up they saw Peggy and Ralph coming in the front door. Sara waved to them and Peggy came over to Sara. "Good morning Sara, Seth, Maggie, Kevin."

"Good morning Peggy, Ralph."

"We were just heading into church, would you like to sit with us?"

Peggy knew Sara better than anyone else. She whispered "Sara, you seem a little distant this morning. Did something happen?"

Sara, knowing she could trust Peggy whispered "Yes, but I can't tell you about it now. I'll tell you later. I don't want Maggie and Kevin to find out about it."

"Does Seth know?"

"Yes."

"Okay. We'll talk later."

They headed into church and sat next to each other. A young couple in front of them, turned around and smiled. When church started Sara found herself distracted even more. She couldn't stop thinking about the man in her bedroom window. Why was he there? Did someone send him? Was she the next person on the killer's list? All of this was going through her mind when the congregation was asked to stand and shake someone's hand. She smiled when she shook hands with people while trying to hide her fear.

Seth could tell Sara was distracted. He knew the last straw was the incident that morning. He knew Sara was a strong woman but this had really unnerved her. When Pastor Jeff started talking about facing fears Sara couldn't handle it anymore. She looked over at Seth with tears running down her face and started sobbing. Maggie heard her sobbing and whispered. "Sara, you alright."

"Yes. I need to leave the service for a few minutes."

"Do you want me to go with you?"

Sara felt panic and terror. "No. I need to walk around for a few minutes."

"I don't want you going by yourself."

Sara started sobbing harder. Seth looked over at Sara. "Sara, do you need to leave the service for a few minutes?"

She nodded her head yes. "Is it about what we discussed this morning?" Again she nodded her head yes. "I'll ask Peggy to go with you."

Sara wrote on a piece of paper "What about Maggie. She's going to be really upset if I don't let her go with me."

"I'll explain to Maggie that it's something personal and you didn't want to bother her with it."

Sara reached for Seth's hand and squeezed it. "Thanks."

Seth whispered in Peggy's ear. "Peggy, Sara's having some problems. She needs to leave for a few minutes. She wants you, not Maggie to go with her. Is that alright?"

Peggy nodded her head yes and she and Sara left together. They got into an office and Sara just started crying. Peggy hugged her until she calmed down enough to talk. "Sara, what's wrong?" Sara told her about the phone call and about the incident earlier that morning. Peggy gasped. "Oh my gosh! No wonder you're so distracted."

"Peggy, I'm terrified that I'm next on the killer's list. Seth's still trying to find the connection between all of these murders."

"Sara, I'm glad Seth's staying with you. I assume he'll be at the school when you come back."

"Yes he will."

"I know I'll feel safer with him there."

"So will I."

"Sara, I get the feeling there's something else you're not telling me. You know you can tell me anything. I'll always be your friend."

"There is something but I'm not ready to talk about it yet. It has to do with Art from the US Bank."

"Seth asked me if I knew him and I told him I knew the name but you're the fourth person who's mentioned his name to me this week."

"Fourth, who are the other three?"

"Seth, Tom and Martha. I saw her at my husband's office the other day. She looks really worn out. She told me Art had been harassing her to go out with him and became infuriated when she started dating Peter."

"Oh no!" Sara gasped, and started crying harder.

"What is it Sara? Did I say something wrong?"

"No. It just brings back some painful memories."

"I'll always be here for you and I'll listen when you're ready to talk about what's bothering you. I love you like a sister Sara and always will. Let me help you if I can."

They hugged each other. "Thanks Peggy; you're a real friend."

"Are you ready to go back to church now?"

"Yes. I think I've calmed down enough."

They walked back into church and sat down. Maggie patted Sara on the hand when she sat down. Sara looked at her and smiled. After church was over they remained in the pews. Sara was still upset but feeling a little better. They decided where they'd go for brunch. As they were getting ready to leave the church Pastor Jeff walked over to them. He'd finished shaking hands with the rest of the people and hoped he'd still find Sara in the church. He was worried about her.

"Hello all of you."

"Hello Pastor Jeff."

"Pastor Jeff, you remember Seth don't you?"

"Sure, he's the man that carried you upstairs and took care of you when you fell ill at Paul's funeral."

"That's right."

"Pastor Jeff, do you remember me? I'm Kevin Sanford, Paul's father."

"Yes, I remember you and your lovely wife Maggie. How are you doing?"

"We're hanging in there but we're really worried about Sara."

"So am I; especially after what I observed in church today. Is something going on I should know about?"

"We aren't sure. Can we walk away from the group for a few minutes so we can speak privately?"

They walked a few feet away. "What's going on Kevin?"

"Sara's been getting calls from someone claiming to be the shooter and the last message stated the next victim will be a woman." Pastor Jeff gasped.

"I hope Sara's still under police protection."

"She most certainly is. As a matter of fact, it was so hard on her having different officers come to the house, we talked to Seth and he agreed to be with her twenty four hours a day. He moved into one of her guest rooms at her home so he can protect her easier. Maggie and I are glad he's there. We trust him and so does Sara."

"I'm glad she's safe, but what about when she goes back to work, or goes out with friends."

"Seth goes where she does. Other than this morning she's never out of his sight except for when she's showering or needs privacy."

"Did Sara agree to this?"

"Yes she did."

They walked back to the rest of the group. "Sara, you doing alright?"

"Yes I am Pastor Jeff. Thank you for asking."

"Sara, I couldn't help notice you seem very distracted today. Has something happened that I don't know about?"

Sara looked at Seth and Peggy. Both of them knew the answer but said nothing. "This is just so overwhelming."

"I understand. If you need anything, don't hesitate to ask."

"Thanks again Pastor Jeff."

"Maggie, Kevin, I'm glad to see both of you again. It's wonderful to have both of you here. When are you two heading back home?"

"Next Sunday afternoon. We want to come to church again with Sara and Seth next Sunday. It's only about a two hour drive home from here. We hate to go home and leave Sara after what she's been through but we know she'll be safe with Seth and she'll be returning to work. She knows we're only a short distance away and we'll come back often and if she needs us we'll be here."

"I'm glad to hear you say you'll come back often. You know you're welcome here any time."

"Thank you Pastor Jeff. It'll be on weekends when we come during the school year and through the summer we might stay several days. Sara will always be very much a part of our lives."

Pastor Jeff smiled. He walked over to Sara and hugged her. "Whatever is bothering you I hope it works out. If you need anything, just ask. I need to go. The next service is getting ready to begin. I'll see all of you next week."

"We'll see you Pastor Jeff."

They walked outside and headed to their cars. They'd decided to meet at the restaurant. "Seth, what did you think of the church service today?"

"I liked it. I like Pastor Jeff. He truly cares about people." Seth looked back at Sara. She still looked like she was dazed but the color was coming back into her face and the joy back in her voice.

"Sara, how did you like the symphony?"

"I had a fabulous time. I think it's the first time I totally relaxed since Paul was murdered."

"I'm glad you had a good time, and I'm glad to hear you're starting to relax. How's your side feeling?"

"A lot better. Dr. Martin will be pleased when I see him on Wednesday. I'm sure he'll allow me to go back to work after that. I really need to get back to work. I miss everyone."

"I know you do but you don't need to go back too quickly. You're still recovering from severe trauma. I'm glad Seth will be in the building with you though."

"So am I."

Seth and Kevin talked until they got to the restaurant. As they were walking Sara stopped. Seth whispered in her ear "It's alright. I'll protect you. I'll be right here." Maggie saw Seth whispering to Sara then squeeze her hand. She knew something was wrong.

They met Ralph and Peggy; they all went into the restaurant together. The waiter took them to a table, Once they were seated the waiter asked them what he could get them to drink. Maggie, and Peggy, ordered iced tea, Kevin and Ralph ordered coffee and Seth and Sara decided to be different and ordered lattes.

The men all started talking amongst themselves and so did the women. "Peggy, have you talked to Carrie since you had all of us over for dinner?"

"Only once why?"

"You know she and Tom hit it off perfectly. They've been together every day since. He bought her chocolates, took her on a carriage ride through the park and last night they met for coffee after he got off of work. She told me he's going with her to her next treatment on Tuesday. She really likes him."

"I know and I'm so glad. I knew she liked him when I invited all of you to dinner and she asked me to find a way to contact him. Carrie deserves happiness too. I didn't know they'd done all that together. That's nice. I'm glad he's going with her to her next treatment. They've been hard on her. She can't wait to get back to teaching."

"I know the feeling. I can't either. This bullet wound is almost healed now and after I go back to the doctor on Wednesday he should let me go back to work the following Monday."

"Carrie's coming back then too."

"That will be terrific."

The waiter came back with their drinks, then gave them menus. They placed their orders and continued talking amongst themselves. "Maggie, I'm really going to hate to see you and Kevin leave. I've really enjoyed getting to know both of you a little better. You're still going to come and visit once in a while aren't you?"

"Yes we are. We consider Sara family and always will. I've enjoyed getting to know both you and Ralph better. I know we knew each other but never got the chance to spend any time together. I'm so glad we've had this opportunity."

"We're both glad you and Kevin could be here for Sara during this horrible time. I think that's made things easier for her. Sara, Seth's so nice."

"Yes he is. I trust him a lot. You should have seen him last night when we went to the symphony. He looked quite dashing in his three piece suit. We'd gone to his place earlier in the day so he could pick it up, especially for that occasion. I had a wonderful time."

Their food arrived and they ate and talked. Afterward, Ralph and Seth paid the bill. Kevin started to offer but Seth looked at him and said "Kevin, we made an agreement remember. I'm going to pay for the four of us today."

"I remember. Thanks Seth."

Carrie was just getting home from church herself when the phone rang. She answered it. "Hi Carrie; it's Tom. I didn't catch you at a bad time did I?"

"No. I just got home from church. I was getting ready to fix myself some lunch. Are you still coming by here this afternoon?"

"Yes I am. Is 3:00 okay for you?"

"Yes. I'll be here."

"Good. I miss you Carrie, I really do."

Carrie was smiling. "I miss you too Tom. Last night was wonderful. I hope we can do that again sometime."

"We will. I've gotta go. I'll see you around 3:00. Goodbye Carrie."

"Goodbye Tom. I'll see you then."

Carrie smiled as she sat at her kitchen table. She never thought she'd feel the way she was again. It felt wonderful.

When Art got up to go to church he woke Rebecca up by slapping her across the face. He ordered her downstairs to fix him breakfast then after they ate Art took Becky into the living room and tied her to the sofa. When he went upstairs to get ready for church she tried to pull free but couldn't. He came downstairs and smiled. "Well Becky, I'm off to church. We'll take care of the unfinished business when I get home."

After Art left, Rebecca tried to pull free and couldn't; she started to cry. Art arrived at his church ten minutes before the service started. He saw Martha in the second pew from the front. He walked over to her and said "Good morning Martha. I was sorry to hear about Peter. Is there anything I can do?"

"Thank you for asking Art. I can't think of anything right now."

"If you need anything just ask."

"I will. Thank you."

As Art left to sit in another pew Martha wondered what was up with him. He hadn't been that nice to her since before she met Peter. She shuddered.

After his church service was over, Art stopped and picked up some food and took it home. When he got home he found Becky asleep. He smiled, then walked over to her and kissed her on the forehead. "Wake up sleepyhead. I brought lunch home. It's time to eat."

Rebecca opened her eyes and gasped as she saw Art standing over her. He untied her hands then walked her into the kitchen. He sat her down at the table, took the food out and put it on the table. They ate quietly.

After lunch was over, he grabbed Rebecca and pulled her to another room. "Now, we're going to take care of that unfinished business I told you about."

Rebecca was terrified. "What are you going to do to me."

"You'll see. It's something I've wanted to do for a long time."

After Seth and Ralph paid for the brunch they decided to go to Sara's for a little while. "Tom's coming by Sara's around 2:00 and I need to be there. I have something I need to give him."

"That's fine Seth. We'd love to come to Sara's again anyway."

"We can enjoy coffee, tea, and some Danish. I also have some pie and cookies left from the funeral."

"That sounds good. We'll see you there."

They left for Sara's house. When they got there Seth got out and walked around the outside of the house. He wanted to see if he could find any evidence of someone being there earlier that morning. He knew he saw someone running away. He hoped he'd find something that might identify him. He found a piece of cloth on one of the bushes outside of Sara's bedroom window. He took his handkerchief and gently pulled the piece of cloth away from the bush. He had an envelope in his pocket and put the piece of fabric in it, then motioned for everyone to come on inside.

Everyone got out of their cars and went into Sara's house. Maggie made a fresh pot of coffee and they sat down and started playing monopoly. In the middle of the game, there was a knock at the door. Seth answered it. "Hi Tom. Come in. I'll get the things for you. I'll be right back."

"Hi Tom." Everyone said."

"Hello. I guess all of you went to church today."

"Yes we did, then we went out for brunch."

"Have you talked to Carrie yet today?"

"Yes. I talked to her earlier. I'm going to stop by her house after I leave here. I have a cell phone I want to give her. I'd feel better if she had one in case something would happen."

"I thought she had a cell phone?"

"She said she did at one time but something happened to it. I got a new phone for her over my lunch hour. I'll feel better when she has it."

They all smiled. They could tell how much he cared about Carrie. Seth came into the room with a folder. "Tom, here's the information I told you about yesterday on the phone."

"Okay Seth. I'll take care of it."

"Tom, could you come into the guest room with me for a few minutes. There's something I brought up on the computer I'd like for you to see."

"Sure. Would all of you excuse me for a few minutes?"

They nodded as Seth and Tom headed to the guest room. When they got there Seth said "Tom, I hated to pull you away from everyone but I have something I need to discuss with you."

"What is it Seth?"

"Remember when I called you this morning about someone peeking into Sara's bedroom window?"

"Yes. I sent two patrol cars around and unfortunately they didn't see anyone out of the ordinary."

He took the envelope out of his pocket and handed it to Tom. "This might help identify who it was."

"What's this?"

"It's a piece of cloth I pulled off of a thorn from the roses beside Sara's bedroom window. That wasn't there yesterday because I checked. I need you to take that back to the station, give it to the lab, have them run DNA samples and check for possible finger prints. Sara's terrified and only you, me, Sara, and the stalker know about this."

"I'll get this back to the lab. Is it alright if I spend a little time with Carrie before I have to go back to the station?"

"Yes, just don't lose that evidence."

"Thanks Seth."

"Tom, you've fallen in love with Carrie haven't you?"

Tom didn't want to admit it but he knew Seth was right. "Yes, I have. Seth, she's like the woman I've always dreamed of. She's smart, funny, beautiful, loving, caring, all the things I want in a woman. I love being with her."

Seth smiled. "I'm so happy for you Tom. Carrie's a wonderful person. Spend time with her when you can. If you really love her, like I believe you do, hold onto her and don't let go."

"Seth, how are things working out for you here with Sara twenty four hours a day?"

"They're going good. I feel so much better knowing someone's in the house all the time and I'm right here if she needs me, and this room, Wow! It's fantastic. Sara and I take turns cooking and cleaning up. I feel useful again. Tom, I wish you could have seen Sara last night at the symphony."

"Did you have a good time?"

"Fabulous."

"I'll tell Mark you enjoyed yourselves. What did you wear?"

"I took Sara to my house and got my three piece suit and wore that but Sara, my goodness, she had to be the most beautiful woman at the symphony."

Tom smiled. "Why? What was she wearing?"

"She had on a blue off the shoulder dress that came just above her knees and she wore a diamond necklace and earrings to match. I couldn't stop staring at her. She was so beautiful."

"Seth, it sounds to me as though you're quite smitten by Sara. I can understand why too. She's very beautiful, very intelligent, witty, loving, caring, and understanding. She's also very hospitable. I really enjoyed being here with her those first few days. Maggie and Kevin are wonderful people too."

"Yes they are but I don't want anyone to know about that piece of fabric until we get some answers back."

"I understand."

"Tom, we better get back out there or they'll think we're plotting something."

They both laughed as they walked into the dining room where the others were. Tom looked at the clock. "Goodness it's 2:45. I told Carrie I'd be there around 3:00. I better get going. It was good to see all of you again."

"Goodbye Tom. We'll see you later."

Art felt satisfied as he walked into his living room, leaving Rebecca in the other room crying. He went into the kitchen and got a drink of water, then sat down and started watching television. After about an hour he went back and checked on Rebecca who was now curled up into the fetal position on the day bed. He leaned down and kissed her and she cried harder.

Art walked to a neighborhood bar, had a few drinks and shot some darts. He talked with his buddies about a rafting trip they were planning for the summer. Back at his house Rebecca lay on the day bed crying. She felt nauseated. Art tied her hands like he had before so she could use the bathroom and when she felt like she was going to be sick she opened the lid

Murder *When the Bell Tolls*

on the bedside commode. She threw up several times. She pulled on the rope trying to get loose. She felt so defenseless.

※

Tom got to Carrie's house at 3:05 and knocked on the door. She answered it with a smile. "Hello Tom."

He smiled back at her. "Hello Carrie. Sorry I'm a few minutes late. Seth had something he needed to talk to me about."

"It's no big deal. Come in. I made a pot of coffee. You can stay and have a cup with me can't you?"

"Yes. I need to show you how this phone works. I programmed in my number at the station, my home phone, and my cell phone, so you can always reach me at any time."

Carrie walked over and got them a cup of coffee. He showed her how to program and work the phone, then he handed it to her. "I'll put this in my purse so I know where it is at all times. Thanks Tom. Help yourself to a cup of coffee. I'll be right there."

As she walked into the living room to put the phone in her purse, Tom helped himself to a cup of coffee and poured a cup for Carrie. She went into kitchen and saw Tom sitting at her kitchen table. She smiled at him and he smiled back. "I poured you a cup of coffee Carrie. I didn't know how you liked it so I just left it black."

"That's fine. I'll fix it like I like it. I like cream and sweetener in my coffee. I just have to reach the sweetener." When she reached up to get it out of the cupboard she felt a sharp pain in her side. She was still weak from the treatments. She dropped the container that she kept the sweetener in. She grabbed her side and grabbed the counter. Tom immediately got up and went to her.

Tom got behind her and put his arms around her and held her next to him, with her back against his chest. "What's wrong? Are you alright?"

When Carrie felt Tom's strong loving arms around her she felt the pain start to ease. She relaxed and leaned back even closer to him. She still couldn't stand without holding onto something but she didn't feel as wobbly as she did before. "Tom, I have this terrible pain in my left side. I get it every so often. The doctor says it's from the treatments I've been taking

and I shouldn't have any of these symptoms after I receive my last treatment."

He hugged her tighter. "Is there anything I can do to help make the pain better?"

"You're doing it."

He smiled, then leaned down and kissed her on the side of her neck twice. She smiled. Then he walked around in front of her so he was facing her. He put his hands on her arms to steady her then he leaned down and kissed her again. He held her closely for awhile. After she felt better, Tom got the things out of the cupboard that she wanted and they sat down and drank a cup of coffee together.

About two hours later he got up and said "I really hate to leave you but I have to get back to the station." He kissed her again. "I'll call you later and check on you."

"I'd like that but, before you leave, why don't you let me fix you a sandwich and something to go with it so you get a chance to eat supper?"

"Carrie, you don't have to do that?"

"I know but I want to."

"I'd appreciate it."

Carrie fixed Tom a huge sandwich and put a pickle, some veggies, a piece of fruit, a truffle, some chips, and a small little note that read: Tom, Thank you for being my knight in shining armor. I'll be thinking about you while you're at work. I miss you and I love you very much. Love, Carrie. She put all of it in a paper bag, then handed it to Tom. She made sure the note was on top when she handed him the bag. He took it, looked at her and kissed her passionately. "I'll talk to you later Carrie. Thank you for the sack supper. It's appreciated. Goodbye Carrie."

"Goodbye Tom."

When Tom started to get into the patrol car, he set the supper, that Carrie had prepared for him, on the front seat. He got into the parking lot at the station and sat in his car. He looked at the photos that Seth had given him. He grabbed the photos, a folder Seth had given him, and his sack supper and headed inside.

Tom walked over to Lt. Marsh and said "Scott, I need for you to find out everyone in New York, and New Jersey that owns this caliber gun. It is extremely important. All of our victims, Sara included, were shot with this caliber weapon. I think that may be a start. I need to go downstairs to the lab and drop off some other evidence that may be helpful in this case. I'll be back."

"I'll start getting those names together Tom."

"That would be great."

Tom went downstairs to the lab. "Hello Tom."

"Hello Dennis."

"What brings you here?"

"Two things actually. I have a piece of cloth in this envelope that Seth found attached to a rose bush at Sara Michaels home. I need for you to run a DNA sample and fingerprints. Also I was wondering if you could try and lift some prints from these photos?"

Dennis gasped when he saw the photos. He knew Sara because his oldest daughter was in her class. "Is something wrong Dennis?"

"It's these photographs. My daughter Lisa has Ms. Michaels as a teacher. I really like Sara. I can't imagine someone doing something like this. Where were these found?"

"Taped to two different doors at Sara's house on a night we went to one of her friends houses for dinner. Seth and Sara got back and Seth found them taped to the doors. Sara doesn't know about them. Seth asked if you could possibly see if there are any prints."

"I'll be glad to if it catches the person who hurt her and the others. Sara's so nice and Paul was nice too. I'll see what I can come up with."

"Thanks Dennis. I appreciate it."

"Tom, what's in the bag?"

Tom hadn't realized he was still carrying the bag Carrie had handed him. "Oh, I forgot I was still carrying it. It's a sack supper that Carrie made for me after I took a cell phone over to her."

Dennis smiled. "We all love Carrie and Sara both."

Tom smiled. "Carrie's very special to me."

"It shows. I've never seen you happier. I'll get right on these things you brought to me."

"Thanks Dennis. I appreciate it."

As Tom headed upstairs he thought about what Dennis had said about Carrie. He was right. She made him so happy.

He realized he was in love with her. Something he thought he'd never find. He got upstairs, sat at his desk and started doing paperwork. At 6:20 he decided to take his supper break. "Scott, I'm going to the break room for supper. If you need me just call in there."

"Will do."

Tom got into the break room and when he opened the sack to eat the first thing he saw was the note Carrie left him. He grinned as wide as he could after he read it. He knew he'd found the woman of his dreams. Now he just had to protect her against this crazed killer. He had no way of knowing Carrie knew Art quite well, especially since he worked where she banked.

⋄❈⋄

Sara and Seth got up and offered to fix supper for everyone. "Oh no thanks you two. That brunch really filled me up."

"Are you sure you don't want anything? I can fix something?"

Ralph looked at his watch. He realized he had some work to do before he went into work on Monday. "Sorry to leave so soon but I have paperwork to do before tomorrow. I want to go to the showing and funeral of Peter Edwards so I need to get this done. I hope you'll excuse us."

"We understand totally. I saw Martha the other day and she told me the funeral was Monday but I forgot to ask what time."

"Well, he's being shown from 9-11 A.M. and the funeral is at 11:00 at the Catholic church downtown."

"Oh okay. Peggy you going?"

"No, I can't get off work."

"Maybe Seth and I'll go just to show our support to Martha."

"That would be nice. I'll talk to you later."

"Bye Peggy, Ralph. I enjoyed today."

"Goodbye all. We enjoyed ourselves too. We'll talk again later."

After Peggy and Ralph left Sara looked at Maggie. "How about you two? Would you like anything to eat? I thought I'd fix soup and sandwiches and some fruit if that would be alright."

Murder *When the Bell Tolls*

"That sounds good Sara. Seth, let me help her. You and Kevin can just relax."

He smiled at Maggie then sat down at the table with Kevin. They started talking. Kevin whispered so Maggie and Sara couldn't hear "Did you get those pictures to Tom?"

"Yes and some other evidence I came up with. Unfortunately the person who took those pictures may not be the killer but they certainly know who it is."

"Will the person who left those pictures be charged with any crime?"

"It's possible. We're looking at stalking charges. I haven't told Sara about the photos yet. She's had so much to deal with I didn't want to upset her anymore."

"I understand. What can Maggie and I do to help?"

"The best thing you can do for her right now is listen and be there for her. She has a lot ahead of her and she'll need you even more then."

"Seth I must commend you on how much you helped Sara this morning at church. I could tell something was bothering her when we met both of you. She seemed distant and frightened. Can you tell me why? Was it nightmares?"

"I'm sorry Kevin. I can't divulge that information. Sara pleaded with me not to mention anything about it and I must honor that."

"I understand. Is she alright now though?"

"She seems to be. Besides, Tom and I are working on it."

Does this have anything to do with the pictures?"

"I'm not sure."

Sara and Maggie were preparing the food. Maggie looked at Sara. "Sara honey, you feeling better than you did this morning?"

"Yes much better, thank you."

"I knew something was wrong this morning I could tell. I was so worried about you. Can you tell me what happened? I want to help."

Sara wasn't sure she should say anything, but she trusted Maggie. "I'm not sure I can tell you." She started sobbing.

Maggie looked at Sara. "Is it that bad Sara? Don't you trust me?"

"I trust you Maggie, I'm so scared and confused. I want to tell you but I don't know how."

"Does Seth know?"

"Yes and he's been a tremendous help with this."

"I'm glad. I really want to help."

"Maggie, if I tell you what happened you have to promise me that you won't tell Kevin and the only people you talk to about this are Seth, Peggy, and me."

Maggie gasped. "I can do that Sara, but is it that bad?"

"Yes it is." Sara took a deep breath then said "Maggie, you remember the phone message I got the other day?"

"I remember."

"Well, to add to all of that, today I was getting ready for church and after we had a cup of coffee I went to put some jewelry and my shoes on. I decided I wanted to wear a different blouse with my outfit and while I was changing my blouse I felt like I was being watched. I looked out the window and saw someone peek into my bedroom window then take a picture while my blouse was unbuttoned. I screamed and ran into the bathroom and they ran. I think Seth saw them running but neither of us saw that persons face. Seth called Tom and he sent some units out to look around." Sara started crying.

Maggie gasped, then held Sara tightly. "Sara, I'm so sorry. I had no idea. No wonder you're so upset."

"Maggie, that's only part of it. What I'm going to tell you now has to stay between you and I okay?"

"Okay. What is it Sara?"

"Maggie, the emotions I was feeling at the time all of this was happening were so bizarre."

"I'd imagine you were terrified and confused."

"I was; but the emotions that were really confusing were the ones I was feeling about Seth."

Maggie looked at Sara with a puzzled look on her face. "Why?"

"When I screamed I only had my blouse pulled shut, then Seth ran into the room. I was so scared and crying that Seth hugged me and Maggie it felt wonderful having his strong arms around me. I felt so safe. I felt that way with Paul too. Maggie I really like Seth; and I think I may be falling in love with him. However; it's too soon after Paul's death to be thinking about something like that but he's so much like Paul. I'm not sure this is right."

Maggie hugged Sara. "Honey, I can understand how you'd feel confused, but Paul's gone and you have to move on with your life."

"Thanks for understanding Maggie."

Maggie and Sara brought the food into the dining room and sat it on the table. They ate, then Maggie and Kevin volunteered to clean up. After everything was cleaned up they played Monopoly until midnight. At midnight Kevin said "Sara, I guess we'll be leaving for the evening. Are you and Seth going to Peter's wake?"

"I think so. I'd feel better if Martha knew she had a lot of support."

"Why don't we bring some food over here tomorrow night and we can finish our game of Monopoly?"

"That sounds good. How about 6:00 P.M. Is that too late for both of you?"

"Kevin and I will be here at 5:30 P.M. We'll see you then."

"Goodbye and we'll see you then."

At 7:30 P.M. Tom called Carrie. "Hello Carrie. Thank you for the supper and especially for the note. I love you too. Are you feeling better?"

"Yes, the pain has eased. That happens every once in a while."

"I haven't stop thinking about you since I read your note. Are you busy tonight?"

"No. I'll be here."

"Would it be alright if I stopped by after work for a little while?"

"I'd like that."

"I get off in about thirty minutes. I can be there in about forty five minutes."

"I'll be waiting for you."

"I'll see you then."

Tom hung up the phone. At 7:50 P.M. Lt. Anderson came in."

"Tom, are you and Carrie getting together tonight?"

"Yes. I'm supposed to meet her after I get off work."

"Go on and get out of here. She'll be waiting for you. I can handle this."

"Thanks Mark. Call me if something comes up."

"I will. Goodnight."

Tom got in his car and drove to Carrie's. She opened the door and smiled as big as she could. Tom put his arms around her and kissed her passionately. She responded the same way. "Come in. I just made a pot of coffee. I just put a coffee cake in the microwave to heat up when you called. I always like to have a little snack before I go to bed. Would you like to join me?"

"Sure, but let me help you. I don't want you hurting yourself this time."

He got the things out that she needed. They sat down at the kitchen table and drank coffee, ate coffee cake, and talked. At 10:00 they watched the news together. As they sat on the couch together Carrie curled up next to Tom. He put his arms around her and kissed her. After the news was over they talked more. "Carrie, I need to ask you something pertaining to this murder case and I hope it won't scare you."

"That's fine. What is it Tom?"

"What can you tell me about Art Hunter and Jack Lake?"

"Jack's a nice man. He works as a manager at the Shop N Save. He goes out of his way to make the customers happy. Art on the other hand is awful, vile, and despicable."

Tom gasped. "How well do you know Art?"

"Quite well. He works at the bank where I have my account."

"Carrie, has he ever done anything to you; I mean hurt you physically in any way?"

"No why?"

"I was just wondering."

"Tom, do you think Art or Jack had anything to do with these murders?"

"Seth and I aren't sure yet but we are exploring every angle."

"I understand."

"Carrie, I have something else I need to say to you."

"Yes Tom, what is it?"

"I never thought I'd find a woman like you and now that I've found you I don't want to let you go. Carrie, I love you. I know this is all so sudden but I don't want to lose you. Would you marry me?"

Carrie gasped then smiled as big as she could. "Oh Tom I love you too. It is sudden but yes, I will marry you." They embraced and kissed each other.

Murder When the Bell Tolls

"I have four weeks' vacation coming this summer or fall. I want to take you to Paris for our honeymoon. Would that be alright."

"Paris? I've always wanted to go to Paris. I never thought I'd get to go. That would be great."

They looked at the clock. It was 11:00 P.M. Tom kissed Carrie. "Honey, I hate to leave but I need to get home so that I can get some sleep."

"I understand. I need to get some extra sleep myself. Tom, please be careful."

"I will. If you need me call; otherwise I'll call you in the morning. I love you Carrie. Goodnight." He kissed her again.

"Goodnight Tom. I love you too."

⋈

Art got home from the bar at 10:30 P.M. When he walked in the door Rebecca started shaking. She was terrified. He walked into the room. "I'm back Becky. I'm going upstairs and change into my pajamas then I'll come down and get you, so that you can sleep too. Tomorrow is a work day remember?"

"I remember."

Art went upstairs and changed clothes. Rebecca had hoped he wouldn't come back but he did. He untied her and stood her up, then leaned down and kissed her. She felt so dirty. "It's time to go upstairs for the night. Get going!" He followed her upstairs, let her use the bathroom, then tied her to the bed. "Goodnight Becky. I put the bedside commode next to the bed. I'll see you in the morning".

He left the room and went into his bedroom. He tried to decide what he was going to say when he called her off work the next two days. He smiled when he figured it out. He rolled over and went to sleep. Rebecca laid in the room and cried. She curled into the fetal position and tried to go to sleep.

Art set his alarm for 6:30 A.M. When it went off he got up and got dressed. He had to be at work by 8:30 A.M. At 7:15 he walked into where Rebecca was, leaned down and kissed her. When she opened her eyes he smiled at here. "Good Morning Becky. It's time for you to get up and fix breakfast for us."

"Art, I have to get ready for work too."

He slapped her across the face and she cried. "You're not going to go to work."

"Art, please I need this job. If I don't show up I'll get fired."

"I've got that covered. I'm going to call you off of work for the next couple of days. I'm going to tell them you had an emergency and needed to leave town for a couple of days."

Rebecca gasped. "A couple of days? Art, why are you keeping me here?"

"I'm not finished doing what I have to do; you're a very important part of that. Now let's get downstairs so you can fix breakfast."

He walked behind her as they went down the stairs. When they got into the kitchen, he untied her hands and let her fix breakfast. After breakfast he forced Becky to clean up. She trembled as he got on the phone and called her off work. As he was getting ready to take her back into the room she plead "Art, I'd really like to wash up and put on some different clothes if you'd let me."

"That's going to have to wait until later. I'll stop and get you some clean clothes. I'll come home at lunchtime and bring you something to eat. After I get home tonight you can wash up and I'll bring you some clean clothes. I'll turn the television on and put the remote close to you and here's another book for you." He tied her hands together then to the table. "I'll see you at lunch. Goodbye Rebecca."

Sara set her alarm for 7:00 A.M. She got up when the alarm went off. She put a robe on over her gown and went into the kitchen to start a pot of coffee. She heard Seth walking around in the guest room. She walked back there and knocked on the closed door. "Seth, you up?"

"Yes, I'm just making my bed."

"I started a pot of coffee. I thought maybe we'd have cereal, fruit, and a Danish for breakfast since we will be eating at Peter's funeral dinner."

"That's fine. I'm changing clothes. I'll be out in a minute."

"I'll get everything ready for breakfast."

Seth couldn't stop thinking about the pictures and the piece of cloth he gave to Tom. He hoped some questions would be answered. He knew he was on the right path to finding the killer; he just hoped he could protect Sara. As he was getting dressed he kept thinking about how beautiful Sara looked that night at the symphony. He realized he was falling in love with her; something he never thought he'd do.

When Seth finished getting dressed he walked into the kitchen. Sara was getting things together for fruit salad. She smiled at Seth. "Good morning Seth."

"Good morning Sara."

"The coffee's ready. Would you mind if I changed clothes?"

"Go ahead. I'm going to get myself a cup of coffee and pour myself a bowl of cereal. I'll make the fruit salad too."

"Thank you Seth. I appreciate that."

Sara walked into the bedroom. She was still nervous about changing clothes in her bedroom so she went into the bathroom. She started daydreaming as she was getting dressed. She realized she couldn't get her dress zipped so she called Seth. He came into her bedroom but didn't see her. "Sara, where are you?"

"I'm in the bathroom. I'll be out in a minute."

She walked out of the bathroom. She had a very pretty navy blue dress on with a little bit of make-up. She was holding her dress closed. "Seth, I hate to bother you but I need your help zipping my dress in the back. Every time I try to reach around and zip my dress I get a stabbing pain in my side."

"It's not a problem." He zipped her dress and stepped back.

"Seth, I need your help with my necklace."

He hooked her necklace for her, then she turned to him. "Thank you Seth."

"You're welcome Sara."

"How's the fruit salad coming?"

"It's ready. I'm getting the bowls out now."

"I'll be out in a minute. Thanks again."

After Seth left the room Sara stood in the room thinking about how wonderful Seth's hands felt on her arms the day before. How gentle his hands were zipping her dress and helping her with her necklace. She felt so safe with him. She couldn't stop thinking about how wonderful it felt to have his arms around her. She went into the kitchen and she and Seth sat down and started eating breakfast. "What time do you think we should leave Sara?"

"I thought we'd get there about 10:30, so we need to leave about 10:00 since the church is uptown and it's a weekday."

"I agree. It may take a little longer to get there."

Once they finished breakfast they both worked together and cleaned up the kitchen, then they sat down and talked. "Sara, I need to check in with Tom, just to let him know we're leaving."

"Okay, that's not a bad idea."

Seth called Tom. "Tom Monroe speaking."

"Tom, it's Seth."

"Good morning Seth. What can I do for you?"

"I wanted to let you know Sara and I are leaving in about an hour, to go to Peter Edward's wake. Did you find out anything from what I gave you yesterday?"

"Not yet. I gave it to Dennis and he was going to run the necessary tests on it. He said it would take a few days."

"I understand, it's just I want to get this guy. I really do."

"So do I Seth. By the way guess what?"

"I don't know but from the sound of your voice something wonderful must have happened."

"It did. Last night after work I went over to Carrie's; we had coffee and Danish and talked. Seth, I asked her to marry me and she said yes. Since I have four weeks vacation coming in the summer and fall that's when we're getting married. I'm going to take her to Paris for our honeymoon."

"Paris? Oh Tom. What did she think of that?"

"She was thrilled. I'm so happy. I never thought I'd find someone like her. I know we haven't known each other for very long but I don't want to lose her. I truly love her."

"I'm so happy for you and Carrie. She's a wonderful person. When did you tell me her last treatment is?"

"Tomorrow; then she doesn't have to go back for six months. I want to be there for her."

"I know you do. I'm truly happy for you and I know Sara will be thrilled."

"Thanks Seth."

"Tom, I'm not sure how long we'll be gone today so I was wondering if you could send a patrol car around the neighborhood every once in awhile. I'd feel better."

"I'll do that."

"Tom, does Carrie know either one of those men I mentioned?"

"Yes quite well. I asked her if either one of them ever hurt her in any way and she said no."

"That's good. I'm worried if we don't find the killer he'll strike again soon if he hasn't already."

"I haven't heard anything yet but I'll keep you informed."

"Thanks Tom and congratulations."

As soon as Seth hung up the phone Sara asked "Congratulations for what? Did Tom get a promotion?"

Seth turned to Sara and smiled. "No Tom didn't get a promotion. He asked Carrie to marry him and she said yes. They're getting married in late summer or early fall. He's taking her to Paris for their honeymoon."

Sara was thrilled. "I'm so happy for Carrie and Tom. He's taking her to Paris? How wonderful. She's always wanted to go there. Paul was going to take me where I always wanted to go on our honeymoon."

"Where is that Sara?"

"Greece and Paris."

"I've always wanted to go to Greece and Paris myself."

"I hope someday I'll still get to go."

"Sara, we better get going if we're going to get to the church by 10:30."

"I'm ready whenever you are."

They walked out to the car and left for the church.

Carrie wanted to go to Peter's wake but when she got up she wasn't feeling strong enough so she decided to stay home and rest. She fixed herself some coffee and ate a bowl of cereal. She didn't feel like getting dressed right away. She felt like lounging around. She thought about Tom and how happy she was. She never thought she'd ever get married again. She smiled a big grin.

Carrie's phone rang around 10:30 A.M. "Hi Carrie; it's Tom."

"Hello Tom."

"Are you getting ready to leave for Peter's wake?"

"No. I'm not going to be able to make it."

Tom could hear anxiety in her voice. "Carrie honey, what's wrong?"

"I'm feeling a little weak and tired today. I think I'll just take it easy today; especially since I have my last treatment tomorrow."

"Are you able to eat anything?"

"Yes. I ate some cereal and drank a cup of coffee. I think it's because I was so excited I couldn't sleep well last night. I thought about you most of the night."

"I thought about you too. I hoped you'd be feeling better today. I'm going to stop by on my lunch hour today and check on you. I'll bring you something to eat so you don't have to cook anything for yourself; you can rest longer that way. I should be there about 12:45 P.M. Is that alright?"

"That would be fine. I'll see you then."

"Carrie, if you need me before then call me. I'll take the rest of the day off and stay with you if necessary."

"Thanks Tom I appreciate it."

"I'll see you around 12:45. I love you Carrie."

"I'll see you. I love you too."

Tom really wished he was off for the day but he knew it wouldn't be long before he could take lunch and go check on her. He opened the files Seth had given him and started looking for more evidence to try and catch the killer.

Art was late for work but he didn't care. All he cared about was getting revenge on the women who had rejected him. He wanted them to suffer like he did. He decided if his boss asked him if he knew anything about why Rebecca wasn't at work, he'd play dumb.

His boss did ask him about Rebecca and he looked at him and said "I walked her to her car on Saturday and she told me about someone being sick in her family but that's all she said. I'm sorry; I can't help you."

The whole day Art tried to concentrate on his job but kept thinking about what he wanted to do to Rebecca when he got home that evening. He remembered he needed to stop at a lingerie shop and pick up some new under garments for her and a nice new dress to let her wear on Tuesday. He pictured what he wanted her to look like. He checked his watch. It was 10:45 A.M. Only one hour and fifteen minutes before he could leave for lunch.

Murder *When the Bell Tolls*

Sara and Seth got to the church in plenty of time. They got out of the car and started walking inside the church. Seth's cell phone rang. "Seth Parker speaking."

"Seth it's Tom."

He could hear uneasiness in Tom's voice. "Tom, is something wrong?"

"Seth, I was wondering if it would be possible for you and Sara to stop by Carrie's on the way back from the wake?"

"That's not a problem, why?"

"Well, I'm a little worried about her. I talked to her a few minutes ago and she said she wasn't feeling very well today. She had an episode yesterday, like Sara had at Paul's funeral, and said it was because she was tired. She promised me she was going to rest. I'm going to take her some lunch when it's my lunch break but I'd really appreciate it if you could stop by and check on her."

"Sure. The funeral's at 11:00. It'll probably be 12:15 before we get to the cemetery and 12:45 before we get back to the church. There's a meal being served so it'll probably be at least 2:00 before we can stop by and Maggie and Kevin are coming to Sara's tonight at 5:30."

"That's fine. I go to lunch at 12:30 and will be at Carrie's from 12:45 until 1:30 at least. I'll tell her to expect you."

"We'll stop by and make sure everything's okay. Tom, I'd suggest you stop by after you get off work tonight and check on her again."

"I will. I'm going with her tomorrow to her treatment."

"I know and Sara and I are both glad of that."

"Seth, do you think it would be inappropriate if I stayed overnight with Carrie in one of her guest rooms?"

"No. It might be a good idea. Remember, that's what I'm doing at Sara's."

"Yes but that's different. She's under twenty four hour protection."

"That's true. Don't worry, we'll stop by. We're heading into the church now. I'll talk to you later."

Sara and Seth entered the church, walked up to the casket, hugged Martha, said their condolences, then took a seat. The funeral service was over in about an hour and everyone filed out of the church and headed for their cars. They all got in their cars and drove out to the cemetery.

Seth looked at Sara who had tears in her eyes. "Sara, you okay?"

"Yes, but this really brings back the memories."

"I'm sure it does. I don't want to upset you anymore but that phone call I got about an hour ago was from Tom. He asked me if we could stop by Carrie's house on our way home from the funeral. He said Carrie isn't feeling well and he'd like for us to check on her."

Sara gasped. "Did he say what's going on with her?"

"All he said was she had an episode yesterday, like you had at Paul's funeral, and she's very weak and tired. He's going to take her some lunch. I told him we'd stop by after the funeral and he's going over there after he gets off work and stay overnight in a guest room."

Sara felt relieved. "That's good. That way neither one of them has to rush to get to her treatment in the morning and maybe she'll relax enough to sleep. She's been through a lot these past four months."

Seth squeezed Sara's hand. "And you've been through a lot in these past two weeks."

Art left for lunch at 12:05. He ran to a corner deli and grabbed some sandwiches and drinks and took them to his house. When Rebecca heard him pull up she turned the television down and shuddered. She dreaded having him there. He walked into the house and walked back to where she was. "Hello Rebecca. I'm home for lunch. I brought us something to eat. Are you glad to see me? I know I'm glad to see you."

Rebecca choked back tears and anger as Art got the food out and put it on plates. He handed her the sandwich and she ate slowly. "Becky, tonight I have a surprise for you I really think you're going to like. I'm going to be home a little later because I'm going to go pick up that surprise, so be waiting for me." She had to keep from choking on her food.

After Art was finished eating he leaned over and kissed Rebecca. I have to get back to work now. I know you're not finished eating so I'll leave your food so you can finish it. Think about me while I'm gone. I know I'll be thinking about you."

Art left Rebecca alone and went back to work. Rebecca's weeping had turned into crying. She curled up into the fetal position and cried harder. Art went back into work as if nothing had happened; however he had a new sense of confidence.

◦⋎◦

Tom left the station early. He headed to the deli to get some soup and a sandwich for him and Carrie. He got his order and at 12:30 was knocking on Carrie's door.

"Hello Tom. Come in."

He walked in and sat the sack of food down on a table next to the door. He put his hands on her arms and looked directly into her eyes. "Carrie, I know I'm a little early but I was so worried about you. Are you feeling better now?"

"Yes. I've been resting a lot and I do feel stronger."

He held her close to him, then kissed her. I'm so glad. I brought us both some soup and sandwiches from your favorite deli."

"It smells good."

Tom found some paper plates and put the sandwiches, pickles, and bags of chips on plates then took all of the food over to the dining room table where he and Carrie sat down and ate.

"Carrie, I talked to Sara and Seth this morning and told them about last night."

Carrie smiled. "What did they say?"

"They're thrilled. I told them you aren't feeling well today and they're going to stop by and check on you after they leave the funeral."

"They don't have to do that."

"They wanted to. They really care about you and so do I." He leaned across the table and kissed her again, then clasped her hand. "Carrie, Seth suggested after I get off work tonight I come and stay all night with you. I think it's a good idea then I won't have to worry so much about you and we won't have to rush to get ready in the morning. I could sleep on the couch if you like. I'll have to stop by my place first and pick up some pajamas, clean clothes and a brush for my hair."

Carrie was shocked but pleased. She smiled at Tom. "Tom, first of all I'm glad you feel like you need to take care of me and second of all you can sleep in one of my guest rooms. You and my late husband are about the same size and height. I couldn't bring myself to get rid of all of his things and luckily I kept some of them. I have some pajamas and some jeans and a shirt I think will fit you. I have a new toothbrush and hairbrush that you can have."

Tom hugged Carrie. "Good, it's set then. I was afraid you'd be upset that I even suggested staying here all night with you."

"I'm glad you'll be staying. I could use some extra support tonight. I always get really edgy the night before I have a treatment."

"I can imagine."

After Carrie and Tom finished their lunch Carrie started cleaning up the kitchen. "Carrie, let me do that. I want you to rest."

"Tom, I think I can handle this."

"That may be true but I really think you should rest. Please Carrie."

"Alright."

Carrie sat down at the kitchen table while Tom finished cleaning up the kitchen. Once he finished he sat down with Carrie. They talked and laughed for a little while. He looked at the clock. "My goodness, my lunch time's over already. Carrie, you going to be alright?"

"Yes, I'll be alright especially since Seth and Sara are going to stop by in a little while."

"I have to get back to the station but I want you to promise me you'll call me if you need me."

"I promise. I'll take it easy until you get here tonight."

"Do you have something you can fix yourself for supper?"

"Yes I do."

"I tell you what. Eat light for supper and we'll order a couple of pizza's and salad's once I get here. We can watch television, a movie, or whatever when I get here. I gotta go honey. I'll see you later. Call me if you need me." He kissed her.

"Goodbye Tom."

Seth and Sara got back to the church after the funeral and headed into the area of the church where the food was being served. They went through the line and went to a table to sit down. When they were almost finished eating, Martha walked over to them. "Sara, Seth thank you both for coming."

"You're welcome Martha. We're so sorry about Peter."

"Thank you both. How are you feeling Sara? The last time I saw you, you had a terrible wound on your side that was infected."

"I'm feeling better and the wound's healing. Thank you for asking."

Martha motioned for some people to come over to her. Four people came over. "Sara, Seth I'd like for you to meet my parents Don and Pam Overby and Peter's parents Thad and Amanda Edwards."

"Hello. We're sorry for your loss."

"Thank you."

"Mom, Dad, Thad, Amanda, this is Sara Michaels. The woman who's fiancé was murdered right before Peter. Sara's a friend of mine and the man with her is Lt. Seth Parker from the NYSPD. Sara's under police protection because she's the only one who's survived the shootings and she's the only one who's caught a glimpse of the killer."

They all gasped, then looked at her empathically and sympathetically. Peter's mother couldn't stop staring at Sara. She wanted to know more about what had happened. "Sara, I hate to sound rude but what did Martha mean by you're the only one who survived?"

"I watched my fiancé slump to the ground; he died in my arms without ever waking up. At the time of the shooting I only remember hearing one shot, but there was two. One killed my fiancé and the other grazed me in the side. I was meant to be a victim, but I survived."

Seth squeezed Sara's hand as the tears flowed down her face. Amanda patted her on the arm. "I'm sorry. I didn't mean to upset you I just wanted some answers. How well did you know Peter?"

"Fairly well. He was my stock broker and he worked in the office with my friends husband. I met him through my friend and through Martha. We got to be friends. Martha, if I can help in any way, please let me know."

"I will, thank you Sara."

"Martha, I hate to leave so early but Seth and I need to stop and check on a friend who isn't feeling well. Again, please let me know if you need anything."

"Goodbye Seth, Sara, thank you both for coming."

They walked out the door and to their car. "I hope Carrie's feeling better."

"Me too. I know Tom's extremely worried about her."

They got to Carrie's about fifteen minutes later. They walked up to the door and knocked. When Carrie answered it Sara could tell she wasn't feeling well. She was pale and weak. "Sara, Seth, come in. Tom told me you were coming; I fixed a fresh pot of coffee if you would like some."

"That sounds good Carrie but let me get it. You need to rest."

While Seth went to get the coffee, Sara and Carrie talked. Sara clasped Carrie's hand. "So Carrie, I hear congratulations are in order."

"Yes. Oh Sara, when Tom asked me to marry him it was like a dream come true. He's such a wonderful man. He's warm, caring, funny, loving, not to mention sexy, and I want to spend the rest of my life with him."

"Carrie, I'm so happy for you; and Paris. Wow! He's taking you to Paris for your honeymoon."

"Yes, that really shocked me. When we were talking that night he was here after Peg's party; we were talking about all the places we would like to go in the world and I mentioned Paris. I never thought I'd get to go there. I'm so excited."

"I would be too."

Seth came back with the coffee and everything to go in it. "Thank you Seth. I appreciate it. Have a seat and join us."

Seth sat on the love seat next to Sara and they talked and laughed for quite a while. At 4:15 P.M. Sara looked at the clock. "Oh my goodness. Maggie and Kevin are coming at 5:30. They're bringing dinner and thought we could finish our Monopoly game tonight. What time is your appointment tomorrow?"

"It's at 10:00. I'm nervous though."

"I bet. If you need anything you let us know."

"I will. Seth, Sara, thanks for stopping by. I feel a lot better now."

"You're welcome. Do you have something you can fix yourself for dinner?"

"Yes. Tom said to eat light because he was going to order pizza and salads when he got here."

Seth and Sara smiled. "Call us if you need us. Goodbye Carrie."

"Goodbye Seth, Sara."

Murder *When the Bell Tolls*

Seth and Sara left and drove back to Sara's.

The bank closed on the inside for the day but the drive-thru was still open until six. Art's boss walked over to him and said "Art, the next two days you'll be working until 5:00. I need you here at 8:30 tomorrow because that armored car comes at 9:00 and I need you to be here to help. I need you here at the same time on Wednesday. I was going to ask Rebecca to do it but since she's out of town I can't. I'm depending on you, alright?"

Art felt special. Someone had finally recognized him for what he could do. He smiled knowing what he had in store for Rebecca.

At 5:00 P.M. Art told his boss goodbye and left for the store to get some new under garments and a new dress for Rebecca, then get something for them to eat. He pulled into the driveway and walked into his house. He heard the television on in the room where he was holding Rebecca. He walked into the room and found her asleep. He touched her shoulder. "Becky, wake up. I have a surprise for you."

She opened her eyes. "Hello Art."

"Becky, I brought supper for us. Let's eat it while it's still hot and then I'll give you the surprise I bought for you."

Becky wasn't hungry. She was miserable. She wanted to go home. They started eating. "Becky guess what happened at work today?"

Becky, trying to humor him asked "What Art?"

"The boss asked me to go in at 8:30 the next two mornings and help the armored car people. He said he was going to ask you but since you're supposed to be out of town for a few days I could do it. He's going to let me off at 5:00 those two nights. Finally, someone who noticed my potential."

After they finished eating, Art cleaned everything up. "Now Becky, it's time for your surprise, but we have to go upstairs for you to get it." He untied her and followed her up the stairs.

Once they got upstairs he said "Becky, I'm going to let you take a shower then you may put these on. I bought these just for you."

She gasped when she saw the under garments he had bought for her. She felt sick. "I'll get you a towel, soap, and shampoo for your shower." She stood in the bathroom, looking at the shower with iron bars around the inside and a thick tile floor. He walked over to the closet and took out the things and handed them to her. "Now, I'll wait outside while you shower and get your underwear on. After you're finished I want you to come out here to me. Now, take your shower!"

She jumped when he ordered her to take a shower. He left the room and closed the door behind him. She undressed, grabbed the things he had laid out for her to use in the shower, then got in the shower. She cried and trembled as she was in the shower. She felt relieved and started to relax. The water stung her wounds but she was so grateful to be taking a shower. She washed her hair, then rinsed off, got out of the shower and dried off. She picked up the under garments and put them on slowly. She shivered as she walked out of the bathroom and into the room where Art was waiting.

Art smiled when he saw her coming out of the bathroom. He walked over to her and grabbed her by the wrists. He pulled her over to the bed, then threw her onto the bed. She trembled in fear. He leaned down and kissed her. She cringed. "There's a couple of good shows on television tonight Becky. I think we should watch them together until it's bedtime. I'll turn the television on."

He turned the television on. It was 7:45 P.M. He knew the show he really wanted to see was on at 10:00 P.M. He tied her hands to the bedside table. "I need to make a phone call. I'll be back right away. You can watch television." He walked into his den and called Jack.

"Jack, it's Art. Everything's going as planned for tomorrow night."

"Art, I don't like this."

"Everything will be alright if you just do as I tell you. I'm working until 5:00 P.M. tomorrow. I'll stop and get dinner and take it home and eat. Be at the park, dressed in a police officer uniform at 8:45 P.M. tomorrow. Look for a woman in a yellow polka dotted dress. Go up to her and talk to her. I'll take care of the rest."

"Art, I don't know."

"Just be there."

"Okay."

Art hung up the phone and went into the room where Rebecca was. He untied her hands, then sat down in a chair next to the bed and watched television with her.

Murder *When the Bell Tolls*

At 5:30 P.M. Maggie and Kevin knocked on Sara's door. Seth answered it. "Come in." He took the food and set it on the table.

"Hello Seth. Where's Sara?"

"She's changing clothes. We had an unexpected stop to make on our way home from the funeral today and we only got home about thirty minutes ago."

"Did something happen?"

"No. We just needed to stop by Carrie's house. She wasn't feeling well and Tom asked us if we could stop by and check on her. He's going over there after he gets off work tonight."

"He's been spending a lot of time with her lately."

"I know. Last night Tom asked Carrie to marry him and she said yes."

Maggie and Kevin smiled. "That's wonderful. I'm sure they'll be very happy."

"I'm sure they will."

Sara came into the room wearing jeans, a blouse and fuzzy slippers. "Hi Maggie, Kevin."

Maggie could see the worrisome look on Sara's face. "Sara, I understand Carrie isn't feeling well. What's wrong?"

"Every once in a while she has an episode, like I did at Paul's funeral, and it makes her really weak and tired. She had one of those episodes yesterday; she just needs rest. I'll be glad when Tom gets over there tonight."

"I'm sorry to hear she's not feeling well. I understand she and Tom got engaged last night."

"Yes they did and she's thrilled."

"Sara, I set the food on the table."

"Oh thank you Seth. All I need to do is get some plates and eating utensils and we can sit down and eat."

Maggie helped Sara get the plates and silverware. Seth and Kevin wanted beer and Maggie and Sara decided on a glass of red wine. They took the drinks over to the table, sat down and started eating.

After they finished eating, Seth and Kevin helped clear the table. Maggie helped Sara with the dishes. It was 8:30 when they got out the Monopoly game to start playing. Before they started playing the game Sara asked "Would anyone mind if I called over to Carrie's to find out if Tom's gotten there yet?"

"Go ahead Sara."

⚜

Tom knocked on Carrie's door at 8:15 P.M. Tom smiled when she answered the door. She smiled. "Come in."

He walked in, embraced her, then kissed her. How you feeling Carrie?"

"I'm a little better. Seth and Sara stopped by earlier. It was so nice to see them again."

"I'm glad they stopped by. I was worried about you. You still look a little pale. Are you worried about tomorrow?"

"A little. Having you here tonight will help ease some of the anxiety."

"I'm glad."

"Tom, I was getting your room ready when you knocked. I need to get you some blankets, and towels yet."

"Carrie slow down. It doesn't have to be done yet. We have plenty of time."

The phone rang about 8:35 P.M. "Hello Carrie, it's Sara."

"Hi Sara."

"Carrie, is Tom there yet?"

"Yes, do you want to talk to him?"

"In a minute. First, are you feeling better?"

"Some. I feel better having Tom here. I was just getting his room ready."

"If you need something, please call. Let us know when you get home from your treatment tomorrow."

"I will."

"Could you let me talk to Tom for a minute?"

"Sure. Here he is."

"Hi Tom."

"Hi Sara. Is everything alright?"

"For now. Is Carrie alright? She looked pale and weak when we were there."

"She still looks a little pale but I think she's a little stronger. I'm going to order some pizza and salads in a little while and we're going to watch television and talk for awhile."

"That sounds good. Maggie and Kevin are here and we're getting ready to play Monopoly. If you or Carrie need anything, just call."

"We will. Thanks for stopping by and checking on her today. I feel better knowing someone else checked on her too."

Murder *When the Bell Tolls*

"Call us tomorrow and let us know when you get back from Carrie's treatment."

"We will. Thanks again Sara."

"Thanks Tom."

Sara, Seth, Maggie, and Kevin started playing Monopoly. "Sara, do you feel better now since you talked to both Carrie and Tom?"

"Yes I do. I know she'll be well taken care of tonight and tomorrow."

"That's for sure."

"Were there a lot of people at the funeral today Sara?"

"Yes actually there were. I was surprised since it was a weekday."

"That surprises me too. Doesn't Carrie have some sort of doctor's appointment or something tomorrow?"

"Yes, she has her last treatment then goes back to the doctor for a check-up six months later. Tom's going with her."

"That's nice. Speaking of doctors appointments, yours is Wednesday right?"

"Yes at 10:00 A.M."

"Good. Elizabeth and Carl have invited us over for dinner on Wednesday night. Kevin and I are going. Do you feel up to going Sara?"

"Yes; I need to start getting out and doing things again especially if I'm going back to work next week."

"She wants us there about 6:00 P.M. if that's alright."

"Seth, do you think that would be alright?"

"I don't know why not Sara."

"Well why don't we plan on leaving here at 5:15 P.M.?"

"That sounds great. I think both of us should drive though in case one of us wants to leave later than the other."

"I agree Seth. We'll both drive."

They continued to play Monopoly. Sara got up and made another pot of coffee. Maggie got up to help her. Kevin and Seth talked at the table.

"Sara, you sure there isn't something bothering you? You seem so quiet tonight. Not as outgoing."

"Maggie, I know I seem quite because something is bothering me; I just can't talk about it right now. It's just too painful."

"Does Seth know about this?"

"No. The only person I talked to about this was Paul."

Maggie gasped. "Is it that bad Sara?"

"Yes it is. Paul was so understanding and loving. He was so easy to talk to."

"Sara, you know you can talk to me about anything don't you?"

"Yes I do Maggie and this is something I'm just not ready to talk about."

"If you ever want to talk about it; I'll listen."

"Thanks Maggie. We better get the coffee back over to the men before they think we went to the coffee shop and bought it." Maggie laughed.

"Here's some fresh coffee."

"Thanks Sara, Maggie. Now we can get down to the business of winning this Monopoly game." They all laughed.

They played Monopoly until about 11:45 P.M. Sara started to yawn. She got up to stretch her legs. "Wow! I can't believe it's that late already."

"Sara, I think we should get going. It's getting late and you need your rest."

"You don't have to leave."

"I know but I think we should. We're going over to Paul's apartment in the morning to clean it out. It'll probably take most of the morning. How about we call you and we'll all meet for lunch at that restaurant where we ate yesterday?"

"That sounds good. I need to get some laundry and cleaning done around here anyway."

"We'll plan on about 1:00. We'll call you first. It might be a little earlier. Paul was a fairly neat person and he had a cleaning lady that cleaned his apartment once a week, so it shouldn't take too long."

"Maggie, Paul had a painting over his couch in his sun room and I was wondering if I could have that painting? It was always one of my favorites because it has dolphins on it and you know how much I love dolphins."

"Sara honey, you may have anything you like from there. You were going to be his wife and I'm sure he'd want you to have it. There's also a silver tea service I want you to have. It was my mothers."

"Maggie, I couldn't accept that. You should have it."

"Sara, I want you to have it."

Murder *When the Bell Tolls*

Sara hugged Maggie. "Thank you so much Maggie."

"You're welcome sweetie."

"Seth, Sara, we better get going. We'll talk to you tomorrow and let you know what time we should meet for lunch."

"Sounds good. Goodnight Maggie, Kevin. Be careful."

"Goodnight you two."

Seth helped Sara clean up the cups and coffee pot. "Seth, I'm exhausted. Do you mind if I go to bed?"

"No, not at all. My body is still trying to get use to being able to sleep every night. I'm used to sleeping in the daytime."

Sara hugged Seth. "Goodnight Seth. Thank you for everything." She kissed him on the cheek then walked back to her bedroom. Seth stood dazed for a minute in the living room then he walked into his bedroom. He smiled. He was glad Sara was doing better.

While Tom was talking to Sara, Carrie got the things she needed and took them into the guest bedroom. She put blankets at the foot of the bed and was hanging towels on the rack when Tom came up behind her and put his arms around her waist. He kissed her on the neck and cheek. "Carrie, please slow down. I don't want you to have another episode."

"I want your room to look nice and I want to make sure you have everything you need."

"Honey, I have everything I need."

Carrie laid a pair of pajamas on the bed. "I hope these fit. My late husband really liked these. He said they were comfortable."

Tom kissed Carrie on the cheek. "They'll be fine. Now, let's go order those pizzas and salads."

Tom ordered the pizzas and salads. Carrie wanted red wine to drink and so did Tom. The pizzas were there in about twenty minutes. Tom paid for the pizzas and salads and took them into the kitchen. He opened the wine and poured each one of them a glass. They ate and talked about plans for their upcoming wedding. After they finished eating, they decided they wanted to watch a couple of movies. Tom put the first movie in and they settled back on the couch. Carrie moved as close to Tom as she could and leaned against him. He smiled and wrapped his arms around her.

The first movie was over at 10:00 P.M. They decided they wanted to watch a program on television. Tom put the movie

back into it's case and they watched a television program. Halfway through the program, Tom looked over at Carrie. She was sleeping peacefully up against his chest. He smiled. After the program was over, he used the remote and turned off the television. There was a blanket next to him so he unfolded it and put it around Carrie to keep them both warm. He leaned down and kissed her on the top of the head, then held her closer to him. He fell asleep too.

At 11:00 Art turned the television off. "Becky, it's time to go to sleep. I have to have my rest especially since I have to get up extra early in the morning so I can be at work at 8:30. I got a big job to do, you know?" He said hauntingly. "You need your rest too since you are going to get up and fix my breakfast. After that I'll give you your other surprise. Goodnight Becky."

Art walked out of the room, turning off the light as he left. He had a smirk on his face as he walked down to his bedroom and got himself ready for bed. He laid out his best suit for work in the morning. He wanted to impress his boss. He set his alarm for 6:00 A.M. then climbed into bed and quickly went to sleep.

Rebecca couldn't sleep. She pulled at the ropes trying to get free. She was terrified. She cried herself to sleep.

When Art's alarm went off at 6:00 A.M. it startled Rebecca. She heard Art walking around. She wondered what type of surprise he had in store for her today. She heard water running and figured Art was showering. At about 6:45 Art walked into the room where Rebecca was. "Good Morning Becky. Well, it's time to go downstairs so you can fix our breakfast." He untied her hands and followed her down the stairs to the kitchen.

Once they got into the kitchen Art got everything out for Rebecca to cook breakfast. "I want you to fix omelets and bacon. Here's everything you need. Now get busy!"

Rebecca mixed up the eggs and made the omelets. She cooked the bacon while the omelets were cooking. She set the food on the table. "Sit down at the table and eat with me."

Rebecca sat down at the table. They ate quietly. Once they were finished eating Art looked at the clock. He had twenty minutes before he had to leave. He pulled Becky over to the sink. "Wash these few dishes then come into the living room where I'll give you another surprise."

She went over to the sink and started washing the dishes. Art walked up behind her and got in her face. She wanted to lean back but was afraid he'd hit her if she did. She finished the dishes then she and Art went into the living room. He went over to the closet and got out the bag with the dress in it. He walked over to Rebecca and handed her the bag. "What's this Art?"

"Look and see."

She pulled the yellow polka dotted dress out of the bag. She looked at Art. "Is this for me?"

"Yes. Try it on."

She did and it fit perfectly. "You may wear that the rest of the day. Today will go much like it did yesterday. I'll bring some lunch home for you and we'll eat lunch together, then I'll bring supper home and we'll eat. After we eat supper I'm going to give you something I think you really deserve then I'm going to take you to the park and let you walk home from there." She just stared at him. "Goodbye Becky, I'll see you at lunchtime."

Becky trembled as she sat in the room. Art tied her hands a little looser than usual but not loose enough for her to get free. She watched television and dreamed of being free and away from Art.

⚜

Sara and Seth both got up around 7:00 A.M. Sara went into the kitchen and started fixing breakfast. "Seth is bacon and eggs okay for breakfast?"

"That sounds good."

"How do you want your eggs cooked?"

"Scrambled. Do you need me to help you?"

"I think I can handle this."

"Do I have time to shower and get dressed before breakfast Sara?"

"Yes. It'll be about thirty minutes before breakfast is ready anyway. When you're finished taking a shower and getting dressed come out to the four seasons room. We can have breakfast out there where the sun is shining brightly."

"Okay. That sounds nice."

Seth went to shower, and change clothes. Sara prepared breakfast. She was just finishing up the food when Seth came out dressed in a nice pair of blue jeans and a buttoned down short sleeve shirt. "It smells good Sara. Let me help you take the food into the other room."

They got into the four seasons' room. Sara set the food down on the glass coffee table. They sat and ate and watched the news on a small television they had. Sara turned the ceiling fan on to get more air. The sun was shining brightly into that room. "Seth, I need to try and get back into my routine so it isn't so hard when I go back to work next week."

"I agree. It'll be a lot easier on you if you start now."

"Would you mind if we took a nice walk around the neighborhood after we finish eating?"

"That sounds like a good idea."

"You know, before Carrie got sick she walked about five miles a day after school and on weekends. I think she's finally started walking again and is up to two miles a day. I used to walk five miles a day myself. Paul walked them with me a lot on the weekends."

"I do a lot of walking in my job too."

They finished eating. "Seth, let me get a running suit on then we can go. I'll shower and clean up after we get back. It won't take me but a few minutes to change clothes."

While Sara changed clothes, Seth took the dirty dishes into the kitchen and stacked them by the sink. He filled the sink with hot soapy water and washed the dishes. He was just finishing up when Sara came out of her bedroom. "I'm ready to go when you are." She looked over and saw Seth drying his hands on a towel. "Seth, did you do up those dishes?"

"Yes I did. I thought I'd help you so when we get back you'll have more time to get ready."

She smiled at him "Thank you Seth; I appreciate it."

It was a little chilly so they both grabbed a light jacket before they left to go walking.

When Tom woke up, Carrie was still sleeping next to him. He wanted to get up, shower, shave, and get cleaned up. He gently moved her over, then kissed her on the top of her head. She opened her eyes and saw Tom sitting next to her. She realized she was on the couch. "Tom, did I sleep here all night?"

"Yes, and so did I. You fell asleep against my chest and I didn't want to wake you so we both slept out here."

"What time is it?"

Murder When the Bell Tolls

"It's 6:00 A.M. Why don't you try to get a little more sleep. I'm going to shower, shave, and change clothes. I'll come and help you with breakfast after that."

"I'm used to getting up at 6:00 anyway when I'm teaching because I have to be in the classroom by 9:00 A.M. but for some reason I'm really tired this morning. I think I will try and get some extra sleep." She leaned back and closed her eyes again.

Tom kissed her on the lips then said "I'll be out in a little while. You just rest." He walked back to the guest room that Carrie fixed up for him and went into the bathroom and showered. He got out of the shower, shaved, then went into the bedroom and put on the clothes Carrie laid out for him. They fit him almost perfectly. He picked up his dirty clothes, folded them neatly and put them on a chair that was in the bathroom, then he walked quietly out to the living room where Carrie was still sleeping.

Tom walked past Carrie, went into the kitchen and made a pot of coffee. He looked in the refrigerator and found what they could eat for breakfast. He wanted to wait to fix breakfast until she woke up. He knew she had to be up by 7:30 so she could eat before they had to leave. They had to leave by 9:15 A.M. in order to get to her appointment by 10:00 A.M.

The coffee was ready so Tom poured himself a cup and sat down at the table to drink it. He heard Carrie stirring in the living room. "Tom, Tom are you here? Where are you?"

Tom walked over to Carrie. She still had her eyes closed. He imagined she was having a nightmare. He touched her shoulder and she opened her eyes. "I'm right here Carrie."

"Oh Tom. I was having a nightmare."

"That's what I thought. You were calling out my name."

"I was? I don't remember what the nightmare was about. Do I smell coffee?"

"Yes, I made a fresh pot and I've set out everything for breakfast. I didn't want to fix it until you woke up."

"Wait; you were going to fix breakfast for us? You don't have to do that?"

"I know but I want to. I want you to get as much rest as you can. Today's going to be difficult on you as it is."

"Yes it is. I probably won't be able to do much for a couple of days but I'll be alright after that."

"How long does it usually take before you feel well enough to do something after you've had a treatment?"

"Two to three days."

"Well since today's Tuesday, that means it'll probably be Thursday or Friday before you feel like doing anything."

"Yes and Monday I'm supposed to go back to work."

"Carrie, I think I should stay here with you until at least next Tuesday night to see how you manage this treatment and your first day back to work. I'm supposed to work Wednesday, Thursday and Friday then be off until next Tuesday. I'd feel so much better if I knew you were alright."

Carrie smiled. "I'd like that. I'd feel better knowing you're here."

"Carrie, let me fix breakfast. You look like you could use something to eat."

"Do I have time to shower and change clothes before breakfast?"

"Yes. It'll be about thirty minutes before breakfast."

"Okay. I'll shower and change clothes."

She smiled as she went back to her room and got ready to shower. She was thrilled Tom was going to stay with her for a few days. She felt weak anyway and would welcome the company. She got undressed and got into the shower. After she showered she put on some perfume, and got into her clothes. She wanted to look as nice as she could. She brushed what little hair she had then tied a colorful scarf around her head. She put on some make-up and went into the kitchen.

Tom smiled when he saw her. "Carrie breakfast is ready. Let's sit down and eat." They ate breakfast, then Tom helped Carrie clean up the kitchen. They looked at the clock. It was 8:30 A.M. they had forty five minutes before they needed to leave. Tom opened the front door and picked the paper up off the porch. He and Carrie sat down and read the paper until about 9:00 A.M.

"Carrie, it's a little chilly outside. I think we should wear a light jacket of some kind."

"I'll get my jacket and I'll get you a jacket that was my late husbands. I'll be right back."

He kissed her. "Okay. I'll be waiting right here."

She left and came back about five minutes later with jackets for both of them. They put their jackets on and walked out to Tom's car. He helped her into the car. She gave him directions on how to get to her doctors.

Once they got to her doctor's office Tom helped her out of the car. She was really nervous. Tom put his arm around her. "Are you alright Carrie?"

"I'm just nervous. I'm glad this is my last treatment."

"I bet you are nervous. I'll be right here with you the whole time. I don't want you to go through this alone."

"Thanks Tom." He leaned over and kissed her.

Maggie and Kevin got over to Paul's plush condominium around 8:30 A.M. They knew they had four hours to do as much work as they could before they needed to leave for Sara's. "Kevin, I'll pack the things in Paul's bedroom, you can take the bathroom."

They got the things packed from those two rooms and met in the living room. It had taken an hour to get both of those rooms done. Maggie looked at the picture above the sofa, then gently took it down and set it in front of the sofa. She got the tea set and put it with the picture. Maggie started weeping as they started packing things away from the living room. Kevin saw a picture that was taken of Paul and Sara shortly before Paul was killed. Maggie held it close to her chest and cried. Kevin put his arm around her and hugged her. She wrapped the picture in bubble wrap to make sure it didn't get broken. She wanted to put that picture on their fireplace mantle when they got home.

At 11:00 they decided to take a break. They almost had everything packed but they wanted to clean the place up before it was ready to have anyone else live in it. Since Paul owned the condo there really wasn't any rush to get it cleaned out. They weren't sure if they'd sell it or keep it or if Paul had willed it to someone. Maggie made a pot of coffee and she and Kevin took a break and drank a cup of coffee. "Maggie, there are two more rooms of things to pack up then all that needs to be done is cleaning and taking these boxes to our car so we can go through them at Sara's or when we get home."

"I'm not sure Sara's up to going through these things yet. We need to give her time to grieve."

"That's true Maggie; however, we need to talk to Sara about what Paul wanted to do with this place once they got married."

"I agree. I think it should be up to Sara to decide what happens to this place."

After they finished drinking their coffee, they started packing up things again. It was 12:20 P.M. when they finally got done packing things up. "Well, everything's packed up. It's 12:20. It's too late to start cleaning but maybe we can do that one day this weekend before we go home. Since we both brought clean clothes, let's take showers and get cleaned up before we meet Sara and Seth."

Carrie was called back for her treatment. Tom held her hand as they walked into the room. "Good morning Carrie. How are you feeling today?"

"Good morning Carol. I haven't been feeling well and I think it's because I'm nervous about today."

"I know you are. I bet you're glad this is the last treatment."

"I am." She looked over at Tom and smiled.

"Who's the good looking man with you Carrie?"

"Let me introduce you. This is Sergeant Tom Monroe with the NYSPD. Tom and I are engaged and planning on getting married in late summer."

Tom smiled at her. "Hello, it's a pleasure to meet you ma'am."

"It's a pleasure to meet you sir."

"Carol, it is okay if Tom stays in here with me isn't it?"

"Sure honey. As a matter of fact we encourage it." Tom squeezed Carrie's hand. "Carrie, are you ready to start your treatment?"

"Yes. Let's get it over with."

"Remove your blouse please. I have a sheet to throw over you for cover."

Tom turned his back to her while she removed her blouse. Once she had done that the nurse helped her sit in the chair that she needed to be in. She put a sheet over her, then Tom went over to her, and held her hand while they started the treatment.

"So Carrie, how did you meet Tom?"

"One of my dearest friends, Sara Michaels, has been under police protection since her fiancé was killed and Tom was one of the officers assigned to protect her. He's now one of the lead officers assigned to these strange murder cases in and around the park. I think the first time I met him was at the wake for Paul Sanford. We started talking and hit it off right there."

"I'm so happy for you Carrie. Tom seems like a nice man."

"He's a wonderful man and a good police officer."

"You're working on the murder cases?"

"Yes ma'am, I am."

"Have they found out anything?"

"I can't discuss an ongoing case but I can say we know all the murders are connected."

"Tom, I'm glad you and Carrie are together. She's a terrific lady. I haven't seen her this happy in a long time. I'm sure the two of you will be very happy together."

"Thank you. I'm sure we will." Tom squeezed Carrie's hand again.

※

Sara and Seth walked about a mile and a half when Sara said "Seth, I have to rest."

"Let's rest for a few minutes then. I don't want you to overdo it and not be able to go back to work on Monday. I know how much that means to you."

"I do want to go back to work. I miss everyone."

"I bet you do."

"Seth, the kids, and the staff are going to love having me back and they're going to love you and love having you there. So am I."

He smiled at her. "I hope they don't think I'm a geek or something."

"They won't. I promise. They're all a great bunch of kids. Nancy Boyd likes you too. I'm supposed to call her after I go to the doctor and let her know if I'll be able to go back on Monday. Peggy told me Carrie's supposed to be going back to work on Monday too. That will be great."

"What's Nancy Boyd like? Is she strict?"

"Yes, but she's very fair and very understanding. I really like her."

"That's good. It makes it easier to work for someone you can get along with."

"I agree."

A few minutes later they started walking again. "Sara, I think maybe we should head back for two reasons. One is you look really tired and need to rest and two it's 11:30. We need to get ready for this afternoon."

Art got to work right on time. He was beaming with pride. He thought his boss had finally learned to appreciate him. He met his boss, who told him how things would go, then he went to the lower level of the bank and waited for the truck to get there. While he waited he thought about Rebecca. He smiled. He thought things were finally going his way.

When the truck got there he helped with the money. He checked it in, put it in the vault, and went upstairs to do his job as a teller. He smiled at people and tried to be nice, thinking it would impress his boss. He kept looking at the clock waiting for 12:00 to get there. He wanted to go home and brag to Rebecca about how his day had gone so far, especially since he was doing her job.

At 11:45 Art's boss told him to go on and go to lunch. "You can take an hour lunch today but be back here by 1:00."

"I will, don't worry."

Art left the bank, went and got food for him and Rebecca, and drove the few blocks home for lunch. He walked into the house and said "Becky honey, I'm home for lunch."

Rebecca cringed when she heard his voice. He walked into the room smiling. "Hello Becky. The boss let me out earlier so I got home sooner but I have to be back by 1:00 instead of 1:15 so we don't have as much time together as I'd like but I'll make up for it tonight. I couldn't wait to get home so I could tell you how my day's going so far."

She felt sick. He was bragging to her about what he'd done so far that day. It was supposed to be her job. What would he do when he finally let her go home, then back to her job? Would she be able to work at the bank with Art still there? She had so many questions and no answers.

While they ate Art continued telling her about his day so far and how proud he was of himself. After lunch Art got the trash together and put it all in one bag. He tied it up and set it by the front door so he could take it out on his way to his car. He leaned over and put his arms around Rebecca and kissed her. He ran his hands over her body then kissed her again. She felt sick. "Well Becky, it's 12:45 I have to leave to get back to work. I'll see you at supper time; oh and remember tonight after supper you'll get something I think you deserve, then we'll go to the park where you can walk home from there."

He laughed his eerie laugh as he walked out the front door. Rebecca was trembling as he left.

Seth and Sara got back to Sara's house at 11:30 A.M. "Seth, I'm going to shower and change clothes."

"Go ahead. I'll be out here drinking a cup of coffee and reading the morning paper."

Sara smiled as she walked into her bedroom. Seth was so much like her late husband Gary and her late fiancé Paul. She really liked him and realized she was starting to have stronger feelings about him. She undressed and got in the shower. After she finished her shower, she got dressed, put on some perfume and jewelry then walked out to where Seth was. "Well, I'm ready to go except for putting my shoes on."

Seth smiled. "You look really nice."

"Thank you Seth. I know I didn't tell you this earlier but you look really nice too." She said almost blushing. "I wonder how Carrie's doing with her treatment. She's always so tired afterward."

"I bet. Tom's with her and that will help."

"Yes it will." Before she could say anything else the phone rang and she answered it. "Hello Maggie."

"Sara, we're just leaving Paul's house now. Sorry we're running a little bit late but we both had to take showers and clean up. We'll be there in about fifteen minutes."

"That's fine. We'll be waiting for you."

"They're running late aren't they?"

"Yes. Maggie said they're just leaving Paul's place now and they'd be here in about fifteen minutes. Seth, I know I would never have been able to do what Maggie and Kevin did. I can only imagine the emotions they went through. It was hard when I packed all of Gary's things up and I was his wife, Paul was their son; that's even harder."

"I know it is Sara. No parent should ever have to bury their child."

About ten minutes later there was a knock at the door. Seth answered the door. "Hi Maggie, Kevin, come in for a few minutes. Sara and I both have to put our shoes on."

When Maggie walked in Sara could tell she'd been crying. She walked over to Maggie and hugged her, then whispered in her ear "I understand."

"Sara, we got that picture and tea set for you. They're wrapped up in a bag in the trunk of the car. We had about five boxes of things to take out of there. We don't want to throw anything away until you have a chance to go through the things and see if there's anything else you'd like to have. I hope you don't mind if I keep a picture of the two of you, that Paul had in a sterling silver frame in his living room."

"I don't mind at all Maggie. You may have whatever you like."

Maggie hugged Sara. "Thank you Sara."

Kevin walked over to them. Sara could tell Kevin had been crying too. Something he very rarely did around other people. "Before we go, I need to bring the boxes from Paul's condo into the house so there's room for everyone in the car. Sara would it be okay if I put them in the other spare bedroom?"

"Sure, you can keep them there for as long as you like."

"I'll get them."

"Why don't I help you?" Seth asked.

"I'd appreciate that."

They talked as they unloaded the boxes, which weren't very heavy. However there was one box that was extremely heavy. "Kevin, how you holding up?"

"I'm doing alright. I think it's finally starting to sink in. I can't imagine how Sara feels after what she's been through. Seth, I don't want Maggie or Sara to hear this so I'll say it while we're outside. I want you to promise me you'll take care of Sara after we leave. I know both of us will worry about her and knowing you're with her will make all the difference to us. We couldn't bear to see anything happen to her."

"Kevin, I promise I'll take care of her. I'll be with her all of the time and go where she goes."

"What if she, Peggy, and Carrie decide they want a ladies night out? They used to do that all of the time."

"Well, Tom and I'll get together and stay within eye shot of the ladies. I'll encourage her to wait until after these people responsible for the murders are caught."

"That would be great." Suddenly Kevin realized what Seth had just said and he looked at Seth puzzled. "Did you just say people?"

"Yes. We believe there are at least two people involved in the murders. One does the killing and the other is just a set-up person."

They went inside carrying the boxes. Maggie found the picture and tea set and gave it to Sara. She took the picture out into the four seasons room and hung it over the fireplace. "Thank you both so much."

"You're welcome. Is everyone ready to go?"

"Yes." They walked out to the car.

After Carrie's treatment was finished the nurse helped her put her blouse on, she took her blood pressure one more time, then hugged Carrie and said "I guess this is it for awhile. I've really enjoyed getting to know you. You're a fantastic person and I hope everything goes well for you from now on. I wish you and Tom the best. Good Luck Carrie."

"Thanks Carol. It's been a pleasure getting to know you too."

"The doctor will be in to see you in a little while. He'll let you know about going back to work and what to expect after this treatment."

"I'm going to miss you Carol. Thank you for everything."

"You're welcome Carrie. Tom, it's been a pleasure to meet you."

"Thank you Carol; it's been a pleasure for me too."

Carol left the room and within five minutes the doctor came in. "Hello Carrie. Who's your friend?"

"Hello doctor. This is Sergeant Tom Monroe of the NYSPD. He's more than a friend. He's my fiancé. We're getting married in late summer, early fall."

The doctor smiled. "Well congratulations. I'm really happy for both of you. Carrie I studied the results of your last tests and I believe the cancer's gone." Carrie grinned.

"So can I go back to work?"

"Yes but not until Monday. I want you to rest the rest of this week. The only side effects you might have from this treatment are tiredness, maybe some nausea, and a slight headache. If you experience any others side effects, call me immediately."

"Okay. I'll do that."

"Doctor, is it okay if she travels out of the states?"

"To where?"

"Paris?"

The doctor smiled at Carrie "Paris? Why Paris?"

"It's where we're going on our honeymoon."

He looked at Carrie and saw how happy she was. "I think so, just come see me first before you go. I'll give you some paperwork in case you have some problems."

"Thank you doctor."

"You're welcome Carrie. Again congratulations. I'm thrilled for you. Let me know when you get ready to go to Paris."

After the doctor left, Tom helped Carrie off of the table then he clasped her hand. As they walked out of the doctor's office everyone said goodbye and congratulations. They walked out to Tom's car. He helped her into the car. It was 1:00 P.M. She leaned her head against the head rest and closed her eyes. Tom looked at her and could see how beautiful she really was but also how vulnerable she was.

They drove twenty five minutes to the deli where she loved to eat on her days off work. He parked the car, then leaned over and kissed her on the lips. She slowly opened her eyes. "I'm sorry, I didn't mean to fall asleep."

"It's alright. I'm glad you could rest. We're at the deli where you like to eat. Are you hungry?"

"I'm starved."

"It's such a beautiful sunny day why don't we eat at an outside table?"

"That sounds good."

They went inside, placed their order then found an outside table and waited for their order. Tom held Carrie's hand across the table. She smiled. She was so happy. Their food came and they started eating. "Carrie, my place isn't far from here. After we get done here would you mind if I stopped and got a few things to take to your house?"

"Not at all. I'd love to see your place."

They finished eating then they left and went to Tom's apartment. It was a very nicely decorated apartment and very neat. "This is nice Tom."

"It's comfortable, but it can be very lonely at times."

"I know. It gets that way at my home too."

"Why don't you have a seat at the table or on the couch and I'll get a few things together then we can go back to your house. I can tell you're getting tired and need to rest."

She sat down on the couch while Tom packed a few things. Carrie fell asleep on the couch. When Tom came out to ask her something he saw her sleeping peacefully on the couch. He didn't want to wake her so he put a blanket over her, went across the room, turned on his computer and worked on the case while she slept.

About an hour later she woke up. "Tom, are you here?"

"Carrie, I'm right here."

"Tom, I'm sorry I fell asleep again but that's what the treatments do to me the first couple of days. What time is it anyway?"

"It's almost 3:30 why?"

"I was supposed to call Sara and Seth and let them know we got back. They're probably with Maggie and Kevin by now."

"We can call and leave a message and Sara can call you back later." He kissed her.

"Did you get everything together you needed?"

"Sort of. I need you to help me pick out something to wear for church on Sunday."

Carrie smiled. They held hands as they headed into his room to pick out some clothes. She picked out a casual outfit and put it in his suitcase. "I have my things together. I guess we're ready to go."

They left and went to Tom's car. He helped Carrie into the car and they drove the ten minutes to Carrie's house.

Sara, Seth, Maggie, and Kevin got to the restaurant and went inside. They were seated and given menus. They decided what they wanted and placed their order. "Maggie, I really appreciate you letting me have that picture from Paul's condo. It means a lot."

Maggie patted Sara's hand. "You're welcome sweetie."

"Maggie, you alright? I know this has been a rough day for you."

"I'm alright. It's been a rough day but it had to be done. The only thing left to do is clean the condo. I think Kevin and I are going to do that on Saturday. We want to get it done before we go back home. I know he had someone who came in and cleaned every week but I'm not sure when she's scheduled."

"She's scheduled to come in Thursday. I know because the night Paul was killed he said the cleaning lady had been there the day before and he wanted to ask her if she could stay a little later the next time because he wanted the carpet in the living room shampooed."

"Since your doctor's appointment is tomorrow, would you mind if Kevin and I went to Paul's condo when the cleaning lady comes and talk to her instead of being there?"

"That's fine. I was going to suggest that Seth and I go over there also."

"That would be great. Maybe we can have a meal together there."

"That's fine."

Their orders arrived and they ate and talked. They left the restaurant at about 3:00 P.M. and headed back to Sara's."

At 4:30 P.M. Art's boss walked up to him and said "Art, you did a great job today. Would you be able to do the same thing tomorrow?"

"Sure, I can be here at whatever time you would like."

"I need you here at 8:00 A.M. I hope that isn't too early?"

"No, that's fine."

"You may go ahead and go home for the night and I'll see you in the morning. Again, great job Art."

Art left the bank feeling better about himself. He thought maybe if he continued to do well he'd get a promotion then after that Sara would want to go out with him. Then he thought about Rebecca. She had disrespected him so badly but Martha had spit in his face one day. He would show them. They would never disrespect him again.

He walked to a Chinese restaurant and ordered take out. He walked back to his car, got in and drove home. He thought about Rebecca the whole way home. He got home and went into where Rebecca was. She looked so innocent in her yellow polka dotted dress. "Well Becky, I'm back. It's time for supper." He got out some paper plates, and eating utensils. He pulled Becky over to the table and pushed her down in the chair. She was trembling. "Let's eat!"

After they finished supper Art looked at Rebecca. He cleaned up from supper and looked at the clock. It was 6:30 P.M. He grabbed Rebecca by the wrists and pulled her upstairs into that dark, cold room. "Becky, I know I promised to take you to the park and let you walk home from there but we have some unfinished business to attend to before we go. First

Murder When the Bell Tolls

of all I need to make a phone call, then I'll come back and we'll take care of that unfinished business."

"Art please just take me to the park so I can go home. I won't tell anyone about this. I promise."

"I'm sorry but I can't do that." He tied her hands to the table by the bed. "I'll be back shortly."

He left the room and went into his den. He called Jack. "Jack, it's Art. I want to make sure that you're still going to be at the park at 8:45 tonight."

"I really don't want to do this."

"Jack, you're not doing anything. I want you to dress in a policeman's uniform and walk through the park. Look for the woman I told you about. She'll be wearing a yellow polka dotted dress and she has strawberry blond hair. Just talk to her like a normal person. I'll do the rest."

"Alright, I'll be there, but this is the last time Art."

After he hung up with Jack, Art walked back where Rebecca was. The anger in his eyes made her tremble harder. He walked over to her and sat next to her on the bed. He reached up and grabbed the back of her hair and pulled her head back."Ow Art, that hurts."

"Good, it's supposed to. You know what our boss said to me today? He told me I did a great job and he wants me to come in even earlier tomorrow and do the same thing. He told me he was proud of me, something you never told me. You never even gave me the time of day. I always tried to be nice to you because I really liked you and you disrespected me with the looks of disgust you gave me. I even overheard you talking to other employees about me; well no more Becky, no more. You'll never disrespect me again."

"Art, what are you going to do?"

"Teach you a lesson you won't forget!" He grabbed her by her wrists and threw her on her stomach on the bed. He tied her hands to the headboard of the bed, then he removed his belt.

After listening to Becky scream for forty five minutes, Art untied her and turned her onto her back. She spit in his face and her slapped her across her face bloodying her nose and lip. She kept screaming and he hit her again. He walked out of the room to clear his head. He had one last thing to do to Becky before they left for the park.

He walked back into the bedroom where Rebecca lay crying. Thirty minutes later he untied her from the bed and pulled her up. "Now, we're going to go to the park and you can walk home from there."

Art pulled her out to his car and shoved her into the front seat. She cringed and bit her lip to keep from screaming. Art put a blindfold over Becky's eyes then they drove to the park. It was 8:30 P.M. when they got to the park. Art parked his car a block from the park and pulled Becky by the wrists to the park. He put her under a tree and untied her hands. He kissed her and whispered. "Goodbye Becky. I'll see you at work tomorrow."

She tried to hit him but since her eyes were covered she couldn't see him. He took her blindfold off. It was just getting dark outside so she saw him running the opposite direction than where his car was. It was chilly and she didn't see anyone at the park except a young couple all the way across the park. She wasn't sure she could walk that far. After being tied up for three days she was wobbly on her feet.

Art hid and waited to see what happened. Jack, dressed in a police officers' uniform was walking around the park. Becky saw him and went over to him. "Excuse me officer."

Jack stopped. He recognized the woman that Art was talking about. "Yes ma'am. How can I help you?"

"Officer I need to file a police report. I was held hostage for three days and..." Before she could finish what she was saying, the church bells began to ring and there was a shot fired. Becky slumped to the ground. She grabbed Jack's hand as she breathed her last breath. Others around the park heard the shot and someone immediately called 911.

Officers were there within a few minutes but Jack was nowhere to be found. He wasn't sure what to think. He wasn't sure whether or not Art had fired the shot or if it was someone else; all he knew was he had to get out of there.

Lt. Anderson and Officer Hand responded to the scene. They gathered the evidence and another officer took it back to the lab for analysis. Officer Hand talked to the witnesses and Lt. Anderson leaned over the body trying to figure out what happened. He cringed when he noticed ligature marks around the her wrists and bruises all over her body. The shooting matched the others but no one had ever been beaten before. Lt. Anderson thought maybe the killer had changed his motive or maybe this wasn't the same killer.

Mark got back to the station and went down to the lab. Since no one was on duty at the time, Mark tagged all the evidence and placed it in the box. He knew since Tom was off he was in charge for the evening. He knew he had to call Tom and let him know about the murder and knew Tom would let Seth know. He knew Seth couldn't leave Sara alone. He walked back into the tiny office off of the lab and called Tom.

"Tom Monroe speaking."

"Tom, it's Mark Anderson. Where are you?"

"I'm at Carrie's. I'm staying here for the next few days; why, what's up?"

"Tom, there's been another murder. A woman."

He gasped. "Where and when?"

"In the park. Witnesses say they heard shots around 9:00 P.M. They also said the church bells were ringing when the shots were fired. Tom, there's something else."

Tom could tell something was terribly wrong."

"What's wrong?"

"Tom, this woman was badly beaten and we're waiting for the results from the sexual assault kit to see if that was the case also."

"Oh dear! Does anyone know who this poor woman is?"

"Her name was Rebecca Segrest. She was a bank teller somewhere. Who's on call at the lab?"

"Dennis. I'll call him for you."

"Thanks Tom. Would you mind calling Seth for me?"

"Sure. I'll call him right away. Do you need me to come in and help with the evidence?"

"No. I can handle it. You enjoy your time with Carrie."

"Thanks for calling Mark. I'll call Seth right now."

Tom had a shocked look on his face when Carrie came back into the room. "Tom what's wrong?"

"There's been another murder."

Carrie gasped. "What poor man was killed this time?"

"It wasn't a man, it was a woman. She was badly beaten and they're not sure if anything else happened."

Carrie was stunned. "Who was it? Do they know?"

"Her name was Rebecca Segrest. They said she worked at a bank somewhere."

"Oh my! I knew her. She was a teller where I do my banking. She was so nice and wouldn't hurt a fly. Why would someone kill her?"

"We don't know but it looks like the same killer that murdered Paul, Peter, and three others."

"I need to call Sara anyway to let her know we got back from the doctors so why don't you talk to Seth then?"

"I better call them now."

Tom called over to Sara's. Sara answered. "Hello Sara, it's Tom Monroe."

"Hi Tom. Are you back from Carrie's appointment?"

"Yes and she did fine. Would you like to talk to her?"

"Yes I would."

"Hi Carrie. How you feeling?"

"I'm a little tired but am feeling pretty good. The doctor said I could go back to work Monday and I can't wait."

"That's great. I'm hoping my doctor will tell me I can go back Monday also. We'll all have to get together and have a soda and celebrate. Is Tom getting ready to go home tonight?"

"No. Actually, he's going to be staying with me until at least Tuesday. He wants to see how I do this weekend and how my first day back to school goes. I'm glad he's here. I feel better knowing that if something happens, he's here."

Sara smiled. "I bet you do. I know how you feel. I feel the same way about Seth."

"Speaking of Seth, Tom needs to talk to Seth. It's important."

"I'll give him the phone."

"Hi Tom; it's Seth. I understand you need to talk to me."

"Yes I do."

Seth could hear the anxiety and fear in his voice. "What is it Tom? Is it Carrie?"

"No. Seth, there's been another murder?"

"What? When?"

"At 9:00 tonight in the park. It matches the same MO except for two things?"

"Which are?"

"The victim was a woman and she was brutally beaten and possibly sexually assaulted."

"Oh my! He wasn't lying when he called Sara."

Murder When the Bell Tolls

Sara heard what Seth had said. She gasped then looked at Seth. She could tell by the look on his face something terrible had happened. Sara started shaking. Maggie looked at Seth and saw a look of horror on his face. She hugged Sara. "Are you with Carrie right now?"

"Yes. I decided to stay here with her until at least Tuesday. I want to see how she does over the weekend and after her first day back to work. Her doctor said she's to do limited activities until Monday. I thought I'd stay here and help, but somehow I feel like I need to be at the station helping with this case."

"Tom, stay with Carrie. I know you're on duty Wednesday, and Thursday then you're off for three days. You need your time off because you may be working longer hours the next few days until we can come up with more evidence. Carrie can stay with Sara and I on the days you're at work if that would make you feel better."

"It would. I don't want her over doing herself and getting sick. Seth, the young woman that was murdered looked a lot like Sara. Her name was Rebecca Segrest. Carrie knew her and said she worked as a teller at the US Bank."

"US Bank? Why does that ring a bell?" Sara started to panic.

"Seth, make sure you're with Sara at all times. I have a bad feeling about this."

"Thanks for the information Tom. If you find out anything more, please let me know. Take care of Carrie."

"I will. When is Sara's doctor's appointment?"

"Tomorrow morning. We're supposed to go to some friends of Maggie and Kevin's for dinner tomorrow. I'll ask Maggie if it's alright to take Carrie if you think you'll be working late."

"Thanks Seth. I appreciate it."

Seth hung up the phone and looked at Sara. She was trembling. "There's been another murder, hasn't there?"

"Yes Sara there has." He walked over to her and put his hands on her arms. Maggie and Kevin could see the compassion and concern in his eyes. "Sara, the victim was a woman who was badly beaten. She worked as a teller at a bank. I don't know much more than that." He didn't want to tell her it was possible the woman had been sexually assaulted until after Maggie and Kevin left. He thought he should talk to Sara about it privately.

"So, the message I got the other day was accurate about the victim being a woman?"

"Yes, I'm afraid so. Sara for the time being I won't let you out of my sight except for the obvious things."

"I understand. I'm really glad you're here all the time. I'll feel a lot safer."

"Maggie, Kevin, I know you heard me talking about Carrie. I'm concerned about her too. Tom may have to work late the next two nights and I was wondering if it would be alright for Carrie to be with us. I know we're supposed to go to Elizabeth and Carl's house tomorrow night for supper but I was wondering if they'd mind if Carrie came with us if necessary."

"I don't know why they'd mind. I can call them and ask them."

"Would you please."

"Sure. I'll do that right now."

Maggie called Elizabeth. "Hi Elizabeth, it's Maggie."

"Hi Maggie. How are you?"

"I'm doing okay. I called to ask you about tomorrow night."

"You're still coming aren't you?"

"Yes, but there's been a change in plans."

"Is Sara not up to coming?"

"No. She and Seth will be there too but I was wondering if you have room for one more person. Sara's friend Carrie may be coming along with us if you don't mind."

"Carrie, do I know her?"

"I'm not sure. She's Sara's friend that's recovering from cancer. She was the pretty woman with the big brimmed hat that came to the showing and funeral."

"Oh, I remember her. She's a teacher with Sara right?"

"Yes."

"Sure, she's more than welcome."

"Thanks Elizabeth. Carrie's a wonderful person and I know you'll really like her."

"Maggie, I detect a bit of anxiety in your voice; is there something going on? Is Sara alright dear?"

"Sara's alright. It's just there's been another murder in the park."

"Oh my. Who's the poor man this time?"

"That's just it. The victim wasn't a man. It was a woman and she'd been badly beaten. What scares me more than anything is the fact that Sara's been getting calls from someone claiming to be the killer and he told her the next victim would be a woman and it was. Sara's terrified"

"I'd imagine she would be."

"Elizabeth, thank you for saying it's alright if Carrie comes with us tomorrow night. She had her last treatment for cancer today and her doctor wants her to rest until Monday when she can go back to teaching. She lives alone and her fiancé Sergeant Tom Monroe of the NYSPD is on duty tomorrow night. He's one of the lead officers on these murder cases."

Elizabeth gasped. "Oh my, I had no idea. Well bring her along with you. We'd love to get to know her better. Give Sara a hug for us and Maggie, we love both you and Kevin. If there is anything you need, don't hesitate to ask."

"Thanks Liz. We'll see you tomorrow night."

After Maggie got off the phone with Elizabeth she told Seth and Sara it was alright to take Carrie with them to the Harris'. Sara was still shaking. Maggie hugged her. "Sara honey, I can't imagine what you're feeling right now."

"I'm just numb. I can't believe this happened."

"I know. There have been two murders since we've been here. Are you going to be alright?"

"Yes. Maggie, Kevin, Seth, would any of you mind if I changed into my night clothes? I'm starting to feel a little dizzy again."

"Go ahead and change clothes."

As Sara walked back to her bedroom she started sobbing. She went into her room and changed clothes. She sat on the chair she had in front of her dresser and cried harder. When she didn't come out after about fifteen minutes Maggie said "I better go check on Sara. She may need some extra help."

When Maggie went into Sara's room she found her weeping at her dresser; she rubbed her hand over Sara's back. "It's alright to be scared Sara. I would be too."

"Thanks Maggie. Would you mind helping me walk out to where everyone else is? I'm feeling a little unsteady on my feet?"

Maggie helped Sara into the living room. Seth could tell she'd been crying. He wanted to hold her and comfort her but didn't. Kevin got up, walked over to Sara and said "Are you alright Sara?"

"Yes. Thank you for asking."

"Sara honey, what time is your doctor's appointment tomorrow?"

"It's at 10:00 A.M."

"Well, why don't we come by here at 8:45 A.M. and we can leave here at 9:15 A.M. That will give us plenty of time to get there. After the appointment, depending on how you feel, we can grab a bite to eat somewhere, then come back here so you can rest then get ready to go to Elizabeth and Carl's. How does that sound?"

"That sounds fine."

"Good."

"Maggie, I think maybe you and I should get ready to go back to the hotel. Sara's really tired and I think maybe she and Seth should talk privately."

"I agree. Sara, Seth we're going to take off now. We'll see both of you tomorrow morning. Sara honey, I hope you can get some sleep. If you need us, just call."

"Goodnight Maggie, Kevin. We'll see both of you tomorrow."

"Goodnight you two."

After Maggie and Kevin left, Sara walked over to the overstuffed chair in the living room, sat down in it and cried. Seth walked over to her and rubbed his hand across her back. She reached out to him and hugged him for support. "Seth, I hoped the message I received wasn't true. I can't believe it happened again. Is the killer ever going to stop?"

Once Sara stopped crying so hard Seth looked at her with compassion, then put his hands on her arms. "Sara, there's something else I need to tell you about the murder tonight."

Sara could tell that this wasn't going to be easy to hear or for Seth to tell her. "Okay Seth, what is it?"

"Sara I don't know how to put this gently so I'll just say it. The woman who was murdered not only was beaten but may have been sexually assaulted also."

"Oh my!" Sara was stunned. "Who was she Seth."

"Her name was Rebecca Segrest. She worked at the US Bank."

Sara gasped. "Did you say US Bank?"

"Yes. Why, does that mean something to you?"

"Only that it's where I used to bank but changed banks because of.." She couldn't finish.

"Sara, what is it? What are you not telling me?"

Sara started crying. "Seth, it's just that US Bank is where Art works."

Murder When the Bell Tolls

"Art? That's why it sounded familiar. I'm going to have Tom send some men over to talk to the other employees at that bank and see what they can tell us about him."

Sara started crying harder. Seth hugged Sara and she leaned against his chest and cried harder. He knew now Art was a person of interest in the murders.

Art rushed home and turned on his television. He wanted to see what they were saying about the murders. He smiled when he heard the reporter say the police were baffled as to why these murders had been committed and who was responsible.

He kicked off his shoes, headed upstairs, turned the television on in his bedroom, changed his clothes and got ready for bed. He wanted to keep up with the latest on the top news story. His smile turned to anger when he saw pictures of the people in the crowd that had gathered. He saw Jack standing there in his police uniform then saw another officer ask him to assist in getting clues. He knew he had to do something about Jack; he wasn't sure what though.

After changing clothes he went into his den and finished a letter he was writing. After he finished the letter he walked into his bedroom, set his alarm for 6:00 A.M., then got into bed and went to sleep.

Carrie was really upset because she knew the victim. She couldn't understand how someone could do that. She looked at Tom. He was on the phone calling Dennis to come into the lab. Once he finished his call he looked at Carrie. He walked over to her, embraced her and held her. She was shaking. "Tom, if you have to go into work I understand."

"No. Mark has things under control. Seth told me to enjoy my time off and to enjoy being with you right now; I'm really enjoying being with you right now. How you feeling?"

"I'm just a little dizzy; which is normal. What isn't normal is I'm starving. I know we just had supper a few hours ago but I could really go for a snack of some sort."

Tom smiled. "I was hoping you'd say that. I could use a snack myself. I noticed you had everything I need to make us some ice cream sundaes. Would you like for me to make us some ice cream sundaes?"

"That sounds good."

"Great. What flavor do you want?"

"Strawberry."

"Strawberry it is. I think I'm make mine strawberry too."

He leaned down and kissed her then fixed the sundaes. He brought them into where Carrie was sitting and they ate their ice cream. It was 10:15 P.M. They decided they wanted to watch a movie then call it a night. Tom put a movie on and they sat together on the sofa.

After they finished their ice cream, Tom got up and cleaned up the dishes then went back and joined Carrie on the sofa. She leaned against him while the movie was on. The movie was over at midnight. Tom leaned over and kissed Carrie.

Carrie smiled at Tom. "Tom, if you don't mind, I think I'm going to go to bed. I'm really tired."

"I don't mind. I think I will too. Let me walk you back to your room."

They walked back to Carrie's room. Tom hugged and kissed Carrie. He watched as she got into bed then he walked down the hall to his room. He smiled while he changed his clothes. He set his alarm for 6:00 A.M. then got into bed and went to sleep.

Seth and Sara sat in the living room. Sara was still very upset. They started talking. "Sara, you going to be okay?"

"I think so. I just feel sick to my stomach. I never thought it would happen." Sara started sobbing. Seth got up and rubbed his hand on her back.

"Sara, this isn't your fault."

"I know it's not my fault but I feel like maybe I could have done something more to help that poor girl."

"Like what? You never knew it was going to happen or even to whom. Don't blame yourself."

"Seth, I'm really hurting. I need some medicine. Would you mind helping me get into my bedroom where my medicine is?"

Seth helped her into her bedroom. While she was taking her medicine, Seth pulled the covers back on her bed. She came out of the bathroom and had tears in her eyes. "Sara, why don't you try and rest?"

"I'm not sure I can rest. I'm so nervous."

"Would it help if I slept in the living room?"

"Yes it would. Could you help me walk to my bed?"

Seth helped her. She got into bed and pulled up the covers. Seth put his hand on her shoulder. "Sara, I'm going to go change clothes then I'll be right out there if you need me."

"Goodnight Seth, and thank you."

"Goodnight Sara."

Seth walked back to his room, grabbed a couple of the files on the case, changed his clothes, then walked out to the living room. He sat in the overstuffed chair and studied the files, trying to find a connection to all of the murders. At midnight he turned out the light and fell asleep.

At around 4:00 A.M. Seth heard Sara up crying and vomiting in her bathroom. He walked back to her room and knocked on her door. "Sara, you alright?"

"Yes. I'm just a little nauseated. I'll be alright. Thanks for asking Seth."

"Sara, do you need my help?"

"No. I'm going back to bed."

"If you need me just call."

"Thanks Seth."

Seth was worried about Sara. He knew something was bothering her and felt it had something to do with the murder cases, but he wasn't sure. He sat down in the chair but dozed. He couldn't sleep. He was really worried about Sara.

Sara, tossed and turned. Every time she closed her eyes she could see Art. It made her even more nauseated. She cried thinking about what he had done to her. She couldn't help wonder if he was in any way connected to the murders.

Art's alarm went off at 6:00. He got up, showered, shaved, and got dressed. He was whistling and singing. He went downstairs, turned the television on to watch the news and eat a bowl of cereal. He smiled when he heard the police still had no leads at all. He smirked, then laughed. He walked out to his car, got in and drove to work.

Once he got to work he was greeted by his boss who was somber and visibly upset. "Hello Art. I'm glad you could make it in."

"What's wrong sir? You look upset?"

"Art, I'm sorry to inform you Rebecca Segrest will no longer be a teller here?"

"Why not. She was fantastic."

"I know; everyone loved her but she was murdered last night in the park. It looks like someone held her prisoner, then brutally beat her and left her in the park, where she was shot in the back of the head."

Art gasped. "That's terrible sir. She was a nice woman."

"Art, I hate to dump all of this on you but I have to replace Rebecca and you've shown me you're capable of taking over her duties. The job is yours if you want it."

Art was jumping for joy inside. He smiled, then said "Yes, I want the job. Thank you for allowing me to have a chance to show you what I can do. I won't let you down, I promise."

"Art, we're taking up a collection for flowers for Rebecca in case you're interested. She didn't have any family around here and her parents are elderly. The company is authorizing me to send them money to pay for travel expenses and hotel accommodations. I need for you to wire the money through Western Union."

"Sure, whatever I need to do sir."

Art's boss gave him the draft to send to Rebecca's parents. Art went down the street to wire them the money. He smirked and whistled as he walked.

※

Tom woke up at 5:00 A.M. He showered, shaved, and put on his uniform. At 6:00 he heard Carrie moving around in her bedroom. He walked into the kitchen and made a pot of coffee. Carrie walked into the kitchen still wearing her gown. She smiled at Tom. "Good morning Tom."

"Good morning Carrie. I got a pot of coffee brewing. What would you like for breakfast?"

"Tom, you don't have to cook breakfast."

"I know, but I want to."

"How about waffles?"

"Sounds good."

Tom fixed breakfast and they sat down and ate. After breakfast was over it was 7:00 A.M. Carrie started cleaning off the table and started washing the dishes. Tom got behind her and hugged and kissed her. She smiled. "Carrie, I love you."

"I love you too Tom."

"What's on your agenda for today?"

Murder *When the Bell Tolls*

"I need to do laundry because I want to wear a particular outfit to go with Seth and Sara tonight."

"You go slow when you do the laundry. I don't want you to overdo it."

"I won't. I promise; besides you need another clean uniform for tomorrow. Do you think you'll be here for lunch?"

"I'm not sure. It depends on how things go with this case."

"I understand."

At 7:30 A.M. Tom hugged and kissed Carrie, then said "Carrie, I have to leave for work. I'll call and check on you throughout the day. I'll let you know if I can be here for lunch. Please don't overdo it."

"I won't. Please be careful Tom."

"I will. I'll see you later. I love you Carrie."

"I'll see you. I love you too Tom."

Seth got up at 6:00 A.M. and walked back to Sara's bedroom. He looked in and saw her sleeping. He could tell she was restless but at least she was sleeping. He walked into the kitchen and got himself a glass of milk then started a pot of coffee. He changed clothes and went back into the kitchen. He heard Sara get up about thirty minutes later.

Sara walked into the kitchen. "Good morning Seth."

"Good morning Sara. How you feeling?"

"Better. Thank you for checking on me earlier this morning. I was really having a rough night."

"I know. I heard you every time you got up. I wanted to help you but I wasn't sure what to do."

"That's sweet Seth. I appreciate your concern. Would you mind if I took a shower and got dressed before I fixed breakfast?"

"That would be fine."

Sara walked into her bedroom and got ready to shower. She couldn't shake that uneasy feeling. After she was done with her shower, she walked into the kitchen where Seth was reading the newspaper. "Sara, since you had such a rough night last night why don't we just have a light breakfast and you can rest a little before Maggie and Kevin get here?"

"That sounds good."

They decided to have cereal and toast. Seth got out the bread and the toaster. He made the toast and Sara got out the cereal bowls and milk. They sat down and ate. Seth could tell something was still bothering Sara. He reached across the table and clasped her hand. "Sara, I know something's bothering you. Do you want to talk about it?"

"I do want to talk about it but I'm just not ready. I just want to get through this day and the dinner tonight."

"I understand Sara. Can you answer me this? Does this have anything to do with Art?"

"Yes it does. Art and my father both."

"Sara, before we go I need to call Tom and have him send some men to the bank, remember?"

"Yes I do."

At 8:30 A.M. Seth called Tom. "Tom, it's Seth. I have some information, about this case, that I thought you might want to know about."

"What is it Seth?"

"Sara informed me late last night the reason US Bank sounded familiar to me was because it's the bank where Art works."

Tom gasped. "I remember that. Carrie told me that too."

"Tom, you need to send a couple of plain clothes officers over to talk to everyone at the bank, including Art to find out what you can. I have a feeling Art's involved somehow."

"I'll do that. Seth, how's Sara?"

"She's shaken up. She had a rough night and she's a little nervous about going to the doctor today."

"I bet. Carrie was nervous yesterday. Carrie told me you and Sara are going to take her with you to Elizabeth and Carl's house tonight for supper."

"That's right we are."

"I'm glad. When I got in this morning I had tons of paperwork on my desk and I'm in the process of..." He stopped. "Hold on a minute Seth. I'm being paged to the lab."

"Tom, whenever you get the results back from the evidence, give me a call on my cell phone."

"I will. What time are you leaving to go to Sara's doctor?" We are leaving at 9:15 A.M. Her appointment is at 10:00 Maggie and Kevin are taking us to get something to eat for lunch then we're going back to Sara's so that she can rest until it's time to leave tonight. I'm glad. After the night she had last night, she could use the rest."

"Seth, take care of Sara. I have a bad feeling about this killer. I really do."

"So do I Tom."

He hung up the phone and walked over to Sara. She was cleaning up and getting ready to go to the doctor. "Sara, why don't you sit down and rest until Maggie and Kevin get her? I can finish up."

"Thanks Seth."

Sara sat down on the sofa and leaned her head back. She closed her eyes and dozed off to sleep.

At 8:45 there was a knock at the door. Seth opened it and whispered "Hello Maggie, Kevin."

"Hello Seth. Why are we whispering?"

"Sara's asleep in the living room. She's ready to go but she had such a rough night she didn't get much sleep."

"If she isn't up to going tonight we can make it for tomorrow night?"

"She wants to go tonight she just needs rest. Maybe when we come back here after lunch she can get some rest."

They walked into the house. About ten minutes later Sara awoke. "Hello Maggie, Kevin. I'm sorry I was asleep when you got here. I didn't get much sleep last night so I thought I'd try to get some rest before we go to the doctor."

"That's alright. You need to rest. Are you ready to go to the doctor or do you need some time to finish getting ready?"

"I just need to get my shoes on and grab a light jacket."

Maggie could tell Sara wasn't feeling well. She wasn't acting like herself. "Sara, you sure you're alright?"

"Yes, I'm alright."

"Sara, would you like for me to go in with you when you see the doctor?"

"Yes. I want you to make sure I get his instructions right."

"That's fine."

They got to the doctor's office and walked inside. There wasn't anyone else waiting so Sara knew she was next. She signed in and waited for her name to be called.

About five minutes later Dixie called her back to an examination room. "Good morning Sara. How you feeling today?"

"Good morning Dixie. I'm a little jittery today. I didn't get much sleep last night."

"Really? Any particular reason?"

Sara looked over at Maggie. "Um, not really."

"Well, I need you to remove your shirt and slacks so we can check your wound."

"Okay."

Once Sara had removed her shirt and slacks, Dixie gave her a sheet to cover up with. Sara started trembling before Dixie even left the room. Dixie whispered "I'll listen if you want to talk?"

"Thanks Dixie."

"The doctor will be here shortly. Try and relax. Everything will be alright."

Two plain clothed police officers and a uniformed officer went to the US Bank. Art was at the Western Union office wiring the money to Rebecca's family when the police got there. The officers talked to all of the employees and one officer was talking to Art's boss when he got back.

When Art got back he talked to another teller and asked "What's going on? Who are those men?"

"Art, they're police officers from the NYSPD. They're asking questions about Rebecca and her relationships with others here and outside of here."

"Really? What were some of the questions they asked?"

"Well they wanted to know if there was anyone here who was upset with her or any customers who may have had a problem with her."

"Oh really? I don't know of anyone who would've wanted to hurt her."

"Neither do I."

"I'm sure the police will want to talk to you Art."

"I don't know what I can tell them but I'll talk to them."

Mark walked over to Art. "Sir, is your name Art?"

"Yes it is. What can I do for you officer?"

"I need to ask you a few questions about one of your co-workers; Rebecca Segrest."

"What would you like to know?"

Mark asked Art all kinds of questions, then the officers left the bank and headed back to the station. Art breathed a sigh of relief when they were gone.

While the officers were at the bank, Tom went down to the lab and talked to Dennis. "Hey Tom, I was just getting ready to call upstairs and talk to you."

"You were? Why?"

"I got back the reports on all the evidence so far in these murder cases. The two sets of footprints that were found at

Sara's home belong to someone with a men's size 11 shoe. The footprints at the scene of the murders belong to someone with a men's size 9."

"The size 9 shoe probably belongs to the man of many disguises. He's been at all of the crime scenes."

"That's not all. The DNA sample from the piece of cloth you gave me that Seth found on the bush at Sara's and a DNA sample from the latest victim's clothes are a match. We don't know from whom but we do know it's from a male."

"So that tells me the killer's stalking Sara for some reason."

"Tom, there's one more thing."

"What is it Dennis?"

"The sexual assault kit from our last victim came back positive."

"Oh no! I have to let Seth know as soon as possible. Sara's in extreme danger. Thanks for the information Dennis. Let me know if you find out anything else."

"I will. Tom, could you tell me why you think Sara's in danger?"

"She caught a glimpse of the shooter as he fled the scene."

"Oh, now I understand. I know Seth will take good care of her. I think he really likes her."

"I know he does. Sara's a very nice woman."

"I know. My daughter really likes her. She said she's so understanding and so nice. My daughter has Carrie as a teacher too and really likes her too."

Tom smiled. "Dennis, you know Carrie and I are getting married late in the summer or early fall."

"I didn't know that. Congratulations. I really like Carrie. How's she doing with her cancer?"

"She had her last treatment yesterday so she's tired and weak but feeling better. I'm staying with her for a few days until after she goes back to work. I want to see how she does after her first day back. She and Sara are supposed to go back on the same day."

"I'm so happy for both of you. I know the rest of the officers like Carrie and Sara a lot."

"I know. Dennis, I was only married for a short time once. My wife was killed in 9/11, remember. I think that's why we're so close. Carrie's the woman I never dreamed I'd find. She's everything I want in a woman and more. I know Carrie's had a rough time the past two years. She lost her husband to cancer eighteen months ago and four months ago she was diagnosed with cancer herself. She told me she spent a year taking care of her sick husband and trying to work. I truly love her."

"I'm so glad to see you happy. This job can get depressing and every bit of happiness you find you need to enjoy it while you can."

"Seth told me that the other day."

"He's right. You're only forty-five years old and you need to enjoy your life while you can."

"I will now that I have someone to share it with."

"How old is Carrie Tom?"

"She's forty-four. I really need to get upstairs and find out if my officers found out anything from the place where our latest victim worked."

"Where was that?"

"US Bank. Why?"

"I was just wondering. I found this in the pocket of her dress."

Dennis handed Tom a piece of paper which read "Remember to be at work at 8:30 A.M. on Wednesday. Boss has big job."

Tom gasped. "This may belong to the last person to see her alive."

"Or to the person who murdered her or both."

"Thanks Dennis; this is a huge help."

As soon as Tom got upstairs Scott and two other officers came in. They reported to Tom. "Well, we talked to everyone at the bank and no one can think of anyone who would want to hurt Ms. Segrest."

"I don't know about that Scott. That man I interviewed seemed a little distant and suspicious."

"Who was that?"

"Let's see. Let me check my notes." He flipped through his tiny notebook. "Here it is. His name's Art Hunter. He's a teller there. He wasn't there when we first got there because his boss sent him to wire some money to Ms. Segrest family to help with traveling expenses."

"Art's boss told me the last time he saw Ms. Segrest was on Saturday when he left the bank at 1:00 P.M. The bank was open until noon then he and Ms. Segrest closed up for the day."

"We need to find out all we can on Art Hunter, his boss, and on our latest victim. Let's get to work."

Sara and Maggie were waiting on the doctor. It wasn't long before he walked into the room. "Good morning Sara, Maggie."

"Good morning Dr."

"Sara, Dixie tells me you aren't feeling well today. Is it because of pain or is it something else?"

"Some of its pain but some of it's something else."

"Let me have a look at your wound."

Dr. Martin used a small pin light to check the wound, then he pushed on the skin around the wound. Sara cringed. "It's still a little tender there I see. That's normal for a wound that deep. It's healing well though." He saw a scar below the wound she had. He touched it and she flinched and tried to move his hand. "Sara, I'm sorry. I wasn't aware that scar was sensitive. It's a little inflamed. You need to use some of the ointment on it too."

He finished his exam. "Sara, I'll step out of the room while you put your blouse and slacks on then I'll come back in and talk with you."

He stepped out of the room and Maggie helped Sara get her blouse back on. The doctor came back in. "Well Sara, your wound looks pretty good. It's healing like it should. You need to continue on your medication for another week, and put ointment on that other scar. Your medication will help reduce the inflammation in your other scar."

"Will I be able to go back to work?"

"Yes you may go back to work on Monday, unless the pain gets worse."

"Thank you doctor."

"Maggie, when are you and Kevin leaving to go back home?"

"We're leaving Sunday evening."

"While you're here I want you to make sure Sara doesn't overdo it. She's healing but if she overdoes it she won't be able to go back to work for another week."

"I'll make sure she takes it easy."

"Good. I hate to ask you this but could you step out in the hallway so that I can speak with Sara alone."

"Okay. Sara, I'll be right outside the door if you need me."

"Okay Maggie."

"Sara, I'm a little worried about that other scar you have. It looks terrible and I've never seen a scar like that before. It looks like you were hit with something extremely sharp. I can tell something's bothering you and you can't talk about it in front of Maggie; that's why I had her step out of the room. Does this older scar have anything to do with what's bothering you?"

"It has everything to do with what's bothering me."

"Can you tell me about it?"

"No. It's too painful."

"Alright but remember I'm a doctor and I'll listen."

"Thank you doctor."

"I won't keep you any longer. I want to see you back a week from Friday after you get off of work. Dixie will set up the appointment for you."

"But I don't get off until about 3:00 P.M."

"That's alright. My office is open and I'm here until 6:00 P.M. If you want to talk to me just call. Don't overdo it."

"I won't. I promise."

"Alright then. I'll see next Friday."

"I'll see you and thank you doctor."

Sara met Maggie. "Sara, good luck going back to work and remember what the doctor said, Don't overdo it. I'll see you next Friday at 4:15 P.M."

"I'll see you then and thank you for your help."

Carrie was upset over the murder of Rebecca but excited about being able to go back to work on Monday. She picked up the phone and called Nancy. "Nancy Boyd speaking."

"Nancy, it's Carrie White."

"Carrie, what a nice surprise. How are you doing?"

"I'm doing okay. I had my last treatment yesterday so I'm a little weak and tired but otherwise doing alright."

"That's great. Are you going to be able to come back to work?"

"Yes; that's one of the reasons I'm calling. My doctor has released me to come back to work on Monday."

"That's great. The kids will have one of their favorite teachers back."

Carrie smiled. "Thanks Nancy. There's something else I wanted to tell you."

"What's that Carrie."

"I'm getting married."

Nancy gasped. "Oh my gosh! That's wonderful. When's the wedding?"

"Either in late summer or early fall. It depends on when Tom can get his vacation."

"Tom? Is that the lucky man?"

"Yes. Sergeant Tom Monroe with the NYSPD. I think you met him at Sara's house."

"I did. He seems like such a nice man."

"Nancy he's everything I want in a man. He's staying with me for a few days because my doctor says I need a lot of rest if I want to come back to work on Monday. Tom's working at least the next two days and he's off over the weekend then he goes back to work on Monday. He'll probably be working long hours though as you probably know there's been another murder."

"I saw that on the news. That poor woman."

"Tom is one of the lead officers on the case and since Seth is staying with Sara twenty four hours a day Tom's in the field. He and Seth work as a team on this though."

"He sounds like a pretty special man."

"He is. I love him dearly."

"I can tell. Have you talked to Sara at all?"

"We talk almost every day since Seth and Tom are working on this case together. Sara's been having a really hard time with that wound on her side."

"What wound?"

"Where she was shot."

Nancy gasped. "I forgot about that."

"How's she holding up emotionally."

"Nancy, Sara blames herself for Paul's death."

"Paul's death wasn't her fault."

"Everyone knows that. I think she knows that too; she just can't deal with it though. I can tell she's coping with it a little more each day. Seth's helping her with it. I think Seth has fallen in love with Sara and I think she's falling in love with him but she's afraid to show it. I think she's afraid she'll lose him or that it's too soon after Paul's death to get involved with someone else. I know I've only known Tom for a couple of weeks and when he asked me to marry him I said yes. For us, it was love at first sight."

"I'm so happy for you."

"Nancy, I know you're busy but I wanted to let you know I'll return on Monday. I think Sara's supposed to be back then too. She had a doctors' appointment today; she'll know after that. I'll see you on Monday."

"I'll see you then. Congratulations again."

Carrie hung up the phone and decided to start doing the laundry. She went into Tom's room and got his dirty clothes and uniform and put them in a laundry basket. She gathered her clothes. She sorted them and put the dark clothes in the washer. She sat down on the couch to watch a television program that she liked. She dozed off to sleep. She was awakened when the phone rang at 11:30 A.M.

She sleepily answered the phone "Carrie honey, it's Tom. Are you alright?"

"Yes. I must have fallen asleep on the sofa after I put a load of clothes in the washer."

"Carrie don't overdo it."

"I won't."

"Honey, would you like some company for lunch? I'll bring us something from that fancy restaurant you like. I can order it now and it'll be ready in about forty five minutes."

"That sounds good. How about some lasagna and a salad for me?"

"Okay. I'll be there in about an hour okay?"

"I'll be here."

Carrie smiled as she walked back to her laundry room to take care of the clothes. She straightened things up a little bit, put on some perfume, then went into the living room and sat down to watch television.

An hour later Tom knocked on Carrie's door. She answered the door with a huge smile on her face. Tom kissed her then went into the house, put the food on the table and embraced Carrie and kissed her again. "Carrie, you feeling better?"

"I am now. Tom, that food smells so good and I'm hungry."

"Good. You need to eat to keep your strength up."

"I set the table in the kitchen. Let's get something to drink and we can eat."

Tom opened the refrigerator and got out the iced tea Carrie had made earlier in the day. He poured each of them a glass and they sat down to eat. "How are things going at work Tom?"

"It's going alright. We've gotten several leads in these murder cases. Carrie, I'm so glad Seth and Sara are going to help you the next couple of nights because it'll probably be 10:00 P.M. before I get here on those nights. I hate having to do that but it's my job."

Carrie leaned over the table and took Tom's hand. "I understand. You're a police officer and I know it's your job; when I'm teaching I put in a lot of long hours grading papers and working on class work, so do Sara and Peggy. I understand there's a serial killer out there you and Seth and the rest of the NYSPD are trying to catch. It's alright. I know I feel safer knowing you're protecting me and other citizens. I love you and always will."

"Carrie, I love you too."

They finished eating and Tom helped Carrie clean up. "Tom, I'll be right back. I have to take care of the laundry."

"Let me help you."

He walked to the laundry room with Carrie and helped her with the clothes. He embraced her and kissed her. He looked at his watch. "Carrie honey, I have to leave in a few minutes. I have to go talk to Jack Lake at the grocery store."

"Jack Lake? Why? Do you think he's involved in these brutal murders?"

"We aren't sure. Seth asked me to talk to him. We have reason to believe he knows something about the murders."

"I can't believe that Jack would kill anyone. His cousin Art Hunter, that's a different story."

Tom was shocked. That was the second time that day he'd heard Art's name mentioned when it came to the murders.

He held Carrie close to him. "I really hate to leave you but I have to get going. Are you going with Seth and Sara tonight?"

"I think so. Sara's supposed to call me with the arrangements. Here's my keys to get in the house in case I'm not here when you get off work."

"Okay, but why don't you call me on my cell phone around 10:00 P.M. and I'll have some idea when I'll be getting off work; maybe I can come get you and bring you home, besides I want to take you on a carriage ride at night."

She smiled at him. "I'll call you at 10:00." She kissed him.

"I have to go now. I'll talk to you later. Have fun tonight. I love you. Goodbye Carrie."

"Goodbye Tom. I love you. Please be careful."

When Sara, Seth, Maggie, and Kevin left the doctors' office, Seth put his arm around Sara's back as they walked to the car. Sara didn't seem to mind and Maggie and Kevin smiled at both of them.

Kevin drove to the restaurant they'd decided on and they went inside. Sara usually sat with Maggie so they could talk but for the meal she decided to sit next to Seth. They ordered their food. "Sara, you haven't said much. Are you alright?"

"Yes. I'm just thinking about what the doctor said."

"Did he tell you you could go back to work?"

"Yes. He said if I didn't overdo it I could go back to work on Monday. He wants me to keep taking my medication and putting ointment on my wound and on an older scar that he seems to thinks may be inflamed also."

"Well that's good."

"Yes it is." Sara couldn't stop thinking about how she got that scar. She trembled when she thought about it. She wondered if that was what Rebecca had suffered at the hand of her killer.

Sara was looking around the deli type restaurant and saw Jack sitting alone in a corner booth. She wanted to get up and go talk to him but wasn't sure if she should. She knew Jack knew her secret and she felt as if he was hiding something else that was important in solving Paul's murder.

Sara kept looking over at Jack. He looked so lost. "Maggie, Seth, Kevin, would you excuse me a minute. I see a friend that I'd like to talk to for a few minutes."

"Sure go ahead."

Seth turned around in his chair so that he could watch where she was going. Sara walked over to Jack. "Hello Jack." She said sweetly.

He smiled. "Hello Sara. How are you doing?"

"I'm doing alright. I miss Paul but I'm trying to move on. Are you here by yourself?"

"Yes. I needed to get away from everything for awhile but I hoped a friend would join me for lunch."

Murder When the Bell Tolls

"I'm here with Paul's parents and another friend, why don't you come join us at our table?"

"Thank you Sara. I'd like that."

Jack got up and walked with Sara to her table. "Everyone this is my friend Jack. He's the manager at the Shop N Save. Would anyone mind if he joins us at the table for lunch?"

"No. Have a seat Jack." Seth, Kevin and Jack were talking and Sara and Maggie were talking. Their food came and they talked while they ate.

At 1:30 P.M. Jack said "My lunch time is over. I have to get back to the store. I enjoyed having lunch with friends. Maggie, Kevin, Seth, I enjoyed meeting all of you."

"It was nice meeting you too."

"Kevin, when are you and Maggie leaving to go back to New Jersey?"

"Sunday evening but we'll come back several times to see Sara."

"Good. We'll have to get together when you do. Good-bye everyone."

"Goodbye."

Kevin paid the bill and they left to go back to Sara's. When they got there Sara noticed the light blinking on her answering machine. She and Seth listened to the messages together. One was from Carrie and the other was from Tom.

"Sara, I can tell you're tired. Why don't you rest for awhile?"

"I will but I need to talk to Seth and I need to call Nancy and Carrie first."

"Alright. What do you have to do to get ready; just change clothes?"

"No. I want to shower and put clean clothes on."

"Okay."

Sara called Nancy and told her that she'd be going back to work on Monday and Nancy was thrilled. Then she called Carrie and told her what time they'd pick her up that evening and what everyone else was going to wear.

After Sara had finished making her calls she looked at Seth and said "Seth, can we go somewhere and talk in private for a few minutes?"

"Sure."

"Maggie, Kevin will you please excuse us for a few minutes?"

"No problem."

Seth and Sara went into the four seasons room. Seth could tell something was really bothering Sara. "Seth, has anyone checked out Jack yet?"

"I think so, why?"

"I get the feeling he's hiding something that might break these murder cases wide open. He's always been nice to me but lately he's been extra nice. I really think he knows something."

"Sara, when I call Tom back I'll tell him to talk to Jack or have another officer talk to Jack and see what we find out. Are you alright Sara?"

"Yes. It's just being around Jack triggered some emotions I didn't know I had."

Seth was really concerned. "Sara, has Jack ever hurt you?"

"No. He wouldn't hurt anyone."

"Okay. That's all I need to know. I better call Tom. I'll call him from my cell phone."

Seth called Tom at the station. Tom told him all of the information he had. Seth's face became ghostly white. "Seth, there's more. Do you remember that piece of cloth you gave me? The one you found on the bush at Sara's."

"Yes, I remember it well."

"Well the DNA from that and the DNA from a smudge on our last victim's clothes and from the semen are a match. That means the killer is stalking Sara."

Seth gasped, then looked at Sara. "Seth, there are at least two people involved in the murders. They are working as a team. Do you want me to put more men in the neighborhood so Sara's more protected?"

"Yes, that would be a big help. Tom I have favor to ask. I was wondering if you could talk to Jack Lake. He's the manager at the Shop N Save. I have reason to believe he knows something about the murders."

"Is he on duty now?"

"Yes, he gets off at 6:00 P.M."

"I'll go talk to him myself Seth. Thank you for helping take care of Carrie."

"No problem. Let us know when you get back tonight. Call me on my cell phone."

"I will. Thanks again."

Murder When the Bell Tolls

After Seth finished on his cell phone he walked over to Sara and put his hands on her arms. "Sara, Tom is going to talk to Jack himself."

"Good. I know Tom will know what to say to him." Seth looked at Sara horrified. "Seth, is something else going on? Are there any leads on the murders?"

Seth didn't know what to say to her. "Sara, I think there's something I better tell you."

"What is it Seth?"

"Do you remember Sunday when you saw someone looking into your bedroom window?"

"Yes I do. It scared me to death. Did you find out who it was?"

"Not exactly but what we did find out could break these murder cases wide open. Sara, after that happened I looked around the outside of the house after church and I found a set of footprints and a piece of cloth. The footprints don't match the footprints at the scene of the crime but the DNA off of the fabric matched other evidence in this last case."

"Well, that's good isn't it."

"Well yes and no."

"I don't understand."

"Sara, the DNA found on the piece of fabric matches some DNA found on our last victims dress but she was sexually assaulted and the DNA from the semen was also a match."

Sara screamed then started to cry. "So that means the killer is after me?"

"Yes, I'm afraid so. Tom's going to increase security in the neighborhood."

Maggie and Kevin ran into where Sara and Seth were. They found Sara with tears running down her face, crying and being comforted by Seth. "Seth, Sara, what's wrong?"

"Everything's alright. Tom just gave me some very important information on these murder cases and…"

"He also gave us some information that I needed to know about and it wasn't what I expected. It shocked me that's all."

"Are you sure?"

"Yes Maggie. I think I'm going to rest in my bedroom for a little while if you don't mind."

"We don't mind; in fact, I'm glad you're going to rest. Do you need some help?"

"I think I can handle this but thanks for the offer."

Sara walked into her bedroom and laid down on her bed. She closed her eyes and drifted off to sleep.

Maggie checked on Sara several times doing the day and so did Seth. "Seth, the information that Tom gave you about the murders; will it help find Paul's killer?"

"Yes, I believe it will. We believe there are two people involved. One is the set-up person and the other is the actual killer. I'm not sure how the victims are selected but I'm working on that. At first we thought it was just random but after this last murder we believe the victims are targeted and we now believe Sara's in a lot more danger."

Maggie and Kevin both gasped. "Why?"

"We have reason to believe the killer is stalking Sara."

"What?" Kevin exclaimed.

"DNA from the latest crime scene matches some DNA I found outside of Sara's bedroom window."

They both gasped. "Do they know who the DNA belongs to?"

"Only a male. Tom's going to increase security around the neighborhood and he and other officers are out talking to witnesses. We'll catch this team of killers because one or both of them will make a mistake."

At 4:00 P.M. Sara finally got up and walked out to where everyone was. "Hello everyone."

"Hello Sara. Do you feel better now?"

"Yes I do. Maggie I was wondering if you could help me get ready for tonight. I need you to help me pick out something to wear then if you wouldn't mind staying in the room while I took a shower; it would be much appreciated."

"I'll be glad to help. See you gentlemen in a little while."

"We'll see you." Seth said and turned to Kevin. "I think I'll get cleaned up too if that's alright with you."

"That's fine."

Kevin helped himself to a cup of coffee while the others were getting ready for the evening. Maggie helped Sara pick out something to wear to Carl and Elizabeth's, then Sara got in the shower. Sara touched the old scar and started to cry. Maggie heard her weeping in the shower and walked to the archway of the bathroom. "Sara honey, you alright?"

Through tears she answered "Yes. I'm okay. I'm almost finished."

"Okay. I'm out here if you need me."

Sara finished her shower, put on her undergarments then went into the room where Maggie was. She was still sobbing. "Sara honey, what's wrong. Are you in pain?"

"A little."

Sara walked past Maggie so that she could get her clothes that Maggie had laid on the chair. Maggie gasped when she saw a very large older scar on Sara's side just below where she had been shot. Sara covered the scar as best as she could. "Sara honey, is that the scar the doctor was talking about that has inflammation in it?"

"Yes it is. It's just a little sore."

"I bet. I've never seen a scar like that before. How did you get it?"

Sara was trying to keep from crying as she got dressed. She didn't want to lie to Maggie but she wasn't ready to tell her what happened either. "I got it one day when I was shopping at the grocery store."

"How did you get a scar like that at the grocery store?"

Sara started crying. Maggie got up and hugged her. "Sara, I'm sorry. I didn't mean to upset you."

"It's okay Maggie."

Sara finished getting dressed. "Do I look okay Maggie?"

"You look very beautiful."

"Thank you Maggie."

"Are you ready to go into the living room?"

"Yes. I guess it's almost time to leave also isn't it?"

"Well, it's only 4:30. We don't have to leave until 5:15 P.M."

"Good, that will give me time to call Carrie and let her know when we're leaving and make arrangements with her."

Sara and Maggie walked out of the bedroom and met Seth and Kevin. "Sara, you look very nice."

"Thanks Seth; so do you. Kevin, I'm going to call Carrie and let her know when we're leaving. Are we going to pick her up or do you want her to meet us here?"

"We'll pick her up. Tell her we'll be there at 5:30."

Sara called Carrie. "Hello Carrie. It's Sara. How you feeling honey?"

"I'm doing better. How are you?"

"I'm doing a little better but I still have some inflammation in my wound and in another scar that I got about a year ago.

One of the reasons I'm calling is to let you know we'll pick you up around 5:30 this evening."

"Okay, great. What are you wearing Sara?"

"I have on a casual pant suit right now."

"Do you think it'd be okay if I wore a pant suit too or should I wear a dress?"

"I think a pant suit would be fine. Maggie and I are both dressed like that."

"Okay. I'll wear my yellow pant suit. Sara, you sound different, you sure you're alright?"

"Not really but we can talk about that later, after we pick you up."

"That sounds good. I'll see you in about ninety minutes."

"I'll see you."

After Sara hung up the phone Maggie looked at her. "Are you sure you're alright and up to going tonight?"

"I'll be alright. I want to go."

"Okay. I need to call Elizabeth and tell her we'll be there about 6:00 P.M."

"That's fine. I think I'll get myself a cup of tea."

"Elizabeth, it's Maggie."

"Hello Maggie. How you feeling?"

"I'm doing alright. I called to talk to you about tonight."

"You are still coming aren't you?"

"Yes, but we're picking Carrie up at 5:30 and will be at your house by 6:00 P.M. I hope that's alright."

"That's fine. I wasn't planning on eating until 6:30 anyway. How's Sara doing?"

"She had a rough night but says she feels up to coming tonight."

"That's good. I guess I'll see you in a couple of hours then."

"Yes you will."

Tom parked in the parking lot at the grocery store, got out and went inside. Once inside he asked a cashier where he could find Jack. She paged Jack and he came to the front of the store. He saw Tom standing there in uniform. "Hello officer may I help you?"

"Are you Jack Lake?"

"Yes sir I am."

"Is there somewhere we can talk privately?"

"Yes; follow me."

They went into a little room in the back of the store. "Have a seat officer." Tom sat on a stool that was there. "How may I help you?"

"You're aware of the murders that have been taking place in and around the park are you not?"

"Yes. What terrible tragedies."

Tom watched Jack's body language. "Did you know any of the victims?"

"I knew all of them. They came into the store all the time. I think I knew Paul Sanford and Rebecca Segrest the best."

"How well did you know Sara Michaels?"

"Quite well. Sara has to be the sweetest person I know. My niece had her as a teacher when Sara's husband Gary was still alive. He was a nice man too. I really like Sara and it bothers me to see her hurting."

"I like Sara too and my fiancé and Sara are best friends. I have a few more questions for you. First of all what size shoe do you wear?"

"Men size 9."

"Where were you last night around 9:00 P.M.?"

"I took a walk."

"Where?"

"I don't remember. I walk a lot to help keep my stress level down."

"When was the last time you talked to your cousin Art?"

"Monday night. He called me here and told me that he'd be working a different time than usual so if I tried to reach him, I'd know where to call him?"

"When was the last time you saw Art?"

"Last week sometime."

"Did he seem different to you?"

"No, not really. He was still as mean and nasty as he always is."

"Well, I think that's it for now. I'll get in touch with you if I think of anything else I need to ask you. You have been a big help. Oh there's one more thing; do you happen to know what size shoe Art wears?"

"No, I'm sorry. If I had to guess I would say a men 11 or 12."

"Thank you for your help."

"You're welcome officer."

As Tom walked out the door he thought to himself. He's hiding something. When I talked to Art at the bank he seemed anxious, and overly friendly. Jack knows something; I just know it. He called into the station. "Lt. Marsh speaking."

"Scott, we need to put surveillance on Jack Lake. He's the manager at the Shop N Save. He gets off work at 6:00 tonight. I want an unmarked car watching the store from the front and an unmarked car watching from the back. Follow him wherever he goes. He knows something and I want to know what it is. I need someone to tap his office phone after he leaves for the day."

"I'll arrange that Tom. Thanks Scott. I'm on my way back to the station. I'll be there in about ten minutes."

Sara went to put her shoes on. Maggie went back with her because she was having a little trouble bending to tie her shoes. When they were back in Sara's room; Maggie looked at Sara. "Sara honey, I know something's terribly wrong. I want to help if I can."

"I appreciate your concern Maggie but I'm just not ready to talk about it to anyone."

"If I can help in any way let me know."

"I will. Thanks Maggie."

Sara had her shoes on, then she and Maggie went into where the gentlemen were. "We're ready to go any time you are."

"I better leave the light on in the living room so that it's not pitch black when we walk in here tonight." Sara turned the light on then they walked to the car.

Sara gave Kevin directions to Carrie's house. Seth kept looking into the back seat to check on Sara. He was worried about her. They got to Carrie's house and Seth and Sara walked up to the door and knocked. Carrie smiled when she answered the door. "Hi you two. I need to grab a jacket and I'll be right there. Wait inside while I get my jacket."

Seth and Sara waited inside and Carrie came back a few minutes later with her jacket on. "Sara, I hope I look alright. I wasn't sure I should have worn this yellow outfit."

"I think you look just fine. The yellow is so springy."

"Thanks Sara, Seth."

They walked out to the car. "Hello Carrie."

Murder *When the Bell Tolls*

"Hello Maggie, Kevin. I appreciate you inviting me to come with you. I realize it's an inconvenience."

"It's not an inconvenience. Elizabeth and Carl are looking forward to having you there. They said they'd like to get to know you better, and we're glad you could come. Sara told us about you and Tom and we're so happy for you."

"Thank you Maggie. Sara don't forget to remind me to call Tom around 10:00 P.M. He thought he'd meet me when he got off work tonight. He said if someone gave him Elizabeth's address he could pick me up so you didn't have to take me home."

"Oh, okay."

They pulled into Elizabeth and Carl's driveway at 5:55 P.M. They headed to the front door. Maggie rang the bell and Elizabeth answered. "Hello all. Come in please."

Elizabeth hugged Maggie and Kevin, then walked over to Sara and hugged her. "Hello Sara, I'm glad you could make it. This must be Seth."

"Hello ma'am."

"It's Elizabeth please; and this must be Carrie. We've heard a lot about you. We met you briefly at the funeral home and talked to you a little at Paul's funeral."

"I remember. Maggie said you and your husband are very good friends and have known each other for years. Sara and I are like that. I've known Sara for about twenty years. We've worked together that long."

"Let me take your coat Carrie. Won't you have a seat in the living room. Dinner will be ready in about fifteen minutes."

Elizabeth hung Carrie's coat in the closet and everyone but Maggie joined Carl in the living room. Maggie followed Elizabeth into the kitchen. Elizabeth hugged Maggie again. "Oh Maggie, I'm so glad you and Kevin could come tonight? How you holding up?"

"I'm doing alright but I'm extremely worried about Sara."

"Why?"

"She had a doctor's appointment today and the doctor told her she could go back to work but that she had inflammation in an older scar just below where she was shot. When I asked her how she got that scar she started to cry. I found out someone's been stalking her. Tom and Seth think all of these murders are related and Sara and another woman may know one or both of the people involved in the shootings. Something happened to Sara when she and Paul first started dating. She told me it was so terrible the only person she talk to about it was Paul. What do you think of Carrie?"

"I like her. She seems really nice. She's attractive too. Have I met Tom Monroe?"

"Yes, he came to the funeral. He's the one who stayed with Sara during the day."

"Okay. I remember. I understand Seth's staying with Sara all the time. How's that working out?"

"Quite well actually. She feels a lot safer with him there. It's easier on her too because she doesn't have to keep adjusting to different officers coming and going. She really trusts Seth and so do we. If anyone can help Sara move on with her life it's Seth. He took her to the symphony the other night and they both had a good time. It was the happiest I've seen Sara since Paul was murdered."

"I'm glad she has Seth to protect her especially since she's being stalked. Hopefully they'll catch the people responsible for these murders very soon."

"I hope so. I know I'll feel safer when they're behind bars."

"I know I will too."

"Let me help you take the food into the dining room."

"Thanks Maggie."

When Carrie and Sara saw the other ladies bringing the food in they went into the kitchen and helped too. Once all of the food was on the table they sat down and started eating and talking.

◈

At 5:05 P.M. Art walked out of the bank and went to his car. He stopped at a fast food restaurant and got some food and took it home. He went into his empty house, turned on his television, sat down on his sofa and began eating his supper. He turned on the news to see if there was any information on Rebecca's murder. He smirked when the newscaster said anyone with information should call the NYSPD. He laughed his haunting laugh.

Art kept his television on while he ate. During the 6:00 news he was startled when the newscaster was talking to Lt. Marsh on the television. He heard Lt. Marsh say they believed there was more than one person involved in the murders and they were working as a team. He also heard him say they were following some leads but had no suspects at the time.

The women were talking amongst themselves and the men were talking amongst themselves too. "So Carrie, I know you said you met Sara where you work. How did you two meet?"

"Sara's late husband Gary was a school psychologist, my husband was a teacher, I was a secretary where Sara worked and Peggy was a teacher there also. Sara, Peggy and I had lunch together and we hit it off immediately as friends and have been friends ever since. Sara took me under her wing and showed me the ropes when I became a teacher."

Sara was preoccupied. She couldn't stop thinking about what Seth had told her about the murders. Her thoughts were interrupted when Maggie said "Sara honey, you alright?"

"Yes. I was just thinking about something?"

When everyone started talking about the murders Sara started feeling nauseated again. "Would you excuse me? I need to walk around for a few minutes."

"Sure Sara, do what you need to do."

Sara got up and walked to the window. She started weeping. Carrie got up and walked over to her. Carrie hugged her. "Sara, would you like to talk about what's bothering you?"

"Yes but not here. I don't want anyone else to hear what I say."

Maggie got up and walked over to them. She saw Sara weeping. "Sara, Carrie everything alright?"

"Maggie, Sara's really upset about something. Is there somewhere she and I can talk quietly."

"I'll ask Elizabeth."

She came back and told them that they could go into the guest room and talk. "Thanks Maggie."

"Sara, is this something I can help you with?"

"No. It's something Carrie and I need to talk about. It has to do with work."

"Okay. If you need me just call."

"We will."

Carrie and Sara walked into the guest bedroom of Elizabeth's home. Sara started pacing. "Sara honey, what is it?"

"Carrie, what I'm about to tell you has to stay between us okay?"

"Sure Sara. It always does."

"Carrie do you remember about a year ago when Paul and I announced our engagement and I went to the grocery store to get some food to make a special meal, that all of us were going to enjoy together?

"I remember. When we all came you were excited but I detected something in your voice that said something was wrong."

"Well, there was something wrong. That day at the grocery store I went down an aisle to get something and Art Hunter was there. He was screaming at Jack. When I told him to stop he walked over to me and said something sexual to me, and I slapped him. He told me that he was going to teach me a lesson I wouldn't forget about disrespecting him and he pulled me into Jack's office and he did just that."

Carrie looked at Sara horrified. "What did he do to you Sara."

Sara pulled her waist band down and said "Do you see this scar? It was caused by the beating he gave me with his belt. The scar was caused by a very special belt buckle he had made." Carrie gasped. "After I found out some of the details of the last murder victim I haven't been able to sleep at night because I keep having nightmares about everything Art did to me in that room."

"Sara something else happened in that room between you and Art didn't it?"

"Yes, but I can't talk about it just yet. Art scares me. I pride myself on being open minded and being able to use good judgment about people but not with Art. He's such an awful man yet I detect that underneath he could be a very caring man if the right woman came along."

"Sara, does anyone know what happened to you that day at the store?"

"Paul knew. I didn't tell him right away because I was afraid I'd lose him. When I did tell him, he was very warm, loving, compassionate, and understanding. Carrie, I can't help but wonder if Art's involved with these murders."

"It's strange you would ask that. Tom went to talk to Jack Lake today and he was asking me about Art the other day. Sara, I'm glad Seth's with you."

"So am I Carrie except I'm having a slight problem with it."

"What's that?"

"I'm falling in love with Seth."

Carrie laughed. "That's okay Sara."

"But it's too soon after Paul's murder. It's only been three weeks."

"I know; however Paul would want you to be happy. He loved you dearly. Sara, you should talk to Seth about this. I know he'd help you, besides he told Tom he's falling in love with you too, but he doesn't want to rush because he wants you to have time to grieve."

Sara started crying again "Carrie, what am I going to do? If I tell him, I may lose him."

"Do you trust him Sara?"

"Yes, I do."

"Do what you think is best."

Carrie hugged Sara. "Thanks Carrie. You're a wonderful friend."

Because Carrie and Sara were gone for so long, Maggie started to worry. She walked back to the room where they were and knocked on the door. "Sara, Carrie, you two alright?"

"Yes Maggie. We're getting ready to come out and join you."

"Okay. I'll wait in the hall."

"Okay. We'll just be a minute."

Sara suddenly started to feel sick again. "Carrie, I'm going to be sick again. You can go on if you want."

"I'll stay here with you."

Sara ran into the bathroom and vomited twice. When she started vomiting Carrie ran into the bathroom to help her. "Sara, you alright?"

Sara nodded her head and tears were running down her face. "Help me over to the sink so I can wash my face off please."

Maggie heard Sara getting sick. "Carrie, Sara, everything alright in there?"

Carrie helped Sara over to the sink then opened the door. "Carrie, what's going on? I heard someone getting sick? Was it you? Are you alright?"

"Maggie, I'm fine. It's Sara that's getting sick."

"Sara, oh my gosh! Is she alright?"

"Yes, she's washing off her face now. Please come see for yourself."

Sara was clinging onto the bathroom sink when Maggie came in. "Sara honey, what's wrong?"

"I'm okay Maggie. It's just a continuation from last night. It's just from the wound. The doctor told me that might happen."

"Are you sure?"

"Yes. Let's go join the others."

When Sara, Maggie, and Carrie returned Seth gasped. Sara looked white as a sheet and he could tell she'd been crying. "Is everything alright Sara?" Seth asked.

"Yes it is."

"No Seth it's not. Sara was vomiting when I went back to check on her. She said it is because of her wound."

Sara looked at Seth. He started to say it wasn't but saw the look of horror on her face. "It could be. She threw up several times last night too."

"Sara honey, do you need to go back to your house?"

"No, I'm okay now. I just need to take some pain medicine."

"I'll get you a glass of water Sara."

"Thanks Elizabeth."

Elizabeth came back with a glass of water for Sara to take her medicine. Sara felt a little better. "Elizabeth, do you need some help with the dishes from supper?"

"Sara, I appreciate the offer but I think you should rest."

"Elizabeth, let me help you." Carrie said.

"Thank you Carrie. I'd appreciate it."

Let me help you too." Maggie said.

Maggie, Carrie, and Elizabeth went into the kitchen and did the dishes. "Seth, Kevin, would you care to join me in the den for a couple games of darts while the ladies clean up? After they finish cleaning up we can play Monopoly."

"That sounds good." Kevin said. "Seth you coming?"

Seth looked at Sara. "No, I think I'll stay here with Sara for a little while. Thanks for the offer."

Kevin and Carl went into the den and Seth moved closer to Sara. He reached under the table and squeezed her hand. She looked up at him with tears in her eyes. He whispered "Are you sure you're alright?"

"Yes."

"Does this have anything to do with whatever has been bothering you the past few days?"

"Yes. That's what's causing all of this."

"Sara, I wish you could tell me what's bothering you."

"I wish I could to but I just can't." He squeezed her hand again.

"I'm here if you need me for anything." She nodded in reply.

Tom went back to the lab. Dennis was still there. "Hello Tom."

"Dennis, I know you're getting ready to go home but I need a favor."

"Sure Tom, what is it?"

"I know Carter's gone for the night but I need to see the body of our last victim again. I need to take a few pictures of that unique scar on her side. I want to see if I can figure out what made that mark."

"Sure come with me."

Tom and Dennis went into the morgue and pulled out Rebecca's body. Tom took pictures of the bruises' and several of the strange looking scar. He noticed the bruises' around her wrists were made with a unique type of rope. He'd have the officers find out more about that rope when the stores opened in the morning.

Tom kept thinking about Carrie and how glad it wasn't her or Sara laying on that slab. He knew that each hour that went by gave the killer even more of an edge. Tom knew it would only be a matter of time before the killer struck again. He needed to review the evidence. He hoped Jack Lake would provide the final clues to this case.

Tom looked at his watch it was 8:45 P.M. He was supposed to get off forty five minutes ago but he knew how important this case was, he was determined to pick Carrie up at Elizabeth's.

Dennis walked out of the back room. "Tom, you still here? I thought you'd be out of here and heading home to see that beautiful fiancé of yours."

"Carrie's with some friends tonight. I asked her to call me on my cell phone about 10:00. I told her I'd meet her there and take her home from there. She knows I'll be working late the next couple of nights, but I also promised to make it up to her when I'm off for three days."

"Tom, I'm leaving for the night. I'll see you in the morning."

"Goodnight Dennis. Thanks for your help."

Tom took the pictures up to his desk and sat down to study all the evidence in the case.

Carrie looked at her watch. It was 9:00 P.M. She started thinking about Tom. She smiled. Elizabeth came into the room. "Well, you ladies ready to beat the guys in a game of Monopoly or do you want to just talk?"

"I wouldn't mind playing Monopoly." Maggie said.

"Neither would I, what about you Sara?" Carrie asked.

"Sara?"

"What?"

"Would you like to try and beat the guys in Monopoly?"

"Sure, why not?"

"I'll go get them." Elizabeth said.

When Elizabeth went to get the men Maggie looked at Sara. "Sara honey, you sure your alright?"

"Yes. I'm just trying to cope with everything right now. I guess reality has finally sunk in."

"Well okay. If you want to talk, I'll listen."

"I appreciate that Maggie."

The men came into the room and they sat down and started playing Monopoly. At 9:45 Carrie took out her cell phone. "I hope no one minds but Tom asked me to call him about 10:00 P.M. He said he would let me know how much longer he'd be and he wanted to pick me up here."

"That's fine Carrie. Go ahead and call him."

"Tom Monroe speaking."

"Hi Tom. It's Carrie."

"Hello Sweetie. Are you doing okay at the Harris'?"

"Yes, but I wish you were here with us."

"What are you doing right now?"

"Playing Monopoly. It's women against the men and the women are winning."

"I need to be there and help the guys out. I'll be leaving work in about fifteen minutes. Can you give me directions on how to get there?"

"I'll let Kevin give you directions."

"Okay. Carrie, I love you."

"I love you too Tom. Here's Kevin."

Kevin gave Tom directions on how to get there then handed the phone back to Carrie. "Carrie, I'll be there in about thirty minutes."

"I'll see you then."

Carrie smiled as she hung up her phone. Tom smiled as he hung up his cell phone too. He wanted to be with Carrie as soon as he could. "Mark, I'm leaving now. I'll leave you in charge. Call me on my cell phone if anything comes up."

"Okay Tom. Be careful and take care of Carrie."

Tom went out to his car, got in and started driving to Carl and Elizabeth's. He couldn't stop thinking about what had happened to Rebecca. He couldn't understand how someone could be so cruel. He cringed just thinking about what Rebecca had gone through. He followed the directions to the Harris' and pulled up in front of their house about 10:25 P.M. He walked up to the door and rang the bell. Carl answered it. "Hello, I'm Sergeant Tom Monroe. You must be Carl Harris."

"Come in Sergeant."

Tom walked into where everyone was. Carrie got up, walked over to him and hugged him. He kissed her gently then said "Hello everyone."

"Hello Tom." Maggie said. "Have you ever met our good friends Carl and Elizabeth Harris?"

"I saw them at the funeral home and the funeral but didn't get a chance to talk to them."

Maggie introduced them. "Tom, won't you sit down and enjoy a cup of coffee and a Danish, or a sandwich?"

"Thank you ma'am. A cup of coffee and a Danish would be very nice."

"I'll get it for you."

Elizabeth got up and got Tom a cup of coffee and a Danish. He sat next to Carrie and held her hand under the table. "Here you go Tom."

"Thank you so much ma'am."

"Please call me Elizabeth."

They talked for a little while and by 11:15 P.M. everyone was getting tired. Kevin got up and said "Well, it's getting pretty late. I guess we should be getting Sara home since she hasn't been feeling well."

"We understand. It was wonderful to have all of you here tonight. We'll have to do this again sometime."

"Thank you for inviting us."

"Maggie you know you and Kevin are always welcome in our home so are Seth, Sara, Tom, and Carrie."

"Thank you Elizabeth." Sara said.

"Sara honey, I hope you start feeling better soon. I know you've been through a terrible ordeal."

"Thank you Elizabeth."

"Carrie, Tom it was nice meeting both of you. We enjoyed your company."

"Thank you Elizabeth. I enjoyed being here; thank you for allowing me to come with Seth and Sara."

"You're welcome and congratulations on your upcoming wedding."

Carrie smiled. "Thank you."

They all left together. Seth and Kevin helped the women into the car then Seth walked over to Tom's car. "Tom, be careful going to Carrie's. Take care of her."

"I will. Seth don't forget what I said earlier. Be extra careful."

"I will. I'll talk to you tomorrow."

Seth headed back to the car and got in. Kevin drove back to Sara's. Sara fell asleep against Maggie. Maggie stroked her hair and hugged her. She was worried about her. "Seth, let me know if she still isn't feeling any better tomorrow. If she's still vomiting I think we should call Dr. Martin back."

"I agree. I'll let you know."

Kevin pulled in front of Sara's house. Maggie touched Sara's shoulder. "Sara honey, you're home now."

Sara opened her eyes and looked around. Seth put his arm around her waist and helped her to the porch. "Seth can you handle her by yourself or do you need for us to come inside with you?"

"I can handle it. What time do you think you'll come by tomorrow?"

"I don't know. Let us call you when we get up in the morning and we can decide then."

"That's fine."

"Sara honey, I hope you feel better. We'll call you in the morning."

Murder When the Bell Tolls

"I'll talk to you then."

Sara and Seth walked into Sara's house. "Thank you for your help Seth. If you don't mind I'm going to get ready for bed. I'm exhausted."

"I know you are. Go ahead. I'll wait out here." As Sara turned to walk to her bedroom she stopped, turned around, walked towards Seth and kissed him on the cheek. Then headed back into her bedroom. Once she got into her bedroom she went into the bathroom and changed clothes. She gasped when she looked at her reflection in the mirror. Before she went to bed she walked to her door and said "Seth, could you come here a minute?"

Seth walked to her door. "Seth, I wanted to tell you goodnight and thank you for not pushing me for answers tonight. I'm not sure what's happening but I think reality's starting to set in. Good night Seth."

"Goodnight Sara. If you need me for anything tonight, just call for me."

Seth watched as Sara got into her bed and pulled her covers up. She turned out her small table lamp and tried to go to sleep. Seth went back to his room and started changing clothes. He thought about how frightened Sara seemed and about the kiss on the cheek. He finished changing his clothes, grabbed a book and got into bed. He looked at the clock in his room. It was midnight.

Sara was having a hard time sleeping. She kept thinking about her conversation with Carrie earlier. She couldn't stop thinking about that awful day in the store. She felt nauseated. She tried to think of something else. She thought about her students and how much she was going to enjoy going back to teach them. She finally fell asleep.

Tom and Carrie got home about 11:30 also. Tom knew something was bothering Carrie. He embraced her, held her and kissed her. "Carrie, I can tell something's bothering you; can you tell me about it?"

"Tom, I'm really worried about Sara?"

"Why?"

Because tonight at Elizabeth's Sara vomited twice and couldn't stop crying. She's terrified because of this last murder and because of something she told me."

"What did she tell you Carrie?"

"I promised her I wouldn't tell anyone. I can't break that promise."

"Okay, but has she talked to Seth about it?"

"No. She said the only person she ever told was Paul."

"Carrie, I'm worried about Sara too. There's new evidence that leads us to believe the killer is someone who knows Sara very well. We believe he may be stalking her?"

Carrie gasped. "Oh no Tom! Is there anything that can be done?"

"We're working on it. I've increased the patrols in her neighborhood and Seth's aware of most of the facts. We'll catch this person Carrie."

"I hope so. I couldn't bear to see anything happen to Sara."

"How did tonight go?"

"It was nice. The Harris' are really nice people."

"They seem like it."

"Tom, Sara told me she's starting to fall in love with Seth but she's afraid it's too soon after Paul's death."

Tom smiled. "I know Seth has fallen in love with Sara. He just doesn't want to push her. He wants to give her time to deal with everything but this killer is making it difficult." He embraced her and kissed her.

Carrie looked up at Tom. "Are you hungry or anything sweetie?"

"No, I'm good. Carrie I know you're tired I can tell. Why don't you go ahead and change clothes."

She kissed him and went into her room and changed clothes. She thought about how his strong loving arms felt around her body and she felt safe. She wondered if Sara would ever feel safe after what Art had done to her. Carrie finished changing clothes and went to where Tom was. He hugged her again. "Tom, I'm not quite ready to go to sleep yet. I think I'll get myself a cup of tea then I'll be ready for bed."

"How about if I change clothes and we have a cup of tea together. After the day I had I could use some time to unwind."

"Okay. I'll fix us both a cup of tea."

Tom went into his room and changed his clothes. He couldn't' stop thinking about Carrie and what she'd said

Murder When the Bell Tolls

about Sara. He knew he needed to call Seth in the morning and tell him about the strange scar the victim had on her side.

Tom came out and saw Carrie in the kitchen making the tea. He walked up behind her and put his arms around her and hugged and kissed her. She leaned back against his chest and smiled. When the tea was ready they both fixed it like they wanted it. "Why don't we go into the living room and sit on the sofa so we can both be more comfortable?"

They sat down on the sofa and set the cups on the wooden coffee table that was in front of the sofa. Carrie told him about how her day went. "Tom, you told me you had a really bad day. Can you tell me about it?"

"Carrie, after I left you I talked to Jack Lake. I know he knows something about the murders so I'm having him followed. It was hard enough doing that but it was even harder when I had to collect more evidence from that poor woman's body. I can't begin to imagine what she went through before she died. All I could think of was you. Carrie, I don't know what I'd do if something like that happened to you. It's bad enough our killer severely beat and sexually assaulted that poor woman, but did he have to kill her too."

Carrie hugged Tom. They both had tears in their eyes. Carrie was thinking about what Sara had told her. Tom saw fear come across Carrie's face. "Carrie honey, what's wrong?"

"I'm not sure. I can't seem to stop thinking about what happened to Rebecca and about what Sara told me. I hope the two aren't connected."

"I'm afraid I don't follow you Carrie. What do you mean what Sara told you could be connected to this murder?"

Carrie realized she'd said too much already. She hadn't meant to say anything. "Tom, what Sara told me was in the strictest confidence. Until there's proof the two may be related, I don't want to say anything."

"I respect that; however Carrie if they are connected Sara needs to tell me or Seth. I promise, we'll keep it confidential."

They both finished their tea. Tom embraced Carrie and held her close to him. "Carrie, I'm so glad you're safe. I love you."

"I love you too Tom. What time do you have to get up in the morning?"

"6:00 A.M. Carrie you don't have to get up with me. I can fix myself a bowl of cereal or something."

"Tom, I'm used to getting up at 6:00 because of teaching. I'll set my alarm and get up at the same time."

"Okay; however, I'm still pretty uptight. Maybe if I listen to some music on my personal CD player it will help."

"Maybe. I'm really tired so I'm going to bed. Goodnight Tom. I'll see you in the morning."

"Goodnight Carrie. I'll see you."

Carrie headed to her bedroom and Tom was still sitting on the sofa with his feet propped up on the coffee table. Carrie smiled as she walked to her room. She closed her eyes but found sleep difficult. She couldn't stop thinking about Sara. She was worried about her. She cringed just thinking about what Sara had told her. She got up and started walking around. She decided maybe a glass of warm milk would help her sleep.

As she walked into the kitchen she noticed Tom was trying to sleep on the sofa. She could tell he was restless also. Tom heard Carrie walking around and woke up suddenly. "Who's there?" He asked, thinking someone had broken into the house.

"Tom, it's me Carrie. I couldn't sleep. I was going to get a glass of warm milk would you like some to?"

"Sure. Let me help you."

Together they made the warm milk and took the cups into the living room. They sat down on the sofa and drank the milk. Carrie leaned over and kissed Tom on the cheek. "Maybe now I'll be able to sleep. Goodnight Tom."

As she got up to go into her room Tom grasped her wrist. "Carrie, please don't go yet. Stay here with me for a little while."

She walked over to the sofa and sat down with her back to him. She leaned against his strong chest. He put his arm around her, leaned down and kissed her on the forehead, then he leaned his head back and closed his eyes. He hugged Carrie tighter. She felt so safe. She closed her eyes and so did Tom. They both finally fell asleep.

When Carrie and Tom both woke up the next morning they both felt better. Tom kissed Carrie. "Good morning Carrie."

"Good morning Tom. I'm going to fix breakfast before I get dressed because I want to take a shower and get dressed later. What would you like to eat?

"Would it be too hard on you to fix bacon and eggs?"

"No, I was going to suggest that."

"I'm going to shower and get ready for work if I have enough time."

"It'll take me about thirty minutes to get breakfast ready."

"That's enough time." He kissed her then went to shower."

As Carrie was finishing up breakfast Tom walked into the room dressed in full uniform. He walked over to her and embraced her. "Carrie, thank you for last night."

Carrie smiled. "You're welcome."

They ate breakfast and Tom helped Carrie with the dishes. "Tom, I'm going to shower and change clothes before you leave, if there's time. Otherwise I'll wait until after you leave."

"There's time. I don't have to leave for another forty five minutes. I'll wait out here for you."

Carrie went to shower. While she got undressed she thought about last night. She smiled. She got into the shower. Once she finished with her shower she got dressed. She was getting ready to put on some make-up when she turned around and Tom was standing in the doorway. She walked to him and they embraced. "Carrie, I just wanted to make sure you were alright."

She looked up at him and smiled. "I'm alright. Will you be here for lunch?"

"Yes. I won't be able to get here for supper though."

"I understand. I'll be looking for you at lunchtime."

Tom kissed Carrie and held her close to him. "I have to leave for work now but I'll call you when I'm leaving for lunch. It'll probably be around 12:15 when I can get away. Is that too late for you?"

"No that's fine."

"Goodbye Carrie. I'll see you at lunchtime."

"Goodbye Tom. I'll see you."

As Tom was walking out the door on the other side of town Art was walking out of his door too. When Art got to work his boss called him into his office. Art's first thought was he was going to be fired. "Art, I have a very special job for you today."

"What is it sir?"

"Rebecca Segrests family is coming into town today. I want you to meet them at the airport. If they're hungry I want you to take them to get something to eat then take them to their hotel. You'll be paid extra for all of this. Her parents will be arriving at the airport at 11:00 A.M. today. Here's an envelope with money in it for whatever the family needs. What you don't spend on food is theirs to do with what they want."

"I'll take good care of Rebecca's family. Thank you for trusting me to do that."

Seth and Sara got up around 8:00 A.M. They were both tired. "Good morning Seth."

"Good morning Sara. How did you sleep?"

"I had a hard time falling asleep but once I got to sleep, I slept well."

"That's good. I was really worried about you. I got up a couple of times and checked on you. You were sleeping then. Did you have any nightmares last night?"

"Yes, but I was able to fall asleep anyway. I thought about how excited I am about going back to school Monday. I miss it and I miss the students."

"I bet you do. Are you hungry?"

"Not really. What about you?"

I'm not that hungry either. I know Maggie and Kevin are supposed to call later so maybe we can make arrangements to meet them for a brunch or lunch."

"That sounds good. I thought maybe we could order pizza for dinner tonight."

"That sounds good. Did Maggie and Kevin have anything planned for today?"

"I'm not sure. I guess we'll know when they call."

"I think I'll shower and change clothes."

"Okay. I think I'll sort the laundry and get a load in the washer."

Seth went to shower and Sara went to sort clothes. She went into her bedroom and sorted the clothes then walked back to Seth's room. She knocked on the door and didn't get an answer. She heard the water running and knew he was in the shower. She grabbed the clothes from his hamper and put them in a basket. She walked back to the laundry room and started a load of colored clothes.

Seth finished his shower, then got dressed. He walked out of his room and saw Sara standing in the laundry room putting clothes in the washer. "Do you need some help Sara?" he asked.

"No, I think I got it for now. I'm going to shower now. If the washer finishes would you please put that load in the dryer and that load of whites in the washer. Don't wash them on hot though. I only use warm water."

"Okay, that's fine."

Sara went into her room to shower. While she was in the shower she ran her hand over the scar that was inflamed. She started sobbing. She knew she needed to tell Seth what happened but she had to do it when no one else was with them. She didn't want Maggie and Kevin to know about it yet. She wasn't sure how Maggie would handle that information. She tried to sort out her feelings and emotions. She knew she was falling in love with Seth but couldn't bring herself to admit it. She'd only known Seth for three weeks, how could she possibly be falling in love already. Love took time, so she thought.

She got out of the shower and got dressed. She went into the living room where Seth was. He looked so handsome in his dress jeans and button down shirt. He smiled. The washer finished and Sara walked to the laundry room and put the clothes in the dryer and put the other clothes in the washer. Sara and Seth worked together to clean up the house.

At 9:45 A.M. the phone rang. Sara answered it. "Sara, it's Maggie. How you feeling?"

"Better thank you."

"You sound out of breath; did I get you at a bad time?"

"No. Seth and I were just straightening up the house and doing some laundry. I wanted to get a lot of those things done before I go back to work Monday. I'll have to do laundry again but at least everything else will be done for a week."

"That's true. Have you and Seth had breakfast yet?"

"No, why?"

"Well Kevin and I saw this buffet restaurant we thought we'd take both of you to for a late breakfast or early lunch."

"That sounds good. Seth and I talked about calling and asking you if that's what you'd like to do."

"Are the two of you up to a little sightseeing today?"

"I'll ask Seth. Seth, Maggie and Kevin want to know if we would like to go to a buffet restaurant and do some sightseeing?"

"Sounds good to me. Are you up to it?"

"I think so. Maggie, that sounds good. Do you want us to meet you somewhere or did you want to come here first?"

"We'll pick both of you up in about an hour. Is that alright?"
"Sure. We'll be ready."

❦

At 9:50 Art left the bank and headed to the airport. He smiled the whole time. He couldn't believe his boss had given him this job. He arrived at the airport around 10:30 A.M. He went to the coffee shop and got a cup of coffee. He loved being in the airport. He liked to watch planes take off and land. He walked to a window with a view and watched the planes.

He watched the monitors to see if the flight was on time. His boss had given him all the information earlier. He saw the plane was actually going to be a few minutes early so he walked to the gate and waited. He saw the plane land. He checked the pocket on the inside of his coat to make sure the money was still there then he waited for Rebecca's family to get off the plane. He held up a sign that read SEGREST FAMILY, in bold print.

An elderly couple came off the plane and saw the sign. "We're the Segrest family. I'm Meredith and this is my husband Cliff. We're Rebecca's parents."

"I'm Art Hunter. I worked with your daughter. She was a friend of mine. Terrible thing that happened to her. I was shocked when I heard about it."

"Thank you Art. It's nice to meet one of Becky's friends. I know she had many because she always wrote about them when she sent us money or when she wrote us a letter. She was such a beautiful person and..." Meredith began to cry. Cliff hugged her.

"Sorry about that Art. It's just Becky was our oldest daughter and we'll really miss her. Her younger brother and two younger sisters looked up to her. They're all grown up but they'll still miss her."

"Are you going to have the funeral here?"

"No, just a memorial service. We're going to have her body flown back home so we can have a funeral there where all of her family is located."

"That makes sense."

"So, what do you do at the bank?"

"I'm a teller but it's my job to help with the money deliveries, money transfers, be a teller, and customer service. Well, we're at my car. Are you two hungry or anything?"

"Yes we haven't eaten at all today."

"Well, my boss gave me an envelope with money in it to pay for lunch for you, and for whatever else you need. Whatever isn't used is yours to keep."

They got in the car and went to a nice restaurant. Art escorted them inside and they sat down at a table. They ordered their food and waited. While they waited they talked about Rebecca and their family. Art listened and tried to be as nice as he could. The food came and they ate quietly.

Tom worked all morning on the evidence in the murder cases. He kept trying to figure out what could have caused that strange and very painful looking scar on the victim's side. He looked at the other files and there was no sign of a scar like that. Why had the killer done that. Was it the same killer or someone different. The motive was the same and the reports came back that all the bullets at all of the crime scenes matched; that meant that the brutality had escalated for some reason.

At 11:00 A.M. Maggie and Kevin knocked on Sara's door. Seth answered it. "Hello Maggie, Kevin, come in."

"Hi Maggie, Kevin. As soon as I get my shoes on we can go."

Once Sara had her shoes on they walked out the door and got into the car. "So Maggie, where is this restaurant?"

"It's about ten miles out of town. We found it the other day when we went sightseeing."

"It sounds really nice."

"I think both of you will enjoy it. Sara, how did you sleep last night?"

"I had a hard time getting to sleep but once I did I slept well."

"Are you feeling better?"

"Yes. I think this is just from all of the stress."

"I hope so. If you start vomiting today or not feeling well let us know and we'll take you home. If you still aren't feeling well tomorrow, I think you should see Dr. Martin again."

"Okay. I'll do that."

Tom looked at the clock. It was 12:00. He looked at Lt. Marsh. "Scott, I'm going to give Carrie a call and go over there for lunch. I'm going to be gone from the office about two hours. I need to check something out after I leave Carries."

"That's fine. I can handle things."

"I need to call Seth too. I'll do that later. Right now I should call Carrie."

Tom called Carrie. "Hi Carrie. It's Tom. I'll be there in about thirty minutes. I'll be leaving here in about ten minutes. Do you need me to stop and get anything?"

"No. I already have lunch fixed for you. Just bring yourself."

"I'll be there shortly."

Lt. Marsh looked at Tom. "Go now. I know she's waiting for you. Enjoy your lunch. I can handle things here."

"Thanks Scott. I'll be back when I can."

"It's alright take whatever time you need."

Tom walked to his car and drove to Carrie's. She greeted him with a smile when she opened the door. He walked in, hugged and kissed her then they sat down at the kitchen table to eat lunch. "Carrie, it smells so good. What did you fix for lunch?"

"I made homemade beef stew and a fresh cherry pie. I was making the salad when you called."

"It looks good. Let me help you."

They got the food and sat down to eat. "Carrie, you feeling better?"

"Yes. How has your day gone so far?"

"It's been hectic. I've been gathering evidence on this case and I need to interview Art Hunter again after I leave here."

"That man is evil."

Tom gasped. "What makes you say that?"

"It's just the way he pushes Jack around and…"

"And what Carrie?"

"Never mind. Just don't believe everything he tells you. He tells people what he thinks they want to hear. I don't like that man. He was always trying to get Rebecca to go out with him and she always refused. She said he was just too picky for her."

Tom thought about what Carrie had just said about Rebecca. "Carrie, do you know if Art ever asked Sara to go out with him?"

"I think he did but I know she never did. She didn't like him much either but said there were times he could be extremely nice and very caring. She always tried to be nice to him."

Murder *When the Bell Tolls*

They finished eating their lunch and Tom helped Carrie clean up. "Carrie, I hate that I have to work late again tonight but I promise I'll make it up to you over the next three days. I have something very special planned for tomorrow. Sleeping in is one."

Carrie smiled. "I agree. I usually sleep in until 7:00 A.M. on Saturday, then do laundry, and clean the house. After I get all of that done, I treat myself."

"How?"

"I go to the ice cream shop and get a double scoop of Rocky Road ice cream in a waffle cone, then I come home and rest for a while then get dressed and go to the mall or go shopping."

"Do you go to the mall alone?"

"Not usually. Sara or Peggy or both usually go along."

"Could I go along with you this weekend Carrie?"

She smiled. "You most certainly can."

Tom hugged and kissed Carrie. "Honey, I need to leave so I can talk to Art then get back to the station. There's a lot of evidence in this case that doesn't make sense but that's where I come in."

"Tom, I wish you didn't have to leave but I understand. Please be careful."

"I will. I'll call you later. There's a chance I may get out of work by 9:00 tonight."

"Okay. I'll be here. Have you talked to Seth yet today?"

"No. I'll do that after I talk to Art."

"Tom, I'm worried about Sara."

"So am I Carrie. I'll talk to you later. I'll call Seth in a little while. I love you."

"I love you too."

Tom kissed Carrie again then walked out the door. He got in his car and drove to the bank to talk to Art.

As Sara, Seth, Maggie, and Kevin waited for their food at the restaurant, Seth's cell phone rang. "Seth Parker speaking."

"Seth, it's Tom. Where are you?"

"I'm in a restaurant with Sara, Maggie, and Kevin. Where are you?"

"I'm on my way to the US Bank to talk to Art again. Carrie said something that makes me think Art may know more than he's saying about the murders."

"Really? Like what?"

"He knew Rebecca Segrest better than he told anyone. He was always asking her out on a date."

Seth gasped. "Did they ever go out?"

"No, she said he was too picky for her."

"Picky, how?"

"I don't know but I plan to find out. How's Sara doing?"

"Better. I don't think she had as rough of a night as she did the night before. She said she still had nightmares but was able to make them go away."

"That's good. Carrie and I are both worried about her."

"So am I Tom. I don't think this is over by far."

"Seth, take care of Sara. The evidence in this case is overwhelming and I'm afraid Sara's in more danger than she ever was."

"I'll make sure she's safe. Tom, find out who else rejected Art; then talk to them and see what you can find out about him. Let me know what you find out."

"I will. Tell Sara hello and that Carrie and I are thinking about her."

"I will. Goodbye Tom."

"Goodbye Seth."

Seth looked at Sara and saw a look of fear on her face. He knew that phone call from Tom had upset her, he just didn't know why. Sara started shaking. Seth looked over at her. "Maggie, Kevin, I need to talk to Sara privately for a few minutes. Would you excuse us?"

"Certainly."

"Sara, please come with me."

Sara and Seth went outside where they knew Maggie and Kevin couldn't hear them. "Sara, what's wrong? I can tell the phone call I just got from Tom upset you, but why?"

Sara trembled. Seth put his hands on her arms. "Sara, does this have anything to do with Art?"

She nodded her head yes. He moved closer to her and hugged her. She cried for several minutes and he tried to comfort her. He had no idea what Art had done to her.

"Sara, I know you're upset and scared but I have to ask you a question. Art was always asking Rebecca Segrest out on dates and she refused. Did he ever ask you out on a date?"

Sara was terrified but answered "Yes he did, but I never went out with him. I couldn't handle his controlling attitude. He was too much like my father and…"

"And what Sara?"

"Seth, I can't talk about it. I just can't."

Seth was frustrated but wanted to give Sara time to deal with everything. Seth was moving closer to Sara when she turned her back and vomited on the ground. Seth rushed to her. "Sara, what's going on?"

"I'm alright Seth. It's just that every time I talk about Art, I become ill."

Seth stood outside with Sara for a few more minutes to let her calm down. He rubbed his hand over her back. "Sara, I'm worried about you."

"Thank you Seth."

"Are you ready to go back inside?"

"Yes but, Seth, please don't tell Maggie and Kevin about this."

"I won't Sara; I promise."

Seth put his arm around Sara's back and they walked inside. Their food was just coming up. "Is everything alright Seth?"

"It is now."

"Sara, you look pale. Are you alright?"

"Yes, I'm alright. The food looks good."

They ate and talked for awhile. After they were finished eating Maggie said "Sara, we thought we'd take you and Seth to the Statue of Liberty and the Empire State Building today if we have time for both. We wanted to take a ferry ride. Is that okay with both of you?"

Seth looked at Sara. "That's fine Maggie."

Kevin paid the bill and they went out to the car.

When Tom got to the bank he asked for the bank manager. The manager came out. "Hello, I'm Sergeant Tom Monroe. We may have met the other day when the police were here after Rebecca Segrests murder."

"I may have seen you. What can I do for you?"

"Is Art Hunter around?"

"No. I sent him to the airport. The bank has paid all bills for Rebecca Segrests family to fly here, stay at a hotel, then fly her body home for burial. We're even paying the funeral costs. Art's picking up the Segrests at the airport and taking them wherever they need to go. I don't expect him back before 2:00 P.M."

"What time does his shift end?"

"5:00 P.M. Usually it's 6:00 but I've had him doing extra things for me the past few days. Things that are usually Rebecca's job."

"Let me ask you a few questions. How does Art get along with his co-workers?"

"Most of them like him. He can be controlling at times and I have to correct him about that."

"How does he respond to that?"

"He usually stomps out of my office in a huff but after awhile he goes back to being the nice guy he can be."

Tom was writing all of the information down on a tablet that he carried in his shirt pocket. "What about the women? How does he get along with them?"

"Most of them talk to him but he was very fond of Rebecca."

"Did any of the women feel threatened by Art?"

"No one has ever said anything. Pat, the woman second from the right always tried to avoid him at all costs."

"Thank you sir. You've helped me a lot."

"You're welcome. Is there anything else I can help you with?"

"No, I think that's all for now."

Tom walked over to Pat and said "Hello. I'm Sergeant Tom Monroe from the NYSPD. I'd like to ask you a few questions about Art Hunter."

She looked at the teller next to her. "Go on Pat. I've got you covered."

"What would you like to know?"

"How well do you know Art?"

"Too well. He kept asking me out so I finally said yes and I wish I hadn't."

"What happened?"

"The date started out nicely. He took me to a nice restaurant, then a movie; it was after the movie that it got strange."

"Why?"

"I was having a really nice time and it was still early so we decided to go for a walk in the park. While we were walking

Murder *When the Bell Tolls*

he started doing things to me that made me feel uncomfortable. When I told him to stop it infuriated him. I've never seen him so angry. He started giving me orders and treating me like I didn't matter. I didn't do something right and he slapped me across the face. After that I did everything he told me to do and I made sure it was perfect. He wanted everything to be perfect. He said my hair had to be perfect, my clothes had to be wrinkle free, all sorts of things. After that night, I've tried to avoid him as much as possible."

"I have one more question then I'll let you get back to work."

"Okay."

"Have you ever seen Art hit anyone else or heard him threaten anyone?"

"No, I'm sorry I haven't."

"That's alright. I know this has been extremely hard on you. I appreciate your time and patience."

"You're welcome officer. Have a nice day."

Even though Tom didn't get to talk to Art he'd gotten a lot of new information. He took that information back to the station and discussed it with the other officers on duty.

Later that day Tom called Carrie. "Carrie, it's Tom. How you feeling?"

"Better. How's the day going?"

"It's going good. I think I'll be able to get out of here by 8:30 P.M. I'll call you when I'm getting ready to leave."

"That sounds great. I'll be waiting for your call."

Seth, Sara, Maggie, and Kevin were having a good time sightseeing. Maggie ran her hand over Sara's back. "Sara honey, how you feeling now?"

"Better. I needed to get away from the house for awhile. I felt like I was being cooped up even though we've gone different places. I think when I go back to work Monday I'll feel more like myself. When I talked to Carrie she said she was going to be going back to work Monday also. Tom's going to stay with her until Wednesday to see how she does with her first few days back. We're both excited."

"I know you are. I know how much you've missed your students and I know you probably would've already gone back to teaching if it hadn't been for your injury."

"I think so too.

Seth looked at Sara and they smiled at each other. He walked over to her and pulled her to the side of everyone else. "Sara, you feeling better?"

"Yes. Thanks for asking."

"I was really worried about you earlier. I hope you realize that you can talk to me about anything."

"I do Seth. I trust you."

"Isn't the view beautiful?"

"Yes. It's breathtaking."

"I agree."

Maggie and Kevin walked over to them. "Are you two alright?"

"We're alright; just enjoying the view."

"It is gorgeous, isn't it?"

"Yes it is."

"Are you ready to move on?"

"Yes we are."

Art finally finished getting Rebecca's family situated for the evening. He got back to the bank around 3:00. His boss came up to him. "Did you get the Segrests settled into their hotel?"

"Yes I did."

"Good, I need to give them a call and see if there's anything else they need. I appreciate you taking care of them today. I couldn't get away with everything I had going."

"It was no bother sir. They're really nice people."

"I'm going back into my office to call the hotel. You may leave at 4:00 today. You'll receive extra pay for your services today."

"Thank you sir."

Art went to his place at the teller's station and counted his money. He tried to act like he was working when in fact he was watching what his boss was doing the whole time.

Arts boss called the hotel and talked to the Segrest family. They praised Art on his professionalism and kindness. They thanked the bank for helping with expenses and thanked Arts boss for his kindness. They told him they were taking Rebecca's body back home to be buried and needed to know where they could make the arrangements. Art's boss told them he'd take care of the arrangements for travel. He told them how to get to the funeral home and who was in charge. They thanked him and he hung up the phone.

Art looked away just as his boss hung up the phone. Someone stepped up to Art's spot and needed their check cashed. He smiled and helped them out. The other tellers were surprised at Art's sudden change of attitude. They couldn't believe he was being so nice to people. Pat thought maybe she should call Tom at the station and let him know about how differently Art was acting. She thought she'd wait until after she got off to do it. She didn't want Art knowing about it.

At 4:00 P.M. Art clocked out and left the bank. He headed home. Pat didn't get off until 6:30 P.M. after the bank closed and the tellers got everything put away. At 4:30 when she was sure Art was gone she pulled Tom's card out of her pocket. She took her break. While she was on her break she called Tom. "Tom Monroe speaking."

Pat was terrified and unsure if she should be doing this but felt it was necessary. "Sergeant Monroe, this is Pat Tracy from the US Bank. You asked me to call you if I noticed anything strange about Art. Well I did. I'd like to talk to you about it if that would be alright?"

"Sure. I can be right over."

"No. I don't want anyone else knowing I talked to you. Art's dangerous. I get off at 6:30 P.M. Would it be alright if I stopped by the station then?"

"That would be great. We'll talk then. Thank you for calling."

"Thank you sir."

Tom hung up the phone. He had a strange look on his face. Lt. Marsh looked over at him. "Tom, what is it? Is something wrong with Carrie or Sara?"

"That call was from a woman at the US Bank. She wants to come in tonight about 6:45 and talk about Art Hunter."

"Tom, are you saying she knows something about Mr. Hunter?"

"That's what I'm going to find out."

Sara, Seth, Maggie, and Kevin decided to call it a day when it came to sightseeing. They were all tired and getting hungry. They got into their car and drove to a nice restaurant.

They went inside and were seated by the waiter. Maggie and Sara excused themselves to go wash their hands. Once they got to the bathroom Maggie asked "Sara, you doing okay honey? This isn't too much for you is it?"

"I'm doing okay. I've had a chance to rest in between time so that's helped."

"How's the nausea?"

"Better. It acts up when the pain starts to get bad. Stress makes the pain worse."

"I would imagine."

After they washed their hands they walked back out and met the men. They ordered their food and talked while they waited. Suddenly Sara started shaking and tears were running down her face. Seth, looked at her dazed. "Sara, what is it?"

"It's Art. He just walked in the door."

Seth turned to look at him. The waiter seated him in a booth near the door. Sara turned ghostly white. "I think I'm going to be sick. Please excuse me." Sara ran to the bathroom. Maggie and Kevin sat horrified.

"Seth, should I go after her?"

"Yes, I think you should. Kevin stay here. I need to talk to someone for a few minutes."

When Maggie got to the bathroom she found Sara vomiting and crying. "Sara, you alright?"

"Yes Maggie, I'm okay."

Sara came out of the bathroom stall and clung to the sink. She splashed water on her face and stood still for a few minutes. Maggie walked over and hugged her. "Sara, what's going on?"

"I'm okay Maggie. Let's go join the others."

Seth had gone over to Art. "Art Hunter?"

"Yeah, who wants to know?"

"Lt. Seth Parker of the NYSPD."

"How can I help you officer?"

"You can start by telling me how you decided to come to this restaurant tonight?"

"It's one of my favorites, besides I was hoping to catch a glimpse of a very beautiful woman who used to come in here often with her male friend."

"Would that woman be Sara Michaels?"

"Are you her new lover?"

Murder *When the Bell Tolls*

Seth wanted to push him against the wall but didn't. Art knew he struck a nerve. "She is beautiful isn't she. She's every man's dream. I've admired her for quite a while."

"If I catch you anywhere near her I'll have you arrested for stalking; do I make myself clear?"

Art smirked "Yes, but I'm not going to stop admiring her. By the way, has she kissed you yet, or have you kissed her?"

Seth pinned Art against the wall. "If you even breathe on her, I swear I'll…" He stopped. He saw Sara come back to the table. "You come near her, I'll arrest you myself."

Seth headed back to the table. Art laughed his haunting laugh as if he had won that round. Little did he know Seth was onto him.

"Sara, you alright?"

"Yes Seth, but why were you talking to Art?"

"We'll talk about that later. Our food's here. Let's eat while it's still hot."

They all ate quietly. Sara could see Art staring at her. It made her very uncomfortable. He couldn't take his eyes off of her. He thought she looked even more beautiful now that Paul was dead. He was upset she had a police officer in her life. He'd win her heart some way, he just knew it.

Everyone finished eating. Kevin got the bill and paid for the food; Seth left the tip. As they were leaving Art came up to them. "Hello Sara. How you feeling?"

Sara felt sick but tried to be nice. "Hello Art. I'm feeling better."

"Good. I was worried about you after that awful tragedy with Paul."

Sara started shaking. "Thank you for your concern Art."

"Aren't you going to introduce me to your friends?"

"I'm sorry, how rude of me." She said halfheartedly. "This is Maggie and Kevin Sanford. They're Paul's parents and you've met Lt. Seth Parker."

"Yes. Lt. Parker and I have met. Mr. and Mrs. Sanford, I'm sorry about the loss of your son."

Before either one of them answered they saw a look of sadness and fear on Sara's face as she began to tremble. Maggie chose her words carefully. "We appreciate your sympathy and prayers. Thank you."

"Art, if you'll please excuse us, we need to get going. Lt. Parker has to get back to work. He took a break to eat with us."

Art started to say something but decided against it when he saw the look of anger on Seth's face. He could tell Seth had deep feelings for Sara. He laughed smugly to himself and smirked. He clasped Sara's hand, looked at her and said "If you ever need anything, just ask."

Sara trembled as they walked to the car. There were woods all the way around the back of the parking lot. Sara was nauseated again. She turned white. "I'm going to be sick. Excuse me." She ran to the woods and vomited. Maggie followed her.

"Sara, you alright?"

"Yes. Do you have any Hand Sanitizer in your purse?"

"Yes, why?"

"May I use it please. I need to wash my hands off."

"Sure, let me find it."

As Maggie looked in her purse for the sanitizer, Sara tried to stop crying. She kept thinking "I've got his filth on my hands. I have to get it off."

She used the sanitizer on her hands then they got in the car and headed back to Sara's. Everyone was quiet on the ride there.

Back at the station Tom was sitting at his desk. At 6:50 Pat came to the station. An officer she didn't recognize came up to her. "Ma'am, may I help you?"

"Yes. I'm looking for Sergeant Tom Monroe."

"Let me take you to him."

"Thank you officer."

The officer knocked on the glass door where Tom and the other Homicide officers were. "Tom, this young lady is asking for you."

Tom smiled. "Pat, come in. Let me get some paper and a pen and we can go back into Lt. Parkers office and talk."

They walked into Seth's office. "So Pat, you said on the phone you have some information about Art you thought I needed to know. Can you tell me what that is?"

Pat was nervous and Tom knew it. "Ms. Tracy, it's alright. I understand how hard this must be. Take your time."

"Thank you Sergeant."

"Ms. Tracy, please call me Tom."

"Only if you'll call me Pat."

"That's a deal." Tom was trying to help her feel more comfortable.

She saw a picture of Carrie. "Is that Carrie White?"

Yes it is. She's my fiancé."

Pat smiled. "I know Carrie quiet well. She's so sweet. I remember when her husband died. How's she doing with the cancer?"

"She had her last treatment Tuesday. She doesn't have to go back for six months. She's doing alright."

"That's good."

"You told me you had some information about Art."

"Yes. Today after you left Art got back from the airport and he seemed different. He's usually rude and obnoxious toward all of us and rude with customers, but he was so nice, so polite. It was frightening. He was whistling and humming the rest of the day. That's not the way he usually is. He's evil, hateful, and demanding. He's so picky when it comes to how he wants things done."

Tom's expression changed. He could hear the fear in Pat's voice. "Pat, you're the third person today that's told me Art was picky. What exactly does that mean? How is he picky?"

"Well, he's a neat freak. I remember one time when Rebecca had some papers scattered on her desk. Art straightened them up then screamed at her about not having things in order. He wants to have every hair on his head in place and his clothes neatly pressed, little things like that. He thinks he's God's gift to women; which he isn't. Who in their right mind would want him?"

"It sounds like he has a serious problem."

"Tom, I'm terrified of him. I don't know what he'll do to me if he finds out I talked to you; probably something like he did to Sara Michaels."

Tom gasped. "Sara Michaels? What did he do to her?"

Pat realized she'd said something no one else knew about. Pat liked Sara. Pat's oldest daughter had Sara as a teacher ten years ago. She wasn't sure what to say. "The police department doesn't know what that evil man did to Sara?"

"No, I'm afraid not. How did you find out about it?"

"Jack Lake, Art's cousin came into the bank one afternoon and he and Art started talking. Jack told Art what he did to Sara was totally unnecessary and she didn't deserve that."

"Do you know what he did to Sara?"

"No, only that it was something horrible. Art told Jack not to say anything to anyone else about what happened between he and Sara. Personally, I think he hit her, and more than once."

Tom was writing everything down. "So, you say Art was being extremely nice? Had he been like that any other time?"

"Yes. When I went out with him; other than that no."

"What time did Art leave work today?"

"Our boss let him off at 4:00 P.M. He's suppose to be back at work at 8:30 in the morning and since it's Friday the bank will be open longer. He won't get off until at least 7:30. He's working the drive- thru."

"What time do you get off tomorrow?"

"The same time as Art. Some of the workers get off at 5:00 but I have an appointment in the morning and won't be able to get to work before 10:30. That's why I'm working later. You won't tell Art I talked to you will you?"

"No. However we'll be watching him more closely. Do you have anything else to add?"

"No. I can't think of anything."

"If you think of anything else call the station. I'm off the next three days but Lt. Marsh or Lt. Anderson can talk with you. Thank you for coming in. You've given me a lot of very important information. Thank you."

"Thank you for listening Tom. Tell Carrie I said hello and congratulations."

"I will. Thank you again. Where are you parked?"

"Right outside."

"Let me walk you to your car."

Tom told Lt. Marsh that he was walking Pat to her car. As he was walking outside his cell phone rang. "Tom Monroe speaking."

"Hi Tom. It's Carrie."

"Hi sweetie. Is everything alright?"

"Yes, I just wanted to see how you're doing and let you know I miss you."

"I miss you too."

Tom assisted Pat into her car. She thanked him then drove off. "Sorry about that Carrie. I was helping a witness out to their car. Where were we; oh yes. I miss you too."

"Tom, what time do you think you'll get off tonight?"

"Well, with this new information I just received it'll probably be no later than 9:00. Is there a reason why?"

"I just wondered because I thought maybe we could order some pizzas, salads, and bread sticks and watch a movie."

"That sounds good. I'll try and be there by 9:15p.m. I love you Carrie."

"I love you Tom." He hung up his cell phone and went back inside.

At Sara's everyone got out of the car and headed inside. Sara was still trembling and exhausted. Maggie looked at Sara. "I think a cup of tea would be nice, would you like a cup of tea?"

"Yes, that would be nice."

"I'll go put the kettle on."

"Sara, let me do it. You need to rest."

Sara sat down on the couch and leaned her head back. She couldn't stop trembling. The tea was ready. Maggie poured the water into cups and everyone fixed themselves a cup of tea. "Sara, would you like to play some cards or Monopoly? It may take your mind off of what's bothering you."

"Sure. Monopoly sounds great."

Kevin got out the Monopoly game and they sat at the dining room table and started playing. About an hour later Seth's cell phone rang. He answered it. "Seth Parker speaking."

"Seth, it's Tom. I just got more information on Art from a co-worker."

"Really? What did he have to say?"

"It was a woman. Her name's Pat Tracy. She's a teller at the bank. She said Art's a neat freak and is usually arrogant and rude with the staff and the public but lately he's been extremely nice. Carrie told me he's evil and Rebecca told her one time she didn't go out with Art because he was so picky. Pat did go out with Art and said it started out wonderfully but ended badly."

"Did she tell you why it ended badly?"

"She said he got angry when she told him to stop doing things to her that made her feel uncomfortable. Seth, there's something else she said that I think you need to hear."

"What's that?"

"She overheard a conversation between Jack and Art about something Art did to Sara. She didn't know what it was but said it must have been pretty bad because Art told Jack to never bring it up again and never to tell anyone else about it."

Seth gasped. "Oh no. We saw Art at a restaurant where we went tonight. Sara got sick when she saw him and when he touched her hand she got sick outside. We definitely need to talk to him again. I told him if I ever saw him around Sara, I'd arrest him myself."

"Seth, I'm off the next three days but on Monday, I'll go back to the bank and speak with Art's boss and Art again and see what else I can find out. How's Sara doing now?"

"She's calmed down but she's still shaking. She saw me talking to Art and asked me about it. I told her we'd talk later."

"Good. Seth, whatever Art did to her it may be a very important clue to solving these murders but don't push her to tell you. If she's not ready we'll figure this out on our own. She's been through enough. Carrie's worried about her."

"I think she really wants to talk about what's happening but she isn't ready. I'm not going to push her. I know she'll tell me when she's ready."

"Seth, I'll talk to you tomorrow. Carrie and I have a big weekend planned, I won't let her get worn out so that she isn't able to go into work Monday. I have to be back Monday anyway."

"Maggie and Kevin are going home this weekend. Sara will miss not having them around but she's looking forward to going back to work too and I'm looking forward to hanging around the school in my new duds. Sara says I'll fit right in."

Tom laughed. "I hope so. I'll talk to you tomorrow."

"Goodbye Tom."

Seth went back to the table to continue playing Monopoly and Tom got ready to leave the station.

✦

Tom finished up his paperwork and at 8:45p.m. he walked out of the police station. He called Carrie. "Hello Sweetie, it's Tom."

Murder *When the Bell Tolls*

"Hi Tom."

"I'm just leaving the station now. I'll be there in about fifteen minutes. You can order those pizzas now or you can wait until I get there."

"I think I'll wait. That way we can get what we want."

"I'll see you in a little while."

While Carrie waited for Tom, she went into her bedroom and put on some perfume. She walked into the kitchen and got things out for when the pizza got there. About five minutes later Tom knocked on her door. She opened it and smiled. "Hi sweetie." He leaned down and kissed her.

Tom walked into the house and embraced Carrie. They kissed each other and held each other for awhile, then Tom said "Carrie, do you still want to order pizza?"

"Sure. Do you want to place the order?"

"Sure. I'll call it in." They decided what they wanted and Tom placed the order. After he hung up the phone he walked over to Carrie. "Carrie, I almost forgot. Pat Tracy from US Bank said to tell you hello."

Carrie smiled. "Pat's so nice. I met her when her oldest daughter had Sara as a teacher and I had her youngest daughter eight years ago in my class. How's she doing?"

"She's doing alright."

"How did you meet Pat?"

"I met her when I went back to the bank to talk to Art. He wasn't there. He was helping Rebecca's family. They flew in and are staying here a few days. They're flying her body back to their home town for burial."

"You talked to her about Art? I bet she had a lot to say."

"She did. Did you know she actually went out with him?"

"No, I had no idea. I can imagine what that was like."

"She said the date started out well but ended badly."

"Let me guess, he started giving orders."

"How did you know that?"

"Sara told me that."

"That's the third time today Sara's name's been mentioned when it comes to Art and this case."

"I'm sorry. I don't follow you Tom."

"Pat told me she overheard a conversation between Jack and Art. It had to do with something Art had done to Sara. You told me you and Sara talked about something Art did to

her and Seth told me about an incident that just happened at a restaurant between him, Art, and Sara."

Carrie gasped. "Tom, is Sara alright?"

"I talked to Seth and he said she was alright but having nightmares and sickness. I have a feeling whatever happened between Art and Sara may be the key to this whole murder case; but let's not talk about that, let's talk about something else like how beautiful you are and about how much I missed you."

Carrie smiled and they kissed each other. They embraced each other and kissed each other again. They started talking then they decided what movies they wanted to watch. There was a knock on the door. Tom answered it. He took the pizzas, tipped the delivery person, then closed the door and set the pizzas on the counter. Carrie went into the kitchen and got herself some pizza and Tom got some too. They both sat down on the sofa and started watching a movie.

Art went upstairs to his den. He continued to write a letter he'd been working on. He stopped long enough to change into his night clothes. He wrote on the letter for about twenty minutes then went downstairs, made some popcorn, and sat down to watch a movie.

He wished he had Sara next to him as he watched the horror movie. He wanted someone to hold onto when the movie got scary. He was frustrated that Sara had Seth with her all the time. He wanted to distract him so he could talk to Sara alone. He thought about Pat and the way she looked at him with disgust earlier in the day and in awe by the end of his shift. That made him angry. He watched the movie until 11:00 P.M. when he finally went to bed.

Jack sat home alone again. He thought about Art and how he was making him help him. He was going to turn himself into Tom but not before he wrote a letter to Art telling him that he wasn't going to help him anymore. He wasn't sure exactly what Art was doing but he knew it wasn't right. He didn't know why Art always wanted him at the scene of a murder but he was going to talk to Tom about it. He liked Tom when he met him. He thought he was polite, caring, understanding, and a good police officer. He knew he'd be fair.

Murder *When the Bell Tolls*

Jack went into the kitchen, got some paper and a pencil, and started writing the letter to Art. He thought carefully about what he wanted to say. After he finished the letter he popped some popcorn and sat down to watch television.

Around 11:00 Maggie and Kevin looked at Sara and could tell she was exhausted. "Sara honey, I think we should go so you can get some rest."

"You don't have to leave."

"We know; but you're exhausted. We can get together tomorrow. We thought we'd clean Paul's apartment on Saturday. You and Seth can have that whole day together to do whatever you need to do also."

"Okay, but what about tomorrow?"

"Didn't you say you wanted to make a donation to Paul's school to start a scholarship?"

"Yes I did. I also want to start a scholarship fund at the school where I teach."

"Would you like to do that tomorrow and go somewhere nice to eat, then come back here and visit?"

"On one condition."

"What's that?"

"Would anyone mind if we barbequed outside for supper for a change. I've been wanting to do that since the weather has gotten nice. Paul and I were going to do that anyway on Memorial Day Weekend. We could invite Tom, Carrie, Carl, Elizabeth, Peggy and Ralph if that would be alright. I'd have to get some things from the grocery store though."

"That sounds great. Would you like me to call Elizabeth and Carl Sara?"

"Yes please. Tell them we'll plan on eating around 7:00 P.M."

"I will. Good night Sara. We'll see you around 10:00 tomorrow morning."

"Good night Maggie, Kevin, we'll see you then."

Once Maggie and Kevin left Sara started crying. Seth hugged her. "Sara, what's wrong? Can you tell me?"

"I was feeling better until I saw Art."

"I know that upset you."

"Why did he have to go to that restaurant? Why?"

Seth hugged Sara again and tried to comfort her. He sensed the fear in her voice. "Sara, I don't want to upset you anymore but I need to ask you a question. Do you know Pat Tracy from the US Bank?"

"Yes I had one of her daughters in my class several years ago. I really like her. Why do you ask?"

"Well, she talked to Tom today and gave him some very startling information about Art. Did she ever talk to you about Art?"

"No. After I stopped banking there I haven't seen her very often. I see her at the store occasionally. I know she's friends with Carrie."

Sara stopped trembling and crying so hard. "Seth, I'm sorry about the tears. I can't seem to control them whenever it comes to Art."

"It's alright Sara. I understand."

"Seth, I'm going to get ready for bed."

"Go ahead. I'll wait out here."

"Thanks Seth."

Sara changed into her night clothes then walked out to where Seth was. "I think I'm going to drink a cup of warm milk so I'll be able to sleep a little better. Do you want anything Seth?"

"I could use a cup of warm milk also. Will you be alright if I change my clothes?"

"Yes, I'll be fine."

While Seth went to change clothes Sara made the warm milk. After Seth changed his clothes he went into the kitchen. They both drank their warm milk, told each other goodnight and went into their own bedrooms.

Seth kept thinking about what Tom had told him about Art. He was convinced Art was involved in the murders somehow. He tried to sleep but found it difficult.

Sara also found sleep difficult. She kept thinking about Art. When she started feeling nauseated she thought about her students. She finally fell asleep.

Even though it was 11:00 Tom and Carrie put another movie in the DVD player and started watching it. Carrie made coffee and they both drank a cup. They were both extremely tired. Carrie leaned against Tom's chest and fell asleep. Tom leaned his head back and fell asleep also.

Murder *When the Bell Tolls*

The movie Art was watching was over. He turned off the television and headed upstairs to bed. He laid in bed thinking about Rebecca and Rebecca's family. He smiled as he closed his eyes and went to sleep.

Since Art didn't have to be at work until 10:00 he slept in. He got up at 7:30, took a shower and headed downstairs to fix himself some breakfast. He cooked himself breakfast, washed up the dishes and sat down to read the paper for a little while. At 9:30 he left for work. He arrived at work at 9:50.

When he got to work his boss came up to him. "Good morning Art."

"Good morning Sir."

"Art, would you come to my office please?"

He went into his bosses office. "Have a seat Art."

He immediately thought the worst. He thought he was about to be fired.

"Art, I was wondering if you're in some kind of trouble?"

"No sir. Why do you ask?"

"There was a police officer here yesterday asking a lot of questions. He talked to me and to Pat Tracy about you. If you're in some kind of trouble I'd like to help you, if I can. You're a very valuable asset to this company."

"Thank you sir. I appreciate the concern."

"Art, if there's ever anything I can do, let me know."

"I will. Thank you sir."

Art left his bosses office and went out to his station as a teller.

Seth got up at 7:30 and was surprised to find Sara asleep on the couch. She'd gotten up during the night and gone out to the living room trying to get comfortable. He tried to be quiet as he fixed a pot of coffee. Sara awoke and sat up on the sofa. "Sara, I'm sorry. Did I wake you?"

"No. It's time to get up anyway."

"What time did you come out here?"

"I think it was around 3:30 A.M. I was having a hard time getting comfortable. I thought I'd be more comfortable out here. It took me awhile but I finally fell asleep. Would you mind if I took a shower and changed clothes before breakfast?"

"Go take a shower. I'll handle things out here."

Sara walked to her room to shower. She laid out her clothes and jewelry and went into the bathroom. After her shower, she got dressed, put on some perfume and jewelry and went out to where Seth was.

"Sara, you look nice. Do you have any suggestions as to what I should wear?"

"Just wear dress jeans or slacks, and a button down shirt."

"Okay. I'm going to shower and change also."

"Okay. How about a bowl of cereal and fruit for breakfast?"

"That's fine. I'll be out in about fifteen minutes."

Sara fixed breakfast while Seth showered and got dressed.

After Seth came out they sat down and ate breakfast. "Sara, I should call Carrie and Tom and invite them over tonight. I'm afraid if I don't call them now, we may not be able to reach them. I know Tom had a special weekend planned for Carrie."

"That sounds like Tom."

Carrie and Tom had gotten up around 7:00 and Tom cooked breakfast for Carrie. They were just finishing up when Tom's cell phone rang. "Tom Monroe speaking."

"Tom, it's Seth."

"Good morning Seth."

"Good morning Tom. How are things going over there?"

Carrie hugged him from behind. He smiled. "They're going good."

Carrie whispered "I'm going to shower and change clothes."

Tom nodded. "Tom, I hated to call you this early but Sara and I were wondering if you and Carrie were free tonight?"

"I was going to take Carrie to a nice restaurant then on a carriage ride but that can wait until tomorrow night. Besides Carrie wants to go to the mall tomorrow. She wants to get some new clothes to go back to work on Monday. We're free I guess. Why do you ask?"

"Sara and I, along with Maggie, Kevin, Carl, Elizabeth, Peggy and Ralph are going to have a barbeque here and we wanted both of you to come. Sara wanted this barbeque because she's trying to go on with her life. I was wondering if you'd come. I know it would be fun. We aren't planning on eating until 7:00 because we know Peggy can't be here before that."

Murder *When the Bell Tolls*

"I'll ask Carrie after she gets out of the shower but I'm sure she'll say yes. Count on us and I'll let you know if things change. I know she wants to do some house work today though. What are you and Sara's plans?"

"Maggie and Kevin are coming over around 10:00 A.M. We're going to go to Paul's school and to Sara's school to present a monetary gift to begin a scholarship fund in Paul's name at both schools. It's Sara's way of honoring Paul."

"That's wonderful Seth. How's Sara doing with the nightmares?"

"I think they're getting worse. We both went to bed around midnight last night and when I got up at 7:30 this morning I found her asleep on the sofa. She said she had a hard time getting comfortable. I had a hard time sleeping myself after that confrontation with Art. I still think he's involved with these murders somehow. If he isn't I think he's the one stalking Sara."

"Take care of Sara. Is there anything Carrie and I can bring tonight?"

"Just bring yourselves. Sara, Maggie, Kevin, and I are going to the grocery store after lunch anyway. There will be plenty of food."

"We'll see you then."

"We'll see you."

Carrie came out of the bedroom with only a robe on. She wasn't sure what she and Tom were going to do so she decided she'd ask him before she finished getting dressed. Tom turned around and smiled. She looked so young and beautiful in her royal blue satin robe. She walked over to him and kissed him. "Tom honey, I wasn't sure what our plans were for today so I thought I'd ask you before I finished getting dressed."

"Sara and Seth have invited us over for a barbeque tonight. I told them I thought it would be okay but I wanted to ask you first."

"That sounds great. What are we supposed to bring?"

"Seth told me nothing but I think we should take something."

"So do I. How about I make a three bean salad and a pineapple upside down cake?"

"That sounds good. Carrie you wanted to know what we're going to do today. I thought since you wanted to get some house work done today I could help you with that, we can make what we're taking tonight, then I want to take you to a nice restaurant for a late lunch. Seth said they weren't eating until 7:00 because they invited Peggy and Ralph and Peggy's working."

Carrie embraced Tom and kissed him. "That would be fine. I'll go put some jeans and a t-shirt on to clean the house and do some cooking. I'll change clothes again after that."

"Okay. I'm going to get dressed also."

They both went into their rooms and changed clothes. Carrie put on jeans and a t-shirt which had the school logo on it and Tom put on jeans and a button down shirt. They met in the living room, embraced, hugged each other then decided what they were going to do first.

Maggie and Kevin slept in. They got up around 7:15. They both showered and got ready to go to Sara's. While Kevin was in the shower Maggie called Elizabeth and invited them over to Sara's that evening. Elizabeth was elated and said they'd be honored to come. "Maggie, is Sara feeling better?"

"I'm not really sure. She seems to be doing better. She was doing fine the other day until she saw someone in a restaurant. She got sick all over again. I'm not sure what's going on but I think this person may be involved in the murders."

"Oh Maggie. Sara must be terrified."

"She is. I hate that we're going home Sunday. I wish we were staying a little longer; at least until they catch this person, but we need to get home. We both know she's in good hands with Seth."

"What time should we be there tonight?"

"We're planning on eating around 7:00. The only reason why it's that late is because Peggy and Ralph are both working and won't be home until around 5:30. We wanted to give them time to get cleaned up or do whatever they need to do first."

"I understand. We'll be there around 6:00. Maybe I can help with the food or something. If not maybe we can talk."

"We'll see you then."

After Maggie and Kevin finished getting ready they drove to Sara's. They knocked on the door, and Seth answered."Good morning Maggie, Kevin, come in."

"Good morning Seth. Where's Sara. Is she alright?"

Murder *When the Bell Tolls*

"She's fine. She's in her bedroom finishing getting ready. We slept in this morning."

"So did we."

"Did you two eat breakfast?"

"Yes. We had cereal and fruit. Sara didn't eat much. I think yesterday was harder on her then any of us thought. I think she had a better night though."

"That's good. I'll see if she needs any help."

Maggie went to Sara's bedroom and knocked on the door. "Yes?"

"Sara it's Maggie. Do you need any help?"

"Yes. Would you mind helping me with this necklace?"

Maggie helped her with the necklace. "Thank you Maggie. I appreciate it."

"Sara, do you feel up to going to Paul's school?"

"Yes I do."

"Well, I talked to Marcus and Nancy and they told me the school will double whatever amount of money is given for the scholarship fund. They're thrilled to know you're doing this. Paul would be proud."

"I know he would. He was a great teacher and a great man. He'll be sadly missed."

"Are you ready to go honey?"

"Yes I am."

Maggie and Sara walked out to where Seth and Kevin were. They got their things together and went to the car. They went to Paul's school first. Sara was nervous and her emotions about Paul's death were still very raw. Sara, Seth, Maggie, and Kevin walked into the school. When they got into the school they started heading toward Marcus' office. One of Paul's students recognized Sara. "Hello Ms. Michaels. How you feeling?"

Sara was stunned but felt good knowing that students from Paul's school cared. "Hello Alex. I'm feeling better. Thank you for asking."

"Are you looking for Mr. Cole's office?"

"Yes. I've forgotten how to get there. When I came here Marcus was usually in the hall or I would bump into him somewhere."

"His office is down the hall a little ways and it sits on the left."

"Thank you Alex. Oh Alex, was Mr. Sanford one of your teachers?"

"Yes he was. I liked him and miss him."

"Alex, this is Mr. & Mrs. Sanford. Paul's parents. Maggie, Kevin this is Alex."

"Pleased to meet both of you."

"Thank you Alex. It's nice meeting you."

"I'm sorry, I'm going to be late for class. Don't forget; down the hall on the left."

"Thanks again."

They walked into Marcus Cole's office. "Hello, may I help you?" His secretary asked.

"Yes, I would like to speak with Mr. Cole as soon as possible?"

"Okay. What's your name ma'am?"

"Sara Michaels."

She gasped. "Sara Michaels? Paul Sanford's fiancé?"

"Yes."

"Welcome. I'm sorry I didn't recognize you. I haven't seen you in awhile. I'll let Marcus know you're here."

She buzzed Marcus' office and told him that Sara was there. He walked out and immediately threw his arms around Sara. "Sara, how you doing my dear?"

"A little better. I miss Paul though."

"I bet you do."

He looked at Seth. "I'm Lt. Seth Parker with the NYSPD; I'm with Sara."

"All of you, please have a seat." They did. "What can I do for you today?"

"Marcus, after Paul was murdered I decided I wanted to keep his love of teaching alive. I want people to remember him for who he was. He loved teaching. He always said he wished there was a way he could give more to his students, especially the ones from poor families so in his honor I am presenting your school with a check worth $2,000.00 to be placed in a scholarship fund for needy families. Maggie informed me the school board and you stated that whatever gift was given the school would double it."

"That's right. We'll add an additional $4,000.00 to the fund. Sara, Paul would be so proud. We at this school, thank you. The students, staff, and board of directors thank you. I'll do the necessary paperwork to get all of this done. Again, thank you."

"It's my pleasure. Even though I teach at another school. teaching children is important anywhere and everyone should get an education. I truly believe that."

Marcus hugged Sara. "I know that. You're a wonderful teacher yourself and this gift will help educate several students who would never have been able to come to school. You're a wonderful person. Please come back and visit us when you can. We'd love to have you. Paul told us once that the students could really benefit from hearing you speak about writing and its importance. Would you consider coming here and speaking to our students about it?"

"Yes, I'd like to do that."

"When are you going to be able to go back to work?"

"I'm supposed to go back Monday. I'm looking forward to it."

"Good luck, and thank you again."

As they headed out of Paul's school, Maggie turned to Sara. "Sara, I'm sure that had to be hard on you. Are you okay honey?"

"Yes. I'm alright."

"Are you up to going to your school now or would you like to stop for lunch first?"

"Why don't we go to my school; besides I need to talk to Peggy and ask her if they can come tonight."

"Okay, let's head over there."

It took about ten minutes to get to Sara's school. When she walked inside she was greeted with numerous hugs and smiles. Nancy Boyd was coming out of her office at the same time Sara was heading in there. Nancy threw her arms around Sara. "Hello Sara. It's so good to see you. How are you feeling?"

"I'm doing okay. I have something I need to give you."

"Really."

"Yes. Could we go into your office?"

"Sure. All of you come in."

Sara was greeted with "Hello Sara." As she walked into Nancy's office.

"Please have a seat."

"Thank you Nancy. You remember Paul's parents Maggie and Kevin Sanford don't you?"

"Yes. It's nice to see you again."

"This is Seth Parker. He's the police officer that will be here with me every day."

"It's a pleasure to meet you sir."

"Please it's Seth, and it's a pleasure to meet you too."

"So what can I do for you Sara?"

"Three things. First could you page Peggy Miles for me and have her come here, second I wanted to let you know I'll be able to come back to work on Monday. My doctor says I have to be careful but I can come back and thirdly I have a surprise for you. I'm here to present you a check for $2,000.00 to start a scholarship fund in Paul's name. I was told the school would double this amount also."

"We'll gladly double that amount. We're so grateful and the students are grateful."

"Paul believed every child should be entitled to an education and I agree. This scholarship plan is aimed at helping needy children get their education. Teaching children is something that means a lot to me and it meant a lot to Paul also."

"We appreciate this. I'll get the paperwork done and the fund will be available immediately."

"Thank you Nancy."

"Let me page Peggy for you."

A few minutes later Peggy came into Nancy's office. "Nancy, you sent for me."

"Yes, there's someone here who needs to talk to you. They're in my office."

Peggy walked in and beamed when she saw Sara. She threw her arms around her. "Oh my Sara! It's great to see you. Are you doing alright?"

"Yes, I'm doing better. The doctor said I'll be able to come back to work on Monday."

"Really, that's great. I'll be so thrilled to have both you and Carrie back."

"I can't wait to get back. I miss everyone."

"We all miss you. Is that why you're here today?"

"Well yes and no. I came in to tell Nancy I'd be back Monday, but I also came for a couple of other reasons. When Paul was murdered I was devastated."

"I can understand that."

"I talked to Maggie and decided I wanted to honor Paul's name by giving our school and Paul's school a check to start a scholarship fund for the needy and worthy students."

"That's wonderful Sara. Paul would be so proud."

"I'm sure he would. But the other reason I'm here is to ask you if you and Ralph are free this evening?"

"As far as I know why?"

"We're having a barbeque at my house and I'd like to invite you and Ralph. We're planning on eating around 7:00. Tom, Carrie, Maggie, Kevin and Carl and Elizabeth Harris are also coming. You don't need to bring anything. We're going to stop at the grocery store on our way home in a little while."

"Sara, you can count on us. We'll be there. I'll call Ralph at work and tell him about it."

"Good. I look forward to having you there."

Peggy hugged Sara. "We're looking forward to coming. It's so good to see you again. We'll see you tonight."

Peggy left to go back to her classroom; Sara and all the rest of them left to go out to their car. Nancy walked with them. "Sara, I'm so glad you'll be coming back. However, if it gets to be too much for you, let me know."

"Thanks Nancy."

They walked out to the car. Maggie looked at Sara. "Are you doing alright Sara?"

"Yes. I'm glad I got to see Peggy again. We've been friends for a lot of years. I'm glad they're going to be able to come tonight. We'll have fun."

"I'm sure we will. Are you ready to get something to eat, then go to the grocery store?"

"Yes. I think so."

⚜

Tom could tell Carrie was getting tired. "Carrie honey, let's stop for today. I think you should rest for a little while."

"Okay. I think I'll fix myself a glass of iced tea."

"Let me get it for you."

Tom fixed her a glass of tea and they walked into her all seasons room. She sat down in a rocking chair and Tom sat in a wing backed chair. They talked and laughed. After a little while Tom got up. "Carrie honey, I promised you I'd take you to a nice restaurant for a late lunch. It's 1:30 P.M. Are you ready to go?"

"Let me change my shoes. These shoes are so hard to walk in."

After she changed her shoes, they walked out to Tom's car. He helped her into his car. Carrie was thrilled when she saw where Tom had taken her. It was one of her favorite places to eat. She smiled. "Tom, this is one of my favorite places to eat."

"I like to eat here too. I don't get a chance to very often but when I'm out this way, I always like to stop here."

"Sara and her late husband and my late husband and I used to come here quite often. I'm not sure if she and Paul had been here yet."

While they were waiting for their food they talked about Carrie's students. Tom could tell how much she loved teaching. He reached across the table and held her hand. She smiled. "Carrie, you really enjoy teaching don't you?"

"Yes I do."

"I'm glad. I bet you're a wonderful teacher. I enjoy being a police officer most of the time; what I don't like about being a police officer is having to tell someone they've lost a loved one and the worst part of being a police officer is when you have to shoot someone. We try not to shoot anyone but sometimes it's the only thing we can do."

"I would imagine that would be difficult. Tom you're a fantastic police officer. I know I feel safer when you're around."

He smiled. "I'm glad. Here comes our food."

Their food got there and they talked and ate. After they finished their meal, their waiter came over to the table to see if they needed anything else. Tom said "Yes, I'd like a hot fudge sundae for me and a waffle cone with a double scoop of rocky road ice cream, please."

"Tom, you didn't have to do that."

"I know, I wanted to. I wanted to treat you because of all the work we did together this morning. I have a special treat planned for you tomorrow and Sunday." Carrie smiled, then squeezed Tom's hand across the table.

At the bank Art was pacing. He couldn't wait until his break. He hoped Pat had a break when he did. He wanted to talk to her and find out what the police wanted to know and who the officer was. At 3:00 P.M. Art took his break. He sat in the break room ate some crackers and cheese, then drank a soda. He kept looking for Pat.

Thirty five minutes passed and he realized Pat wasn't coming. He needed to talk to her but didn't want everyone to see him. He decided that since they worked together tomorrow he'd talk to her after work. He might even take her out to dinner.

Pat was supposed to take a break when Art did but she and another friend switched break times so she could go on a break with her good friend Maya. She wanted to stay as far away from Art as she could.

Art came back from break and looked at Pat. She felt a cold chill going up her spine. She shivered. Art went back to work and didn't even notice Pat wasn't there until he looked up and noticed Maya was gone also. He figured they both took their break together. That was alright though. Art knew what he had to do.

When Pat and Maya got back from their break, Pat thanked her other friend for switching with her. She looked over at Art and he smiled at her. She felt sick. She wondered if he knew she'd gone to Tom and told him how differently he was acting.

While Sara, Maggie, Kevin, and Seth were at the grocery store, they saw Jack. Sara thought he looked tired and worn. She liked Jack. He came out of his office and walked over to her. "Hello Sara. How you doing today?"

"I'm doing better. You remember Kevin and Maggie; Paul's parents don't you?"

"Yes. You allowed me to eat with all of you. I also remember Lt. Parker. Hello sir."

"Hello Jack. I noticed you've been holding your side a lot. Are you in pain?"

"Some. I cut myself on one of the shelves the other night when I was stocking them."

"Have you seen a doctor?"

"No, not yet. I was hoping it would get better. I guess I should go Monday and have it checked out."

"I think that would be a good idea."

"Sara, is there anything I can help you with?"

"No, I think I can find everything alright, but thanks for asking Jack."

They finished their shopping and left the store. They went to Sara's and Maggie helped Sara prepare the food, while the men got the grill started and iced up the soda and beer. Maggie made tea and coffee. Sara looked at Maggie and said "Maggie, I'm worried something might go wrong tonight. I hope I don't say the wrong thing."

"Sara honey, everyone that's coming tonight knows what you've been through the past few weeks. They certainly won't judge you."

"Thanks Maggie. I needed to hear that." Maggie hugged Sara. "I'm going to see if the men need anything."

"Let me know so I can take it to them."

"I will Maggie."

Carrie and Tom got back to Carrie's house about 3:30 P.M. Tom hugged Carrie. "Carrie honey, I need to shower then I'm going to put on some clean clothes. I'll be out in a little while."

"Okay. I need to stir my salad and check on the food we're taking this evening. I'll change clothes after you get finished."

"Okay. I'll be out as quickly as I can." He leaned down and kissed her then went to shower.

Carrie started rushing around and getting the food ready. She suddenly felt very dizzy. She grabbed onto the kitchen counter and stood quietly for a few minutes. She sat down to catch her breath. After a few minutes she got up and finished what she was doing.

Tom came into the kitchen, and hugged and kissed her. He looked concerned. "Carrie honey, you alright? You look a little pale."

"I'm alright. I was just trying to do too much. I'm going to change clothes now. I'll be back in a little while."

Tom watched with concern on his face as she walked into her bedroom. She'd laid out what she wanted to wear so that she didn't have to rush. She started changing clothes. She felt really dizzy and suddenly she just collapsed. She yelled "Tom, I need your ..." and that was all she was able to say before she passed out."

As she felt herself starting to collapse she grabbed onto a table. The table crashed to the floor; Tom ran into her bedroom. Carrie laid quietly on the floor, clad only in a bra, and underwear. Tom knelt beside her and stroked her hair. "Carrie honey, it's Tom. Can you hear me?"

She started to moan. Tom bent down and kissed her forehead. She didn't realize what had happened. She opened her eyes. "Tom, what happened?"

"You don't remember?"

"All I remember is that I started feeling dizzy and… she looked down and realized she was only half dressed. She felt her cheeks get red. Her robe was at the foot of her bed. Tom got it for her and handed it to her. He helped her up. She was really unsteady on her feet. Tom helped her over to a chair. She sat down. "Thank you Tom. I appreciate it."

"It's not a big deal. How you feeling now?"

"Better. I'm not as dizzy. I think I was just trying to do things too quickly. The doctor told me I'd have to do things slower for awhile until I get my strength back. I just wanted to get those things done."

"Carrie, I think you worked too hard this morning. Are you sure you're up to going tonight? I can call Seth and Sara and tell them you aren't feeling well."

"I'm up to going I just have to slow down."

"Okay, but if you start feeling bad tonight, let me know; I'll bring you back here."

"I can do that Tom. By the way would you mind handing me my shirt please?" He handed her the shirt. "Thank you Tom. I'm so sorry about what just happened. I'm a little embarrassed you found me this way."

"You don't have to be sorry or embarrassed. You passed out while you were changing clothes. I didn't think anything of it. Seth had the same situation happen to him with Sara the other night, when she was changing clothes and screamed because she saw a prowler outside her window. Carrie, you have no idea how many times we, as police officers, have had to respond to calls and find people in their underwear, pajamas, or even nude. I think they're just as embarrassed as you are. We're trained to treat them like anyone else. It isn't a big deal, however, I don't remember anyone being as beautiful as you." She blushed again. He hugged her and kissed her.

Peggy got home before Ralph. She showered and was changing clothes when Ralph got home. He said hello to her, then he showered and changed his clothes. Peggy made a green salad to take to Sara's. "What time are we supposed to be there Peg?"

"Sara told me they were eating at 7:00 P.M. I wanted to get there a little early to help with preparations if we can."

"Well, it's 5:45. If we leave in fifteen minutes that would get us to Sara's by 6:15. Are we taking that salad?"

"Yes. I just put it together. I feel like we should take something."

They got into their car. "Ralph, it was wonderful to see Sara at school today. She still looks a little pale but she's anxious about coming back to work on Monday. It was nice to see Maggie, Kevin and Seth also."

"I bet you were happy to see Sara. You said she looked pale, was that from the pain of her wound?"

"No. According to Seth, Sara's been having reoccurring nightmares and some sort of illness. He didn't go into detail but she did look very pale. She didn't seem as numb as before. I think she's finally able to move forward in her life. I'm afraid she's really going to feel lost when Maggie and Kevin go home this weekend."

"I'm sure she will."

Carl and Elizabeth were the first of the guests to arrive at Sara's. They hugged Maggie and shook hands with Kevin. They both walked over and hugged Sara. "Sara, we're so glad you invited us."

"I'm glad you were able to make it on such short notice. Carl, Elizabeth, you remember Lt. Seth Parker don't you?"

"Yes, the very polite gentleman from the other night. Maggie said you're staying with Sara until they catch that awful person responsible for the murders."

"Yes ma'am I am. I'm staying in one of her guest bedrooms."

"Please, it's Elizabeth and Carl."

"Okay."

"Carl, would you care to join us out here while the women are inside. There's soda and beer in one of the coolers."

"Thank you."

"Carl, I'll be inside with Maggie and Sara."

The women continued getting the food ready. Elizabeth had brought a jello salad, and a warm casserole. Maggie turned the oven on warm and put it in there. "Sara, how you feeling today?"

"Better; thank you for asking. I felt so bad about what happened at your house the other night; I just wasn't feeling well."

"I could tell dear. You looked pale. You've been through a lot these past few weeks. I'm glad you're feeling better."

They talked a little while longer when there was another knock at the door. Sara answered it. It was Peggy and Ralph. Sara smiled and invited them in. They took the salad into the kitchen. Ralph joined the men outside and Peggy joined the woman. "Sara, I was so glad to see you today. I can tell you're feeling better. I'm so glad you invited Ralph and I tonight."

"Peggy, have you met Elizabeth Harris? She and her husband Carl are very dear friends of Maggie and Kevin."

"Hello. It's a pleasure to meet you Elizabeth."

"It's a pleasure to meet you too."

"Sara, are Tom and Carrie coming?"

"Yes. They said they were."

"I'm surprised they aren't here yet?"

"Well, maybe they are running a little late. Carrie hasn't been feeling well since her last treatment and maybe that has something to do with it too."

"Maybe. I'm so thrilled to know that she and Tom are getting married."

"Me too. Sergeant Monroe is a very nice man. I know they'll be very happy together."

"That's obvious."

Tom and Carrie finally arrived at Sara's. They knocked on Sara's door. "Hi Sara. Sorry we didn't get here before now but I wasn't feeling well."

"I understand. Come in. Tom, the men are out back if you'd like to join them. There's soda and beer in a cooler out there. Help yourself."

"Thanks Sara." He hugged Sara then whispered "Are you alright?"

Sara nodded yes and Tom went out and joined the men.

"Hello Carrie. It's nice to see you again."

"It's nice to see you too Elizabeth. Is there anything I can help with?"

"If you feel up to it would you mind getting some Chinet plates out of my pantry. They should be on the second shelf from the bottom."

Carrie opened up the pantry door and took out a stack of plates and took them over to the where they had set the rest of the food. "Sara, I can't thank you enough for inviting me."

"I'm glad you could come. You said you weren't feeling well earlier; are you feeling better now?"

"Yes. I think I was trying to do too much too fast. That happens every once in awhile."

"Carrie, Sara tells me that you're going to be able to go back to work on Monday also, is that right?"

"Yes and I'm thrilled. I've missed everyone and missed my students."

"What grade do you teach?"

"I teach seventh grade history and science."

"That sounds interesting. It sounds like you really like it."

"Most of the time I enjoy teaching but there are things like grading students on their work that I really don't like to do but it's necessary."

The women talked and finished preparing the food. Seth came in and said he needed to get some more ice for the cooler and that the grill was ready for the meat. Maggie and Sara took the meat to them. Kevin put the meat on the grill and Seth seasoned it. Carl, Tom, and Ralph were playing darts in the four seasons room. Sara smiled at Seth. He could tell she was nervous. He looked over at the other men and said "Kevin, could you watch the grill for a few minutes?"

"Sure Seth."

"Gentlemen, would you please excuse me? I need to talk to Sara privately for a few minutes." Seth and Sara walked over to some trees in her yard, out of ear shot of everyone else. "Sara, you alright?"

"Yes. I'm just nervous. Maybe this wasn't such a good idea."

"Sara, Maggie, Kevin, and I will be here if anything happens. All of these people are your friends. They're not going to judge you if you get upset or start to cry. Given what you've been through, it's perfectly normal."

Sara clasped Seth's hand. "Thank you Seth. I needed to hear that." They talked a little while longer then Sara went inside to finish up the meal.

Pat left work around 6:30 P.M. Art was busy with a customer so he didn't see her leave. When he realized she was gone he asked another co-worker where she was. He was infuriated that she was gone and he hadn't had a chance to talk to her.

Murder *When the Bell Tolls*

He couldn't wait to get off work. His boss let him leave at 7:15 P.M. "Art, I'll see you at 7:30 in the morning okay?"

Art gave him a smirk. "Yes sir. I'll be here."

Art went home, grabbed something to eat, watched a little television, took a shower then went into his den. He wanted to finish a letter he was writing so that he could put it in the mail on Monday. He finished the letter but didn't put it in the envelope just yet. He wasn't sure if he needed to add anything or not; he would know after the weekend.

Everyone was having a great time at Sara's. Sara was actually laughing and smiling. Everyone decided they wanted dessert and either coffee or tea. Maggie and Sara went inside to get it. "Sara, it's nice to see you smile honey. You're actually enjoying yourself aren't you?"

"Yes I am. Elizabeth's so nice. Maggie I was afraid I'd done something to offend her especially after I got sick at her house the other night."

"Sara, Elizabeth didn't think anything of you getting sick. She was worried about you. We talked about that when I called her and asked them to come tonight. She has four grown children and nine grandchildren. She knows what's it's like when one of them is ill. She really likes you Sara and she likes Seth and the rest of your friends. Elizabeth and Carl are really nice people; they've always been there for us when we needed them."

"Maggie, thank you for introducing them to me. I like both of them. I hope even though Paul is gone now all of us can remain friends."

"I'm sure we can. Sara you'll always be like family and I'm sure Elizabeth and Carl will feel like that too. They adored Paul and watched him grow up. They were thrilled, like we were when they found out the two of you were getting married. They wanted to know all about you and couldn't wait to meet you. Unfortunately the circumstances in which they met you were not what anyone expected."

"No they weren't but I'm still glad I met them.

As Sara and Maggie were getting ready to take the desserts out to everyone, Tom and Seth came into the house. "Let us help you with those."

"Thank you both."

Everyone ate their desserts and continued talking. At 11:00 Ralph and Peggy said "Sara, we hate to leave this party but Ralph has to go into the office tomorrow so we better go home and get some sleep. Thank you for inviting us. We had a great time."

"Thank you for coming. We enjoyed your company."

Elizabeth and Carl were the next ones to leave. "Sara, we had a wonderful time. I'm glad we got the chance to know you and your friends better. We're going to have to do this again sometime."

"Yes we are. I enjoyed getting to know you better. Thank you for coming."

Maggie was stacking up dirty dishes next to the sink to wash. Sara looked over at her. "Maggie, you don't have to do those dishes. You're a guest. I can do those."

"Sara, why don't you let me help you?"

Before Sara could say anything, Carrie walked into the kitchen and said "Sara, there are a lot of dishes. Why don't you let us help you. It would go faster; besides I feel like I need to do something to help."

"Carrie, Maggie, I appreciate your offer but you're guests here. I couldn't expect my guests to do the dishes."

"We want to help."

"Well, okay. I'll wash and you two can dry and help put the dishes where they belong." Sara said.

"Alright, that's fine."

Seth, Tom, and Kevin sat in the living room and started talking. Sara filled the sink with warm soapy water and Maggie grabbed two towels and handed one to Carrie. Sara started washing the dishes. Suddenly she felt faint. She grabbed the sink and stood there for a minute. Maggie looked over at her. "Sara, you alright?"

"Yes. I'm just a little dizzy. All of this has been overwhelming."

"I'm sure it has. Why don't you sit down in one of those chairs and Carrie and I will finish up?"

"I should be helping."

"Sara, just stay there and rest." Maggie and Carrie finished up the dishes. Sara sat at the breakfast bar and held onto the counter.

Maggie motioned for Seth to come into the room. Seth walked into the kitchen. "Maggie, what's up?"

Murder *When the Bell Tolls*

"It's Sara. I had her sit down and rest because she said she was feeling dizzy. She said it was because all of this is overwhelming but Seth, I'm not so sure. Could you talk to her?"

"Sure. I'll go talk to her." He walked over to Sara and put his hand on her shoulder. "Sara, I understand you aren't feeling well again. What's going on?"

"All of this is just overwhelming. All of my friends were here and it made things easier but reality is setting in and I realize what happened that awful night three weeks ago. Oh Seth, I feel awful. I couldn't stop it even if I wanted to. Everything happened so fast and now Art is…"

Seth gasped. "Sara, what about Art?"

"It's nothing. It's just something I have to deal with."

"Sara, if you need help with it, I'll be glad to help you."

"Thanks Seth I appreciate it."

Maggie and Carrie finished the dishes right as Seth was going back into the living room. Tom could tell Carrie was starting to get tired and he could tell Sara was exhausted. "Sara, Seth, Maggie, Kevin, I think it's time Carrie and I went home. She's had a rough day and Sara, I can tell you're exhausted. We had a great time and are so glad you invited us."

"I'm glad you were able to come. Carrie, enjoy the rest of your weekend with Tom. I'll see you on Monday at school."

"I'll see you on Monday. Thank you for inviting us."

As they walked out the door, Kevin looked at Maggie. "Maggie, I think maybe we should get ready and leave too. Sara's exhausted and really needs some rest. We have a big day planned tomorrow anyway."

"Maggie, Kevin, thank you for your help today. I really appreciate it."

"You're welcome Sara. We're cleaning Paul's condo tomorrow so if you need us for something, call us there. You and Seth enjoy the day together and try to relax. We're hoping to be over there by 9:30. Seth if something happens through the night please call us. We're worried about her. Sara, we'll call you tomorrow night when we get back and make arrangements for church Sunday."

"Okay. I'll talk to you tomorrow night." Maggie hugged her then walked out the door with Kevin.

"Seth, I'm going to change into my night clothes."

"Alright. I'll be right out here."

Sara trembled as she changed clothes. She couldn't stop thinking about the last murder. It was extremely cruel and brutal. After she changed her clothes she walked into the living room and told Seth goodnight. He told her good night then headed back to his room to get ready for bed himself. He checked on Sara before he went to bed. She was sleeping soundly.

On Saturday morning Art got up at 6:00 A.M. He showered, shaved, then went downstairs to eat breakfast. After breakfast he left for work. When he arrived at work he saw Pat at her station counting money. "Good morning Pat." He said cheerfully.

"Good morning Art."

He started counting his money. He wanted to be ready for customers when the bank opened at 8:00 A.M. Although he was counting and sorting his money he kept looking over at Pat. He felt the anger building inside but remembered he had to be polite to everyone, including Pat.

Art's boss walked over to him. "Well Art. Are you ready for your vacation ?"

"Yes. I'm glad to be getting away for a few days."

"Do you know where you're going yet?"

"No, I haven't decided that yet."

"I know you'll be missed around here. No one will be able to do the job like you do."

"Thank you sir." Art started feeling needed. He was ready for the bank to open.

Maggie and Kevin got up, got dressed then ate breakfast at their hotel. After breakfast they left the hotel and headed to the store to buy cleaning supplies. It was about 8:45 A.M. Maggie decided to call Sara. She was really worried about her. "Seth answered the phone. "Hi Seth, it's Maggie. How are you this morning?"

"I'm doing alright. How are both of you?"

"We're doing alright. We're heading to a store to buy some cleaning supplies. How's Sara?"

"I think she's doing okay. She said she slept fairly well last night but she still seems a little shaky. Would you like to speak to her?"

"Yes, I would. Thanks Seth."

"Good morning Maggie."

"Good morning Sara. How you feeling honey?"

"Better. Yesterday was just a little more than I was able to handle. I thought I could handle a barbeque but I wasn't ready. I'm hoping I'm going to be ready to go back to work on Monday."

"I hope you are too. Do you two have anything planned for today?"

"I'm not sure. We talked about going shopping then to a movie or just shopping."

"That sounds fun. We're on our way over to Paul's condo. If you need us call us there."

"I will."

"Sara, you sound different. Are you sure everything's alright?"

"Yes, everything's fine, really."

"We'll talk to you later about church tomorrow."

"I'll talk to you then."

When Sara hung up the phone she had tears running down her face. Seth ran his hand across her shoulders. "What's wrong Sara?"

"It's just Maggie and Kevin are cleaning Paul's condo. I started thinking about Paul and all the great times we had together there. I cry just thinking about it and about what happened to Paul."

Seth put his arm around Sara's shoulder and hugged her. "I understand how you feel Sara; I truly do."

They talked for a little while then decided they wanted to go do some antiquing. They got dressed and left to go to the antique shops.

Tom got up earlier than Carrie. He went into the kitchen, fixed coffee, then fixed breakfast. He was just finishing breakfast when Carrie walked into the kitchen. "Tom, something smells good. What is that?"

"I fixed coffee and I made ham and cheese omelets, with hash browns."

"That sounds fantastic. I know I'm going to enjoy this breakfast."

"I hope so. It's ready."

He leaned down and kissed her, then served her breakfast. She smiled. "Thank you Tom."

He sat down and they ate together, then they cleaned up the kitchen. "Carrie, how you feeling today?"

"Better. I slept really well last night."

"So did I. Carrie you were sleeping peacefully when I checked on you earlier this morning. I had a wonderful time at Sara's last night."

"So did I. Sara's always a gracious hostess and we always have fun at her home."

"Carrie, I have a big day planned for us today."

"Really?" She smiled. "And what does that entail?"

"First of all I thought I'd take you to the mall since you said you'd like to find a new dress and shoes, then secondly I'm going to take you to a lovely restaurant for dinner, followed by a surprise."

"I like surprises."

"I know. I also know you'll love this one."

They embraced and kissed each other. "Carrie, would you mind if I wore dress jeans and a buttoned down shirt today?"

"Not if you don't mind me wearing jeans and a nice blouse?"

"I don't mind."

They both went to change their clothes. Carrie wanted to wear something casual and not too dressy but nothing too casual. She picked out a short sleeve baby blue satin shirt to wear with her jeans. She walked out to where Tom was. He smiled a huge smile. "You look fabulous Carrie. That blouse really brings out the color in your eyes."

"Thanks Tom. You look quite handsome yourself."

"Are you ready to leave?"

"Yes I'm ready." They left to go to the mall.

At the bank, Art was waiting on customers. He kept looking over at Pat. He had to talk to her. He had to know what she told Tom.

Pat felt nervous when Art looked at her. She wished he'd just do his job and stop watching her. She wondered if he knew she'd talked to Tom.

At 10:00 Art was scheduled for a break. He walked over to Pat and tapped her on the shoulder. "I'm getting ready to go on a break in about fifteen minutes. I was wondering if you'd like to join me."

Murder *When the Bell Tolls*

Pat looked at Art. She didn't want to be anywhere near him but was afraid to tell him no so she said "Okay, I'll go on break with you."

Art smiled. "Good. I'm glad you said yes. I'll enjoy the company."

※

Maggie and Kevin got to Paul's condo about 10:00. Maggie sobbed as they walked inside. They set the things down, looked around deciding what to do first. Maggie noticed Paul had some laundry that needed to be washed so she put a load in the washer. She went into the kitchen and fixed a pot of coffee. She emptied out the refrigerator then cleaned everything in the kitchen, including the oven. Kevin swept the foyer floor and the bathroom floor, then he mopped them. They continued cleaning.

They took a break from cleaning around 11:00 and called a Chinese place to order food for lunch. They talked a little while until the food arrived. They ate lunch and talked about Paul. "He really loved Sara, and I know she loved him. They would've been so happy together." Kevin said.

"I know they really loved each other. Sara's having a really hard time dealing with Paul's murder and frankly so am I. I hope Sara can move forward with her life."

"So do I. I think her going back to work on Monday will be a big start. I know she'll be nervous."

"I know. Even Carrie told me she herself would be nervous. I really like Carrie. I'm so happy for her and Tom. I know it seems like a whirlwind romance but I can tell they really love each other. I believe in love at first sight and those two had that happen. They've both been married before anyway so it's not like they're young kids."

"I agree. I like Tom Monroe. Sara told me he's very nice and treated her with respect and dignity."

"I know Paul would want Sara to be happy."

"I know that too."

"Kevin, I don't know if you're aware of this but Sara's falling in love with Seth. She's afraid to let him know because she thinks it's too soon after Paul's death. She told me he's so much like Paul. She said she feels safe with him and he's treated her with the utmost respect and is so compassionate and understanding. I have a feeling their relationship will continue to grow into a romance. I think she's seeking approval from us that it's alright to fall in love with someone else, especially this soon after Paul's death."

"Maggie, I know Paul would want Sara to be happy and I know he'd tell her it's alright to fall in love again. I'm sure when you have someone with you twenty-four hours a day it's easy to become friends and eventually romantically involved. I really like Seth. I think he and Sara would make a wonderful couple and I know he'd treat her right. Paul would approve, I'm sure."

"I think she's afraid we won't consider her family anymore if she and Seth would eventually marry, but we both know that's not so. Sara will always be part of our family."

"I know that. Maggie, I think you should talk to her and reassure her of that. Let her know Paul would be pleased to know she found someone who will treat her right and love her for who she is."

Tom and Carrie left around 10:00 A.M. to go to the mall. They went to different shops looking for just the right thing when Carrie saw what she wanted hanging in one of the store windows. She and Tom went into the store. She tried on the outfit and told the clerk she'd take it. She purchased a knee length white dress with red polka dots, a floppy white hat with a big red bow and red pumps. She smiled when they walked out of the store.

"Carrie, I really like that outfit. I think it'll look really nice on you."

"Thanks Tom. I was planning on wearing it to church tomorrow."

"Good. I'm anxious to see that outfit on you."

They shopped for a little while longer then Carrie said "Tom, I need to take a break. I'm starting to feel a little weak."

"Why don't we go to the coffee shop and get a cup of coffee? That might help both of us; unless you're hungry?"

"I could eat a sandwich. Why don't we get a bite to eat in the food court? Maybe that will perk me up. Besides, I have one more shop I need to go to before I'm finished shopping."

They went into the food court, grabbed a sandwich, potato chips, and a cup of coffee. They ate and talked for quite awhile.

Seth and Sara decided to take a break from shopping. They stopped at a deli and got some sandwiches. They sat down at the tables outside and enjoyed eating. They talked for awhile and decided they'd go to the early show, then go home and play some cards. They finished their lunch then shopped more.

∽✼∾

Art went into the break room. He heated up what he brought to eat and watched the door waiting for Pat. He took his food out of the microwave, then sat down to eat. He kept looking over at the door hoping Pat would come soon.

Pat finally walked into the break room. She trembled as Art walked over to her. "Hello Pat. I'm so glad you decided to take your break with me. It's gets pretty quiet when there's no one in here but me."

"I know. I noticed that the other day, when I took my break by myself."

Pat got her food out of the refrigerator and sat down with Art to eat. "Art, I understand you're going on vacation starting as soon as you get out of here today."

"Yes, I am."

"Do you know where you're going?"

"No. I haven't decided. It sort of depends on what my cousin Jack is doing."

"Is he going with you on vacation?"

"No, but I'm having him watch my house and get my mail for me while I'm gone."

"That's nice. Jack's a nice man."

Art's break was over. "Well, my break time is over. I'll talk to you later Pat. Thank you for sharing your break time with me. It means a lot."

Pat swallowed hard. "You're welcome Art."

Art walked to his teller's station and started working again. Ten minutes later Pat came out. One of Pat's friends looked at Pat then looked at Art. "Pat did anything happen during break?"

"No. Art was nothing but nice. I'm really worried. That's not like him."

"No kidding. I can't believe you actually went out with him."

"Neither can I. I wish I hadn't."

"What time do you get off Pat?"

"I'm working until 3:30. Art and I are scheduled to close together today."

"Oh my. Be careful."

"I will."

Around 11:30, right after Art's break, his cousin Jack walked in. "Hello Art."

"Hello Jack. What brings you here?"

"Art, I have to talk to you. I can't help you anymore."

"Jack, let's go into an office and talk more privately." They walked into an office and Art closed the door. "Okay Jack, what's this about?"

"Art, I can't take this guilt anymore. I feel like I'm losing my mind."

"Jack, calm down. I tell you what. I'm on vacation starting at 3:30 today. I'll be busy the rest of the day and part of the day tomorrow. Why don't we meet in the park Sunday evening around 9:00 P.M. and we can talk?"

"Well okay, but where should we meet?"

"Under that big oak tree next to the fountain."

"Okay, I'll be there."

Jack walked out of the bank at 12:15 P.M. He headed over to his store.

The bank closed for the day. It was now 3:20 in the afternoon. Art and Pat were finishing up. Art and Pat walked out the door and to the parking lot. Before Pat could get in her car, Art grabbed her by the arm and pulled her into his car. He covered her mouth so she couldn't scream. Once they were in his car he locked the door from the inside. "Pat, I would like for you to join me tonight for dinner. We'll go back to my place and talk."

"Art, I'm not dressed for dinner. Wouldn't you rather I go home first so that I can shower and look nice just for you?"

Art smiled but said "You look fine just like you are."

Pat started to panic. She wanted to get away from Art but he had the door set for child safety and no one could open the door except from the outside. She could only imagine what would happen.

While Art was taking Pat to his place, Seth and Sara were heading to a restaurant to eat an early dinner and go to the show. Sara was feeling better and looking forward to a night out. They got to the restaurant and the waiter showed them to

Murder *When the Bell Tolls*

their table. Once they were seated, Seth looked at Sara. "How are you feeling Sara?"

"Better. I've had a lot of fun today."

"So have I. I'd been wanting to get these bookends for a long time. I'm a big collector of classic ships and airplanes."

"You know I'm a collector of dolphins."

"I like dolphins too."

"Seth, I want to thank you for being so understanding these past few days. I don't know what is happening to me. It just seems so unreal."

Seth reached across the table and clasped Sara's hand, then looked at her very compassionately. "Sara, I care about you and I'm here to help."

Sara felt her cheeks turning red. She smiled and said "Thank you Seth." She realized she was falling in love with Seth and was trying to keep those emotions to herself at that moment.

They ordered their food, then talked while they waited for their order. They talked about their work and about the things they had in common like the theater, music, and a couple of board games.

Art and Pat got to Art's house. He walked around the outside of the car and unlocked her door and helped her out. They walked into his house. Pat looked around. "This is a nice place Art. How do you keep everything so neat and organized?"

"I try not to make too much of a mess. Having a woman around would help; I know I would enjoy the company. Tonight I'm going to fix you a nice home cooked meal and we can talk. After dinner, we can watch a couple of movies."

"How am I going to get home tonight Art?"

"You're not. You're spending the night with me; did I forget to tell you that?"

"Yes you did. I'm a Sunday school teacher and need to be at my church in the morning."

"Well, you need to call them and tell them you won't be there because you'll be busy."

Pat gasped. "Art, I can't tell them that. They'll want to know if something is wrong."

"Just tell them something has come up and you can't make it. Now, let's go into the kitchen so that I can fix our dinner."

Art fixed dinner for them and they sat down at his dining room table and ate. "Pat, I understand there was a police officer at the bank Thursday asking questions. Our boss said he talked to you."

"Yes he did."

"What did he want to know?"

"He asked about you and about the other workers."

"What did you tell him?"

"That I knew you fairly well and that I hadn't noticed anything different about you, that was until now."

"Oh so now you notice. Before you didn't give me the time of day. I thought after we went out the first time that it wouldn't be our last. You broke my heart when you kept telling me no, just like Sara Michaels, Martha Burns, and Rebecca."

Pat gasped. "What does that have to do with those three ladies?"

"All of them, except Sara disrespected me and I've made them pay. I have loved all of you and all any of you have ever done is turn me down. I'm not good enough for you, well, that's going to change; you'll see." Pat was terrified.

Tom and Carrie had gone to a nice restaurant to eat. Carrie felt exhausted from shopping so sitting in a restaurant having someone wait on her was wonderful. Tom smiled at her, then clasped her hand. She looked around. "Tom, everything in here is so unique and so lovely. I've never been to this place."

"I thought maybe you would enjoy this place, especially since they wait on you, instead of you having to get up and serve yourself. I thought you deserved a special night at a nice restaurant."

"It is very nice Tom. I love it."

Tom clasped Carrie's hand and they continued talking until the waiter came and took their orders. Once their orders were placed they continued talking. "Tom, I'm worried about Sara. She looks really tired."

"I'm worried about her too but I know Seth will take good care of her."

"I wonder if the nightmares she has been having are getting any better. I know she's worried about talking to Seth about something."

"Why?"

Murder *When the Bell Tolls*

"Tom, I shouldn't tell you this but I'm going to. Sara's falling in love with Seth and she's afraid if she tells him about Art he will walk out of her life."

"Carrie, I know you've told me that Sara told you some of what happened between her and Art. I respect you for not telling me what she said, but you really need to convince Sara she needs to tell Seth about it. I can guarantee that whatever it is, he won't walk away from her. He has fallen in love with her and he really cares about her and that will never change."

"Tom, since Sara is going back to work Monday, I'll talk to her about it. She and I have always been able to be straight forward with each other and respect each others' opinions and feelings."

"Are you nervous about going back to work Carrie?"

"A little. I'll have a classroom helper with me at least the first week to try and get me back on track to where the students are in class work and homework. Nancy has tried to keep me up to date with that but after Paul's murder I lost track of things. Sara has been the only thing on my mind, except you of course."

He smiled. "I know the feeling. Finding this serial killer was all that was on my mind until I met you. I love you Carrie."

"I love you Tom."

The food arrived; they ate and talked. After they finished eating, Tom paid the bill, then left a tip. They left the restaurant. Once they were out of the restaurant, Tom and Carrie walked to the car hand in hand. They got to the car and Tom embraced Carrie, held her close to him and kissed her, then helped her in the car. "Carrie, are you ready for your surprise?"

"Yes, I am."

"Good. I actually have two surprises for you but we need to get back to the park for the first one."

"The park?"

"Yes."

As Tom and Carrie drove back to the park, Seth and Sara arrived at the movie theater. "Sara, would you like something from the snack bar?"

"Yes. Some buttered popcorn and a large diet soda."

Seth ordered an extra large tub of buttered popcorn and two drinks. Once they got their snacks they headed into the theater and took their seats. "I heard this is supposed to be a really good movie. It's supposed to be really funny. I thought we both would enjoy laughing a little."

"I know I would." Sara said. "I don't think I've ever cried so much as I have these past two and a half weeks."

"Sara, it's understandable."

Art and Pat finished eating. Art got up and pulled Pat to her feet. He pulled her into the living room. "I got a movie that I thought we could watch together." Pat had no idea what type of movie it would be. She hoped it wasn't horror or porn. "Now, before we watch the movie you will remove your shirt, skirt, pantyhose, and shoes then join me on the couch."

Pat gasped and then said. "No. I will not remove my clothes for anyone unless I decide to do it myself."

Art got furious. He grabbed Pat's arm and squeezed it. "You will remove what items of clothing I told you to remove or I'll remove them for you then make you pay dearly for disobeying me."

Pat was terrified and did what he asked. Art smiled when he saw her. "Now, walk over to me." She trembled as she walked over to him. When she got over to him, he pulled her down onto the couch. He handed her the phone, "Now, get on that phone and call whoever you need to and tell them you won't be there tomorrow. If you say anything other than an emergency has come up, I promise you, you'll be sorry."

Pat called a friend of hers. "Hello."

"Hello Sheila, it's Pat."

"Hi Pat. It's nice to hear from you. Are you ready for tomorrow?"

"Well, that's what I called you about. An emergency has come up and I'm afraid I won't be able to be there."

"I'm sorry to hear that. Is there anything I can do?"

Pat thought about what to say. "I don't think so. Thanks for understanding Sheila."

"It's okay but you sound funny? Would you like me to come by your house this evening?"

Pat started to panic. "No. Um that's okay. I'll be alright. I'll talk to you later in the week okay?"

"Okay, but if I can help in any way, let me know."

Before Pat could say anymore, Art grabbed the phone away from her. He sat the phone down on the cushion of the couch and slapped Pat across the face. She screamed. "Shut up Pat. You had that coming."

On the other end of the phone Sheila was screaming "Pat, Pat, are you alright? What's happening?"

Art picked up the phone. "I don't know who you are but your friend won't be around for quite some time. She'll be busy with me paying for her sins. If you pursue this conversation farther you will suffer the consequences. Goodbye."

Art slammed the phone down and pulled Pat down onto the couch. "Now, we are going to watch the movie then I will escort you upstairs where you will be allowed to shower and change into the outfit I bought for you. If you try to run, you'll be sorry."

Pat was too terrified to try and run. She sat on the couch as Art put the movie into the DVD player. He came over to the couch and sat down next to Pat. They started watching the movie. Art put his arm around Pat. She shuddered. He leaned over and kissed her. She knew better than to resist him because of her earlier experience with him. The last time they were together she slapped him for kissing her and he slapped her back, along with what he called spanking her. She cringed thinking about that experience. She dreaded what he might do now.

"Your lips feel so good on mine but not as good as Sara Michaels."

"What does Sara have to do with this?"

"You haven't figured that out yet have you?"

"No. All I know is Sara is a very sweet lady and my daughter loved her when she had her for a teacher."

"I forgot you have two adult daughters. How are they doing?"

"They're doing good. Why do you ask?"

"No reason, just curious."

When the movie was over Art got up from the couch and pulled Pat up. "Well Pat, now I will escort you to where you may take a shower. After your shower, you will put on the outfit I bought for you, model it for me then you and I will take care of some unfinished business. Let's go."

Art grabbed Pat by the wrists and pulled her upstairs and took her into his bedroom. He took her into his bathroom. "You may shower in here. There are towels on the rack. I will bring your outfit in while you are in the shower. Go ahead and get undressed to shower."

"May I please undress the rest of the way in private?"

Art was angry but looked at Pat and said "I'll step out for now; get undressed and make it fast!"

Art walked out of the bathroom and got the outfit for Pat to wear. He heard the water in the shower begin. He opened the door just a crack to see if Pat was in the shower yet. He smiled when he saw her completely nude with her back to the door. He watched her step into the shower and waited a few more seconds to enter the bathroom again. When he took the outfit into the bathroom he could see her silhouette thru the glass door of the shower. He smiled, set the outfit down then said "Pat, the outfit for you to wear is laying across the sink. You better be wearing it when you come out."

Pat trembled and replied "Okay Art. I'll be finished in a few minutes."

"Good. I'll be waiting in the bedroom."

Pat finished her shower then got out and dried off. She gasped when she saw the outfit that Art had put out for her to wear. She cried as she put the outfit on. She felt so humiliated. After she was dressed she walked into the bedroom and found Art sitting on the edge of the bed. He smiled then grabbed her by her wrists and pulled her over to the bed. "That outfit looks wonderful on you, now it's time to take care of the unfinished business I talked about."

"What's the unfinished business Art?"

"You need to find out what happens when you disrespect and reject me. Rebecca had to learn too. Both you and Rebecca are helping me decide what I need to do to Sara to earn her love and respect."

Pat gasped. "Rebecca? Art what did you do to Rebecca? Was it you who brutalized her so badly? Did you kill her?"

Art wouldn't answer. He grabbed Pat by the wrists and said, "Get on the bed on all fours!" She did. "Now, I'm going to tie your hands to the headboard and we'll get started."

"Art, what are you going to do to me?"

"You're going to get what you deserve!"

Tom and Carrie got to the park. He parked the car, leaned over and kissed Carrie then handed her a ring box. "What's this?"

"Open it up and find out."

When she opened up the box she saw the most beautiful diamond ring she had ever seen. She started to cry. "Tom it's beautiful."

"I wanted to give you an engagement ring so that others know it's official. I love you Carrie."

"I love you too Tom."

"Now comes the next surprise."

They walked across the park to where a fancy horse and carriage were waiting. Tom looked at Carrie. "Your carriage awaits Madame."

Carrie had tears of joy in her eyes. Her late husband wasn't able to take her on evening carriage rides or able to do much of anything else after he got sick so she was thrilled. She remembered how romantic the evening rides with her husband used to be. Tom helped her climb in then he got in. He leaned over and kissed her. "Are you surprised Carrie?"

"Yes I am. Thank you Tom."

The carriage ride began. Carrie moved closer to Tom. He put his arm around her and she leaned against him. The driver guided the carriage around the park. Halfway through the ride Tom kissed Carrie. "Are you alright darling?"

"Yes. This is so romantic."

"I think so too and you're so beautiful in the moonlight." He kissed her again. "Are you enjoying the ride?"

"Yes and you look quite handsome yourself." Tom smiled.

When the carriage got to the spot where Paul was killed Carrie and Tom both shuddered. Carrie shook her head. "It's such a shame that something like that had to happen."

"I agree. Sara is such a lovely person and I feel honored knowing her."

"She is a wonderful person and so are you Tom."

They kissed each other and moved closer to each other. It was getting chilly outside so they snuggled closer to each other until the carriage ride was over. Once the ride was over Tom helped Carrie out of the carriage and they walked to the car. "Carrie, I could use some coffee and maybe something to eat. How about you?"

"That sounds wonderful."

Tom and Carrie drove to an ice cream shop and went inside to eat. Tom looked at the menu. "I would like a cup of coffee and a double scoop of peach ice cream in a waffle bowl for myself. Carrie what would you like?"

Carrie felt like a teenager on her first date after the carriage ride. She couldn't stop thinking about how wonderful it was. Tom could tell she was daydreaming so he put his hand on hers. "Carrie honey, the waitress would like to know what you would like."

She looked over at Tom and smiled, then looked at the waitress and said "I would like a cup of coffee and a double scoop of rocky road ice cream in a waffle bowl also please."

"I'll get that right to you."

"Thank you ma'am."

They talked while they waited for their order. When their order arrived they ate their ice cream and drank some coffee. "So Carrie, did you like your surprise?"

"I loved it."

"I thought you would. I felt so bad about having to work late the past few nights with this last murder and I wanted to make it up to you. I had hoped it would all work perfectly and it did."

"Tom, I do understand that your job requires you to work extra hours and that's alright. I can handle that. My job as a teacher doesn't just end in the classroom either. I have lessons to prepare and papers to grade. Even though my late husband and I were both teachers we made a rule. We always allowed at least two hours a day for just us. That meant watching a movie together, going on a carriage ride, whatever at least until he got sick and that along with my job took up all of my time. Tom we need to make that same promise to each other now, especially since I'm going back to work on Monday. I know there's only a month of school left but it will be extremely busy and I want us to be able to have time together."

"I agree. We need to make time just for us." They kissed each other, then left to go to Carrie's.

Seth and Sara had enjoyed the movie and both laughed a lot. They walked out of the theater and headed to Seth's car. He helped Sara into the car. "Sara are you ready to go home?"

"Yes I am." As Seth was driving Sara said "Seth, I really enjoyed the movie. It made me laugh."

"It did me too. Are you hungry Sara?"

"Not yet."

"Well, I have an idea. Since it's early yet, why don't we just go home, play some cards and if we get hungry order something?"

"That sounds wonderful. That way I can shower and get in my night clothes."

"That sounds good."

They headed home. Once they got home, they walked inside. The light on the answering machine was blinking so Sara decided to check her messages. She heard "Sara honey, it's Maggie. Kevin and I got home around 6:00 P.M. We discussed our plans for tomorrow and decided we would meet you and Seth at your house around 8:00 A.M. for church; after church we want to take you out for lunch. Please call me back at the motel and let me know if these plans are alright. Thanks sweetie. We love you."

Sara smiled. "Seth, do you think that's too early or not?"

"No, call them back and let them know that's fine."

"Hello Maggie, it's Sara."

"Hi sweetie. Are you doing okay?"

"Yes. Seth and I just got back from the movie so I'm returning your call. 8:00 A.M. is fine for in the morning."

"Good. Did you and Seth enjoy the movie?"

"Yes we did. We went shopping and ate an early supper before the movie. We're going to play some cards and order something if we get hungry. Did you get done what you wanted to do?"

"Yes and everything else from Paul's condo is yours, including the condo."

"What do you mean including the condo?"

"We heard from Paul's lawyer and he left the condo to you. He was planning on renting it out after you two were married. It was supposed to be a surprise wedding present."

Sara was shocked. "Wow! I had no idea."

Maggie laughed "Sara honey, you can decide what you want to do with the condo at a later time. It's clean though so you don't have to worry about that. Honey, we'll see you at 8:00 tomorrow okay?"

"Okay. Thanks for the information Maggie."

"You're welcome."

Sara hung the phone up and looked at Seth with a shocked look on her face. "Sara, what's wrong? Are Maggie and Kevin alright?"

"They're fine. I just found out that Paul left his condo to me. He was planning on renting it out after we got married. It was supposed to be a surprise wedding gift."

"That is a wonderful surprise. Do you have any idea what you're going to do with the condo?"

"Not yet. I can't even think straight right now. I feel so confused."

"Well, you can deal with that later. Are there any more messages on the machine?"

"No, that was the only one."

Seth smiled. "I'm glad; that means Tom was able to spend the day alone with Carrie. I wonder what the surprise was that he had in store for her?"

"I wonder too. Seth, I'm going to shower now. Go ahead and get the cards"

"Alright."

Sara walked to her bedroom to shower. She finally had a good day where she didn't cry as much. She got undressed and got into the shower. After she took a shower, she dried off and dressed into her night clothes, then went into the dining room where Seth was. "I'm finished with my shower now. Would you like for me to make a pot of coffee?"

"That sounds good. I think I'll go shower now."

"I'll start the coffee and meet you in the dining room."

"Alright."

Seth went into his bedroom to shower. He took a shower, then dressed in his night clothes also. He met Sara in the kitchen. They both poured themselves a cup of coffee and went into the dining room and started playing cards.

Carrie and Tom got to Carries and went inside. They hung their jackets up on a coat rack by the front door. Tom embraced Carrie and kissed her. She kissed him back. "Carrie, it's still early would you like to watch a movie or something?"

"Watching a movie sounds great. I need to relax after that very busy day. Tom, I really enjoyed today."

"So did I. I promise you there will be a lot more of those days after we're married too." Carrie smiled, then Tom kissed her again.

Murder *When the Bell Tolls*

"Tom, would you mind if I changed into my night clothes before we watch the movie?"

"No. As a matter of fact, I think I'll do the same thing."

They both went into their bedrooms to change clothes. Tom changed quickly into his night clothes and headed out to the living room. He passed Carrie's room on the way there. She had left her door open a crack. She had her back to the door when he looked in to make sure she was alright. She was only wearing her underwear. Tom smiled, then continued walking into the living room. He put a movie in the DVD player and waited for Carrie to come in.

Carrie walked into the living room and sat down next to Tom on the sofa. He turned the movie on. They snuggled close together and watched the movie until they both fell asleep in each others' arms.

Pat spent three hours screaming and begging Art to stop hurting her. He looked at her and said "This is only the beginning my dear. This is just for disobeying me. You still have to learn what happens when you reject me and what happens when you tell people things you shouldn't."

"Art please I'm sorry. It won't happen again."

"I know it won't. I'm going to make sure of that my dear Pat. You will be branded for the rest of your life."

"What does that mean Art?"

"You'll find out tomorrow after I get back from church. Now, it's getting late. Here's what's going to happen. You will be sleeping in my bed with me. I will allow you to sleep for two hours, then I will awaken you and you will find out what happens when you tell people things you shouldn't, then I will allow you to sleep until morning. In the morning, I will untie you, take you downstairs, set you in a chair, let you eat breakfast, then use the restroom, then I will take you into a room where you will remain until I return from church with our lunch. I will have a portable toilet next to you so you may use the restroom when you need to. When I return for lunch you will eat lunch, then we will come back up here and you will find out what happens when you reject me and talk about me behind my back."

"Art, I promise. I won't do that again. I'll tell people that you are a very warm and loving person and that any woman should be proud to go out with you." Pat said gasping from tears and from the pain.

"That's a great gesture but it won't prevent you from finding out what happens when you reject me and talk about me behind my back. Now let's get some sleep."

"Art, could you please untie me from the bed so I can get comfortable?"

"I'll untie one of your hands but that's it." He untied her left hand and shoved her down on the bed. "Now go to sleep or we'll continue our unfinished business now"

Pat laid down and sobbed into her pillow. Her whole body ached. She had no idea how bad the back side of her looked, she just knew it hurt.

Sara and Seth were enjoying their game of cards. Seth looked at the clock. "Sara, it's 10:15. Are you hungry or anything?"

"Yes I am. I was going to ask you if you were hungry."

"Why don't we order a large pizza and have it delivered?"

"That sounds good. I'll call in the order."

Sara called in their order and they told her it would be about thirty minutes. They continued playing their game until the pizza arrived. At 11:00 the pizza was delivered. Seth paid the person, tipped the person and brought the pizza over to the table. "I'll get some paper plates to put this on."

Seth got plates and they ate and continued their game. They talked and laughed. Around midnight they both decided that it was time to go to bed. Seth walked Sara back to her bedroom then he went into his room and got into bed. He laid in bed and thought about how wonderful it was to finally see Sara smile and laugh; then he thought about how much he wanted to get the people responsible for Paul's murder. As he closed his eyes he thought about how wonderful of a day he'd had. It had been a long time since he enjoyed himself that much. He went to sleep quickly.

Sara got into bed. She thought about how much enjoyment she'd that day. She was finally starting to feel like herself again. She smiled when she thought about Seth and how much fun the two of them had. She closed her eyes and fell into a peaceful sleep.

Art had set his alarm to go off in two hours. When his alarm went off Pat jumped and trembled in fear. Art got up, went into the bathroom, grabbed what he needed and came out. He pulled Pat's head up by her hair. She was crying and he laughed an eerie laugh. "Well my dear Pat, it's time to settle some more unfinished business. After the next hour you will know what happens when you reject me. You will find out tomorrow what happens when you talk about me behind my back and tell people lies about me. You will realize what a mistake it was."

Pat plead with Art. He didn't listen and Pat screamed and begged for Art's forgiveness for the next hour. Art untied Pat's other hand then he yanked her up off the bed. He allowed her to use the restroom, then he pulled her back into bed with him where he continued hurting her. After another hour he pulled her up again, then he forced her to lay down on the bed on her stomach and he tied her hands to the headboard again. "It's time to go back to sleep. I need to be up by 7:00 so I can get to church by 8:30 A.M. Goodnight Pat. Sleep well. I'll see you in the morning."

Pat trembled and cried into her pillow as she tried to sleep. She was lying next to a mad man and there was no way out.

Seth's alarm went off at 6:00 A.M. He got up and got ready for church. He wanted to let Sara sleep as long as he could. He finished getting dressed and looked at his clock. It was 6:20. He walked back to Sara's bedroom and looked in. She was sleeping so peacefully he hated to wake her. "Sara, it's 6:30 A.M. You have to get up and get ready for church. Maggie and Kevin will be here in ninety minutes."

Sara sat up in bed. She looked at Seth, who was standing in her doorway. "Seth, is it really time to get up?"

"Yes it is. I'm ready to go. I'll wait out here for you."

"Thanks Seth." When Seth went into the living room Sara got up and started getting ready for church. She walked out to where Seth was, walked over to him and kissed him on the cheek. He smiled. "Seth, I wanted to say thank you for a wonderful day yesterday. I'm finally beginning to feel like myself again."

"That's great. I know how hard this must be for you."

"It is. I just hope it doesn't get harder when Maggie and Kevin go home this evening. I'm going to miss having them here. They have been such a big help through all of this but now that I'll be going back to work I would feel so bad because I wouldn't be able to spend more time with them. They are such wonderful people."

"Yes they are. I like them. I can tell how much they care about you and I'm sure you can talk to them anytime you want. I can say for sure that when we catch the people responsible for these murders, Maggie and Kevin want to know about it and be here for the trial."

"I know they do. I can't blame them. After all one of the victims was their son." Sara kept looking at Seth. "I'm sorry for staring but you look so handsome in that outfit."

"It's alright to stare Sara. You look beautiful in your outfit too." He hugged her. "Maggie and Kevin should be here soon."

When Tom woke up at 6:00 A.M. he kissed Carrie on the forehead. She opened her eyes and smiled. "Good morning Carrie."

"Good morning Tom. What time is it?"

"It's 6:00 A.M. I'm going to shower and shave before church."

"I'm going to go change my clothes too."

Tom helped her up, then he kissed her. Tom walked into his room and got into the shower. Carrie got out her new dress and put it on. After she finished getting dressed she went into the kitchen and made a pot of coffee. About ten minutes later she felt Tom wrapping his arms around her waist then kissing her on her neck. She turned around and he kissed her again. She smiled. "Carrie, that dress looks beautiful on you. Are you going to wear the hat you bought too?"

"Yes, I still feel a little uncomfortable about my hair. It's coming back in but I'm not ready to go without a hat."

"Do I smell coffee?"

"Yes, I made a fresh pot. Would you like a cup?"

"Yes, but let me get it."

They both got a cup of coffee, then Carrie took some fruit out of the refrigerator. They ate some cereal and fruit before they left for church.

Art's alarm went off at 6:00 A.M. Pat started trembling. Art leaned over and kissed her. "Good morning sleepy head. It's time to get up for breakfast." Art got up and got dressed for church.

Pat didn't want to get up. She wasn't even sure she could walk after what Art had done to her. He untied her from the bed, let her use the bathroom, then pulled her downstairs. He fixed breakfast for them, then cleaned everything up. He pulled Pat into the room where he was going to keep her until he got home from church. He forced her to remove her underwear then he pushed her down on an old couch in the room. She screamed and he slapped her across the face. She started crying. "My dear Pat, you will stay in this room until I return from church. When I get back we will eat lunch and then we will conclude our unfinished business. Right now I need to shave and finish getting ready for church. I'll be back in a little while."

Pat cringed when she moved and bit her lip to keep from screaming. Art went upstairs and finished getting ready; then he went downstairs into the room where Pat was. He leaned over and kissed her. He turned the television on. "I'll see you later my dear."

When Art walked out the door Pat tried to pull free from the couch. She cried and cringed every time she moved. She finally stopped trying and fell asleep. She felt safe for the time being.

Maggie and Kevin arrived at Sara's around 7:50 A.M. They knocked on the door and Seth answered it. "Good morning Maggie, Kevin, come in. We're just about ready."

Maggie saw Sara come out of her bedroom. Sara was actually smiling. Maggie smiled to. "Good morning Sara."

"Good morning Maggie."

"Sara you look a lot better today. You look more rested and a lot happier."

"I feel a lot better. Seth and I had a wonderful time yesterday shopping and going to the movies. We came home and played cards until midnight. I feel more like myself again."

Maggie hugged Sara. "I'm so glad you are feeling better. It's good to see you smile. I'll feel better going home knowing that you're doing better. I told Kevin I hate to leave this evening but we really need to get back home."

"I hate to see both of you go. You've been such a tremendous help to me during these last two and a half weeks. I'll miss both of you dearly, however, I would feel bad because I wouldn't be able to spend as much time with you as I would like after I go back to work on Monday."

"I'm so glad that you are feeling up to going back to work. I know that will help a lot. I want you to call us Monday night and let us know how your first day back goes and on Friday to let us know how your first week went. You can call us anytime though, you know that."

"I know. I'll miss you though."

"Is everyone ready to go now?"

"Yes, let's go."

They all got into the car and headed to Sara's church. When they got there they went down for doughnuts and coffee. Everyone talked to the four of them. Ralph and Peggy had gone early also. "Sara, Maggie, it's good to see you this morning."

"It's good to see you too Peggy."

"Maggie, Sara tells me you're going to be heading home tonight. That's too bad. We'll miss you. It's been a real pleasure getting to know you. We have enjoyed having both of you here."

"Thank you Peggy. It's been a pleasure getting to know all of you. We'll miss all of you too."

"Sara, are you excited about coming back to work tomorrow?"

"Yes I am. I know Carrie's excited also."

"Seth will be at school with you won't he?"

"Yes. Seth goes where I do. I'm glad too. Seth and I had a really nice day yesterday. We shopped, ate at a nice restaurant, went to a movie, then went home and played cards until midnight. I'm actually starting to feel more like myself again."

"I'm so glad. You've been through so much."

At 8:50 people from the first service started coming down for coffee and doughnuts. Pastor Jeff made it down also. He saw Maggie and Kevin and went over to them. He shook their hands. "Maggie, Kevin, it's good to see you again. I wasn't sure when you said you were leaving to head home."

"We're leaving early this evening. It's two hours home and we want to be home before midnight tonight. I'm not really sure what time we're leaving because we're taking Sara and Seth out for lunch after church then going back to Sara's for a little while. We're all packed and have our suitcases in the car. We're supposed to return the rental car to the dealer in New Jersey by tomorrow."

"How did you get to the airport in the first place?"

"The car rental agency at the airport came and picked us up, took us to the airport in Florida, then met us at the airport in New York with this car."

"We're glad you're here and you'll always be welcome here. If I don't see you after church, have a safe trip home."

Murder *When the Bell Tolls*

"Thank you Pastor Jeff." They all went up to church and sat together.

Art walked into his church. Several people said hello and good morning to him and he told them good morning. He was all smiles because he was on vacation and he knew he was going to get away for a few days. He knew that no one knew where he was going. He sat down in the pew and listened to the service. It was about rejection, pain, guilt, and forgiveness. He thought about Pat and Sara. He had forgiven Sara but he wanted her for himself. He wanted to forgive Pat, he just couldn't. He just knew that she had told Tom something awful about him and he couldn't forgive her for that. She had to pay for her sins.

Art was so deep in thought that the person next to him tapped him on the shoulder when the offering plate was passed. He took the plate and smiled at them. He placed a five dollar bill in the plate and passed it to the next person. He started getting anxious. He wanted the church service to be over.

When Carrie and Tom walked into Carrie's church everyone smiled. They all came up to Carrie and said good morning then Carrie introduced Tom to everyone. They all smiled, shook his hand, and congratulated both of them. One of Carrie's other friends said "Carrie, you look great and Tom's so handsome. He seems really nice."

"He is. He's been helping me do a lot of things since I had my last treatment. I go back to work tomorrow."

"I bet you're excited."

"I am. Sara is coming back too. It'll be good to have her back too."

"How's Sara doing?"

"Fairly well. She's under twenty four hour police protection. Lt. Seth Parker is staying with her constantly. He's living at her home in one of her guest bedrooms."

"I'm glad. She probably feels a lot safer."

"She does. I know I feel safer when Tom is with me."

"I would imagine especially since you were friends with Paul and with the latest victim Rebecca Segrest."

Tom clasped Carrie's hand. "Are you ready to go into church Carrie?"

"Yes, let's get a seat." They walked into church and sat down.

After the service was over Carrie introduced Tom to her pastor. "Pastor Francis, this is my fiancé Sergeant Tom Monroe."

"It's a pleasure to meet you Tom. Did I hear that you are a sergeant?"

"Yes. I'm a Sergeant with the NYSPD."

Pastor Francis looked surprised. "NYSPD? How did you and Carrie meet?"

"We actually met through Sara Michaels, Carrie's best friend."

"Sara Michaels, I know that name but I don't remember from where?"

"She's a teacher who works with me and her fiancé Paul Sanford was murdered in the park three weeks ago. Sara is the only person to get a glimpse of the possible shooter?"

He gasped. "That's where I've heard the name. Carrie, how is Ms. Michaels doing?"

"She's doing a lot better. Both of us are returning to work tomorrow. Sara is under constant police protection. Lt. Seth Parker will be with her at all times. He's staying in a guest bedroom in her home."

"I'm glad someone is with her at all times."

"So are we."

"Have you two set your wedding date yet?"

"No. It will be sometime this summer though."

"Let me know as soon as you can so I can clear my calendar."

"We will."

"Have a blessed day you two and Carrie I hope your return to work is good. I'll pray for you."

"Thank you Pastor Francis. I'll see you next Sunday. Tom has to work."

"I understand. Be careful out there Tom; and welcome to our church family."

He shook Tom's hand. "Thank you Pastor."

Carrie and Tom left the church and headed for their car, walking hand in hand. Carrie hadn't been this happy in awhile. They got in the car and drove to Carrie's.

Seth, Sara, Kevin, and Maggie were just getting out of church also. Everyone came up to them and wished Maggie and Kevin a safe trip and told them they were glad to know them and they were welcome any time. Ralph and Peggy hugged Sara and Maggie, and shook hands with the men. "Maggie, Kevin, would you like to come to our place for lunch before you leave this evening?"

"Thanks for the offer but Kevin and I are going to take Sara and Seth out for lunch, then go back to Sara's for a little while, then head home."

"What time are you leaving?"

"Probably around 6:00 P.M. We'll stop on the way home at a diner about an hour from our home and eat dinner."

"We're all going to miss you."

"We'll miss all of you too. Thanks for everything Peggy, Ralph. Maybe when we come back to see Sara we can all get together again."

"That would be nice. We look forward to it."

They walked out of the church, went to their cars and went their own way. Kevin drove to a nice restaurant. They went inside and waited to be seated. Once they were seated they ordered their food. They talked while they waited.

Art practically ran out of the church when the service was over. He got in his car and drove to a deli two blocks from his house. He ordered the food, got the order, then got in his car and drove home.

When Art got home he went to the where Pat was. She was sleeping soundly. Art smiled. He walked into the kitchen, then set the table. He smiled as he walked into where Pat was. He shook her several times until she awoke. She opened her eyes. "Hello Pat."

Pat swallowed hard. "Hello Art."

"I have lunch ready. I'll untie you and we'll go into the kitchen and eat lunch."

He untied her and helped her up. She cringed. He walked behind her into the kitchen. He forced her to sit in a wooden chair. She bit her lip to keep from screaming in pain. They started eating. "Pat, you will never guess what the sermon at church was about today."

"What was it about Art?"

"Rejection, pain, and forgiveness. All of which I intend to make you feel. So far you have felt rejection today when I left you here alone. After lunch you will feel physical pain because of it and tonight you will be forgiven. Let's eat our lunch."

Carrie and Tom got home. It was 12:30 P.M. "Carrie honey, are you hungry?"

"Yes I am. I thought I would fix some sandwiches, chips, veggie sticks, and fruit for lunch and fix lasagna for supper. Would that be alright?"

"Everything sounds great except I was hoping we could make our lunches into a picnic in the park. I have a blanket in my car we can sit on and I even have a Frisbee in there. I wanted to do that tonight but it really looks like rain. So what do you think Carrie? Does a picnic in the park sound alright to you?"

She walked over and kissed him gently. "It sounds great, however, I want to change clothes first."

"I think that's a good idea. I want to change my clothes too."

They both went to change clothes. Tom put on a pair of jeans and a t-shirt, then headed toward the kitchen to get the food ready. As he walked past Carrie's room he stopped. Her door was ajar slightly. Carrie was standing, with her back to the door. Clad only in her bathrobe. Tom could tell Carrie was having problems. He knocked on her door. "Carrie honey, are you alright?"

"Yes, I'm just a little dizzy. I'll be alright. I'll be out in a few minutes."

"If you need me, just ask. I'll be in the kitchen getting the food ready."

"Okay. I'll be out shortly."

Tom went into the kitchen and began preparing the food. Carrie came out dressed in jeans and a short sleeved shirt. She went into the kitchen and helped Tom prepare the food. After the food was prepared, they put it in the picnic basket, grabbed their jackets, grabbed the blanket out of Tom's car then walked to the park.

When Tom and Carrie got to the park he spread the blanket on the ground and Carrie sat the picnic basket on the blanket. They sat down and started eating their lunch. While they ate they watched the children laugh and play and other couples just walking through the park.

Seth, Sara, Maggie, and Kevin got their food. They talked and ate. After they finished eating, Seth insisted that he pay the bill. "This is on me. Maggie, Kevin, you both have been such a big help for Sara and for me. The least I can do is pay the bill for this lunch. I'm going to miss both of you but I'm looking forward to a whole new experience when I go to school with Sara."

"I know you will have a whole new experience, but it will be rewarding. Those kids are wonderful and so is Sara. Seth, we appreciate you paying the tab for lunch."

They left the restaurant and went back to Sara's. It was around 1:00 P.M. when they walked into her house. "Sara, there are a few things that need to be discussed before we go home. I think it would be better to do it now while we're all together."

"That's fine."

As they were sitting down at the dining room table Seth looked at them and said "I think I'll go change my clothes. I'll be in the guest bedroom if you need me."

Sara, Maggie, and Kevin discussed a lot of things involving Paul's estate and his will. "Sara, we know this is hard for you that's why we decided to do it while we are all together. We'll notify Paul's lawyer that everything has been taken care of. There's one other thing that we want to discuss with you though."

Sara suddenly looked concerned. "What is it Maggie?"

"Sara, Kevin and I know how Seth feels about you and we know how you feel about him. We want you to know that it's alright if you fall in love with Seth. I know you think it's too early after Paul's death, but sometimes emotions speak louder than words. You can't help how you feel about him. Seth is a fantastic person and we want you to know that you have our support and blessing when it comes to Seth. Sara honey, it is alright to love again. Paul would want you to be happy."

Sara, with tears running down her cheeks, hugged Maggie and Kevin. "Thank you both so much. I needed to hear that. I was so afraid that you would think it was wrong because it's only been three weeks since Paul was murdered. I was afraid that both of you would think I didn't have respect for Paul or that I didn't really love him, which is not true. I loved him dearly."

Maggie put her hand on Sara's arm. "We know how much you loved Paul and how much he loved you. It's not disrespectful to fall in love again after you lose someone you love, even if it's three weeks later. It means you're moving on with your life. You'll always be a part of our family and so will Seth, Carrie and Tom. Always remember that. We love you Sara."

"Thanks Maggie, Kevin. I'm really going to miss both of you."

"Sara, think of it this way. You'll be working full time, trying to get back into a regular routine; and you and Seth will have more time to get to know each other better, and when they catch the killers, I'm sure there will be a trial. You're going to need Seth with you to help you get through it."

"Will both of you come back here for the trial?"

"We'll both be here. We wouldn't miss it."

"I'm going to get Seth and ask him to join us. Why don't we have some coffee and play some cards?"

"Sounds good."

Kevin walked back and asked Seth to join them. Maggie made a pot of coffee and they sat at the dining room table and started playing cards.

Art and Pat finished eating lunch. Art pulled Pat up from the chair, pulled her close to him and kissed her. She cringed. He threw her against the cabinet and she fell and hit her head. She screamed and began to cry as blood poured out of her wound. He pulled her up from the floor. "Now my dear, you are going to find out what real pain is."

"Art please don't hurt me anymore. I'm sorry if I hurt you in any way. It won't happen again. Art Please!" Pat begged as he pulled her upstairs.

Once they got upstairs he threw her across his bed. "Get up and get on all fours!" He screamed. She did what he asked and he tied her hands to the headboard.

Three hours later Pat had finally stopped screaming. Art untied her and took her into the bathroom. He turned the shower on, undressed her, and forced her into the shower. She screamed the whole time. "I have a new outfit for you to wear after you get out of the shower."

She gasped when she saw what little bit of her body the outfit covered. She dried off then Art pulled her into the bedroom again and forced her to put the outfit on. After she was dressed, he tied her to the bed again. He went downstairs to get himself a snack and realized it was almost supper time. He decided he wanted to change what he had written in his letter so he went into his den and wrote a different letter. He smiled when he was finished with it. He put it in an envelope, addressed it, put the proper postage on it then placed it on top of his suitcase so that he remembered to take it with him when he left later that evening.

Carrie and Tom had finished their lunch and decided to take a walk around the park before it started to rain. They were halfway around the park when the rain began. Tom helped Carrie put her jacket on and pulled up the hood for her, then he put his jacket on. They walked a little faster and tried to find a little shelter, hoping the rain would ease up enough to walk back to Carrie's. They found some shelter and stood and talked. Carrie laughed. "I know I probably look like a drowned rat. My hair always frizzes when it gets wet. Oh well, I don't mind, it's just a little water."

Tom smiled back. "Even if you do look like a drown rat you look like a beautiful one. I think the rain is easing up, let's try and get back to your place before it really starts raining again."

Tom and Carrie walked as quickly as they could. They decided to stop at a coffee shop along the way. "Coffee may help warm me up."

"Me too. I'll take a large cup."

They got some coffee and sat down to drink it and wait out the rain. Everyone at the park was scrambling for shelter. The rain continued. Carrie and Tom stayed at the coffee shop for several hours and talked. Around 5:00 P.M. the rain eased up enough for Tom and Carrie to walk home.

Once they got home Tom looked at Carrie "Honey, you need to get out of those wet clothes and get into something drier or you'll get sick. Why don't I start making the lasagna and you change clothes?"

"Tom, honey, you need to get out of your wet clothes into something drier too. I'll start the lasagna as soon as I finish changing clothes."

"Okay." He said as he kissed her.

Maggie, Kevin, Sara, and Seth were playing cards. They heard the rain hitting the windows. "Maggie, it's 5:30 P.M. I guess we better get ready to leave for home, especially since it's raining now. Sara, remember what we talked about earlier and thank you for the hospitality. Seth, thank you for taking care of Sara. We appreciate it."

"Thank you both for everything. I'll remember what we talked about. I appreciate it. Have a safe trip and call us when you get home."

"We will. It might be 10 or 11:00 P.M. though."

"That's alright. I want to know when you get home."

Maggie and Kevin hugged Sara. "Seth, take care of her please."

"I will. Be careful."

After Maggie and Kevin left to go home Sara felt tears running down her cheeks. She felt sad and very unsure of herself. Seth hugged her. "Seth, I feel so lost without them here."

"I know, but I think that will change when you return to work tomorrow."

"I think so too. I think I should get some supper started for us. How about some sandwiches and soup or would you prefer spaghetti?"

"Soup and sandwiches are fine. Let me help you."

Sara and Seth fixed supper together then sat down, ate and talked. After they finished they cleaned up the kitchen and went to watch some television. They wanted to see how long the rain was going to last.

Tom walked out of his room wearing only a pair of shorts and he was drying his hair with a towel. Carrie came out of her room wearing a purple silk robe. They went into the kitchen and fixed supper together. When the lasagna was done they ate and talked. After supper they cleaned up the kitchen then went into the living room and turned on the television.

They snuggled next to each other as they watched the news. The weather forecast called for rain the next three days. "Well, I was going to wear my new outfit to school tomorrow but with this rain I'll have to wear something else." They put a movie in the DVD player and watched it.

Art went upstairs to where Pat was still tied to the bed. She was sobbing. He got behind her and ran his hands all over her body. "Pat, you have a little more pain to endure then I will decide if I want to forgive you."

"Art please. I can't take anymore. I'm sorry. If you let me go home I promise I won't tell anyone what happened here these past few days. I'll take a few days off work until the bruises heal a little. No one will ever know what happened. Please let me go Art."

Murder *When the Bell Tolls*

"I can't do that until I'm satisfied that you've learned your lesson and until I leave my mark on you."

The rain had suddenly turned into a thunderstorm. Art laughed an eerie laugh. "This is perfect. Pat, I love storms don't you?"

"No, actually I'm frightened by them."

"There's really nothing to be afraid of." Art said as he picked up Pat's towel from the floor and placed it in the clothes hamper. He leaned down and kissed her again. "Now my dear Pat, let's get our unfinished business over with then you can rest."

Pat screamed for the next ninety minutes then Art looked at her. "Well my dear, you can rest now. I have a couple of things I need to do then I'll make my decision about whether or not I forgive you."

Art left the room. Pat was powerless to move. She knew that Art was involved in Rebecca's death. She trembled in fear.

Art went to his car and put his suitcase in the trunk, and the letter on the front seat. He wanted to make sure he mailed it in the morning; after he was out of the area. He laid a big piece of plastic on the floor of the garage then grabbed one important thing out of his car, then went into the house to where Pat was. He walked into the room. He grabbed Pat's hair and pulled her head up to look at him. He slapped her across the face. She screamed. "You deserved that; now you will get the rest of what you deserve."

Pat screamed as loud as she could but the clap of thunder drowned out any sound that someone outside might hear. After Art had finished doing what he wanted to do to Pat, she lay motionless on the bed, drenched in blood. Art picked up her body and took it out to the garage and laid her body on the plastic. He picked up her body and the plastic and placed them on the back seat of his car. He went back inside his house and watched television for an hour.

At 8:30 P.M. Art went out to his car. He opened the back door and checked on Pat. She was still breathing but barely. He started his car up, drove to the park and parked two blocks away. He opened the back door, took Pat's body out and carried her to the park. He laid her down on the ground in front of the oak tree where he was supposed to meet Jack.

He walked back to his car, got what he needed then walked over to the church and waited for Jack.

Pat opened her eyes for a few minutes. She tried to get up but she was too weak. She kept trying to get up. Art watched from a distance. At 8:55 P.M. he saw Jack walking over to where Pat was laying. Jack walked over to her. "Oh my goodness! Ma'am, are you okay?"

"Please help me. I'm too weak to get up."

As Jack bent over to help Pat the church bells began to toll. Suddenly two shots rang out and Jack and Pat laid motionless on the ground. Art walked out of the church before the bells finished tolling. It was 9:10 P.M. when Art got into his car and starting driving to his undisclosed location.

The rain became a very heavy rain that lasted for several hours. Seth and Sara had decided to light a fire in the fireplace and watch television. Carrie and Tom lit the fireplace also. They decided to watch another movie. They ate popcorn and watched movies until they fell asleep.

The rain had stopped and the sun was coming up. It was 6:30 A.M. A couple walking through the park stumbled upon the bodies of Pat and Jack. The woman screamed; her husband called 911 and the police arrived on the scene five minutes later. Lt. Marsh, gasped when he saw the bodies. He knew it was the same killer. The police roped off the area and began their investigation. Lt. Marsh talked to the couple that found the bodies then called the coroner's office.

Tom and Carrie both got up at 6:00 A.M. Tom went into his bedroom and put on his uniform. Carrie changed into a nice pants outfit. They went into the kitchen and ate breakfast.

"Tom, I'm so nervous about going back to work today."

"I bet. You've been off for a long time and been through a lot in that time."

"Yes I have. I can only imagine how nervous Sara is about going back to work. I'm glad Seth will be with her."

"So am I. I need to call Seth and Sara and see if they could bring you home today. I'm going to take you to work though."

"I can drive Tom."

"I know, but this way I can spend more time with you before I have to go back to work."

"That sounds wonderful." Carrie said before she hugged and kissed Tom.

"I'm going to call Seth now."

When the alarm went off at Sara's she got up slowly. She got dressed then went into the kitchen. She made a pot of coffee, then went to see if Seth was up. She knocked on his bedroom door. "Seth, it's 6:45 are you up?"

"Yes. I'm getting dressed. I'll be out in a few minutes."

"Okay. Is cereal alright for breakfast?"

"That's fine."

Seth came out and he and Sara sat down and ate breakfast together. "Sara, are you nervous about going back to work today?"

"A little but I'm excited too. Having you there will help a lot."

"What time is your lunch break?"

"It's at 11:50-12:30. Is that alright?"

"That's not a problem."

"I usually eat there unless I'm in the mood for a salad or a deli sandwich."

"That's sounds fine."

They finished their breakfast, and were cleaning up the dishes when the phone rang.

"Seth, it's Tom."

"Hello Tom. How are you doing this morning?"

"I'm doing alright. I have a favor I would like to ask."

"Sure, what is it."

"I am going to take Carrie to school this morning and I was wondering if you would mind bringing her back home."

"Not a problem. We'll bring her home.

"Thanks Seth."

Sara and Seth left for the school. When they arrived they were greeted by Nancy. "Welcome back Sara."

"Thank you Nancy. You remember Seth, don't you?"

"Sure. I'll show you where your office will be while school is in session. I've also made arrangements for you, Sara, and Carrie to have lunch at the same time. We're very glad to have you here. The students are looking forward to meeting you."

"I'm looking forward to meeting them. I'm a little nervous though."

"Let me show you your office."

Sara and Seth followed Nancy to an oversized room that was to be Seth's office. "Wow! This is nice. Thank you."

"Sara, why don't you show Seth where your room is?"

"Okay Nancy."

As Sara and Seth were walking to Sara's classroom, they met Peggy in the hall and started talking. Right before they walked into their rooms they heard Carrie and Tom talking to Nancy. "Carrie, we're so glad to have you back."

"I'm glad to be back."

"I've arranged for a student teacher until you feel up to teaching alone; then we're planning on making that person a classroom assistant. She's really nice Carrie and I'm sure you'll get along just fine. Would you like to meet her?"

"Sure. Is it okay if Tom comes with me?"

"Sure."

When they got to Carrie's classroom, Tom's phone rang. "Tom Monroe."

"Tom, it's Scott Marsh. I know you're coming into work but we need for you to come to the park instead of the station."

"Why the park?"

"Tom, two more bodies were found. A man and a woman. The woman has been physically tortured and has the same mark on her left hip as the last victim."

Everyone heard Tom gasp as he heard the news. He looked at Sara then Carrie. "I'm at the school with Carrie. I'll be there in a few minutes."

Tom hung up his phone. Seth saw the color go out of Tom's face. "Tom, what is it?"

"Seth, Carrie, Sara they just found two more bodies in the park. A man and a woman. Same MO with the woman. She was brutalized and he left his mark on her as well. Carrie, it may be late when I get home tonight."

"It's okay honey; just be careful."

Tom hugged and kissed Carrie. Tom whispered "Seth, take care of Sara and Carrie please."

"I will. Do they have any ID on the victims?"

"I'm not sure. I'll know when I get there. Carrie, I'll see you later. I love you."

"I'll see you later Tom. I love you too."

"Tom, call me on my cell phone as soon as you find out something."

"I will. I'll see you later."

As the women went into their classroom, Seth went to his office. He could see Sara's room from his office. Students

Murder *When the Bell Tolls*

started coming to class. Carrie and Sara were greeted with hugs, tears, and applause.

Tom got to the park and met Scott. "Scott, where are the bodies?"

"Over by the oak tree."

Tom walked over to the tree and gasped in horror when he saw Pat's body. "Oh No! It's Pat Tracy and Jack Lake. What did he do to her?"

"Tom, you know the victims?"

"Yes. The woman is Pat Tracy, she was a teller at the US Bank and the man is Jack Lake, the manager of the Shop N Save. I interviewed both of them the other day. Pat came to me to talk to me about Art and Jack was Art's cousin. Who found the bodies?"

"That couple over there. They were out walking this morning."

Tom walked over to the couple and talked to them for awhile, then he looked at Pat's lifeless body. He felt tears running down his face. He leaned down and touched Pat's face. "I'm so sorry I didn't protect you. I promise you we will find the person who did this to you." He walked over to Jack's body and leaned over it. As he was looking over Jack's lifeless body he saw a piece of paper sticking out of his pocket. He took a handkerchief out of his pocket and picked up the piece of paper.

Tom gasped when he opened up the piece of paper and read it. On the paper was a letter addressed to Art. The letter read: Art:

I couldn't face you so I thought I would write you this letter. I told you the other day that I couldn't do this anymore and I won't. I can't stand by and watch you hurt people like Sara Michaels. I really like Sara and I liked Paul too. You hurt Sara twice and I won't stand by and let you hurt her again. I'm going to the police and I'm going to tell them everything about these murders. I can't let you hurt anyone else especially Sara.

What you did to Sara was awful. She hasn't been the same since. You said that all of these people who died got what they deserved because they disrespected or rejected you. Who are you to judge. Art please stop whatever it is you're doing. If you don't want to stop that's your choice but I will not help you anymore.

Sincerely,
Your Cousin Jack

Tom almost dropped the letter. He remembered that Carrie had told him something happened between Art and Sara but she wasn't sure what. Had Art hurt Sara like he had hurt the last two victims? He had to find out more of what happened to the victims. Tom knew that Art was involved in the shootings, he just didn't know how yet.

Tom walked over to Scott. "Is there any evidence that we can use?"

"Yes, there were two fresh footprints in the mud by the tree. One belongs to our male victim and we haven't determined who made the other print. We are making a plaster cast of it now. It looks to be a men's size 11-12 shoe."

"We have foot prints and this letter I found on Jack's body."

Scott gasped when he read the context. "Tom, do you have any idea what Jack was referring to when he talked about Art hurting Sara ?"

"I'm not sure. Carrie knows a little but before I upset Sara or Carrie I want to get everything together that we have on these murders and see how they connect. If I find that the contents of this letter are important, I'll talk to Sara and see what I can find out. For now though, I don't think it's wise to do that."

The bodies were taken away and some of the officers stayed behind to collect more evidence. Tom and Scott went back to the station to make out reports and study the evidence they had so far.

Art had driven almost all night. He stopped at the border of New York and Canada to mail the letter he had on his front seat. He drove into Canada and spent the night. He got up early the next morning and drove to a house that he had rented for several days. He had made arrangements with the owner to let him use the home four times a year. He pulled into the home and unpacked. He went inside, showered, shaved, changed clothes then drove to a local restaurant for breakfast.

While Art was at the restaurant the news was being broadcast on the television. The reporters were talking about the murders. He smiled. He ate his breakfast then went back to the house he was using. The house sat on a lake so he grabbed his fishing gear, went out in a boat and did some fishing. He smiled and whistled as he sat in the boat.

Murder *When the Bell Tolls*

Sara, Carrie, and Peggy were upset about the recent murders. Sara threw herself into her work. Her kids were hugging her and welcoming her back. Carrie found herself having to ask her helper for more help than she had planned. Carrie was still very weak but getting stronger. Sara looked out her door and saw Seth sitting in his office doing some paper work. At lunchtime Sara, and Carrie met Seth. "Seth, have you heard anything from Tom yet?"

"No. I'm sure that he is still gathering evidence. So ladies, what is on the menu for lunch?"

They looked at the menu then went down and got their food from the cafeteria. They sat in the teachers' lounge. Several other teachers walked in and welcomed Sara and Carrie back. Sara introduced Seth to everyone and they welcomed him. As they were eating their lunch Seth's cell phone rang. "Seth Parker."

"Seth, it's Tom. Sorry it took me so long to get back to you but we've had a lot of evidence to gather."

"Tom, do you have an ID on the bodies?"

"Yes, I'm afraid so. The women is Pat Tracy, and the man is Jack Lake."

"Jack Lake? The manager of the Shop N Save?"

"Yes. Seth, the rain washed away a lot of the evidence but we managed to collect two sets of footprints. One belonged to Jack and we made a plaster cast of the other set. So far all we know is that the footprints are from a man's size 11-12 shoe. We know the woman was extremely brutally beaten and shot. We don't know if she was sexually assaulted yet. Jack was shot once in the back of the head. Seth, I just talked to both of them about Art and now they're dead. I know Art is involved somehow."

"I know he is to. Let me know what else you find out."

"I will. How are Sara and Carrie doing?"

"They're doing okay. We're at lunch now."

"Seth, I'll call you as soon as I know more."

"Thanks Tom."

Sara and Carrie both looked at Seth. "Seth, what happened to Jack?"

"Sara, Carrie, one of the victims that was found this morning was Jack Lake. The other was a woman named Pat Tracy."

"Oh no!" Sara said. I had her daughter in class a few years ago."

"So did I. She was a wonderful lady."

"Sara, did you hear from Maggie and Kevin last night?"

"No. I think they may have gotten home a little later than they wanted to and didn't want to call that late. I'm sure they'll call me tonight."

"I'm sure they will once they hear about the latest murders."

They talked and ate until their lunch was over. They took their trays back to the cafeteria and headed back to their rooms. "Seth, I'm glad you and Sara are taking me home. I feel safer knowing that I don't have to drive. I'm feeling a little tired now anyway."

"Are you going to be able to handle the rest of the day Carrie?"

"Yes but if I can't Dolly can. She's been helping me a lot today."

"That's good. Don't hesitate to ask her for help."

"I won't. Sara, how are you holding up?"

"I'm doing alright. My students have been great today."

"So have mine. Seth, thank you for walking me to my classroom. I'll see you after school."

"I'll see you. If you need me you know where to find me."

Seth walked Sara to her class. He could tell that the latest murders had really upset her. "Sara, are you sure you're alright?"

"Yes. It's just so disturbing to hear that such a sweet man as Jack was murdered."

"I know. Tom feels really bad about all of this too."

"Why?"

"He interviewed Pat Tracy and Jack last week."

"He was just doing his job."

"I know. Sometimes though, when things like this happen it really makes you wonder if it's all worth it."

"Seth, I only have two more classes to teach today; I need to do some paperwork after my last class."

"Okay. I'll wait here for you to come to my office." He clasped her hand. "Sara, I know you're worried. I'll be right here."

Sara found it really hard to concentrate the last two hours of teaching. When the bell rang for school to be over she was relieved. She looked into Seth's office and saw him writing something down. Carrie and Peggy walked down to Sara's room. "Hey Sara are you ready to call it a day?"

"In a few minutes. I need to finish writing something down first."

"We'll meet you in the hallway."

Sara finished then met Carrie and Peggy in the hallway. "Well ladies how did your first day back go?"

"It went fairly well. I found myself getting tired very easily."

"How's Dolly working out for you?"

"She's so sweet and a great teacher. I like her. How did your day go Sara?"

"It went alright. I had a hard time concentrating those last two hours but I did alright. I think it'll take awhile to get back into the routine I had."

"I'm sure it will."

The women went and met Seth. He walked Peggy to her car then helped Carrie and Sara into the car. He drove Carrie home. When they got to Carrie's house, he and Sara both walked her up to the door and made sure she got in safely. "Carrie, are you going to be alright?"

"Yes. I have some things to do around here until Tom gets here."

"Well if you need something you call us okay?"

"Okay, I will."

Carrie walked into her house, took off her shoes, hung up her jacket, fixed herself a pot of coffee, grabbed the newspaper, sat down at the table and began reading the paper and drinking her coffee. She grabbed a pencil and started working the crossword puzzle. Around 5:00 P.M. She fixed herself something to eat and turned on the television. She watched the news and listened to the reporter talk about the murders. Carrie shuddered at the thought that what had happened was only a few blocks away from her home. She thought about Sara.

Evidence from the crime scene had come in all day. Dennis was busy putting the evidence together and running the necessary tests to try and determine who had killed Pat and Jack. Dennis called Tom on the phone. "Tom, it's Dennis. I found something in the evidence that I think you should see."

"I'll be right down."

Tom headed to the lab and met Dennis. "What did you find out Dennis?"

"First of all, the female victim was sexually assaulted numerous times and brutally beaten. Secondly take a look at her left hip. It's the same mark as the other victim. I already took photos of the mark. I found skin and hair underneath her nails. She must have fought back. I'm running a DNA sample now. Also the shoe prints found at the scene were an exact match to another set of shoe prints from another crime scene."

"Another crime scene? I wasn't aware that any shoe prints were found at any of the other murders."

"They weren't. The shoe prints are an exact match from Sara's stalker."

Tom gasped. "What? Are you sure?"

"We checked them twice." Before Tom could say anything another piece of evidence came in. "Tom, look at this. It's the DNA results from the crime scene this morning, the last murder, and from the piece of cloth found at Sara house."

Tom gasped. "Oh my gosh! They are an exact match."

"I'm afraid so. Tom there's something else. We found a fingerprint on the inside of our female victim's leg. We're running the prints through Aphis right now. That's all I have for now. I wish we had more."

"This is a great help Dennis. Thank you."

Tom took the report upstairs and started going over it. Tom took the letter he had found on Jack out of his pocket and read over it again. He knew that Art was involved and he was going to prove it. He was going to talk to Art again and see if he could get some answers. He put the letter in the evidence file and studied the other evidence they had.

Tom called Seth. "Seth Parker"

"Seth, it's Tom. I have some information about the murders I need to relay to you."

"What is it Tom."

Tom told Seth all of the information he had then saved the worse for last. "Seth, there's more." Tom sighed.

"Tom, what is it? What's wrong?"

"Seth, do you remember I told you we found two sets of shoe prints at the crime scene?"

"Yes I remember, why?"

"Well, we know one set belongs to Jack and the other set belongs to someone else. Someone who wears a men's size 11-12 shoe. Seth, that second set of shoe prints are an exact match to a set of shoe prints found at another crime scene."

"I don't remember reading in the evidence files about another set of shoe prints found at any of the other murder scenes."

"That's because there weren't any found at any other murder scenes; they were found at Sara's house."

"What?"

"Seth, they're an exact match to the shoe prints we found outside Sara's bedroom window. We believe that that set of prints belong to the killer. Where's Sara now?"

"She's fixing supper."

"Make sure you don't let her out of your sight until we apprehend this person."

"I won't. Tom, please keep me informed."

"I will. Seth, was Carrie alright when you took her home?"

"Yes, she said she was tired but she was alright."

"I'm going to call her in a few minutes and check on her. I don't think I'll get out of here on time tonight. I have a lot of evidence to go over before the trail gets cold. I have some leads to follow tomorrow and will see where that goes. Thanks for taking care of Carrie."

"It was our pleasure. We'll talk to you later."

Tom hung up the phone then called Carrie. "Hi honey, it's Tom."

"Hello Tom. How are things going at work?"

"They're going alright. I don't think I will get out of here at 8:00 tonight, it'll probably be more like 9 or 10. Are you alright?"

"Yes, I'm just tired."

"I bet. I want to hear all about your first day back to work when I get there tonight."

"Tom, have there been any leads in these murders?"

"Yes and I'll follow up on them tomorrow. We'll talk about that later. Carrie, I talked to Seth and Sara. Sara seems to be alright so far. I'm going to ask Seth and Sara if they would mind bringing you home again tomorrow. I'll take you and pick you up the next couple of days when I'm off. I would feel safer knowing that someone is with you right now."

"Tom, is there something you're not telling me?"

"Yes because I can't right now. I promise, I'll talk to you about it when I get there. If you need anything call me."

"I will. I love you Tom."

"I love you too Carrie. I'll call you when I'm leaving the station."

Sara and Seth were both in the kitchen cooking when the phone rang. Seth answered it. "Hello Seth, it's Maggie. How are you?"

"I'm fine. How are you?"

"Kevin and I are fine. We're home now. I apologize for not calling last night but it was late when we got home and I knew you both were tired and had to get up early this morning, so I waited until now to call. How's Sara?"

"She's doing okay. We're both in the kitchen fixing supper. Would you like to talk to her?"

"Yes please."

"Sara honey, it's Maggie. How are you?"

"I'm doing alright. Are you and Kevin alright? I got worried when we didn't hear from you last night."

"We're fine and we're home. It was late when we got home and I knew you were exhausted so I wanted to wait until today to call you. How did your first day back to work go?"

"It went alright. It was hectic but my students hugged me and welcomed me back. I really missed them."

Maggie and Kevin had been gone all day doing things and hadn't heard about the murders until Kevin turned on the television to watch the news. Kevin dropped the remote and Maggie gasped when she heard about them. "Sara honey, are you sure you're alright?"

"Yes it was just a really busy day."

"Sara, may I talk to Seth again for a few minutes?"

"Sure, here he is."

"Seth, Kevin and I just heard about the murders last night. Wasn't Jack Lake the man who ate lunch with us when we were there?"

"Yes he was. Sara doesn't want anyone to know but this has really affected her. She couldn't concentrate after she found out who the victims were."

"How's she holding up?"

"Alright so far but I haven't told her what I found out from Tom."

Maggie gasped. "What did he tell you?"

"Maggie, I can't discuss that with you over the phone. Tom said they have some leads and he's going to check them out tomorrow."

Murder *When the Bell Tolls*

"I understand. Please let me know what you find out and if we can help in any way."

"I will. Thanks Maggie. We're glad you both made it home safely."

"We're glad to be home. Tell Sara we love her and we'll be back whenever she needs or wants us. Goodbye Seth."

"Goodbye Maggie."

After Seth hung up the phone he and Sara sat down and ate supper. They talked, laughed, and ate. After they finished eating and cleaning up Sara looked over at Seth and said "Seth, would you mind if I took a shower and got into my night clothes?"

"No I don't mind. After you finish I think I'll do the same thing then we can play a game, watch a movie or whatever."

"That sounds good." Sara left and went to shower. Seth walked around the inside of the house checking to make sure everything was alright. He couldn't stop thinking about what Tom had told him about the shoe prints. He shuddered thinking about it.

Sara came out after her shower. She was clad in a gown and robe. She went into the kitchen to get herself a cup of coffee. Seth couldn't stop staring at her. She was so beautiful. He finally said "Well Sara, it's my turn to shower and get changed. I'll be out shortly."

"I'll fix a fresh pot of coffee while you shower and change. I think we should finish that Monopoly game we started last night."

He smiled at her. "Okay, but we start from scratch."

"Deal."

After Seth had showered and changed clothes he came into the dining room. "The coffee's ready, do you want a cup?"

"I'll get it Sara."

He got himself a cup of coffee and they sat down at the dining room table and began their game of Monopoly.

At. 6:00 Art decided he had done enough fishing for one day. He brought the boat back to the shore, got out and walked into the house. He wanted to shower and shave, go into town, get groceries, then come back and fix himself something to eat.

As he undressed he listened to the news on the radio. The press wasn't releasing a lot of information but they did release their names. Art smiled as he got into the shower. He knew Jack wouldn't be extra baggage to carry around anymore.

Once Art had showered and gotten dressed, he walked out to his car, then drove into town. He went to a local grocery store and started a conversation with the manager. "This is quiet an establishment you have here sir. I like it."

"Thank you sir."

"Please my name is Art. I'm renting the house on the lake. I come up here about five times a year."

"It's a pleasure to meet you Art. My name is Sam."

"Sam, where's a good place to relax and unwind around here?"

"There's a bar down the street and a movie hall around the corner."

"Thanks Sam. Have a good night."

Art took his groceries back to his house then fixed himself something to eat. He looked at the clock. It was 8:00 P.M. He decided to go to the bar and have a few beers before he went to bed. He got in his car and drove to the bar.

Tom called Carrie at 9:00. "Hi Carrie. I'm on my way out of the office. I'll be there in about fifteen minutes. Do you need me to pick up anything for you?"

"No. I just need for you to get here safely. I'll see you in about 20 minutes."

"Okay. I'll see you."

After Carrie hung up the phone with Tom, she went into the kitchen, got some food ready to heat up for Tom, then she went into her bedroom and laid out the clothes she was going to wear in the morning, and laid out her night clothes also.

About twenty five minutes later Tom was at Carrie's door. Carrie opened the door, embraced him, and kissed him. "I'm glad you're here Tom."

"I'm glad to be here. How are you feeling honey?"

"I'm doing alright. Are you hungry? I can heat up what I had left from supper if you like."

"That would be wonderful."

Carrie heated up the food, then served it to him. "Thanks honey."

"Tom, I wanted to wait until you got here before I took a shower because I'm.." she stopped. She wasn't sure she wanted to tell him she was still feeling woozy.

Murder *When the Bell Tolls*

"Because you're what Carrie? Are you starting to feel dizzy again?"

"Yes, but I think it is because today was really hectic. Would you mind if I took a shower now and got into my night clothes? I won't be but about twenty minutes."

"That's fine. I need to shower myself after I eat. I'll be alright if you want to take a shower. Call me if you need me."

Carrie went into her bathroom and took a shower. When she got out she started feeling dizzy again. She sat down on the edge of her bed for a few minutes. She felt a little better when she started putting her gown on. She finished getting dressed then walked over to her dresser. She was shaken up by the murders, especially since she knew both of the victims. She needed to feel Tom's arms around her for a long time so she dabbed on some of his favorite perfume, then walked out to the living room where he was waiting for her.

When Carrie walked into the living room Tom smiled. He walked over to her and held her close, then kissed her. He could smell the scent of her perfume. He held her closer and kissed her again. "Carrie, you look so beautiful and that perfume you're wearing is one of my favorites."

"I know, that's why I'm wearing it. Tom, this has been such a trying day and I really need you. I need to feel your strong arms around me so that I feel safe."

He hugged her and held her close, he ran his fingers through her hair. Then he leaned down and kissed her again. "Carrie honey, I need to feel you close to me tonight also. I need to hold you like I'm never going to let you go, but I need to shower first and change into something more comfortable. I want to be able to hold you as close to me as I can and I can't do that in this uniform. I promise I'll be back in twenty minutes."

Carrie kissed him and smiled. She clasped his hand. "Go shower and get into something comfortable; I'll fix us a pot of coffee."

"That sounds good. When I come back, you can tell me all about your first day back to work."

Tom went into his room and took a shower. He debated on what he should wear for night time. He decided on a pair of lounge pants and a t-shirt. As he walked into the living room, Carrie was carrying a tray with a coffee pot and cups into the living room. She set the tray on the coffee table in front of the sofa and they both sat down. Tom couldn't stop staring at Carrie. He couldn't imagine how he would feel if something happened to her.

"So Carrie, how did your first day of school go?"

"It went great. It felt so good to be back but I found myself having trouble doing little tasks. My student teacher Dolly is wonderful. She helps a lot. My students hugged me and welcomed me back and so did the rest of the staff; they did that to Sara also." Carrie sensed that something was wrong. "Tom, what's wrong honey? I know today had to be a horrible day for you. Can you tell me about it?

Tom told Carrie everything he knew saving the worst news for last. "Carrie, there's one more thing. We found two sets of shoe prints at the scene. One belonged to Jack the other someone else. That second set of shoe prints are a perfect match to another crime scene."

"That means you can place this person at at least two murder scenes right?"

"Well no. The second set of prints matched the set of shoe prints found outside Sara's bedroom window."

Carrie gasped. "Oh my gosh! It's possible that Sara does know who the killer is and she's unaware of it."

"Yes. Sara's in extreme danger. I told Seth about this but he said he wasn't going to discuss the shoe prints with Sara yet because he wasn't sure she could handle it."

"I agree. She had a really hard time with these last two murders and it might make it worse if she knew that she's being stalked by a killer."

Carrie stood up to go get more coffee. Tom stood up and pulled Carrie next to him and hugged her tightly. She smiled. It felt wonderful to be held that tightly but she also sensed that there was something Tom hadn't told her. "Tom, when I talked to you earlier, you said that there was something that you hadn't told me about these murders. Was it about the shoe prints or is there more?"

Tom had tears in his eyes, "Carrie, these two innocent victims are dead because of me. I should never have pushed them so hard for answers."

Carrie hugged Tom. "Their deaths are not your fault. Why would you say that?"

Murder *When the Bell Tolls*

"I interviewed both of them about Art Hunter and now they're both dead."

"Art Hunter? Do you still think he had something to do with this?"

"I know he did. Carrie, I want you to read this." He handed her the letter he found on Jack.

Carrie gasped in horror as she read it. "Tom, where did this come from?"

"I found it in Jack's pocket. Carrie, do you have any idea what Jack means when he says Art hurt Sara enough and that what he did to her was awful?"

"No Tom I don't. I'm sorry honey."

He hugged Carrie who had tears in her eyes. "It's alright."

"Tom, this is not your fault. You were doing your job. You're a good police officer." She kissed him.

He put his arms around Carrie and hugged her tightly again. "Carrie, after what I saw today I want to hold you close to me and not let you go."

"Was it that bad Tom?"

"It was awful. I've never seen anyone so brutalized as Pat was."

Carrie cringed, then ran her hand across Tom's back. "Honey, I love you."

"I love you too."

"Tom, it's a little chilly in here. Would you mind if we built a fire in the fireplace and sat on the sofa with only the light from the fire?"

"That sounds wonderful. I'll make the fire."

"Tom, I'll be right back. I need to get something out of my room."

While Tom built the fire Carrie went into her room and reapplied more perfume. She got some slippers for her feet. When she walked into the living room it was lit only by the fireplace. She walked over to Tom. He held her in his arms. They talked for awhile then they kissed each other. Tom sat on the sofa and Carrie sat next to him. She leaned against him. He held her close to him. They kissed each other and hugged and held each other into the early morning hours. They fell asleep in each others' arms.

Seth and Sara played Monopoly until about 11:30 P.M. They looked at the clock. "I think maybe we should try and get some sleep."

"I guess you're right Seth. I don't know if I will be able to sleep though."

"Sara, would you feel better if I slept out here in the chair?"

"I hate to have you do that but yes I would feel safer."

"I'll walk you to your room then I'll sleep out here. To be honest with you, I would feel better if I slept out here myself."

Seth walked Sara to her room, told her goodnight, watched her get into her bed, then he walked to his room, grabbed a pillow, some blankets, a book and his slippers. He walked into the living room and curled up in a chair and tried to fall asleep.

Seth found sleep difficult. He couldn't stop thinking about what Tom had said about the shoe prints. Who was this person and what did they want with Sara? He needed some answers. He hoped Tom would be able to give him some after he followed up on the leads.

Sara had a hard time sleeping too. She couldn't stop thinking about Pat and her daughters. She really liked Pat. She tossed and turned and finally went to sleep.

Art got back to the house he was renting about 11:30. He went into the kitchen and made himself a snack, sat down at the kitchen table and ate it. He smiled when he thought about all the things he wanted to do to Sara when he finally had her for his own. He couldn't stop thinking about how beautiful she was. He wondered how she would react within the next few days. He laughed, then finished his snack, washed up his dishes and went to bed.

Art laid in bed and thought about Pat and what her last hours with him were like. He beamed with pride. He had never felt so much in control as he had then. He could still hear her begging for him to stop. He could hear her sobbing and screaming. He closed his eyes and fell asleep quickly.

Seth and Sara got up when the alarm went off at 6:00 A.M. They got dressed then met in the kitchen. "Good morning Sara."

"Good morning Seth."

"How did you sleep Sara?"

"Once I got to sleep, I slept good. I had a hard time sleeping. I couldn't stop thinking about Pat's daughters."

"I had a hard time sleeping too. I couldn't get this case off of my mind. I need to call Tom. He said something yesterday about bringing Carrie home again the next two days. He said he would bring her home on his days off. Besides, he's having a hard time with these murders."

"Why?"

"He thinks he could have prevented them."

"How? No one knew when this person would kill again."

"I know that. I'll call him."

When Carrie and Tom woke up they were still in each others' arms. Tom leaned down and kissed Carrie. She smiled at him. "Carrie, I wish neither one of us had to go to work today but we do so I guess I'll go change into my uniform."

Carrie got up and headed into her bedroom to change clothes too. They walked hand in hand until they got to Carrie's room. She walked in and closed the door slightly. Tom walked to his room, but stopped a few times on the way to look back at Carrie's room. They both changed clothes and met in the kitchen. Carrie started fixing scrambled eggs. The phone rang and Tom answered it. "Hi Tom, it's Seth. How are you doing this morning?"

"I'm doing okay. I had sort of a rough night sleeping last night but I feel okay."

"I had a hard time sleeping too. I couldn't stop thinking about what you told me. I worried about Sara all night."

"I know the feeling. Carrie and I slept in each others arms all night."

"Speaking of Carrie; would you like Sara and I to bring Carrie home again tonight and tomorrow?"

"That would be great. I have leads to follow up on in this case and I'm not sure how long I'll be."

"We'll bring her home."

"Thanks Seth. I'll let you know what I find out."

"Please do."

After Tom hung up the phone he went into the kitchen and helped Carrie with breakfast. They sat down and ate, then cleaned up the dishes. It was 7:45 A.M. They had to leave in thirty minutes to get to the school and have her in the classroom by 8:30 A.M. They both finished getting ready. Tom held Carrie in his arms and kissed her. "I'm going to miss you today. I hope everything goes alright for you. I will think about you."

"Tom, I'll think about you too. Please be careful following those leads."

"I will. It's time to go. It's still raining so I guess we both need umbrellas."

They grabbed umbrellas and headed to Tom's car. The rain was fairly heavy when they got into the car.

Sara and Seth grabbed an umbrella and headed to Seth's car. They got in and drove to the school. Tom and Carrie arrived at the same time that Sara and Seth did. They walked in together. Tom kissed Carrie and told her goodbye, then he walked over to Seth. "I promise, I'll call you as soon as I find out anything."

"Thanks Tom."

As Tom headed to the police station all he could think about was talking to Art. He wanted answers. He got to the police station and found there were three messages left for him from people who knew the victims. He called them back and got more information about the victims, some of which was very important.

Tom was going over the evidence again when a young woman walked into his office and knocked on the door. He raised his head up. "Yes ma'am, may I help you?"

"My name is Chloe Tracy. My mother Pat was murdered yesterday in the park."

Tom felt himself getting choked up. "Please come in. Have a seat. How can I help you?"

"I was wondering if you had any leads as to who may have killed her."

"We have a few and we are going to follow up on them."

"I hope one of your suspects is Art Hunter."

Tom gasped. "Art Hunter? Why?"

"Well, about two years ago Art kept pressuring my mom to go out with him and she refused every time until she couldn't stand it anymore. She went out with him and told me she wished she hadn't."

"You're mother told me it was awful, that it turned ugly quickly. Did she happen to say how?"

"She said that he forced her to do what he wanted to do and when she refused, he beat her. I think he did other things to her too but I know he beat her. She came home the next morning with bruises and marks all over her. When I asked her what happened she said she told Art no and he told her he had to punish her and he did."

Tom cringed. "Chloe, has Art ever done anything to you?"

"No, but he's a bad man. Mom told me that all the women at work were afraid of him."

Murder *When the Bell Tolls*

"Chloe, this is important, do you think Art could ever kill someone?"

"Yes I do."

"I'm sorry about your mom. Is there anything you or your family needs?"

"Just for you to catch the person who did this to our mom and …" She started to cry. Tom put his arm around her shoulder and hugged her.

"We're going to get this person. I promise. When we do they will be punished. I promise."

"Thank you sir."

"It's Tom Monroe, Chloe."

"Tom Monroe? Are you the man who is going to marry Ms. Carrie White?"

"Yes I am."

"It's a real pleasure to meet you. Mom told me how happy Ms. White is. Congratulations."

"Thank you Chloe. If you or your family needs anything please feel free to ask."

"I will. Thank you again Tom."

After Chloe left, Tom walked over to Scott Marsh and said "Scott, I have a couple of leads I need to follow up on. I'll be at the US Bank talking to their employees, Art Hunter in particular. Call me on my cell phone if something comes up."

The bank was crowded when Tom got there. He waited for the crowd to leave then he walked up to one of the tellers. Her eyes were red and swollen from crying. Tom felt the knot form in his stomach too. "May I help you sir?" the young woman asked.

"I'm Sergeant Tom Monroe from the NYSPD. I was wondering if I could ask you a few questions about Pat Tracy and Art Hunter."

"What do you want to know about that jerk Art Hunter?"

Tom sensed the hostility and thought carefully how to word his questions. "I need for you to tell me all that you can about him."

"Well, first of all he has a huge temper. I can't stand him; he forces us to accept him or he threatens us."

"How does he threaten you?"

"He grabs us by the hair and gets in our face. He catches us in the break room and swats us on the butt, he even burned a former employee with her own cigarette. He has quite a temper. Pat was terrified of him."

"That's my next question. Why do you think Pat went out with him?"

"I think it's because of the physical things he did to her when they had to close the bank together."

"Physical things; like what?"

"She never said but I know that one day after she closed the bank with Art she had a lot of bruises on her arms. It looked like someone held her down."

Tom cringed. "Did Pat and Art close the bank together a lot?"

"Yes and it was mostly on Saturdays."

"Did they work together last Saturday?"

"Yes and I remember Pat saying that Art was acting differently."

"Was he acting differently?"

"Yes he was being extremely nice."

"Thank you. You've been extremely helpful. Is your boss here?"

"Yes he is. He's in his office. It's right over there."

Tom walked over to Art's bosses office and knocked on the door. "Hello Sergeant Monroe. Please come in." What can I do for you?"

"I need to ask you some questions about Pat Tracy and Art Hunter."

"Certainly. I'll try and help anyway I can. What would you like to know?"

"I met Pat the other day and she told me several disturbing things about Mr. Hunter. How was their work relationship?"

"They got along alright as far as I know. I never had to talk to either one of them about their conduct with each other. Pat was a good worker, person, and friend. She'll be sadly missed. She didn't call off work except for an occasional illness or one of her children were sick. Art on the other hand, that's a whole different story. I've talked to him, warned him and even told him he would be fired if he continued coming in late and being rude to the customers. I let him do Rebecca Segrest job. I told him he could do it until she got back and when she was murdered I let him continue doing the job. His attitude changed toward everyone. It's like he's a different person."

Murder *When the Bell Tolls*

"Is Mr. Hunter here today?"

"No I'm sorry he's not. He's on vacation for a week. He's supposed to be back on Monday."

"Where did he go on his vacation?"

"He wouldn't tell anyone where he was going. I asked him several times and he told me he wasn't sure where he was going, yet last year all he talked about was that he was planning a vacation for this year."

"Did he leave a number where he could be reached or anything?"

"No, nothing. Do you think he may be involved in these murders?"

"Yes we do. Can you give me his home address?"

"Certainly, let me look it up."

The boss checked his computer and got the information, then handed it to Tom. "Sergeant, I'm sorry I couldn't have been more help."

"You've been a big help. Thank you for your time."

Tom left and went to the store where Jack had been the manager. He talked to all of the employees that were there. One of the employees said. "Are you sure it was Jack? It would be easy to tell because of his strawberry birth mark on his cheek."

Tom stopped writing. "What did you say about a birthmark?"

"Jack has a strawberry birthmark on his left cheek, above his ear."

"Thank you very much, all of you. I'm truly sorry about your loss."

Tom left the store and headed back to the station. At the station he headed to the lab to talk to Dennis. "Tom, I'm glad you're here. I have some information for you."

"What is it Dennis?"

"The DNA report is back on our second female victim. The DNA we recovered from both womens sexual assault kit are an exact match to the DNA we found on the piece of cloth at Sara's. We checked Jack's DNA to see what came up and we found something I thought you might find interesting. Jack's DNA and the DNA found at the crime scene have similar aphelia's."

"Which means what exactly?"

"That someone related to Jack is your killer. It could be a brother, cousin, nephew or son."

"Dennis, did you take pictures of the bodies after they were brought in?"

"Yes, why?"

"Did Jack have a strawberry birthmark on his left cheek, above his ear?"

"I'm not sure. Let me call Carter and ask him to check the body."

"Ask Carter to take a picture of the victims face please."

Dennis called Carter and told him what they needed. Carter said "I'll be up with the photos in five minutes."

Tom and Dennis talked until Carter got there. Tom gasped when he saw the birthmark. He knew he had probable cause to bring Art in for questioning after he returned from vacation. He had enough evidence to get a search warrant for Art's home, garage, and vehicles.

Dennis saw the look of concern on Tom's face. "Tom what is it?"

"I think I may know who the killer is but I can't be certain until I go over the evidence again. I need to talk to Seth too. Thanks for your help Dennis."

"You're welcome."

Tom went upstairs, sat at his desk, and opened the evidence folders again. He looked for statements from people. He found Sara's statement about the raggedy dressed man. He gasped when he saw that she stated that he had a strawberry birthmark on his cheek, above his ear. "Oh no! Was Jack the raggedy dressed man that Sara saw? I need to ask for that warrant."

Tom called a judge he knew and told him the situation. The judge said he would issue the warrant within the hour. Tom looked at the clock and realized it was lunchtime. He came out of his office and asked the other officers if they wanted anything from the deli. He wrote down their orders then he turned to Scott. "I'm going to go to the deli but first I'm going to see Judge Abrams about a warrant to search Art Hunter's house, garage, and vehicles."

"Tom, let me go with you."

"Alright. Stan, you're in charge while I'm gone. If Carrie calls tell her to call me on my cell phone."

Murder *When the Bell Tolls*

"Alright."

Tom and Scott went to pick up the warrant. They picked up the warrant, thanked the judge, stopped at the deli, then went back to the station. Once they ate Tom started assigning officers to go with him and Scott to Art's home.

Tom, Scott, and two other officers left for Art's home. Tom took out his cell phone and called Seth. Seth, Sara, and Carrie, were eating their lunch in Seth's temporary office when Tom called. "Seth Parker."

"Seth, it's Tom. I wanted you to know that Scott Marsh, myself and two other officers are on our way over to Art's home right now. Judge Abrams signed a warrant based on the DNA evidence gathered."

"Why, what turned up?"

"The DNA found on both female victims and the piece of cloth from Sara's house are an exact match. Carter took a sample of Jack's blood when he did the autopsy and several aphelia's match that DNA, meaning that someone related to Jack is possibly the killer."

"Oh my. Art is Jack's cousin."

"I know. That's why we're starting there first."

"How does Art feel about the warrant?"

"He doesn't know. He took a vacation and no one knows where he went. He refused to tell anyone where he was going. Seth, I know Art is involved in this somehow."

"I do too. Let me know what you find out."

"Seth, please take care of Sara and Carrie."

"I will."

"Seth, could I talk to Carrie for a few minutes?"

Seth handed his cell phone to Carrie. "Hello honey, how are you doing?"

"Carrie, it's so good to hear your voice. I'm doing alright but today has been a very troubling day. I can't wait to get to your place tonight. How's it going for you today?"

"It's going a little better than yesterday. I don't feel as weak. I think what happened last night helped a lot. I hope it happens a lot."

Tom smiled. He really enjoyed the night before also. Sitting by only the light from the fireplace, talking and enjoying each others' company, then falling asleep in each others arms. It was wonderful. "Carrie honey, I hope it happens a lot also, only maybe we'll do things differently once in awhile."

"Sounds good honey. Do you think you'll be home early tonight?"

"Yes. I'm going to leave the station at 8:15 tonight. I should be at your house by 8:30. Carrie honey, I have to go. I'll see you tonight. I love you."

"I'll see you tonight. I love you too."

Carrie hung up the phone and handed it back to Seth. They finished their lunch and Carrie headed back to her classroom. Sara stayed with Seth for a few more minutes. Seth clasped Sara's hand. "Sara, are you alright?"

"Yes. Did I hear you say Art's name when you were talking to Tom? Is he involved with these last murders?"

"We don't know. Sara, try not to worry about it. All of our officers are questioning everyone involved in Pat and Jack's life right now, looking for answers."

"Okay but Seth, please don't keep me in the dark if something comes up about who murdered Paul."

"Sara, I promise as soon as we have anything involving Paul's murder I'll let you know."

"Okay." Seth hugged Sara before she went back to her classroom. She felt different. After she got into her classroom she couldn't stop looking over at Seth. She felt so safe with him.

Tom and the other three officers pulled into Art's driveway. Two of the officers went to Art's garage and Tom and Scott picked the lock on the front door and entered. "Scott, you look downstairs, I'll look upstairs. Yell if you find anything."

"Okay."

Scott went into the kitchen first. He was amazed at how immaculate the kitchen was. Art wasn't married but yet everything was in its' place. He looked in the trash cans and found a wadded up piece of paper. He took it out and found Pat's name on it. He knew that she had been there recently. He put the piece of paper in an evidence envelope and continued looking around. He finished in the kitchen, then went into the living room. He didn't find anything there but when he went into a tiny little room off of the living room, he gasped. There was blood on a chair and on the floor and it looked like someone had been drug thru it. He took some pictures, then went upstairs to join Tom.

Scott started yelling for Tom. "I'm in the master bedroom Scott."

Murder When the Bell Tolls

"Tom, there's a room downstairs that I think you should look at. There's blood on a chair and on the floor. It looks like someone was dragged thru it."

Tom got on his radio and contacted his officers in the garage. "Did you find anything?"

"Yes, we found the piece of plastic that was cut off to lay the victims' body on."

"Bag it and we'll take it to the lab. If you're finished we need you inside."

"Scott, could you go downstairs and let the officers in. I'll head to the next…" He stopped. Out of the corner of his eye a piece of clothing caught his eye. He picked it up from under a chair, which had a skirt on it. He felt sick when he picked it up. He recognized it as Pat's. There was blood on it. "Oh No. I think we've found our primary crime scene. Go let the officers in, I'll collect the rest of the evidence from this room."

Scott headed down the stairs and as he did he noticed blood droplets on the stairs. "What happened in this house?"

He let the officers in and they went upstairs to collect evidence. Tom pulled the covers back on the bed in the master bedroom and gasped. There was blood on the sheets as well as the headboard and a night table next to the bed. He also found epiphyllous on the headboard. He scraped them into a Petri dish and marked it as evidence, then he took a sample from the sheets.

He went into the next bedroom and almost got sick. There was a strange odor that he couldn't distinguish. He turned on the light and gasped. He started taking pictures, and collecting evidence. The other officers found little evidence of any activity until they walked into the den. Tom walked over to the desk. The trash can was filled with wadded up paper. Tom took a piece out and opened it up. He gasped. He knew that somehow the letter he found on Jack's body and the letter he had just found were connected. They finished collecting the evidence, then left the house and headed back to the lab.

Tom took all of the evidence to the lab. "Carter, Dennis could you put a rush on this."

"Sure, I'll stay here as long as it takes."

"Thanks Dennis, Carter."

Carrie walked to Sara's classroom after school. Seth walked up to them. "Are you ladies ready to go home?"

"Yes, it's been a long day."

"Seth, Sara, would you mind if we stopped by the fruit stand on our way home. I need to get a few things before Tom comes over tonight. The grocery store was out of some of the ingredients I need to make a surprise for Tom."

Seth and Sara smiled. "What are you making for him?"

"A Lemon Sponge cake, served with ice cream and fresh peaches and strawberries."

"That sounds good. We'll be there in about five minutes."

Seth pulled up to the fruit stand. Carrie got out. "I'll be back in a few minutes."

"Carrie, I think I'll come with you."

Sara got out of the car to. Seth watched as the ladies walked over and picked out what they wanted, watched as they paid for the items then they got back into the car. "We're ready to go Seth."

He started driving. He looked over and saw that Sara had bought some fresh peaches, grapes, cherries, and onions. He smiled at her. They got Carrie home. Seth and Sara walked Carrie to her door. "Sara, are you alright. You've been very quiet today."

"I'm okay. I 'm just trying to get back into a routine. Seth and I stayed up and played Monopoly last night. I just need some sleep."

"I know what you mean. Tom and I stayed up pretty late talking."

"Carrie, I'll see you at school tomorrow. If you need anything before Tom gets back just call."

"I will. Thank you both for everything. I really appreciate it."

"You're welcome. We'll see you tomorrow."

Carrie, got inside and put her groceries on the counter. She took her shoes off, hung up her coat, then went into the kitchen. She thawed out a beef roast in the microwave, then placed the roast in the oven. While the roast was cooking, She mixed up the cake and got it ready to bake. She went into her bedroom and laid out her night clothes.

Carrie went into the kitchen and took the roast out of the oven, then put the cake in and set the timer for forty minutes. She looked at the clock. She decided to shower and change clothes before Tom got there then finish cooking and look at her mail.

Murder *When the Bell Tolls*

Sara and Seth walked in the door at around 5:00. Seth grabbed the mail out of the box and set it on the dining room table. Sara took off her shoes, they hung their wet coats up on a rack by the door, then Sara went into the kitchen and began cooking supper. She fixed a pot of coffee to start with. "Seth, I thought maybe we could have spaghetti tonight and maybe some pork chops tomorrow is that okay?"

"Sure, that's fine. Do you need any help cooking? If not, I'd like to shower and change clothes."

"I can manage for now, however after the spaghetti cooks, I'll need your help to drain it. The pot is just too heavy for me to lift right now."

"That's fine. I'll shower, change clothes and be out here in about fifteen minutes."

"Okay. That's fine." Sara poured herself a cup of coffee and put the spaghetti in the pot of boiling water. She set the timer for fifteen minutes. She fixed salads, and fresh fruit, and got out some brownies she had in the freezer. She thawed them in the microwave.

About fifteen minutes later Seth came into the room. "Seth, you're just in time to help drain the spaghetti."

He helped Sara then he saw the salads and the start of fresh fruit being cut up. "What can I do to help?"

"I'll finish cutting up the fruit if you wouldn't mind opening that jar of spaghetti sauce, pouring it into a bowl and putting it in the microwave for about three minutes."

"I can do that." Seth opened the jar, poured the sauce into a bowl, covered it with a paper towel, then placed it in the microwave for three minutes. When everything was ready they sat down at the dining room table, and talked and ate. "Sara, this is terrific."

"Thank you Seth, but you helped to."

"I know but you did most of the work."

"I don't mind. I love cooking."

They talked for a little while longer then they cleared the table and did the dishes. Afterward Sara looked at Seth and said "Seth, I'm going to shower and change into my night clothes if you don't mind; then maybe we can watch television or play a game."

"That sounds good Sara. Go ahead and shower. The mail is on the table by the door. I put it on the dining room table but moved it when we ate."

"I was wondering where the mail went. I'll take it with me and look at it after I shower and change clothes."

"Let me get it for you." Seth handed her the mail and she headed into her bedroom.

Sara set the mail on the end of her bed, got undressed, then got into the shower. She let the warm water soothe her tense body. After she was finished with her shower she wrapped a towel around her head to dry her hair, then got dressed into her night gown and robe. She started going thru the mail. She threw away the junk mail and found that she had two bills and a letter addressed to her with no return address but a postal stamp from New York. She set the letter aside and opened her bills. She sighed and then put them in a separate pile.

Sara looked at the strange letter carefully. She didn't recognize the handwriting and noticed that every letter was made with exact precision. She opened the letter and began to read it. She dropped it on the floor in horror. She covered her mouth to muffle her scream. She now knew that Art was involved in the murders. She started shaking. She bent down and picked up the letter to finish reading it. She trembled the whole time.

The letter read:

Sara,

I have loved you for so very long but you always ignored me. That day at the store when I whispered what I wanted to do to you and you slapped me, that was the day I realized how much I wanted you for my own and that I would stop at nothing to have you.

What I did to Becky and Pat is what I want to do to you, except I don't want you to die. I want you for my own. I want to be able to make love to you every night and hold you in my arms. You are so beautiful.

When I look back on that day in the store, you know I had to punish you for slapping me. I guess I didn't punish you severely enough or you would never have fallen in love with Paul.

Paul had to die because he stood in my way. Peter had to die because Martha had to find out what happens when you disrespect me, and Becky and Pat, they disrespected and rejected me. All of the others dated or were married to women who disrespected me. They got what they deserved.

Murder *When the Bell Tolls*

If you continue to reject the idea of going on a date with me Sara, I will have to punish you again and again until you say yes. Think about it, because you my dear will be next.

Sara found herself gasping for air, terrified. She grabbed the dresser and tried to get her bearings. She felt lightheaded and nauseated. All she could think about was what Art had done to her in the store. Had he written that note? He had to. He and Jack were the only ones' who knew about that awful day and Jack was dead when the letter was mailed.

Sara was still trying to get her bearings when Seth knocked on her bedroom door. "Sara, are you alright?"

Sara swallowed hard and said "Yes. I'll be out in a few minutes."

"Okay."

Sara stood in the middle of the room and cried for several minutes, then stumbled over to her bed. She grabbed the bills and the letter. She carefully put the letter in her purse. She didn't want anyone to know about that awful day at the store and the two weeks that followed. She walked into the living room with the bills in her hand. Seth looked at her concerned. "Sara, you look pale, are you sure you're alright?"

"Yes. I'm just a little tired."

"So am I. Did you go through the mail?"

Sara felt panic building up. "Yes, I threw the junk mail away and brought the bills out here so I remember to pay them Friday."

"Well, I can set up the chess board if you like."

"Seth, normally I would say that's great but tonight I don't think I could concentrate enough to play chess. How about Monopoly or cards?"

"Monopoly it is."

Seth set up the game and they started playing. Sara found it hard to even concentrate on that.

Carrie got out of the shower and put her robe on. She heard the timer go off for her cake. She went into the kitchen and took the cake out of the oven. She fixed the rest of the supper. She looked at the clock. It was 7:15 p.m. The phone rang. "Hi Carrie. It's Tom. Are you doing alright ?"

"Yes. I'm doing fine."

"Good. I'll be leaving here in about forty five minutes and be there in about an hour."

"Good. I have supper waiting for you and I even have a surprise for you."

Tom smiled. "Good, I can't wait to get there."

"I'll be waiting for you honey."

"I'll see you in an hour."

"I'll see you."

Carrie smiled when she hung up the phone. She finished cooking the meal, lit the fireplace, lit two candles on the kitchen table and turned off the rest of the lights. She turned on the radio so they could listen to some music while they ate. She sat down at the table and tried to relax.

Sara couldn't concentrate. She got up and started pacing. Seth was worried. "Sara, what's wrong? You seem distracted."

"Seth, I need to call Carrie and ask her something; may be then I will feel better."

"Okay."

"Seth, I'm going to the four seasons' room and use the phone. I'll be back shortly."

Sara walked into the four seasons' room and called Carrie. Carrie was deep in thought when she heard her phone ring. "Carrie, it's Sara."

"Hi Sara." Carrie sensed anxiety in Sara's voice. "Sara, what's wrong?"

"Carrie, I have to ask you a very important question."

"Sure Sara, what is it?"

"Did you tell anyone about what I told you about Art?"

"The only person I talked to about it was Tom and I only told him you said something bad happened between you and Art. I never told him anything else. When he asked me what Art had done to you I told him I didn't know and I don't. Why?

"I received a letter from someone in the mail talking about what happened between Art and I ;and they told me I'm next. Carrie I'm so scared."

"I bet. What did Seth say about the letter?"

"I haven't told him yet. I'm afraid to tell him because I'll have to tell him about what Art did to me and I may lose Seth forever."

Carrie gasped. "Sara, you've fallen in love with Seth, haven't you?"

Murder When the Bell Tolls

"Yes. I've tried not to but the more time I spend with him the more I find myself loving him. When he puts his strong arms around me I feel so safe."

"I know how you feel. I feel the same way about Tom. Sara, I know from talking to Tom that Seth is very much in love with you. He has tried to be as professional as he can but he fell in love with you after being with you at Paul's funeral. I think you should tell him about the note."

"Carrie, if I do that, then I have to tell him about what happened between Art and I."

"Sara, if he loves you he'll understand. He's a police officer, I'm sure he would be very professional about it."

"I hope you're right. I think I'll wait until tomorrow to tell him. We are both extremely tired tonight."

"I am to but I have a surprise for Tom."

"That's right, did you get your cake baked?"

"Yes I did. I made a roast, tossed Greek salad, carrots and potatoes, along with the cake for supper."

"That sounds good. I'm sure he'll be surprised."

"I'm sure he will but that's only the first part of his surprise, the second part is a secret."

Sara had to smile. She knew Carrie and Tom really loved each other. She thought about what Carrie had said about the letter. "Carrie, thank you so much for all of your help."

"You're welcome."

"Do me one favor. Please don't tell anyone about this letter until I talk to Seth tomorrow night. I'm afraid of what might happen."

"Alright. Try and get some rest tonight and I'll see you at school tomorrow."

"I'll see you then."

Sara hung up the phone and walked into where Seth was. "Sara, is everything alright?"

"Yes. I just needed to talk to Carrie about something and she helped me with it."

"I'm glad. You don't seem as nervous as you were earlier." Seth clasped Sara's hand and looked her in the eye. "If you need to talk about anything I'm here. I'll listen. I do care about you and I- -I love you."

Sara gasped. She didn't know what to say. "Seth I love you to. There I said it. I know it's too soon after Paul's death to think about it but Seth, I've fallen in love with you."

Seth hugged Sara and held her close to him. Tears rolled down her face. His strong arms helped her feel so safe. She relaxed and started to feel like herself again. She looked at Seth then said "Let me finish knocking your socks off in our game of Monopoly."

Seth smiled. "Alright but let's call it an early night."

"I agree."

About thirty minutes after Sara called Tom got to Carrie's. He smiled when she opened the door. He hugged and kissed her. "Something smells great."

"I have supper ready for us. I hope you like it."

Tom sat down at the table, Carrie got the food and placed it on the table. "Carrie this looks so good."

After they finished eating, Carrie said "Tom, I have a couple of surprises for you. One is this cake I made for you. It's your favorite. Lemon Sponge cake."

Tom kissed Carrie. She served him a piece of cake and whispered in his ear about the other surprise. He looked up at Carrie and beamed. Carrie served him the cake. "Tom, I need to go into my bedroom for a few minutes. I'll be right back."

Tom ate his cake while Carrie went into her bedroom and dabbed perfume on her neck, wrist, and breasts. She walked out to where Tom was waiting for her. "Carrie, the cake was delicious."

"Thank you Tom."

He embraced Carrie and kissed her. They sat down on the sofa and held each other tightly. Even though Carrie was trying to make the night as romantic as she could she couldn't stop thinking about Sara. She knew she could trust Tom with the information. Tom sensed that something was bothering her. "Carrie, honey what's wrong? Have I done something to frighten you?"

"No, what you are doing is wonderful it's just that about thirty minutes before you got here I got a call from Sara. Tom, she was terrified."

"Why? What happened?"

"She got a letter in the mail today and it really upset her."

"What was in the letter that upset her so badly?"

"I'm not really sure. All she told me was that it went into detail about what happened between her and Art."

"Art Hunter?"

"Yes why?"

Murder *When the Bell Tolls*

"Carrie, I went to interview Art at the bank today and was informed that he is on vacation for a week and no one knows where he is. I talked to several other employees and they told me they were afraid of him. We have reason to believe that he is involved in these murders. We also believe that there will be more murders when he returns."

"The next person could be Sara."

"What did you say?"

"I said according to the letter Sara received she's next."

"Oh my gosh! What did Seth say?"

"She hasn't told him yet."

"What? She needs to tell him."

"I told her that. Tom, something terrible and awful happened between Sara and Art. You know that from the letter you found on Jack. I think it's worse than any of us know. Sara asked me not to tell anyone about the letter until she had a chance to talk to Seth tomorrow night. She's really scared and trying to do like she always does and deal with it alone. Tom, I'm scared for her. I don't want to lose her. You have to promise me you won't talk to Seth about it until Sara tells him tomorrow night."

"I won't but why is she waiting to tell him?"

"She's fallen in love with Seth and she's afraid she'll lose him if she tells him."

"That's ridiculous. That will make Seth want to protect her even more. I would hope that if something like that ever happened to you that you wouldn't hesitate to tell me about it. There's nothing that would change how much I love you and care about you".

Carrie smiled. "I love you to Tom. Thanks for listening. Sara means so much to me."

"I know she does. However let's continue where we left off."

"Alright, but let me go get a blanket and stoke the fire."

Carrie came back with a fleece blanket and sat next to Tom and picked up where they left off.

Sara and Seth continued playing Monopoly. Sara still had a hard time concentrating. Seth looked at Sara and could see fear and pain in her eyes. "Sara, are you sure you're alright?"

"Yes but I think I'm going to go to bed now. I'm really tired."

"So am I. I think a good nights' sleep will do both of us some good." He walked Sara to her room, hugged her and helped her into her bed. "Good Night Sara."

"Good night Seth. I'll see you in the morning."

After Seth left the room, Sara tried to sleep. She closed her eyes but found sleep difficult. She kept seeing Art's face and found her mind wandering back to that awful evening at the store. She trembled and began to cry.

Seth found sleep difficult also. He kept thinking about Sara. He knew something was wrong. He kept thinking about the evidence that Tom had told him about. When he finally relaxed enough he thought about Sara. He also thought about his late wife. He knew that she would want him to be happy, and he was with Sara. He finally fell asleep.

Sara was still having problems sleeping. She got up and walked around trying to clear her head. An hour later she laid back down. She thought about Paul, then about Seth. She knew that Paul would want her to be happy but she felt like it was too soon after Paul's death to feel like she did about Seth. She couldn't help how she felt. She thought about how wonderful it felt having Seth's arms around her and how much she enjoyed being with him. She was finally able to fall asleep.

Seth woke up when his alarm went off at 5:30 a.m. He shaved and got dressed, then went into the kitchen and made coffee. He looked at the clock. It was 6:10 a.m. and Sara wasn't up yet. He started to worry. He walked to her bedroom and looked in. She was still asleep but he could hear her sobbing quietly. He walked over to her and touched her on the shoulder. She opened her eyes slightly."Seth is that you?"

"Yes Honey, it's 6:20 a.m."

"Oh No! I overslept."

"Relax Sara. I made coffee. I'll get breakfast started while you get dressed."

"Thanks Seth."

He hugged her, then went into the kitchen and fixed scrambled eggs and toast while she got dressed. Once Sara was dressed she went into the kitchen. "Seth, that smells good. I'm sorry I had to ask you to fix breakfast."

"It's not a problem. I used to fix breakfast for Marie and I on my days off."Sara smiled at him.

They ate then cleaned up. Seth rubbed Sara's shoulder then said "Sara, when I woke you this morning, you were sobbing. Is everything alright?"

"Yes. I was just having a bad dream. I was thinking about the night Paul was killed. I can still see that strawberry birthmark on the raggedy dressed mans' face. I had a really hard time sleeping last night until I thought about our conversation last night. Thinking about that helped me sleep."

Seth smiled. "I know, it helped me fall asleep also. We better get going if we're going to get to school by 8:30."

Tom woke up at 5:45. Carrie was lying next to him on the sofa. He smiled, then went to change clothes. After he changed clothes, he went into the kitchen and made coffee. Carrie awoke around 6:10 a.m. "Good Morning Carrie."

"Good Morning Tom. Is that coffee I smell?"

"Yes, I made a fresh pot."

He walked over to her, held her in his arms and kissed her again. "I better get dressed if I'm going to be at the school by 8:30."

Tom kissed Carrie again then said "Go get dressed. I'll heat up some Danish and get some cereal for us."

She smiled at him; he hugged her again and ran his hands over her back. She smiled then went to get dressed.

She smiled as she got dressed. Last night had been wonderful. She looked out the window and saw that the rain had finally stopped. She decided to wear her new outfit to school that day. She got dressed and thought about Sara. Carrie had a wonderful night cuddling, snuggling, and talking with Tom but she wondered what kind of night Sara had. She could only imagine that sleep was probably difficult for her. She was anxious to talk to her.

She finished getting dressed then walked out to where Tom was. "Carrie, you look really nice in that outfit. I think you made a good choice."

"Thank you Tom. I decided to wear it today since the rain has finally subsided."

"Carrie, what time is your lunch again?"

"11:50-12:35. Why?"

"I thought maybe I would stop by and eat lunch with you today."

"That would be nice. Do you think you can get away from work with this case?"

"I'll make time."

"We better go if we're going to get to school on time."

As Seth and Sara were getting ready to leave Sara said "Seth, I forgot something. I need to go back to my room and get it. I'll be out in a second."

She went into her bedroom and looked in her purse for the letter she had received. She wanted Carrie to read it and see what she thought about it before she talked to Seth about it. She walked to where Seth was and they left for the school.

Sara was quiet on the ride to school. She kept thinking about the context of the letter she was carrying. She couldn't stop thinking about how cruel Art had been and about what he had done to her. She looked over at Seth. She felt tears welling up. She looked outside the rest of the way to school. Seth put his hand on her leg. "Sara, are you alright?"

"Yes. I'm just a little tired, that's all."

"Aren't you supposed to go back to the doctor about your side this week?"

"Actually, I'm supposed to go Friday after school. He wanted me to work a week before I went back. He said after a week he would be able to tell if there were going to be any lasting problems."

"What time is your appointment?"

"3:45 p.m."

"Okay. I'll remember that. One of your students wants to come by and chat with me for awhile the next couple of days and I told her that was fine. She said she is writing a story about someone being arrested and she needed some police details."

"That's fine. I'm glad the students are getting to know you. I think it will benefit them as well as you." Sara was trying not to cry.

They pulled into the parking lot at the school. Seth helped Sara out of the car. He could see tears in her eyes. "Sara are you sure you're up to working today? If you're not, I'm sure Nancy will understand."

"I'm okay. I need to work today. I really do."

"Alright but if you start feeling like you need to leave let Nancy know and I'll take you home."

"I will. Thanks Seth."

As Seth and Sara were walking into the school, they saw Carrie and Tom pull up. They waited for them. "Good Morning Seth, Sara. It's good to see you both."

Murder *When the Bell Tolls*

"Good Morning Carrie, Tom. It's good to see both of you as well. You both look absolutely elated this morning."

"We are. We set our wedding date. It's going to be July 3. It's a Friday night. We'll be leaving for Paris on that Saturday."

Sara tried to smile thru tears. Carrie looked at her, then went over and hugged her. She whispered "Sara, are the tears because of what we talked about last night?"

Sara nodded her head yes. "Carrie, I brought the letter for you to read. After you read it, I need it back. I want to put it where no one else can see it."

Sara secretly handed Carrie the letter. Carrie put it in her skirt pocket. She had an hour break before Sara. That was when she was going to read it. "Carrie honey, I have to leave for work. I'll see you at lunchtime."

Carrie walked over to Tom and kissed him. "I'll see you then. Be careful today. I love you."

"I love you to Carrie" He leaned down and kissed her again, then whispered. "I really enjoyed last night."

She smiled, then whispered back "So did I."

"Tom, did I hear you say that you are meeting Carrie for lunch?"

"Yes, I'm going to bring her something from the corner deli. Do you want me to bring you and Sara something?"

Seth looked at Sara. "Do you want something from the deli?"

"Yes. Get me a Roast Beef on Rye with Mayo and a pickle."

Tom wrote down the orders. "I'll see all of you at lunchtime."

"Goodbye Tom."

Seth walked Carrie and Sara to their classrooms, then went into his office. Nancy had asked Seth if he could get materials together for an assembly presentation to the entire school by Friday. She wanted him to talk about crime. How to prevent it, how to fight it, and how to report it. He started working on that when he went into his office.

When Tom got into the station he pulled all of the files on the murder cases. He looked at the notes that Seth had made, then he compared the evidence. When he saw the notation about the man with the strawberry mark he knew he would have to question Sara. He needed to know if Jack's birthmark was the one she saw. If it was he knew that Jack had to be the set up man. He found more evidence that placed Jack at several of the murder scenes. He pulled both Art and Jack's financial files up on the computer and found nothing but when he pulled Art's personal file up he found something very interesting. He found out that Art had a criminal history. He had been charged with three separate counts of assault but every time the charges were dropped. Tom put the files down and went back to the lab.

At the lab he talked more to Carter and Dennis. He found out that the killer actually made a huge mistake. He left a bite mark on one of Pat's breasts. An impression of the mark was made, pictures were taken and the evidence was entered into the file.

Carrie's break time had come. She had about thirty minutes before her next class started. She pulled the letter out of her pocket. She was horrified after reading the letter. She sat in shock. The bell rang and students began to come into her class. She folded the letter up and put it in her desk drawer until she would be able to see Sara. She greeted her students with a smile but her heart was aching.

Tom came back to the school about ninety minutes later with everyone's lunch. Carrie went and got Sara. She secretly handed the letter back to Sara, who turned around, went back into her classroom, and placed it in her desk drawer. "Sara, you must be terrified."

"I am. I just don't know what to say to Seth."

"Sara, I talked to Tom about the letter?"

"What? I asked you not to say anything."

"Sara, all I told Tom was that you got a letter in the mail and it really upset you. He wanted to know what it was about and I told him I didn't really know except that it had to do with something that happened between you and Art. Sara, what happened that night at the store? Can you tell me?"

"I can't tell you. I don't even know how I'm going to tell Seth. Carrie, I love Seth and I told him that last night. He told me that he has fallen in love with me to. Carrie, I don't want to lose him."

Carrie touched Sara on the hand as they approached Seth's office. "You aren't going to lose him. It'll all work out."

They all met and sat down to eat. They talked and laughed together until it was time for Tom to get back to the

Murder *When the Bell Tolls*

station and time for Sara and Carrie to get back to their classrooms. Tom hugged and kissed Carrie before he left then he hugged Sara. He whispered in her ear. "If you need to talk, I'll listen."

Sara nodded. "Thank you for everything Tom. The lunch was fantastic."

"You're welcome. Thank you for taking care of Carrie. Carrie honey, I'll see you tonight after work."

"I'll see you."

Tom left and the women went back to their classrooms. Sara was really nervous about that letter. Carrie touched her hand. "Sara, it'll be alright. Tom and I will stand behind you."

"Thanks Carrie."

"Sara, I really think you should make a copy of this letter."

"Don't you think Seth will get suspicious if I go to the copying machine right now?"

"No, just put some others papers with it and he won't have any idea what you're doing. Sara, it's important."

Sara placed the letter on top of some other papers and walked past Seth's office to the copying machine. He smiled at her and she smiled back. She trembled as she made a copy of the letter. She felt tears rolling down her cheeks. After the copy was made she went back to her room, placed the letter in her desk drawer, then tried to teach her class. She had a hard time concentrating. One of her students asked her after the class was over if she should go get Seth. "No, it's alright honey. I'm just having a difficult time adjusting to everything."

"Lt. Parker is so nice Ms. Michaels. We all like him."

Sara smiled. "Yes Becky he is nice."

"Are you sure you don't need me to bring him here. You seem distracted."

"No. It's okay really. Lt. Parker and I need to talk later. Where's your next class Becky?"

"Down the hall. I have Mrs. Miles."

"Oh. I didn't know that. Would you ask her to come down here for a few minutes please?"

"Sure."

Sara's student went to her class. "Hello Becky."

"Hello Mrs. Miles. I have a request for you."

"What is it dear?"

"Ms. Michaels wanted me to ask you if you would go to her room for a few minutes right now."

"I'll be right back."

Peggy walked into Sara's room and found Sara with her back to the door trembling and holding the letter in her hand. Peggy knocked on the door. Sara jumped. "Sara, one of my students said that you requested me to come here. Is everything alright?"

Sara couldn't answer. Tears were running down her cheeks. Peggy walked up behind her. "Sara, what's wrong. Are you alright?"

Sara turned to Peggy and started crying. "No, I'm not."

Peggy hugged Sara as the tears rolled down her face. Seth had been doing paper work and he looked up to check on Sara and saw Sara trembling. Sara told Peggy about the letter. "Peggy please don't say anything. I haven't told Seth about it yet."

"What? Why not? You know he would help you."

"I know but I'm in love with Seth and I don't want to lose him." Peggy looked at Sara stunned. "Peggy, I didn't mean to say that. It just came out."

"That's alright. I'm happy for you Sara. Paul would want you to be happy."

"You don't think it's too soon after Paul's death for me to fall in love again?"

"Sara, love just happens. I'm sure having Seth with you twenty four hours a day has helped both of you get to know each other better. Seth is a fantastic man and a good police officer. Carrie will tell you that. Sara, it's alright, just let love happen; don't try to stop it. You deserve happiness."

"Thanks Peggy. My students will be arriving soon. I need to pull myself together so I can teach this last class."

"Sara, you're going to tell Seth about that letter aren't you?"

"Yes, within the next day or so."

"Alright. I won't say anything but you have to promise me that you'll tell Seth about that letter by the end of the week."

"I will, I promise."

Peggy hugged Sara again and left for her class. As students began coming into Sara's class, she tried to compose herself. Seth could tell she was having a hard time. He walked over to her class. "Sara, may I see you in the hall for a few minutes?"

"Class, I'll be right back."

Murder *When the Bell Tolls*

Sara stepped into the hall. Seth clasped Sara's hand. "Sara, is everything alright? You seem distracted and nervous today. Are you in pain?"

"I'm not is pain I'm just having a hard time coping today."

"That's normal. I experienced the same thing when my wife died. Are you going to be alright until the end of class?"

"Yes, once I start teaching I'll be fine."

Seth squeezed Sara's hand. "I'm here if you need me."

"Thanks Seth. I appreciate it. I'll see you after class."

Tom started going thru the evidence again. He made more phone calls then made some notes. He needed to find Art. He and some of the other officers called bus station, airlines, and the train station putting them on alert for Art. If he was spotted they were to call him or one of the other officers. He gave strict orders that the media was not to be contacted until he said so. He didn't want to spook Art.

The more Tom looked at the evidence the more he knew that Sara held the key to what Jack meant in his letter to Art. Tom was convinced that Art was the prime suspect in the murders. Tom was off the next three days. He had to talk with Sara again. He needed to see the letter she received.

Tom looked at his clock. It was 3:45 p.m. He knew that Sara and Carrie were probably getting ready to leave from the school. He called Carrie on her cell phone. "Hi Carrie, it's Tom."

"Hi Tom."

"Are you getting ready to leave the school?"

"In about thirty minutes. Sara has some paperwork to finish up. She had a rough day. Tom I read that letter. It's horrible. I'm worried about her."

"So am I Carrie. I'll be home earlier than usual tonight. I'm taking a couple of hours off. Why don't we go out to a nice restaurant for dinner, then catch a movie. The movie you have been wanting to see is playing at the theater in town. I thought we could catch the 8:00 show then go back to your place. How does that sound?"

"Great. I'm looking forward to it."

"I'm bringing home the files from this case. I'm afraid I'm going to have to talk to Sara and try and get more information about the night Paul was killed."

"Is that necessary?"

"I'm afraid so. I'm not going to do it tonight. I thought maybe Thursday night because I have a surprise for you for Friday and I'll tell you what it is tonight, when we are at dinner."

"Sounds Great. What time should I expect you?"

"Around 5:30 p.m."

"I'll be ready."

As Carrie hung up the phone, Seth and Sara came to her room. "Are you ready to go Carrie?"

"Yes I'm ready."

They left and headed to the car. Seth helped the ladies in then he drove to Carrie's. "Seth, several of my students have said they got a chance to met you today and they really like you."

"I like them to Carrie. They are a great bunch of kids. Nancy has asked me to put together some information to present for an assembly on Friday."

"How's that going?"

"Fairly well."

"That's good. Tom called and said he was going to take off early today and take me to dinner and a movie."

"That sounds good. Is he still staying at your place?"

"Yes and I hope he never leaves. I feel so safe with him there."

Sara smiled. "I know how you feel."

"Having Tom there and having someone to talk to and cook for helps my big house not feel so empty. I really love Tom and enjoy his company."

"He feels the same way about you Carrie." They pulled up to her house. They got out and walked Carrie to the door, then into her house. After they were convinced she was safe, Sara and Seth left for Sara's house.

Seth looked over at Sara. "Are you alright Sara?"

"Yes. It was just a very difficult day today."

"That's what you said earlier. Why don't we do the same thing that Tom and Carrie are doing except skip the theater and maybe watch a movie at home."

"That sounds great. Once we get home, I'll shower and change clothes, then we can go."

"Alright. I want to change clothes also."

They got home a few minutes later. Seth helped Sara out of the car; they walked into the house. Sara saw the light flashing on her answering machine. She had two new messages. "Seth, why don't you change clothes first. I want to get myself a cup of coffee. Would you like a cup?"

"Yes, but I'll fix it after I change clothes. I'll be back shortly."

Sara fixed herself a cup of coffee, then walked over to listen to her messages. One message was from Maggie asking for Sara to call back when she could and let her know how things were going and the other shook her up. It was from the killer. The message was "My dear Sara, by now you should have received my letter. I hope you are thinking about what I said because I will follow through on my promise.

Sara stood horrified with tears running down her face. When she heard Seth walking into the room she wiped her eyes. "Sara, what's wrong?"

"Nothing, I just listened to my messages. One was a wrong number and the other was from Maggie. Hearing her voice was wonderful."

Seth, being the police officer that he was, detected that Sara wasn't telling him something but he didn't push. "I'm going to fix myself that cup of coffee now."

"I'll go change clothes now. I'll be out in a little while."

Seth went into the kitchen and Sara went into her bedroom. She couldn't stop the tears. She changed clothes, then sat on the end of her bed took the letter out of her purse and reread it. She cried harder. Seth had gotten as close to her bedroom door as he could without her knowing about it. He heard her sobs and knew that something was terribly wrong. He knew what he needed to do.

Sara came out a little while later. "You look really nice Sara."

"So do you Seth."

"Are you feeling well enough to go?"

"Sure. Where are we going?"

"Only to one of the finest Seafood places in the area."

"Sounds good. Let me get my purse."

She walked into her bedroom again. She took the letter out of her purse and placed it in a drawer in her dresser. She joined Seth and they left for the restaurant.

Carrie had gotten home, took off her shoes, then got into the shower. She smiled as she thought about the night before. She got out, dried off, applied perfume and make-up, then got dressed She dressed in something semi-casual yet comfortable.

She went into the living room, grabbed a book, curled up on the sofa and waited for Tom to get there. At 5:25 p.m. Tom arrived. She opened the door and let him in. They kissed each other. Tom smiled when he smelled the perfume. "Carrie, you look lovely."

"Thank you Tom."

"Let me go change clothes, then we can go."

Tom changed quickly. He smiled thinking about the night before. It felt so wonderful to wrap his arms around Carrie. He truly loved her. He dressed in semi-casual, then he went and joined Carrie. "Are you ready to go honey?"

"Yes I am."

They got into the car and Tom drove to a nice Mexican restaurant close to the theater. Carrie smiled as they walked into the restaurant. The waiter seated them and they placed their orders.

"Tom, this place is wonderful. I haven't had real Mexican food in a long time."

"I thought you might like it. This gives us more time to eat then go to the show." Carrie smiled. Tom clasped her hand across the table. "How did your day go Carrie?"

"It was hectic but went better than Monday. Sara had a really bad day though because of that letter."

"Where is that letter now?"

"Sara has it."

Their food came. They talked while they ate. After they finished eating they still had forty five minutes before the show started. "Carrie, would you like to get to the show early and get a seat, or do you want to sit here and talk."

"Why don't we go to the theater so we can get a good seat."

"Alright." They got to the theater and walked in. Carrie and Tom sat in the back of the theater. Tom put his arm around her and kissed her several times. The theater filled up quickly.

While Tom and Carrie were enjoying the movie, Seth and Sara were enjoying a wonderful Seafood Dinner. "Sara, how do you like this place?"

"It's wonderful. I have never heard of it. How did you find it?"

"A friend told me about it. I haven't been here in five years. I had hoped they were still open; I had another plan if they weren't."

Sara smiled at him "Why am I not surprised."

He smiled. They finished eating; he paid the bill. They walked to the car, and drove home. When they got inside they hung up their coats. Seth said "Sara, why don't I make a pot of coffee or would you prefer tea?"

"Tea would be wonderful. I'm a little chilled. Would you mind if I took a shower and changed clothes before we watched a movie?"

"No, go ahead. I'll fix the tea."

Sara walked into the bedroom and got ready to shower. She opened her dresser drawer and took out the letter. She reread it again and shuddered, then felt tears running down her face. She showered, then got into her night clothes. She walked into the living room where Seth had the tea, setting on a tray. She smiled. "Thank you Seth."

Seth put a DVD in the player and turned on the movie. Sara made some popcorn. They ate it and watched the movie. After the movie they sat and talked until midnight.

Carrie and Tom got home about 10:30 p.m. "Tom, I'm going to get into my night clothes and then get myself a cup of tea."

"That sounds good. I think I'll do the same thing."

Carrie went into her bedroom and changed into a gown and walked into the kitchen to get a cup of tea. Tom walked out in boxer shorts and a t-shirt. He smiled at Carrie. "Do you need help with the tea honey?"

"No, I think I can get it. Just sit on the sofa and I'll bring it to you."

He sat down and she brought the tea over. They talked for awhile, then Tom started stretching his back and neck. "What's wrong honey?"

"My back and neck are stiff from the stress."

"Turn your back toward me and I'm see if I can't help you relax those muscles."

He smiled, kissed her, then turned around. Carrie massaged his back, shoulders and neck. "That feels a lot better Carrie. Thank you."

"Why don't you let me massage your neck and help with the stress?"

She smiled then moved closer to him. He massaged her neck and shoulders then kissed her again. She snuggled next to him; they talked and laughed together until they both fell asleep.

Sara couldn't sleep. She kept thinking about that letter and phone call. She kept thinking about how she was going to tell Seth. She trembled. She got up and walked around for about an hour, then went back to bed.

Seth heard her walking around and got up to check on her. He walked to her bedroom, and whispered "Sara, are you alright?"

"Yes. I'm just having trouble sleeping."

"Why don't you let me fix you a cup of warm milk or hot cocoa? Maybe that'll help."

"Hot cocoa sounds good Seth."

Seth fixed Sara a cup of warm cocoa. She sat in the overstuffed chair and drank it. Seth sat in the chair next to her. "This is so good. I think it's just what I needed. Thank you Seth."

"You're welcome Sara."

"I'm going to go back to bed and see if I can get some sleep."

"Goodnight again Sara. If you need me just call."

"Goodnight Seth."

Sara headed to her bedroom and got back bed. She drifted off to sleep but her sleep wasn't peaceful. It was riddled with flashbacks. She started sweating. She threw off her covers, grabbed a pillow, clutched it close to her chest, started weeping, and tried to sleep. She thought about Seth and relaxed enough to go to sleep.

Seth slept lightly listening for Sara. He found sleep difficult also. He got up and walked into the living room, curled up in the overstuffed chair, threw a blanket over his feet, then drifted off to sleep.

Tom and Carrie both woke up when Carrie's alarm went off. Tom kissed her. "Good Morning Carrie."

"Good Morning Tom."

"Carrie, why don't you let me fix breakfast while you get ready for school?"

"That sounds good. I'll be back shortly." She kissed him and headed into the bedroom. While she changed clothes and got ready for school Tom fixed breakfast. When Carrie went into the living room she could smell eggs and toast. "That smells so good and I'm hungry this morning."

Murder When the Bell Tolls

"So am I. It's ready, why don't you sit at the table and I'll serve you?"

Carrie sat down, thrilled to have someone waiting on her. Tom handed her a plate then he helped himself and they sat down and ate. After they were finished eating Tom started clearing the table. "Carrie, don't worry about the dishes. I'll do them while you're working. Besides, I remember I forgot to give you your other surprise last night, so close your eyes."

She did and when she opened them she saw two tickets to a show on Friday night. She smiled. "Tom, this show has been sold out for weeks. How did you get tickets?"

"I have a friend who works in the ticket office and he told me about them. I thought I would surprise you with these tickets."

She kissed him. "You did. Thank you."

"You're welcome."

"What night is the show anyway?"

"Friday. The show starts at 8:00."

"I will be picking you up today and tomorrow."

"I'm glad. I just hope Sara has a better day today. She has had a rough week. I can't imagine what it's like for her to come back after that awful murder."

"I hope she does to."

Seth got up when his alarm went off. He got dressed, then went into the kitchen and fixed breakfast. At 6:20 a.m. Sara still wasn't up. Seth got really worried so he went into her bedroom to wake her. She wasn't in her bed; then he heard her vomiting and crying in her bathroom. He knocked on her bathroom door. "Sara honey, it's Seth. Are you alright?"

"Yes I'm alright. I'm just finishing up. I'll be out in a few minutes."

"I have breakfast fixed. Are you up to eating?"

"I'll only have toast and some coffee."

"Is there anything I can do?"

"No, I'll be out in a minute."

"I'll wait for you in the kitchen."

Sara finished getting ready and went into the kitchen. "Sara honey, you look really tired and worn. Are you sure you're up to going to work today?"

"I'm sure. I'm just really tired."

"I bet. What time did you finally fall asleep?"

"It was around 2:30 a.m."

Seth cringed. "I didn't sleep very well myself last night. Let me fix you some toast."

Seth fixed her some toast and coffee; they sat down and ate and talked. After they finished they gathered their things and left to go to the school.

On the ride to the school Sara leaned her head back and closed her eyes. Seth looked over at her and smiled. She looked so peaceful. He put his hand on her shoulder and she smiled, without even opening her eyes. When they got to school, they met Carrie and Tom. They walked inside together.

"Sara, is everything alright? You look exhausted?"

"I didn't sleep well last night."

"Are you going to be up to teaching today? If you aren't I'm sure Nancy would understand."

"I'm up to teaching. I need to teach, especially after last night. Carrie how are you feeling?

"I'm feeling a lot better than I was Monday. I think a lot of Monday was the jitters."

"I had them too. I'm glad you're feeling better."

"Thanks Sara."

Sara clasped Carrie's hand. "Carrie, can we talk later, privately?"

"Sure. I have a few minutes before my students get there now, would you like to talk now?"

Sara turned to Seth. "Seth, Carrie and I need to discuss something privately. She has some time now. I'm going to go with her if that's alright."

"That's fine. I'll be in my office if you need me. Otherwise I'll see you at lunch."

"Carrie, I'll pick you up after you get off."

"It should be about 3:30 p.m."

"I'll see you then. If you need me before then, call me on my cell phone. Goodbye honey."

"Goodbye Tom. I'll see you later."

Seth walked into his office while Sara and Carrie went into Carrie's room. Sara started trembling and sobbing. Carrie walked over and hugged her. "Sara what's wrong?"

"Carrie, the reason I'm having problems sleeping is because I can't stop thinking about that letter."

"Have you talked to Seth about it yet?"

Murder When the Bell Tolls

"No. To make matters worse there was a message on my machine yesterday from the author of this letter."

Carrie gasped. "How do you know that?"

"Because the caller said to think about the contents of the letter and to remember that I'd be next."

"Oh Sara. That's terrible. What did you tell Seth?"

"I told him it was a wrong number. Maggie called also. Carrie I don't know if I can tell him; I'm so scared. I need to feel his strong, loving arms around me and his gentle voice telling me it will be alright but…" Sara stopped. She was crying so hard. Carrie held her next to her and cried along with her. Sara was startled when one of Carrie's students asked "Mrs. White, Ms. Michaels, is something wrong?"

Sara tried to compose herself but couldn't stop crying. "Sara, let me call Nancy in her office and ask her if Dolly could fill in for you this hour. She's a good teacher and I think you could use a little extra free time right now."

"Okay. Maybe it's the right thing to do but what am I going to tell Seth?"

"I'll have Nancy tell Seth that you took the hour off because you weren't feeling well and that you needed to rest. I think he'll understand."

"Alright, call her but at least let me get back to my class first."

Carrie clasped Sara's hand. "It'll be alright. I'll help you as much as I can."

"Thanks Carrie."

Seth watched as Sara walked to her classroom. He could tell that something was terribly wrong but he knew her students would be getting there shortly. He watched as she sat down at her desk. She buried her head in her hands and cried.

Carrie called Nancy and told her that Sara needed someone to teach her first class because she wasn't feeling well, and suggested that Dolly do it. Nancy agreed, then told Carrie she was going to Sara's room to talk to her."

Seth watched Sara's room and when he saw Nancy walk in he knew something was wrong. Nancy walked into the room and saw Sara with her head in her hands crying. "Sara, it's Nancy. I asked Dolly to fill in for you for at least this hour. What's going on?"

"Nancy, I'm just really tired. I've been having problems sleeping. I keep seeing Paul's murder over and over in my head."

"Why don't you go to the teacher's lounge or Seth's office and try and relax?"

"Okay. I'll go to Seth's office. I could use the rest."

"I'll walk you there."

Nancy walked with Sara to Seth's office. He got up and looked at Sara very concerned. "Seth, Sara needs to stay in here with you for at least an hour. She isn't feeling well and I think she could use a little rest."

"That's fine. She had a rough night anyway. I'll take care of her."

"Sara, will you be alright?"

"Yes, thank you Nancy."

Nancy left and Seth helped Sara into a chair. He turned his chair around to face her. "Sara, what can I do to help?"

"Could you have someone get me a glass of ice water please?"

Seth called down to the cafeteria and had them bring Sara a glass of water. She searched in her purse until she found her pain medication. She took it then sat down in the chair and tried to relax. Seth felt helpless. He clasped Sara's hand. "Are you going to be alright?"

"Yes. I appreciate you letting me stay here and not questioning me about why. It means a lot Seth."

He clasped her hand tighter. "I'm here for you. You know that."

She smiled at him. "I know that."

The bell rang for the class to be over. Sara get up slowly and started walking toward the door. "Sara, do you think you're going to be able to teach this next class?"

"Yes. I'm feeling better. The pain medication is working."

"This is the first time all week that you've had to take any medication. Is the pain starting to get bad again?"

"It's not too bad; I think it's just from all of the stress of coming back to work and being on my feet all day. I think a good night's sleep will help."

"Maybe. Your doctors' appointment is tomorrow isn't it?"

"Yes, right after school. I need to let Carrie and Tom know that."

Murder *When the Bell Tolls*

"I'll tell him today. I think he's off again tomorrow anyway so that shouldn't be a problem."

"Seth thank you again."

"You're welcome Sara. Let me walk you back to your class."

The students smiled as they saw Sara and Seth walking to Sara's class. The students liked Seth and Sara both. They were glad they were both there. Sara walked into her class and thanked Dolly for filling in for her. "Dolly, please don't leave. I would like for you to stay. I'm still not feeling well and I could use the help today."

"Sure Sara. That's not a problem."

Seth left the class and walked back to his office. Tom had laid out the evidence from all of the cases on Carrie's dining room table. He was going over the evidence again. He kept going back to the letter that was found on Jack, the birthmark, and the shoe prints. Tom called Seth. "Seth Parker speaking."

"Seth it's Tom."

"Hi Tom. Are you enjoying your day off?"

"Yes and no. I'm going thru the files on this case and Sara seems to be the key person to answer some questions. Do you think it would be alright if I spoke with her within the next few days? I can't do it tomorrow night because Carrie and I are going to see a show."

"Sure come by anytime and bring Carrie along if you like."

"I'll call you first. Is Carrie doing alright today?"

"Yes. She's been helping Sara out today."

"Seth, I want to ask you a question?"

"Sure Tom. What is it?"

"Do you think it's wrong for me to move out of my apartment and move in with Carrie? I would feel better if I could be with her most of the time. I love her dearly and I love being with her."

"I don't see anything wrong with it, especially since the two of you are going to get married in a couple of months. I worried about that to when I first moved in with Sara."

"Thanks Seth."

Seth hung up the phone and looked into Sara's room. She seemed to be doing better. She looked over at him and smiled. He smiled back. At lunch Carrie and Sara went to Seth's office. They talked and ate. After lunch was over Seth looked at Carrie and said "Carrie, I need to talk to Sara alone for a few minutes. I'll walk you to your class though. Sara, please wait in my office."

Seth walked Carrie to her class, then went back to his office where Sara was. He closed the door, something he normally didn't do unless a student asked him to. "Sara, I know you need to get back to your class but I need to tell you Tom called. He wants to talk to you about something to do with this case. He asked if he and Carrie could come by sometime in the next few days. I told him yes."

"I don't know what else I can tell him."

"He said he may have to talk to you. Two more things before you go back to class. Tom is going to ask Carrie if it would be alright if he just moves in with her. He feels that she needs a lot more help than she'll admit. She's still pretty weak."

"I agree. They really love each other and I know Carrie told me she hopes he doesn't leave. She loves having him there. You said there were two things. What's the other thing?"

He walked over to her and hugged her tightly. "Sara, I just wanted you to know that I care about you. I thought maybe you needed this to help you feel better."

She looked at him with tears in her eyes and said "I did and I still do. Seth I really need you right now."

He held her at arms' length. "Sara, I'll be there for you. Please trust me."

"Seth, I do trust you, but now is not the time to tell you what is happening. I promise I'll tell you all about it later."

"Alright, but remember I'm in here if you feel like it can't wait. Motion for me if you need me."

"I will. Thank you Seth." She kissed him on the cheek as he watched her walk in to her class.

Tom sat and ate lunch. He left the evidence on Carrie's dining room table, took a shower, changed clothes, then walked to a nearby ice cream shop and bought a half gallon of Rocky Road ice cream and a half gallon of Black Cherry Ice cream. He also bought whipped cream and some cherries. He walked back to Carrie's and put the ice cream in the freezer. He checked the time and realized it was time to leave to go pick Carrie up.

Tom got to Carrie's school about ten minutes before the class was out. He went to Seth's office and knocked on the door. "Hey Seth."

Murder *When the Bell Tolls*

"Hey Tom. How's it going?"

"Alright. How's it going for you here."

"I really like it. These are a great bunch of kids. Tom are you going to pick Carrie up tomorrow also?"

"Yes. I have the day off. Why?"

"Sara has a doctors' appointment after school tomorrow to check her wound. I hope it's doing okay. She had to take pain medication today."

"I'm sorry to hear that. Carrie and I have tickets to a show tomorrow night."

Sara and Carrie walked out of their classrooms. Tom walked over to Carrie and hugged and kissed her. "How are you feeling Carrie?"

"Okay. I didn't have as bad of a day as I thought I would."

"That's good. Sara, I understand you haven't been feeling well today. Are you feeling better now?"

"Yes. I think it's just the stress of being on my feet all day."

"Hopefully that's all."

"Carrie, are you ready to go?"

She hugged Sara then said "Yes. Sara, I'll see you tomorrow."

"I'll see you both. Goodbye."

"Goodbye Seth."

"Goodbye Tom, Carrie. We'll see you."

After Carrie left Seth walked over to Sara, who was now trembling. She needed to feel Seth's strong arms around her. "Sara, you're trembling. What's wrong?"

"Can we go into your office for a few minutes?"

"Sure."

They walked into his office. "Sara, what is it?"

"Seth, please hold me. I need to feel your arms around me, please."

He gladly responded by hugged her and holding her. He stroked her hair. He kissed the top of her head. She finally stopped trembling. "Sara, what's wrong. Please tell me. I want to help."

"This isn't the place. Tonight after supper, we'll discuss some things. I promise."

"Alright, that's fine. Are you ready to go?"

"Yes."

Seth and Sara headed home. Sara kept thinking about that letter that she had in her purse. She felt like the words You're Next were tattooed into her brain.

Tom and Carrie got to her house and walked in. "Sorry about the mess on your dining room table Carrie but I'm trying to make sense of these murders."

"It's alright. We can eat in the kitchen tonight anyway."

"I bought us some ice cream, whipped cream, and cherries to make sundaes for dessert tonight."

"That sounds wonderful. I'm going to go shower and change clothes, then I'll fix us something for supper."

"Take your time. I thought we would order Chinese tonight so that we have some time for ourselves."

She kissed him. "That sounds wonderful. I'll shower and be out in a little while."

She showered and changed clothes. She put jeans and a t-shirt on and headed out to where Tom was. Tom was making a salad when Carrie walked past the dining room table and gasped. She saw a picture of the marks left on the female victims, and caught a glimpse of the letter that was in Jack's pocket. She picked both of them up and said horrified "Tom, where did you get this picture of this unusual mark?" Tom stopped everything he was doing and saw the fear and pain in Carrie's eyes. "Tom, did you talk to Sara?"

"No why? Carrie, what's wrong" ? She started crying and trembling. He walked over to her. "Carrie honey, what is it?"

"It's that mark. It's very unusual."

"Yes I know. That mark was found on both of the female victims left hips. We don't know what caused that mark."

Carrie got ghostly white. Tom looked at her. "Oh No! Sara!"

Carrie collapsed on the sofa. Tom walked over to her. "Carrie, are you alright?"

"I am but I'm not sure Sara is."

"What do you mean?" Carrie was crying and Tom hugged her.

Once Carrie stopped crying so hard she looked at Tom and said "Tom, I've seen that mark before."

He gasped. "Where?"

"On Sara's left side. Just below the bullet wound. That's the mark that got infected along with the bullet wound."

Tom sat stunned at what he had just heard. "Oh my ! Carrie are you saying that what happened to the last two victims, happened to Sara?"

"I'm not sure what Art did to Sara?"

"Art? Art Hunter?"

"Yes. He's the one who gave her that mark."

"Oh my! That's what Jack was referring to in that letter. Art was in on the murders. I need to talk to Sara and Seth right now."

"Tom, I want to go with you. Sara may need some moral support after this."

"I agree. Let me call Seth and tell him we're coming."

When the phone rang Seth answered it. Sara was in the shower. "Seth. It's Tom. I need to come over right now and speak with Sara if that's alright."

"It's fine. She's in the shower then we were going to eat some dinner. Why don't you join us?"

"That would be nice but I think Sara will need you more than ever after we talk. Carrie's going to come with me. We'll be there in about thirty minutes."

"Alright. I'll tell Sara."

Sara got out of the shower and walked into the living room. She had gotten into her night clothes and put on her slippers. "Well Seth, I guess we should order dinner."

"Sara, we might want to wait on dinner."

"Why? It's 5:30 aren't you hungry?"

"I'm hungry but Tom and Carrie are on their way over. Tom said he needs to speak with you right away. He's bringing Carrie along."

"Alright. When will they be here?"

"In about twenty minutes."

A little later Tom and Carrie arrived. Seth let them in. Tom had a small file under his arm when he came in. "Hello Seth, Sara."

Carrie hugged both of them. Tom shook Seth's hand and then walked over to Sara. He put his hands on Sara's arms and looked her in the eyes. She could see concern and compassion in his eyes. "Sara, could we go somewhere and talk privately?"

"Is it necessary to do this in private?"

"Yes."

"Let's go into the all seasons' room and talk."

Before they went into that room Tom looked at Carrie and said "Ask her Carrie."

"Sara, where's the letter?"

"It's in my purse in my bedroom."

"Sara, I need to see that letter."

"Carrie, it's in the side pocket of my purse."

"Seth, have you seen the letter Sara got in the mail the other day?"

"No. I didn't know anything about it?"

"Carrie, bring it to me and let me see it."

Sara and Tom sat on the sofa. "Sara, I know this is hard for you but I really need your help. I need for you to look at a couple of photos and a letter and tell me if you recognize anything."

"I'll do my best."

Tom showed her the pictures of the birthmark, and the odd mark left on the victims. She turned ghostly white and started shaking, tearing were running down her face. Carrie walked in with the letter, sat by Sara and hugged her. "Sara, it'll be alright. Tom will help you."

"Sara do you recognize that birthmark?"

"Yes, that was the mark that I saw on the face of the raggedy dressed man."

"What about this other photo? Do you recognize this mark?"

Sara started crying harder. Carrie rubbed her hand across Sara's back. "It's okay Sara. You can trust him."

"I recognize that mark because I have one like that too on my left side."

"Sara, who gave you that scar?"

"Art Hunter."

"Sara, I want you to take a closer look at the birthmark. Do you recognize the face?"

She gasped. "It's Jack Lake."

"And the mark in these photos are from the last two female victims."

Sara almost passed out. "Oh No! Were they....?" She couldn't continue.

"Were they what Sara? Sexually assaulted? Yes they were. Here are some of the photos from the folder."

Sara couldn't stop crying. Tom touched the top of her hand. "Sara, do you think Art is capable of doing this?"

"Yes, especially after what he did to me."

"Can you tell me about what he did to you?"

"No, it's just too painful."

"We can place Art with at least the last two victims and outside your bedroom window."

"Oh No! He was my stalker?"

"I'm afraid so. Carrie, may I read the letter Sara received?"

She handed him the letter. He was horrified when he read it. Tears filled his eyes. He looked at Sara, then touched her hand. "Sara, Whatever happened must have been horrible. I'm so sorry that it happen to you. Did you tell anyone what Art did to you?"

"Only Paul."

"Sara, I hate to put you through this, but I need for you to read this letter. She did and gasped.

"Where did you get this?"

"It was in Jack's pocket when he died. We think he was going to turn himself in for his role in the murders, then tell us everything he knew about what Art had done. Art got to him first. We have reason to believe Art is the murderer."

"What happens now?"

"When we find Art, we're going to arrest him on eight counts of murder and leave it to the courts to decide his fate."

"What do you mean when you find him? He works at the US Bank."

"We're aware of that except he left for a vacation sometime over the weekend and no one knows where he is."

Sara started crying uncontrollably. "Carrie, would you mind staying with her while I get Seth and fill him in on what we know?"

"That's not a problem."

Carrie hugged Sara and tried to comfort her. Tom went into the kitchen and talked to Seth. Seth turned ghostly white when Tom showed him the pictures and both of the letters. "It's no wonder Sara had been crying so much lately."

"I'm not surprised. Seth she needs your support right now."

"Have you called into the station and told the officers about Art?"

"No."

"Why?"

"Seth, we have a problem. Art left on vacation over the weekend and no one knows where he went. I have put guards on the airport, bus station, and train station and no one has seen him. It's like he just vanished."

"When is he due back to work?"

"On Monday; I'm going to have Scott get an arrest warrant. On Monday we'll go to the bank and arrest Art on eight counts of murder and three counts of sexual assault. Seth, I think you need to go where Sara is, she really needs you now."

Seth and Tom walked out to where the ladies were. Carrie had finally gotten Sara calmed down. "Carrie, thank you for staying with me and helping me through this difficult time."

Seth and Tom walked into the room. "Sara, thank you for your help. I hated putting you through that. If you need anything, just ask."

"I will Tom. I know you did what you had to do and it's alright. I'll be alright."

"Sara, we'll find Art and arrest him. I promise you."

"Thank you Tom."

"Sara, we'll talk to you later. I'll see you at school tomorrow."

"I'll see you."

After Tom and Carrie left, Sara got up and started walking around. "Sara, Tom told me that he showed you some pictures from the last two crime scenes and you were able to recognize some things that blew the case wide open. I had an idea that Art was the killer but I had no idea that he had pulled Jack into it. Jack seemed nice but I always felt like he was hiding something. Now I know what. Are you alright?"

"Yes. I just need to process the information Tom just gave me."

"If you want to talk about it I will listen."

"Thanks Seth. I appreciate it. Why don't we eat supper?"

"How about I order something for us ? I think you need to relax."

"That's fine."

Carrie and Tom stopped and got some Chinese food on the way back to Carrie's. Once they got to Carrie's they went in and started eating. "Carrie, I have something I want to ask you?"

"What is it Tom?"

"Carrie, I'm thinking about telling my land lady that I will be moving out in two weeks; that is if you wouldn't mind me moving in with you permanently."

Murder *When the Bell Tolls*

She hugged and kissed him. "Oh Tom, I would be thrilled to have you move in with me. I enjoy your company and my big house won't feel so empty. Besides it will give us more time to spend together and get to know each other better."

"I agree."

The food Seth ordered arrived. Seth got the plates out; they sat down at the table and ate. Sara was shaking inside. "Seth, isn't there any way someone can find out where Art is before Monday?"

"Tom has everything covered as far as that goes. The arrest warrant will be issued tomorrow and Tom and Scott will pick Art up at the bank on Monday."

"What if he makes bail?"

"It'll be alright. Tom assured me that they'll increase patrols at the school. I'll talk to Nancy and inform her about what's happening so that they can be on alert."

"Thank you Seth. I'm just so scared."

"I know." He said and hugged her. It's alright to be afraid."

They finished their meal, cleaned things up, then started playing some cards.

Tom and Carrie finished eating their supper, then went in to watch television. They snuggled against each other. A little later, Tom got up and fixed the sundaes. They ate the sundaes, watched television and fell asleep in each others' arms.

Sara and Seth played cards until around 11:00 p.m. they both went into their bedrooms and got into bed. Sara had a hard time sleeping. She couldn't get the vision of that awful day in the store out of her head, then she kept seeing Paul slump to her feet. She started crying hysterically. She got up, went into her bathroom, splashed water on her face and tried to calm down. Seth heard her walking around. He got up and walked to her room. He heard her crying and knocked on the door. "Sara, are you alright?"

"Yes, I'm just having a hard time sleeping. I can't get those images of those poor women out of my mind."

He held Sara close to him and tried to comfort her. She finally stopped crying. "Seth there's something I need to talk to you about."

"What is it Sara?"

"I don't know how to tell you this." She started trembling. "Seth, the reason I could tell Tom that I know about that unusual mark is because I have one of those too. Art left that mark on me about a year ago when I was in the grocery store."

Seth gasped. Sara started crying harder. "Sara, what did Art do to you?"

She cried harder as she told him everything. He looked at her horrified. "Seth, I'm sorry I didn't tell you about it earlier but I'm in love with you and I was afraid you would walk away from me after I told you about this. I wanted to make sure Art was implicated before I said anything. I'm sorry."

Sara was crying hysterically when Seth, with tears in his eyes and a horrified look on his face threw his arms around Sara and held her close to him. Once Sara stopped crying so hard, Seth put his hands on her arms and looked her in the eyes and said "Sara honey, I love you and I would never walk away from you because of that. Art is an evil, sick man who deserves to go to jail. None of this is your fault. I'll always be here for you. My number one priority is you. My job as a police officer comes second behind that. Does anyone besides me know what Art did to you?"

"I only told Paul."

"You didn't tell Tom, Carrie, or even Maggie?"

"No. I didn't tell anyone else. Seth, I'm so scared. I don't want anything to do with Art."

"I know that. We just have to trust Tom and the other officers to take Art into custody."

Sara gasped. "Seth, I just realized that someone is going to have to contact Maggie and Kevin when Art is arrested. How am I going to tell them what Art did to me?"

"Why don't we tell them together?"

"Thank you Seth."

"Sara, you're so tired. Why don't you go back to bed and try and get some rest? I'll go in the living room and you can call me if you need me."

Sara got into bed and Seth went into the living room. Neither one of them slept much that night.

Tom woke up around 5:30 a.m. He looked over at the other end of the sofa and saw Carrie sleeping peacefully. He smiled, got up, showered and changed into casual clothes. He thought about Sara and wondered how she made it through the night. He knew what needed to be done to get

Art. He would wait until Scott got on duty and call into the station. At 6:30 he walked over and kissed Carrie, then rubbed her arm gently trying to awaken her. She opened her eyes and smiled at him. "Good Morning Tom."

"Good Morning Carrie. I'll get breakfast started if you want to get dressed for work."

She smiled, kissed him, then went to get ready for work. When she finished getting dressed she walked into the kitchen and met Tom. They sat down and started eating. "I hope Sara's alright."

"So do I. Carrie, I hope you know that I hated having to do that to her. The information she provided will put Art away for the rest of his life."

"I know, I just hope she talked to Seth about what Art did to her. I know he'll understand it's just that she's in love with him and she doesn't want to lose him."

"She won't. He's very much in love with her to. He's also a very good officer and a very compassionate and caring person."

"So are you Tom Monroe. I can't wait until tonight. I'm so excited."

"So am I. I'll pick you up after school."

"Are you ready to go?"

"Yes I am."

Seth woke up early. He got up at 4:45 and found Sara standing in the all seasons' room. The early morning light was shining on her strawberry blonde hair; he couldn't help noticing how beautiful yet vulnerable, she looked. He walked up behind her and put his arm on her bare shoulder. "Sara, what are you doing up so early?"

"I couldn't get back to sleep. I kept seeing Art standing there, then I saw images of my father one day when I made a mistake."

Seth stroked Sara's hair. She turned to face him. "Sara, I promise, I won't let Art hurt you ever again. I mean it."

She hugged him and he held her tightly against his chest. After a few minutes Seth put his hands on Sara's arms. He looked into her eyes, he lifted her chin up then kissed her very passionately. She responded with a kiss of her own. Then she started shaking again. He held her in his arms for awhile then said "Are you up to going to work today?"

Debbie Creamer

"Yes. Having you there will help and I won't think about my doctors' appointment as much either."

"Sara, are you afraid to go back to the doctor?"

"No. It's just that Dr. Martin wants to know how I got that scar and what tool made it ;I just can't tell him."

"I know Bob will understand if you say you aren't ready to talk about it. He won't push. I'll be there with you."

"Thanks Seth."

After they had changed clothes, Seth made breakfast. They sat down and ate, then Seth and Sara left for the school.

Once they got to school, they met Tom and Carrie. "Good Morning Seth, Sara."

"Good Morning Tom, Carrie."

"Sara, how are you feeling?"

"I'm feeling a little better but I'm still really scared."

"I bet. Sara, again I'm so sorry."

"It's alright Tom. You did what needed to be done."

"Sara, I understand that you have a doctors' appointment after school today."

"I do. It's at 3:45p.m."

"Good luck with that. Carrie, don't forget, I'll pick you up at 3:30."

"Tom, why don't you join us for lunch today? I'll pay for everyone."

"I think I might just do that. Thanks Sara."

"Tom, I'll see you later."

"I'll see all of you at lunch. I love you Carrie."

"I love you Tom."

Seth walked Carrie to her classroom, then Sara. When he got Sara to her class he clasped her hand. "Are you alright?"

"Yes. I'll be fine. Thanks for understanding Seth. It means a lot."

"You're welcome Sara." They walked into her classroom and continued talking then Seth put his arms around her and hugged her. He raised her chin up and kissed her. Suddenly behind them they heard someone clear their throat.

They turned around. Sara was embarrassed when she saw Nancy standing there. Nancy smiled. "Sara, I wanted to see if you were feeling any better today."

Seth clasped Sara's hand as she faced Nancy. "Yes, I had a rough night but I'm feeling better. I have a doctors' appointment after school today. Hopefully he will say that everything is healing like it should."

"Hopefully he will. I'll let you get things ready for your class. I'll talk to you later. If you need anything, you know where to find me."

"Thanks Nancy."

As Nancy was leaving Seth said "Nancy, I need to talk to you for a few minutes. Would it be alright if I met with you in your office after school begins?"

"Sure. I'll be waiting."

Seth hugged Sara again. "Sara, everything will be alright. She needs to know about Art."

"Seth, you don't have to tell her about what Art did to me, do you?"

"No, that's just between us."

"Thanks Seth."

Seth left Sara and went to Nancy's office and knocked on her door. "Seth, come in. Have a seat. What would you like to talk to me about?"

"Nancy, I thought you might want to know that we have a suspect in all of the murders."

She gasped. "You do? Who?"

"Art Hunter. We can place him with two of the victims and other evidence leads us to believe that he is the mastermind and murderer. His set up man was Jack Lake."

"Jack, the last victim?"

"Yes." Seth told her some of the evidence that they had. Nancy gasped. Then he told her about what was happening with Art.

"Oh my. How's Sara handling this?"

"She's having a hard time. Art wrote her a letter telling her she's next; that's part of the reason she's having such a hard time concentrating. She didn't get much sleep last night. She cried most of the night."

"I would imagine. I'm sure having you there with her has helped."

"It has. She's a wonderful person who I've fallen in love with."

"I can tell. I know Sara thinks a lot of you and from what I saw I would say she's fallen in love with you to. If she needs anything tell her to ask."

"I will. Thank you for being so understanding Nancy."

"You're welcome."

Several students stopped by to talk to Seth during the day. The assembly was scheduled for after their lunch so Seth was busy getting things together. Seth checked on Sara several times thru out the day. Around 11:45 p.m. Tom arrived at the school. He went into Seth's office. "Hi Tom. The ladies will be here shortly. Have a seat."

"Seth, how's Sara doing?"

"She's doing alright. She told me about what Art did to her. She cried most of the night. I have been really worried about her today. I hope this weekend will go a lot easier for her."

"So do I. I wanted to tell you I got the warrant for Art's arrest."

"Good. Tom, do you have his house covered?"

"No. I got his address from his boss though. I'll get someone to cover his house. He has to come home sometime. We'll be at the bank Monday to serve the warrant."

"Good. I know a lot of people will be happy when he's in custody."

Carrie walked to Sara's room. "Are you ready to go to lunch?"

"Yes, just let me grab my purse."

They walked out the door and headed toward Seth's office. "How are you feeling Sara?"

"Better. I told Seth about what Art did to me?"

"You did? What did he do?"

"He was so understanding. He told me he would never walk away from me over this. After he said that something happened that I was prepared for and was glad it happened." Sara told Carrie what happened and Carrie hugged her. Carrie told Sara about Tom moving in with her permanently. Sara smiled. "I know you and Tom are very happy."

"We are. Speaking of Tom, he did make it for lunch."

They all met in Seth's office and had lunch. "Tom, I'm giving a presentation today for the school about crime and punishment. Could you stay for a few minutes after I walk the ladies back to their classrooms? I need your input on the information I have put together."

"Sure but only if you will allow me to walk along with you."

"Sure."

Murder *When the Bell Tolls*

Seth and Tom got the women to their classes. Tom kissed Carrie before they walked Sara to her room. "Tom, could you excuse me a minute. I need to talk to Sara alone."

Tom stepped in the hallway. Seth hugged Sara. "Are you alright Sara?"

"Yes. I want to get things together before the assembly."

"I know you do, but try to relax."

"Seth, before you go could you hug me just one more time?"

He hugged her, then leaned down and kissed her. Tom happened to look in the room at that time. He smiled. He knew they both finally realized how they felt about each other. Seth came out and they went to his office. "Seth, when is this presentation?"

"In about twenty minutes. Here's what I have written down."

Tom looked it over then said "I think you've got it all covered. How much time are they giving you for the assembly?"

"I have an hour."

"That's about right. Did you happen to talk to Nancy about Art?"

"Yes and she said the school will help in any way they can."

"Good. I want to pick up a couple of things before I come back and pick Carrie up, so I'm going to call Scott and tell him to place an officer at Art's home. I want this dirt bag. I really do."

"So do I."

Tom called Scott and told him what he needed for him to do, then he went and picked up a couple of things to surprise Carrie. Seth got ready for the assembly.

Seth asked Nancy to keep an eye on Sara until her class went into the gym. Seth set his things up and looked around for Sara. He got worried when he didn't see her. She smiled at him when she finally walked into the gym.

The assembly went well. Nancy watched as Sara and Carrie walked to their classrooms. Seth went into his office. He checked on Sara as he waited for school to be over. Seth saw Tom arrive at 3:10 p.m. Tom went into Seth's office and they waited for school to be over. "Seth, How did the assembly go?"

"It went well. Were you able to talk to Scott Marsh?"

"Yes. They sent an officer over there now, and Mark Anderson will be there over the weekend. Seth, Mark asked if he could work overtime Monday and help us bring Art in."

"Yes. We need all the man power available on this case. I have authority to use however many man hours are necessary to solve this case."

School was over and the ladies went into Seth's office. "Hi Tom."

"Hi Sara. How are you feeling?"

"Nervous. I'm a little concerned about what the doctor will tell me today."

"I bet you are. How is the pain?"

"It's better."

"I'm glad. I was worried about you."

"Thanks Tom."

"Thanks for your help this week Carrie. I really appreciate it."

They hugged each other then walked out the door. Tom and Carrie went to Carrie's and Seth took Sara to the doctors'. She signed in and waited for the doctor. She started shaking. Seth clasped her hand. Dixie called her into the examining room. She walked back with the nurse and went into the room. She started trembling. "My goodness Sara. Are you alright?"

"No. I'm terrified."

Dixie gasped. "Of what?"

The doctor walked in before she had a chance to answer. He walked over to her. "Sara, you're trembling. Are you in pain?"

"No, just nervous. Would it be alright if Seth comes in here with me?"

"I don't see why not except for the fact that I need for you to pull your waist band down so that I can examine that scar. Dixie, would you have Seth come back please?"

Dixie took Seth into where Sara was and she stopped shaking. Dr. Martin looked at Seth. "Seth, is something going on with Sara that I should know about? I mean she is my patient now."

Seth told the doctor about the letter Sara had received and they had a suspect in the murders. He didn't disclose the name because they didn't want to spook Art. "That's why

Murder *When the Bell Tolls*

Sara is shaking so hard. Sara, you need to try and get as much rest as you can. The stress from being on your feet and the emotional stress are causing this wound to heal slower than it should. It's healing, just not as quickly as I would like. I want you to keep your feet elevated for at least two hours a day and rest. I want to see you back in two weeks this time. Maybe by then the wound will be healed. Take pain medication as needed. If you need more medication, call. I'll call you in a refill. Please try and relax this weekend Sara."

"I will. Thank you doctor."

"Seth, take care of her. That infection could turn into a very serious problem. It looks better but she's struggling with it. Call me if she develops any symptoms like she had before or if the pain gets worse. Otherwise, I'll see both of you in two weeks."

"Thank you again doctor."

Sara made an appointment for two weeks, then she and Seth walked out to the car. "Sara, I'm glad that the wound is healing but I agree, You need rest."

"I can't rest as long as Art is still out there."

He hugged her. "I know honey. I won't be able to rest much either. I think the best thing any of us can do is try and enjoy the weekend and forget about Art for awhile."

"Could we start by stopped at my favorite coffee shop; the one where Carrie, Peggy, and I used to go all the time?"

"Sure. Let's go."

They drove to the coffee shop. Since it was nice outside they sat at a table underneath an awning. Seth got their drinks and Sara watched the people walking by. They talked while they drank their coffee. Seth held Sara's hand across the table. "Sara, why don't we stop by the store and I'll get everything I need to fix you the best steak dinner you've ever had?"

She smiled. "That sounds good."

They stopped at the store. Sara felt an emptiness when she walked in. They got the things they needed, paid for them, then went back home. "Things aren't the same in the store without Jack. It seems empty."

"I'm sure it does. I didn't know Jack very well but I know everyone liked him."

"Seth, do you need my help with anything?"

"No. I have everything covered. You rest."

"I think I'll shower and change clothes alright?"

"That's fine."

Sara went into her bedroom and showered. She put on her gown and robe and went into where Seth was. When he saw her he smiled. "Are you sure I can't do anything?"

"There is one thing you can do."

"What?"

"This." He said as he grasped her in his arms and kissed her. She smiled. "Thank you Seth. I needed that."

"So did I; I want you to rest now and put your feet up."

She grabbed a book, went into the living room, sat in a chair, and put her feet up. Seth looked over at her and smiled. "You like your steak Medium Well don't you?"

"Yes, I do."

Sara read her book while Seth cooked. When it was time to eat, Seth and Sara went into the dining room and sat at the table. "Wow Seth! This looks great."

They ate and talked, then Sara helped Seth clean up. "That was a fantastic meal."

"I'm glad you enjoyed it."

"I wonder how Carrie and Tom are enjoying their evening".

"Me too. Carrie told me that Tom is going to move in with her now but keep the lease on his apartment until the end of next month so he can get his things moved out."

"I know both of them will be happier that way."

"Yes they will. I know I feel better having you with me all of the time especially now with Art roaming free." Seth kissed Sara and held her close.

Tom and Carrie enjoyed a wonderful dinner then headed to the show. They took their seats and waited for the show to start. During the intermission they got up, walked around, and got some refreshments. Tom held Carrie's hand as they walked back to their seats.

They really enjoyed the show. After the show they went back to Carrie's. Tom had picked up a bottle of wine earlier in the day and had placed it in the refrigerator. He kissed Carrie then got out two wine glasses. Carrie looked at him puzzled. "I bought some wine earlier. It should be chilled enough now. Why don't you go ahead and change clothes and I'll get the wine poured?"

Carrie smiled as she went into her bedroom to change clothes. Tom had just finished pouring the wine into the glasses when he heard "Tom, could you help me for a minute please."

Murder *When the Bell Tolls*

Tom walked into her bedroom. "Tom, could you please help me undo this clasp?"

He helped her with the clasp, leaned over and hugged and kissed her. Carrie smiled. Tom's gentle hands on her bare back felt wonderful. Once he got the clasp undone he kissed her again and started to leave the room. "Tom, thank you."

He went back into the living room. He lit three candles and set them on a table in living room. He set the glasses on the table and walked toward his room. He looked in on Carrie. She was completely naked but had her back to the door. She was reaching for her gown. Tom said "Carrie honey, I'm going to change clothes to. I'll be out in a minute."

Carrie took her time putting on her night clothes. She put on some perfume, then decided to wear only a gown. She heard Tom walking down the hall. Tom went into the living room and sat on the sofa and Carrie came in shortly after that. They talked and drank the wine. Tom set the alarm for 6:30 a.m. While Tom was up he brought the wine bottle into the room and poured each one of them another glass. They talked for a little while longer. Carrie kissed Tom then they hugged and kissed each other for quite awhile before they drifted off to sleep.

Seth and Sara talked late into the evening. Sara started to yawn. "Sara, why don't you try and get some sleep. I know you must be exhausted."

"I am exhausted but I don't know if I can sleep. I'm worried about telling Maggie and Kevin about all of this. I need to call Maggie tomorrow anyway."

"Sara, when you call them I need to talk to them. I'll tell them that Art is going to be arrested and booked on murder charges. Now try and get some rest."

He walked Sara back to her bedroom. "Seth, are you going to sleep in your room tonight?"

"No. I'm going to sleep on the sofa in case you need me."

"Good. I feel better knowing you are closer to me if I need you."

She got into bed. "Goodnight Sara. I'll be in the living room if you need me."

"Goodnight Seth. Thank you for being so understanding."

Seth leaned over and kissed her. "You're welcome honey. Yell if you need me."

Debbie Creamer

Saturday morning came too early for Tom. He looked over at Carrie. She was sleeping peacefully next to him. He got up slowly. He smiled then put his nightshirt over her. He walked into his room and changed clothes. He walked into the kitchen and got himself a bowl of cereal and made a cup of instant coffee.

Tom sat at the kitchen table and started reading the paper. A few minutes later he felt arms around his waist. He looked up and saw Carrie. She bent down and kissed him. He stood up and hugged, then kissed her several times. "Tom, I wish you didn't have to go to work today."

"I wish I didn't either. I would rather stay here and continue where we left off last night and then take you anywhere you want to go."

"I really loved last night. The show was fantastic and the wine was wonderful. Being in your arms all night was wonderful to."

"I loved that myself. I love you Carrie."

"I love you to Tom. Are you going to be able to come here for lunch or supper?"

"I am hoping to be here for lunch."

"I'll have something ready for you to eat then."

He kissed her. "Carrie, I have to get to work. Please be careful. I'll see you around 12:45 p.m."

"I'll see you then."

When Tom left, Carrie went into her room and got dressed. She thought about the night before and smiled. After she finished getting dressed she started cleaning her house.

Seth and Sara both slept in. They got up around 9:00 a.m. Sara fixed breakfast. They ate and then cleaned up the kitchen. "Sara, it's raining again. I know we talked about taking a walk in the park but we can do something else indoors. How about going to an indoor mini golf course."

"That sounds fun."

"We can go this afternoon."

"I guess I better call Maggie."

"Maggie, Hi it's Sara. Sorry I haven't gotten back to you sooner but I've been so busy, since I went back to work."

"How's work going?"

"Okay. It was rough a couple of days but I'm handling it."

"That's good. How's Carrie doing?"

Murder When the Bell Tolls

"She's doing great. She had to have help the first couple of days after she came back to work but she's doing alright now. Tom has been staying with her too and that helps."

"Yes it does. How's Seth doing?"

"He's doing alright. He took me to the doctor yesterday and stayed with me during the exam."

"What did the doctor tell you?"

When Sara told Maggie about what the doctor had said, Maggie sensed fear and pain in Sara's voice when she asked "Sara, I can tell something is wrong. Can you tell me about it?"

Sara started crying as she tried to tell Maggie about what was happening. Seth took the phone from her and started talking to Maggie.

"Maggie, it's Seth."

"What's wrong?"

"Sara has been under a lot of stress because of the last two murders. The police department has issued an arrest warrant for Art Hunter."

"Art Hunter? I've heard that name before."

"Yes so have a lot of people. Art Hunter was Jack Lake's cousin. He works at the bank that our last two female victims worked at. His DNA was found on both of the victims and also on a piece of cloth from another crime scene."

"How does Sara fit into all of this?"

"She broke the case wide open."

"How did she do that?"

"Apparently, Art was obsessed with Sara. He wrote her a letter and told her how much he wanted her for himself and what he would do to her if she didn't respond." Maggie gasped. "He also told her she was the next victim."

Maggie screamed and dropped the phone. Kevin picked up the phone and handed it back to Maggie. "Seth, I'm putting you on speaker phone. Could you repeat what you just said about Sara?"

When he did he heard a huge gasp. "Have they arrested Art yet?"

"No. No one knows where he is. He left on a vacation over the weekend and no one knows where. Tom has the airports, bus station, train station, and even his house under surveillance. Tom and several other officers are prepared to arrest him as soon as he shows up, even if it's where he works."

"Are the police sure they have the right man?"

"We know that Art is involved in the murders because Tom found a note on Jack, written to Art about Sara and about what Art had done. Also photos taken of the victims reveal a very strange mark on the female victims. Sara was able to give us information about that mark."

"Seth, is that the mark she has on her left side? The other one that got infected?"

"Yes it is. She said that Art Hunter gave it to her."

"She told me she got it in the store one evening when she was shopping."

"She did. Art was there that night." Maggie gasped.

"Seth, Kevin and I will be there on Wednesday."

"That'll be fine. However, if Art is apprehended, he will be booked on Monday, and go before a judge on Tuesday. If he pleads guilty the judge will sentence him right then, if he pleads not guilty then that's a different story."

"Well then, we'll be there on Tuesday. Sara honey, is there anything you need?"

"No. Seth has been helping me with everything."

"That's good but I still sense a bit of tension in your voice. Is there something you're not telling me?"

"Maggie, when you and Kevin get here Tuesday, there's something I need to tell you and I can't do it over the phone."

"Alright. We should be there by 1:00 p.m. Tuesday. If something changes please let us know."

"We will. We'll see you Tuesday."

Carrie thawed a chicken in the microwave, then put it in the oven. She cleaned her house while it baked. She put a load of clothes in the wash, then sat down to take a break. She had picked up one of the files that Tom had left there accidently. She couldn't stop staring at that mark. She cringed just thinking about what she was afraid Art had done to Sara. She was deep in thought when the phone rang.

"Carrie honey, it's Tom. I'll be coming home for lunch in about an hour. Will that be okay?"

"Yes. I have lunch almost ready."

"Good. I look forward to it."

I thought I would call Sara."

"That would be nice. I'll see you in an hour."

"I'll see you."

Carrie called Sara. "Hi Sara, it's Carrie. How are you feeling?"

"I'm feeling a little better."

"Good. What did your doctor say?"

Sara told Carrie what the doctor had said, then told her she had just talked to Maggie and Kevin and Seth told them that there was an arrest warrant issued for Art's arrest. "They said they would be here on Tuesday."

"It'll be good to see them again. I wish we all could get together under different circumstances though. It seems that every time we get together it's because of these murders."

"I know. I haven't told them anything about what Art did to me and I haven't told them I finally told Seth how I really feel about him. We actually kissed for the first time last night and it was fabulous. For the first time since Paul was murdered I actually feel like myself."

"That's good. It means you are moving forward. What are your plans for this afternoon and evening?"

"Seth and I are going indoor mini golfing then going to do some shopping, then eat at a nice restaurant. What are your plans?"

"I'm not sure. Tom is coming home for lunch in a little while and I assume we will discuss what we're going to do tonight."

"Well, if you don't have anything to do would you like to go along with us? You can talk to Tom and see what he says. We will be leaving around 2:30 p.m. Tom is welcome to meet us at the restaurant if he likes."

"Thanks Sara. I'll ask him."

After Sara hung up the phone she and Seth did some laundry, cleaned the house, then sat down and ate lunch. "Seth, if you wouldn't mind, I really would like to shower and change my clothes before we go."

"That's fine. I think I'll do the same thing."

Carrie was getting some tea out of the refrigerator when Tom walked thru the door. "Hi honey."

"Hi Carrie. Something smells good."

"I made baked chicken with stuffing. I hope that's alright."

"It's fine. How have you been this morning?"

"I've been okay. I've missed not having you here though."

Tom hugged and kissed her several times. "I've missed you to. Did you talk to Sara?"

"Yes. She and Seth are going to an indoor mini golf course and then out to a restaurant for dinner. They would like for me to join them and have you join us after you get off work at the restaurant. Seth said he would call you and tell you which restaurant if you want to go."

"I think it would be a great idea for you to go. I'm going to be getting off by 8:00 tonight so call me and let me know where to meet you. I wish I could go to the mini golf course with you. I love mini golf."

"I wish you could to. Maybe we all could go together to an outdoor mini golf course after this case is over with."

"That sounds great. Right now though I just want to spend my lunch with you."

Carrie smiled as she set the food on the table. They sat, ate and talked. After they were done eating Tom helped Carrie with the dishes, then he embraced her and kissed her. "That was wonderful."

"Thank you Tom. I enjoyed making our lunch. It's always nice to have someone to cook for besides yourself."

"I know. I never fix much when I cook for myself."

"I'll call you and let you know what restaurant we're going to so that you can meet us there."

"That would be nice. I have to go back to work now."

He kissed her. "I'll see you at the restaurant Tom. I love you."

"I love you Carrie."

After Tom left Carrie called Sara and Seth and told them she would like to go along. They told her they would pick her up around 2:45. She rushed to finish getting ready and at 2:45 Seth and Sara were knocking on Carrie's door. "Hi Seth, Sara, come in. I just need to get my shoes on and then I'll be ready to go. Tom came home for lunch and I just got done cleaning everything up. It was wonderful to have him here."

"I know it is. I love having Seth with me because I love to cook and having to cook for just one person isn't always fun. I enjoy Seth's company."

"I enjoy Tom's company also. We talked about his trip to Thailand and my trip to England."

"That's right. I forgot that you and your late husband went to England about ten years ago."

After Carrie got her shoes on they went out to the car, got in and drove to the mini golf course. They talked about a lot of different things along the way. They went inside, got what

Murder *When the Bell Tolls*

they needed and began playing the course. They laughed and had a really good time. After they got done playing mini golf Sara and Carrie wanted to go to a store to look for something. Seth went with them. The ladies were like two kids in a candy store. Seth laughed to himself.

They walked out of the store and each of the ladies had three packages. Carrie took out her cell phone. "Seth, I need to call Tom and let him know where to meet us for dinner."

They decided where they wanted to eat. Carrie called Tom and told him to meet them there after he got off work. "Carrie, are you enjoying yourself?"

"Yes but it would be more fun if you were here, but I understand that you have to work. How's work going?"

"It's going alright. I can't stop thinking about you. I'll be glad when I can get out of here and meet you three. I'll see you about 8:30 p.m."

"We'll see you then."

Sara, Seth, and Carrie got to the restaurant about 7:45 p.m. They went to their table and ordered drinks. They told the waiter they wanted to wait until Tom got there to order. They talked while they waited. At 8:20 p.m. Tom walked into the restaurant. Seth waved for him to come over. "Wow Tom ! You made good time."

"Mark got there early and took over for me. I haven't been to this place in years. I wonder if the food is still as good as is always was."

"It is. Paul and I were here about a year ago and the food was excellent."

"Good. Have you ordered already?"

"No, we were waiting for you."

They motioned for the waiter to come to the table. They ordered their food and while they waited they talked. "Tom, how is the search for Art going?'

"We have all the bases covered and no sign of him yet. I just hope the press hasn't caught wind of this yet."

"I haven't spoken to anyone except Carrie about it."

"Yes and Nancy knows about it."

"She won't say anything."

"Seth, Tom, I do have one request regarding the press. I promised Alan Master from the NY Post, that he could have an exclusive when we found out anything."

"Then he will. After we arrest Art, I will personally call him and have him come down to the station. I'll give him the story myself."

"Thanks Tom."

Their food got there; they talked, ate, laughed and cried together.

When they got ready to leave Seth paid the bill. Tom handed him some money for he and Carrie's food. "Tom, it's on me."

"Seth, you don't have to do that."

"I know but I want to. You've been working so much and we really enjoy having you with us. It's a pleasure to pay for your meal. Carrie, do you want to ride home with us or with Tom?"

"I'll ride home with Tom. Thank you for taking me with you today. I had a wonderful time."

"So did we Carrie. Tom, take care of her."

Sara and Seth left right after Carrie and Tom. The rain had finally stopped and the stars were shining in the sky. Sara, I know it's later than we had planned but how about that walk now."

"Okay, but I would like to get my jacket first."

Seth got Sara's jacket out of the car and they started walking. Seth reached for Sara's hand. They walked along the path stopping after they had walked about a mile. Seth put his arm around Sara and leaned over and kissed her on the cheek. She turned and faced him and they embraced and kissed for awhile. They walked back to the car, got in and drove home. "Sara, what church service are we planning on going to tomorrow?"

"How about the service we usually go to. I think we can get up and get ready in time."

"So do I. I really like your church and the people there are so nice."

"Yes they are. They really like you to. Maggie told me that."

Seth smiled, then kissed her again. They got ready for bed and each one of them went into their own bedrooms and got into bed. Sara felt safe as she closed her eyes and drifted off to sleep.

When Tom and Carrie got home, Carrie fixed a pot of coffee. She and Tom sat down at the kitchen table and each drank a cup. "Carrie honey, you look exhausted."

"So do you Tom. I think a good night's sleep will help both of us."

"I agree. Are you planning on going to church tomorrow?"

"Yes, but it doesn't start until 10:00 so I have a little extra time to get ready."

"Carrie, why don't you go change clothes while I shower and change clothes?"

"That sounds good."

Carrie went to change clothes and Tom took a shower. They came back into the living room. Tom embraced Carrie and they kissed each other. "Tom, I'm going to go to bed if you don't mind."

"I don't mind. I'm going in my room and go to bed myself."

They kissed each other then went into their bedrooms. Carrie took off her robe and got into bed. Tom found sleep difficult. He couldn't stop thinking about Art. He tossed and turned for about an hour. He got up and walked down the hall, looked into Carrie's room and saw her sleeping peacefully. He walked back to his room and got into bed. He thought about Carrie and about how much he really loved her. He finally drifted off to sleep.

On Sunday morning Tom got up and got dressed for work. He fixed a pot of coffee and grabbed a couple of Danish. He was sitting at the kitchen table reading the paper when Carrie walked in and hugged and kissed him. "Good Morning Carrie."

"Good Morning Tom. Did you find something to eat for breakfast?"

"Yes. I ate a couple of Danish and I made a fresh pot of coffee. How are you feeling this morning?"

"Much more rested. I had a hard time getting to sleep. I was so worried about Sara. When I did get to sleep I slept well."

"That's good. I had a hard time sleeping to. I was worried about Sara to. I wish we knew where Art was. I think he decided not to tell anyone where he was going because he knew that we would figure out it was him. That horrible letter he wrote to Sara. It makes me wonder what he did to her and why?"

"I wonder why too. I know she told Seth though."

"I'm glad she did. He needs to know so he can protect her." He kissed Carrie then said "Honey, I have to leave for work now. I'll call you later and see how you're doing."

"Okay. That would be great. Church gets out at 11:30 p.m. What time is your lunch?"

"Anytime I can get away."

"I'll talk to you later then."

"I'll talk to you."

When Tom walked out the door Carrie got dressed for church, then drank a cup of coffee, ate a roll, and read the paper until it was time for her to leave.

Sara and Seth both got up and got dressed. They met each other in the living room. Sara was trying to remain calm. She was still very nervous about what she had told Seth. Any doubt about how Seth felt about it was washed away when he walked over to her, embraced her, and kissed her several times. "Sara, you look lovely. I like that dress on you. It brings out the color in your eyes."

She smiled. "Thank you Seth. You look quite handsome also."

"What time do we need to leave?"

"In about fifteen minutes unless you don't want to go for coffee hour."

"I like going to coffee hour. I get to meet people that way."

Seth looked outside. "It's beautiful outside. I don't think we need jackets."

"Well' I'm ready to go if you are."

"I'm not quite ready yet. There's one more thing I need to do yet."

"What's that?"

"This." He said as he embraced Sara and kissed her several times.

She felt wonderful inside. She knew that she was allowing herself to feel again. She smiled, then kissed him back. "I'm ready now."

"Me too."

They got into the car and went to church. They went to coffee hour. Peggy and Ralph were there. "Hi Sara, Seth. How are both of you today?"

Sara looked at Peggy and said "We're both doing okay."

"I'm glad. I was really worried about you, especially Friday."

"Friday was not a good day."

Murder When the Bell Tolls

"Seth, what's going on with the murder case?"

"I can't disclose much information but I can tell you that there has been an arrest warrant issued for someone in this case that we believe is the killer."

Peggy gasped. "Have they arrested this person yet?"

"No, they can't find them. He is due back in town tomorrow."

Sara started shaking. Seth put his arm around her and whispered "It's alright. I'm right here. I'm not going anywhere."

"Seth, if this person is the killer what happens next?"

"Well, they'll go to an arraignment and if they plead not guilty there'll be a trial, if they plead guilty they'll be sentenced by the judge the next day, which should be Wednesday."

"That's great. So will you leave the school and go back to working out of the station?"

"No actually I will go back to the station but not until the school year is over."

"That's good because the students really like you."

"I like them a lot too."

They walked around and talked to other people until it was time for church. They went into the church and sat down. After the service Pastor Jeff walked up to them. "Seth, Sara, it's nice to see both of you. How are things going?"

"Fairly well. Going back to work was hard but I have enjoyed it."

"Any news on the case."

Seth, knowing that Jeff wouldn't say anything said "Yes. The police department has issued an arrest warrant for Art Hunter."

"Art Hunter? Doesn't he work at the US Bank where Pat Tracy worked?"

"Yes. Rebecca Segrest worked there also. We believe he is the man who Sara saw running from the church across from the park."

"Oh My. Sara, you must be terrified."

"I am, but having Seth with me at all times makes it easier. I feel safe with Seth."

Seth reached for Sara's hand. Pastor Jeff saw the love in their eyes. He knew they had fallen in love with each other. "Does the police department believe that Art is responsible for all of the murders or just the last three?"

"He is being charged with eight counts of murder and two or three counts of felony sexually assault and torture."

Pastor Jeff gasped. "Oh My. You said they haven't arrested him yet. Why?"

"They can't find him. Apparently he left on vacation and told no one where he was going. The police have his house, the airports, bus station, and the train station under surveillance."

Jeff looked at Sara; she was shaking. "Sara, I know this is difficult for you. I'll pray that they find Art before he hurts someone else. I know you are in good hands with Seth. Go in Peace."

"Thank you Jeff."

As Seth and Sara were getting out of church Carrie was going into her church. She went in and sat down. Another one of her friends sat next to her. "Where's Tom today?"

"He's working. He should be here next weekend."

"That's good. He is so nice and so handsome Carrie. I'm so happy you found someone like him."

"So am I. He is so good to me. He cooks for me, calls me throughout the day, he's always coming up with surprises too. I love him so much."

"I can tell he loves you to."

After her church was over she decided she was going to surprise Tom. She went to the corner deli and got sandwiches, chips, pickles, cookies, and ice cream sandwiches. She got in her car and drove to the police station. When she walked in everyone greeted her and smiled. She walked to where Tom's office was and looked in. He was on the phone so he didn't know she was there. She knocked on his door and he raised his head and smiled. "Carrie, what a wonderful surprise."

"I brought some sandwiches and ice cream. I thought maybe we could have lunch together outside."

Tom looked at Scott and several other officers. "Tom, go be with Carrie. We've got this covered. If something comes up we'll call you."

Tom put his arm around Carrie. They walked to a nearby bench and sat down to eat lunch. "I'm so glad you came by. How did church go?"

"It was nice. How has your day been?"

"Quiet so far." He leaned over and kissed her. "I'm so glad you're here. I was thinking about you."

Murder *When the Bell Tolls*

"I haven't stop thinking about you since you left for work this morning. Have you told anyone that you're going to be staying with me from now on?"

"Only Seth and Scott. However, I don't care if the whole world knows. I want to be with you. I want to spend the rest of my life with you. I love you."

"I love you too Tom and I feel the same way."

"Seth told me that after this case is over he is going to recommend that I work Monday thru Friday nine to five. It would be a promotion."

"I would love that."

"So would I."

Tom's lunch hour was over. He walked Carrie to her car, and hugged and kissed her. "I'll call you later."

"Okay."

Carrie was heading home when she saw something in a store window that she really wanted to buy. She parked the car and went into the shop. While she was in the shop she saw Sara and Seth across the street. They had gone to the deli themselves for lunch. She walked out of the store and called them over.

They all went shopping together. "Sara, how are you feeling?"

"Better. I had a hard time sleeping last night. I kept thinking about what Art did to me."

"I would imagine. Sara, that dress looks great on you. I remember how hesitant you were to buy it."

"I told her the same thing. Have you talked to Tom since you've been out of church?"

"Yes. I stopped by the station and we had lunch together. We sat on a bench about two blocks from the station."

They both smiled. "What are your plans for the rest of the day Carrie?"

"I'm going to finish cleaning my house, watch the baseball game on television, cook Tom a wonderful dinner, take a shower, and wait for him to get home. What are your plans?"

"Sara wants to take a walk in the park and maybe take a carriage ride, then I think we'll go home finish the laundry, watch the rest of the ball game or maybe the race, and I think I'm going to put something on the grill for supper. After supper we talked about playing darts, then maybe some cards. We don't want to stay up to late."

"I agree. When are Maggie and Kevin coming back?"

"They'll be here Tuesday."

"Are they going to stay at the same hotel as they did last time?"

"I'm not sure. I'm going to ask them if they would like to stay with us at least until the sentencing and or trial is over. I do still have an extra guest room."

"That sounds so nice. I have a couple of extra bedrooms too if you need them."

"Thanks Carrie. I appreciate the offer. I'm sure Maggie and Kevin will too."

They all started walking toward their cars. "Carrie, we'll see you later. If you need us call."

"Thanks you two."

Carrie got in her car and drove home. She thought about Tom then she thought about what she was going to fix for him for supper. She drove to the grocery store to pick up a few things. She had the same feeling that Sara did when she walked in. The store had a sadness about it. It wasn't the same. She thought "How could Art do that to his own cousin. Why Jack?"

She got her groceries, then drove home. She put her groceries away, kicked her shoes off, changed her clothes, put a load of clothes in the washer, and turned on the ball game. She finished cleaning her house, then started making a very special dinner for Tom.

Sara and Seth drove to the park. Sara started trembling as they walked. When they got to the tree where Paul died, Sara stood quietly until the church bells began to toll. Sara started crying hysterically. Seth held her in his arms and tried to comfort her. She could remember everything that happened now. She remembered that she did catch a glimpse of the man in black running away and it was Art. "Seth, it was Art that killed Paul. I know it was."

"I believe you, but how can you be so sure?"

"Remember when I told you about the man in black running away?"

"Yes, we thought it was the killer."

"It was. I caught of glimpse of his face. It was Art. He ran with a limp and he was carrying something in his hand."

He held her closer to him as she cried harder. Once Sara had stopped crying so hard they walked across the park and got into a carriage and took a carriage ride. Sara was still shaking. She moved closer to Seth and he held her close to him and kissed her. She relaxed and enjoyed the ride. After the carriage ride, they got in their car and went home.

When they got home they both took off their shoes, and went into their rooms and changed clothes. Sara came out and made a pot of coffee. Seth turned the radio station to the race. He helped Sara get a load of clothes in the washer, then he went outside and got the grill started. She looked over and noticed the light flashing on her answering machine. She started to listen to the message but stopped. Instead she said "Seth, could you come inside for a minute please?"

Seth walked inside. "Sara, what's wrong?"

"I was wondering if you would mind listening to the message on the machine with me."

"Sure, but is there a problem?"

"Well yes. I'm afraid that the other night when I told you about Art. I didn't tell you or Tom about the last message on the machine."

"Sara, what was it about?"

"I'll let you listen to it."

Sara and Seth listened to the messages. The new message was from Peggy. She wanted Sara to call her. After that message Sara played the call from Art. Seth gasped. "Sara, no wonder you were so terrified. I wish you would have told me about the call. I would have understood and I know Tom would have to."

"I was just so scared and I wasn't sure that it was Art until after I got the letter."

Seth put his hands on Sara's arms. "Sara, I promise, I'll do whatever it takes to protect you. I love you and will be here for you. You can talk to me about anything. I understand now why you have been having flashbacks."

"Seth, you are still going to be with me when I tell Maggie aren't you?"

"Yes. I want to be there to support you." He kissed her again.

"Thank you Seth. I'll call Peggy back now and then I'll fix the salads and get the potatoes ready to put on the grill."

"Okay. I'm going to check the grill and see if it's ready yet." He hugged and kissed her then went outside to check the grill.

Sara picked up the phone. "Hi Peggy. It's Sara. I got your message and I'm returning your call."

"I'm glad. How are you feeling?"

"Fairly good. Seth and I enjoyed a quiet lunch together, then we ran into Carrie and did some shopping. We just got home a little while ago. Seth is cooking on the grill for dinner."

"That sounds great. I'm worried about you though. Once this case is solved are you going to be alone again?"

"I hope not. Seth is going to stay with me until the end of the school year."

"That's only five more weeks. What happens after that?"

"I don't know. We haven't talked about that. I guess we'll deal with it when the time comes."

"Sara, do you have plans for next weekend?"

"I'm not sure. It depends on what happens with this case. Maggie and Kevin are going to be here on Tuesday."

"Well, we thought maybe we all could get together for a potluck or something."

"I'll talk to Seth and see what he says. I'll ask Maggie and Kevin too."

"That sounds great. Let's see what happens."

"Sara, you've fallen in love with Seth haven't you?"

"Yes I have. He's a wonderful person."

"I know he is. I hope things work out for both of you. You deserve to be happy."

"Thanks Peggy. I'll keep it in mind. I'll talk to you tomorrow at school."

"I'll talk to you."

Sara hung up the phone and went out to where Seth was. She kissed him and he stopped what he was doing and embraced her and kissed her. "Sara was everything okay?"

"Yes. Peggy is having a potluck next weekend and wanted to know if we could come. I told her we had to wait and see what happens this week."

"That's good. I just hope this isn't a long drawn out thing. Art is guilty. I know it."

Sara started shaking again. "I know he's guilty too Seth, but I'm worried about what he might do to me if a jury finds him not guilty."

"I'll protect you." She smiled at him. "Why don't I come in and help you with the potatoes."

Murder When the Bell Tolls

"Okay."

They went inside. Sara looked at the clock. It was 7:00 p.m. "Seth, would you mind if I called Carrie and checked on her?"

"Go ahead."

Sara called Carrie. "Hi Carrie, it's Sara. Are you doing alright?"

"Yes. I'm finishing up supper for Tom. He called and said he should be home by 8:15. Did you go on a carriage ride today?"

"Yes I did and it was wonderful. The walk in the park really upset me because of the memories but the carriage ride helped relax me. Seth must have kissed me fifty times. He makes me feel so special inside."

"You are definitely in love Sara. That's how Tom makes me feel too. Sara is something bothering you?"

"Yes. It's something I remembered from walking in the park. When Seth and I were standing under the tree where Paul was murdered, the church bells tolled. I remember seeing a person in black running from the church. I also remember catching a glimpse of his face. It was Art. He was carrying something in his hand."

Carrie gasped. "Did you tell Seth that?"

"Yes and he's convinced that Art is the killer."

"So is Tom. Have you heard anything more ?"

"No but I'm worried about what might happen if a jury would find Art innocent?"

"I know that Seth and Tom would protect you. I don't think any jury in their right mind would find him not guilty."

"I hope you're right. I'll let you go since Tom will be home in about an hour. I'll see you at school tomorrow."

"I'll see you then."

Sara hung up the phone and went into the kitchen and helped Seth fix the potatoes.

Art was almost home by 7:00 p.m. He had planned on being back to his home by 9:00 or 9:30. Since it would be dark by then he wanted to go by Sara's and see if he could catch a glimpse of her from her bedroom window.

Art kept driving and got within fifteen miles of his home about the time Tom got to Carrie's. As he kept driving he saw police cars everywhere. He had no idea what was happening. He drove to Sara's and didn't see anyone. He drove around the block hoping to see if she was out in her backyard. He saw her and Seth embracing and became furious. "Sara you will pay for what you are doing." He thought to himself.

He drove to his house and passed several more police cars. He knew something was wrong but didn't know what. He didn't want to be seen so he drove to Jack's house. He didn't see any police anywhere and since he still had a key he let himself in and bolted the door behind himself. He smiled. He found a flashlight and held it down low. He found some candles and lit them. He walked upstairs with a candle. He showered and because he and Jack were about the same size he slipped into some of Jack's clothes. He went downstairs carrying a flashlight. He kept checking out the window to see if he saw anyone. He snickered. He thought he was home free.

Tom got to Carrie's. He kissed her and embraced her. "Carrie something smells wonderful."

"I made breaded pork chops, with mashed potatoes and gravy, green beans, fruit and homemade bread."

He kissed her again. She got out two plates and they sat down and ate. "Carrie this is fantastic. How did you get all of this done in that short of a time?"

"I wanted to surprise you."

"You did"

"Tom, I need to tell you something. I talked to Sara several times today but when she called me a little earlier she told me something that could convict Art for sure."

Tom looked at her very serious. "What was it Carrie."

"The night Paul was murdered, Sara said she saw someone in black running away from the church. She told me she caught a glimpse of his face and that it was Art and he was carrying something in his hand."

"That would make sense because she identified the birthmark that Jack had as the man in the raggedy clothes. They were in on this together. However I think Jack was an unwilling participant. Art must have used something against Jack to get him to participate."

"Tom, Sara's concerned about what might happen if a jury would find Art not guilty."

"Seth and I will protect her. No jury in their right mind would find him not guilty. We have enough evidence to put him away for a long time for criminal sexual assault and kidnapping."

"That's a relief."

"I wish we could find him."

"So do I."

They finished eating, then watched some television. Carrie had already taken a shower so she changed into her night clothes. Tom took a shower and changed into his clothes for the night. They talked for awhile. "Carrie honey, I can tell your exhausted. You have to work tomorrow. Why don't you try to get some sleep?"

"Tom, you have to go to work to. You need your rest to"

"Carrie, right now I need to do some thinking. You go on and go to bed. I'll go in my room later."

"Alright. Good night." She kissed him.

"Good night." He kissed her back. She walked into her room and got into bed. She couldn't sleep. She kept thinking about Art. She shuddered thinking about what he had done to those women. She got up and walked into the kitchen to get herself a cup of cocoa. She glanced over at the sofa and saw Tom, sound asleep. She fixed her cocoa, sat at the table and drank it, then walked over to Tom and covered him up with a blanket. She kissed him on top of his head then went back into her room and tried to sleep.

When it got later Art decided to try again to catch a glimpse of Sara. Jack's house was three blocks away from Sara's. Art grabbed his flashlight and headed to Sara's. He got there and saw that there were still lights on. He sat down on the ground underneath her bedroom window. He knew he could see under the curtains from there.

Seth went and changed his clothes first, then he looked over at Sara and said. "Honey, you are so tired. Why don't you go change clothes and get ready for bed?"

Sara got up and went into her bedroom. Art saw her walking and saw her turn on her light. She got her things out of the drawer. As she undressed Art stared underneath the curtain. She was more beautiful than before. He watched as she put her gown on and walked across the room to get her robe. He couldn't stop staring. He slipped in the mud and went to grab onto the ledge on the window. Sara saw him and screamed. Seth came running. Art ran as fast as he could back to Jack's house. He ran inside, turned off the flashlight and bolted the door. He went upstairs and blew out all of the candles and sat in the dark, smiling thinking about Sara's naked body and what he wanted to do to her.

Sara was crying and trembling when Seth got to her. She ran to him and he held her. "Sara, what's wrong?"

"Seth, Art was just outside my window."

"What? Are you sure it was Art?"

"Yes I'm sure. He must have been sitting underneath the window and he slipped in the mud. It was when he grabbed the window ledge and looked in that I knew it was him. He smiled at me and when I screamed he ran."

Seth took out his cell phone and called the station. "Mark Anderson speaking."

"Mark. It's Seth."

"Hi Seth. How are you?"

"I'm doing alright. Mark, I have a problem."

"What's that?"

"Sara was changing clothes and there was someone outside her bedroom window. When they slipped she looked out and saw that it was Art Hunter."

"Art Hunter? Is she sure?"

"Yes. She screamed and he ran."

"Do you know which direction?"

"No. Sara is too shaken up to tell me that."

"Tom was afraid something like this might happen. He said he had a feeling that Art would make his presence known when he got back and that it would be aimed toward Sara. Is Sara alright?"

"Yes, she's just really scared and I can't blame her. Is there a police unit at Art's home?"

"No, but they are a few houses down. They can see if he comes or goes."

"He must be hiding out somewhere, but where?"

"Seth, it's almost midnight. Do you think we should call Tom?"

"I would call him if someone spots him again otherwise wait until morning. Nothing can be done until Art is found."

"Seth, I'm going with Tom to the bank tomorrow to present the arrest warrant."

"Tom told me. I'll be with Sara and Carrie at the school. Let me know what happens. Let me know if you find the scum tonight. If you do I want to personally tell him what I think about what he has done."

"I am sending a K9 unit out there to see if we can pick up his scent."

"Thanks Mark."

Seth took Sara into the living room and sat her on the sofa. He held her next to him and she cried and trembled. He kissed her on the cheek. "You're safe now Sara. It'll be alright."

Seth got her a cup of tea and sat next to her. She was rocking back and forth, terrified. Seth saw the flashlights outside. He walked into the all seasons' room and opened the door. He could see Sara the whole time. "Seth, it's just us. The dog's have picked up a trail. Hopefully we'll find him tonight."

"Let me know if you do."

Sara sat next to Seth on the sofa and cried. He held her close to him. He got up and turned some soft comforting music on to try and help her sleep. At 5:00 a.m. the phone rang.

Seth was startled but answered it. Sara was sleeping restlessly on the sofa. "Seth, it's Mark. I wanted to call and let you know we found Art inside Jack Lake's home. It seemed he still had a key. He's on his way to be booked now."

"Have you called Tom yet?"

"No. I'm going to call him now. Art probably won't be done with booking for several hours. We'll call you at the school when he's been processed."

"Thanks Mark."

"How's Sara?"

"Sleeping. She will be relieved to know he is in custody and being booked. She's terrified."

"I bet. I wanted to tell you one other thing. We found photos of the day Art hurt Sara. He must have forced Jack to take pictures of the brutality. He had it in his wallet and he had a sticky note attached to it that read: the best day of my life. We also found Pat Tracy's locket in his pocket along with something of Rebecca Segrests'."

Seth gasped. "Oh My. Is there anything I can do to help right now?"

"Just take care of Sara."

"I will. Call me on my cell after the scum has been processed."

"We will."

"Thanks Mark."

"I'm going to call Tom now Seth so I'll talk to you later."

Seth looked over at Sara and saw her trembling. He walked over to her and sat next to her on the sofa. He leaned down and kissed her. She opened her eyes. "Seth, what time is it?"

"It's 5:20 a.m."

"Why are you up so early?"

"I had to answer my cell phone."

Sara sat up quickly on the sofa. "Seth, what is it? Was there another murder."

Seth clasped Sara's hand. "No. Lt. Anderson called to let me know they found Art and have taken him into custody. He's on his way to be booked right now."

Sara sighed. "Oh thank goodness. That helps me feel better. When do you think he'll be arraigned?"

"Tomorrow morning."

"Does Tom know yet?"

"No. Mark is calling him now."

"I can't go back to sleep so I think I will get up and shower now and change clothes."

"I'll make some coffee and change clothes myself."

Tom's cell phone rang at 5:30 a.m. "Tom Monroe."

"Tom, it's Mark Anderson. I'm sorry to have to call you so early but I thought you should know we arrested Art Hunter about ninety minutes ago."

Tom gasped. "How did you find him."

"He totally messed up when he went to Sara Michaels house and watched her through her window. When she saw him she screamed and he ran to Jack Lake's house. It turns out he had a key and he was going to hide there until he went into work. I sent out the K9 unit and that was how we tracked him down. He's at the station being booked right now."

"Does Seth know?"

"Yes. I called him first since he called in about Art stalking Sara."

"I can understand that and he is the lead officer on this case. How's Sara?"

"He said she was sleeping."

"I hope she was able to get some sleep. Do you need me to come down there now?"

"No. It's going to be a while before he gets finished with booking."

Murder *When the Bell Tolls*

"Did he say anything?"

"Only that if he gets out the he will show Sara how a real man treats a woman." Tom cringed. "Also we found a locket of Pat Tracy's in his pocket, something of the Segrest woman's and pictures of the night he hurt Sara at Jack's store. Tom, They're awful."

"I'll be in around 7:50 today. I want to talk to Art and see if I can find out why he did this."

Tom heard Carrie walking around in her room He got to her room and looked in. She was getting dressed for school. He knocked on the door. "Good Morning Carrie."

"Good Morning Tom. Did I hear you talking on the phone just now?"

"Yes you did. It was Mark Anderson. He called to let me know that they found and arrested Art early this morning."

"That's great. Now Sara can breathe a little easier, at least until the trial."

"I don't think there'll be a trial. They found a locket that belonged to Pat Tracy on him, along with something of Rebecca Segrests' and photos of the night he hurt Sara."

Carrie gasped. "There were pictures? Sara never told me that."

"She may not know about it. Art is being booked as we speak. I told them I would get to work about ten minutes early today because I really want to talk to Art and find out why he did it."

"I'll be fine at work a few minutes earlier. Seth and Sara will probably be there early to." He kissed Carrie several times.

"Honey, I don't know what time I'll get home tonight because of this case. I'm afraid that the press might hound you."

"It's alright. I can handle it."

He kissed her again. "I know you can."

They went into the kitchen and Carrie fixed a pot of coffee. Tom fixed breakfast. They sat down and ate. They finished then cleaned up the kitchen. After they had cleaned up the kitchen they left for the school.

Sara and Seth both showered and got ready to go to the school. Seth had already made a pot of coffee so Sara fixed breakfast. They sat down and ate, then cleaned up the kitchen. "Seth, do you think there will be a trial?'

"No. If Art is as smart as he appears he will plead guilty. There's overwhelming evidence that he committed the crimes. The only thing the judge or jury has to consider is if he is found guilty will he serve eight consecutive life terms." Sara started trembling. "It'll be alright. He has to stay in jail until he is sentenced anyway. I won't let him hurt you again Sara."

"Seth, what about the press. Do they know about this yet?"

"No. I'm sure Tom will take care of that."

"I promised Alan Master an exclusive."

"I'll call Tom and tell him that. I like Mr. Master. He seemed really nice when he was here with you the first time."

They left for school and met Tom and Carrie on the way inside. "Carrie, you're here earlier than usual this morning."

"Yes I know. Tom has to be at work a little earlier today. Are you doing okay Sara?"

"Yes. I'm still scared but I feel relieved."

"I can imagine."

"Seth, Sara I'm glad I caught you this morning. I'm on my way into work now. Art has confessed to all of the murders and sexual assaults of Pat, Rebecca, and Sara. The officers have informed me he will be booked later today and arraigned tomorrow afternoon. How are you doing Sara?"

"Alright, just scared."

Tom hugged her. "I know you are. I can understand that."

"Tom, has the press been notified about any of this yet?"

"Not yet but I'm holding a press conference at 10:00 this morning."

"Tom, I have a favor to ask. Sara talked to a reporter from the New York Post and promised him and exclusive when anything was about to break. His name is Alan Master. I was wondering if you would call him before the rest of the press finds out about it."

"Sure. I'll call him as soon as I get to the station. Would you mind bringing Carrie home tonight? I have no idea what time I'll get out of the station tonight."

"Sure, we'll take her home."

"Thank you both. Carrie honey, I'll see you sometime tonight."

"I'll see you."

"Seth, Sara, thanks again. Seth, I'll call you after we have Art booked and awaiting arraignment."

"Thanks Tom."

Seth walked the ladies to their classrooms. He made sure Carrie was okay, then he walked with Sara to her room. Once they were inside Sara broke down. She cried and Seth held her. "Seth, I'm sorry for the tears but I've been so scared and this has all caught up with me."

"It's alright to cry Sara. I understand. However, I think we should inform Nancy about what has transpired."

Seth picked up the wall phone and called Nancy's office. She came to Sara's room. Sara was still sobbing. "Seth, Sara, what's going on? Sara are you alright?"

"I'm okay Nancy."

"Nancy, I wanted to let you know that Art was captured and taken into police custody early this morning. He has confessed to all eight murders and five other charges also. Sara was the key for us to crack this case. Art was obsessed with her and he was also obsessed with getting even with people who he felt wronged him by rejecting him. Sara rejected him once and as I told you before she was next on his list. She is safe for now. I talked to Tom and he said that Art was being booked and then held until his arraignment tomorrow afternoon. He will be sentenced on Wednesday."

"I'm glad he is where he belongs. I think you, Seth, Carrie, and Peggy should take Wednesday off and go to the sentencing. I think it will give you closure Sara and Carrie needs to be there to support Sara. I'll make arrangements to have two subs come in on Wednesday. Dolly will fill in for one of you."

"Thanks Nancy. I appreciate it. Paul's parents are coming in Tuesday anyway but I think I better call them and tell them they need to be here by tomorrow morning."

"Do what you need to do. I'm glad he can't hurt anyone else."

"So am I."

Tom got to the station. Mark Anderson walked over to him. "Tom, there's something I think you should see."

He took Tom into a vacant office and popped a DVD into the player. Tom gasped as he saw Sara being brutally beaten while she was restrained and Art screaming at her and spitting on her. "Where did you get this?"

"We found it at in Art's house."

"Has anyone else seen this?"

"No."

"I need to make a phone call." Tom got on the phone and called the New York Post. "Hello. New York Post. Walter Mason speaking."

"Hello. I need to speak with Alan Master please."

"Alan Master."

"Hi Alan. I'm Sergeant Tom Monroe with the NYSPD. Sara Michaels and Lt. Seth Parker asked me to call you. Sara informed me that she promised you an exclusive if anything would break in these murder cases."

"She did promise me that."

"Well, I'm informing you now. We have arrested someone and he has confessed to all eight murders and several other charges against him. We have overwhelming evidence against him. I'll be giving a press conference at 10:00. However I would like for you to come to the station and talk with me so I can give you the details first."

Alan was thrilled. He had only been a reporter for two years and didn't get a lot of big stories so he said "I'll be there in fifteen minutes. Thank you sir."

Alan hung up the phone and his friend Walter looked at him. "What was that about Alan?"

"I just got an exclusive interview with the Sergeant involved in these murders. I've been waiting for this for a long time."

His friend was happy for him. "That's great. Good luck."

When Alan Master arrived at the station, Tom walked out to where he was. He introduced himself them took Alan into a empty room so they could talk. "Sergeant Monroe, I want to thank you for this opportunity. It is an honor to meet you."

"Thank you Mr. Master. What I can tell you about this case is that we have arrested Mr. Art Hunter in connection with these brutal murders. When he was arrested a few hours ago he confessed to all of the murders."

"Did he say why he did it?"

"He said it was because he wanted to prove that he could make a name for himself. He wanted to prove that he wasn't a nobody."

"How does Sara Michaels fit into all of this?"

"Sara held the key that broke the case open. She actually saw the suspect running away from the scene on the night Paul Sanford was murdered. She also identified the birthmark on our latest male victims face as the birthmark she saw on the man of many disguises. We have reason to believe that he and our suspect were working together on these murders. We also believe that Jack Lake was an unwilling participant."

Murder *When the Bell Tolls*

Alan was writing everything down. Now here's the exclusive: Sara Michaels was going to be the next target. Mr. Hunter stated in a letter written to her that he would do whatever it took to get her for his very own. We also have a DNA match to Mr. Hunters. It was found on the last two female victims and on a piece of cloth found underneath Sara's Michaels bedroom window. He was also stalking her."

"How's Sara?"

"She's terrified but relieved that Mr. Hunter has been arrested and is being held without bond until his arraignment tomorrow afternoon."

"I like Sara. She's really nice."

"Yes she is."

"Thank you sir. I appreciate the exclusive."

"You're welcome young man. You're welcome to stay for the press conference in about forty five minutes."

"No. I think I'll go back and get this ready for print. Thank you again."

Alan went back to the newspaper and wrote up his story. He smiled the whole time. He was grateful to get the interview. His friend Walter asked "So Alan, what is Sergeant Monroe like? I've heard he's really strict."

"He's really nice and very compassionate. He's a good officer."

At 10:00 a.m. the press was waiting outside the police station. Tom went out and addressed them "Ladies and Gentlemen of the press: As you are all aware of Mr. Art Hunter has been taken into custody and is being held without bond until his arraignment tomorrow afternoon."

The press threw out questions to Tom and he answered them as well as he could. Seth and Nancy had set up a television in Seth's room so they could watch the press conference. They listened as Tom talked about the brutality of the murders and then about the items found on the suspect. They watched as he walked away from the camera with tears in his eyes. Seth was proud of him. He knew that wasn't easy. Nancy looked at Seth and asked "What happens now?"

"Well since he has admitted to being guilty the judge will hear what his lawyer says tomorrow and set a time for the sentencing on Wednesday."

"Seth, after all of this is over you aren't going to leave here are you?"

"No. I will be staying until the end of the school year."
"What about Sara?"
"Nancy don't tell her yet but I have a big surprise for her."
"Okay. I won't say anything, but can you tell me what it is?"
"I'm going to ask her to marry me?"
Nancy gasped, then smiled. "That's wonderful."
Before they could finish their conversation Seth's cell phone rang. "Seth Parker."
"Seth, it's Tom."
"Good job at the press conference."
"Thank you Seth."
Seth could hear the hesitation in Tom's voice. "Tom is something wrong?"
"Seth, I don't know how to tell you this so I'll just come out and say it. During a thorough investigation of Art's home and car, one of the officers found a tape which I think you should see. You alone."
"Okay Tom but why?"
Tom was trying to compose himself and Seth could hear the tears. "Seth, Art made a DVD of the night he hurt Sara. Seth, it's awful. I almost got sick when I saw it."
Seth gasped. "Where is the DVD now?"
"It's in my desk drawer. No one except Mark and I have seen it."
"Seth how's Sara?"
"She's alright. Scared, but alright. Art actually admitted to killing all eight people?"
"Yes he did and it's on tape."
"Good."
"Seth, what would you like for me to do with this tape?"
""Bring it by Sara's tonight. I have a DVD player in my bedroom. I'll watch it tonight after Sara is asleep. I'll give it back to you in the morning."
"Okay. Sounds good."
"I have to call Maggie and inform her about the change. I'll see you tonight Tom."
After Seth hung up the phone with Tom he called Maggie and told her that they should come earlier. "I know. We saw the press conference. We'll be there by 9:30 tomorrow morning. I'll stop by the school and let you know when we arrive. We'll be staying at the hotel that we stayed at when we were there before."

"Sara and I were wondering if you would like to stay with us? There's plenty of room?"

"That sounds fabulous. I'll talk to Kevin and let you know this evening. Are the two of you going to be home?"

"Yes. Sara hasn't been sleeping well and with good reason, so we planned on staying in, ordering pizza, and watching some movies."

"I'll call you about 7:30 is that too early?"

"No, that's fine."

"Is Sara alright really?"

"Yes, she's just scared; and with good reason."

"I would imagine. I'll talk to you later. Thanks Seth."

The bell rang for lunch. Carrie walked down and met Sara. "How are you holding up Sara?"

"I'm doing alright but I'm still nervous. Maggie and Kevin will be here tomorrow and I'm going to have to tell them about what Art did to me?"

Carrie gasped. "Are you going to be able to do that?"

"I'm not sure but Seth said he would be with me when I did. I just hope they understand."

"They care about you. I think it will hurt them because they didn't know about it when it happened but also glad to know that you trusted Paul and them enough to tell them."

Seth met the ladies halfway. "Ladies, are you ready for lunch?"

"Yes. I'm starved." Carrie said.

"I'm hungry to. Let's go get our food."

They all went to the cafeteria and got their food, then went into the teachers' lounge to eat. "Sara, I haven't had a chance to talk to you much with everything that is going on. Nancy and I watched the press conference. Carrie, Tom did a great job. I talked to him and he said to take care of both of you. I told him I would. Sara, he is particularly concerned about you and frankly so am I. I know this has been hard on you."

"So do I Sara. If there is anything I can do for you please let me know."

"Sara, Carrie, When I talked to Nancy earlier she suggested that both of you, myself, and Peggy should take off Wednesday and go to the sentencing. I think it will help you get closure Sara."

"I agree but I'm surprised Nancy said that."

"So am I but she cares about you Sara, we all do."

Sara started sobbing. Seth reached across the table and clasped her hand.

They finished eating and were getting ready to go back to their classes when Seth said "Sara, I almost forgot. I talked to Maggie and told them they needed to get here earlier tomorrow. She said they would be here by 9:30. She said they were going to stay at the hotel they stayed at before and I invited them to stay with us. I hope that was alright?"

"It was. I was going to do that anyway. I'm not sure they will want to stay with us after they find out about what Art did to me." Sara started to cry. Seth walked over to her and hugged her then kissed her. Carrie smiled.

"Sara honey, I think Maggie will be very understanding. I liked her from the first time I met her."

"Thanks Seth."

Seth walked Carrie to her classroom and waited until she got inside. He waved to her then walked Sara to her room. Sara still had about ten minutes before the students started coming to her class. Seth embraced her and kissed her several times. "Sara, everything will work out. You'll see. I'll be with you when you talk to Maggie."

"What about Kevin. How am I going to tell him?"

"You're not. I'll tell him. Sometimes things like that are better received if a police officer tells them."

"I understand. Thanks again Seth."

Seth smiled as he left Sara's classroom and headed back to his office. He was worried about Sara. He cringed thinking about the fact that Art had made a DVD the night he hurt Sara.

When school was over. Carrie walked down to Sara's classroom and found her trembling. "Sara honey, what's wrong. Are you still worried about talking to Maggie?"

"No. I'm just worried that Art will get off and then he will be free to do to me what he wants."

"Sara, Seth is not going to let that happen. He loves you. I could see that at lunch today. You said that you told Seth what happened and he didn't walk away from you. That should tell you something."

"It does but Wednesday scares me. Please tell me that you'll be there."

Murder *When the Bell Tolls*

"Sara, Seth, Tom and I will be there. I haven't seen Peggy but I'm sure she'll want to be there also. We're all friends and we've been thru a lot together. Friends stand by friends thru good and bad."

"I know you're right Carrie; I'm just afraid of what people will think when they find out about what Art did."

"Sara, I don't know everything Art did to you but whatever it was, it wasn't your fault."

"Thanks Carrie. I needed to hear that."

They were still talking when Seth came to Sara's classroom. "Are you ladies ready to go home?"

"Yes we are."

They walked to the car. They talked on the way to Carries'. When they got to Carries' they walked her to her door and watched her go inside, then they got back into the car and headed home. Seth reached for Sara's hand and clasped it as he drove. Sara leaned back and tried to relax. "Sara honey, I know you had a rough night last night so I thought tonight we could order some pizza, eat in, and watch movies."

"That sounds wonderful."

"Tom is going to stop by. He has a couple of things we wants me to see from this case. I told him to drop it by and I would return it to him sometime tomorrow."

"That's fine."

They got home. Sara took her shoes off, then went into the kitchen and fixed a pot of coffee. Seth walked up behind her and put his arms around her waist and kissed her. She leaned against him for comfort. She turned around and he kissed her several more times. She smiled. "That was wonderful."

"There's more where that came from." She smiled. He pulled her close to him and kissed her again. "I love you Sara. I have tried to hide how I feel about you because I know you think it's too soon after Paul died but I can't hide it anymore. I love being with you. I love talking to you, holding you, touching you and kissing you. I can't help how I feel."

Sara had tears running down her cheeks. "Oh Seth. I feel the same way. I have been holding back because of what Art did to me. I was so scared and so afraid you would leave me. Seth I love talking to you, being with you, laughing with you and I feel so safe and so much love when I'm in your arms. I love it when you hold me and kiss me. It feels wonderful.

However, now that this ordeal with Art is almost over I guess you'll be moving back into your house, and I'll only get to see you occasionally."

"I thought I would stay here at least until the end of the school year, if you wouldn't mind."

She smiled. "I would be thrilled."

He hugged and kissed her again.

Art had been booked and was sitting in his jail cell when Tom went back to talk to him. Art smirked when he saw Tom. "Well, Well, Well, if it isn't the infamous Tom Monroe. When is your buddy Seth Parker going to be here? I can't wait to see him so that I can tell him how he needs to treat that sexy little woman of his." He laughed his eerie laugh as Tom felt his angry building up. "What's wrong? Do you think that Sara is still the innocent victim? Well she's not. She got what she had coming to her."

Tom lost his temper and grabbed Art's shirt through the bars of his cell. "Listen Scum bag. I never want to hear you talk about Sara Michaels like that again." He let go of Art's shirt and tried to calm down.

"I see I struck a nerve. Good. Now let me see if I can really make your day. That little woman of yours needs to be treated like I treated Sara the day she rejected me."

Tom grabbed Art again and said "You ever lay a hand on Carrie and I'll make you wish you hadn't."

"That sounds like a threat."

"No threat, it's a promise."

Tom left before he punched Art. Tom wasn't the violent type but Art made his blood boil.

When Tom walked out from where Art was some of the other officers that had heard his conversation looked at him and said "Are you alright Tom?"

"Yes. I just want Art to get what he has coming to him."

"We all do. His arraignment is scheduled for 1:00 tomorrow afternoon."

"Good. I'll be there."

Tom went back to his desk and sat down. He looked at the clock. It was 6:30. He picked up the phone and called Carrie."

"Hi Honey, it's Tom. I'm just calling because I miss you and wanted to make sure you were alright."

"I miss you. I'm alright. I'm just reading a book and I'm going to start fixing supper in about an hour."

"Carrie, I have to stop by Sara's and drop something off for Seth and then I'll be home."

"That's fine. I'll be waiting for you. I love you Tom."

"I love you Carrie."

Seth and Sara both took showers and changed into their night clothes. Seth called in the pizza order then they decided which movies to watch. The pizza got there about 7:00. They were almost finished eating when the phone rang. Seth answered it. "Seth, it's Maggie. I talked to Kevin and he said we would be delighted to stay with you. Are you sure it's alright with Sara?"

"Yes. Let me put her on the phone."

"Maggie?"

"Hi Sara. How are you doing sweetie?"

"I'm doing alright. I'm relieved that Art is in jail but will be more relieved when he is found guilty and goes away for a very long time."

"I agree. Sara is there something else going on?"

"No Maggie. Everything's fine."

Sara started sobbing and Seth walked up behind her and ran his hands across her back. "Sara, Kevin and I are delighted that you and Seth have asked us to stay with you. We'll accept the offer if it's alright with you?"

"It's fine. I'll get the other guest bedroom ready for you tonight."

Seth took the phone from Sara and said "Maggie, Tom is coming by tonight to give me a couple of things pertaining to this case. I'll ask him what time you should be in the court room tomorrow."

"Sounds good. We'll see both of you tomorrow. I'll come by the school and get a key to the house."

"Okay."

Seth hung up and they finished their pizza. Sara got a tall glass of iced tea for both of them. They were getting ready to start the movie when there was a knock on the door. Sara answered it."Hello Tom. Please come in."

"Hi Tom."

"I'm sorry for the intrusion but I had a few things I needed to give Seth from this case."

"It's not a big deal. We both decided to take showers and get into something more comfortable. Would you like a cup of coffee or glass of tea?"

"No thank you Sara. I need to get home to Carrie. She's waiting for me."

Sara smiled. "I know she is. Tom, I'm so glad the two of you met. I haven't seen Carrie this happy in three years."

Tom smiled. "I'm glad we met. I really love her."

"We know."

"Sara, is there anything you need?"

"No. I'll be fine."

After watching the DVD and listening to Art, Tom couldn't stop staring at Sara. She was so beautiful yet so vulnerable, just like Carrie. He cringed thinking about the contents of the DVD. He felt even more angry at Art. He handed Seth two pieces of paper with the DVD between them. "Tom, I'll get these back to you tomorrow."

"Okay. Seth, can I talk to you alone for a minute?"

Seth looked at Sara. "Go in the all seasons' room. It's private there."

They went out there while Sara used the bathroom. Tom looked at Seth and with tears in his eyes said "Seth, I'm sorry about the tears but when I look at Sara and think about this DVD my heart aches. Seth this is so graphic. I have never seen anyone go thru what Sara did and be able to hide it from everyone."

"Is it that bad Tom?"

"Yes."

"Tom, what are you not telling me?"

"I talked to Art tonight and I almost hit him. He made it a point to tell me that Sara got what she deserved then he said Carrie needed it to. Seth that man is sick."

They saw Sara walk back into the room. They walked back into the room also. "Sara, Seth, I need to get home to Carrie. I'll see both of you tomorrow at school."

"Goodbye Tom."

After Tom left Seth and Sara sat down on the sofa and started watching a movie. Seth put his arm around Sara and she leaned against him. He kissed her several times during the movie.

Tom walked in to Carrie's and found her in the kitchen finishing up dinner. He embraced her and kissed her several times. She could see the look of horror and pain on his face. "Tom, what's wrong. You seem different. Is it this case?"

"Yes Carrie it is. I just took a DVD over to Sara's for Seth to watch."

"What's wrong with that?"

"It's a DVD of the night Art hurt Sara."

Carrie gasped. "I didn't know there was a DVD. Where was it found?"

"In Art's house during our search. It was laying on a table next to the television set. It was label "The Best Night Of My Life with my Dream Girl."

Carrie gasped. "Tom, how bad is it?"

"It's horrible and so graphic. I've never seen anyone go thru what Sara did and not tell anyone. That had to be terrifying. Trying to deal with it on her own had to be even worse. I don't know how Seth will handle it. I'm not sure how I would handle it if that were you. Art is sick."

Carrie ran her hand across Tom's back. He pulled her down to him and kissed her. She put the food on the table and they ate. After they ate Tom looked at Carrie and almost cried. "Carrie honey, would you mind if I took a shower and changed clothes?"

"Go ahead. I can get the kitchen cleaned up. Besides. I thought I would have something special for dessert tonight."

Tom kissed Carrie again before he went to shower. She cleaned up the kitchen then went into her room and changed her clothes. She came out and met Tom in the living room. He had poured himself a tall glass of tea. "Carrie, would you like some tea?"

"Yes, but I'll get it."

She got herself a glass then walked over to the sofa and snuggled up next to Tom. He put his arms around her and held her as tightly as he could. He kissed the top of her head. "Tom honey, do you want to talk about what's bothering you?"

"Carrie it's what's on that DVD that's bothering me and the fact that Art is so proud of what he did. He told me that Sara got what she deserved then he told me that you needed that to. Carrie I could never hurt you like that. I love you. I just need to feel you in my arms right now."

Carrie felt so safe and Tom's arms felt wonderful around her. "Tom, can you tell me what part of the DVD bothered you the most?"

Tom told Carrie about what was on the DVD. Carrie gasped. "Oh My! I can't imagine how she kept that from everyone. How could anyone be so cruel?"

"I don't know. I don't understand that myself. Carrie I almost punched Art tonight when he said that then told me that you needed that to. I never lose my temper like that but something about him just got under my skin."

Carrie hugged Tom. "It's okay. You're human you know."

"I know but that's unprofessional."

"That may be; but he isn't a normal person. He's a serial killer with no remorse."

I wanted to kill him myself when he said that. To make matters worse when I went to Sara's I was hoping that Seth would answer the door. That wasn't the case. Sara answered the door and Carrie I have to tell you; I couldn't stop staring at Sara. I couldn't help thinking how she must have felt. She looked so lovely yet so vulnerable, and Art took advantage of her kindness and understanding."

"What's going to happen with this information about Sara?"

"I'm not sure. That will be up to her and Seth. We can charge Art with another count of criminal sexual assault, and torture or we can leave it alone. If for some unforeseen reason we can't put Art away for murder we can for criminal sexual assault."

"Tom, I can only imagine how you feel but you have done all you can. It's in the hands of the judge now."

"Thanks for saying that Carrie."

She snuggled closer to Tom and they talked more, then Carrie got up and made them some dessert. They talked and ate then snuggled more before they both fell asleep in each others' arms.

After the movie had ended Sara was exhausted. She looked at Seth and said "Seth, I'm really tired. I think that I'm going to go to bed now."

"Okay. Before I go to sleep I need to look over the things that Tom brought so I can return them to him in the morning."

Seth got up and helped Sara stand up. He embraced her and kissed her. He walked her back to her bedroom and helped her into bed. He kissed her again. "Good Night Sara. If you need me call."

"Good night Seth."

Seth walked out of Sara's bedroom and headed to his bedroom. He got the things that Tom had brought and went over the papers and signed what he needed to, then he put the DVD in the player and turned it on. He gasped and watched in horror as he saw Sara being abused and tortured by Art. He cringed. It made him sick to watch what was happening to her but he knew he needed to see it. He was relieved when it was over. He checked the time when he started the DVD and the time when it was finished. The DVD lasted forty five minutes. He felt tears running down his face. He very seldom cried but this was one time he did. He couldn't imagine how Sara felt at the time. He was furious at Art.

Seth got up and walked around the room. He now understood why Sara was afraid to tell Maggie and Kevin what happened. Sara hadn't even told him everything. He felt hurt but realized how hard it was for her to tell him what she did tell him. He wanted to go to her and hold her and never let her go. He wanted to make sure that nothing like that ever happened to her again. He wanted to talk to her more about what happened and let her know he supported her, cared about her and mostly that he loved her and that this was not her fault.

He leaned back on his bed and closed his eyes. He couldn't sleep. He kept thinking about Sara. He got up and walked to her bedroom. She was tossing and turning, and talking in her sleep. He heard her say "I'm sorry Art. It won't happen again. Please stop. It hurts." Then she was quiet. He walked over to her bed and she was still tossing and turning. Then he heard her say "Seth, I'm sorry. I know I should have told you. I'm so sorry. I love you but I don't know how you can love me. I'm damaged."

Seth covered his mouth and gasped. He had no idea that she felt that way. He didn't see her as that. He loved her for her. She started moaning. He touched her shoulder and it startled her awake. She jumped. "Seth?"

"Sara honey, you were talking in your sleep. I thought I heard you call my name so I came to see if you were alright?"

She was shaking. "I was having a bad dream, that's all."

"Sara, you were having a flashback. It happens to a lot of people who have been thru what you have. It's your body's way of helping you deal with it and move forward, but you can't do it alone."

"Seth, I'm really having a hard time sleeping. My wound is bothering me too. Would you help me to the sofa? I think I might be more comfortable out there."

Seth helped Sara to the living room, then helped her to the sofa. He grabbed a couple of blankets for her. Seth sat next to her. She was trembling. "Seth, I'm scared. Would you please hold me?"

He hugged and held her until she stopped trembling. He kissed her and held her tighter. The Moonlight was shining on her hair and Seth thought about how beautiful she looked. He felt the anger at Art building up as he held her closer to him. He could still see her trembling as Art tortured her body. He ran his hands over her body gently and held and hugged her until they both fell asleep.

When morning came Tom and Carrie both awoke and got ready for work. Carrie fixed breakfast and they sat down and ate. "Tom, are you feeling better this morning?"

"A little. I'll feel better when Art has been convicted and put in jail."

"So will I. Sara told me Maggie and Kevin are coming in today."

"When I talked to Seth he said they were coming in at 9:30 today and they were going to swing by the school and pick up the keys to Sara's house."

"What time is the arraignment?"

"1:00 this afternoon. His lawyer met with him last night after I left and is going to be there today at 10:00. I hope he doesn't pull a stunt like he did last night because today I may not be able to refrain from punching him."

Carrie hugged and kissed Tom. "I think you'll be alright Tom. Just think about me if you start to feel like you're getting angry at him, think about the past few nights we've had together and how much we've enjoyed them."

"They have been wonderful and are only going to get better."

"I know they are." They kissed each other again.

Seth woke Sara up. "Sara honey, it's 6:15. It's time to get up and get ready for work."

Murder When the Bell Tolls

She got up and started headed toward her bedroom to change clothes. Seth went into his room and changed. They both came into the kitchen. They decided on Cereal and toast so Seth made the toast while Sara made coffee. They sat down and ate. Seth couldn't stop staring at Sara. His heart ached for her. Sara got up and walked into the kitchen. She stood at the sink and trembled and cried. Seth walked over to her and held her closely. "Sara, it's almost over. I'll be right here with you. We'll get thru this together." She finally stopped trembling.

"Sara, I'll be right back. I have to get those things for Tom." She waited and he came back with the things he needed. They left for school. When they got to school they met Carrie and Tom. Tom looked tired and worn. Seth knew this case had gotten to him. "Good Morning Tom, Carrie."

"Good Morning Seth, Sara."

"Tom, you look tired."

"I didn't get much sleep last night."

"Neither did we."

"Seth, I was going to call you and let you know what time the arraignment is today but everything just got so hectic."

"I understand. Ladies could you excuse us for a few minutes while I talk to Tom. You can wait in my office if you like."

Sara and Carrie went into Seth's office and sat down. Sara was still shaking. Carrie hugged her. "Are you okay Sara?"

"Yes. I just had a night of bad dreams and memories."

"I can imagine."

Tom and Seth were talking. "Tom, I cried and almost got sick watching this DVD. I had no idea how bad it was. Sara only told me some of what happened and I know that was very difficult for her to do."

"I cried and almost got sick myself when I saw it. I almost punched Art yesterday because of it to. Seth, it's your call about what you want to do about this DVD."

"I don't want to put Sara thru any more pain than she has already been thru. If you can add charges without having Sara testify or making a statement that would be great."

"I'll see what can be done. He needs to pay for what he did to her."

"I agree."

"Tom, I'm sure Maggie and Kevin will tell me what happened at the arraignment. I'll see you at the sentencing tomorrow. We'll take Carrie home tonight."

"Thanks."

Seth walked into his office where Sara and Carrie were talking about Carrie's upcoming wedding. Seth smiled because he knew something they didn't. He was happy to see Sara smiling to. He walked Carrie to her classroom then walked Sara to hers. He hugged and kissed her. "Sara, try and relax. Everything will be alright."

Seth walked back into his office as the classes began. At 9:45 Maggie and Kevin walked into Seth's office. "Maggie, Kevin, it's a pleasure to see you again."

"It's good to see you to. How's Sara?"

"She's scared but doing as well as can be expected. You can see her in her classroom as soon as the class is over."

"Good."

Seth told them what time they should be at the courthouse then handed them a spare key to Sara's. They waited around until the bell rang for the classes to be over for that hour. Maggie walked into Sara's class. "Hello Sara."

"Maggie. It's good to see you again."

Maggie hugged her then said very concerned. "Sara, you look pale. Are you sure you're alright?"

"Yes maam. I couldn't be better."

"I got the key from Seth. We'll go to the arraignment then meet you back at the house. After the sentencing tomorrow if he is found guilty we'll have a celebration. I think you could use some happiness about now."

Students started coming into Sara's class and greeting her and Maggie. "Sara, I'll let you go. We'll let you know what happens and we'll see you later."

"Goodbye Maggie."

Classes continued after Maggie and Kevin left. They drove to Sara's and put their things in the hall. They were hungry so they left and grabbed themselves something to eat before they went to court. They got to the court room around 12:30 and found a seat. They were amazed at how quiet the room was.

When it was time for Sara and Carrie to go to lunch Sara started shaking. "Carrie, the arraignment starts in a few minutes. I wish I could be there to hear what Art has to say."

"Sara, you can be glad you aren't there. I'm sure he'll have a lot to say and none of it will be good."

Murder When the Bell Tolls

"I guess you're right. I just wish I could have talked to Maggie and Kevin more before this."

"I know. You can talk to them tonight though."

Seth met the ladies halfway. They got their food and sat in the teachers' lounge and talked. Sara wasn't hungry. She was worried about the outcome. Seth and Carrie tried to reassure her that everything would turn out okay. They finished eating then Seth walked Carrie back to her classroom then he walked Sara to her room. She was still shaking, he hugged her. "Seth, I'm just so worried. Will you let me know if you hear anything?"

"Yes. I will."

"Thanks."

Seth went back into his office. About thirty minutes later his cell phone rang. "Seth Parker."

"Seth it's Tom. I've got good news and bad news."

"What happened?"

"Well, the good news is Art plead guilty on all eight counts of murder and on the kidnapping charges."

"That's great but what's the bad news?"

"Art yelled across the courtroom that the victims deserved to die and that anyone in that courtroom that rejected or disrespected him would die also. He also said that he made an example of Sara by doing what he did to her and that the next time he would finish what he started and she would end up like the last victim."

"Oh My! What did Maggie and Kevin say?"

"They were shocked and asked me what Art meant by that statement. I didn't know what to tell them except that they needed to talk to you."

"Thanks Tom. When's the sentencing?"

"10:00 a.m. tomorrow morning. The DA is asking for life. His attorney is asking for 50-75 years."

"Either way he will be put away for life. I'll let Sara know. Thanks again."

Seth wrote down on a piece of paper that Art plead guilty and that he would be sentenced in the morning. He walked down to Sara's classroom and knocked on the door. She answered and smiled. "Sara, I thought you would want this."

"Thanks Seth. I'll talk to you later."

He walked back to his office. He felt better knowing Art would be put away for a long time, he felt like he should get life for what he had done to Sara and the other female victims. He thought about Sara and how this was going to affect her. He knew she was going to need a lot of support and love and he was willing to give her both. He relaxed and waited for school to be out.

Sara opened the piece of paper and sighed a sigh of relief. After school was out Carrie walked down to Sara's room. "Sara, did you hear anything?"

"Yes. Art plead guilty to all of the murders. He will be sentenced at 10:00 tomorrow morning. Have you talked to Peggy yet?"

"No, but she's on her way here."

Peggy arrived and Sara told her the news. "That's good news. He's where he belongs. He's a sick man."

"Maggie wants to have a small celebration tomorrow night after the sentencing. I'll let all of you know what time and where."

"Okay."

Seth met the ladies. "Seth, Sara told us the good news. We're so happy."

"So am I."

Sara noticed the look on Seth's face. "Seth is there something you haven't told us?"

"Sara, we'll discuss it later."

"Alright."

"Are you ladies ready to go?"

"Yes we are."

Seth watched Peggy walk to her car and then he, Carrie, and Sara got in the car. Seth and Sara watched Carrie walk into the house then they started heading home. "Sara, would you mind if I stopped by my house for a few minutes. There's something I need from there."

"No problem."

They got to Seth's house. He helped Sara out of the car. "Come inside with me Sara."

She went inside and was amazed. His house was very neat and organized. But needed a woman's touch. "Sara, let me see if I can find what I'm looking for then I want to talk to you about something that happened in the courtroom today."

Sara looked scared. "Sara, it's alright. I just want to talk to you before we go back to your house and Maggie and Kevin are there."

Murder *When the Bell Tolls*

Seth went into his old bedroom and found his late wife wedding ring and the box it was in. He placed it in his pants pocket then went into the room where Sara was. She started shaking. He hugged her "Sara honey, it's alright. I just want to tell you what Tom told me happened in court today. I think you should hear this before you see Maggie and Kevin."

Sara gasped. "Why? What happened?"

Seth told Sara what Art had said. She started crying "Oh no. He didn't."

"I'm afraid he did Sara. Tom told me that Maggie and Kevin asked him what Art meant by that and he said to ask me."

"Seth, I don't know if I can face them."

"Sara, they love you and care about you. I know they'll understand. I'll be with you the whole time."

"Okay."

"I found what I was looking for so are you ready to go?"

"Yes."

Seth and Sara went back to Sara's. When they got there Maggie was fixing supper and Kevin was reading the paper. Sara started trembling as soon as she walked in the door. "Hi Sara, Seth. I thought maybe you two would be late so I started fixing dinner. I stopped at the store after the arraignment and bought some steaks. I hope that's alright."

"That sounds good. Do you need some help with that Maggie?"

Maggie looked over at Seth. "Sara, I could use some help. Why don't you fix the salads and Seth, you can take the steaks out to Kevin so he can put them on the grill."

Sara helped Maggie and Seth took the steaks out to Kevin. He stayed outside and helped him cook but checked on Sara periodically. Once the steaks were done The men brought them in and everyone sat down at the dining room table and ate. Once they finished eating Sara said "Thank you so much for getting the steaks. They were really good."

"You're welcome Sara. I thought that maybe you could use a break. You look so tired."

"Thank you for your help Seth."

"You're welcome Kevin."

Maggie and Sara cleaned up the dishes, then went to where the men were. "It'll be nice not having to rush off tonight. I think we're both tired from the drive here. It was worth it to see Paul's killer caught. Speaking of which, Sara we were wondering if you could clear up a matter for us. Art said something about finishing what he started with you. What did he mean by that?"

Sara started shaking and crying. She looked over at Seth for guidance. Maggie saw the terror on Sara's face. "Sara, what did that man do to you?"

Sara started crying harder. Seth, not even considering that Maggie and Kevin were there, walked over and hugged Sara and kissed her. "It's time to tell them Sara. I'll be right here."

Seth stood behind Sara as she told Maggie and Kevin about what Art had done to her. Kevin hit the table with his fists and got up. Maggie just stared horrified at Sara. Sara ran to her bedroom and closed the door. She laid on her bed and cried like a child. A few minutes later there was knock on Sara's bedroom door. "Go away."

"Sara honey, it's Maggie. May I come in?"

Sara walked over and opened the door. "Sara honey, I'm sorry about the way I reacted out there. I just wasn't expecting that. Seth told us that Paul knew about it."

"He did. He was angry at Art but very understanding with me. He told me it wasn't my fault."

"For goodness sake. It's not your fault. It just floored me. Honey, why didn't you say something before now?"

"Maggie, I was afraid you wouldn't understand or that you wouldn't want to be around someone who's damaged goods."

"Sara, you are not damaged goods. Something awful happened to you and we want to help you in any way that we can. We care about you. None of this effects how we feel about you." Maggie hugged Sara. "After what I saw of this Art fellow I hope he rots in prison."

Maggie and Sara were still talking when Seth knocked on her bedroom door. "Sara honey, is everything alright?"

"It is now."

He walked over to Sara and kissed her passionately. Maggie smiled, she was so happy for Sara that she was moving forward. She knew this had to be very difficult for her. "Honey, we're going to play some Monopoly. Do you feel up to it?"

"Yes, but could I shower first?"

"Sure. We'll be waiting for you." He hugged her and whispered in her ear. "Wear the royal blue gown. It's my favorite." She smiled.

Murder *When the Bell Tolls*

"Sara, I'll go out with everyone else while you shower. We'll see you out there."

"Okay Maggie."

As they were leaving Sara said "Seth, could you stay a minute? I need to ask you something?"

"Sure. Maggie I'll see you and Kevin out there in a few minutes."

After Maggie left Sara walked over to Seth and threw her arms around him. He smiled. "Seth, what I wanted to ask you was why don't I wait until Maggie and Kevin go back home again to wear your favorite gown. The royal blue is my favorite to. Maybe I'll wear the green one tonight and then we'll see about the blue one."

He smiled, then kissed her and embraced her. "That's fine. Sara, I hated the fact that you had to go thru that tonight."

"It's okay. I'm glad I did. It was difficult but now I don't have to hide it from my friends and family. Thank you for your help Seth."

"You're welcome honey."

"I'll be out in a few minutes."

Sara took a shower while the others set up the game. Maggie made iced tea and poured it into glasses. Sara came into the room dressed in her green knee length satin gown, with the robe over it and sat down to play monopoly. She sat next to Seth. They played monopoly until midnight. Sara got up and said "I think I'm going to go to bed. I'm exhausted. I know we don't have to get up as early tomorrow morning but I'm tired. She hugged Maggie and Kevin, then Seth got up and walked her to her bedroom.

When they were in her room Sara put her arms around Seth and hugged him tightly. He kissed her and ran his hands down her back. She smiled. He helped her into bed, kissed her again then went out with the others.

Tom called Carrie at 7:30 and told her he would be home in forty five minutes. She smiled. Tom was off the next day and they were going to the sentencing. She knew she had enough time to shower before Tom got home. She hoped he had a better day. She took a shower, then dressed only in her robe. She put perfume on, then went into the kitchen and finished dinner.

Debbie Creamer

Tom got home around 8:15. He smiled when Carrie greeted him. He embraced her and held her close. "Hi honey. I'm so glad you're home."

"I'm glad to be home. I missed you today. After what happened in court today I couldn't stop thinking about you. I was so glad you were safe."

"Yes I was safe. I thought about you to. I made something special for you for supper. I hope you like it."

Carrie opened the oven and took out the food. She had made meatloaf, baked potatoes, and corn on the cob. Tom smiled. "That looks good. I'm starved."

They sat down and ate. After they finished eating Tom helped Carrie clean up the kitchen. Tom kissed Carrie. "Honey, I'm going to shower and change clothes. I thought maybe we could play Yahtzee."

"That sounds good. I made a fresh peach cobbler for a snack later."

"That's sounds wonderful. I'll be back in a little while."

Carrie set things up to play the game while Tom took a shower. She thought about how wonderful it was having him there and how wonderful and special he made her feel. She smiled when she thought about being in his arms. She was so deep in thought that she didn't hear Tom come back into the room. He put his arms around her waist, embraced her and kissed her. She laughed, then turned around and kissed him. They sat down and played the game.

About ninety minutes later they put the game away and ate the cobbler. After they finished eating the cobbler, they decided to watch a movie on television. They snuggled next to each other and started watching the movie. "Tom, I almost forget. Sara told me that Maggie said that after the sentencing tomorrow, they would like to have a celebration and we are invited. It will be at Sara's and it's supposed to be us, Peggy, Ralph, Sara, Seth, Maggie and Kevin. I don't know what time yet. Are you interested in going?"

He held her close to him. "Yes, but right now the only thing I'm interested in is you." He kissed her and she giggled like a school girl. He smiled. They talked for awhile then they fell asleep curled up next to each other.

Seth, Maggie, and Kevin, talked a little while after Sara went to bed. "Seth, are you sure Sara is doing okay. She looks pale?"

"She'll be alright with help from all of us. She has tried to carry this burden alone and she isn't able to do that anymore. I know I'll stand by her and help her get through this." He had tears in his eyes as he turned to Maggie.

Maggie looked at Seth, then clasped his hand. "We'll stand by her to. We care about her and want to help."

"Maggie, Kevin I want to tell you something. I've fallen deeply in love with Sara. I want to spend the rest of my life with her. I care about her and I hope that you will give us your approval because Sara is a fantastic woman and so very smart. I love being with her."

"Seth, before you go any further, we give you our approval. We want Sara to be happy. We can tell how much she loves you by her actions. I know she's tried to hide it from everyone but we can see the sparkle in her eyes when she talks about you. She cares about you to. The only thing we ask is that you take care of her."

"I will. I think I'm going to bed myself but first I'm going to check on Sara."

"That's a good idea. We're going to bed ourselves. Goodnight Seth. We'll see you in the morning."

"Goodnight you two."

Maggie and Kevin went to their bedroom and Seth went back to check on Sara. She was struggling to sleep. Seth sat down in the chair next to her bed and held her hand. She opened her eyes. "Seth?"

"I'm here Sara. You're safe." She smiled as she closed her eyes. Seth leaned down and kissed her. He put his head down on the bed and they both fell asleep.

Everyone had agreed to meet for breakfast before going to the courtroom. Maggie and Kevin were the first ones' up at Sara's. They showered and got dressed. Kevin walked back to Seth's room and found it empty. "Maggie, Seth isn't in his room. We better check on Sara."

They walked back to Sara's room and found Seth, still holding Sara's hand, asleep in the chair next to the bed. Sara was sleeping peacefully. Maggie hated to wake either one of them. She looked at Kevin and whispered "They really do love each other. It obvious." Kevin nodded his head.

Kevin walked over and touched Seth on the shoulder. He awoke. "Did you sleep in here all night?"

"Yes. Sara was having nightmares and I was trying to comfort her. I must have fallen asleep."

Maggie smiled "I'm glad you took care of her. I hate to wake her but we are supposed to meet the others in ninety minutes."

"I'll wake her." He rubbed his hand on her arm. "Sara, honey, it's Seth. It's time to get up."

Sara opened her eyes. "Seth, Maggie, Kevin. What time is it?"

"It's 6:45 a.m. We are supposed to meet the others in about ninety minutes."

"Okay. Let me shower and change clothes. Maggie could you help me pick out something to wear today?"

"Sara Honey, I'm going to take a shower and change myself."

"Alright. I'll meet you in the living room."

Seth and Kevin headed to the living room and Maggie helped Sara decide what to wear. "Maggie, would you mind staying in here until I finish getting dressed?"

"Sure."

Seth headed to his room. He laid out a nice casual outfit. He shaved then got into the shower. He was worried about Sara. He knew that the day was going to be hard on her.

Sara got into the shower. After she finished she came into the bedroom and put on the outfit Maggie had laid out for her. Maggie gasped when she saw the mark on her left side. "Sara honey, is that mark from Art?"

"Yes it is. That's the other mark that got infected."

"Sara, I'm truly sorry about my reaction last night. It just really shocked me."

"It's alright Maggie. I guess I should have told you about it sooner but I didn't know how. I was scared."

"I understand. You know you look very nice. Sara, Seth, Kevin and I had a lovely conversation last night after you went to bed. He loves you very much and from what I've seen I think you love him to."

"I do. I tried not to fall in love so soon after Paul's death but Maggie I couldn't help it. Seth is warm, compassionate, funny, loving, and not to mention very attractive. He's so much like Paul."

"Sara, Paul's gone. Seth's here now. It's obvious how much the two of you love each other. Kevin and I couldn't be more happy for both of you."

"Thanks Maggie." Sara looked at the clock. "I guess we should get going if we're going to met the others."

Maggie and Sara started to go out of Sara's room. "Maggie, thanks again for everything."

She hugged Sara. "You're welcome."

They walked into the living room where the men were. Seth smiled at Sara. "Are the two of you ready to go?"

"Yes we are."

Tom and Carrie both woke up early. They showered and changed their clothes. Tom was shaving when Carrie walked into his bedroom. He smiled when he saw her. He walked out of the bathroom and hugged and kissed her. "Good Morning Carrie."

"Good Morning Tom."

"Carrie you look really nice today. I like that outfit on you."

"Thank you Tom. I just came in to tell you that I'm getting myself a cup of tea and was wondering if you would like anything."

"I don't think so. As soon as I get my shirt on, I'll be out there."

"Alright. I'll go fix me a cup of tea."

"Carrie, are you alright honey?"

"Yes. I'm just worried about Sara."

"I know. So am I."

Carrie fixed herself some tea. After Tom had finished getting his shirt on he went into where Carrie was. He hugged her then kissed her on the cheek. "Carrie, I know how you feel about Sara. I'm worried about her to. I know Seth is to. I just hope that everything goes well in court."

They left to meet the others. When they pulled into the restaurant parking lot Peggy was just getting out of her car. "Hi Carrie, Tom. How are the two of you?"

"Alright. I'm worried about Sara."

"So am I. She has been thru so much. I hope they put Art away for life."

"So do I especially after what he said in court yesterday?"

"What was that?"

"You don't know?"

"No. All I know is that Nancy came to me and said that I should be with all of you today. I agreed and when I talked to Seth yesterday at school he said we were all meeting for breakfast."

Carrie told Peggy what Art had said. Peggy gasped. She and Carrie were talking when Sara and Seth got there. They got out of the car and walked toward the others. "Good Morning all."

"Good Morning Sara, Seth, Maggie, Kevin."

"Peggy is Ralph coming?"

"No, not right now. He couldn't get away from the office since he is working short because of Peter's murder." Sara cringed.

They went inside and sat down. They ordered their food and waited. "Maggie, how was the trip back?"

"Better than the last time. We drove this time and it was much easier. We got here about 9:15 yesterday morning. We went to the arraignment yesterday."

Sara started shaking. Seth put his arm around her. "Sara, are you sure you're up to this? We don't have to go you know?"

"I'm up to this I'm just nervous and scared."

"I would imagine."

Their orders got there and they all ate. They paid the bill then headed to the court room. Sara started shaking harder. Seth took them in the side entrance to protect them from the press. Family members from almost all of the victims were present in the court room. They were all talking with each other. They walked in and took a seat next to Martha Burns family. They were all talking amongst themselves when Art entered the room wearing the traditional Orange Prison jump suit. The room was so silent that you could have heard a pin drop. Art saw Sara and smiled. Sara felt sick. Seth put his arm around her. "Are you okay?"

"Seth I need to go out in the hall and get some air for a few seconds."

"I'll go with you." He told Maggie and Tom where they were going. They went in the hall and Sara just started crying hysterically. Seth hugged her tightly."

"Seth, I'm sorry. I never expected to react like this."

"Sara, it's perfectly fine to react like you did. Art is a sick man, remember that."

Murder *When the Bell Tolls*

Sara took a few deep breaths and looked at Seth. "Alright, I'm ready to go back in and sit down."

"Are you sure?"

"Yes."

They went in and sat with the others. The judge entered the room. The Bailiff opened the door and admitted the press. The judge looked at Art with disgust. "Mr. Art. Hunter. You have been found guilty by your own admission to eight counts of murder, two counts of kidnapping, and three counts of criminal sexually assault. It's my job to hand down your sentencing. Art Hunter I sentence you to eight consecutive life sentences with no chance of parole for each of the murder charges. I also sentence you to another 150 years for two counts of kidnapping, three counts of criminal sexually assault and three counts of torture. Do you have anything you would like to say before I direct the bailiff to have you taken back into custody?"

Art looked over at Sara and said "Sara Michaels, this is all your fault. All you had to do was love me. If you would've loved me I wouldn't have been rejected and disrespected by all of these other people. All of them, you included got what they deserved. Sara you deserved more. I would've given you everything and treated you like any man would treat a woman. This is all your fault!"

Sara was trembling. She sunk in her seat and started crying hysterically. Seth was trying to comfort her and so were Maggie and Carrie. Art continued "Seth, I hope you know what kind of sleazy woman Sara is. I should've killed her when I had the chance."

Tom had to hold Seth back. The court room was buzzing. The judge used his gavel to quiet everyone down. "Bailiff, get that prisoner out of here before I start adding more years to his sentence."

As the bailiff was having Art escorted away the judge looked over at Sara and said "Ms. Michaels, I would like to see you, Lt. Parker and Sergeant Monroe in my chambers please."

"Yes Your Honor."

They joined the judge in chambers. "Ms. Michaels, first of all let me say how sorry I am about all of this. I had no idea that he would do that. His Attorney asked me yesterday if he could say something after he was sentenced but I had no idea what it would be when I allowed it. I'm truly sorry."

Seth finally got Sara calmed down. Sara looked at the judge and said "It's alright. Art is the kind of sneaky person who would pull a stunt like that."

"Yes and his attorney was aware of that also. His attorney will pay dearly for that stunt. Ms. Michaels, will you be okay?"

"Yes sir."

"Lt. Parker, Sergeant Monroe, I want Ms. Michaels to be under constant police protection until Mr. Hunter is safely behind bars. She may still be in danger."

"That won't be a problem sir. I'm staying with her all of the time anyway because of medical problems and because the police feared she may be in danger."

"I'm glad but what type of medical problems are you having Ms. Michaels?"

Before she could answer Seth looked at the judge and said "Art shot her when he shot her fiancé. The wound got infected and after it healed the mark that Art gave her got infected."

The judge gasped. "You were the third assault victim. I never knew who it was I was just told by the DA there were three victims and one hadn't been killed. Ms. Michaels, I truly am sorry. I can assure you Art will not be able to hurt you again. You may all go."

"Thank you sir."

As they were leaving they saw Alan Master getting ready to leave the building also. Sara was still crying hysterically. Alan glanced back and saw Sara. He put his things away and walked over to her. "Hello Sara."

"Alan. I don't feel much like talking now after having my name racked across the coals."

"It's alright. I'm not going to ask anything except are you alright?"

"Yes, just humiliated, but thrilled that he'll never be able to hurt anyone again."

"I would guess. I'm so sorry that something like this had to happen to someone as nice as you."

Sara smiled. "Thank you Alan, we're having a celebration later at my place. We're celebrating that this is finally over. You're welcome to join us if you would like, and bring your wife along."

"Thanks Sara. What time should we be there?"

"5:00 p.m. Will you be off by then?"

"Yes. I'll see all of you then."

Murder When the Bell Tolls

"Good. We look forward to having you there,"

"Sara. Ralph and I'll be there. I better get back. I told Nancy I would try and come back and work the rest of the day."

"I'll see you this afternoon."

"Sara, Carrie and I have a couple of things we have to do but we'll be there at 3:00."

"Thanks for coming with us today Tom, Carrie it is appreciated."

Carrie hugged Sara. "You're welcome honey."

Sara, Maggie, Kevin, and Seth, got in the car and went back to Sara's. Since it was close to lunchtime Maggie fixed lunch for everyone. They sat down and ate, then Sara laid down and tried to rest. Seth, Maggie, and Kevin talked for a little while then they started getting things together for the celebration.

Sara got up at 2:20. At 3:05 Tom and Carrie got there and helped finish things up. Peggy and Ralph got there at 4:35 and Alan Master and his wife arrived around five. They all ate and talked.

After dinner Seth served his famous dessert. After they ate dessert he turned to Sara and said "Sara, I have something very special for you." He handed her a velvet blue box. They all looked at each other and smiled.

Sara opened the box and gasped. It was a beautiful 14 carat gold ring with a 1 carat diamond. "Sara, I love you, will you marry me?"

Sara was speechless. She looked at her friends than looked at Seth. Tears of joy filled her eyes and she said "Yes, Yes, Yes. I'll marry you. I love you to."

They both stood up, embraced and kissed each other. Everyone applauded. "Sara we're so happy for you."

"I'm so happy to. Everyone here will be invited."

"Seth, how about you, Sara, Carrie and I get married at Sara's church, with both of our pastors, on the same day. We can all go to Paris together."

"Paris, here we come."

Made in the USA
Charleston, SC
09 July 2010